THE ROOTS
OF EVIL

Quintin
Jardine
THE ROOTS
OF EVIL

HEADLINE

First published in 2020 by
HEADLINE PUBLISHING GROUP

1

Cataloguing in Publication Data is available from the British Library

978 1 4722 5591 4 (Hardback)
978 1 4722 5593 8 (Trade paperback)

Typeset in Electra by Avon DataSet Ltd, Arden Court, Alcester, Warwickshire

Printed and bound in Great Britain by
Clays Ltd, Elcograf S.p.A.

Headline's policy is to use papers that are natural, renewable and recyclable
products and made from wood grown in well-managed forests and other
controlled sources. The logging and manufacturing processes are expected to
conform to the environmental regulations of the country of origin.

HEADLINE PUBLISHING GROUP
An Hachette UK Company
Carmelite House
50 Victoria Embankment
London EC4Y 0DZ

www.headline.co.uk
www.hachette.co.uk

This book is for Mia Abernethy Teixidor, *una llum de la meva vida*, and for Rex Masato Jardine, Granddad's Number One Boy, who is the other.

Both men heard the first chimes of midnight . . .
but neither heard the last.

One

'Happy New Decade, my love,' Sir Robert Morgan Skinner murmured to his wife, as the fireworks lit the darkness outside, and he had finished shaking hands with everyone around him, as tradition demanded. 'May it bring you all you wish for.'

'The last one did pretty well in that department,' Professor Sarah Grace replied. 'It brought a few surprises too.' She inclined her head towards a pair who stood a few feet away from them, watching the scene through the bay window of the golf club's first-floor dining room. 'For example, if you'd told me this time last year that those two would be here, let alone as a couple, I'd have sent you for a cognitive test.'

'How many times?' he murmured. 'My daughter and Dominic Jackson are not a couple. They are house-mates, no more than that.'

'So you say.'

'So Dominic assures me.'

'Are you telling me you asked him?' she chuckled.

'I didn't have to. Before Alexis moved in with him full-time, he came to me and asked if I had any objection. He told me something she'd kept from me herself, that she hadn't been able to settle back into her flat after she was attacked there.

More than that, he said that psychologically she was on the edge. He believed she had never had a really close friend outside of family, and that it was telling on her. The more success she had in her career, the more it contrasted with what she perceived as failure in her private life. She felt empty inside.'

'But everybody loves Alex,' Sarah protested.

'Everybody but Alex herself, it seems,' Bob murmured. 'I said what you just said, but Dominic was adamant, that her self-esteem was at a critical point. "She's never failed at work," he told me, "so when she perceives that she's a failure as a person, she has no idea how to cope with it. Let her move in with me, Bob, and I will be the friend she needs so badly . . . but nothing more than that, I promise you." Given that the man has an honours degree, a masters and a doctorate in psychology, I wasn't about to argue with him, so I agreed. And it's worked. Look at her, for Christ's sake! Compared to how she was, she's blooming.'

Sarah looked again at her stepdaughter. 'I'll grant you that,' she admitted. 'Why didn't you share this with me at the time?' she asked.

'You were away at that forensic pathology conference in Paris when it happened. By the time you came back she'd moved in. I told you then what the arrangement was.'

'And I doubted you then. This is Alex, remember.'

'Her mother's daughter? Is that what you're saying?' His voice was low; his smile was not reflected in his eyes.

'No, I didn't mean that at all,' she said, hurriedly. 'But I do know her; we are close.'

'Not so close you can't accept that she's capable of sharing a house with a man but not a bed?'

'And can you? Really?'

'I believe her. So should you. End of story.'

'That story, okay.' As the fireworks climaxed, she glanced once more at Alex's huge companion. 'I wonder what this crew here would say if they knew his history, that all those qualifications of his were gained in prison doing a life sentence for murder, under another name?'

'They would say nothing, because he's here as my guest. God knows what they would think,' he conceded, 'but trust me, nobody would utter a word.'

'Not in your presence,' she said, 'but as soon as you left the building, the place would be chattering like a tree full of starlings. This is a golf club, for heaven's sake. Rumour and innuendo spread faster than on Facebook in places like this.'

'Yeah, maybe they do, but nobody is going to find out this secret. Dominic keeps a low profile professionally, and the circles he moves in, nobody's likely to link him with Lennie Plenderleith.'

'Until Alex calls Dominic as an expert defence witness in a High Court trial,' Sarah suggested. 'There are still plenty of advocates and a few judges who were around when he was there last.'

'Yes, but he's changed a lot since then; the beard, the change in body shape since he stopped pumping weights.'

'He's still two metres tall.'

'That's not as exceptional as it used to be.'

'Isn't there a parole officer who knows who he is, or was?' Sarah argued.

'They would be bound by confidentiality,' her husband countered, 'but Dominic doesn't have to check in anymore. Yes, he's still on licence as a life-sentence prisoner, but the terms of that licence are as limited as they can be. He has a passport; he can go anywhere he likes without asking permission or informing anyone.'

'How about the USA? My home country is very choosy about who gets in. He'd be required to declare his personal history, and withholding information from US immigration is never a good idea.'

Bob grinned. 'We let your president into the UK.'

'Our president doesn't have any murder convictions.'

'There are those who would say he doesn't have convictions of any sort.' His attention was caught by the three-piece band shuffling back into position. 'Come on, kid, let's dance the night away.'

'Give my feet a break, Twinkletoes,' his wife groaned. 'They've suffered enough for one night.'

'Are you suggesting I'm not a *Strictly* candidate?'

'I'm not suggesting anything, I'm telling the world out loud: cops can't dance.'

As she stepped away from the window, Alex heard her. 'That's a given,' she agreed. 'I did my level best with him, but my old man has no sense of rhythm, none at all.'

'How about you, Dominic?' Sarah asked.

'I don't think that dance floor's big enough for me,' he laughed as they approached. 'Besides, I think it's time to run the gauntlet and drive home. If I'm not pulled over between here and Edinburgh, at one a.m. on January the first, it'll be a sad reflection on the state of policing in modern Scotland.'

'But don't let us drag you away, Pops,' Alex insisted. 'This shindig still has a while to go, by the looks of things.'

'No, I think we're done.' Bob glanced out of the window. 'All of a sudden it's chucking it down out there. If you are going, maybe you could drop us off at home, and wish your brothers a Happy New Year in the process.'

'Brothers?' she repeated.

He grinned. 'You don't think Jazz is going to be in bed, do you? Mark certainly won't be, and Ignacio doesn't have the clout to make them. Trish would lay down the law if she wasn't spending Christmas with her folks in Barbados, but the boys won't take it from him. Besides, I promised him that we'd be back in time to let Pilar and him catch up with some pals at a party.'

'I haven't met the girlfriend yet,' Alex observed. 'They're on the same uni course, yes?'

'That's right, she's a would-be chemist too. She's from Madrid; her father's a banker, and her mother's Norwegian. The mum did her degree in Edinburgh too; she got a two one in chemical engineering at Heriot Watt.'

'Do you think it's serious between them?'

'Ignacio's in love,' he conceded, 'and the lass seems smitten too, but everybody does when they're twenty. You've heard me talk about my old Uncle Johnny . . . he wasn't really my uncle though; he was my dad's best pal. He was a man of many sayings and one was that you shouldn't look at your girlfriend, you should look at her mother, because that's what she's going to look like in twenty-five years or so.'

'He sounds like a real old sexist pig,' his daughter declared. She glanced towards her stepmother, who was making her way to the toilet. 'Mind you, if that's true, my little sister's boyfriends will be impressed when that time comes. Sarah looks fantastic with the new silver hair. I'm still getting used to it.'

'Yes,' he agreed, 'me too . . . and it's natural!'

'You're kidding me!'

'No, she's been covering grey streaks for a few years now. One day, after we'd been out for dinner with Mario McGuire and Paula, on a whim she copied her and spent a small fortune having all the dye removed. What you see is pretty much how it looked.'

'Maybe I should try it,' Alex mused.

'No way!' her father said. 'You're far too young. Plus, your Grandma Graham didn't start to go grey until after your mother died, and you're very like her. If you did have the tint taken out, you'd be wasting your money.'

'I'm also very like you,' she pointed out, 'and you were grey in your mid-thirties.'

'True,' he conceded, 'but I still say don't do it. One's enough.' He nodded towards the door where Dominic was waiting. 'Let's go . . . once I've said goodnight to the Captain. Got to observe the formalities.'

'When will it be your turn for that job?'

'Never. I was a cop for thirty years, love, and I finished at the top of the tree. I'm an autocrat to my bootstraps, not a committee man. In fact, I rage against those, like Jimmy Proud did, God bless and keep him.'

Skinner said his farewell to the golf club captain and his party, joining his own on the back stairway that led out to the car park. He recovered an umbrella from his locker, sheltering his wife and daughter from the bite of the cold rain as they bustled back to Dominic Jackson's massive SUV.

It was a short distance to the Skinners' home, no more than three minutes' walk, but they were both grateful not to have to make it as the rain grew heavier, battering on the roof of the Mercedes G Class. Their driver pulled up as close to the door as he could, and all four leapt out and into the porch of the modern villa. As Bob had expected, only their two youngest children, Seonaid and Dawn, were in bed; Mark and James Andrew were still awake, but both were flagging. Alex kissed her half-siblings . . . Mark was half her age and Jazz was twenty years younger . . . then she and her escort disappeared into the night, as Bob and Sarah went upstairs to change out of their formal clothing into casual.

'Who are you first-footing?' Skinner asked Ignacio, his oldest son, as he came back down.

The young man stared at him. Clearly, the phrase meant nothing to him.

'Christ,' he lamented. 'Did your mother tell you nothing of your Scots heritage when she was bringing you up in Spain? Traditionally, the first person across your threshold in the new year should be a tall dark handsome man. In an ideal world he'll be carrying a lump of coal and a bottle of whisky.'

Beside Ignacio, his girlfriend Pilar Sanchez Hoverstad laughed. 'I don't think I would let anyone in if he was carrying a bottle of whisky,' she said. 'Vodka, yes, or maybe schnapps.' She pulled a face. 'But not whisky, never. And what is coal?'

'Yes,' Ignacio echoed. 'What is it?'

'Seriously? You mean . . . ? Fuck! I give up. Where are you going?'

'To our friend Ronnie's house. She lives on Goose Green, where you used to live with Alex.'

'Ronnie? She?'

'Veronica, Dad, Veronica Goodlad. She's at uni too, studying English.'

'Well, you'd better get moving,' Bob said, 'or she'll have graduated by the time you get there. Have you got a bottle of anything to take with you?'

7

'Two,' Pilar replied. 'Spanish wines; a Tempranillo and a Verdejo.'

'Very nice,' he murmured. 'Can I come?'

'The hell you can,' Sarah retorted, as she re-joined them.

'Nah. You're right. I'm too old for all-nighters. On you go, you two, but don't forget to be back for the Loony Dook at midday.'

'What's that?' Pilar asked.

'A swim in the sea on New Year's Day, on Gullane beach. It's become a tradition.'

'In the sea?' she gasped. 'Nacho, you never told me that. All you said was to bring my costume, that we were going to swim. I thought you meant in a pool.'

He nodded. 'I know, they're crazy here. You don't have to, really.'

'No, I will,' she insisted. 'If my mother was here, she would. She is very proud of being Norwegian. I have her blood so I must too.' She looked up at Bob. 'Are you doing it?'

'Yup. Jazz too.'

'I don't know about that,' Sarah murmured.

'Try and stop him.'

'I think he's beyond my control,' she admitted.

Bob escorted his oldest son and his partner to the door, returning to the living room with a brandy in one hand and a bottle of Corona in the other. He handed the goblet to his wife and settled down beside her on the sofa. 'Want to watch Jools Holland?' he asked.

'Tomorrow maybe; it has less attraction now that I know it isn't live. Mind you, I'd like to be in the audience when they record it. Could you fix that for next time? You've got contacts everywhere.'

8

'Not quite,' he corrected her. 'I have contacts in the media, in the security service and in the police. None of those will cut much ice with the producers of the *Hootenanny*.'

'What about your former wife's actor boyfriend? He's got cred with them, surely.'

'Maybe,' he acknowledged, 'but given that I once offered to make Aileen a pair of earrings with his nuts, he might not be too willing to use it. Ask me in six months and I'll see what I can do.'

'Who knows where we'll be in six months? I've been following the press coverage of the new coronavirus in China after I read a piece on a pathology website ten days ago or so. Unless they find a quick and effective treatment, and very fast, that could become global. If it does, the consequences are anyone's guess. Who's to know what'll happen?'

He frowned, and his mood darkened. 'Who was to know a couple of years ago what would happen with Jimmy Proud? Hell no! More recently than that, could I have imagined Alex being attacked in a secure penthouse apartment? Hell no! Could I have foreseen what would have happened to poor Carrie McDaniels?' He shuddered.

'Go back those two years,' she countered. 'Could we have imagined that now we'd have a beautiful second daughter? Not really. Or that you'd be chair of InterMedia UK? I didn't see that coming. Or that you would be back in the police?'

'I'm not back in the police,' he corrected her. 'I'm mentoring rising CID officers. As for InterMedia UK, that's only a division of the parent company, and it's at the pleasure of my friend Xavi.'

She sipped her brandy and smiled. 'Your friend Xavi Aislado: the only man I know who's as big as Dominic Jackson.'

Bob nodded. 'That's why he was a goalkeeper, until his knee packed in on him. Big Iceland, they used to call him at Tynecastle. Strange thing is, I never saw him play. I only knew him as a young journalist.'

'How did you two get close? Did you feed him insider information?'

He raised his eyebrows. 'And put my career in jeopardy? I don't think so. The fact is, Xavi tells people I saved his life. I didn't; I turned up after he'd been shot, and I got him to hospital, but it was never life-threatening.'

'That's not what he means when he says that,' Sarah argued. 'He told me that if you hadn't turned up when you did, he might have put another bullet in his head and you'd have found three bodies instead of two.'

'He may say so, but he wouldn't have done that. Yes, what happened was tragic, but he's too strong a character.' He sighed. 'That's another story, though. Let's look forward today. Have you made a New Year resolution?'

She laughed. 'Yes, I resolve to dissect the next person who calls me "Lady Skinner". I'm an American; we don't do titles.'

'Of course, you do!' Bob declared firmly. 'Half of your compatriots refer to themselves by their job titles. Chief this, Coach that: look at *Blue Bloods* on the telly, everybody round the table has a title; it's a status thing. You do it yourself, Professor Grace.'

'Yes, I do, because I've worked damn hard to attain the status. Lady Skinner makes me out to be an appendage of my husband. It's archaic, it's . . . it's . . . anti-feminist!'

'Enlighten me, do.'

She raised her brandy goblet. 'Certainly, Sir Robert.

Suppose I had been honoured, not you. Suppose I'd been made a dame.'

'You can't be; you're a US citizen.'

'Piss off, Skinner, just suppose, for the sake of argument.'

'I don't want an argument.'

'You asked me to enlighten you; let me. If I'd been made a dame, that's the female equivalent of a knight, right?'

He smiled and eased himself closer on the sofa. 'If you say so. I've never really thought about it.'

'I do say so. So there I am, Professor Dame Sarah Grace. What are you?'

'Bob.'

'What else, idiot?'

'Whatever you'd like me to be. How about Chief Skinner? That's what they called me whenever I visited the States.'

'But what would everyone else call you, instead of Lady? What's the male equivalent?'

'Gent? That's how it works with public toilets.'

'Nothing!' she cried, her nostrils flaring. 'There is no gender equivalent to the courtesy title given to the wife of a knight . . . or to a husband,' she added, with a flourish. 'It's all right for the little wife, but it would be demeaning for a male to walk in his wife's shadow . . . or his husband's? Is that not sexism, is it not a denial of feminism? Go on, tell me.'

He put his head against hers. 'The only thing I will tell you is that when you have a certain amount to drink, and get argumentative, you also get very horny. So what say I display my masculinity . . . ever notice that there's no such word as maleism? . . . by carrying you upstairs, Lady Skinner, and we carry on this discussion in a more intimate setting?'

A few strands of her silver hair fell over her right eye. 'Are you suggesting that we bring in the new year with a bang?'

'Perceptive as always.'

'And you'll concede that I'm right?'

'Whatever it takes.'

She put her arms around his neck. 'In that case, Sir Robert, I'm all . . .'

He was in the act of lifting her from the sofa when they were interrupted by the powerful voice of P!nk, Skinner's ringtone. He paused, looking Sarah in the eye.

'Go on,' she sighed. 'You've never been able to just let it ring, and you never will.'

He laid her back down, took out his mobile, glanced at the screen and took the call. 'Deputy Chief Constable McGuire,' he growled, slowly, 'if you're pished and calling to wish me a Happy New Year, you can stick it up your arse.'

'I'm not drunk but I wish I was, Bob. Happy New Year, of course, but it's off to a lousy start.'

The tension in his normally unshakeable friend's voice snapped him into full wakefulness. As she looked up at him Sarah saw his eyes narrow and his mouth tighten. 'What's up?'

'I don't want to tell you over the phone. How steamin' are you? How heavy a night was it at your golf club do?'

'It was okay, but on the quiet side, as these formal events usually are.' He glanced at his Corona and saw that it remained more than half full. 'I'm okay; not okay to drive, but every other way.'

'Can I send a car for you? There's one in your area.'

'Seriously?' Skinner checked his Rolex. 'At five to two on New Year's Day?'

'Seriously. Could Sarah come too?'

He felt a ripple of apprehension. He realised that McGuire

was asking for her as a pathologist, not as his partner. 'Not a chance of that,' he replied. 'Get someone else if that's necessary. Kids,' he explained. 'Ignacio's gone out and Mark's still too young to be left in charge.'

'How about Alex?'

'She's gone too. Look, Mario, I'll come if you really think it's necessary.'

'Bob, you'd have killed me if I hadn't called you. I'll send the car right now.'

He blinked as the call ended, shaking off the last of his drowsiness. Sarah stood. 'You really have to go out?' she asked. 'Is this a set-up? Have you and your chums planned a stag New Year? Or are you being lured into one?'

'My chums are all too serious for that, plus, if it was a ruse, he wouldn't have asked for you and your little bag of tools. No, it's a mystery, and I have a feeling that when I get to where I'm being taken, I'm not going to like it at all.'

Two

The police car pulled into Skinner's driveway within three minutes of McGuire's call ending; by that time he had donned a padded, hooded rain garment that he had bought one cold October night in Barcelona, but barely used since. He slid awkwardly into the back seat behind the uniformed PC driver and her companion, an older man with sergeant's stripes whom he recognised from his time as chief constable in Edinburgh. He cursed himself inwardly for being unable to put a name to him.

'Been busy?' he asked, making conversation in the hope of prompting a recollection.

'No, sir,' the sergeant replied. *Auld*, Skinner remembered, with a surge of relief, *Bertie Auld, a crazy Rangers supporter even though he had been named after a Celtic legend*. 'It's no' like the old days.' He paused. 'Well mibbe's it is in the town. I'm not used tae East Lothian.'

Eyes met in the rearview mirror. 'Do you know what this is about, Bertie?'

'No, sir. The DCC never said. He just told us tae pick up Sir Robert and bring him into Edinburgh, toot sweet, blue light if we need to.'

'Where in Edinburgh?'

'Haymarket, sir.'

'Eh? Haymarket what? The station?'

'No,' Auld replied. 'He said they'd meet us at the War Memorial, that was all.'

'They?' Skinner repeated.

'Him and the chief.'

He was taken by surprise. 'Maggie too! What the hell? Has there been a military coup?'

The car slowed as they entered Aberlady. As always there were cars parked on either side of the road, but only one other moving vehicle, a Nissan Leaf, travelling slowly and making its way carefully through the space. 'Do you think we should be stopping him, Sarge?' the young driver asked.

'We don't have grounds, PC Gregg,' Auld told her. 'He hasn't hit anyone, he's taking care not to, and it isn't an offence to do fifteen miles an hour.' He had hardly finished speaking when the car clipped the wing mirror of a wide pick-up truck. 'That, on the other hand . . . Show him some blue, Janice, and pull him over.'

The Nissan pulled into the kerb, past the last of the parked cars, the police vehicle stopping in front. Auld stepped out; the PC made to follow until Skinner intervened. 'No, wait here, Constable. I'll go; I know that registration. She's one of us.'

He moved quickly to join the sergeant who stared in surprise as he moved past him leaning over beside the driver's window as it opened. 'Noele,' he said, 'are you okay?'

'Sir? What are . . .' There was a pause as the woman composed herself. 'I'm okay, Bob, just a bit shaken up. That fucking pick-up shouldn't be allowed to have unfolded mirrors that wide.'

'Agreed, but what the hell are you doing here, and who's looking after the wee one?' He paused, turning to Auld. 'Do you know DS Noele McClair?' he asked. 'She works with DCI Pye and DI Haddock on Serious Crimes. Our kids are best mates.'

'Very good, sir,' the veteran sergeant said quietly, 'but has she been drinking? There's lights on in that house over there and people are lookin' at us. Bloody social media, ye ken.'

McClair replied for him. 'I had a glass of Prosecco with my mother at the bells, Sergeant, and I gave myself a breath test before I left the house.'

'Why did you leave the house, exactly, Noele?'

'Duty, sir. I had a call from Sauce. He said I'm needed. He did offer to have me picked up, but I said I'd rather be in control of my own movements.'

'Did he tell you why?'

'No, just to meet him at Haymarket. I imagine he meant the divisional office at Torphichen Place.'

'This gets stranger and stranger,' Skinner murmured. 'That's where I'm heading, at the request of the DCC. Noele, don't worry about getting home, that'll be taken care of. Park up, come with me and let's get there as fast as we can.' He glanced at Auld. 'Use all the blue lights you've got, Bertie.'

Three

The rest of the journey into Edinburgh passed by almost entirely in a silence that was broken only by the chatter of the police transmissions on the patrol car radio. The road traffic was as quiet as Skinner had expected it to be, and the broadcast transmissions were routine, none of them offering any clue to the reason behind the summons to the capital.

As they entered the city, PC Gregg turned left at the Willowbrae traffic lights, then right into Duddingston Village, choosing the road through Holyrood Park, where they saw the first of the revellers, their number growing steadily as they carried on into the Cowgate and beyond through the Grassmarket.

'We're coming this way, sir, because Princes Street's cordoned off for Hogmanay,' the driver explained. As a mere detective sergeant, McClair seemingly did not merit an explanation.

'It takes us nicely down to Haymarket,' she observed, asserting her presence.

Skinner sensed an edginess in her, one that he felt himself. McGuire's call, and its nature, was unlike any he could recall either receiving or making in his career. His unease grew as they turned out of Grove Street into Morrison Street. It was empty, but for a black Range Rover, beside which stood two people recognisable to everyone in the police car, even out of uniform.

Mario McGuire signalled that they should pull in behind his car. Chief Constable Margaret Rose Steele was by his side.

'Where's Sauce?' McClair wondered aloud, as they came to a halt. 'I'm supposed to meet him.'

'Let it play,' Skinner told her, as he opened the door. The rain had become sleet, and the temperature made him thankful for his choice of overcoat. 'He'll be somewhere. Hasn't it occurred to you that you're not the only DS on his team? In fact, you live further away from base than any of them, you're off duty and yet he called you.'

She offered a nervous smile. 'He's always saying I'm the best.' She slid along the back seat and stepped out beside him.

'Thanks for coming,' the chief constable said, as she approached them. 'We didn't expect you both to arrive together.'

'But you knew DS McClair was coming?'

'Yes, she was called in on my instruction.'

'Even though she's a single mother like you? There must be a powerful reason for that.'

'All four of us have got young children,' she retorted. 'We should all be with them, but this . . . Well, it overrides that.'

'Even for me? I'm a civilian, remember.'

'Neither of you are here because you're cops,' McGuire said, beckoning. There was something in his eyes that Skinner could not read, for all the years he had known the man. 'Come on and we'll show you what this is about.'

They fell in behind him as he led them a few yards down Morrison Street, pausing as they reached its junction with Torphichen Place, where the West End Police Office was located. As they turned the corner, Skinner tensed. Beside him Noele McClair gasped.

A crime scene tent had been set up at the entrance to the station. It was large, covering the pavement and half the roadway. At its entrance a ginger-haired man was climbing into a disposable tunic.

'He's here?'

McGuire nodded. 'Aye, Bob; for this one, accept no substitutes.'

Arthur Dorward was head of the Scottish Police Authority's Forensic Services Unit, and he was not a delegator. For major incidents he was usually the first on the scene. He turned as they approached, frowned, then stepped inside the tent.

'He's not happy about a Hogmanay call-out either, it seems,' Skinner murmured.

'Who would be?' the chief constable replied. 'We all need to be suited and booted,' she continued, accepting a package from a crime scene technician.

Skinner shed his overcoat and donned the sterile garb as quickly as he could, only to find that McClair had a problem. She was wearing a skirt. 'Sauce never said,' she protested.

'That's okay, Noele,' McGuire assured her. 'Nip into the station and change in the ladies.'

'Mario,' Skinner barked as she left them, irritation overcoming him. 'What the fuck is this?'

As he spoke a tall young man emerged from the tent, grim and white-faced. His ears had escaped from his sterile cap. He stopped short when he saw his former chief and continuing

19

mentor, his eyes widening. 'Are you going to tell me what this is about, Sauce?'

Detective Inspector Harold Haddock's mouth tightened until it was no more than a slash across his face. He shook his head and looked away, then retraced his steps.

'I've had enough of this,' Skinner growled. He made to follow, until Steele put a hand on his arm.

'Please, Bob, wait for DS McClair. She's going to need you, as a friend.'

Scowling, he obeyed her, biding his time until the DS returned, her change of clothing completed, then stepped through the opening into the covered enclosure, with her following behind.

The area was bathed in cold, bright white light. At its centre was a car, a blue estate; a sheet had been placed over the windscreen and roof, against glare from the floodlights, he supposed. It looked vaguely familiar to Skinner, but he was unable to place it . . . until Noele McClair spoke.

'That's Terry's car,' she cried out. 'It's my ex-husband's car. What's it doing here?'

'That's the thing, Noele,' Sauce Haddock replied. 'It was dumped here at twelve forty-one. The driver jumped out, got into the passenger seat of a car that was following him and it got the hell out of here. He was wearing a black balaclava, so we never got a look at his face.'

'But why?' she asked, her anxiety building. 'What's this about?'

'This is the reason,' the chief constable said. She stepped up to the car and pulled the covering sheet away exposing some of the windscreen.

Reflected light blazed off the glass, blinding them all for a second, until Skinner moved past McClair, up to the vehicle, and looked inside.

The front seats were unoccupied but two male figures were sprawled in the rear. He jerked the nearside door open and leaned inside. He knew Terry Coats, the detective inspector who had lost his career for sailing too close to the wind, the husband who had lost his wife and daughter for going far beyond it. He recognised him at once, even with a third eye in the middle of his forehead from which a single trickle of blood ran down his nose, across the stubble on his upper lip and into his mouth.

He stood, turning to face Steele and McGuire, fury in his eyes. McClair had moved up behind him, but he held his position, blocking her view of what was inside the car. 'What the fuck!' he hissed. 'I thought I'd trained some tact into you two. Obviously you skipped a couple of lessons, to be pulling this stunt.'

'I'm sorry, Bob,' the chief constable replied. 'It was my call, not Mario's. Neither of us have ever experienced anything like this, so I felt your advice was essential.'

'You must have skipped the self-confidence lesson as well, Maggie. Okay,' he continued, calming a little, 'I'll take that as a compliment, but why bring Noele here?'

'What was the alternative? Having a police car call at her house, with her child there? Sauce knew that her mother would be there for New Year, so I thought it was best if she was brought to the scene.'

'You got that fucking wrong!' he yelled at her, in a way that he never had when she had been an officer under his command.

McClair looked up at him. 'The scene of what, Bob?' she asked, quietly.

21

He sighed. 'Terry's in there, lass, and he's dead. He's been shot.'

The colour fled from her face, in an instant. Her cheeks seemed to collapse into themselves, giving her a skeletal look. She leaned against him, and he put his arms around her. 'What's the silly bugger done now?' she murmured, into his chest.

'That we will find out, Noele,' he promised her. 'I'm sure he'll have left a trail. From what I knew of the man, he didn't do subtle.'

'Can I see him?' she asked, her voice tremulous. 'I mean, we'll need a formal identification, won't we?'

'You can do it at the morgue, before the autopsy. But it's not "we". You can't be involved in the investigation.'

'Why not?' she said, bitterly, disengaging herself and looking back at Steele, McGuire and Haddock. 'We were divorced.' She paused. 'Or do you have to eliminate me as a suspect? Is that it?'

'The thought never crossed our minds,' Haddock replied. 'You're too close; that's all, Noele, you must know that. I will need to talk to you though, about Terry's movements, associates, stuff like that.'

'I won't be able to tell you much, Sauce. I only see Terry,' she gulped, 'only saw, him when he came to pick up our Harry every other Saturday.'

'We may have to go further back than that.'

'But not now,' Skinner declared firmly. Even in her distress, McClair had the impression that he had effectively taken command. 'You've done what you saw as necessary, Maggie. Now do what's decent and have Bertie Auld take her back to Gullane right away.'

'Back to my car,' she corrected him, as the first tears began to fall.

'No, back home. You're not driving tonight. PC Gregg can drop Sergeant Auld off in Aberlady; he can take your motor back.'

'He can't,' she murmured. 'He's not insured.'

'He is, as a police officer. Don't you worry about that; let's just get you home to Harry and your mother. And if you need someone to look after the wee fella in the next few days,' he added, 'you can drop him off at mine. Sauce,' he ordered, 'take her back inside to change, then straight to the car.'

As Haddock obeyed his instruction, Skinner, still bristling with anger glowered at the two senior officers. 'I can see why you wanted me here,' he conceded, 'but bringing her here was miles over the top. You could have told me about Coats, and I could have gone to see Noele at home.'

'I agree, Bob, we could, and in hindsight, we should,' McGuire was grim-faced, as tense as before. 'But there's more. You need to look in the other side of the car.'

Puzzled, he did as the DCC asked; he walked round behind the vehicle, and once again opened the rear passenger door and leaned in. As he did, he noticed for the first time the rank smell of death with which he had become familiar during his police career, a mix of blood, sweat and human waste.

The other occupant was slumped sideways, restrained only by the curve of the back seat. He wore a heavy knitted sweater and faded denim jeans. Skinner recognised his trainers as Air Jordan, James Andrew's choice of Christmas present, and seriously expensive, the top of the Nike basketball range. The man also had been shot, but through the back of the head: that was all too obvious as the bullet had exited through the left eye, taking all of it away, turning the socket into a mess of gore and bone chips.

He stood once again. 'Yeah,' he said with a shudder.

'Look again, Bob,' Maggie Steele told him.

He did so, forcing his gaze away from the awful wound and fixing it on the undamaged section of the slack-jawed head. He stared at the body for several seconds; as he did so, a cold hard fist seemed to grip his stomach and twist.

'Aw my God,' he gasped. 'Is this for real? It can't be. How the fuck . . . this is Griff Montell?'

'Yes,' the chief constable confirmed. 'Inspector Griffin Montell. You recruited him as chief in Edinburgh, and you have a personal connection with him through his friendship with your Alex. We need to know how he wound up dead in the same car as Terry Coats, and we're hoping you can help us find out.'

Skinner's head swam, as he recalled his history with the dead man. It was an exaggeration to say that he had recruited him, but he had approved his transfer from his police force in South Africa and had made the best use of the skills outlined in his service record by putting him straight into CID, without any pointless acclimatisation in uniform. Montell had more or less been driven out of his home country when a failed marriage had left him with court-awarded child support costs that he could not have met on a Rand-based salary. The solution he had chosen had been to move to Scotland where the conversion rate from sterling allowed him to do that easily.

Montell was a colourful character, as well as being a good detective. Skinner's daughter Alex had been attracted to him when they were neighbours in Stockbridge. And there had been a third person in that block, he realised.

'What about Spring?' he asked. 'She's his next of kin. Has she been told?'

Montell's twin sister had emigrated with him. She was gay, and her romance with Superintendent Mary Chambers had caused family and professional friction for a while; indeed it might have cost Montell his job if Skinner had not been there as a moderating influence.

'She doesn't live in Edinburgh full-time any longer,' McGuire told him. 'She moved in with Mary, and after she retired they bought a flat in Pretoria, where she and Griff grew up. That's where they spend the winter. I know this because Mary told me. I have her mobile number, so I'll try that. If it's switched off I'll ask the police there to track her down and get her to contact me, and I'll ask her to break the news.'

'What about his ex-wife and kids? You might have contact details for her on his personal file. She'll have to be told.'

'Again, that's a job for the morning. I might ask Mary to do that too.'

'Meanwhile I've got to tell Alex,' Skinner murmured.

'Were they still . . . ?' Steele ventured. 'We all know that when she was attacked in her home, Griff was there. He was injured protecting her, wasn't he?'

'If you're asking whether they were still sleeping together,' Skinner retorted, 'not so far as I know. It wasn't a steady thing. Griff was a friend, and if she was lonely or low, she could give him a call.'

'She'll need to be interviewed,' the chief constable said.

Something about her manner brought Skinner's temperature to boiling point once again. 'She'll need to be consoled,' he snapped, 'and that's my job, mine and Dominic's.'

'You mean Lennie,' Steele observed.

'No, I don't, Maggie. Lennie's in the past; Dominic Jackson is a different person altogether.'

The chief constable frowned. 'I'm a sceptic when it comes to rehabilitation,' she declared. 'I'm not convinced by people who claim to have reinvented themselves in prison.'

'Across the board, neither am I,' he fired back, 'but I knew the big fella before you did, and I liked him. The fact is you don't really know him at all, and you never did. Many of us are moulded as people by our social circumstances; I'm one of them . . . and so are you. So was the young Lennie Plenderleith, but he didn't have my good fortune. He wasn't born into a middle-class professional family so he was never spotted by the education system. In his case, his father was a brute and he was brought up that way.' He paused, recovering his temper. 'The prison service doesn't do IQ tests on inmates as a matter of course, but I had them run one on Lennie and it was off the fucking scale.'

'You never told me that,' she said.

'No,' he agreed. 'Nor did I tell you that I visited him a couple of times a year when he was inside, in the Governor's office so the other prisoners didn't twig and mark him down as a grass.'

'No, you didn't; not even when I was your executive officer. You didn't trust me?'

'It wasn't a matter of trust, Mags, it was private, between me and Dominic, that's all. However, I do trust him to take care of my kid, and that's all you need to realise now.' He paused. 'No, not quite, you also need to realise that if anyone in the media ever makes a connection between him and Lennie Plenderleith and I find out that it came from the police, I will find the source and I will end their career. Now,' he barked, abruptly, 'can we get indoors, sit down with the SIO . . . Sammy Pye, I assume . . . and work out how this double-murder investigation will proceed.'

To McGuire and Steele, it was as if Bob Skinner had never left the service. Automatically he had slipped into command mode. Automatically, they obeyed. The DCC nodded and led the way into the police station. They removed and discarded their sterile clothing in the reception area, then climbed one floor to the station commander's office, which Steele had occupied herself earlier in her career, before the old Edinburgh force had become part of the unified Scottish police service.

'Mario,' she said, as the door closed behind them, 'text Sauce and ask him to join us. You were wrong about Sammy being SIO, Bob; he's on extended sick leave and Haddock's filling in for him as Serious Crimes commander in Edinburgh.'

'What's his problem?'

She hesitated; he realised that she was considering what she could tell him. 'Within these four walls, he's been diagnosed as having motor neurone disease,' she replied. 'Don't breathe a word, though: not even Sauce knows. He thinks it's a virus.'

'Fuck,' Skinner sighed. 'What a New Year this is turning out to be. Poor Sammy, we've all known him since he was a . . .' He stopped in mid-sentence as there was a knock at the door.

Haddock came into the room without waiting for a reply; he was still wearing his paper suit. 'Chief, sir, gaffer,' he said. 'You wanted me.'

'Yes, Inspector,' McGuire replied, 'we do. We have an investigation to launch, and you're in charge.'

'Me, sir?'

'Who else? It's a serious crime; that's what it says on your office door, and you're in charge of the team.' He hesitated.

'Okay, Sauce; we know you're relatively new in rank and inexperienced, but the chief and I have got faith in you. By the same token, we're not going to leave you exposed to everything. The media will swallow its collective tongue when it learns that a police officer and a former cop have been executed like this. I'll front up all the public statements and briefings, and Allsop's team in the press office will deal with one-off questions, so you won't be in the spotlight at all, until the day that you make an arrest. Then, you can go out front. You can run the inquiry out of this office if you like, with all the personnel you need. If the investigation goes beyond Edinburgh, you'll have the support of Serious Crimes wherever necessary. They'll report to you, regardless of the rank of the senior officer. On top of that, Sir Robert will be there in the background, acting as a mentor, as he's done in the past.'

Skinner started, but McGuire forestalled him. 'I don't need to ask you, Bob, do I? You're as keen to find the person who pulled that trigger as we are.'

'No, you don't need to,' he agreed, 'but you and I won't be seen together, Sauce. When we meet, it won't be here, and we won't be observed. I'll help you every way I can, but if I'm seen to do so, it'll undermine your authority, in the eyes of the press, and possibly of your own team. Now,' he continued, 'what's your first priority?'

'Process the crime scene,' Haddock replied immediately.

'You don't know where the crime scene is,' Skinner pointed out. 'One was shot in the back of the head, the other,' he touched his forehead, 'right there. Coats might have been killed in the car, but Griff wasn't, no way. Even if he'd been leaning forward so that the gunman could get a shot off, if that had happened there would have been debris all over the place, blood, bone fragments, brain tissue. Earlier you described the car being dropped off. I take it you've got CCTV footage.'

'Yes, there are three cameras; one covers Torphichen Place, one's on Dewar Place Lane, and the third looks at the rear of the building and the car park.'

'What about the other vehicle? What do you have on that?'

'We have a registration,' Haddock told him. 'Problem is it belongs to a Vauxhall Insignia, three years old, owned by a leasing company in Bristol. The car on camera is a Renault Megane.'

'You'll be able to narrow that by looking at the style of the vehicle, model details and so on.'

'I'm not holding my breath, gaffer. Before you ask, I've ordered a search of all available street camera footage, for both vehicles. If we get lucky . . .'

'Don't call it luck; call it the result of proper police procedure.'

McGuire grunted. 'We'll be sure to do that at the press briefing. But if we do get lucky,' he continued, 'we'll find footage of the driver and the passenger getting out and they won't have bloody helmets wrapped around their coupons.'

'Which makes that your top priority, Sauce,' Skinner added. 'The next being to process the vehicle and get every trace of DNA from it. You're bound to find traces of wee Harry, Terry and Noele's son, in there, but it'll be so similar to his dad's that you won't need to take a sample from the wee chap. Likewise, Noele, for hers is on the database for elimination purposes. Again, add on the luck factor and you might find someone who's on the system for the wrong reasons.' He paused. 'That's what we're thinking,' he said. 'Now, tell us, as the SIO, what's in your head?'

'Okay,' Haddock replied. 'Once all the by-the-book stuff is done, we're going to be trying to find out how the hell Terry Coats and a uniformed police inspector came to wind up dead in the same car.'

His mentor nodded. 'Yes, you will be,' he agreed, frowning. 'And maybe I can help you. When you were investigating the murder of that bothersome blogger, Austin Brass, you had Terry Coats in the frame as a potential suspect.'

'That's right. We had him under observation and you and I tracked him to a hotel out by Edinburgh Park. We wondered what he was up to; it turned out it was an air stewardess that he was banging on the side. That was when he and Noele went their separate ways.'

'Correct. What you don't know is that, after she kicked him out, Terry turned up at my house full of hell and looking for trouble. I had to,' he paused, 'calm him down. When I'd done that, and he'd come to his senses, he came out with a bizarre story.' He laughed, softly. 'He said he'd been working under cover.'

'Under duvet, more like,' McGuire grunted.

'I knew the first part of that,' Haddock added. 'You told me at the time that you'd had to deck him.'

'I didn't have to,' Skinner admitted, 'but he took a punch at my boy; that's as big a line as you can cross. What you don't know is the tale he spun me. His excuse was that he'd come upon what he said was a money-laundering operation, converting stolen Krugerrands through an airport shop, after they were smuggled in by flight crew on a certain airline. He told me that he'd checked the background with a guy he knew . . . Griff Montell. He said that Griff had mentioned a big gold robbery that had happened during his time on the South African force.

I thought it was bullshit, but I told him he should take the story back to Griff. At the time he was upset about being moved off CID, and I thought that on the off-chance there was anything in it he might see it as a way back in.' He frowned. 'Then I got wrapped up in the Brass investigation, and in the other thing that followed it, and what with Alex being attacked and everything, Coats and his story went right out of my mind until now.'

'Can you remember the details?' the DI asked.

'That's what I'm trying to do, put them together in my head. I didn't make any notes at the time. I was too busy persuading myself not to give him more of a doing for hitting Ignacio. The cabin-crew girlfriend's name was Aisha Karman, he said, and she was one of those laundering the money. She worked on an airline called Wister Air. I remember that because it struck me that I had never heard of it. Yes,' he nodded, 'it's fitting together now. Aisha from Wister Air would make purchases in the store but rather than use cash or card she'd pay in Krugerrands.'

'That was the tale?'

'As much of it as I can remember,' Skinner said.

'Well,' McGuire observed, 'I think we can be fairly certain that if he did go back to Griff, he never took it to CID, otherwise I would have heard about it. And yet they were found dead together.'

'We need to search both their homes,' Haddock said. 'Their phones, their diaries, everything.'

'Agreed. Get on with it.' The DCC turned to Skinner. 'Bob, Griff and his sister lived next door to your Alex, didn't they?'

'That's right; overlooking the Water of Leith. She told me he still lives there.'

'Do you know if he had any female involvement, other than being friendly with Alex?'

'I know he used to have a thing with Alice Cowan, the officer we had to let go, but I haven't heard of anyone since then . . . other than Alex, when the pair of them felt like it.'

'Still.' McGuire frowned. 'Sauce, add Cowan to your interview list. They might have kept in touch.'

'She's on the list already,' the young DI replied, boldly. 'But interviews are the second phase. Before them I need to get SOCOs into Griff's flat, and into Coats' home as well. They're working in Griff's office as we speak. When they're done there, I'll go through his papers myself.'

'Do you know where Coats lived?' Skinner asked.

'No, but I can get that from Noele.'

'I suggest that you try his employer first, rather than troubling her. Coats worked in security at Edinburgh Airport. Anyway, its management is going to want to be told that one of its senior people has been bumped off, rather than reading it in the *Evening News* online. In fact, you might want to do that right now; you'll be putting Arthur Dorward's people in Coats' office too. Before they get there, it needs to be sealed off.'

'You're right, gaffer. We have patrol officers full-time at the airport. I'll tell them to do that and put a guard over the door. That isn't something we can leave to the airport staff. Until we know what Coats was up to, and who else was involved, I suppose they'll all be persons of interest.'

'True,' Skinner agreed, 'but you might find there aren't all that many of them. In effect it's our patrol officers who are the real security people. Have you got a pathologist on site yet?' he asked.

'Yes, she arrived just before I came up here. Her name's

Emily Badger. She's new, which I guess is why she copped the on-call slot on Hogmanay. She brought an assistant; I just hope she's up to it. I wish Sarah could have come.'

'It's as well for you she didn't, without being told what she was walking into, like I wasn't. She knew Griff well and she'd met Terry Coats. That would not have been good and I would not have been pleased,' he shot a sidelong glance at McGuire, who wore a sheepish expression, 'as in very not pleased.'

The chief constable intervened, rapping the desk that once had been hers. 'People,' she exclaimed, 'even as we sit here, this thing is expanding. Sauce, you'll need more personnel than you have, especially with DS McClair not being available to you. Things are quiet in the west just now, so I'm going to take a chance that they don't heat up. I'm going to second Charlotte Mann and Cotter, her DS, to you, with a couple of detective constables as well.'

'Lottie's a DCI, ma'am,' Haddock pointed out.

Steele smiled, faintly. 'In that case you'll need to be very nice to her. As Mr McGuire said earlier on, you will still be the SIO.' She glanced at the DCC. 'Mario, you advise them please, and make sure they understand the chain of command.' She stood. 'Okay, unless anyone has something else they need to ask, let's get on with the job. I'm going home, but I'll be available and I will,' she emphasised the word, 'expect to be updated.'

'Do you want a car home, Bob?' McGuire asked as she closed the door behind her.

'Not yet, Mario, thanks. I'll stick around for a while. When we get into Griff's office another pair of eyes might be helpful. In fact, I'll probably stay here until it's a reasonable time to go and see Alex. But, listen,' he added, 'what are you going to do about the media? Even on the first of January, traffic being diverted away from a large police office won't go unnoticed. Are you going to get Peregrine Allsop here from wherever he fucking nests?'

'Hah! Our Head of Communications is in Australia, would you believe. I called Jane Balfour, our new Edinburgh assistant, as soon as I got word of this. She sounded half cut, even though she was supposed to be on call, so I told her to get her act together and get along here for eight o'clock. Meanwhile all media calls come straight to me. So far there have been none, but you're right, anytime now it has to happen. "Police incident, no threat to life, more details later." That's all I'll say for now.'

'That'll hold them, for a while at least,' Skinner agreed. 'Once you get Ms Balfour in place make sure she knows that I don't exist in the context of this investigation: just in case she sees me around. I don't want my name being leaked to any journo pals.'

He rose. 'We'll leave you to get on with it, Mario, if we may. Sauce, this office has a canteen . . . or it used to. It's probably closed today, but there must be a coffee stock somewhere. I'm in need.'

As he had predicted, no staff were working in the small canteen, but there was a coffee machine. 'Costa,' he muttered. 'Always fucking Costa.' Nevertheless he made himself a latte with two extra shots. Haddock settled for tea. They sat at a table in the empty room.

'You all right, son? You were as white as a sheet when I got here.'

Haddock drew a breath and nodded. 'It was a shock, no question,' he confessed, 'but I'm holding myself together.

I could ask you the same thing. You knew Griff better than I did.'

'I've had thirty years' practice at holding it in, but that,' he jerked his thumb in the general direction of the door, 'that out there, it had me close to losing it.' He glowered at the DI. 'It was bad enough trying to involve Sarah in it, although I can understand it, she's the top pathologist in this part of the country. But calling Noele in to look at the father of her kid with a hole in his fucking head . . . not for repetition, but DCC McGuire and I will be having a further conversation about that.'

'That wasn't him,' Haddock said quietly. 'That order came from the chief constable herself. Big Mario wasn't there at the time. I could hardly question her, gaffer, could I?'

'Are you sure about that? Could she and Mario have spoken about it before?'

'No, or I doubt that it would have happened. I heard them discuss calling you; I was in the commander's office while they closed the street off. He said that he needed you there, and that while he didn't think you would both come, he'd ask if Sarah was available. She said that if there was a choice it should be Sarah, but he overruled her. He said no, that he needed you here. Then he went out; she was quiet for a bit and then she told me to call Noele and get her here. I sort of looked at her for a second, but she just said "Now!" as in "Don't say a word, Haddock." This is nothing really new, gaffer. The whisper is that the DCC is taking all the big decisions at HQ, and that she seems to have lost her self-confidence. I hope that's not true. It was the chief who spotted me when I was a plod, and she was in that office along the way. It was her that helped me develop. I've done better than most folk think I should have, and I know it, but it's thanks to her.'

'Don't sell yourself short, son,' his mentor said. 'You deserve to be where you are. I know they called Sammy Pye "Luke Skywalker" because he was such a high-flyer, but you'd have cruised past him on the runway.' He sighed; realising that he had made a mistake by referring to Pye in the past tense. He glanced at his companion, but he gave no sign of having noticed. 'But Maggie,' he continued, 'ah, that's not so good. You're telling me it's just a whisper, but before you know it whispers can turn into shouts.' He paused. 'Mind you, those can often be unfounded too. It might just appear that way; we both know what a forceful character Mario McGuire is.'

'Yes, but he also hears everything,' the DI countered. 'If he knew that sort of talk was in the air and there was nothing in it, he'd have squashed it.'

'True,' Skinner conceded.

'Can you do anything about it?'

'Me? I'm not the chair of the Scottish Police Authority, Sauce.'

'No, but you made her, just as she's made me. You could talk to her.'

'I could, but . . .' He finished his coffee, then returned to the machine and made another. 'This might bear out a theory of mine, Sauce,' he said as he resumed his seat. 'I suspect that the chief's job is so big now that each holder has a shelf life. Even before unification, I think that was true. I was chief in Edinburgh, and then in Strathclyde, even if it was only to shut up the shop and hand over to the national force. One of the reasons why I didn't apply to be its chief constable, apart from disagreeing profoundly with it, as I still do, was that I felt my time was up. I wasn't afraid of it; I looked at the terms, at the length of contract, and I doubted that I had it in me to see it out. Look at what happened to Andy Martin. He was gone inside two years, leaving behind him a trail of enemies who'd once been friends . . . including me, but that had fuck all to do with the job. Maggie's been in post for not much longer. Okay, she hasn't been abrasive, as Sir Andrew was, but she may have gone too far in the other direction. She's always been reserved; her upbringing may have something to do with that, but we do not go there. She's a brilliant police officer and she was the outstanding candidate when the job came up, but it may be that the inevitable limelight's been too much for her. I know for a fact that she turned down the damehood that was offered after she was appointed. On top of all that, she's a widowed mother, who lost her husband and survived cancer while she was carrying her child.' He looked the younger man in the eye. 'You said that I could talk to her. If I did that it might be to persuade her that there would be no shame in resigning and going home to look after wee Stephanie. How would you feel about that?'

Haddock was silent for a few seconds, considering the question. When he replied, he was hesitant. 'Selfishly?' he began. 'It would depend on who took over. It would have to be advertised nationally, and I don't know that I trust the Authority to get it right; I wouldn't like to see somebody parachuted in from England who's never walked a beat north of the border in his life. The DCC? Absolutely. ACC Mackie? Okay.' He glanced at Skinner. 'You, if you applied for it? No reason why not. You're still years short of retirement age.'

His mentor laughed, quietly. 'You can forget that one. I would still have a very short shelf life, plus I've gone in another direction. I have commitments elsewhere with InterMedia, for which incidentally I get paid a serious amount of money, twice the chief constable's salary for a part-time job.' He winked. 'Oh yes, I have an avaricious side. No,' he continued, 'not me. You're right, there would be a danger of the wrong appointment being made, but . . . while I'm not a member of the Police Authority, I do know the chair, and quite a few of the members, and I've got some influence I think. I'm fairly confident that an in-house appointment would be made. Mario is the outstanding home candidate, no question. Brian Mackie? No. Brian's an excellent manager, excellent senior officer, but he's not a leader, not a general. But let me throw another name at you. Neil McIlhenney.'

'I don't know him. That said I know of him; anyone who's moved to the Met from here and has done as well as he has, yes, he has to be in the game. But would he want it? Isn't he a . . . ?'

'Deputy Assistant Commissioner? Yes. Will he go all the way? No. Louise, his wife, has given up stage acting, so he's not constrained by her career. I doubt that he'd go against his best mate, but if Mario didn't want it, you never know.'

'Will you talk to the chief?' Haddock asked.

'I'll have to think that through,' Skinner declared, killing his second coffee and blinking as the caffeine hit. 'Meantime, let's see if you and I can get into Griff's office yet.'

Four

Ignacio Watson Skinner stood in the doorway of the garden room, looking at his stepmother in surprise. He was slightly drunk, but less so than Pilar who clung to his arm as her world swam around her. Sarah was on the sofa, peering at her iPad. An empty goblet, a Corona bottle with a sad piece of lime at the bottom, and a mug with the word '*Profesora*' emblazoned around it, one of his Christmas gifts, were on a small table beside her.

'Is it that late?' he slurred. She looked round, startled, as he spoke. 'Have you been to bed and up already? Has Dad crashed?'

'No to both of those,' she replied. 'I haven't been to bed yet, I was going but I had a New Year message from the international medical examiners' body. It's a bit of a downer, about the new virus that's been identified out in China. It sobered me up; if it's even half true, we could be in for a very nasty year.'

'Where?'

'Everywhere.' She smiled and checked her watch. 'When I was your age, I'd still have been going at New Year's. Come to think of it I suppose I still am.' She checked the goblet; it was empty. 'No, maybe not.'

'If Dad is not upstairs,' Ignacio began, 'where is he?'

'He was called out, by the police. A car came for him and took him up to Edinburgh. I don't know why, but I do know there's a body involved, because they asked for me too.'

'Ohhh,' Pilar murmured. 'Nacho.' Her olive complexion had turned significantly pale.

Sarah recognised impending disaster. She rushed across, peeled the young woman from Ignacio's arm, and half-carried her into the cloakroom toilet. He looked on as the door closed, a soft grin on his face.

He was still smiling when his ringtone sounded. He checked the screen before answering. 'Mum,' he said, 'we spoke already. Are you drunk too?'

'I don't drink anymore,' Mia Watson replied. 'Ignacio, have you heard from your stepfather in the last hour?'

'From Cameron? No, why should I? I spoke to him with you, at midnight. What is wrong?'

'He's vanished,' she exclaimed her voice rising. 'Gone. Disappeared. We were at the Hogmanay celebrations in the hotel. I left around quarter to one; my ears were starting to hurt it was so loud. He said he was going to have a cigar in the garden, then follow me back to the house. When he hadn't shown up an hour and a half later, I went back there to dig him out; the thing was over by that time and all the guests had gone to their rooms or been taken home by the courtesy bus. I couldn't find him, Ignacio; he wasn't there. I sent all the staff out to look for him in the grounds, in case he'd been taken ill, but nobody could find him.'

'Did you call the courtesy-bus driver?' her son suggested. 'Maybe he went on it, to make sure everyone got home. It's the kind of thing Cameron would do.'

'The bus is back. He was never on it.'

'Is his car still there?'

'Yes, both of them. Ignacio, there isn't a trace of him. It's as if he's been abducted by aliens.'

Five

'He was neat,' Haddock observed.

'You haven't spent enough time in uniform,' his companion told him. He had donned another sterile suit, after the DI had asked the crime scene officers to take a break to give them access. 'Neatness is obligatory, with the station commander on the prowl all the time. Unlike your average CID office, which is a fucking shambles.'

'Maybe in your day . . .'

Skinner beamed. 'My day . . . Jeez, slide the Zimmer over will you. Listen, if a CID office is spotless, it means everybody has time to keep it that way and that means you're not doing the job properly. What are we looking for here?' he asked, moving on.

'Anything that links Griff and Coats.'

'I doubt that would be in plain sight.' He looked at the immaculate single-pedestal desk. The only paper on it was a printout of the station's duty rota over the Christmas period. He leaned over and tugged the smaller of the two drawers; it slid open easily, revealing nothing more than a box of tea bags, three pens, a comb, a pair of nail scissors, tweezers, a pack of Kleenex tissues, a tin box which claimed to contain

42

a multipurpose credit-card-sized tool, and a spectacle case bearing the RayBan logo. He opened it and found a pair of glasses; he took them out and held them up. 'I never knew he needed these,' he murmured.

'Reading glasses,' Haddock said. 'He didn't like to be seen wearing them. I called in here one day unannounced. He whipped them off sharpish.'

Skinner examined them, weighing them in his hand. 'He still shelled out for lightweight designer frames though. You won't get much change out of four hundred quid for these. I know this because I looked at them or something similar last year and wound up going for a cheaper option. How old was Griff? I can't remember.'

'Thirty-nine.'

'My reading glasses came with my forty-ninth birthday, when I realised that my arms weren't long enough anymore.' He moved across to a tall metal locker at the back of the room; it was locked, but he took the tweezers from the desk and had it open in less than five seconds.

The DI whistled. 'How often have you done that?'

'Not a lot since I was at your rank. If you don't have that skill, acquire it; you'll save a hell of a lot of time trying to find keys.'

He looked into the locker. It contained two uniforms on hangers, trousers and tunics, one of which bore the epaulettes of an inspector, square silver pips. Alongside them were a casual jacket and a pair of jeans, hung upside down, weight to the bottom. He took them out and examined them.

'Hugo Boss,' he murmured reading the jacket label. 'And going by the logo, these jeans are Armani. I bought a pair of those in Girona; a hundred and seventy euros. Maybe I'm out of touch; an inspector's on just over fifty grand these days, but . . .'

'Griff was single,' Haddock pointed out.

'So are you. Okay, you live with Cheeky, but she's an accountant, a good earner, and I don't see you wearing gear like this. Marks and Spencer, as I recall, last time I saw you without sterile clothing. And you don't have a couple of kids to support, as Griff has in South Africa.'

He replaced the clothing and peered into the locker once again, looking at a shelf above the rail. 'What's here?' He removed several items. 'Photo album.' He flipped it open. 'His kids. Paracetamol. Deodorant. Condoms. Johnnies in a police-office locker?' he exclaimed. 'Was he banging somebody in this building? Better find out, Sauce, as discreetly as you can. And . . . what the . . .' He paused and held up a cardboard square. 'A pay-as-you-go SIM card,' he murmured, curious. 'What the fuck would a uniformed police inspector be doing, Sauce, with this in his private locker?'

The DI exhaled, loudly. 'I don't know, gaffer, but I need to find out. How do you get a warrant on New Year's Day to access somebody's bank account?'

'You waken a sheriff and get him to sign it; or her. Then you hope they don't hold it against you in the future. Justice never sleeps, chum; it never sleeps.'

Six

Skinner checked his watch as he stepped from the police car into the drizzle, outside the block that held Dominic Jackson's duplex home. It showed eight fifty-two. Deeming that to be a reasonable hour to call his wife, he dug his phone, awkwardly, from his padded raincoat and pressed 'Home' on his favourites list.

It was James Andrew Skinner who answered the call, not his mother. 'She's still asleep, Dad,' he said. 'Where are you?' The boy sounded puzzled by his absence. There was no one awake to tell him about his departure, Skinner guessed.

'I had to go out on business,' he explained. 'I'm just about to go to Alex's. What are you doing for breakfast?'

'I've done it,' his son replied. 'Mark and I had cereal and French toast. I had to make it, as usual. He's bloody useless.'

'Language, Jazz.'

'Sorry, Dad, but he is, you know that. The last time he tried to make toast he set off the smoke alarm.'

'You have a point,' he conceded. 'Did you feed the girls too?'

'Of course, although Dawn had porridge, not cereal, and juice. Seonaid cleaned up after her.'

'Good for her. If you want to score some Brownie points you might make your mum some French toast too. And coffee.'

'Why would I want Brownie points, Dad? I'm a Scout.'

'You know what I mean, smartarse.'

'Language, Dad,' James Andrew retorted. 'I'll do it, but I'll get Seonaid to check whether she's awake.'

Skinner smiled as he re-pocketed the mobile, but it left his face quickly as he pressed the videocall button labelled 'Jackson, Consultant psychologist'.

Another male voice answered, but deeper and darker. 'Bob? What's up?'

'I need to see Alex. I'll explain when I get up there.'

'I'm not sure she's awake,' Jackson said. 'Come on in and I'll give her a shout.'

The lift took him to the top floor quickly; it was littered with festive detritus, relics of the city's famous and notoriously commercialised Hogmanay celebrations. The door to the duplex penthouse was open as he stepped out, his host waiting within.

'Coffee, I guess?'

'God yes, Dominic. Please.'

'Anything else?'

'No thanks. I won't be hungry for a while.'

'So what's up?' Jackson asked again. 'Something big. I can see it in your eyes. You've got the thousand-yards stare.'

Skinner sighed. 'I'm sure I have. I'd be worried if I didn't.'

'What's the matter, Pops?' his daughter asked, from behind. 'Have you and Sarah had a barney?'

He turned. She was wrapped in a thick dressing gown over cotton pyjamas and wearing white slippers which bore the logo of a Barcelona hotel. As she saw his face, her expression changed, and her mood.

'What is it?' she asked anxiously. 'Is it one of the kids? Is it Aunt Jean? That's your death look,' she said. 'I know it.'

'No family, love, no family,' he replied, softly. 'It's Griff Montell. He was dumped outside the Torphichen Place police station just after midnight, in a car with another man. They'd both been shot in the head.'

In an instant, she went ghostly white; her hands flew to her mouth, pressing inwards, hard. 'No!' It was a muffled hiss. She turned to Jackson, then paused, turning back to her father. Then she stopped, as if unable to choose between them, spun round and half-ran across to the doors that opened on to the deck. She jerked them apart and stepped outside, oblivious to the rain as it grew heavier.

Skinner followed and put his arms around her, drawing her gently back inside. She buried her face in his chest as, for one of very few times in her adult life, she let others see her cry.

'Surely not,' she whispered, when she had regained her self-control.

'I'm afraid so, love.'

'Why?'

'That's always the first question.'

'A serving police officer?'

'I know.'

She looked up at him red-eyed and angry. 'I think I'll accept that offer to go to the Crown Office,' she murmured. 'I want to prosecute the people who did this.'

'The Lord Advocate who'd let you do that hasn't been born yet, Alexis.'

'I'll put coffee on,' Jackson said. He looked as shocked as his housemate.

'Thanks,' Skinner said, 'and maybe a shot of brandy in Alex's if you've got any. Sod the hour.'

'Why are you involved, Pops?' she asked, as he sat her in an armchair. 'Did they send you to break the news?'

'No, that was my choice. Mario called me in; I've been there ever since. Sauce is the SIO, and I've been asked to lurk in the background.'

'Is Sauce going to want to talk to me?'

'I'll do that for the moment,' he replied, 'although he probably will later. We needn't do it now though, if you don't feel ready.'

'No, make it now,' she insisted, 'while my blood's up.'

'Okay, if that's what you want. You should gather yourself together.'

'Yes. I'll throw some clothes on.'

She left him, returning a few minutes later, wearing black, polo neck and trousers. A *subconscious choice?* he wondered.

At the same time Jackson arrived with coffee on a tray, three mugs. He separated one and handed it to Alex. She sipped it and nodded.

'Do you want me to leave you to it?' he asked.

'Hell, no,' she declared. 'I need you here.'

Her father took a slug from his own mug, nodding approval. 'Thanks, Dominic. I like Colombian. When did you last see Griff?' he asked his daughter, continuing without a pause.

'Two weeks ago,' she answered briskly, back in control. 'We met for a pre-Christmas drink at the Dome.'

'How did he seem? What was his mood?'

'It was a bit mixed. He was bright and brash, but not quite full on. A shade distracted. Eventually I asked him what was

48

up. He said, "Ah, nothing really. Fucking uniform; I find it constraining." His exact words.'

'Was that all he said about it?'

'No. I told him he should ask to be reassigned, but that made him turn quite morose. He said there were no vacancies for detective inspectors, not where he wanted them. "Sure, if I wanted to go to Inverness," he said, "I might get back in there, but I don't really fancy investigating sheep rustling in the Orkneys." Then he was quiet for a while. I said, "Come on, what else is bugging you? Out with it." It all came out after that. First he said that his face didn't fit with Mario, or with you . . .'

'Me?' Skinner exclaimed. 'What the hell have I got to do with it?'

'He thought you still pulled Mario's strings, that he was your puppet. "Super-Mario-nette," he called him. And he reckoned that you had a down on him because of me, and the relationship that we had.'

'Well, he was wrong, wasn't he?' he said. 'You're a big girl, you're in the same situation I was when I was your age, single, not really looking for a permanent relationship, but not dead from the waist down either. You and Griff, you were like me and . . . well, Allison Higgins to name one. Didn't you tell him that?'

'As a matter of fact, I did, but he said that no father has the same rules for his daughter that he had for himself. Griff's got, had, a daughter, remember. He thought he was on your shit list. Latterly, Griff thought he was on everybody's shit list.'

'Even after he saved your life when those guys broke into your flat? He still thought I had marked his card?'

Alex nodded. 'Even after,' she confirmed. 'But that wasn't

the only reason why he thought his CID career was over. He said that everything seemed to be moving very fast as the new national police service bedded in. A few people were zooming up the ladder, and all the senior posts were gradually being filled by people who'd be in them for years. He named a few; Lowell Payne, who was a sergeant not so long ago and now runs counter-terrorism in Scotland, Lottie Mann . . . he said she'll be a detective superintendent before her DCI badges have lost their shine . . . Sammy Pye, Sauce Haddock, who he said is being fast-tracked to succeed Mario eventually, and even Noele McClair, Sauce's DS. Then he talked about his time in South Africa, before he relocated; that's something he did very rarely. He said it was different there, that things were much more set, that, okay, corners were cut but that criminal investigation was a settled community . . . one big happy family, he said, even if a bit of interbreeding went on.'

'That sounds pretty racist for Griff,' Skinner said, 'hell, it sounds racist for anybody.'

'No, I don't think he meant it that way; I didn't see it in that way, not at the time and not now. He meant something different, I'm sure, but I don't know what.'

'He probably meant that the in-crowd looked after each other,' her father murmured. 'Maybe I used to do that too,' he admitted. 'That night, did he mention Terry Coats?'

'Who's Terry Coats?' she asked, puzzled.

'Noele McClair's ex.'

'Was he the guy who turned up at your house and punched my brother?' Alex asked. 'I never knew his name; Ignacio told me about it, but he never said who it was, just that it was somebody with a beef against you. I asked him if you barbecued it, and he said that you did, more or less. And no, Griff never mentioned him either. Why should he?' Her mouth fell open, for a second. 'Ahh . . .' she whispered then fell silent. 'I can think of a reason, of sorts. To get Griff out of his mood, I suggested that he get hammered. He wasn't completely averse to that proposition, so he had a few expensive cocktails.'

'Did he splash the cash often, or were you paying?'

'We split it. Griff wasn't tight in any way, he offered, of course, but I always insisted we go Dutch. Anyway, he had a few more than usual, but he had hollow legs so he wasn't falling over or anything like that. I had a couple too, and I got . . . cool, let's say.' She glanced at the floor, momentarily. 'We hadn't been together since the night of the attack. No particular reason on my part, but we just hadn't. Anyway, I suggested that we might go back to his place, to round off the night and maybe extend it into next morning.' She paused. 'Dominic and I have an agreement that I don't bring men back here.' She looked at Jackson.

'That's right, Bob,' he confirmed. 'Alex proposed that from the off, and I agreed that it might be best, for a few reasons.'

'It doesn't cut both ways,' she added, 'but the only woman who's ever come here since I moved in has been the cleaner.'

'Not even as clients?' Skinner asked. 'You consult here; it even says so at the door.'

'No way; if I had a proper office and a female receptionist, yes, I'd have female clients here, but I don't so it wouldn't be wise.'

'I get it. Carry on, Alex. He never mentioned Terry Coats, but he did mention Noele on his list of promotion rivals.'

'Yes. He'd mentioned her before, as someone he knew through the job and then again that night, when he was sounding off. But the funny thing was, or it struck me as funny eventually, was that when he listed her, he just called her "Noele", didn't use her surname.'

'What made it funny?'

'I'll get there, Pops. When I suggested that we go back to his place, he was embarrassed. I'd never seen that from him before, never, so it took me by surprise. Then he said, "No, Alex, better not, it wouldn't be right." I jumped straight to the conclusion that he thought that Dominic and I . . .' She let the sentence tail away unfinished. 'I told him that he'd the wrong idea about us. But he said "No, I haven't, it's more from my point of view." He looked sort of coy and finally I caught on. "You've got somebody else," I said, and he nodded, and said, "Yes, I have. Are you upset?" Of course I said no, that I wasn't and I meant it. And then, half-pissed or not, the Skinner brain clicked into gear, and I thought back to what he'd said earlier and I said out loud . . . although I don't think I meant to . . . "It's Noele, isn't it? Noele McClair." He just smiled and nodded.' She frowned, as she replayed their conversation. 'Is that why you asked me about Terry Coats? Did you know that Griff was sleeping with his ex-wife?'

He stared at her in silence, more surprised than he had been in longer than his memory stretched. 'No,' he told her, 'I hadn't a clue. I asked you about Coats because he was the other man found dead with Griff in that car. And what I am thinking now is that I am so fucking glad I didn't let Noele look inside!'

Seven

'This lock is Fort Knox, pal,' the locksmith said. 'I know; I fitted it. In fact, I fitted the whole security system.'

'He had a security system?' DI Haddock exclaimed. 'I thought the building was secure.'

'It is, but only at the door on the street through the video entry system. Mr Montell had his own. That CCTV camera to the side of the front door, that's his.' He pointed to a corner of the corridor in which they stood. 'So's that one. There's cameras inside too, all monitored through the Cloud. The alarm's state of the art; it's got sensors on this door and all the windows; serviced every year. This front door's new too. Some of them in this building you can practically push open. No' this one. The frame's bolted into the wall so it can't be jemmied out. This lock,' he said, as he opened it, 'they call it a Doormaster. It's as good as you'll get. Between you two and me, I did the security locks on the chief constable's house. This set-up's better than hers. Voila,' he boomed as he opened the door. 'Wait a minute, one more thing to do.' He stepped into the hall and punched a code into a panel set on the wall. 'There you are, it's disarmed; Mr Montell can do that remotely, arm and disarm.' The locksmith smiled as the DI and his colleague followed him inside. 'I don't suppose you're gonnae tell me what he does, this guy, for you to get a warrant on the first of January to search his house. Drugs? Arms dealer? Jeweller?'

'You're right, Mr Francis,' the DI agreed. 'I'm not going to tell you. Now, I'd like you to step outside and wait in the hall, in case we need you again.'

'Oh, you will, trust me. I'll be here. The main room's straight ahead.'

The two detectives slipped on paper overshoes and gloves, then followed his direction into the apartment's spacious reception area.

The Water of Leith meandered under the window, making its way towards the port from which it took its name. Its level was high after the heavy rainfall of the previous days, but it was still well short of being a torrent. Broken twigs, vegetation and the inevitable single-use plastic were carried by on its surface, drawing a grunt of disapproval from Detective Sergeant Tarvil Singh.

'Folk that do that should be in fucking jail,' he growled.

'What?' Haddock asked.

'Chucking milk bottles in the Water of Leith.'

The DI smiled at his righteous indignation. 'The prisons wouldn't be big enough.'

'Maybe we could reintroduce transportation to Australia. There must be enough space, going by the number of Aussies working in pubs around here.'

'Come away from the window, Tarvil,' Haddock said. 'You're like an eclipse of the sun standing there.'

The massive Sikh obeyed. 'What are we looking for here, Sauce?' he asked.

'When we find it, we'll know. Anything that will connect

Griff and Terry Coats. Anything that will tell us where they might have been last night when they were killed. We've been through Griff's work diary, and through his whole office computer. There was nothing on it that wasn't police business.'

'Last night?' Singh repeated. 'How do we know for sure when they were killed?'

'Emily Badger, the pathologist, was confident that they died not long before the bodies were dumped. They were still warm and there was no sign of rigor when she examined them. So far, the forensic team haven't found anything that gives us a clue to where they were shot, but it's early days for them. One question I need to answer is, why was Griff here at all? He was signed off on leave from last Friday night until a week on Monday, and he told Sally McGlashan, the South East area commander, that he was going to South Africa to visit his sister and Mary Chambers, and to catch up with his kids.'

'But did he say when?'

'Yes. He told her he'd a flight booked on Saturday night.'

'It's Wednesday now. Could he have been there and back?'

'In theory yes, but would you go to the southern hemisphere at the end of December for just a couple of days? Jackie Wright's in the office already; I've asked her to check whether he actually had a flight booked. I've decided to run the inquiry out of Fettes rather than Torphichen Place. It's logical; that's our base and we've got more facilities there.' He paused, looking around the room, frowning. 'Wait a minute,' he said softly. 'It's cold in here, Tarvil, isn't it? I've still got my coat on but it's freezing.'

'Now you mention it . . .' the DS agreed.

Haddock stepped back into the hallway, where he had noticed a thermostat. 'This is set to ten centigrade,' he called out. 'It's a holiday setting, just to make sure nothing freezes. That's consistent with what he told Chief Inspector McGlashan. And yet he was still in Edinburgh. How come?' He re-joined Singh. 'Another mystery, but let's get started, see what this place tells us.'

Together they opened each drawer and cupboard in the living area, emptying each one out. They found nothing but table linen, place mats and crockery, everything in order, everything arranged logically. Similarly, the drinks cabinet contained nothing more than a range of liqueurs and glasses, and a cocktail shaker.

'Kitchen?' the DS suggested. 'You can read the book of my life in mine. Everything gets stuck in a clip behind the door.'

Haddock grinned and nodded. 'With us, it's a jar. Let's have a look, but this room's just like his office, im-fucking-peccable. If that's the same . . .'

The kitchen was a galley shape. The sink was below the window, which also overlooked the river; there was a combined washer dryer and a dishwasher plumbed in beneath. The wall above the work surface was fitted with cupboards for the length of the space until they reached a large fridge freezer. Above a chopping block, next to the hobs, an array of knives hung on a magnetic strip. But there was no clip behind the door, no credit card receipts in a jar, no visible evidence of occupation.

'This could be a show flat,' Singh observed, contradicting himself as he opened the fridge to find butter, cheese, an unopened carton of orange juice, half a dozen bottles of Peroni, and on a rack, a bottle of Prosecco and two of a white wine with a distinctive label. 'No milk,' he said.

'Let's see those.' Haddock stepped alongside him and took

one of the wine bottles from the rack. He examined the label. 'Chateau Vartely,' he murmured.

'Aye?'

'Moldovan, Tarvil. It's unusual; I only recognise it because somebody gave me a bottle for Christmas. It was at the Fettes party. I took it home and stuck it under the tree, but the label fell off, so I don't know who it was from.'

They searched the cupboards one by one, finding nothing other than tinned and packaged food, more crockery and utensils. They were about to move on when Haddock glanced at the washer dryer. 'He's forgotten to empty it,' he said, pulling the door open and removing the contents, in a bundle. He selected an item and held it up. 'Tommy Hilfiger shirt.' He tossed it back in the pile and chose another. 'Armani boxers. Wouldn't you . . . Eh?' He spotted two other garments and held them up, peering at the labels. 'Frilly knickers, black. One matching bra, thirty-eight C cup. I doubt that these were Griff's.'

'No, wrong size,' Singh growled.

'That and they're Marks and Spencer.'

'Do you reckon they're Alex Skinner's?'

The DI gazed at him, unsmiling. 'It won't be me that asks her,' he said. 'Come on, let's look in the bedrooms.'

They returned to the hall, where they saw four doors. Closest to the entrance was a cupboard that contained the heating boiler and other standard items, including an iron and board and a Dyson vacuum cleaner. *Top of the range,* Haddock noted mentally. They moved on to the bathroom, finding nothing in it other than two towels on a rail and soap in a dispenser.

The third door was secured by a circular Yale lock. 'I'll get Mr Francis back in,' the DS said.

'Let's check the bedroom first. I guess it must be Griff's.'

It was an en-suite, again with a river view. The wardrobes were fitted to make the most of limited space, and the bed was king size. It had a printed duvet, avoiding the need for a cover; its pattern was a version of the South African flag. Singh opened a pair of double wardrobe doors, looked in, and began to examine the contents. It contained ten shirts by Pink on hangers, four suits, two of them with the labels of a private tailor, three casual jackets, one of them in supple tan leather, four pairs of trousers, hung upside down, a white tuxedo and a heavy winter overcoat. Two further hangers and a trouser clip were unused, side by side on the rail. Beyond them were a pair of denims, ladies' size, and a grey midi dress.

'Our man Griff had a fair clothing budget.'

'That bears out what we found in his office locker,' Haddock confirmed. He took the denims from the rail and held them up. 'M and S again. You can forget them being Alex's. They're too short; she's at least five nine. We have to go over everything again, Tarvil. We need to find this woman, whoever she is.'

'Is there a bar code on those jeans? On the label?'

'Good call,' Haddock muttered, examining the garment. He found what he was looking for beneath the washing instructions, took a photograph and sent it to DC Jackie Wright, with a message. 'Check if we can establish from this where this garment was sold. If possible, see if we can link it to a card payment. I need to know the buyer; it'll be a woman.'

The next wardrobe contained open shelves, stacked with socks, boxers, neatly folded casual shirts, and a few female undergarments including nylon tights, still in their wrapping. 'She wasn't a live-in, whoever his woman was,' the DI murmured. 'Does the bathroom tell us anything?' he called out to Singh, who had moved into the en-suite.

'It tells us what the empty hangers in the wardrobe do,' the sergeant boomed, 'that he had left for a trip. There's no shaving gear, or deodorant, or aftershave. However,' he continued, lowering his voice as he re-joined his colleague, 'there's these.' He held up, between his gloved fingers, a pink toothbrush and a small black cylinder. 'There's no toothpaste, so I'm assuming that Griff took it, and his own toothbrush, and that this is hers. As is the lipstick. We might get prints off them.'

'We'll get prints off the whole fucking flat,' Haddock pointed out, 'and if she's on file we'll trace her, but good thinking nonetheless.'

'Not just a pretty face.'

'Not even. Let's check the last room.'

They summoned the locksmith; he was smiling. 'I told you that you'd need me again.'

'Can you get in?' the DI asked.

'It's my job,' he replied. 'If my customers lose their keys, and it happens, they come to me for replacements. You cannae just walk into a shop and have one done. This looks like any other Yale but it's not.' He stepped up to the door, selected a key from a ring and opened it. 'This is his office,' he announced.

The room was smaller than the others. The window had a Venetian blind but the slats were open far enough for them to see that it faced downriver, rather than overlooking it. There was a wall-mounted TV, a small sofa, and a Cyrus music system that Singh, an enthusiast, knew must have cost at least two thousand pounds, but the space was dominated by a fitted workstation, with the same facing as the bedroom units, that housed a twenty-seven-inch iMac.

Haddock touched the computer. 'We need to get into that.' He glanced at Mr Francis. 'I don't suppose you've got his password as well?'

'Naw, you're on your own there,' he paused, 'but you'll need to get into this too.' He stepped past the detectives and opened a door in the workstation, revealing a safe. 'I don't have the combination for this boy either . . . but you can get in with a key in an emergency, if you know where to find the keyhole.'

He knelt, awkwardly, because he was a bulky man, sorted through his keyring once again, then rolled the maker's name upwards, revealing a slot. 'You find the odd idiot who'll burn out a dozen drill bits trying to get into one of those things,' there was a click and the safe swung open, 'but this is all you have to do.' He pushed himself to his feet. 'I'll leave you to it again. Is that me done?' he asked.

'Yes,' the DI said, 'if you leave us the keys you used.'

'Mmm.' Doubt showed on his face. 'I don't know about that. Mr Montell won't be very pleased when he comes back. Does your warrant mean that I have to?'

'No, it doesn't, but that's irrelevant. Mr Montell won't be coming back, Mr Francis, because he's dead, but not a word of that outside this building, and not a word about what went on here. Understood?'

The locksmith nodded. 'Aye, no worries. I value the work I get from the police. Okay, you can have the keys.'

'That's good. Just one more thing before you go. When did you fit all this stuff?'

'Two years ago; this was a bedroom before. Gimme time and I can give you the date that I done it.'

'It must have cost a bit.'

'Oh yes.' He grinned. 'A fair few grand, with all the bits and installation. I shouldnae tell you this, ken, but I gave him a discount for cash. I'd still love to know what he did, but I don't suppose you're goin' tae tell me.'

'I can't do that, but thanks for your help. Enjoy the rest of your day.'

Mr Francis unwound three keys from his selection and left, closing the front door behind him.

As soon as he was gone, Haddock dropped to his knees in front of the safe and looked inside. It contained a thick brown envelope, a plastic food container, and on a shelf near the top, two watch boxes and a cloth bundle, all of which he removed. Branding on the boxes showed that one was a Rolex and the other a Breitling. The former was empty, but the latter contained a steel and gold timepiece with a jewel-encircled black face that weighed heavily in the DI's hand as he examined it. 'Breitling Galactic,' he read, from a booklet in the box. 'Not much change out of ten thousand for that, if any, I'll bet.'

Singh bent, picked up the bundle, and unwrapped it. 'Holy Moses,' he murmured. 'What the fuck is going on, Sauce?' The pistol looked small in his huge hand, but deadly nonetheless. 'This is a Beretta, fifteen-shot magazine, one of the most popular handguns in the world and one of the best. I know that because I did a firearms course a few years back, and this is what we used. What is a uniformed police officer in the West End doing with one of these?'

'Or this lot.'

The DI looked up at the sergeant from his kneeling position. Before him lay the brown envelope, ripped open to reveal two thick stacks of banknotes, and the food container, its lid removed, displaying stacks of coins, each one around an inch in diameter.

'What are those?' Singh asked.

'These are Krugerrands,' Haddock replied.

'Are they chocolate?'

'Not from the weight of the box; no, these are the real thing. Each one of these is worth around a thousand quid, maybe a shade more.' He sighed. 'You know, I was hoping that we'd be able to lock up here and go home to catch up on some of the sleep we've missed. No such fucking luck. I have to get the DCC down here, and somebody else too, somebody who's going to be kicking himself when he sees these.'

Eight

'Yes?'

The woman who opened the door had to be in her sixties, Skinner guessed, but she could have been his own age from the smoothness of her complexion. However, there was no doubting her hostility as she frowned at him, a frown that turned into a glare as she saw the police car in the courtyard of the converted steading.

'It's all right, Gran,' a much younger voice called out from behind her. 'It's my friend Seonaid's dad, Mr Skinner.'

'Ah.' Noele McClair's mother's posture eased, but only a little. 'Come in,' she said, grudgingly. 'Harry,' she called out to her grandson, 'back to the kitchen. You're not getting off with peeling the potatoes.'

He tried to place her accent; it was Glaswegian, but refined, Kelvinside, or possibly even more up market, Bearsden.

'Is Noele . . . ?' he ventured.

'She's in the living room. I told her to go to bed but she said she couldn't.'

'Has she told you why she was called out?'

Lines of pain appeared around Mrs McClair's eyes. 'Yes, she has. Harry doesn't know yet, so be careful. I'm fair blazing mad that my daughter was put through that; I hope you had nothing to do with it, or that young Haddock.'

'I didn't,' he assured her, 'and Sauce wasn't in a position to prevent it. For what it's worth I agree with you. It was a misjudgement by senior officers, albeit in a very stressful situation.'

'I hope you told them,' she said, firmly.

'I did, make no mistake. Not that I have any influence any longer.'

'That's not what I've heard.' She opened a door at the end of the hall. 'Dear, Mr Skinner's here. I think he just wants to make sure you're all right.'

'More than that,' he whispered. 'I think she's going to need you again after I've gone.' He moved past her quickly, into the living room.

Noele McClair stood as he entered, out of courtesy rather than deference. He waved a hand, signalling her to sit down again and joined her, taking an armchair beside a floor-to-ceiling picture window. 'How are you doing?' he asked. 'Has it sunk in yet?'

'I don't really think so,' she sighed. 'Maybe it will after I've done the formal identification. We'll see. At the moment my main worry is how to tell Harry. He worships his father. He's only seven, Bob, it'll crush him.'

'It won't. My Alex went through the same thing, and she came out all right. You'll need to keep him close for a while, now and when the people who killed Terry are brought to court. If Sarah and I can help in any way, you only have to ask, no notice required.'

She smiled at him, her eyes filled with tears. 'Look at me,' she croaked, with a strange stifled laugh. 'I'd washed my hands of the bugger. We were divorced, and I was over him.

Or I thought I was; now here I am unable to stop crying.'

For a second or two, he found himself wanting to get out of there, to leave her with her grief without piling on even more. But he was held in place by the thought of how she would react if she heard the further news through the media, or even in casual conversation with a CID colleague.

'You don't have to do the formal identification,' he pointed out. 'You're not his next of kin any longer; Harry is, although obviously he's too young. Are Terry's parents still alive? Does he have siblings?'

'His dad died when he was young. His mother remarried and moved to Norway. I have no idea how to contact her. There's a sister though, Beatrix. She lives in Paisley. But she's flaky. She's bipolar and on medication. I don't think she'd be up to doing that. No, Bob. I'll do it. She doesn't have support, but I do, of a kind. I haven't mentioned this to anyone, anyone at all, not even my mum, but I'm in a relationship.'

'I know,' Skinner said softly.

She blinked the tears away and stared at him. 'You do? How would you?'

'My daughter told me.'

'Seonaid? But she could only have heard from Harry, and I haven't let anything slip to him because I'm not sure how he'll take it.'

'You misunderstand me. My oldest daughter: Alex. She had a drink with Griff Montell just before Christmas; he let it slip then. I'm sure he didn't mean to, but Alex is a defence advocate, and she's very good at cross-examination.'

He felt the moment approaching. He was full of trepidation, unsure how to go on, until finally his expression betrayed him.

'There's something else, isn't there,' she said. 'Something I don't know. Something that made you come here rather than phoning me.'

Still he prevaricated. 'Did Terry know about Griff?' he asked her. 'Did you tell him?'

'Hell no!' she exclaimed. 'Why would I do that? He never told me when he was shagging that air hostess. He was out of my life. Look, Bob, between you and me, the first thing I did when the divorce went through was join an online dating site and get it all out of my system. Not for long though; having sex with strangers isn't my thing. Griff's different, though. He's nice, he's funny and I like him. So must you; after all he protected Alex from those intruders, and got himself cut in the process.'

'Yes, he did.'

'I wish he was here now,' she sighed, 'but he's gone to South Africa for a couple of weeks, to visit his sister, and his kids.'

'No.'

She stared at him, finally clear-eyed.

'What do you mean, no? He left at the weekend.'

Skinner stood abruptly. He walked out of the living room, and through to the kitchen. 'Mrs McClair,' he said, 'I need you through here. But not Harry.'

She followed him without a word. When they returned Noele was on her feet. 'Bob, what's up? Why are you really here? And why are you asking about Griff? Are you going to tell me he shot Terry?'

'Please,' he said, 'sit down again. Noele, I'm here because there were two bodies in the car you saw this morning.' He faltered for a second or two, as his own emotions threatened to overcome him, but he carried on, albeit with a slight tremble in his voice. 'The other one was that of Griff Montell.'

For a second or two Noele McClair lost control of her bladder. She fell against her mother who eased her on to the sofa, with the good sense to remain silent. She stared up at Skinner, yet through him as if he was not there.

'That's not true,' she protested, finally. 'You're mistaken. It was somebody else. Griff's in South Africa, I tell you.'

'Believe me,' he told her with utter sincerity, 'I wish that he was. I've known him for longer than you have, and I will never be able to describe to you or anyone else what it felt like to look into that car.'

'No, but I think I can imagine. Bob . . .' She fell silent, words beyond her.

'I'm going to leave you now, Noele. Your mother will look after you, but if you want to talk to me later, I'm only a phone call away. In fact, if you need me to come back I'll do that. For now, if you would like a sedative, or sleeping tablets, I can arrange for a police surgeon to issue a prescription and have them delivered to the door. Say the word.'

'Why not, dear?' her mother said. 'It sounds like a good idea.'

'Thanks,' she replied, 'but no. I need to keep a clear head for Harry. He's got to be told before this becomes public knowledge, and that could be today.' She looked up at Skinner. 'You could do one thing for me, though; take him home with you, tell him he's to have lunch with Seonaid; Mum or I will pick him up this afternoon. I need to get cleaned up and get my act together in general. When he comes back, I'll be ready to tell him about his dad.'

'I'll do that with pleasure,' he told her. 'He can even have a hurl up the road in a police car. Wee boys love that.'

She gave him a watery smile. 'I don't think I want to be in

one, ever again. That's me finished with the job. There's one thing I know for certain; I will never be able again to walk into a violent crime scene without being taken back to this morning.'

'I can understand that,' he agreed. 'But don't be in a rush to hand your warrant card in. You're best out of CID, sure, but I'm sure that the chief can arrange a transfer to a quiet posting in uniform. Let me talk to her, please. We both know she owes you one, and I won't be slow to tell her.'

'Okay, but don't commit me to staying.'

'Fine. Now, Mrs McClair, would you like to round up Harry and meet me outside.'

He was waiting by the police car, on the point of calling Sarah to tell her that there would be one more for lunch, when his ringtone sounded. 'Sauce,' he barked as he took the call, 'what is it now?'

'Gaffer, can you come back into town? There's something I need you to see.'

'Eh? No fucking chance. If it's urgent give me a WhatsApp video call and show me. Quick about it, though. I have a lunch guest to take home.'

Nine

'What did he say when he saw them on his phone?' Mario McGuire asked. He was standing in the kitchen of Griff Montell's home, while crime scene technicians worked in the other rooms.

'It wasn't repeatable, not with the SOCOs here,' Sauce Haddock replied. 'It was along the lines of him cursing himself long and loud for not taking Terry Coats' story about the Krugerrand smuggling seriously, and not following it up with Montell after Coats mentioned his name as the pal who'd told him about the South African bullion robbery. He reckons that if he'd done that, or taken it to you, the whole thing would have been uncovered then and Coats and Griff would still be alive.'

'Maybe so, maybe not,' the DCC growled. 'Has it occurred to him that if he had followed it up with Montell, he might have been the one dumped in the back of a car? No,' he added quickly, 'don't answer that. It's a stupid question; he thinks he's bulletproof, even though he has a scar on his leg as evidence to the contrary.'

'I've never heard about that.'

'You wouldn't. Secret squirrel stuff; I got shot on the same operation myself, worse than him, but not at the same time.'

'And they say this job isn't dangerous.'

'It isn't, for nearly all of us,' the DCC said. 'There's just the odd one that keeps on looking for it, or the unlucky ones like Stevie Steele. Did Bob say anything else, other than the self-recrimination?'

Haddock nodded. 'Yes, he said we should check with the National Lottery. He said it's possible to buy Krugerrands on the bullion market, and he suggested that's the sort of thing a rich South African might do. He told me that I should check all possible sources of Griff's obvious wealth, before assuming he was bent.' He grinned. 'I said I didn't need telling that.'

'How many coins were in the box?'

'I didn't empty it out, but looking at the number in one stack, I reckon there are at least two hundred and fifty.'

'Fuck me! That's a quarter of a million in folding money. How much cash was in the envelope?'

'Eighty-eight thousand and a few hundred; all in used notes.'

'Lottery win, my arse. Go ahead and check it like Bob said, but I can tell you now that Inspector Montell did not win the jackpot. I'm equally certain that he didn't have a rich uncle who snuffed it and left him loaded. We need to set you up with an interview with his twin sister. I'll arrange that through Mary Chambers when I manage to speak to her. Her mobile's going to voice mail. Alex Skinner needs to be interviewed as well,' McGuire added. 'Gently, mind, but we need to ask her to recall everything that he's ever said to her. It might have a relevance that wasn't apparent at the time.'

'Agreed, sir,' the DI acknowledged. 'I'll ask DCI Mann if she'll take that on. They know each other. Alex acted for Lottie in a custody hearing a while back, when her husband tried to take her kid from her.'

'I remember that one; he was another bent cop. Jesus, Sauce, I tell you I'm going to go through this force like an industrial strength laxative. We can't keep having surprises like this.'

I'm going to, Haddock thought, *not the chief constable.* He filed the remark in his memory bank as he continued. 'There's someone else who needs to be interviewed, boss; one that I am definitely going to do myself. Noele McClair.' He explained Skinner's discovery that she and Montell had been in a relationship. 'The clothing Tarvil and I found here, the personal effects: they're hers.'

'Oh my God,' McGuire exclaimed. 'How many fucking worms are in this can? Sauce, sorry but you will not interview her, you're too close. You take Alex, and have Mann and Cotter interview Noele. You know her, they don't. They shouldn't do it at her place either. They need to bring her into Fettes and do it in formal surroundings.'

'If you say so sir, but why? This is Noele, we don't need to play her by the book surely. She's a victim by association.'

'Maybe, but she's also a person of interest, until I decide that she's not. From what you're saying, she's been here, she shared Griff's bed, she hung her dress in his wardrobe beside his designer gear. Has she ever been in his office? Did she know about the stash of gold and the cash? Most of all, did she know about that firearm you found? Take nothing for granted, Inspector, nothing at all.' He stopped abruptly, then grinned, self-consciously. 'Listen to me!' he exclaimed. 'I'm sorry, Sauce. I know you don't make assumptions as a rule, and I can't really fault you for doing that with your DS. I'm as shocked by this thing as everybody else, but it's no excuse for me to patronise one of my best detective officers.'

The DI shrugged. 'No worries, sir; you were right. I can't be blinkered. I'll do what you say.'

'What about the pistol?' the DCC asked.

'I've spoken to Arthur Dorward about that,' Haddock said. 'They'll test fire it and run a comparison through the database to see if it's been used in any crimes. I suppose there's a chance that Griff had a firearms certificate, and I'll check that out, but something tells me I won't get a result. That'll raise another question. Where did he get it? All the weapons in the police armoury are checked in and out; I can't believe it would be one of ours, although from what Tarvil said, I know that we do have that weapon in our stock.'

'It could have been handed in during an amnesty. The last one was only a couple of years ago. It's not impossible for an officer to have trousered a gun when nobody was looking and made the paperwork disappear.'

'Not impossible, sir, but trousering a box of ammunition as well might have been more difficult. I found one in the safe; it wasn't full. Neither was the magazine in the pistol. It holds fifteen rounds but there were only thirteen there. That worries me.'

'Me too, but could it have been target practice?' McGuire suggested.

'I thought about that, but . . . if that's what he was doing would he take only two shots?'

'Good point. Let's see what the database tells us. Meantime, is there anything else you can tell me? We've given the media the holding statement we agreed, but we need to go back to them before the day's out. I'm thinking five o'clock. When I saw "we" I mean me. Assuming that I've contacted Spring Montell by then, I intend to announce the names.'

Haddock nodded. 'Do you want me there?'

'The point of me doing it is to shield you; if you feel strongly you should be there that's up to you, but if you are, you'll have to field questions. It wouldn't look good for the SIO to be hiding behind me. And if you don't have any answers . . . well, that wouldn't look good either.'

'I don't at this moment,' the younger man admitted, 'and unless somebody walks in and confesses, I won't have any this evening either. As you know, I have Jackie Wright looking at all available traffic CCTV. She checked in just before you arrived. So far, she has Coats' car first appearing at the Western Corner at twelve twenty-one, and she can track it all the way from there to the police station. The second car, the Renault Megane, was following close behind; it got caught by a red light at Palmerston Place. The driver actually stopped, believe it or not, and whoever was in Coats' car waited up for him. It was safe enough, for there wasn't a soul on the street, and not another vehicle to be seen. After the drop, the pick-up car went through Haymarket, turned into Coates Gardens and after that went completely off the radar. The driver was either lucky or they'd done a very thorough recce before doing it for real. It could be anywhere now.' The DI sighed. 'You know what? I have a wild theory that right now it's parked in the place its owner left it, with its original plates back on, and he or she is none the wiser. It's the perfect day of the year to do that. Steal a car after ten on Hogmanay in a quiet street, and there's a better-than-even chance it's not going to be noticed, far less reported, until the owner surfaces next lunchtime. I got Jackie to check for any Renault Megane reported stolen this morning in Edinburgh, the Lothians and Fife. So far there hasn't been a single one and I'm betting there won't be. We need to find that car, for the

DNA that'll be inside it; barring a lucky break, the only way we can do that is by finding every Megane in the city and beyond. And that's going to be a fucking nightmare, because that's one of the most popular models in Britain. There'll be hundreds of them that are driven by locals, but are leased, with registration documents that show the name of the legal owner. It's impossible, sir. Yes, it's best if I'm not at the press conference. It's a Ronan Keating situation: best say nothing at all.'

McGuire nodded. 'I agree with that. There's one flaw in your thinking, though, Sauce. If you're going to steal a car for a job, why bother to change the registration plates? I reckon that any time now we'll have a sales rep calling the one-one-one number to complain that his have been nicked. And that means . . .'

'That they used their own car for the job,' Haddock moaned. 'I really am knackered. I should have worked that out by myself.'

'We're all knackered,' the DCC said. 'Don't worry about it. But it does mean that, unless by some miracle you find the theft or the disposal of the plates on a street camera somewhere, you are indeed going to be checking the ownership of every bloody Megane in the country.'

Ten

Sarah and Seonaid were waiting in the doorway when the police car dropped its passengers in the driveway. Skinner had made his warning call, without explaining the reason for Harry's visit. As his daughter took her friend off to the play room, he led his wife into the kitchen and talked her through his stressful night and morning.

'Oh my,' she gasped. 'Poor Noele. That's the whammiest double I've ever heard of. Her ex and her boyfriend in the same hit. She has to be the link; she has to be.'

'I don't see that,' her husband said. 'As far as I can see, nobody knew about her new relationship, other than Alex, not even her mum. Terry didn't, at least not from her. What passed between him and Griff Montell we may never know. How they came to die together, we may never know. Anyone ruthless enough to execute a serving police officer, and an ex-cop, is going to be thorough as well when it comes to covering their tracks.'

'Emily bloody Badger,' Sarah hissed. 'She's the rawest of the raw, only on call because I decided that nothing serious ever happens on Hogmanay in Edinburgh because everybody's too busy having fun or having their pockets picked. She gets pulled in on the most significant double homicide in the city in living memory and it doesn't occur to her to call her boss. I have to get in on this, Bob. I have to take over the autopsies. Emily's fine technically, but she's nowhere near ready to be an expert witness in a High Court trial. It's your turn to look after the kids. I have to get into the city.'

Bob nodded. 'I get that, but are you fit? You had a few drinks last night and very little sleep afterwards. It's more important that these post-mortems are done correctly than that they're done today. Sauce is the SIO, you should talk to him and agree a timetable.'

'Okay,' she agreed. 'I'll do that . . . once I've filleted Dr Badger for not putting me in the picture.'

'Maybe you should pause on that one,' Bob suggested. 'Call the mortuary and instruct them that nothing should be done until you get there. That's all you need to do for now. When you put Badger right it would be better in sorrow than in anger.' He surprised himself by yawning. 'Look at me,' he said. 'I need sleep even more than you do. Let's feed the kids, and ourselves, then we can take turns for a siesta.'

'Sounds like a plan, but first . . . you might want to speak with Ignacio . . . although he and Pilar have crashed as well, in his apartment.'

'What's his problem? He hasn't got her pregnant, has he? I'm not ready to be a grandpa, not with two kids at primary school and one at playgroup.'

'I hope not,' she said, severely, 'given the state she was in when they got back this morning! The problem does involve a grandpa, though. Ignacio's mother called him in a panic while I was holding Pilar's head over the toilet bowl. Her husband did a disappearing act in the middle of the night. But after the time you've had, you don't need to be getting involved with that. I expect he'll have sobered up and come home by now.'

Bob frowned. 'Two things wrong with that picture,' he observed. 'One, Cameron McCullough doesn't drink much. I've seen him in his hotel; there's always a glass in front of him but it's rarely empty. Two, Mia doesn't panic; she's a Watson. It's not in her genes. You look after the kids, get them fed. I'd better call her.' He checked his watch; it showed twelve thirty-five. 'Fuck, I've missed the Loony Dook too!'

'Mark and James Andrew didn't. Jazz insisted on going and shamed his brother into going with him. Don't worry, I made them both wear their wet suits. You go do what you have to do. I'll phone the mortuary, check with Haddock and then get lunch underway.'

Skinner moved into the garden room, phone in hand. As he looked out across the Bents, he saw two black-clad figures running up the slope towards the house. Part of him was guilty about not being with them, but his sensible side admitted to relief. Sea swimming on the first of January was pure bravado, he acknowledged, and nothing else.

He went to Mia McCullough's mobile number in his directory. As his thumb hovered over the screen, his mind went back to the time they had met, he a newly promoted detective superintendent, she a daytime presenter on a popular Edinburgh local radio station, not Mia Watson but Mia Sparkles, with a devoted following of early teenagers, of whom his daughter Alex had been one. She was the last surviving sibling of a trio, born into a brutal criminal family; he had visited her at the radio station while investigating the killing of her brother and there had been unavoidable chemistry. Their relationship had been entirely unprofessional on his part; it had also been brief, one night, but long enough to produce Ignacio. She had been pregnant, unknowingly, when she left town in a hurry, disappearing from the potentially fatal repercussions of an act of treachery, and had brought up their son in Spain without ever considering telling his father of his existence, until it was in her interests to do so, and until the boy was in the kind of trouble from which not even Skinner could extricate him unscathed. Mia had settled back in Scotland and had gone back to her old occupation, radio, landing a job on a Dundee station owned by the city's wealthiest man, Cameron 'Grandpa' McCullough. He had his own colourful story, which included an acquittal on murder and drugs charges after the mysterious disappearance of the principal Crown witness, and the narcotics in question. He had laughed out loud when he had been told of their marriage. There had been an inevitability about the events of Mia's life and so it had been entirely predictable. And yet it had been successful; Cameron and Mia McCullough were an undoubtedly devoted couple and Skinner's misgivings about his son's new stepfather had been overcome.

He hit the WhatsApp call button and waited. She answered within ten seconds, taking him by surprise by switching the call to video. Her hair was wrapped in a towel, and she wore no make-up, but she was as striking as ever. He saw the tension in her eyes, the tightness of her mouth, and knew from those signs that the crisis, whatever it was, had not been resolved.

'Grandpa's gone AWOL, I'm told,' he began.

'Completely off the fucking grid,' she exclaimed. 'His phone's off; the cars are all still there. I've had hotel staff search the whole estate but there's no sign of him, neither hide nor hair. I don't know what to do.'

'Have you called the police?'

'No, not yet. If I reported him missing, I wouldn't trust that lot not to leak it. You know how much they love him,' she added, her voice heavy with irony. 'He's a man in his sixties, fit and well, with no worries. What are they going to do? Laugh up their sleeves, probably, but otherwise nothing.'

'They'd have to take it seriously, Mia,' he assured her. 'Do you want me to make the call?'

'No way. It would leak to the *Sun* for sure. I'm taking a chance that it won't leak to the *Saltire*, by talking to you.'

'I wouldn't do that,' he said. 'Besides, it isn't a news story. How can I help?'

'To be honest I don't know.' The lines around her eyes deepened. For a moment, to his surprise, he thought she would cry. 'Bob, the best I can hope for is that the phone rings and I get a ransom demand. The worst I can hope for . . .'

'No, no, no, Mia. You're getting way ahead of yourself. Kidnapping for ransom is very rare in this country; if that's what this is, it would be even more unusual. If I was looking to extort money from Cameron, I'd be kidnapping you, not him. It would be much easier and much less of a physical risk.' He paused. 'That said, we need to look to your security. What arrangements does the hotel have?'

'It's well protected. There are cameras in all the corridors, the rooms are secure and we have a janitor who used to be in the Parachute Regiment.'

'Right. If Cameron doesn't come walking in later on today smelling of cheap perfume and claiming to have no memory of the previous twelve hours, I want you to move in there. Let's give it twenty-four hours. If I'm wrong and it is a kidnap, you should have had contact by then. If not, I will come up with my apprentice and take a look at the scene.'

'Your apprentice?' she repeated.

'Our son. That's always assuming I can peel him off his girlfriend by then.'

'Girlfriend? What girlfriend? He never told me he has a girlfriend.'

He laughed. 'When a young man begins to have regular sex, the last person he's going to discuss it with is his mother.'

On his screen, he saw her nostrils flare. 'If that's the case,' she exclaimed, 'I hope he's a fucking sight more careful than you were!'

Eleven

'This place is a tip,' Tarvil Singh observed. 'I've seen tidier scrapyards.'

'I doubt that he was expecting visitors,' Sauce Haddock said. 'When I lived on my own, I let things slide from time to time.'

The sergeant picked up an empty food container, held it to his nose and sniffed. 'Lamb Balti,' he guessed. 'Letting things slide is one thing; this is more like an avalanche. I don't know how Noele put up with this guy for as long as she did. Griff must have been a culture shock. Did Coats own the place?'

'Yes, he bought it after the divorce from Noele was finalised. The SOCOs got the address from his employer, and the key from them too. There was a spare in his office at the airport.' Terry Coats' home was a small semi-detached villa in Corstorphine, to the west of the city, convenient for his place of employment. Haddock guessed that it was around a hundred years old.

'The SOCOs are done here already? That must be a record for Dorward's crew. He usually makes them do everything twice. They might have cleaned up for us.'

'All they really had to do was establish that this wasn't the crime scene,' the DI pointed out. 'The place is tiny, and they aren't as fastidious as you.' The living room was no more than fifteen feet square and the furniture was minimal; two armchairs, a gateleg table, a small sideboard and a television on a stand. Haddock looked around the debris. 'There's nothing personal at all, apart from that one photo of his wee boy on the sideboard. This is sad, Tarvil, when you think about it. We're looking at the life of a forty-one-year-old man, and this is all there is?'

'What's even sadder,' Singh retorted, his size compressing the room still further, 'is that he doesn't even have a toilet brush. Have you been in that bathroom? Holy Moses, what a mess. And the bedrooms! One thing's for certain, if he was still shagging that cabin-crew woman you caught him with, he wasn't bringing her here.'

'Nonetheless,' the DI insisted, 'we will still search the place. The SOCOs might have been over it, but they weren't looking for the same things as us. Again, we want to find anything that links him and Montell, or anything else that we don't know about that might point us at whoever killed the two of them. Of course . . .' His voice tailed off, the sentence unfinished, his forehead narrowing.

'What?'

'It's just . . . Tarvil, I'm thinking, we've been assuming that Montell and Coats were acting together in this enterprise, whatever it was. But what if they weren't? Griff's lifestyle showed unexplained wealth, but this is the home of a man with barely a pot to piss in. I assume that the split from Noele left him with hefty child support to pay; he seems to have been struggling, rather than raking it in.'

'Aye, so?'

'Well, we know that Griff was booked on a flight from

Edinburgh to Johannesburg via London on Saturday evening. We know that he checked in for it, but he never boarded the flight. Coats worked at Edinburgh Airport. Could he have intercepted Griff when he arrived there? Might they have been rivals in some way rather than partners? Do something for me, while I go through this place. Get in touch with British Airways and find out whether there's an unclaimed suitcase lying in Jo'burg off that connecting Heathrow flight.'

'Technically a bag isn't meant to fly without its owner,' Singh said.

'Mistakes happen. Do it anyway.'

Haddock began to search the little house, examining everything, looking under cushions, shaking every discarded magazine in case something had been stuck between the pages. He found nothing out of the ordinary other than a Ninjago magazine that he guessed Harry had left on a visit. He moved to the sideboard. It revealed a twenty-four-piece dinner set, a bottle of Famous Grouse, three-quarters empty, a miniature chess set and two crystal glasses. Their weight told him that they were quality pieces. He moved upstairs. The bathroom was untidy, but clean, apart from the toilet. The suite might have been an original fitting; it was a pale green colour that made Haddock wince. There were two bath towels on a rail, and a hand towel on a ring beside the basin. The shower was a hose-type attachment over the bath, contained by a plastic curtain. Coats appeared to have been a blade shaver; a Gillette disposable stood in a glass, on a shelf above the basin with a brush beside it. Haddock touched it and felt residual dampness. He winced at the thought that the man who had used it was in a refrigerated drawer in the City Mortuary. Leaving the bathroom, he went into the second bedroom. It showed no signs of use; indeed, with its smoothed and folded bedspread, it was the neatest room in the house. He wondered if Harry Coats had been allowed to stay overnight with his father on his court-approved visits. The main bedroom was a complete contrast. Discarded clothes were piled in a corner. Rather than look through them he kicked them, then shuffled them apart with his right foot to satisfy himself they were concealing nothing. There were two bedside tables but only one reading lamp, with a USB socket in its base, into which a mobile phone cable was plugged. The place smelled ripe; he pulled the drawn curtains apart and threw open the window, letting in the crisp winter air to flush out the muskiness. He opened the wardrobe and again was struck by the contrast between Coats and Montell. There was one suit . . . he checked the label; 'Slater', he murmured . . . two pairs of trousers, one of jeans, a shiny leather jerkin and a sports jacket. The shirts looked over-laundered, the underwear in two boxes was a mix, some of it with BHS labels. On the floor were a pair of New Balance trainers, three pairs of shoes, and leaning against the back wall, a laptop, a Dell Inspiron that Haddock judged to be the newest and most expensive item in the apartment. He reached in to pick it up, wrinkling his nose against the odour of stale clothing. He was familiar with the keyboard layout, owning a similar model himself.

'What's that?' Singh asked from the doorway as he switched it on.

He turned to face him, displaying it. 'Computer. Did you get through to anyone?'

'All the way. There is an unclaimed case in Johannesburg; it came off last Sunday's Heathrow flight and the barcode says it was routed all the way through from Edinburgh.'

The DI smiled. 'Progress. It needn't mean a hell of a lot, of course. Griff may have checked it in to lay a false trail, but it tells us that he was at the airport, and it gives us a shot at picking him up on camera.'

'Do you want me to check that?'

'Yes, but not right away. Go and knock some neighbours' doors first and see if you can establish when Coats was last here. Even if nobody saw him, find out when his car was seen last. While you do that, I'll check in with the DCC. He'll want to know everything there is to know before he sees the press at five.'

Twelve

Mario McGuire looked out across a space that had been the gym of the Edinburgh police service before it was superseded by unification. He had expected a smaller turnout, during what was a two-day public holiday, but there were a dozen recording devices and four microphones on the desk behind which he sat and at the back of the room five TV cameras on stands. One of the latter belonged to his own media department, an innovation by Peregrine Allsop, the director, that Sir Andrew Martin, the former chief constable, had approved without consulting his senior colleagues. Its purpose, McGuire believed, was to strengthen the control of Allsop's department over police communications by allowing him to highlight officers' failings. The director was in the DCC's sights, but Maggie Steele had been reluctant to face the flak that his removal might provoke. He had no such qualms.

The press officer, a small dark-haired woman seated on McGuire's left, leaned towards him. 'I'll introduce you,' she whispered. She made to rise but he put a hand on her arm.

'It is all right, Ms Balfour,' he told her. 'I know every reporter in this room. I don't think we need that.'

'The Director says . . .' she began, but by that time he was on his feet.

'Good evening, ladies and gentlemen,' he began, projecting his voice as the buzz of conversation died away. 'Thank you for coming. You'll be aware by now, I think, of an incident earlier today in the centre of Edinburgh. It's with regret that I tell you now, that not long after twelve thirty this morning, a car was abandoned outside the West End police station in Torphichen Place, at Haymarket. Its driver was taken from the scene by another car. On examination, the bodies of two men were found in the back seat of the vehicle; each had been shot in the head. They have been identified formally and next of kin have been informed, so I can tell you that the deceased were Mr Terry Coats, aged forty-one, formerly a detective inspector with the now defunct Strathclyde Police, latterly employed in the security department of Edinburgh Airport, and Inspector Griffin Montell, aged thirty-nine, a serving police officer stationed at the West End office. Enquiries into their murders have begun, under the direction of acting Detective Chief Inspector Harold Haddock, the senior investigating officer. He has nothing to report at this stage, which is why he's not here, so any questions you can fire at me. I just want to say that DCI Haddock and I, and many of the investigating team, knew Griff Montell as a friend and colleague and are shocked by his death, but I promise you that our enquiries will be conducted dispassionately and efficiently.' He paused, looking around the room as voices were raised in competition for the first question, then pointed to a man in the front row. 'Jim.'

The chosen reporter leaned forward. 'Jim Finney, Sky News. DCC McGuire, obviously you knew Inspector Montell, but did you also know Mr Coats personally?'

'No, I didn't, because I wasn't Strathclyde myself, so our paths didn't cross, but I can tell you that he was the former husband of one of our serving officers, Detective Sergeant Noele McClair. She's part of the Serious Crimes Unit based in Edinburgh, in this building. Obviously she's been recused from this investigation.'

'Can we talk to her?' a BBC reporter seated close to Finney asked.

'That will be up to her, Lisa. I'll consult with her and see how she feels about that. However, she has a child, yes, Mr Coats' son, and he has to be protected. What I do not want to happen is for her to be door-stepped, mob-handed, or even approached at her home by individuals.' He gazed around the room. 'Should that happen, and I am happy to say this on camera, there will be hell to pay. I want her and her wee boy left alone. What I will do is ask her if she's prepared to issue a statement. If she is, it'll come through Ms Balfour here, our press officer.'

'You said "former husband",' Jim Finney said. 'They were divorced, yes?'

McGuire nodded. 'Yes, last year.'

'Were they on good terms?'

'I have no idea, but I don't regard that as having any relevance to this investigation. Do you hear me, Jim?'

'Loud and clear . . . not that you're saying anything.'

'Can I ask, Mr McGuire,' a sharp voice interrupted, 'what these two men were doing in the same car?'

The deputy chief constable managed to keep his feelings from showing on his face. Jack Darke, the crime correspondent of the *Saltire*, would not have made a list of his hundred favourite journalists. 'That's one of the first questions that DCI

Haddock's team is trying to answer,' he replied. 'When we know that, we might come closer to knowing who put them there.'

'Do you have any lines of enquiry at all?'

'Several, Jack, and as always we're going to keep them to ourselves until it's in the public interest to share them.'

'Did Coats and Montell ever work together? Montell was a detective sergeant before he was promoted into uniform.'

'They never served on the same force,' the DCC said.

'That doesn't answer my question,' Darke shot back.

McGuire shrugged. 'As far as I'm concerned it does.'

'Why did Coats leave the police?'

'He chose to. My understanding is that he was offered a uniformed posting that he didn't like, and that was behind his decision.'

'It had nothing to do with him being bent?'

There was a collective intake of breath. All eyes in the room fastened on the *Saltire* journalist, and then on the DCC, as if expecting a volcanic eruption.

None came. Instead McGuire nodded and said, quietly, 'Mr Darke, I'm not going to respond to that, because I know you're trying to provoke me into throwing you out of this briefing. But I know also that your knowledge of police matters is encyclopaedic, and that there's an underlying reason for your question. So why don't you enlighten us, or are you going to keep it for a front-page exclusive?'

The reporter leaned back in his chair and pocketed his recorder. 'I might just do that, Mario.'

'That's your right,' the Deputy Chief Constable agreed. 'Mind you,' he added, 'it's mine to offer a little background information to everyone here. The dead can't sue but there are things a kid might not want to read about his dad when he grows up.' His gaze swept across his audience. 'It's not correct, ladies and gentlemen, to say or imply that Mr Coats was corrupt. However, he was accused by a website called Brass Rubbings of having protected from prosecution a valuable source of criminal intelligence. He did that, yes, but it's in no way unique. Sometimes good detectives have to compromise when it comes to intelligence-gathering; they might decide to let a small fish stay in the water to catch a big one. In this case, unfortunately, the website named the informant, and he was found dead shortly afterwards. That was the background to Terry Coats being moved out of CID, and to his decision to resign. I tell you all this in clarification. It's a matter of public record, so feel free, all of you. With that, I'm drawing this to a close. You'll be briefed when we have something positive to tell you, until then Ms Balfour here is your contact for questions.'

'You're a big Irish-Italian bastard, McGuire,' Darke hissed after him as he left.

He stopped, turned, and looked back. 'Aye,' he said. 'And don't you forget it.'

Jane Balfour followed him through the door behind the desk. 'That was nicely done, sir,' she said when they were out of earshot of the journalists. 'That was the *Saltire* man, wasn't it? I haven't had much to do with him, but when I have he's always aggressive.'

'If he gets too bad, let me know. His boss is a friend.'

'June Crampsey, the editor?'

'No, her boss. I agree with you about Darke, but there are guys like him in every walk of life. June Crampsey knows him well enough, but she also knows that he's a good reporter with contacts everywhere. He gets more exclusives than anyone else in that room we've just left.'

'Contacts within the force?'

'Of course; the force, the courts, the prison service, the legal profession. I know of a few of them.'

'Couldn't you shut them down?' the press officer asked.

'I could, but I don't want to. It suits me to have a back channel to Jack. If there's information I want to get to him and I do it through you, he'll be suspicious. If I feed it through a trusted source, it's accepted.'

'Does he pay his informants?'

'Not cops. I don't know about the rest but not our people. That I would shut down if I heard about it . . . and I would hear about it.'

Jane Balfour smiled. 'I think I can learn from you, sir.'

'Feel free,' he said. 'But don't call me "sir". You're not a cop. Mr McGuire will do for now; when you get to know me better you can call me Mario, but not in front of the troops.'

'And you can call me Jane, in front of anyone you like.'

'Fine. Is there anything you need to know or want to ask me? I need to brief a couple of people.'

'I didn't know that Mr Haddock was an acting DCI. Do you want me to issue a press release?'

'No need. I've just told the media. Sauce doesn't know himself yet. I did that on the hoof, so to speak. I'm bringing someone of that rank on to the team, and it occurred to me that I should make clear his authority as SIO. He'll be acting in the rank for as long as Sammy Pye is off, but realistically until he's retired on medical grounds. Once that happens, we'll see about permanency. This hasn't been shared with your department, but Sammy's diagnosis precludes recovery.

It's a matter of how quickly the disease progresses and that's uncertain.'

'I don't know Mr Pye, I'm afraid.'

'That's a pity. A lot of us go back all the way with Sammy. He's a big loss.'

'Pardon me for asking,' Balfour ventured, 'but does DCI Haddock's temporary promotion need to be approved by the chief constable?'

'Yes, but I'll tell her. I'm the Head of CID, as well as her designated deputy. You haven't met her yet, have you?'

'No.' She smiled. 'Mr Allsop doesn't encourage other ranks to mix with the higher-ups. I'm only here because he's away.'

'Don't be so sure of that. My view, which I think you'll find carries more weight than Mr Allsop's, is that you're the person on the ground in this part of Scotland. When you speak, it's not on Perry Allsop's behalf, but on the chief constable's, so the two of you should meet. I'll try to make that happen, Jane, as soon as I can. Meanwhile, my door's always open to you.' He frowned. 'Thanks for your help in there. Now I really must go.'

He made his way back into the main building, and through to the Serious Crimes office suite. The room was crowded. He looked around for newcomers. One of them was easy to find. Detective Chief Inspector Charlotte Mann was a large and formidable woman who had made her reputation in the hard school of Glasgow CID. In her early days as an officer she had been entered into a boxing tournament at a police smoker against a male opponent and had despatched him in less than a minute. In contrast her colleague, DS John Cotter, was at least four inches shorter and more lightly built. Tyneside born, he had chosen to serve in Scotland and had been picked out as someone with prospects, placed with Mann after her mentor, the legendary Detective Sergeant Dan Provan had retired to a life of happy domesticity . . . with her.

'Lottie,' McGuire exclaimed. 'Thanks for answering the call. You too, John.'

She gazed back at him, her right eyebrow slightly raised. 'I wasn't aware it was optional, sir. But I'd have been here regardless,' she added. 'I knew Terry Coats in the Strathclyde days. Conceited arsehole, but a good detective. He didn't deserve what happened to him, then or now. Once a cop always a cop as far as I'm concerned.'

'Did you ever meet Montell?'

'No. He transferred into your old force from overseas, didn't he? That made him very much Edinburgh. I did hear about him, though, getting cut defending Sir Bob's daughter. How's she taking it?'

'How would you expect? They were close; never a couple, but close.'

'And Coats's wife? How's she? I met her, after Terry had jumped ship from Strathclyde, not long after she made CID. I thought she might have brought him under control, but apparently not.'

'Controlled him in what way?' Cotter asked.

'Women,' Mann replied. 'Terry would have shagged anything with a pulse; and maybe without, if there was nothing else available. He knocked Noele up when she was a plonk. He did the decent thing, marrying her . . . at least that's what we all thought at first. Well, maybe not all of us,' she reflected. 'Dan reckoned that he only did it because her father, Bert McClair, was a South Lanarkshire councillor, and served on the Strathclyde police committee. Right or not, nothing changed with Terry; it didn't surprise me at all when Sauce and Sir Bob caught him in the act. Speaking of Sauce,' she exclaimed, looking past McGuire towards the door.

Haddock swept into the room, his coat over his shoulder and a laptop computer tucked under his arm. Singh followed, closing the door behind them. 'Sorry I'm late, sir,' the DI said. 'Coats' place took longer than I thought it would.' He waved the laptop. 'There was nothing there of any significance, only this. We'll see what it has on it, but I'll tell you one thing, he and Griff weren't riding the same gravy train.'

'What does that mean?' Mann asked.

'It means that we found signs of unexplained wealth in Griff Montell's office and at his home,' the DCC explained.

'And signs of unexplained poverty in Coats's,' Haddock added. 'Jackie,' he called out, 'have we got into Griff's computer yet?'

'Sorry, Sauce,' DC Jackie Wright replied. Griff Montell's computer was on her desk, taking up much of the available space. 'It's beyond me; I've tried all sorts of passwords based on date of birth, his service number, kids' names, everything obvious. I'm going to have to call in the IT people.'

'Have you tried "Alexis"?'

'No, why should that work?'

'It probably won't; it's Alex Skinner's given name, that's all.'

'Okay.' She turned back to the keyboard and punched in the letters, carefully. 'No luck,' she reported.

'Try it backwards,' McGuire suggested.

She did; as soon as she pressed the 'Enter' key the wallpaper disappeared and a photo of Alex herself filled the outsize screen.

'And here were we all thinking they were just good friends,' McGuire exclaimed. 'Not as far as Griff was concerned, it seems. Sauce, when you speak to Alex, I don't think that's something she needs to know.'

'Are you sure about that, boss?' Haddock asked. 'We don't know how Alex really felt about Griff, but we've had an insight into how he saw her. Isn't she entitled to know, and have we got the right to keep it from her?'

The DCC sighed, long and loudly. 'You know, you are right,' he said. 'I've known Alex since I was a plod, and she was maybe thirteen. The first time I met her was at a crime scene in Infirmary Street Baths. The big fella had brought her along because he'd had no option; he asked me to look after her while he was inside. She didn't really need looking after, even then, but I did, and in a way I've been looking after her ever since. We all have, and that's what I was doing there. You handle it any way you like; the purpose is to extract from her as much information about Montell as she has, that we might not. Have you arranged to see her yet? If not, do so now, and make it first thing tomorrow. We've all been up long enough today.'

'What about John and me, sir?'

He turned to Mann. 'I need you two to interview Detective Sergeant McClair. There's no sentiment in this situation; she and one of the victims had an adversarial relationship, so she needs to be approached on that basis, regardless of who she is. Noele will understand that, I'm sure.'

'What do I do if she asks for a lawyer?'

'You refuse,' he told her. 'She isn't entitled, because she won't have been cautioned; she'll be interviewed as a witness. That said, if she wants a Police Federation rep, I have no problem with that. The objective is simple; find out how much she knew about Terry's life. His associates, his love life, his financial position.'

'For example, why he was living in a dump,' Haddock added.

'That bad?'

'Ask Tarvil. He's pretty fastidious; he was for having the place fumigated.' The big Sikh grunted confirmation.

'Okay, deal with that too, Lottie. Was Coats under pressure, and if so what might he have done to relieve it?'

'What about exploring his relationship with Montell when we talk to her, sir?' Cotter asked.

'Yes,' McGuire agreed, 'but very carefully. It's emerged that Noele was in a relationship with Griff herself. Ultimately you're trying to find out how much she knew about both of them. Did each of them share information with her that was common to them both? Did they both drop the same names, people, places, events?'

'Or did she drop their names to someone else?' Mann said.

The DCC and the Haddock stared at her.

'What?' she exclaimed. 'No stone left unturned. No possibility left unexplored. We want to know everything about the victims; those rules apply to her too.'

'Okay,' McGuire conceded. 'Now, acting DCI Haddock . . .' The young detective stared at him. 'Look, Sauce, you are in practice, so it should be made official . . . can we talk about priorities? You're the SIO, what are they?'

'Interviews with Alex and Noele,' he replied. 'There's an argument that we treat them both the same, i.e., interview both on police premises, but I'm not going to go there, one, because there's no connection at all between Alex and Terry Coats and, two, because I don't fancy the heat it would draw from a certain quarter. Once we have everything we're going to get from them, we look at all the video we can find, from the traffic cameras, street cameras around the homes of both men, and security footage from the airport. We've established that Montell checked a suitcase on to his Saturday flight, routed through to Johannesburg, but that he never boarded the aircraft. Various possibilities occur to me, but do any of you have thoughts? DCI Mann?'

'When did he drop the case off?'

'Don't know yet, that's one of the things we'll look at on the airport CCTV. Why?'

'It could have been several hours in advance of flight time. If so, he could have been meeting someone before he caught the plane, and heard something that made him miss it. There are three hotels close to that airport; Dan, my Jakey and I stayed in the Moxy when we flew out of Edinburgh in October. There would have been plenty of time for him to go there before he went airside.'

'That's true,' Haddock agreed. 'If you and John could check them all that would be good. If you get something, excellent. If not, I would like you to visit airport security. Check if Coats was working on Saturday; if so, ask them whether he put any sort of an alert out for Montell.'

'What about our own people? We have patrol officers there.'

'That's right, Lottie, round the clock . . . which makes it unlikely that he was abducted from there, but chances are some of them might have known Inspector Montell by sight and recognised him on Saturday afternoon.' He nodded. 'While you're doing all that I'm going to be speaking to Sir Robert. He told me about a yarn that Coats spun him about bullion robbery in South Africa and gold coins being smuggled into the country and changed in an airport shop. He thought it was nonsense at the time, but he's changed his mind now. Just as we're doing with Alex and Noele, I need to press him to remember as much of the detail as he can. Once I've done that, I'll have the difficult task of speaking to Griff's twin sister, Spring. The DCC contacted her in South Africa through her partner . . . you two may not know, but she's a retired chief superintendent who used to be Griff's boss. She was serving when the relationship began, and he created a hell of a row when he found out, but he got used to it once he calmed down. Whether that translated into regular social contact, that's something I need to find out. I'm doing it by video link at eight tomorrow before I see Alex; that's been arranged by the DCC. We're an hour behind them, so she'll be awake and as ready for it as she's going to be.'

'Speaking of which,' the deputy chief constable declared, 'let's all go home and get some sleep. This is the most eventful New Year's Day I've ever had, and I can't wait for it to be over.'

'Me too,' Haddock conceded. He reached for the coat that he had thrown over a chair, only to be interrupted by a shout from DC Wright.

'Sauce! I think you should see this on Inspector Montell's iMac.'

'Can it wait?' he asked, then corrected himself, knowing his curiosity meant that it could not. 'Of course not. What is it?' He stepped across to her workstation, with McGuire and the two Glasgow detectives close behind.

'There's a folder on here of recordings from his security system. This one's from last Saturday evening, timed at twenty-two forty-nine. It's from a camera mounted on the outside of the building, and . . . look.'

A hazy image was frozen on the screen; it showed the street outside Montell's apartment, deserted, with no one in sight. Wright's hand was cupped over a computer mouse; she clicked it and the recording began to play, rain lashing down, ripples showing in the puddles by the side of the roadway. As they looked on, a figure appeared, walking into view, its back to the wall-mounted camera. The new arrival was wearing a long, dark, hooded raincoat. 'Male or female?' John Cotter murmured.

'You tell me, Sarge,' Wright replied, freezing the picture once more. 'You can't tell from this. Look there, whoever it is, they're wearing calf-length wellies, and those are pretty much unisex.'

Haddock leaned forward. 'What's that he or she's carrying? I can't make it out.'

'It's a plastic bag, Co-op.'

'So somebody's been shopping?'

'Maybe,' the DC agreed, 'but . . .' She hit the 'Play' icon once more; they watched the subject step up to the door, punch a code into the panel and slip inside.

'Okay, so somebody arrived in the pissing rain. What do the inside cameras show? There are four of them; entrance hallway, kitchen, living room, and bedroom.'

'That's the thing, Sauce. They don't show anything. They were all disabled at the time. They didn't have motion activation, so they had to have been turned off. I can see from this that the system allowed him to do that remotely; but by and large they were never switched off, nor even when Noele was there. I found some footage of her that I will only show you privately, if you think it's necessary, and even then only with an order from the chief constable. They were switched off half an hour before whoever it was arrived, then back on an hour later.'

'If that's so, I wonder why he didn't disable the street camera,' Haddock observed.

'It's possible that he tried, only the weather got in the way of the signal.'

'Maybe so, but evidentially there is nothing to show us that whoever that person was had anything to do with Griff. Is it possible that the weather could have interfered with the storage system of the internal camera footage? Mr Francis said it was stored on the Cloud.'

'As backup, that's right, but it's also stored on the computer; that's where I've got this from, so the weather isn't a factor. Griff seems to have been in the habit of erasing it after three months, and relying on the Cloud for longer term. And you're right, we don't have anything visual that links him with the person we saw. However,' she paused, 'we have this.' She went back to the computer and fast forwarded the street camera recording. The detectives watched as its clock raced, until she slowed it with a move of the mouse. 'About now,' she said. 'Watch.'

They did; the rain was as heavy as before, with no one braving it until the door was opened from the inside and the same figure stepped out, wrapped up against the weather, with the hood pulled down. 'There's no way of telling whether the face is being hidden deliberately,' Wright said, 'but from this angle, and the body shape, I would say that the person is a male. I have two begged questions. The first, could that be Inspector Montell himself? The second, where's the Co-op bag?'

McGuire looked down on her; he shook his head. 'No to the first. I'd say that's too short to be him and not wide enough in the shoulders. As for the bag, who knows?'

'I do,' Tarvil Singh replied, loudly. 'In Montell's office,' he said, 'I remember seeing a placky bag, blue and white. I remember because it was out of place. Everything else in his office was as neat and tidy as the rest of the house, a monument to OCD, yet that thing was just lying there, discarded and never picked up. That's right, Sauce, isn't it?'

'Absolutely,' Haddock confirmed. 'It was empty; I know because I knelt on it when I looked in the safe. It'll still be there, and maybe there's a chance Arthur Dorward's people will be able to tell us what was inside it.'

Thirteen

'I'm knackered,' Sarah whispered, leaning against her husband on the garden room sofa. There was a sitting room in the house itself, but they never used it other than to watch television. 'You knackered?'

'I won't know until I try to sleep,' he confessed. 'I've seen things today that will be with me for a long time.'

'You've seen such things many times before. Too many, I know,' she added.

'Rarely involving people I know, though; when I see those, they never go away. You'll autopsy them both tomorrow, but I suppose it'll be different for you. If you brought things home in your head I'd be peeling you off the ceiling through the night.'

'You want the truth?' she murmured. 'Sometimes I do just that. Children: I'm a mum so I associate with the people who've lost them. Burns victims, they're bad, and there was an acid attack a few years ago that will always be fresh in my memory. We're taught to be dispassionate, but they can't train all of the human reactions out of us. Terry Coats, I'll be okay with him, but honestly, I don't think I'll be able to banish all thoughts of the Griff Montell that I met with Alex.'

'Maybe you should,' Bob said. 'Going by the things in his

locker, and the stuff that I'm told Sauce and big Singh found in his house, there was a hell of a lot about the guy that we didn't know.'

'What things?'

'Designer clothes, a wardrobe full of them. Cash, plenty of it. Gold coins worth six figures. A burner SIM card; I can't think of a legitimate reason for a cop to have one of those. Most worrying of all, there was a gun; a pistol. There's no record of him ever having a permit for it. Yet Sauce told me it was clean. The serial number was intact; most illicit weapons, they've been removed. It looked like a standard police firearm, but it isn't. Not one of ours . . . theirs . . . at any rate.'

'Could he have bought it in South Africa and brought it home with him?'

'Packed in a suitcase that's going to be X-rayed? Somehow I doubt that.'

'Is it that big a deal?' she asked. 'I come from a nation of gun owners, so maybe I look at it from a different angle. There are gun nuts in every walk of life.'

'I know there are, but unlicensed possession is illegal in this country; you can go to jail. A serving police officer found with one almost certainly would. That's a heavy deterrent, yet Griff still had one. It was a hell of a risk; I'm afraid that when Sauce finds out why he had it, we're not going to like it.'

Sarah glanced up at him. 'Don't fly off the handle at this but . . . do you think there is the slightest chance . . .' She hesitated.

'That Alex knew about it? I admit that question crossed my mind; I feel guilty about harbouring it, but I'm certain she didn't. I believe that if she'd found out about it she'd have told him to hand it in. She'd have forced him, in fact, given him an ultimatum. She's an officer of the court and she takes that seriously.'

'Did you ask her about the clothes and the other stuff when you saw her this morning?'

'I only knew about the things in his locker then,' Bob told her. 'I decided that the time wasn't right, so I didn't mention them. Sauce is going to interview her properly tomorrow. I'm sure he'll talk her through everything. One thing I do know. When they did have one of their occasional get-togethers, it was always at her place. As first that was because his sister lived with him. After she moved out, Alex made a point of keeping it that way. She insisted that she saw him only as a friend and an . . .' He stopped short.

'And an occasional shag?' his wife suggested.

'If you want to put it that way, yes. The way she put it to me was that she didn't want to get her feet under his table even once.'

'Noele had no such qualms, from what you said.'

'No,' he agreed, 'and from what Sauce told me half an hour ago, there's video evidence of that, and more.'

'Jesus,' she protested, 'he didn't! Did he?'

'Constant video monitoring, according to Jackie Wright. Nobody's saying he got his rocks off watching it, but it's there, on his computer and apparently up in the Cloud.'

'Oh my God, if someone hacks into it. Can't Sauce delete it?'

'In the circumstances, I suspect that he'd need the permission of the procurator fiscal to do that.'

'Did she know? Was the camera obvious?'

'Apparently not. It was built in to the alarm system's motion sensor.'

‚'Bloody hell, Bob, does ours have that?'

'No, I was offered that option when it was fitted, but I declined. I even made the installer show me the inside of each sensor before he put them up.' He grinned. 'Maybe I've been hanging around the spooks for too long.'

'You and Sauce were on the phone in the office for quite a long time,' Sarah remarked. 'What were you talking about?'

'He quizzed me about the story that Terry Coats spun me, the day that Noele slung him out and he turned up here looking for trouble. The more I think about it the more significant it becomes and the more I regret not taking it seriously. I think I've recalled all the detail now and given him a proper line of enquiry. Coats claimed that the girl we caught him with was part of a scheme to import stolen Krugerrands into the country. She was cabin crew and, with others, would bring coins from South Africa into Edinburgh among her possessions. They'd then be spent in a shop. To me, it sounded crazy at the time, but in fact it's so fucking simple, it's dazzling. They'd be accepted as currency, at a ridiculously low value, and that would be it, they'd be in the country, seemingly legitimately, to be disposed of on the open market.'

'But why do this? Why not simply sell them in South Africa?'

'Because they were stolen. According to Coats, years ago there was a robbery there, in which a huge quantity of Krugerrands were taken. The haul was so big, possibly twenty, thirty million sterling, possibly even more, that the thieves may have sat on them for years before they started to move them on. The source of the information about the robbery was a South African chum of his . . . Griff Montell. His knowledge of the smuggling operation, he said, came from a contact in the shop.'

'How many smuggled coins are we talking about?' she asked.

'No idea. It depends how many people were involved, as well as the woman Coats mentioned.'

'The shop must have been in on it, surely.'

'Very much so; that and the airline Coats' girlfriend worked for; it was called Wister Air. I'd never heard of it, but I did a quick google this evening and it was there, although it doesn't fly to Edinburgh anymore. He never mentioned the name of the shop but he did say that both were owned by a Russian.'

'How many staff were involved in the smuggling?'

'I have no idea, but if Sauce can find Terry's girlfriend, she might know.'

'And Griff, how did he tie into all of this?'

'And how did he happen to have a stash of Krugerrands in his safe, along with nearly ninety grand in cash? My big worry is that Griff didn't simply know about that gold robbery, but that he was part of it.'

Fourteen

Sauce Haddock rubbed his eyes with both hands; they felt as if half a beach had been washed into them overnight. He blinked hard to clear his vision, then shrugged his shoulders as if to shake off the weight that fate had dumped on them. He and Cheeky, his partner, Cameron Davis by her Sunday names, the latter coming from her stepfather, had been planning to grab a last-minute holiday break in the Canaries. In the wake of the double murder investigation, that had been postponed until Easter, and maybe later if Sammy Pye had not recovered from his mystery illness by then. He suspected that the DCC knew what the problem was, and the fact that it had not been shared with him made him worry about the man who was both his boss and his friend.

'You ready to go?' Tarvil Singh asked him, breaking into his thoughts. 'You're miles away.'

He blinked again. 'Sorry, these early morning starts are worst in the winter. Are we sure they'll be there?'

'The DCC said so, but there's only one way to find out.' The DS opened Zoom on Haddock's computer and placed the call. For around thirty seconds they stared at their own weary faces on the screen, until they shrank to a box on the top right corner and were replaced by two women. The older of the two was familiar to them both; Mary Chambers had been the first woman to make Chief Superintendent rank in the old Edinburgh force. She could have gone on to command rank in its replacement, but she was of the Bob Skinner school and had wanted no part of it. With thirty-seven years' service, she had taken her pension and gone into a happy retirement with her younger partner, helping her run the online graphic design business that she had set up. Neither detective had seen her since then; each was surprised by the change in her. The severe box haircut had gone, replaced by a longer look from which the grey had been banished by a glossy auburn colouring. The stiff white shirt they remembered had been replaced by a sleeveless yellow blouse. A medallion hung around her neck and her interlocked fingers were adorned by several rings. Most surprising of all, she wore eye make-up and a pale pink lipstick.

Spring Montell was her junior by almost twenty years but appeared to be catching her up. She and Griff had been identical twins, facially and, to an extent, in build. She wore a black T-shirt; unlike her partner, she was without make-up, her eyebrows were un-plucked, and her grey-flecked black hair was pulled back in a ponytail. Even in her bereavement her appearance came as a shock to the DI. Having known her only by name, he had read too much into that and had expected a slight, ethereal, womanly figure rather than the version he saw on the screen.

'Good morning, lads.' Chambers' greeting sounded slightly tinny, but her voice came through clearly. 'You look bloody terrible, if you don't mind me saying so. In case you were wondering, I'm going to sit in on this,' she announced; her tone did not invite discussion. 'Spring's still pretty fragile, and if I think at any time she's not up to this, I'm going to pull the plug.'

'That's fair enough, Ms Chambers,' Haddock said.

'Sauce, it's Mary, okay? You've grown up and I've grown older.'

He smiled. 'Fair enough, Mary. Spring,' he continued, 'we haven't met. I'm Detective Inspector Harold . . .'

'I know who you are, Sauce,' she said, cutting him off. 'Griff used to talk about you. He called you the Chosen One, and I don't think he was being kind. And you'll be DC Singh; from the way he described you, there can only be one of you. Or is it DS now?'

He nodded. 'It is. I managed to fool the promotion board.'

Haddock leaned forward. 'Have you told the family, Spring?'

'I told my ex-sister-in-law. She was shocked, but not hysterical. They really did part badly. Apart from her, there's nobody to tell.'

'Hold on,' Chambers exclaimed. 'You told me you had a cousin in Cape Town. What was his name again? I can't remember.'

'Tom,' Spring said, a little irritably. 'Tom DuPlessis. I haven't seen him for years, so I haven't called him, but the story made the front pages this morning, so he'll know. Did you see my brother's body, Sauce?' she asked, sharply.

'Yes, I did, in the car when it was dumped outside the police station.'

'Did he . . . ?' She frowned. 'Was it . . . ?'

'He never knew what hit him, Spring,' Haddock replied. 'He was shot once in the back of the head; at close range, the pathologist said. It would have been instantaneous.'

'Was he killed in the car?'

'No, somewhere else; we don't know where yet. We're working on it.'

'I'm sure you are. Why were they left outside the police station?'

'Our guess is that whoever did it was making a statement, to us, the police, I suppose. They must have known that he was stationed there.'

'And are you thinking it was related to something he was working on?' she asked. 'Because I don't see how that could be. Griff felt that his police career had become a waste of time. When he applied for promotion he assumed it would be to detective inspector, but instead the last chief constable, Martin, stuck him in a uniform and gave him a box of pencils to push. My brother knew why he did that too; he told me so often enough.'

Haddock leaned forward, making his on-screen image bigger. 'What did he believe, Spring?'

'He reckoned that he was being vindictive; he believed that it had to do with him sleeping with Alex Skinner, with her being Martin's woman.'

'Ex at the time, I think you'll find,' Haddock corrected her.

'Not always, I think you'll find yourself,' she countered. 'Griff and I shared everything towards the end. We learned that lesson from the fight we had when I teamed up with Mary. He'd talk to me about his love life all the time. He'd talk to me about everything. There were occasions, he told me, when Martin had really pissed Alex off, that she'd phone him, and he'd go along to her place. She'd fuck his brains out, he said, just to let off steam. His promotion happened after they split; he knew that Martin couldn't block it, but he did him all the damage that he could. Griff was convinced that Martin had known everything that went on in Alex's life, even after they broke up. He was even convinced that he'd had her watched.'

'Did he ever mention this to Alex?' Singh asked.

'He may have done, I'm not sure. But he was sure of it; he believed the guy had it in for him, big time. Where is Martin now?'

The sharpness of her question seemed to take Chambers by surprise. She laid a hand on her arm. 'He's in America, love, lecturing in one of the top universities. He left the country after he quit the job; he said he wanted some space.'

'So what? He has children; he's probably home for Christmas.'

Haddock intervened. 'Spring, I have to tell you that Sir Andrew Martin is not a suspect in your brother's murder. Whatever grievance he might have had against Griff, I doubt that he'd ever heard of Terry Coats, the man who was killed with him. Have you? Did he ever mention him to you?'

'That's who the other man in the car was?' she exclaimed. 'Griff told me that he had a new girlfriend, another police officer. Her name was Noele; he said that she was a single mother, the ex-wife of a guy he knew slightly, and he said that his name was Terry Coats. He'd been a cop, he said, but that was all. What's his history?'

'He served in the Strathclyde force, but never in our lot; when he died he was employed in security at Edinburgh Airport. Noele, his ex, is my sergeant; naturally, she's excluded from the investigation.'

'And they wound up dead together? That's weird.'

'It is,' Mary Chambers agreed. 'Do you have a connection between them, other than the woman?'

'Possibly,' he replied. 'Spring, did Griff ever talk to you about a robbery in South Africa around ten years ago in which a shedload of gold coins was stolen?'

Her eyes widened as she stared at him. 'Did he talk to me about it? He was involved in it. He was a victim. He and his partner were the police escort when it happened. It was on the outskirts of Pretoria; they had picked up a consignment from the Rand refinery in Jo'burg in an armoured van, and they were escorting it to a bullion warehouse when they were ambushed on a quiet stretch of road. Griff was shot in the shoulder and in the head; his partner was killed and so were the van drivers. The money's never been recovered.'

'That's true,' Chambers confirmed. 'There's a chap in my bridge club here who was on the force at the time. He told me all about it; I knew some of it, of course, from Spring.'

'Did they have any leads?' Haddock asked. 'We heard that Russians might have been involved.'

'You know how it is, there were all sorts of conspiracy theories; Russians, the Mafia, there was even one nutter who insisted that the CIA had done it to raise cash to fund covert operations in Africa. I doubt that anyone will ever know for sure.'

'Did your card-playing friend fill you in on the details?'

'As much as they ever found out. Most of it was speculation; Griff was the only survivor and he was out of it for most of the time. He stepped out of the police vehicle; one of them shot him before he could even draw his firearm. Fannie, his partner, tried to pull his own gun as he was being hauled out of the car. The robber shot him in the side, then shot Griff again, in the head . . . or so he thought: the bullet knocked him out but it didn't penetrate his skull. The doctor who treated him said he was the luckiest man he'd ever seen. After he recovered they gave him a medal and promoted him into CID.'

'It left a mark on him, though,' Spring added. 'He was different after it. His behaviour changed at home; Annelise, his wife, got the rough end of his tongue . . . nothing else, mind . . . until finally she looked elsewhere. They got divorced, she got hefty child support . . . even though she married an accountant who earned five times what Griff did . . . and that was when he decided he had to look for an international transfer.'

'And you went with him?' Singh asked.

'I decided it was best,' she replied. 'I never liked Annelise. Left to my own devices, I might have done her some damage for the way she treated my brother.'

'What about your parents? Were they happy with both of you leaving?'

'My father left us when we were children. My mother died when we were twenty.'

Haddock leaned forward once more, looking directly into the camera rather than at the screen. 'Did Griff find it easier to make ends meet in Scotland?'

'Of course. He was paid in sterling and that buys a lot of rand. Annelise, the cow, actually went back to court to try and get more, but she was laughed right out of there.' She smiled, savagely. 'Tough shit on her now,' she said.

'Do you know if Griff left a will? We couldn't find one in his flat.'

'Try our lawyer, Edgar Matthew at Smith and Green. We made wills when we bought the apartment. We had a joint life policy to cover the mortgage, and they underlined that arrangement. I amended mine to leave everything else to Mary. He left his half of the flat to me and any balance to Lisa and

Andre, his children, not that there'll be much left, I guess. Griff had expensive tastes, in clothes . . . and women.'

'Is that so?'

'It always was; he was always after the extra buck when we were young.'

'Mmm,' the young detective murmured. 'Mary,' he said changing tack unexpectedly, 'suppose you wanted to smuggle something out of South Africa, something bulky, but very valuable. How would you go about it?'

'Bulky, but valuable,' she repeated. 'A bit like me? It's not something I've ever considered, but off the top of my head, I'd find someone on a container ship, or an oil tanker, or maybe even a cruise liner and bribe him to help me shift it. It would probably have to be an officer; ordinary seamen would be subject to scrutiny. You think about here, you think about smuggling diamonds, but that's not what you've got in mind is it, Sauce?'

'No, it's not. I'm thinking about gold, coins to be precise. Krugerrands to be even preciser. I'll be frank with you both. Griff's home has state-of-the-art security, installed after you moved out, Spring.'

'Come on,' she exclaimed, 'he has an alarm system. He fitted it because he was living on his own.'

'He fitted it because he had a safe, Spring. Were you never there after you moved out?'

'Of course I was, but only to visit. He made my room into an office, so I didn't go in there. If he had a safe, so what? We do, here and in Edinburgh.'

'Do either of them contain a quarter of a million in gold and eighty-eight thousand in cash? Because that's what we found in Griff's. I'm going to ask you straight out . . . sorry,

Mary, both of you . . . do either of you know anything about it?'

Chambers screwed up her face in sheer astonishment. 'How much?'

'Two hundred and fifty Krugerrands. The cash was in your classic brown envelope. Plus one other item: a handgun. Spring,' he asked again, 'do you know anything about this, anything at all?'

She drew a breath. 'Nothing at all, I swear.'

'How about the cousin you mentioned? Were he and Griff close?'

'Fairly; closer than he is with me. I never hear from him.'

'I'd like contact details for him, if you can let me have them. Also, Mary, can you ask your bridge pal if the police report on the robbery is still readily available or if it's archived?'

'I'll call him as soon as we're finished,' she promised, 'I have his mobile. He was pretty senior; he was a Brigadier, I think. The South African Police Service has military-style ranks,' she explained. 'If it helps, I can ask him for advice on how to go about getting it.'

'Thanks.' He hesitated, then went on. 'This is pure speculation, but can you ask him something for me? What types of weapon do South African police officers carry?'

'Will do. Why do you want to know?'

'Because I read too many detective novels,' he replied. 'Either that or I've been around Bob Skinner too long. If he was sitting here, he'd want to know too. One last thing,' he added. 'When Griff didn't show up, did you try to contact him?'

'Show up?' Spring Montell exclaimed. 'What do you mean by that? Where was he going to show up? When?'

'He was booked on a flight to Johannesburg out of Heathrow, on Sunday. He was signed out for a couple of weeks' holiday and told his station commander that was where he was headed. His suitcase made it, but he didn't.'

'If that's the case, Sauce, he didn't tell us.' She dabbed at her left eye as a tear appeared. 'But that's not unusual. Griff always was a surprising guy.'

Fifteen

'Thank you for agreeing to come in, Detective Sergeant. We've met, but if you don't remember I'm Detective Chief Inspector Charlotte Mann. This is DS John Cotter.'

'You're not easily forgotten, DCI Mann,' Noele McClair said. 'Good to meet you, John. Now, are you going to tell me why I'm here rather than you coming to me?'

'With your child being at home, we thought it might be best,' Mann replied.

'With respect, ma'am, no you didn't. I'm here because someone higher up the chain told you to do it that way. Sauce is the SIO but he would have spelled it out for me; that leaves only two, the DCC and the chief constable herself, but he's the boss in all but name when it comes to criminal investigation. I'm here,' she continued, 'because I'm a person of interest. I had relationships with both victims, one past, one current. I'm your only link between them at the moment; if you weren't interviewing me formally you'd be falling down on the job.'

'Do you want to have a rep present?' Mann asked. 'If so, I can postpone this for a while.'

'Christ, no,' she declared. 'You're going to be asking me about things I'll want to stay within this room. Fire away.'

The DCI nodded. 'Fair enough. I would like to record this, but only with your consent.'

McClair replied by leaning across the desk and switching on the recorder. 'Let's do it.'

It was Cotter who began the questioning. 'DS McClair, for how long were you and Mr Coats married?'

'Ten years. Out of those, a couple were okay; after Harry was born.'

'What were the problems with the marriage?'

She whistled. 'Where do I begin? His ego for a start; he really did think he was the Special One. He was a good cop, no question, but he thought he was better than that. Terry thought that rules were for other people, and that corners were there to be cut. He also thought that a chain of command involved body piercing. That's what did for him in the end. When Brass Rubbings came for him he was up shit creek, because he didn't have the fallback of blaming it on somebody else. If you have an informant you know is an active criminal, you don't let him run without getting the approval of someone higher up. Right, DCI Mann?'

'Spot on.'

'Okay,' Cotter continued. 'His ego, and what else?'

She frowned. 'His cock; now that was a problem, for the second half of our marriage and probably longer. I could never be sure where it had been, then latterly, when things were really bad, it wasn't in me often enough. Sorry if that embarrasses you, John, but you want a full and frank disclosure.' She paused. 'Truth is, I put up with it for longer than I should have; but when Sauce and Bob Skinner caught him with that trolley dolly in a hotel, and it became public, well that really was one too many. I should have done it years earlier. I am so much better off without him. Personally, and financially too.'

Her bitterness took the sergeant by surprise. 'Even without his salary coming into the house?'

Noele McClair laughed out loud. 'I think you mean without his gambling debts taking the shoes off our son's feet, and the food out of his mouth.'

Lottie Mann intervened. 'Terry was a gambler?'

'An addict. It was always in him and it just got worse and worse. I had to hide my credit cards from him. I had to divert my salary into a personal account rather than our joint, and I had to ask the bank to remove the overdraft facility on that, because it was still bleeding me dry. The bank wasn't fucking interested of course; they wouldn't do it without his signature as well. When we got divorced they had to. Under the terms of the settlement we were each liable for half the overdrawn amount. I cleared mine by switching it to my personal account. I have no idea what he did. I'm sure you'll find out, once the banks reopen for business tomorrow.'

'What was he like to live with?' the DCI asked. 'Sauce and Tarvil went through his place. They said it wasn't fit for pigs.'

'Good analogy. If Terry had seen two pigs, he'd have bet on which one was the faster. He was a slob. He'd throw stuff on the floor, leave empty beer cans lying around, and expect me to clear up after him . . . which of course I did, without complaining nearly often enough.' Her mouth tightened. 'One time I did go mental, though. Harry had left a toy on the floor, a wee Ninja warrior figure. Terry stamped on it, broke it, and told him that would happen any time he left something lying around. The wee man was crying, and I just ripped into him. I don't think I'd ever been so angry with anybody in my life.'

'Suppose Terry hadn't been caught being unfaithful,' DS

Cotter asked, probing, 'would you have split up, or would we be interviewing you as a widow?'

She looked him in the eye. 'There's a fair chance you'd be interviewing me as a murder suspect . . .' She broke off and grinned. 'Oh silly me,' she chuckled, 'that's what you're doing just now.'

'No,' Mann said, firmly. 'We are not doing that. Nor do I believe we would have been. My ex was as bad as yours, but I never actually thought about caving his head in with the pepper mill.' A flicker of a smile showed in her mouth but did not make it to her eyes. 'Okay, maybe I did once or twice, but I wouldn't have done it, for Jakey's sake, and nor would you for Harry's. DS McClair, we just need to know everything you know about your ex and about Inspector Montell. Is there anything you can tell us about Mr Coats after your separation and divorce? Was he still involved with that woman, Aisha Karman, for example?'

'I have no idea, although I doubt that he could have afforded her with the child-support payments. That's one thing Griff and he had in common, but Griff was up to date with his, unlike Terry. I had little or no contact with him after the divorce, other than when he called to pick up Harry every other Saturday. When he did, we never spoke for any length of time. I really did loathe him.'

'When did your relationship with Inspector Montell begin?' Cotter asked, taking back control of the interview.

'At the end of August, beginning of September,' McClair replied. 'I had to go to Torphichen Place to interview a suspect. Sauce had been called away, so he took the other chair. We'd never met before. He was out of CID by the time I transferred to Edinburgh and moved to Gullane. Once the business was done we went for a coffee in the canteen. He mentioned that he knew my ex, sort of; that their paths had crossed before police unification, and that he'd heard Terry had quit rather than be booted from CID and posted to a desk job in the back of beyond. He said that he sympathised with him, that he'd fallen foul of a chief constable too.'

'Did he explain that?'

'Not at the time. I asked him what he meant but he just smiled and said, "Conflict of interests". Later on, he told me about him and Alex Skinner, and how he was injured in her flat, defending her. He said that she'd moved in with somebody, and that their thing was over . . . not that it had ever really been a thing in the first place.'

'Apart from that first occasion,' Cotter continued, 'did he ever mention Terry? Did he give you any indication that he had met him recently?'

'No, none at all. If you're going to ask me how they came to be in the same car after they were killed, I can assure you that it's a complete mystery to me.'

'I was,' the DS confirmed, 'but before that, can we talk more about your relationship with Inspector Montell. How serious was it?'

'I can only speak for me,' she told him, 'but on a scale from one to ten, I would say seven with a real possibility of upward movement. Immediately post-divorce, I had no intention of taking another marital risk, but the more time I spent with Griff the more that started to soften. He was the complete opposite of Terry in every way, kind, thoughtful and generous.' She winked at Mann. 'He was also spectacularly good in bed. I never knew what an orgasm was with Terry; he was one of those guys who didn't realise that women are entitled to come too, or maybe he just didn't know we can.' She leaned back. 'I have this theory . . . fuck no, this profound belief . . . that every young man should be given a copy of *The Joy of Sex*, or something similar, on his sixteenth birthday. I'm pretty sure that Griff was.'

'Who knew about the two of you?'

'I don't think anybody did, until he had to tell Alex Skinner. We were very careful; we were both cops, and we knew that if one colleague found out, so would everyone else in a very short time.'

'Officers found female garments in his home. Can we assume that they're yours?'

'Yes, I kept a couple of things there. I stayed over a few times; my mother would look after Harry, and I'd spin her a yarn. If we were going somewhere after work, dinner, theatre and the like, I needed things I could change into.'

'Were you happy with him?'

She looked at her hands, steepled on the table. 'Happier than I'd ever been.' Her eyes moistened. 'Now it's all been ripped away. Bastards!' she hissed.

Mann edged forward, and Cotter withdrew, slightly, as she took over. 'Did you ever have any thoughts about Inspector Montell's lifestyle?' she began.

'Not really; it was modest. We didn't go to any flash places, no weekend at Gleneagles, or anything like that. If I read you right you're talking about his dress sense, the designer clothes that he liked. I teased him about that; we had a laugh when he confessed that he shopped in an outlet place in Livingston, where they do seconds and the like much cheaper that the real thing.'

'Did you ever go into his office? You must have noticed

there was a lock on the door. In fact, you must have noticed the security in general.'

'The alarm system? Of course; the monitor sensors were just about everywhere. I asked him about it; he said it was just part of being a cop, and I got that. As for the office, no, I never went in there. I had no reason to, and I had no reason to ask him about it.'

'No, of course not,' the DCI conceded. 'In all your time together, did Griff, Inspector Montell, ever mention your ex-husband?'

'No,' McClair said, firmly, 'and neither did I. I didn't want Terry near my new relationship in any way.'

'He didn't give you any hint that they might have been in touch?' Mann persisted.

'No, never. Griff and Terry had absolutely nothing in common. One was a gentleman, the other was an arsehole.' She paused, anticipating the next question. 'I know, and yet they both wound up dead in the same car. I hope you do find out how, but it won't be through me. I have no idea.'

'We will, eventually.'

'Do you have any lines of investigation?'

'We do, but I'm not going to divulge that just yet. Instead . . . look, the two of you were intimate. Apart from the injury that he sustained during the incident in Alex Skinner's flat, did Inspector Montell have any other scars?'

'Yes, he had one big one, on his right shoulder, front and back. It was from a gunshot wound he sustained when he was a police officer in South Africa.'

'Did he tell you how it happened? I'm assuming that you asked him.'

'Sure, but he wasn't wounded in action; it was a stupid

accident and he was embarrassed by it. We did a scar comparison one night; my caesarean, my appendix, his shoulder. I said that mine were boring, but that his must have a story behind it. "Oh yes," he said. He told me that he went out hunting one evening with his patrol partner. His name was Fannie, I think. He said they were after deer and separated to flank a herd. But the light wasn't too good; he made a sudden move and Fannie mistook him for an antelope. I told him I didn't believe him but he swore blind that it was true.' She peered at Mann. 'It was . . . wasn't it?'

'Not according to our information. Did he ever tell you about a robbery in South Africa, when a consignment of gold coins were stolen from a hijacked van?'

'No, ma'am,' she insisted, 'he didn't. That's not something I would have forgotten.' She paused and gasped, her mouth falling open slightly. 'But Terry said something that comes right back to mind. When I found out about his affair with the airline woman, and told him he was gone for good, he tried to talk me round. He said it was all connected to stolen Krugerrands. I told him he could spend the rest of his life thinking up crazy excuses, I wasn't buying any of them and he could fuck right off. He protested, swore it was true, but I yelled at him that he and the truth were total strangers and he should get out of my life. Could it actually have been true? And suppose it was, how would it connect to Griff?'

'If his story was true,' Mann replied, 'it's just possible that the coins he spoke about came from the robbery I just mentioned. How would it connect to Inspector Montell? I have no idea. But I do know that he was part of the escort of the consignment, that he was the only survivor, and that's how the wound from the so-called hunting accident really happened.'

Sixteen

'And here I was thinking it had been a quiet Hogmanay,' PC Andrea Newman sighed, as she drew the car to a halt. 'Where did she say he was?'

'Just before the thirty sign, the ops room,' PC Ronnie Hamilton, her partner, replied.

She looked along the narrow highway. 'What did the informant say? That she saw a bloke sleeping it off in a field?'

'Aye. She said she saw him from her kitchen window.' He pointed across a field to a group of houses that backed on to it. 'She had to have been over there, for there's no other buildings with a view of this stretch of road. That's at least three hundred yards away. She's either got great eyesight or great binoculars. I don't see anybody? Do you, Andrea?'

'Not on this side of the fence, that's for sure. If she did see someone, he's probably woke up and gone home . . . although,' she wondered, 'how would he get here in the first place. If he was walking towards Howgate, he's come from a fair way off. If he was walking away . . . he was a candidate for hypothermia.'

'Maybe a patrol car gave him a lift part way and left him to walk the rest, to sober him up,' Hamilton suggested.

'Strictly against the rules, Ronnie; you know that, after that man froze to death years ago.'

'Some of the folk we've had transferred in don't know that story; they might be a bit lax with those rules. Whatever, he's clearly not by the roadside, as we were told, he's not playing Worzel Gummidge in the middle of the field . . .'

'But he could be lying behind that wee row of trees on the other side of the fence,' Newman pointed out, peering in that direction. 'Come to think of it, I'm sure I can see a shoe; let's find if there's anything in it.'

The copse was only a few yards short of the speed limit sign. She led the way towards it and climbed nimbly over the wire fence. Her bulkier colleague made no move to join her. 'Is it muddy over there?' he called out.

'No, it's okay. Ronnie, there's somebody here right enough.' She moved towards the figure, stretched out at the base of the trees. He was well dressed, in a thick camel coat. The shoes that had caught her eye were patent leather, reflecting the weak late-morning sunshine. 'Come on, sir,' she called up, 'the party's over, it's time to call it a day. Your pretty balloon is well burst . . .'

The man was lying face down; leaning over, she turned him on to his side . . . then recoiled. 'Oh shit,' she muttered.

The fence wire sang as Hamilton put his weight on it. 'You need to stay on that side, Ronnie. This fella's not waking up any time soon. Move the car along to the other side of the trees,' she tossed him the keys, 'and bring some tape if we've got it. We're going to need CID here, medical examiner, the works. This man's been shot.'

Seventeen

'He was always well dressed, Sauce,' Alex Skinner said. 'You know that. You worked with him when he was in CID.'

'That was a couple of years ago,' Haddock pointed out. 'I remember him being smart, but I don't remember ever noticing a designer label on his shirt. There was barely anything else to be seen when we went through his house. But your father told me you made a point of never going there, so you won't have seen it.'

'That's what I let my dad believe, but the fact is, Griff never invited me. The last time I saw him, I suggested it, but he put me off. He told me he was involved with someone else; I accepted that, and I was happy for him. I was in and out of the place often enough when we were next-door neighbours, but Spring was there then so I never stayed overnight. If we were having, let's call it a sleepover, he'd come into my place; then my life got complicated for a while and I moved. After Spring left, when we were both single again, I thought that might change, but no, he never once asked me there. The opposite; he would suggest that he come to mine. Mind you I was with Andy Martin for some of that two-year period, so it didn't arise for a while. When that ended, I turned to him for comfort and a little joy.' She smiled.

'Are you sure about that?' he asked, quietly.

'About what?'

'When you were with Andy, didn't it arise?'

She gazed at him for a while, then sighed. 'Maybe, once or twice. It got frustrating at times; in hindsight I could sense Andy drifting away from the relationship. He'd say it was just work, but finally, after being stood up a couple of nights on the trot, I called Griff and asked him if he could come over. He was hesitant at first. He knew I wasn't asking him over for a coffee, and I guess he was worried that screwing the chief constable's girlfriend might not be a great career move. Lust overcame logic, though . . . it always did with us.' Her voice faltered for a second.

'Just the once?'

She shook her head, quickly. 'No, more than that,' she admitted; then she grinned. 'You've been talking to his sister, haven't you? You and she probably think I'm a right slapper, but I'm not, I promise. There isn't a man had breakfast in my apartment, or anything else, other than those two.'

'You're right,' he confirmed. 'I did talk to her. She said that Griff blamed those times for him being moved out of CID. He was sure that Andy Martin had found out and was getting even with him. He even thought that Andy had been having you watched. Do you believe that?'

'Not all of it. I could accept that Andy was jealous of him and that, yes, he might have bumped him into uniform out of sheer personal spite. But having me watched? No, absolutely not. If I'd suspected that . . . and I'm not stupid, I'm a cop's daughter plus you have to be aware of what's happening around you in my line of work . . . I'd have done one of two things. I'd either have squared him up myself, or if I'd been feeling evil enough, I'd have set my dad on him. He knows a couple of things about Andy that he wouldn't want being leaked.'

'And yet those two used to be best friends,' Haddock observed.

'Used to be, Sauce, until Andy's incredible ambition got in the way.' She took a breath, frowning. 'People think he's gone for good, you know, but I don't. My guess is he's just on sabbatical. Aileen de Marco, my former stepmother, used to be a big fan of his. Now that she's taken her political bandwagon down to Westminster, she has influence with the Mayor of London, and he has a big say in Metropolitan Police appointments, so watch this space.' She paused. 'Are you warm enough, by the way?'

They were seated on two Adirondack chairs on Dominic Jackson's deck, taking advantage of a break in the rain and the unexpected morning sunshine. The DI gave an almost imperceptible nod, burying himself deep in a heavy leather jacket. 'I'm good,' he said. 'How long are you going to stay in this place?' he asked.

'That's open-ended,' she replied. 'I realised that I was damaged when I came here; I was as much a patient as I was a lodger. I'm good now. The tenant in my place by Holyrood Park is moving out in three months, when his contract in the Scottish Parliament ends. I could move back then, but Dominic says he likes having me around, that I keep him from getting morose. He shared accommodation with several hundred men for several years, remember. He'd tell you himself that he has trouble adjusting to living completely on his own.' She grinned. 'We'll see how it goes. Do you think Griff had trouble adjusting,' she asked, 'after Spring moved in with Mary Chambers?'

The question took him by surprise, but the answer came easily to him. 'The opposite,' he said. 'The first thing he did was fortify the place.' He described the security system that he and Singh had discovered.

'He never mentioned any of that to me,' she assured him. 'A little over the top, surely. What the hell was he protecting, apart from those designer clothes you were asking about?'

'Lots,' Haddock replied, moving on before she could press him. 'Alex, did you and he ever talk about anything other than work?'

'I never talked about mine. Him cop, me criminal defence lawyer; it wouldn't have been appropriate. He didn't either, but come to think of it, he didn't really talk about anything. We'd discuss current affairs, the latest movies, who'd been slagging who off on social media . . . I remember us trying to work out what exactly the fuck an Instagram influencer is and not coming up with an answer . . . but, beyond that, nothing much. Our relationship was physical, not philosophical.'

'He had a scar on his shoulder. Did he ever tell you about that?'

'He said that Spring shot him accidentally with a crossbow when they were both kids.'

'And you believed that?'

'Why shouldn't I?'

'No reason,' he conceded, 'but the truth is he was shot while he was a police officer in Pretoria. There was an armed hijack, and he was wounded. He never mentioned that?'

'Never.' She smiled, lightly. 'Sounds like we weren't as close as I thought.'

'How did he seem when you were with him? Was he happy, sad, up, down?'

'Same old, same old. Mind you, the last time we were together, the night I had the break-in and he got hurt, he'd been a bit unsettled before it happened. His mind wasn't on the job, so to speak; he wasn't really with me. I got a bit annoyed about that, I asked him what the matter was. The way he reacted, it really pissed me off. That's when I got out of bed and went into the kitchen for some juice, and was surprised by the two intruders.'

'The way he reacted,' Haddock repeated. 'How was it, what did he say that annoyed you so much?'

'It was dismissive for a start; it was as if he wasn't for sharing, at least not with me. As for what he said, I have no idea what that was, because he said it in Afrikaans!'

Eighteen

'I notice you didn't tell her about t' gold in Montell's safe,' DS Cotter remarked. 'Or the gun.'

'I didn't think she needed to know that,' DCI Mann replied. 'That information stays within the investigating team, and Noele McClair isn't part of it. More than that . . .'

'Are you saying she's a suspect?' he asked.

'No, but she's still a person of interest. The two men in her life died together, John, and she remains a possibility as the link that brought them there, even if she isn't aware of it. It's evident that she hated Coats's guts, but we don't really know anything about the true nature of her relationship with Montell, other than what she's told us.'

'We do, surely. DI Haddock told us that he brushed off Ms Skinner because he was in a relationship with DS McClair. I've never met the woman, but I saw her on telly once, after she got one of her clients acquitted in the High Court. In Montell's shoes I wouldn't have been doing that lightly . . . and I'm bloody married!'

Mann treated him to a rare smile. 'If that ever found its way back to Mrs Cotter . . .'

He tapped the side of his head. 'Don't worry, boss, it's all in here. I've always been more cautious than brave.'

'That makes you an exception then, Sergeant. In my experience men don't consult their brains at all when making decisions like that.' She rose from the comfortable chair that she had commandeered and walked across the CID room. 'DC Wright,' she said, 'any joy accessing those bank accounts?'

'Surprisingly, ma'am, yes,' she replied. 'I thought I might have to wait until tomorrow, but no. I have Coats' and Inspector Montell's, and I've been promised Noele's once my TSB contact clears it with the right level of management.'

'What do they show?'

'Terry Coats's Bank of Scotland account is very much what I expected. He was chunkily overdrawn; a little over one third of his net salary went out again in child support and pretty much all of the rest goes in mortgage, credit-card and interest payments. He had two credit cards with the bank, both nearly maxed out and an Amex card that isn't, but a lot of retailers don't take them. I don't know how the guy survived.'

'No other in-goings other than his pay? DS McClair said he was a gambler, but they don't lose all the time. Are we sure he doesn't have any other accounts? He wouldn't have been the first guy who tried to hide assets from his ex-wife. I can tell you that from experience.'

'I can't be certain of that,' Wright admitted. 'I started my search based on the information I had from his employer; same with Inspector Montell and Noele. Once I've got through that first phase I can widen the trawl.'

'My ex had help from his parents in trying to stitch me up, until Alex Skinner threatened them with a court-enforced audit of their assets, and with HMRC as well. That's not her usual line of work, I know,' she added, 'but her father asked her to do me a favour. Have you checked tax records too?'

'No, ma'am, but they're all on PAYE so I wouldn't expect them to be self-assessed. I'll have a look, though.'

'Do that, but don't prioritise it. Now, what did you learn from Montell's banking?'

'About as much as I learned from Coats's. He was paying much less in child support, and he seemed to manage it better. He made the payments using a banking app called Revolut. It lets you do currency exchanges at market rate and transfers funds instantly. He was never overdrawn, used credit cards to manage cash flow rather than borrow, and was able to transfer small sums regularly from his current account to a savings account. He had fourteen and a half thousand in that.'

'That sounds too good to be true,' Mann observed.

'He didn't own a car,' Wright countered. 'Think about it; a car is a big liability, unless you run a banger and don't use it very much. Even then you're going to be hit by bills for maintenance, MOT, insurance, all the things you need to do just to keep it legally parked on the public highway. If you're free of that, and a lot of single people who live in cities are, you have a hell of a lot more disposable income.'

'True. More to spend on designer clothes, maybe, but DS McClair said he told her he shopped for them in a cut-price place in Livingston. Take a look at his credit-card spend and see if it bears that out.'

'I have done already, ma'am. I looked specifically for clothing-store purchases but I didn't find any. Wherever he bought them he must have used cash.'

'He had plenty of that, going by what DI, sorry, acting DCI Haddock,' Wright thought that she detected a faint trace of irony in her tone, 'found in his safe. What about . . .'

'Anything to explain it?'

'Stop reading my mind, Jackie, but yes.'

Wright shifted in her seat. 'I've given it some thought,' she admitted. 'We know that Griff, Inspector Montell, possessed a significant holding in Krugerrands; let's assume that it was legitimate, there being no firm evidence that it wasn't. It could have been a legacy, it could have been a lottery win that he kept quiet about and invested in gold. They found two hundred and fifty; the cash in the safe might have come from the sale of others. If it did, you'd think there would be a record of their disposal, but I can't find any in his banking records. That would suggest, supposing that's what happened, that every one of them was sold privately, for cash. Who would buy them?'

'Jewellers?'

'They might, but more likely he'd have gone to a bullion dealer. There are a few of them around Edinburgh, and I will speak to them all. I've called a couple already but they're closed for the holiday. Tomorrow's Friday, so they might not open until Monday.'

'That's good work, DC Wright,' Mann said. 'Have you ever fancied transferring to Glasgow?'

Nineteen

'Who's the SIO?'

The question reached the detective from the other side of the small copse. He took two long steps to his right so that he could see the source. His exceptional height made his sterile coverall a tight fit; 'One-size' it said on the packet but he was close to being an exception. 'I am,' he said. 'DI Jack McGurk. Who's asking?'

'Dr Emily Badger, duty pathologist,' a sharp-featured, dark-haired woman replied. She gestured to her companion. 'This is my assistant, Denzil Douglas.'

McGurk thought that he caught a flash of resentment in the man's eyes. Douglas was a forensic examiner attached to the pathology department, and the two had met before. 'Hi, Denzil,' he called out. 'I thought you'd have escaped New Year duty, given your seniority.'

'There is only me, Jack,' he grumbled. 'Cuts.' He nodded towards the man who stood beside the DI. 'Hi, Lance. Happy New Year, guys, by the way. We'll maybe forego the handshake, though.'

'Has life been pronounced extinct?' Badger asked briskly as, suited for action, she slid between the wires of the fence.

'Technically not,' Detective Sergeant Lance Anderson told her. 'That said, the worm that's just crawled out of his ear makes it better than even money that he's dead.'

'Leave her alone, Lance,' McGurk murmured. 'She's a bairn. I take it Professor Grace is otherwise engaged,' he said, raising his voice to address the young pathologist.

'Yes, she is,' Badger replied. 'She pulled rank on me, she's doing the post-mortems on the two men who were found dead yesterday outside the police station. I'd expected to be asked to assist but instead I was diverted here.' She moved towards the body on the ground. 'He hasn't been moved?'

'No,' the DI confirmed.

'Not at all? What about the people who found him?'

'They were police officers, brought here by a call from that house over there.' He pointed across the field. 'They knew better than to disturb the body any more than they had to. The informant, she assumed he was a New Year drunk.'

'If so, he's had his last drink. Are we thinking suspicious death? Nobody said when I was called to the scene.'

'Take a look, Doctor.'

She crouched beside the body. As McGurk looked down at her he saw her frown. 'Have you seen this?' she asked.

'Us? Not close up. We've played it by the book and waited for you.'

'Then take a look now.'

He lowered himself down with surprising ease, turned the dead face towards him and peered at it through his varifocals. 'Very efficient,' he whispered. 'Double tap; two shots in the middle of the forehead. Very special forces.'

'So I'm told,' she said, 'and quite a coincidence. One of the men I examined yesterday was killed in almost exactly the same way.' She reached to the back of the head, running her gloved hands over it. 'No exit wound; nor was there with the other one. That means the bullets are still in there, as they were with him; no sorry, as it was, the Torphichen Place man having been killed by a single shot. You should be able to run a comparison.'

'Oh bugger,' the DI sighed. 'It means more than that. It means this just moved above our pay grade.'

'Divisional commander?' Anderson suggested.

'No,' McGurk said, 'above his too. This one goes straight to the deputy chief.'

Twenty

'Ten more minutes and I would have started without you,' Sarah Grace said, as Haddock and Singh came into the examination room of the mortuary, wearing gowns, hats and rubber boots.

'Sorry, Prof,' the DI replied. 'My last meeting went on for longer than I expected.'

She nodded. 'I know who you met. She called me after you left. Was it fruitful?'

'Yes, in that it left me with another question. No, in that I've no idea how to answer it.'

'The answers here are pretty obvious,' she took a breath, 'but my job has to look at all present factors, and determine what is and what isn't relevant.' She turned to the mortuary assistant. 'Mary, let's begin with Drawer Six.'

The detectives waited as the woman left the room; two minutes later she was back, wheeling a height-adjustable trolley bearing a stretcher laden with a white body bag; as she unzipped it, they saw it contained the remains of Griff Montell. Between them, she and the pathologist eased the burden on to the middle of the three steel examination tables.

Professor Grace switched on an overhead microphone. 'The

subject is an adult white male,' she began, 'aged thirty-nine, found dead in Torphichen Place, Edinburgh, in the early hours of the first of January. Rigor has passed, and the scene of crime examiner's report indicates that death occurred very shortly before the remains were discovered. I am now making the Y incision.'

As she went to work with a scalpel a smell seemed to explode into the examination room. Tarvil Singh had witnessed more than one examination in his police career, but unknown to Haddock, he had never made it beyond that point. 'Sorry, Sauce,' he muttered, as he turned and headed for the door.

'It's better that he keels over outside than in here,' the pathologist said. 'I doubt if the three of us could get that one off the floor.'

Haddock's reply was forestalled by the sound of his phone. He looked at the screen. 'Sorry, Sarah,' he muttered as he accepted the call, 'it's the DCC. Sir?'

'Sauce.' Even in addressing him, McGuire's tone was urgent. 'There's an incident out at Howgate. Know it? Village near Penicuik. Uniform called it in, and Midlothian CID responded; big McGurk. A body; male, middle-aged, well-dressed and very dead, dumped behind some trees on the edge of a field. The new pathologist, Badger, attended; when she saw two bullet holes in the middle of the forehead she told Jack it reminded her of Terry Coats and he called me straight off. It's possibly, maybe probably, unrelated to yours but it needs to be assessed by you until we know for sure.'

'Either way, boss, it's a serious crime. That's what we do, isn't it?'

'Yes, but at this moment your team is focused completely on

Montell and Coats. If you decide they're not linked, leave it with Jack. Where are you just now?'

'That's the thing, sir. I'm at the mortuary witnessing the post-mortems. Tarvil's here, but he's outside throwing up his last three curries. So I can barely leave him.'

'Not again!' McGuire laughed. 'He's a legend for that; I should have warned you. Leave it with me; I'll send Mann and Cotter, and tell Lottie to report to you from the scene. One thing you can do for me though. Ask Sarah to make space in her schedule to do another, tomorrow morning. I'll arrange for the victim to be taken into Edinburgh.'

Twenty-One

Few men made Lottie Mann feel small, but Jack McGurk did. She had heard of him from Bob Skinner, who had described him as 'a very good detective officer, but probably lacking command potential'. He looked commanding enough to her as she and Cotter arrived at the crime scene. There were so many vehicles lined up on the narrow Bonnyrigg road that they had to park on the other side of the roundabout that formed the junction with Penicuik, Auchendinny and the village of Howgate itself. Their way was briefly blocked by an officious uniformed constable but a flash of the DCI's warrant card, and a glare, prompted him to stand aside.

'DI Haddock might have told us to bring wellies,' Cotter complained as they surveyed the crime scene.

'You're from fucking Tyneside, John,' she laughed. 'You don't have any wellies. Me neither, but I do wear sensible shoes, and I do carry these.' She produced two pairs of disposable overshoes from her bag and handed one to the DS. Donning them, she climbed the fence and approached the tall figure in the field.

'DCI Mann,' he called out, 'I'm . . .'

'I know who you are, Inspector, the DCC briefed me. This is my DS, John Cotter.'

McGurk nodded a greeting, downwards; Cotter was a foot shorter than he was. 'This is my sergeant, Lance Anderson,' he said, introducing the bearded man by his side. 'That over there is the pathologist, Dr Badger. She's the reason I called in Special Forces. She thinks it might be related to the Griff Montell murder.' He winced. 'That's a bastard. I knew Griff well. We went out on a couple of double dates, him and Alex, me and my wife, before Martin binned his wife and kids and weaselled his way back into Alex's life. How's she taking it? She's a good act, Alex. She and Griff were never altar-bound, but I always thought that was a shame, for they made a nice couple. I've rarely seen two people more comfortable together.'

'In that case you'll know how she's taking it better than I will,' Mann told him. 'I haven't seen her since I've been through here. Sauce has been handling that; he's the SIO in DCI Pye's absence on sick leave. I do know Alex though. She did me a favour once in a domestic matter.'

'Domestic?' McGurk repeated. 'That's not her line, is it?'

'Her old man asked her to help me, and she did. She rammed it so far up my ex and his bully of a father that they've been speaking in high-pitched voices ever since. Down to business though, what have we got here?' She glanced at Badger. 'A young pathologist with a vivid imagination, or should I take this seriously?'

'No and yes, I would say. She came from Torphichen Place to here in successive days. Maybe that scene was too fresh in her mind, but my gut says it's a stone that needs turning.'

'Let's talk to her. Dr Badger!' she called out.

The pathologist looked towards her, then turned as the four

detectives approached. 'Who's next?' she asked cheerfully. 'The chief constable with his shiny hat?'

'The chief constable's a woman, and she's not given to wearing the official headgear. DCI Mann and DS Cotter, Serious Crimes. What can you tell us?'

Badger winked. 'I can tell you that he's dead; that's for sure.'

'If he wasn't, you might be,' Mann growled. 'I had an early start this morning, plus I'm never at my best when standing a few feet away from a cadaver. I'm told you're new to field work; don't assume it's like what you see on telly. There's no room for comedians in situations like this.'

The young pathologist flushed, glanced away and bit her lip.

The man beside her intervened. 'Leave her alone, Lottie. You're right, she's new, and she's had a pretty rough baptism, three gunshot victims in two days. We can all get a bit flippant when we're nervous. Don't worry, I'll break her in. She's learning all the time; for a start she knows now that a crime scene technician isn't a pathologist's assistant. Isn't that right, Emily?'

Dr Badger sniffed, but smiled weakly. 'Yes.'

'So, Denzil,' the DCI continued. 'You're the wise old head around here. What have you got from the scene so far?'

'I can tell you one thing. The Torphichen Place drop-off was a day and a half ago, right? The post-mortem examination will confirm it, but this man's been here for longer than that, a day more, maybe two. I'm going by the animal and insect depredation that's evident on the body. It's been cold, not sub-zero but enough to keep maggot infestation to a minimum, but plenty of other species will have been tucking in. It's evident to me that he wasn't just dumped here, chucked over the fence.

The position of the body makes it obvious that he was placed here carefully. You're the detectives, but you'll be supposing that it was done so that he wouldn't be seen from a passing car.'

'Agreed,' Jack McGurk said. 'Nor by farm workers either; this field's used for potatoes just now. It hasn't been touched since the last ploughing in the autumn and it won't be until the next crop gets planted. You were going through his pockets, Denzil, just before our colleagues got here. Did you find anything to identify him?'

The technician shook his head. 'No, and I wasn't meant to either. There's nothing in his pockets, no wallet, no phone, no coins. He's well dressed, though. That camel coat he's wearing, it could be a Crombie, but the label's been ripped off. It's the same with the suit, but that's expensive too. The shoes? Patent leather, thick leather sole, steel-reinforced heels. He's had a manicure too, fairly recently.'

'How about his underwear?' Cotter asked.

'I'll leave that to you. He shat himself when he was killed.'

Twenty-Two

'How was your day?' Sarah asked, as she came into the kitchen where her husband was in the midst of preparing evening meals for the four children. 'Quiet, I guess.'

'In the context of my normal days, yes,' Bob replied. 'I had one call from Jack Darke, the crime reporter on the *Saltire* trying to complain about Mario McGuire stitching him up at the media briefing last night. Other than that and one Happy New Year call from Xavi Aislado in Girona, all I've had to cope with is Seonaid having a screaming fight with her younger brother, Dawn having a dose of the squitters, and having to send Mark down to the Co-op because the milk was off. Sure; quiet.'

She laughed. 'Nothing you haven't handled before, though.'

'No, but concentrated into a short time-frame. It's fucking Pimm's o'clock, I'll tell you that.'

'What did you say to the man Darke?'

'I told him that I know what happened at the briefing, and that he was lucky Mario took it easy with him. His beef was that he thought he had an exclusive angle on Terry Coats, and that Mario spilled it to the entire room. I told him cheerfully that in my day I'd have nailed his balls to the wall for shooting his mouth off like that. Then I pointed out to him that in a way it's still my day, in that the position I hold with InterMedia makes me his two-up boss, and that it's my signature on his contract of employment, not June Crampsey's. I reminded him that his value to the *Saltire* is linked entirely to the quality of the stories he produces, and that in turn is tied to his maintaining good relationships with the police service at all levels. Then I suggested that the fact he's generally regarded as being an arse-wipe kind of works against that. Finally, I told him that if hear of him being anything other than courteous while representing the paper I'd terminate the aforementioned contract. Then I hung up.'

'Will he take that?' Sarah asked. 'Can he complain to his trade union?'

'Till he's blue in the face, but it won't do him any good. He has no friends there either from what I hear. I emailed June afterwards and told her to give him a written warning, to make it official.'

'You enjoyed that, didn't you,' she challenged him. 'You took the InterMedia job on partly as a favour for a friend, but you've grown into it and it's grown with you. You like the authority it gives you, it's part of you, you can't help it.'

'Maybe so,' Bob conceded, then he smiled. 'Maybe I will take that job.'

'What job?'

'One I was offered ten days ago. You know I have friends in Westminster after that thing McIlhenney and I sorted out a wee while back?'

She nodded. 'Friends who just won the election.'

'That's right. I had a call from one of them, offering me a job. Home Office minister, with a seat in the House of Lords.'

'What!' Sarah exploded. 'And this is the first time you tell me?'

'Sorry,' he said, contritely. 'I promised I'd take time to consider it; discussing it with you is the next part of that process.'

'And?'

'What do you think?'

'I don't know. If it's what you want . . .'

'I don't,' he told her. 'Leaving aside the fact that it would cost us at least three hundred grand a year, because I couldn't combine it with the InterMedia job, leaving aside the fact that I voted Yes at the Indy referendum and will do so again given the chance, it would mean reporting to the current Home Secretary, and if that isn't my worst fucking nightmare, it's definitely high in the charts. I won't put it that way when I turn it down but turn it down I will. Happy with that?'

'Utterly.' She stepped up to him and hugged him. As she did so she noticed a large corner of the kitchen work surface. 'What's that?'

'It's a new year present from Xavi. All the directors get one. Take a look.'

She had to stand on tiptoe to open the lid and peer inside. She gasped, then jumped back. 'Jesus! What is it?'

Bob reached past her and lifted the gift from its container. 'Jamon Iberico,' he announced. 'Spanish ham, complete with stand and knife. A hundred and fifty quid's worth there. You can carve, Professor Grace.'

'No chance,' she snorted. 'I don't do delicate. I'm a butcher not a surgeon.'

'Speaking of which,' he said, 'how was your day? Pretty grim, I guess.'

'Very. And I have another booked in for tomorrow, another

gunshot victim found in Midlothian somewhere: I forget the name of the place. They don't know whether it's connected or not, and I won't be able to tell them unless the bullets I recover match the one I took from Terry Coats.'

'Nothing at all from Griff?'

'Not as much as a fragment. The one thing I do know is that they weren't shot with the same gun. The bullet I took from Drawer Five . . . it helps me to think of them by mortuary numbers rather than by name . . . was a standard nine milli-metre. Whatever killed Drawer Six was much bigger than that; something the size of Dirty Harry's weapon. Remember?'

He nodded. 'A forty-four Magnum, the most powerful handgun in the world.'

'Don't quote me the rest of that, please. It's almost true. You saw the mess it made; it took a big chunk of his brain with it. I didn't spend too much time on either of them, just enough to establish that Drawer Six was exceptionally fit for a man of his age, whereas Drawer Five had the beginnings of an oesophageal tumour that might well have finished him in a couple of years.'

'Do you think he knew?'

'At that stage, maybe not. He might have experienced general discomfort, but not enough for him to seek urgent treatment. Enough of that, though. You know I don't like bringing the likes of that home with me.' She eased him to one side, along the work surface. 'Here; let me take over or these kids are never gonna eat. What about Ignacio and Pilar?'

'They're going to eat with us; I asked them. I thought it would be nice for us to get to know the girl a bit better, given that she's Spanish and everything.'

'Everything including shacking up with your son.'

'Out here maybe, but . . .'

'No,' she insisted, 'up town as well. In theory there are three of them sharing the flat, but in practice the third party, a girl, lives with her boyfriend. Her parents don't know, of course. They're from Horsham, in Sussex.'

'How do you know all this?'

'Alex told me. Ignacio talks to her a lot. Go on, Bob, get out of here, get yourself a beer.'

He was in the process of obeying that instruction when his phone sounded. He accepted the call while uncapping his Corona and headed for the garden room. 'Mia,' he said, a little wearily. 'How goes? Is your old man home smelling of cheap Chanel Five, with his tail between his legs and a brilliant cover story? Myra, Alex's mother, used to come home smelling of Aramis or Paco Rabanne, and I, the great detective, never worked it out.'

'No, he's not!' she shouted in his ear. 'Skinner, will you take this seriously! My husband has disappeared. He's missing. I'd hoped you'd help me, but you're just like all those other cops, you couldn't care less.'

Contrition was not one of his more common reactions, but the anxiety in her voice got to him. 'I'm sorry,' he said, at once. 'We've been dealing with something serious here too. If you've seen the papers today you might guess what it is.'

'I've seen nothing today, no news at all. I haven't even listened to my own radio station. What is it?'

'Two guys have been murdered in Edinburgh. One's a police officer, the other used to be; I knew them both. One of them was friendly with Alex.'

'Oh.' Her voice softened. 'I'm sorry about that. How friendly?'

'Friendly enough for her to be pretty distraught. Did Ignacio ever tell you about the attack in her apartment?'

'Yes, he did. Was this the guy who protected her?' she asked.

'That's him.'

'In that case I can understand Cameron not being at the top of your list. But I really am worried about him, Bob. If you think about the life I led and the family I grew up in, that should tell you something.'

'It does,' he conceded. 'You've got my full attention, and concern. Has anything happened, since yesterday?'

'Yes,' she replied. 'We have this guy. His name is Vito Tremacoldi; officially he's on the security staff of the hotel, unofficially he's Cameron's minder. He's been with him for a few weeks. He's never obvious but when Cameron wants him to be around, he is. If Cameron ever needs a driver, like if we're ever going to a party, or even out for dinner, he's the man who takes us.'

'Did you vet him? Is he clean, or does he have a history?'

'He has a security background, Bob. That's all Cameron told me. He's a real Italian, not one of the Scots kind like your friend McGuire.'

'Only half of him,' Skinner reminded her. 'I thought Cameron only employed local heavies.'

'Vito isn't a heavy, he's a professional,' Mia assured him. 'You're doing what everyone always does, you're tarring him with his dead sister's awful past. You know as well as I do that she was the real criminal in the McCullough family, not him. She had some mental people around her, and she was a pure-bred psychopath.'

'In other words, she could have been a Watson,' he murmured.

'You'll never let me forget that!' she snapped, then surprised him by chuckling. 'Although I must admit that when I was told about her, my mother did come to mind. No, I promise you, Vito is very much on the up and up. He even has a couple of medals from his days in the Italian army.'

'Okay, that's Vito,' Skinner said. 'Go on.'

'He's disappeared too.'

'Why are you only telling me now? That makes a difference.'

'I'm telling you because I've only just found out. Vito has a room in the hotel that he uses when he's here, but he has a place across the river where he stays usually, a show home on one of Cameron's house-building developments.'

'Does he have a family?'

'He's only just joined us, so I don't really know, but he didn't bring anybody with him. He wasn't at the Hogmanay celebration in the hotel,' she said. 'Cameron said he didn't need him and that he should take a few days off, so when he vanished after the party, I never thought to contact him, not until today. I rang him, landline and mobile, and got no reply to either. I'm really worried, Bob. I want him found, sure, but I want it done discreetly. Cameron is who he is; he's wealthy, he's as low profile as he can manage, but he owns the fucking radio station, so all the media will be on to this if it leaks. Some of Cameron's business interests are sensitive; there could be commercial damage if this gets out. Help me, Bob, please.'

He drew a deep breath, and exhaled slowly, thinking. 'Okay, Mia,' he replied. 'I'll do what I can but be aware that if I have to involve the police I will. If that happens, it may go public.'

'Understood.'

'Right. Tell me everything you know, more than that, everything you suspect, anything he's ever done that you might

152

not be sure about. My gut is still saying that he's done a runner for entirely personal reasons and that when you find out, you might not like them.'

'If that's so,' she said, 'God help him. You're right. I am still a Watson.'

Twenty-Three

'W ho stole your scone?' Tarvil Singh asked, seeing the frown on the DI's face as he walked into the office.

'Don't ask,' he replied. 'Family business.' He was still focused on a call he had received earlier that morning from his mentor.

'Sauce,' Skinner had said. 'I need a favour. Make a note of this registration.' Later, Haddock realised that it had not even occurred to him to question the request. 'It's a Jag F-Pace; the registered keeper is Black Shield Lodge PLC, but the driver is a man called Vito Tremacoldi. It's gone missing and so has he. Does the name mean anything to you?'

'I can't say it does, gaffer. Should it?'

'Not necessarily, but it might mean something to your partner. He works for Cheeky's grandpa, and the two of them have gone off the radar at the same time. Mia's asked me to find him, without any big public fuss if possible. If that car shows up anywhere, I want to know about it. I could get this information from my friends in Millbank, but I'd rather not go to that level. Will you do this for me? I'll understand if you don't.'

'No, I won't do it for you, Sir Bob . . . but I will do it for Cheeky. Should I tell her?'

'That's your call, son. But in your shoes I'd be trying to imagine the fallout from not doing that.'

'That might not be pretty,' he had conceded. 'Leave it with me.'

Of course he had told Cheeky, as much as he knew, and of course she had phoned her stepmother to ask what was going on. She and Mia McCullough lived in a state of fragile truce not unlike that between the two Koreas, and the fact that she had been kept out of the loop for twenty-four hours did not sit well with her. Once he had brokered a tentative cease-fire, he had made the call through the central traffic control, telling the duty officer that the vehicle was wanted in connection with a potential abduction, all responses directly to him. With his fingers crossed that word of his enquiry would not find its way upstairs, he had headed for the office.

'It's like a ghost town out there, isn't it?' the DS continued. 'Officially this is the first working day of the year, but there's hardly any bugger about. They're up and at it in South Africa though. Jackie had a call from police headquarters in Pretoria five minutes ago; a guy was looking for you. His name's Major Pollock and she put his number on your desk.'

Haddock grunted his thanks and headed towards his office, stopping on the way at DC Wright's desk. 'Jackie,' he said, 'I want you to know that I appreciate the work you're doing for us. I need someone here in the office that I can rely on to do the boring stuff. With Noele being off, it's all the more difficult for you. You're covering a lot of the slack. Please, please, please, pass those sergeant's exams!'

She grinned. 'That's my blind spot, boss, but I'm trying.'

'Did Major Pollock say what he had for us?'

'Not in detail, but he sounded keen. When I called last

night with your request for information, on the contact number Mary Chambers gave you, they put me on to a sergeant. She sounded fairly disinterested, just said, "Okay, I'll get back to you." I was expecting just that, her to call me; instead I got a senior officer. I offered to pass on a message to you but he said no, that he needed to talk to you, preferably by Zoom or Skype.'

'What the hell's Zoom?'

'It's a video-conferencing tool. It's the future, Sauce.'

'I'll sooner stick to the present,' he chuckled. 'I can just about work Skype but I suppose I should keep up with the times. Did Mary have anything else for me?'

'Yes, sorry. She said she put your question to her friend, and he said that police sidearms would generally be a nine millimetre, but the make could be one of several. Helpful?'

'Slightly. Anything else? How about Griff's cousin? Any joy with him?'

A quick frown creased her forehead. 'None,' she answered. She glanced up at him. 'He's very hard to catch, but I may be getting closer. I left messages on his landline and mobile numbers yesterday, and I sent him an email, but nothing's been acknowledged. However, I did a search for him on social media and came up with a Tom DuPlessis who lives in Cape Town, and according to his 'About' info, works for a shipping company. Griff and Spring Montell are listed among his Facebook friends, so I guess that's him.'

'What sort of shipping company?'

'Cruise liners; I googled it. It's called Oceanic Magic.'

'Call them,' Haddock instructed. 'I want to find this bugger.' She reached for her computer mouse as he headed for his office.

The note that Wright had left on his desk gave him detailed instructions on how to contact the South African policeman by Zoom. He followed them step by step and waited, gazing at his own image on the computer screen until it was replaced by that of a square-headed, crew-cut man in his mid-forties, wearing a uniform shirt, with epaulettes of rank on display.

'Detective Inspector Haddock?' he began, quizzically.

'That's me,' he said.

'Sorry, I was expecting someone older.'

'You should see the portrait in my attic,' Sauce quipped, then moved on as the other man's face showed blank bewilderment. 'Thanks for responding to our request,' he said. 'I didn't expect a call, just an email.'

'It's better this way,' Pollock retorted. 'Better to make eye contact; it reduces the risk of misunderstanding. I have to tell you that when your message came across my desk, I had a hell of a shock. I knew Griffin very well; I was his supervisor when he was a cadet, and later he worked under me in the detective division here in Pretoria; I was his lieutenant. I was sorry when he decided to emigrate, but I understood the reason for it. He had little or no option but to leave, and I was more than happy to give him a reference when I was asked for it. The family court gave him a hard time after his marriage breakdown, it really did.'

'So I gather, from his sister and others. I knew him, but not that well. Why did the breakdown happen?'

'He didn't talk about it much,' the major replied. 'I don't believe there was a third party involved. Griffin changed after the incident; he became darker, not quite the open, cheerful guy he had been before. These days you might call it

PTSD, but back then we were all too butch to talk about that. Part of my job now involves officers' mental health; it's a serious issue.'

'You mentioned the incident,' Haddock said. 'I take it you mean the gold robbery. I knew nothing about that until it came out in the discussion I had with his sister and her partner. I doubt that anyone in our force was aware of it, not even Bob Skinner, who approved his transfer.'

'Skinner,' Pollock repeated, 'I remember that name. He was the guy who asked for the reference.' He frowned. 'I suppose I might have mentioned the robbery, but Griffin had put it behind him by then and so I decided just to let it lie. It wouldn't have disqualified him. Plus, of course, it was in his service record. How could I forget that?'

'What can you tell me about the robbery? How was it pulled off?'

'We never did know for sure, not all of it, but we found a tracker on the bullion van afterwards. The route from the Mint was changed every time; there were several they could use, never the most direct way, all on roads that were rarely used. The choice was at the discretion of the escorting officers, but that day, with the tracker on the van, that was irrelevant. How it got there, we never did find out. Our suspicion was that it was put there by either the driver or his mate before they left the Mint, but they were both shot dead so it couldn't be confirmed. If one of them was involved, he never collected his share. Griffin was lucky; he was shot twice but survived. I visited him in hospital.' He touched the side of his head, drawing a finger across it. 'The second gunshot ploughed a furrow, right along there. It was at close range, too.'

'The gold was never traced, I'm told,' Haddock said.

'Fucking untraceable, wasn't it? As soon as it was off the scene and out of its boxes.'

'How much was stolen? I've heard a couple of figures.'

The major raised his eyebrows. 'That doesn't surprise me. The Mint claimed that ten thousand coins had been lost. They said that they were never moved in quantities larger than that, but actually an audit revealed that to be bullshit. In fact, there were thirty-five thousand Krugerrands in the van. It was one of the biggest gold robberies ever.'

'You're telling me that upwards of thirty-five million sterling, current value, was taken?'

'That's right. The financial crash happened just after the theft, so the haul was worth a hell of a lot more than that for a couple of years.'

'What happened to it?'

'The belief was that nothing did, that the thieves put it away somewhere. It was too much to fence; if they had tried, even in small parcels, we have underworld sources that would have let us know if important quantities of Krugerrands suddenly appeared. Again,' Pollock admitted, 'we have nothing more than theory, and that is that most of it is still out there.' He paused. 'Look, Detective Inspector, I'm puzzled. Why are you so interested in this, and why are you asking for a copy of the police file? Be honest with me, please.'

'I will,' Haddock said. 'I'll be completely frank. The fact is, we've got no obvious suspects for these murders. We know that Griff and Terry Coats had encountered each other when Coats was still a cop, although they were in different forces. We've discovered also that Griff was in a developing relationship with one of my officers, who happened to be Coats' ex-wife. Other than that we have nothing that puts them together . . .

except . . . Coats worked in airport security and claimed to have uncovered a smuggling operation there, with gold coins being brought in by flight crew of a specific airline and routed through a certain airside shop. That's how we first heard about the robbery, from Coats; he claimed that he had been told about it by Griff Montell. Yet Griff never mentioned it to any of his colleagues.'

'I can understand that,' the South African said. 'It was a painful memory for him.'

'Given what Coats said about the smuggling operation, can I ask, was there ever any suggestion of Russian involvement in the hold-up?'

'None at all; we didn't have any fucking clue who might have been involved, and that remains true, we still don't. If your investigation uncovers anything, please, please let us know. That robbery is still a big stain on our reputation.'

'Of course we will,' Haddock said. 'Are you okay with giving me a copy of the investigation file?'

'Sure. It's all digital, so no problem. It includes investigator reports, the text of a statement by Griff, crime-scene photographs and all the forensics.'

'Thanks. Can you remember, where were the van driver and his mate killed?'

'They were inside the cab, but they'd opened the door. The assumption was that they'd decided to give up and save their skins, only the robbers didn't intend to leave any witnesses. They hadn't a chance. Somebody emptied an Uzi magazine into them.'

'The same weapon as wounded Griff and killed his partner?'

'No,' Pollock said. 'All the bullets were nine millimetre, but the one that was taken out of Fannie DeWalt came from a different firearm than the one that shot the van crew. We never did find the cartridges that hit Griffin. The shoulder wound was through and through; the head shot we guessed hit the roadway and fragmented. You got an email for me?' he asked.

Haddock spelled out his online address letter by letter. As he finished, the door of his tiny office opened and Wright entered. 'I called Oceanic Magic,' she whispered. 'Tom DuPlessis is their baggage controller. He didn't turn up for work yesterday morning or today. The company can't find him either.'

'Maybe I can get them some help,' he murmured in reply. 'Meantime, get on to them and find out their cruise schedules over the last few years, where they sailed from, where they docked, everything you can.'

He turned back to the computer, to see Major Pollock's concentrated frown as he clicked his mouse. 'There,' he declared, 'that's the report off to you.' He had barely finished speaking when an incoming email notification popped up on Haddock's screen.

'Great,' he replied. 'Thanks for that. I'll study it, and if I have any more questions I'll get back to you. Meanwhile, Major, there's one more thing I wonder if you can do for me. I need to speak to Griff's cousin. His name is Tom DuPlessis, he lives in Cape Town, and he works for a cruise line called Oceanic Magic. My problem is that he's not responding to any messages, and he's missing from work.'

'Are you thinking this might be connected to Griffin's murder?'

'I have no reason to, but you and I both know what we detectives think of coincidences.'

'Absolutely. Until they're proven, we don't believe in them.

Email me the contact details you have for him, and I will order a search for him, country-wide. It's been good to meet you, Detective Inspector Haddock, even if you haven't come out and told me exactly what's in your mind. Level with me: you suspect that Griffin was involved in the robbery in some way, do you not?'

Sauce sighed. 'I wish I didn't, but yes, you're right.'

Twenty-Four

'When will the pathologist be here?' Lottie Mann asked, impatiently.

'The post-mortem's down for twelve noon,' Denzil Douglas reminded her. 'Professor Grace will be here by eleven forty-five, I'd guess, but not much earlier. If you've got time on your hands, Chief Inspector, there's a coffee place in the bookshop round the corner.'

'I'll get by,' she said. 'You can spend some of the time filling me in on what you got from the body.'

'The shitty drawers were Levi's. They'd left the label on those; no surprise, all things considered. As I established at the scene there was no identification on the coat, suit and shirt. However, the shoes he was wearing came from a company called Crick and Son, of Jermyn Street in London, and from the look of them they're hand made. I've sent them to the company by courier and with a touch of luck they'll be able to match them to a last and tell us whose it was.'

'Last?' John Cotter said.

'It's the mould of the customer's feet, that all his shoes are made from. Very expensive.'

'You might say he was well-heeled.'

Douglas stared at the detective.

'Well-heeled?' Cotter ventured. 'Wealthy?'

'Whether he was or not, he's been soled down the river by somebody,' Mann drawled, as Sarah Grace came into the room.

Twenty-Five

'I wish my office was like this,' Sauce Haddock remarked, looking around the spacious glass-walled room.

'I still wish, sometimes, that my office was like yours,' Bob Skinner countered. 'Then reality bites, and I hear the goose-steps of the march of time. Do you want a coffee?'

'Thanks, gaffer, I need one.'

'For fuck's sake, Sauce, as I keep telling you, call me Bob.'

The DI smiled. 'I will when I feel comfortable with it.'

'You didn't just come here for a view of a miserable rain-sodden January Edinburgh,' Skinner said, as he handed his visitor a mug.

'No,' he conceded. 'I'd rather we talked about Grandpa away from the office. I've had no reported sightings of Tremacoldi's car, and nobody's heard from him. Mia's been calling him and so has Cheeky. His phone's going straight to voicemail, and they've been leaving messages, but neither's had any joy. The thing that worries me most is him not getting back to Cheeky. If he's had a strop with Mia that she's not telling us about and gone away for a while to cool down, that I would understand, but him not calling his grand-daughter, that is something else.' He glanced up at Skinner.

'Do you think I should be making this official?'

'That depends how much heat you want to risk. If it was leaked and the *Courier* in Dundee picked it up, the *Saltire* would have to follow. That fucker Jack Darke would be on it like a flash. If he found out there's a connection between Cameron and me through Ignacio and Mia . . . that's if he doesn't know already . . . he'd be all over it. If I tried to shut him down, I wouldn't put it past him to leak that to the rest. It's been a little over two days since Grandpa left the reservation, he's a middle-aged man and with his minder Tremacoldi being gone too there's no reason to fear for his safety. Hold off, I'd say, and let's see how it falls.' He took a mouthful from his own mug. 'How's the investigation going?' he asked.

'In a direction I never expected,' Haddock admitted. 'It's clear that Griff was seriously up to something. He told Chief Inspector McGlashan, and he told Noele, that he was going to South Africa last Saturday, and he even checked in for his evening flight and dropped his bag, but he never got on board. We've got him on camera in the airport, landside, three and a half hours before flight time, then we lose him . . . until about half twelve on New Year's Day, when he and Coats turned up dead.' He sighed. 'The stuff we found in the safe, that really threw me, and now I know about his involvement in the robbery . . .'

'What do you mean by that?'

The young detective updated his mentor on his discovery, from Spring Montell and later from Major Pollock, of the dead man's part in the drama of the unsolved bullion hijacking. 'I've read the report. There was only one thing in it that I wasn't told by Pollock. The route they took from the gold refinery to the depository was decided on the day by the officer in charge of the escort vehicle. That was Griff, as he had seniority. There were six options; the one he chose went over a stretch that was off highway. You can see the entrance and exit on Google Earth street view, but not the track itself. That runs for maybe a mile until it re-joins the roadway. That's where the robbery happened. I've logged the file and attachments on to the investigation database, but I can email it to you if you want.'

'A bit fucking late for that, since this is the first I'm hearing about it,' Skinner exclaimed. 'Why was it left off his application when he came to Edinburgh? Be sure it was, Sauce; I would not have seen that and forgotten about it. Why did Pollock not tell me in the covering letter that came with it? Why was there no mention of it in his service record?'

'Pollock told me that he didn't think it would affect the transfer,' Haddock explained. 'He said it was such a traumatic experience for Griff that he wanted to help him to put it behind him, to leave it in South Africa. He was shot twice and left for dead.'

'But he wasn't fucking dead, was he? And if you're right and he did want to forget it all, why would he tell Terry Coats about it? That's where we first heard about it, from Terry when he was caught shagging the air hostess. Have you found her yet?' he asked, suddenly.

'She's still on our to-do list. I've asked Jackie to trace her, through the airline.' He grimaced. 'The DCC's been good, giving me extra manpower, but I could sure do with having Noele back. Fuck me, I could do with Sammy Pye getting over his bug, and taking the load off me.'

'Neither of those things will ever happen, Sauce,' Skinner said, quietly. 'It'll take a real effort to keep Noele in the job at all, and as for Sammy,' his face darkened, 'it's no bug, I'm afraid. Don't press me about it, but you can take my word for it, he's not coming back.'

The DI stared at him. 'Seriously?' he whispered.

He nodded.

'The place is falling apart, gaffer.'

'Then it's up to the likes of you to hold it together. Who's handling the Howgate murder?' he asked. 'I saw a *Saltire* news feed just before you arrived, but of course I knew about it from Sarah. Who took the media briefing? All it said was that it was a police spokesperson.'

'The new press officer, on the DCC's orders. Pending the autopsy, we're still calling it a suspicious death, but only for the media. Two shots in the forehead.'

'The second one usually rules out suicide,' Skinner observed, grimly. 'Do you think it links to Griff and Coats?'

'I'm not thinking anything. I don't have the luxury of speculation. I can only deal with what I can prove.' He glanced at his mentor. 'What do you reckon?'

'Given the time-frame, I'd be assuming it does until I knew different. Have they identified the victim?'

'Not yet. From what I've heard from Lottie and Jack McGurk, someone wanted to make it hard for us. But we'll . . .' He broke off as his mobile sounded. 'Jackie,' he said as he took the call, then fell silent, listening. 'Thanks,' he said eventually. 'I don't know where that takes us, forward or back.' He turned back to Skinner. 'The count rises. Jackie's just off the phone to the Wister Air HR department. Coats' bird, Aisha Karman, went missing last November. She flew into John Lennon Airport in Liverpool, coming from Amsterdam. She was supposed to join a flight from Manchester to Cape Town next day but never showed up. She was booked into a hotel called the Grange, at Manchester Airport, but didn't turn up there. The airline waited for three days and then reported her missing to the police in Liverpool and they've heard nothing since.'

'When did we catch her with Terry Coats?'

'A few months before that.'

'I reckon you should get in touch with your Scouser colleagues,' Skinner suggested, but in a way that made it sound like an order, 'and request that they get the finger out.'

Twenty-Six

'There you are, Mr Douglas,' Sarah Grace said, as she handed two small containers to the technicians. 'Two bullets retrieved from the brain of Drawer Three. They're the same calibre as the one I took from Drawer Five yesterday. It's up to you to determine whether they were fired from the same gun.'

'Thanks, Prof,' he replied. 'Do you have anything else for me? I've taken fibre samples from all of his clothing, and the shoes are off to London. If that's all there is, I'll head off to the lab.'

She turned to Mann and Cotter. The DCI was paler than she had been an hour before, but her colleague seemed unperturbed. 'Drawer Three was a healthy male, aged somewhere between fifty and sixty, or possibly a year or two older. He was physically fit, a non-smoker and his liver shows no sign of excessive alcohol consumption. His last meal was battered haggis and chips, consumed very shortly before death, with Irn Bru on the side. His bladder evacuated itself when he died, as did his bowels, but Scotland's national drink hadn't made it that far. Wherever he died, I'd say it wasn't far from a fish and chip shop.'

'Vinegar or sauce?' Mann asked.

The pathologist smiled at Cotter's puzzled expression. 'She's asking me, Sergeant, whether he was from Edinburgh, and liked brown sauce on his supper, or from the west of Scotland and took vinegar. Tribal customs that you obviously haven't caught up with. The answer, DCI Mann, is vinegar, but don't read too much into that. Now what may be good news,' she continued. 'I had the body X-rayed and that revealed that the man had a plate in his right femur, put there to repair a bad fracture, around five years ago. I've removed it; it was made in England, but that's not definitive, for these things are exported all around the world. However, it had a serial number, and I'm hopeful that the manufacturer will be able to tell me where it was implanted, and into whom. His killer tried to remove all identification; he was careless when he left the shoes behind, but there's no way he could have known about the plate.'

'Killers,' Mann said, quietly. 'We saw the victim in situ. There's no way that he was put there by one person alone unless he was the size of Drew McIntyre.'

'Who's he?' Cotter enquired. 'One of your Glasgow villains?'

'National hero, more like,' his boss replied scornfully. 'He's a wrestler. How about time of death, Professor,' she continued. 'We know he was there for a while, but how specific can you be?'

Sarah frowned. 'Looking at the physical and other factors, rate of decomposition, and the beginnings of saponification in the area of the body that was resting on a very wet surface, my estimate is that he died some time on Saturday. Looking at insect invasion, and animal depredation, I believe that the body was dumped not long after he was killed. On the assumption that it wasn't done in the daylight hours, you're looking at Saturday night or Sunday morning.' She paused, looking Mann in the eye. 'There's one thing about the body that I haven't mentioned, and it could be important. Three fingers on the left hand were broken, fresh fractures, untreated. That suggests there was a struggle before he died; either that, or the man was tortured.'

Twenty-Seven

'I don't know why they reported it to us, mate.' Haddock was sure he could hear the officer on the other end of the line stifle a yawn. 'If she was booked into a hotel in Manchester, like you say, they should have reported it to the Mancs, shouldn't they?'

'That's a debate for another day, Constable,' the Scot said, failing to keep his irritation from his voice. 'What I'm asking is if she's still on your books as a missing person.'

'Let me look, then. Kaufman, F, no, that's a bloke. Yeah, here she is; Karman, A, female. The file's still open, so she's still missin', as far as we know. Happens from time to time, mate, especially with cabin crew on the smaller airlines. The pay's crap, they line up a better job in one of the countries on their routes and next time they're there, like, they just bail out. Where's this girl from? South Africa? Yeah, I could see that havin' happened.'

'Maybe you could, Constable Lynch, and maybe you're even right, but has your force actually done anything to locate this woman? Even something as basic as circulating her photo?'

'We don't have one, mate.'

'Fuck me!' Haddock gasped. 'Even I've got one and I've only started looking for her today. I'll email it to you. I need

173

this woman; she's a potential witness in a double-murder investigation.'

'Then you better talk to my boss, mate.'

'That would be Detective Chief Inspector Mate, and yes, that would be an idea.'

'Very good, sir,' the Liverpudlian said stiffly. 'If you'll hold on for a minute, I'll see if she's available.'

The minute stretched into a second, and then a third. He was on the point of hanging up when a female voice came on the line. 'DCI Haddock? I'm Inspector Jamie Ellis. You need our co-operation, I'm told.'

'Acting DCI; DI really. I only used it to light a fire under your doorkeeper.'

'Bert Lynch?' she chuckled. 'Sorry about that. He's a year and a half off retirement and he doesn't give one.'

'If you think about having a whip round to send him off early, let me know. I might contribute.'

'He gave me the bones of the story, would you care to flesh them out?'

'Sure. I'm the SIO on a double murder in Edinburgh; one of the victims was a serving police officer, the other an ex-cop. I'm trying to trace a South African woman, Aisha Karman, age twenty-eight, last seen in Liverpool in July. She worked for an airline called Wister Air, but dropped out of sight somewhere between John Lennon Airport and the Grange Hotel, Manchester. Her employer reported her missing, and from the little that PC Lynch could tell me, she still is.'

'She's a potential witness in a cop murder, you say.'

'Yes.'

'Okay,' Inspector Ellis said, decisively. 'I'll dig out the file and put a team on it. Don't worry, PC Lynch will not be on it.

If she's anywhere in the North West we'll find her. Is she likely to co-operate?'

'Maybe not,' Haddock admitted. 'She's suspected of smuggling stolen gold into Scotland, so she might not be too keen to talk to us.'

'Can you give me grounds to hold her?'

'I'm pretty sure I can find a sheriff who'll give me a warrant that lets me bring her back to Scotland, but that'll hold for as long as it takes her to brief a half-decent solicitor. The source of my information was one of our murder victims, so he won't make a very reliable witness.'

Twenty-Eight

'How much progress have they made, Mario?' the chief constable asked, as her deputy came into the room. Outside, the street lights lit the evening, as she finished tidying her desk, and readying herself to go home.

'On tracing the perpetrators?' he replied. 'Frankly, none. On uncovering stuff that we never knew or suspected about Inspector Montell, remarkably well.' He briefed her on the discoveries made in his apartment, on the security that had been installed, and on the facts about his South African service that Haddock had uncovered.

'Jeez,' she sighed. 'You think you know people. Although,' she continued, 'I can't say that I ever really knew Montell. He was a fixture, always there with a smile when one was needed and a word, and yet, now I think back, it was all superficial. He was like a mirror; when you looked at him you never really saw anything of him, just a reflection of yourself.' She shuddered. 'How many people do I really know, I wonder?'

'How many can you know, Maggie? You have going on for eighteen thousand officers under your command, and on top of that about five thousand civilian staff. If you knew any more than three or four per cent of them on a personal level it would be a miracle. Even remembering that many names would be an achievement.'

'I wasn't talking about my officers,' she retorted. 'I meant people in general. Mario, you know me better than any man alive; we were married, but I never let you get close. In the end, I drove you away and you were happy to go. That's how I am. I have a barrier built into my personality and it's impenetrable. Yes, Stevie got inside my wall. Stevie made me happy, Stevie gave me a child. And then Stevie opened that booby-trapped fucking door in that fucking house and Stevie died.' Her face contorted with the pain of the memory. 'I know now I should have had counselling after it happened, but instead I had cancer, then I had Stephanie and I rebuilt my wall around us both. Since my sister went back to Australia to pick up her career again, and I put Steph into day care, we've been completely alone. When you called me to the crime scene in Torphichen Place, I could only go because you sent an officer to stay with her. How many friends do you think I have? People to call up for a chat, people to meet for a drink. None. I'm not kidding, none. I am completely absorbed in myself and my daughter, and that's how I feel most comfortable. At work, I'm exactly the same, introspective, and I can feel myself shrinking. When I took over this job, I hoped I would expand into it. Before, when I was climbing the ladder, it was okay, because I had my little box of things to do and that was manageable. When I became Andy Martin's deputy, it still was, because Andy never delegated anything to me. Then I became chief, and overnight the box was enormous. I've managed for a while, but gradually it's begun to eat me. I've been pushing more and more in your direction and Brian Mackie's and Doreen Irons'. You're running the fucking force now, Mario; I know it, you know it and so does anyone who operates at our level. Yes, occasionally I will try to assert myself; for example on Wednesday morning, when I summoned DS McClair . . . fuck, I'm sitting here trying to remember her first name . . . to the crime scene to identify we had the body of the father of her child. That was an awful thing to do but something inside me said, "It happened to me, so you can face up to it too." Inevitably, I'm taking it home. When I got back on Wednesday morning I shouted at Steph. I don't remember ever doing that, ever. She cried, and so did I and that's when I knew, Mario, that I can't do this anymore. I'm resigning. I'm all my kid's got and she deserves far more of me. Fuck it, so do I!' She looked up at him from her chair, as the tears began to stream down her face.

He stepped across, sat on the edge of her desk, and took her hand. 'I'm sorry, love,' he said, gently. 'I should have realised how bad it was and helped you before now. You do have friends, you know; you've got Paula and me for a start, and big Bob and Sarah, and Brian, and Sauce, and everybody who's been alongside you all these years.' He frowned. 'This is my fault, Mags. You talk about driving me away, and maybe you did, but I didn't go that far. When Stevie died, I should have been there for you far more than I was, but just like you, I was too wrapped up in myself.' He pulled a tissue from a box on the desk and handed it to her. 'Dry them, go on, and tidy yourself up, while I tell you what's going to happen. You're not resigning, you are going on sick leave. You've got mental-health issues and, like any other officer, you'll be assessed by a police-service doctor, and we'll go by the findings. Agreed?'

She nodded and gave him a watery smile. 'If you say so, big guy.'

Twenty-Nine

'Aw no,' Cheeky Davis moaned, as her partner's phone sounded by the side of their bed. 'With this thing going on I wasn't expecting you to have a Saturday morning off, but it's ten past eight.'

'Not for this guy,' Sauce replied, drowsily. 'He's in Pretoria, and they're an hour ahead of us.' He accepted the call. 'Good morning, Major Pollock.'

'I'm calling from home, Inspector,' the South African said. 'I thought you'd want to know this right away. We've found Griffin's cousin. He was stopped late last night by a patrol car about fifty kilometres from the Namibian border. He said he was going on holiday, but the officers didn't believe him, since he had virtually no luggage beyond an overnight bag. He's being brought straight to Pretoria by car but it's a long way, well over a thousand kilometres. As soon as I have him here, I'll arrange for you to talk to him, maybe tomorrow morning if that suits.'

'Thanks,' Haddock replied. 'I'd prefer it if you let him sweat for a few hours.'

'Sure, would you like us to tell him what you're going to be talking about?'

'Yes, please. I want to interview him about certain matters that have arisen from his cousin's murder, including an allegation of gold-smuggling, money-laundering and abduction.'

'Abduction?'

'That's possible. We're looking for a potential witness. Her name is Aisha Karman; she worked for an airline called Wister Air, until she left them six months ago, without notice.'

'What's her nationality?'

'She has a British passport, but she was educated in Port Elizabeth, South Africa.'

'Then she could have come home. I'll do what I can to help you find her. Plus, give me everything you have on DuPlessis or suspect about him and I'll look into that as well. Anything else?'

Yes,' Haddock said, 'one more thing. Why was there no mention of the gold robbery on Griff's service record when he applied to join the Edinburgh police?'

'What are you talking about? I told you, there was.'

'Not according to Sir Robert Skinner, our former chief constable; he vetted him and approved his appointment. He wouldn't have forgotten something like that.'

'Then Griffin must have doctored it himself. That's all I can suggest. After the robbery, he had a lot of "Hero cop" coverage. He didn't like attention like that.'

'Obviously,' the DI agreed, 'and maybe there was a reason for it. Thanks, Major. We'll speak tomorrow.'

He returned the phone to his charging stand, and rolled over . . . only to find himself alone. Cheeky was standing by the side of the bed tying the cord of her pyjama bottoms.

'Come on, babe,' he pleaded. 'Get back in, I don't have to get up for another fifteen minutes.'

She looked down on him, imperiously. 'Make that half an hour and I might be interested.'

He reached out for her pyjama cord.

Thirty

'You'd think that road from Glasgow would be quiet on a Saturday morning, John,' Lottie Mann complained, as they strode into the area of the Serious Crimes office that they had commandeered.

'It's much the same on Tyneside,' her DS pointed out. 'Down there, every bugger seems to head for the Metrocentre at weekends.' He looked around the room. Jackie Wright was at her desk, but otherwise it was empty. 'Fucking typical, we've come the furthest and yet we're almost the first in. Remind me, why are we here?'

'We're trying to find the killer of a police officer,' she reminded him, as she lowered herself into an unyielding chair. 'And there's always something to do. For example, there's the phone records for both our victims.' She reached out a hand. 'Let's have a look at them.'

Cotter shrugged. 'I've been through them, boss; both Montell's and Coats's. There's nothing on either that ties them together, other than obliquely.'

'What do you mean by obliquely?'

'I found an exchange of WhatsApp messages between Montell and DS McClair in which Coats's name comes up.

Specifically, she refers to, quote, that cunt of an ex of mine, unquote, in the context of him failing to pick up her son and making her miss a date with Montell. Yes, we've been told by DI Haddock that Coats told him and Sir Robert that he knew Montell from previous police service, but there's nothing in the messages to indicate that McClair was aware of them being acquainted, far less in regular contact. However, there is plenty of evidence of Coats's gambling habit. There's loads of phone calls to bookies, and his emails show an online history of bets being placed, and even notification of winning bets, albeit very rarely.'

'Aye, fine, John,' Mann said, 'but we're no closer to putting those two men in each other's company. And until we can do that, we're no closer to whoever did them in, so we're contributing nothing to the main investigation. That's what you're telling me really.'

The DS agreed. 'That's what I'm telling you, ma'am.' Then he smiled. 'But that was the bad news. Do you want the good?'

'Please,' she sighed, unimpressed. 'Anything to brighten my day.'

'I've got an email here from Denzil Douglas, the pathology forensic technician. He's had a lightning fast response from Crick, that shoemaker in Jermyn Street he was on about. He says they've identified the customer; his name is, or rather it was, Anatoly Rogozin.'

'Say that again?' the DCI snapped.

'Anatoly Rogozin,' he repeated.

'Fuck! It couldn't be.' She stared at him, then snatched her phone from her pocket, scrolled through her contacts and called a number.

'Lottie,' Bob Skinner answered. 'What can I do for you?'

Thirty-One

'Are you good, Lexie?' Dominic Jackson asked his house-mate.

'I've been better,' Alex Skinner admitted. 'But I was a lot worse before I moved in with you. Do you know,' she said, 'that you are the only person who's ever called me "Lexie"? Not even my dad ever called me that. I like it, but why do you?'

'One,' he replied, 'it suits you, two, it gets you out of yourself. You had a faint touch of locked-in syndrome when you came here, in that you were obsessed with Alex and all the issues she had. Lexie's a different woman; you like it, and I think you like her a bit more than you were liking yourself.' He winked. 'But you're both the same really.' He paused. 'Can I ask you something serious now? How did you really feel about Griff Montell?'

'Honestly? I don't know anymore. He should have been the man of my dreams. He was kind, considerate, brave, funny, attentive, hung like a donkey, and very good in bed . . . two things that rarely go together in my limited experience. I heard a joke the other day: "What's the difference between a clitoris and a golf ball? A man's prepared to spend ten minutes looking for a golf ball." Griff? All I can say is he wasn't a golfer. I've

184

never had a shopping list when it comes to men, but any who don't live up to my basic expectations don't last long. If I'd had one, he would have ticked all the boxes and added a couple more. I can't imagine why his wife left him.' She frowned. 'Why didn't I fall in love with him? Maybe I did at the beginning, but it didn't develop; it settled into something that I can only describe as comfortable. Looking back on it now, it occurs to me that . . . this is going to sound vain . . . I was irked with him because I realised that he didn't mind me not falling head over heels for him. He was all the things I said, made me feel good in many ways, but he never once used the "L" word. He never showed any signs of falling in love with me. I told myself "That's fine, it's cool, it's uncomplicated," but inside, I was hurt, suffering from a bruised ego, but unable to do anything about it. Maybe I did love him, Dominic,' she exclaimed, 'but the one thing I do know is that he didn't fucking love me!'

He looked at her and saw her eyes mist over. 'He didn't love anyone,' he told her. 'He couldn't, literally. What you are describing to me is a man with what psychologists tend to diagnose as an antisocial personality disorder. Everything you've told me, and what I've been told by the deputy chief about his personal tastes, the things Sauce found in his home, and the way he protected it, they all bear that out.'

'Mario spoke to you about him?' she asked, surprised.

'Yes. He's given me a commission; he wants me to draw up a psychological profile of Griff.' He glanced at her with a shy smile. 'It's the first one I've had from that level in the police service.'

'I thought you were wary of accepting those.'

'I am, but there's no possibility of me being called as a witness with this one, as the subject's dead. There can't be a trial.'

'You're going to say he had a personality disorder? Griff?'

'That's what I'm seeing. He reminds me of a man I met in prison. He was utterly charming, the most popular man on the wing in a place where that sort of behaviour can have you marked down as a grass or a . . . you know. He was good company; I spent quite a bit of time talking to him in the gym. He was clever, articulate and highly intelligent. In society he'd been a senior university lecturer in mathematics. And he'd killed four women by the time he made the one mistake that had led him there. I made him a case study in one of my degree dissertations. He was a very high-functioning psychopath. The Inspector Montell you're showing me is exactly the same.'

'Griff? Really?' Her tone was sceptical.

He smiled again. 'Are you thinking that it takes one to know one?'

'No,' she protested, but in truth the thought had crossed her mind.

'You were,' he insisted, 'but don't be embarrassed for I've considered that very question. The first profile I ever did was on myself, and I got an A for it. My conclusion was that I am neither a sociopath nor a psychopath. I did hurt people, yes. Eventually I did worse. But I did it because I'd been hurt myself as a kid. It was the world I'd grown up in and it was what I'd been shown as a norm, but I felt empathy for the people I was hurting, with only a couple of exceptions. When I was convicted, I was called a psycho by one of the tabloids, but I never was. I knew the difference between right and wrong, and crucially I actually did care about it.'

'Are you saying that Griff didn't?'

'Precisely. And more; I read Griff Montell as someone who might have been a very dangerous man.'

Thirty-Two

'Sir, are you up to speed with the murder investigations that we're all working on?' Lottie Mann began.

'Reasonably so,' Skinner replied. He was slightly out of breath and the wind noise in the background made her suspect that she had caught him in the middle of a run. 'Sauce is talking to me,' he continued, more evenly, 'with the deputy chief's approval, and of course I'm getting feedback at home, given that my wife did the autopsies on them both.'

'She also did one yesterday morning.'

'That's right. Are you going to tell me they're connected?'

'No, I'm not, but we've identified the Howgate victim and the name I've had thrown at me got my attention big time and it will yours too, I guess. Rogozin. Remember him?'

'Dimitri Rogozin? Yes, of course I do,' Skinner exclaimed, 'and the thing I remember most about him is that he's dead!'

'That makes two of them. We've managed to identify the man who was found shot dead and dumped out of the city, in Midlothian. Your wife's third new year autopsy. His shoemaker put a name to him, and that's what it is: Anatoly Rogozin. We're just at the beginning of trying to find everything we can about him, but Crick of Jermyn Street has just told us in an email that his shoes are delivered to an address in Chelsea, and payment comes from a platinum Amex card.' She paused, but Skinner sensed that she was simply building up to the headline announcement. 'That card,' she announced, with something akin to triumph, 'is billed to Merrytown Football Club, of our very own Scottish Premier League. Its principal shareholder, as we both know, is your friend, Cameron McCullough. We're going to need to talk to him, sir. Do you know where I can find him?'

He stayed silent for a few seconds, digesting what she had told him before replying. 'My acquaintance, Lottie,' he corrected her, 'but it's a hell of a good question. I'd like to know the answer myself.'

'What do you mean?'

'Grandpa McCullough went missing around the same time as the bodies were dumped in Torphichen Place. He hasn't been officially reported as a misper . . . shit, I've always hated that term and here I am using it . . . but there's a location request out for his minder's car.'

'What?' she gasped. 'Does that make him a suspect?'

'On the face of it, no, because he was in his hotel in Perthshire immediately before he vanished. But what you've told me about the dead guy in Howgate makes me a hell of a lot more keen to find him. It's time I dug out that Special Constable warrant card that Maggie Steele gave me. You and Cotter and I need to head up to Tayside.'

Thirty-Three

Tarvil Singh was never at his most sociable in the morning, and he knew it. In his earliest days as a police officer there had been those who said he was never at his most sociable in the afternoon either. That had been an advantage on Saturday afternoon duty at Edinburgh's football grounds, but after surprising himself by securing a transfer to CID, he had worked on his social and communication skills His preference was still to speak to no one until ten o'clock had gone, but as a detective officer that was difficult to manage.

When the office door opened and Sauce Haddock stepped into the room it was five minutes past his silent zone. He glanced at his watch, a gesture that some senior officers might have seen as insubordinate.

'I know,' the DI said. 'I had domestic matters to take care of before I came in. Let's just leave it at that.'

'Aye, sure,' Singh chuckled. 'You had to make her breakfast; and it'll probably be an expensive dinner the night as well? Where'll it be? Ondine? The Honours? The Ivy?'

'Oh no; they're for when Cheeky's paying. She makes more than I do, Tarvil. Tonight, it'll be lemon chicken at the Loon Fung.'

The sergeant felt himself salivate. 'Ohhh! Lucky bastard.'

'I hope so. The table's booked for seven o'clock. Whether we make it, that'll depend on how today goes.' He glanced around the room, nodding greetings to Wright and the two other officers on duty. 'What about Mann and Cotter?' he asked. 'Are they not here today?'

'Been and gone,' Singh told him. 'They're following up some info on the Howgate incident. I heard her talking to someone, then a few minutes ago they headed for the door. They never said where they were going, and I . . .'

'Let me guess. It being short of ten o'clock you never asked them?'

'Something like that,' he grunted, as Haddock stepped past him and into his little office.

The DI sighed as he sat at his desk. His lateness was attributable, in part, to the need to reassure Cheeky that her grandfather was surely okay, having taken his new minder with him to wherever he was going. 'Right now, love, he's probably standing on the first tee of a country club in Malaga, or maybe even Miami, with three other guys. You know he's taken up golf.'

'I know,' she had admitted, 'because you played with him and you told me how bad he was. Grandpa doesn't like being second best at anything.'

'He's a lot worse than second best. Give a kangaroo a golf club and it would have a better swing than him.'

'Which is exactly why he wouldn't swan off on a golf tour. Sauce, the truth is he only took up the game in the hope that it would make him closer to you, because you're going to be the father of his great-grandson . . . some day!' she had added quickly.

'Some day?'

'Sauce!'

The smile left his face as his mobile sounded and he saw the name on the screen. Arthur Dorward was famously phlegmatic on his better days; at weekends, he was notoriously dour.

'Mr Haddock,' he growled, 'I'm calling you from the crime campus at Gartcosh. I can only hope you're somewhere equally grim.'

'I'm at Fettes,' he replied. 'Does that qualify?'

'Fuck, yes. The ugliest building in Edinburgh, even worse than the mortuary,' he hesitated for a second, 'which, in a way, brings me to why I'm calling you. That gun you sent us for test-firing and comparison purposes, the Beretta. You said it was just for elimination, right?'

'Yes. It came from Griff Montell's safe. He was a naughty lad to have it, but that hardly matters now.'

'You might say that, and I can confirm that it was not the weapon that killed Mr Coats.'

'No,' the DI said. 'I knew from the start that it couldn't have been, given the timeline. Sorry, Arthur, I suppose that was a waste of resources.'

'I'll accept an apology any time, son; even when it's not warranted. The Beretta might not have done for Coats, but it did account for the man we now know as Anatoly Rogozin.'

'What man, Arthur?' Haddock exclaimed, puzzled.

'Jesus,' Dorward chuckled, 'and you're the SIO. Do you not read your own investigation files, or speak to your own officers? He's the guy they found behind the trees in Howgate. Denzil Douglas emailed it to big Lottie's new gofer last night.'

'It's the first I've heard of it. The pair of them are out of the office, but maybe they've left me a note. Who is he, this Rogozin?' he mused.

'That may be what they've gone to find out. But,' he continued, 'leave him to one side for a moment. As I told you, he was killed by Montell's gun; it's up to you lot to find out who pulled the trigger, but given that you found it in his safe, it only points one way. To back that up, remember that Co-op bag you sent me?'

'Yes. We saw it being taken into the building on Saturday night on Griff's monitor camera, although we don't know who was carrying it.'

'Whoever it was, the gun was in it. We found significant quantities of the same lubricant that was used on the pistol inside the bag. Are you sure it wasn't Montell himself that was carrying it?'

'I haven't ruled that out a hundred per cent,' Haddock admitted, 'but the build is wrong. Griff was bulkier than the person on the video recording. But in the light of what you're telling me, maybe we should test all of Coats' clothing for traces of that oil.'

'Test the body too. That stuff's pervasive; if he got it, say, on his hair it could still be there.'

'I'll do that. I'll ask Sarah to have one of her people take another look. Thanks, Arthur. I'll be in touch.'

'Fine, but hold on, we're not done yet. We're thorough here at Gartcosh. We cover everything, including the South African crime report that you added to the investigation file yesterday, the one about the bullion robbery where a police officer was killed and Montell survived. You might find this hard to believe, Sauce, but that cop was killed by the same weapon that took out Howgate Man.'

Haddock sighed, deep and long. 'You know, Arthur,' he said, 'given what's happened this week I'm not surprised at all.'

192

Thirty-Four

'I was expecting something bigger,' Lottie Mann remarked, as Skinner drew his car to a halt outside a modest cottage-style dwelling on the Black Shield Lodge estate. 'McCullough's a squillionaire, as we all know.'

'It's all they need,' he replied. 'They've got all the facilities of a five-star hotel just up the road.'

John Cotter looked around as he stepped out of the car. 'This is a big property,' he said. 'Are we sure he's not hiding out in the woods, sir?'

'If he was, his wife would have rooted him out by now, with a fucking machete. Cameron's a formidable bloke, but they're well matched.'

As he spoke the cottage door opened, framing Mia McCullough. She had aged well, Skinner reflected. The memory of their brief liaison twenty-odd years before had never faded, nor had his instinctive attraction to her. He was a man who had always admitted to his weaknesses, and she had been one of them. Sarah, on the other hand was his strength and as he looked at his one-time fling he felt a surge of love, paradoxically, for his wife.

'Three of you?' she exclaimed as they approached, with an

accusatory glare. 'From your text I thought it was just you, Bob. I take it these are not social workers come to give me emotional support.' She looked directly at Mann, ignoring Cotter entirely.

The DCI returned her gaze, unsmiling. She knew that Dan Provan, her former CID, and now lifetime, partner would have fired back an instant response, but that was a skill he had been unable to pass on, so she restricted herself to a slightly raised eyebrow as she introduced herself and her sergeant.

'Lottie and John are part of the team investigating the Edinburgh New Year murders,' Skinner explained as she escorted them indoors. 'They're not investigating Cameron's disappearance . . . which has now been given semi-official status, by the way; they're looking for the car . . . but something else has come up. If he was here they'd be asking him about it, but he's not, so . . .'

'So you're settling for second best.'

'Put it any way you like, Mia.' He smiled, trying to ease the tension. 'Coffee would go well.'

'You think this is fucking Starbuck's?' she retorted, then relaxed slightly herself. 'There's a pot on the hob, but it's the servants' day off, so we'll have to help ourselves.'

'Does she really have servants?' Cotter whispered as they followed her into the kitchen.

'Only one, John, and he's missing,' Skinner hissed.

To their surprise, Mia McCullough was not alone. 'This is Cameron's daughter, Inez Davis,' she said, introducing an unnaturally blonde middle-aged woman with narrow, furtive eyes and painted but well-chewed fingernails. 'Cheeky's mum,' she added. Skinner recognised her; on the occasion of their first meeting she had been in police custody. She glanced at him briefly without holding eye contact. 'She doesn't like me calling her my stepdaughter, since I'm only two months older than her.'

'Where's my dad?' Inez asked the officers, abruptly. 'I've asked my daughter's polisman boyfriend, but he was no use.'

'He's occupied elsewhere at the moment,' Mann told her, 'as are we. Your stepmother,' she looked her in the eye as she used the term, 'has probably told you that the circumstances of your father's disappearance don't justify the excessive use of police time.'

'If it was anybody else it would,' she complained. 'You lot have always had it in for my father.'

'Shut the fuck up, Inez!' Mia sighed. 'You've never given a damn for him before, so don't start now.'

She turned to the visitors, handing each a mug, leaving them to add milk if they chose. 'Right,' she said, as the sergeant stirred his sugar, an addition which drew a look of contempt from Skinner, 'what's the emergency, and,' she added, 'what are you doing here, Bob? I know they never did cut the umbilical between you and the police, but it is Saturday and you don't deal with the small stuff.'

'I'll let DCI Mann explain,' he replied.

'As Sir Robert said,' Lottie began, 'we're part of the Serious Crimes squad investigating the killings of Terry Coats and Inspector Griffin Montell.'

'Neither of whom I know, or had even heard of until a couple of days ago.'

'I appreciate that, Mrs McCullough, but a couple of days ago a third man was found dead. He'd been shot and his body was dumped too, but outside Edinburgh. It was partially hidden and attempts had been made to hide his identity, but one item was left behind. From that we were able to establish that he was a man named Anatoly Rogozin.'

The faintest flicker of surprise broke through Mia McCullough's mask of impassivity. 'Go on,' she murmured.

'We're seconded to Edinburgh,' Mann continued, 'but normally we're based in Glasgow. A while back, before John joined me, I investigated the murder of a man pulled out of the River Clyde, near the Squinty Bridge. He was identified as the chairman of Merrytown Football Club, of which your husband is the majority shareholder, and his name was Dimitri Rogozin. I hope you'll understand, Mrs McCullough, that when a second Rogozin turned up dead in Scotland, where members of that clan are not exactly thick on the ground, it got my atten—'

'His brother,' Mia snapped, cutting her off abruptly. 'Anatoly was Dimitri's brother. You'd find out soon enough so I'll save you the trouble of chasing it down. But don't ask me why he was in Scotland because I can't help you there.'

'Was he involved with the football club?' Skinner asked. 'I did some googling earlier on and, as far as I can see, the bulk of the shareholding is still shared between Cameron and Rogotron, the investment company that he and Dimitri jointly owned. When I was involved, Dimitri was chairman but Cameron was the principal owner, with fifty per cent of the shares personally, and twenty five per cent through Rogotron.'

'That's true,' she conceded. 'But . . .' She stopped, frowning.

'Come on Mia,' he said, 'we'll find out. It won't be easy since Rogotron is foreign-registered, but we'll get there in the end.'

She nodded. 'I suppose. No, he wasn't involved with the club; when Dimitri died, Anatoly expected to inherit his share in the club, and he told Cameron that he intended to buy him out. You'll remember that Dimitri was a pompous little arsehole, nothing to him at all behind the bluster and the bodyguard. Anatoly, though, he was a different animal altogether and not one that Cameron wanted anything to do with. So . . . let me get this right . . . yes; Rogotron was constituted in an unusual way; Cameron and Dimitri were fifty-fifty owners, and there was a clause in the articles that said that in the event of the death of either one, the survivor had the right to buy his shareholding, at a figure set by the auditors. So instead of Anatoly taking over Merrytown, Cameron did, completely.'

'How did Anatoly react to that?'

'Badly. Threats were made, but you probably know, Bob, maybe all of you do, that my husband isn't a man you can threaten. In the end, Anatoly thought better of it and went back to running his other interests.'

'He had an Amex card in the football club's name,' Skinner said.

She nodded. 'I know. Cameron gave him that. He called it a fuck-off present. It has a spending limit and it's valid for three years.'

'And yet he did come back to Scotland,' Mann said. 'And when he did, he wound up dead. And just after he was killed your husband decided to go away for a few days, without telling anyone, even you.'

Mia sighed. 'I know what you're going to say, but no, I won't let you. Cameron didn't kill him.'

Skinner laughed. 'That's the thing. We know he didn't, which makes me wonder even more. Why the hell has he done a runner?'

Thirty-Five

Although the image on the computer screen was shaky, it was recognisable as Major Pollock. However, the background had changed, from a drab office wall enhanced by a framed photograph of Nelson Mandela to bright sunshine and a verdant landscape. The sound was different also; snatches of conversation in a language that Haddock did not understand, but assumed was Afrikaans.

'Inspector,' the South African exclaimed, 'I wasn't expecting to hear from you again; not today anyway. I'm at my golf club; we tee off in ten minutes.'

'Sorry,' he replied. 'Zoom invitations seem to go everywhere. I can call you back. I'm a golfer myself; the last thing I'd want would be some bugger interrupting my practice routine by calling me about work.'

Pollock laughed. 'I don't practise. I just go out and try to hit the damn thing straight. I play off nineteen. You?'

'Single figures,' the Scot replied, modestly.

'It would be good to play sometime. You'll be welcome here if you ever visit Pretoria.' He glanced away from the camera. 'From what I can see here,' he said, 'that ten minutes is stretching into fifteen at least. Two guys in a four-ball in front

198

have just found the water off the tee. Go ahead and ask me what you want.'

'Tell, not ask,' Haddock said. 'Are you sure? It might put you off your game.'

'My game's past praying for, Inspector. Go ahead.'

'Okay, if you insist. Some of this is theory but it's based on fact. Can I ask you something? What are your storage and recording arrangements for patrol officers' sidearms?'

'The officer is responsible for his or her firearm.'

'When it's issued is the serial number logged?'

'Yes.'

'When someone leaves the service or changes job what happens to it?'

'It would be reissued, and the serial number would be logged out to the new carrier.'

'Sure, but would the number be checked when the gun is surrendered?'

Major Pollock frowned. 'No, probably not,' he admitted. 'What are you getting at?'

'If I sent you the serial number of the Beretta we found in Griff's safe, could you check it against your records?'

'Yes, and I will do. Now tell me why.'

Sensing his impatience, Haddock replied, bluntly. 'Griffin Montell killed his partner, Officer DeWalt. The image in your robbery file matches the gun we have. Naturally enough, nobody ever thought to check Griff's weapon during your investigation, but even if they had, I don't believe it would have told them anything, unless they had also checked the serial number against that of the weapon issued to him. I believe that Griff helped stage the robbery. He told his accomplices where to wait, in the quietest stretch of track he could find. When they got there, he shot DeWalt straight away. The gun that he used was replaced by an identical firearm . . . not difficult, it's the choice of international police services . . . and taken from the scene, but returned to him later, for his own security.'

'What do you mean by that?'

'My belief is that as long as he had the gun, he felt he was safe. He didn't trust anyone else to dispose of it, because he didn't want it turning up anywhere by accident, and he didn't want to take the chance of being blackmailed.'

'What about his own wounds?'

Haddock stared into the computer camera rather than at the screen, knowing that he was looking Pollock directly in the eye. 'One of his co-conspirators did that; a flesh wound in the shoulder, then he aligned the weapon against the side of his head and fired the grazing shot. Griff was a tough guy, remember.' He paused. 'His medical records here in Scotland show something interesting: a slight deafness in his right ear. Not enough to incapacitate him or make him unfit for service, but noticeable.'

'Okay,' the major conceded. 'But what about the tracker that was found on the armoured van?'

'Easy. It was put there at the scene. It was never in the Mint.'

'You realise you're making my colleagues look sloppy for missing all this in their investigation?' Pollock said.

'I don't think so,' the DI replied. 'I would have made the same assumptions they did. I'd never have thought to check the serial number of Griff's service weapon, or to give him a gunshot residue test. They found an officer dead and another one down at the scene, and they acted accordingly. After the event he did nothing wrong either. He didn't draw attention to himself; he took his reward, a transfer to CID, and sat on his money until he was able to leave the country legitimately, on a job transfer. Once he was clear of South Africa, he was able to move his Krugerrands to Britain.'

'Mmm,' the South African murmured. 'What you're saying, it's a terrible accusation, but it makes sense to me. Maybe the man DuPlessis can shine some light on it.'

'Maybe he can,' Haddock said. 'Like I said, much of it's conjecture, but at the centre of it, Griff's gun killed Officer DeWalt. Everything flows from that. It killed a man in Scotland too. His name was Anatoly Rogozin, but I have no idea how he fits into the story, or even if he does.'

'I'll check it out for you, if you text me the spelling and everything you know about him.' He glanced off camera. 'We're up next, Inspector. My partner isn't going to be very pleased with my game today, but that's nothing new . . . she's my wife.'

Haddock grinned. 'No way would I play golf with my partner,' he chuckled.

'I don't have the choice,' Major Pollock sighed. 'You know,' he said, as he began to move and his image became shaky once more, 'one thing I don't understand. Why didn't they shoot Griffin between the eyes rather than upside the head? That would have been the obvious thing to do.'

'I agree,' the DI concurred. 'I can't work that one out either. If I ever do, I'll let you know. Good luck out there. By the way,' he added, 'missing the water off the first tee sounds like a good plan.'

Thirty-Six

'Sod it,' Jackie Wright murmured, as she studied the Civil Aviation Authority website. 'If you were registered in the European Union, you'd show up here but you don't, so where the hell are you?' Frustrated, she closed the window. 'Marlon,' she called to a detective constable who had been seconded to the team from Glasgow with Mann and Cotter, 'I'm struggling here. I'm trying to find the ownership of an airline called Wister Air. It's got a foreign permit to fly into the UK, but that doesn't tell me its base.'

'What about its own website?' he suggested. His accent was heavily Glaswegian but with West Indian undertones.

'I've tried that. It tells me everywhere it flies to, what I can eat on board and what the special offers are on its duty free, but nothing else.'

'Does it have a corporate section? Most companies do, for investor relations.'

'Not that I could see.'

'That suggests it's privately owned.'

'If you wanted to protect your privacy,' Wright asked, 'where would you register a business?'

Big eyes stared at her. 'I'm Marlon Honeyman, a boy fae

Castlemilk. How the hell would Ah know that?' Then he smiled. 'But if I was a clever bastard who'd done a degree in business studies before I joined the polis, I would probably look at somewhere offshore.'

'If your business had South African links, which haven might you choose?'

'It wouldn't be African, but otherwise pretty much anywhere. It would depend on how much privacy I wanted. Jackie, leave it with me. I'll have a look and see what I can find.'

Thirty-Seven

'Inspector Haddock? Jamie Ellis, Liverpool. I think I've traced Aisha Karman.'

Sauce beamed at her image on the computer screen; her message asking for a Skype meeting had taken him by surprise. 'That's excellent. Do you have a location for her, and can I speak to her?'

'Yes and no,' the officer replied. 'She's in cold storage at Manchester City Mortuary, so I don't think you'll get a word out of her.'

'Shit,' Haddock hissed, as an unspoken fear became reality. 'Are you certain that it's her? How long has she been there?'

'We're absolutely certain. She's been there two months, but she looks brand new. The photo you sent puts it beyond doubt. Her body was dumped on a quiet road just north of Bolton and found by a dog-walker within twelve hours of her death. She'd been shot once in the head at close range, but there wasn't a scrap of personal identification on her, which stymied the CID investigation from the beginning. DCS Jones on the Manchester force is dead chuffed with you, by the way,' she added, 'for taking a big black smudge off her record, just by telling us who she was. I've been seconded to work with her on the investigation. Before you say anything, they might have identified her from the missing-person report in Liverpool, but,' she shrugged, 'they didn't.'

'There was no potential identification at all?' Haddock asked. 'Not even clothing?'

'She was naked; her prints weren't on any database, nor was her DNA.' Inspector Ellis raised an eyebrow. 'However, we do have someone else's. She had sex shortly before she died. My Manc colleagues believe that he stripped her, shagged her and shot her . . .' she paused '. . . hopefully in that order.'

'The donor DNA. No match, I guess?'

'None, anywhere. Our investigators have searched databases internationally. Are you going to make DCS Jones even happier by telling us who he is?'

'I'm not going to promise that, but I do know of a man who was in a relationship with Aisha Karman, here in Scotland.'

Her eyes widened. 'Could you get a DNA sample from him? Do you have grounds for doing that? Do you even need grounds in Scotland?'

'We have the same rules as you do. Once a suspect has been arrested, we can take it with or without consent. In this case, that's not going to be an issue. The man I'm talking about is as dead as Ms Karman, and currently occupying similar accommodation in the Edinburgh morgue. We need to work together on this, Jamie. I'm going to send you a photo of my suspect. If I'm right the DNA puts him together, obviously, but I'd like to paint a complete picture of what happened. Quid pro quo, I'm also going to need to see your investigation file, including all the forensics. Most important of all, you said Aisha was shot so: did you recover the bullet?'

Thirty-Eight

'This gets worse, Sauce,' Tarvil Singh remarked, as Haddock finished briefing him on his calls with Major Pollock and Inspector Ellis. 'We started off with two dead men in Edinburgh, and now we've got five victims in three countries. D'you fancy giving DCI Pye a call and telling him how fucking lucky he is to be missing this?'

'That would be cruel,' the DI told him. 'Sammy would love this. He'd see it as a path to glory and switch into full Luke Skywalker mode, the last of the Jedi.'

'You do know we used to call you R2D2, don't you?'

'No,' he admitted, 'but I prefer that to being half of our official nickname, The Menu.'

'How long's he going to be off?' the big DS asked.

'How should I know?'

'Because you always do. And,' he added, heavily, 'the fact that you're not saying makes me think this is not man flu that he's got.'

'I prefer it when you don't think, Tarvil.'

'I get it. You're telling me not to ask.'

Haddock nodded, then drew two fingers across his mouth in a zipper gesture.

'Boss!' Jackie Wright's call forestalled any comeback. 'Can Marlon and I have a word?' The Glaswegian DC stood behind the desk, with a blue folder pressed to his chest.

'If it's relevant,' the DI replied.

'Your office?'

'Hell no, it's barely big enough for me. We'll use the meeting room. Tarvil, you come too.' He led the way through a door at the far end of the suite into an area that was dominated by the view through its picture window of Fettes College, the great grey Victorian faux-chateau that seemed to have been imposed on Edinburgh, its grandeur emphasising the awful drabness of the police building.

'Every time I look at that thing,' Singh remarked, 'it makes me think of Mervyn Peake.'

'Who?' Wright asked.

'Gormenghast,' Honeyman said.

'Fuck me!' Haddock whispered, as they took seats. 'Right Jackie,' he said, 'what do you and Marlon have for us?'

'It's him, not me,' she replied. 'Marlon, you did it, you tell him.'

He nodded his shaven head, almost dislodging the glasses that were perched on the bridge of his nose. 'I've been chasing Wister Air,' he began, 'the airline name that's mentioned by Sir Robert Skinner in the statement he gave us. He alleges that Coats claimed to him—' He halted in midsentence as Haddock held up a hand. 'Sir?'

'Bob Skinner doesn't allege things, DC Honeyman,' the DI said. 'He tells you things, and you take them on board. You don't question them or doubt them in any way; you act on them. Besides, I was there at the time, more or less, so I know what Wister Air is and how it fits into the story. Go on.'

The detective's mouth tensed at the reproof; he continued, stiffly. 'I've been investigating the company, sir, and I've established that its head office is in Cape Town, South Africa. It flies mostly tourist routes, and that's the market it chases. In Britain it operates out of Edinburgh, Manchester, Liverpool and Stansted, and in Europe it flies from Schiphol, in Amsterdam. It appears to have very little interest in business travel. It makes its money flying British and Dutch holiday-makers to Cape Town, where their pounds and their euros go a hell of a long way.'

'That's interesting,' Singh observed, drily, 'but who owns it?'

'That was harder to pin down,' Honeyman admitted. 'I looked at company registration in South Africa, in the UK and in Holland, but no joy. I looked at some other popular places, including Liechtenstein and the Cayman Islands: nothing. Then I looked at North Cyprus.'

'Is that really a country? I thought it was an occupied territory.'

'To most of the world it is,' the DC agreed, 'but it's recog-nised as a state by one country, Turkey, and to them, it's the Turkish Republic of North Cyprus. It's got all sorts of inter-national embargoes on it, but it is possible to use it as a corporate base. Wister Air was registered there, by an outfit called TCOC, as an offshore company in 2010; it has two shareholders, Anatoly Rogozin Enterprises, based in Monaco, and Lente, spelled like the six weeks before Easter but with a final e.'

'What's that?'

'Nothing that I can discover. It's just a name. I can't get anywhere with that. There are two directors of Wister Air, Rogozin himself, and a Northern Cypriot nominee. That's a common device to get round local requirements.'

'What about Lente's assets?' Haddock asked.

'Shielded,' Honeyman replied. 'Whoever set this up with Rogozin didn't want to be known, and they've made a bloody good job of it.'

Thirty-Nine

'Just occasionally, Mario, there are times when I'm really glad I'm retired,' Skinner declared.

'I hear what you're saying, Bob,' the deputy chief constable replied. 'But they don't last long, fortunately. What you're doing as a mentor for Sauce and other young people, that's invaluable, and I like to think it's a unique resource for our force.'

'Bollocks! You could do that yourself; you've got the experience and you have the skills.'

'No, I couldn't,' McGuire insisted, 'because I'm too fucking busy. You were dead right to walk away from the unified police service. It has fundamental flaws. We all grew up as cops. Those of us who made it to command level had to become managers. At local or regional level, most of us got by even without specialist training, but that's not the case now.'

'You're doing fine,' Skinner said, but his voice lacked conviction and he knew it.

'For now, maybe, but that won't last. The job eats you. It devoured Andy Martin . . .'

'He was swallowed by his own ego!' his friend protested.

'You know that's not true. Andy was one of the best police

officers you and I ever met, but he was a fucking detective. He was used to focusing on specific issues, mostly one at a time. He couldn't handle the breadth of the responsibility. It affected him in every way. He became remote from people he'd worked with all his career and he became dictatorial. He turned from a pleasant guy into a grade-A shit, and when he finally packed it in his former friends had a farewell party, only he wasn't invited. Now I'm sitting here in the senior command office which might as well be in fucking Stromness, and I'm . . .' He stopped, in mid-sentence.

'What?'

'Ach, nothing. Forget it, Bob.'

'Like hell I will,' he said. 'Let me take a stab at what you were going to say: you're sitting there and you're seeing the same thing happening to Maggie.'

'You know me too well. Yes, you're right. She's taking some time off, Bob, at my suggestion . . . actually, my insistence . . . after having a chat with our senior medical officer. Nothing will be announced, but she won't be around for a while.'

'And if she doesn't come back?'

'I don't like to think about that, but one thing I know for certain: I don't want the bloody job. Nobody in their right mind would, not if they wanted to stay that way.'

'Can I help?' Skinner asked.

'There's one thing you could do,' McGuire replied. 'I've spent some time with the NYPD, as you know, and I'm convinced that we need to adopt the New York system, a Police Commissioner who isn't a cop necessarily, but who has oversight of the whole system, with hire and fire powers. He or she would be appointed by Clive Graham, the First Minister, and would appoint their own advisory team on management matters; operationally we'd go back to the old set-up, with ten or a dozen areas each with a chief, responsible to the commissioner. It would spread the load, the public would like it and I think we'd all do a better job.'

'I agree with all of that,' he replied. 'But what can I do?'

'Use your media clout. Run the proposition on the *Saltire*.'

'Hold on a minute. I'm not the editor; June Crampsey is. That would be her shout.'

'So ask her if she'll do it,' McGuire persisted. 'I bet she will; her dad's a retired cop. I'm sure he'd persuade her if it was needed.'

'Let me think about it,' Skinner said, 'but I'm not putting the paper up to be shot down. I won't do it without sounding Clive out first. It might be seen as a climb-down by government, and you know how much politicians hate that.' He took a deep breath and continued. 'Now, what you told me earlier. Run it past me again, but at normal speed this time.'

'The Torphichen Place investigation; it's like that virus, spreading everywhere. Sauce has just finished briefing me. The latest is that the woman Coats told you about has been found in the mortuary in Manchester, with a Jane Doe label on her toe. Their CID have been able to trace her move-ments from John Lennon Airport to a hotel near the airport in Manchester.'

'That's progress. How did she die?' He paused, with a quick intake of breath. 'Let me guess, she was shot in the head.'

'Got it in one. The bullet's being couriered up to Gartcosh right now. They thought they had a DNA sample too, but that's been corrupted.' McGuire hesitated. 'But that's not all,' he added. 'Sauce has established that the gun in Montell's safe didn't only shoot Anatoly Rogozin, it also killed his partner in the Pretoria gold robbery. I've just been given a profile by Dominic Jackson which suggests that Griff might have been a high-functioning psychopath. It looks as if that's no longer in doubt.'

Forty

'If there is any news about Grandpa, you will tell me, won't you?' Cheeky asked, as Sauce handed her a bacon sandwich. 'I had my mother on the phone yesterday afternoon,' she added. 'He barely speaks to her but somehow she found out that he's missing.'

'She found out from me,' he confessed. 'I called Inez yesterday, on the off-chance that he had been in touch with her. She said he hadn't, and I didn't tell her anything, but . . .'

She grimaced. 'But . . . she seized on it as an excuse to phone me. The last thing I want to do is let that woman into our lives, Sauce. She's a disaster, just like my Aunt Daphne was . . .'

'Nah,' Sauce countered. 'From what I've been told by Bob Skinner and others, including your grandpa, she's not in the same class as Goldie was. She was flat-out dangerous. Inez is just an idiot, or so they all reckon. The puzzle is how she had a daughter like you. Your brains must come from your dad.'

'My dad,' she repeated. 'I'm in my late twenties and all I know about him is that he had the brains to disappear off the face of the earth when Grandpa found out that he'd knocked up his fifteen-year-old daughter. He brought me up, you know, Grandpa did, him and Granny Abby.'

'I know, you've told me, and so has he. He tolerated your mother, but since that time when she and Goldie got you involved in one of their scams, she's been banished into the outer darkness, or to put it another way, managing the radio-station canteen.'

'In that case why did you bother phoning her?'

'Because despite it all, she is his daughter, and she might occasionally speak to him. And she's your mum, so I can't pretend she doesn't exist any more than you can.'

She sighed. 'I know. That doesn't mean she'll get anywhere near her . . .'

He gazed at her, caught by her hesitation. 'Near her what?'

'Oh nothing. Go on, get to work, since you say you have to.'

'Not until you tell me what you thought better of saying.' He grinned. 'You might as well; I'm a professional interrogator, love.'

She frowned, then looked up at him. 'You do love me, don't you, Harold?' she asked, earnestly.

'With all my heart,' he promised, 'even when you call me Harold. Why?'

'I'm late.'

His mouth opened then closed again, then opened and closed once more. 'How late?' he was able to ask, finally.

'Two weeks, and that's not Tom Jones disease: it is unusual, I promise you.'

'Bloody hell, I thought you were on the . . .'

'So did I, but I asked a doctor and she said that every month you take it, even without missing one, there's about a half of one per cent chance of you falling pregnant.' She smiled nervously. 'Do you really have to go to work?'

'Yes, I do, there's a guy in a cell in Pretoria waiting to talk to me. I can't do it from here because there have to be two officers on the call.'

'In that case,' she instructed, 'find a chemist once you're finished, and bring back a test kit.'

First things first, Haddock decided as soon as he fastened his seatbelt. He sent a message to Major Pollock, delaying his video meeting by half an hour, then headed straight for the Gyle Shopping Centre, where he was confident that he would find a pharmacy, even on the first Sunday of the year. Having no idea which of the tests on offer was the most reliable, he chose the most expensive. The checkout lady smiled at him. 'Good luck,' she whispered.

He was about to counter, 'What makes you think it would be?' when he realised that he might never have been happier in his life.

His mind was still full of domesticity when he arrived at his office, and his imagination was out of control. It took a fleeting vision of enrolling his twins at Fettes College to force him back to the day's business.

Jackie Wright had more than earned a day off, although it had needed an order to make her take it, but Marlon Honeyman was on duty, gazing fixedly at a computer screen, oblivious to Haddock's nod of greeting. Tarvil Singh, on the other hand was deep in a copy of the *Observer*.

'Are we in that?' the DI asked.

'What?' he looked around, momentarily startled. 'Us, no, we don't rate the English Sundays. No, I was reading about the new flu they're having in China. It's not too clever.' He looked more closely at his colleague. 'What are you so happy about? It's bloody Sunday. Are you so wrapped up in this that you've forgotten that?'

'It's your cheery face, Tarv. It does it every time. Have you got the South African on stand-by like I asked?'

'Yes,' the DS replied. 'I sent an invitation to the address that Pollock gave us. The custody officers wanted to know how long they should hold the guy. I told them to ask their boss. That was right, wasn't it?'

'Spot on. We don't have jurisdiction and I don't see us wanting him as a witness. Go on, call them back.'

As Haddock pulled up a chair beside his, Singh went to his keyboard and reactivated the Zoom meeting that he had set up. To their surprise the face that appeared on screen was familiar, that of Major Pollock, and he was in uniform.

'Good morning, guys,' he began. 'You probably weren't expecting to see me, but things have changed here. I've had a team of officers investigating movements on cruise vessels operated by Mr DuPlessis' company, and it's proved very interesting. It seems that he and a couple of colleagues have been providing what I'll describe as discreet transport services for sensitive consignments.' He grinned, but grimly. 'In other words, the buggers have been smuggling. You asked me specifically about a consignment that Griffin might have received a couple of years ago, but in fact we've uncovered more than that, for people other than him with nothing to do with your investigation. So today, we're both going to be interviewing him. After that I'll decide whether he'll be kept in custody. As yet, he doesn't know what I know, so be ready for me to jump in when the moment's right.'

His hand covered the camera, the source computer was swung around and the two Scots found themselves looking as a middle-aged man was brought into the room. He had a black V-shaped hairline, a sharp nose and a loose, nervous mouth.

'Mr DuPlessis?' Haddock began. As he spoke, a flashback from the morning found its way into his mind, and he had to push it back.

'That's me,' the man on screen replied.

'I'm Detective Inspector Harold Haddock, in charge of the Serious Crimes team in Edinburgh, Scotland, and this is my colleague, Detective Sergeant Singh. We're investigating the murder of our colleagues, Inspector Griffin Montell, and another man. I believe Inspector Montell was your cousin.'

'Yes, he was. Our mothers were sisters, but we weren't close.'

'I believe that his mother is no longer alive.'

'That's correct,' DuPlessis confirmed. 'Mine is, but she lives in Buenos Aires with her second husband. He's a rugby coach,' he added.

'When did you last hear from your cousin?'

'I can't remember. We never communicated much.'

'Try, Mr DuPlessis,' Singh growled.

The sight of the massive Sikh leaning forward to fill the screen seemed to alarm the South African, but not enough to shake his claim to forgetfulness. 'I can't, okay.'

'When we searched your cousin's apartment after his death,' the DI continued, 'we were surprised by some of the things we found. Specifically, there was a significant amount of South African gold coins, far more than you'd reasonably expect to find in the home of a working cop. There was a lot of cash, more than a year's salary for his rank. And there was a firearm, a Beretta handgun, a type regularly carried by police officers around the world.'

DuPlessis shrugged. 'Why are you telling me? Like I said, I hardly knew the bloke.'

'Is that really true?' Major Pollock asked, breaking into the investigation. 'You see, Tom, my people in Cape Town have been making enquiries at your workplace, Oceanic Magic. They have interviewed a woman called Dee Gosford: she's a chief engineer and under questioning she told them . . . confessed would be a better term . . . that a couple of years ago you asked her to take charge of an item for you, and take it to Southampton where it would be offloaded at night, when the rest of the world was asleep. She was paid five Krugerrands for her trouble. She couldn't identify the man who collected the consignment, not unnaturally, because it was dark, but her physical description is a fair match for Griffin Montell.'

'It had nothing to do with me,' DuPlessis snapped, gaining confidence. 'It's her word against mine, and you don't sound like you can prove a damn thing.'

'Give me forty-eight hours,' Haddock retorted, 'and I will.'

'You better believe that,' Pollock added. 'When he does, and when we can tie you to that box, you will be in deep trouble. We, the three of us, have established that the firearm we know to have been in that box was used to kill a serving South African Police officer. The fact that you handled it makes you an accessory to his murder. Twenty-five years without parole, buddy, is not something I would be taking as lightly as you seem to be.'

'Fuck!' DuPlessis shouted. 'What are you trying to pull here?'

'I am telling you like it is. There isn't a single officer in the South African Police Service who has forgotten about Constable Fannie DeWalt, and every one of us is righteously angry that nobody has ever been convicted for his murder. You will help us put that right, Tom DuPlessis.'

'I never knew about the fucking gun! Or anything else!'

Okay, yes, a couple of years ago Griff contacted me when he was over here on holiday, and told me he had something he wanted to get out of the country and over to Britain before his ex-wife got wind of it. He asked me to get it across on one of the liners. He knew we did that; quite a few people do, but what we take on board is harmless. We don't move drugs or anything like that.'

'Did Griff tell you what was in the box?'

'He told me it was money, and I didn't ask any more. He paid me in gold coins, fifteen of them. I gave Dee five.'

'How did you get the box?' Haddock asked.

'He brought it to me. I think he had it in safe storage, long term. That's all, I swear. You need me to give evidence to anybody, I will.' He looked away from the camera, across at Pollock. 'Is that it? Are you happy now? Can I get out of here? I got to get back to work, man.'

The major laughed. 'I tell you what. You give me a record of everything you've ever moved out of the country, and the people you've moved it for, and I might think about releasing you. As for going back to work, I think you'll find that after what they've found out about you, Oceanic Magic don't want to see you again.' He looked off to his right. 'Officers, take Mr DuPlessis back to his detention cell, and give him a pen and paper, so that he can write as if his life depends upon it, because that might very well be the case.' As he was being removed, Pollock turned back to Haddock and Singh. 'Can you guys really prove that Griffin collected that box?'

'I hope so,' the DI replied. 'I can promise you we'll have a bloody good try.'

Forty-One

Sauce Haddock wanted nothing more than to step into his car and drive home, his purchase in his pocket and ready for use. He was elated and nervous at the same time, and yet he knew that professionally his day was not over.

As soon as he had ended the Pretoria video conference, he had called the DCC's home number from his landline to update him. As he hung up, on impulse he phoned his mentor.

Skinner's mood brought him back down to earth. 'I can't believe I got it so wrong about a man. I recruited him, I advanced him in the service, and all the time he was a thief and a killer.'

'Me neither, gaffer,' Haddock admitted. 'I don't know whether to feel pleased that we've helped the South Africans solve a twelve-year-old crime or gutted that we've been betrayed by one of our own. I do know that in terms of the purpose of the investigation, I know fuck all. I can't tie Coats and Griff together and until I do that I'm not one step closer to finding out who killed them. Now I've got the Rogozin murder, and Griff's apparent involvement, muddying the waters, and on top of that . . .' He paused as an idea, not previously considered, crossed his mind. 'As you and Lottie found out yesterday,

Grandpa McCullough knew Anatoly Rogozin; he turns up in Scotland, he's killed and a couple of days later Grandpa disappears. I'm asking myself, did Grandpa know Griff? Is it possible that after their clash over the Rogotron shares Grandpa saw Anatoly as a threat and had Griff take him out?'

'No,' Skinner said, firmly. 'I don't see that for a second. If Cameron had done that he'd have established an unshakeable alibi, and he wouldn't have drawn attention to himself by disappearing afterwards. To cover that base, though, you might ask Mia where he was on Saturday night.'

'Shit!' Haddock whispered. 'I don't need to. He did set up the perfect alibi; it's me. On Saturday night he and Mia took Cheeky and me to the restaurant in the Caley Hotel. Vito Tremacoldi drove them down from Perthshire; he had a bistro meal in a place across Rutland Street.'

'Do you know when Rogozin arrived in Scotland?'

'Yes, I do now. Rogozin had an address in London. DC Honeyman, our secondee from Glasgow, has him coming into Edinburgh on a flight from London City that afternoon, Saturday, around the same time that Griff was dropping his bag for his trip to South Africa.'

'A trip he never made,' Skinner pointed out. 'I take it you've . . .'

'Gaffer, we've been crawling all over the airport CCTV for Saturday afternoon. Apart from one sighting of Griff at the bag drop there's nothing.'

'And Coats?'

'A man of fucking mystery; we know where he lived but that's it.' As he spoke, his attention was grabbed by Marlon Honeyman's waving left hand. 'I have to go,' he said. 'I think I'm wanted.'

He replaced the handset and stepped out of his room, walking across to the DC's desk. 'What's got your attention?' he asked. 'What the hell are you doing here anyway?' he added. 'There's no overtime allocated and even Lottie's taking the day off.'

'I want to get into Inspector Montell's personal records, sir, and I got sidetracked yesterday.'

The DI nodded. 'Thanks. It's appreciated, and it won't go unacknowledged. From that hand signal, you've found something.'

'I may have. Montell booked a trip to South Africa for last weekend, as we know. That was paid for with a credit card. I got that information from British Airways at the same time as I traced Rogozin, because it's generally quicker doing it that way than accessing it through the bank. The thing that's interesting me is that he was booked on the last shuttle, yet he dropped his bag in the afternoon. As it turned out, he missed the flight, but why would he do that, drop his bag so early?'

'Because he knew that Rogozin was coming and he intended to be waiting for him?' Haddock suggested.

'That's what I'm thinking.'

'In which case, how did he know, and what was the connection between them?'

Honeyman smiled. 'That's above my pay grade, sir, I'm just a computer nerd. However, leaving that aside, the reason I wanted to talk to you, I found something interesting on his debit card. We have Montell checking in his case at nine minutes past three, we have Rogozin disembarking from his domestic flight at twenty-four minutes past. Then, at three forty-seven Montell makes a payment on his debit card to Lothian Buses. Do you know how much a single ticket costs on the airport bus?'

'Four and a half quid. My partner and I caught it last October.'

'In that case he bought two tickets.'

Haddock patted the DC on the shoulder. 'Progress, at last,' he declared. 'There are security cameras on all Lothian vehicles. If we can find out where they got off, we may be in business.'

'Very good, sir, but how does it help us find out who killed Montell and Coats?'

'I've got no idea, Marlon, but there's a story unfolding before us. All we can do is read it and hope that in the end it tells us. Now get yourself back to Glasgow. Accessing the bus camera's a job for tomorrow. You've done enough for today, and I've got another detecting job to do.'

Forty-Two

Edinburgh was back to work on the first Monday of the new year, after the extended break that invariably follows a Tuesday Hogmanay, but Sauce Haddock was almost oblivious of the traffic as he waited for the lights to change. Cheeky's pregnancy test had been positive; to be even more certain they had done a second, with the same result.

They had agreed they would tell nobody until she could make plans at work. She was a senior audit manager with her firm, and her schedule was set out for the full year, with each client having a reporting deadline. He wanted nothing more than to go off on holiday at the first opportunity. The August trip to Madeira that they had booked would have to be cancelled as Cheeky's pregnancy would be too far advanced to allow air travel. And then there was the housing question. They had been considering moving for a while; they were agreed it should be out of the city, but not about the direction. Thousands of new homes were under construction or planned for East Lothian, but Sauce had a hankering for Fife.

'You could leave the police,' she had suggested, deadpan over dinner, 'go and work for Grandpa.'

He had dropped his fork. 'Are you serious?'

She had flashed him the happiest smile he had ever seen, then laughed out loud. 'No. I'd sooner you became a monk.'

'We're a bit late for that.'

His grin became a frown as a horn blast came from the car behind, for a second too long to be acceptable. He drove off slowly; on the other side of the crossing he flashed a concealed blue light but decided to do no more than that. 'Your lucky morning, pal,' he murmured as he beamed once more, into the rearview mirror.

He was still smiling as he walked into the CID suite, until he saw that the deputy chief constable was waiting for him in his office. He had not been expecting a visit from McGuire and hoped that it did not signal a problem, but he relaxed when he stepped out to join him. 'You lot,' he announced in a voice loud enough to carry round the crowded room, 'are moving out of here for a while. The DCI's office is a joke and the rest of you are all crammed in. DI Haddock, you're moving into that virtually redundant meeting room, until DCI Pye comes back. The cubicle's getting knocked down and the layout re-planned. The joiners will be in as soon as this investigation winds down. Sauce, come with me please.'

He led Haddock into what was to become his new accommodation. 'Close the door, will you? What I said there about Sammy coming back, that was for their benefit. I think we both know the truth. I should tell you also that you'll be seeing less of me, for a while at least. The chief's going to be taking a period of sick leave and I'll be standing in for her. That means I won't be getting involved on the ground, and certainly not at the ridiculous level of micro-management that you've just seen. ACC Lowell Payne will be taking on more tasks in addition to the counter-terrorism and organised crime briefs. He'll be your go-to boss from now on, well, for a while at least. Do you know him?'

'No, we've never met.'

'You'll get on,' McGuire assured him. 'He's not one of those ramrod-straight guys. You won't be snapping to attention all the time. He's also from the west: it concerns me that this force has been a bit Edinburgh-centric in its early years; that's something that both Mrs Steele and I are looking to correct. As an aside, he's Alex Skinner's uncle, married to her mum's sister; I doubt he would be if the big man didn't rate him. You can expect to see him within a couple of days, but he won't sit on your shoulder.'

'Is this thing starting to fall apart, sir?' Haddock ventured. 'First Sammy, Griff and what we're finding out about him, and now the chief?'

The DCC frowned and for a moment Haddock thought he had gone too far. He was relieved when he sighed. 'There is the potential for it, Sauce, that I will admit; but I'm damned if I'll let it happen. Sammy's problem, that has nothing to do with the job. Mrs Steele's, well, maybe that has; she's been diagnosed with stress and depression although that's for senior officers' ears only. It won't be made public; the media department won't be told the detail, only that it's medical and she's entitled to the same privacy as anyone else. But aside from all that,' he continued, 'I only really came in here before heading for the Chateau d'If, as I like to call our headquarters, to tell you that Dorward rang me last night to advise me that his guys put in an extra shift yesterday. A bullet was couriered up to Gartcosh from Manchester; Arthur's senior ballistic man examined it microscopically and compared it with the one dug out of the Howgate victim. It's a match. What exactly does that mean? I didn't like to sour Dorward's triumph by telling him I didn't fucking know.'

'It means I should have spoken to you myself over the weekend, sir,' Haddock confessed. 'Remember Bob Skinner and I catching Terry Coats with an air hostess, and the story he spun?'

'Yes. I even remember her name. Aisha, wasn't it?'

'That's right, Aisha Karman. We went looking for her, only to find that she went missing a couple of months back, somewhere between the Mersey and Manchester. She turned up as soon as I sent her picture down there, unidentified in a mortuary drawer. You've just confirmed my hunch, that she was killed by Griff Montell's gun.'

'But how would he . . . ? If she was Coats's bird . . .'

'That's what I'm hoping to find out. I still haven't put Coats and Montell together; I haven't proved a physical link between them, but this gets me right on the edge of it.'

'Then crack on, Acting Chief Inspector. It would be good if you could tie that up by the time ACC Payne makes contact. I'll be seeing you.'

Haddock looked at the door for several seconds after it closed behind the deputy chief. He felt his earlier elation drain from him, as he was seized by a disturbing feeling that an era was coming to an end. Maggie Steele had been a considerable early influence on his career; she had been his mentor just as much as had Bob Skinner in more recent times, and he was deeply concerned by her situation. His gut feeling was that she would not be back, and that another command regime had hit the wall, leaving an uncertain future for everyone in the police service. Bringing himself back to the present, he looked around the room that McGuire had decreed would become the Serious

Crimes commander's office, and took an executive decision.

'Tarvil,' he called out, stepping back into the suite, 'I'm not waiting for the joiners, I'm moving in there now. Help me move my kit.'

'Okay,' the DS replied. He looked across the suite at two detective constables who were trying to appear as inconspicuous as they could. 'Joe, Tyson. Move the DI's desk, his computer and his other stuff from the chicken coop into the big room. You call that delegation, Sauce,' he said. 'You'll never be as good at it as me.' He picked up his phone and hit the zero button. 'DS Singh, Serious Crimes East, Fettes. From now on all calls to the DCI's extension should go to the one in the squad conference room. That's right, from now until further notice. Got that? Good.' He turned back to Haddock. 'Can I move into yours in the meantime, until they knock it down?' he asked.

'No chance. You'd suffocate in there. Jackie,' he called to Wright, 'do you want it for as long as it's there? You'd benefit most from the quiet.'

The DC stared at him. 'Seriously? Yes, please.'

'Get moving, then. Tarvil, I'll be in there; they can move around me. Since you'll have time on your hands, I need you to follow up on the dates we got from the guy DuPlessis yesterday.'

'What are you going to be doing?'

'Being the boss, big fella, being the boss. I think you call it delegating.' He smiled. 'I might never be as good as you, but you're going to lose about ten kilos watching me try.' He heard laughter behind him as he returned to his new office.

'Where do you want the desk, sir?' one of the DCs asked him from the doorway.

'Beside the phone point, back to the window. I don't want to be looking at fucking Gormenghast all day.'

He took a seat at the far end of the table and called Cheeky on his mobile. 'Hi, how are you doing?' he asked.

'Fine.'

'You're not sick or anything?'

He heard her laugh. 'I don't think I'm at that stage yet.'

'Have you told your boss yet?'

'Sauce,' she said, 'in terms of the whole process, we've barely wiped the sweat off our foreheads. I'll tell her when I think the moment's right, but I'll decide when that is. You're not going to phone me every morning, are you?'

'I'll try not to. Will we go looking at houses at the weekend?'

'Do you expect your investigation to be finished by then?'

The question brought him back to reality. 'That's a point. It's going all right just now though; I ticked another box this morning. I'll let you go, but just one more thing. When your grandpa resurfaces, do you want to tell him yourself or do you want me there?'

She laughed. 'I'll tell you what. Let's hold off on that until I'm wide enough for you to hide behind me.'

'I'm expecting him to be hiding behind me from Mia. See you later, love.'

As he ended the call his mind turned to another matter. He and Cheeky had discussed marriage a few weeks before. They had decided that while it was definitely in their future, there was no rush, as they had no plans to start a family for a couple of years. 'Maybe Grandpa will have a view on that too,' he whispered to the empty room.

Forcing himself back to the business of the day, he retrieved the number of Inspector Jamie Ellis from his phone memory and called her. 'DI Haddock,' she answered in a cheery accent that reminded him of *Coronation Street*. 'Did my package arrive?'

'Yes, and it's been acted upon. The gun that killed Ms Karman has been around. It's linked to two murders; the first was about twelve years ago, in Pretoria, South Africa and the other one was last week in Howgate, Scotland . . . that's to say,' he added, correcting himself, 'the body was found there, but we believe he was killed somewhere else.'

'Can you match the firearm to anyone, or is it one of those that can be rented?'

'I wish it was,' Haddock sighed. 'It was found among the possessions of a former colleague of ours, Griffin Montell, who was murdered on New Year's Day, along with another man, Terry Coats. That's my investigation.'

'How did it get from South Africa?' the inspector asked.

'It was smuggled across to him as part of a consignment.'

'That was risky, was it not?'

'Not the way he did it.'

'Mmm,' Ellis murmured. 'Could you forward an image of this man? My colleagues in Liverpool have struck it lucky. They've traced a private-hire driver who's used by Wister Air, her airline. He remembers picking Ms Karman up at John Lennon on what we believe was the day she disappeared, and taking her to the Grange Hotel near Manchester airport. But,' she added, 'he also remembers that as she got out of his car, she was hailed by a man, and instead of going into the hotel, she went across to talk to him. He said that she was animated, excited, as if she was pleased to see him.'

'Poor woman,' Haddock said. 'The excitement didn't last long. I am guessing that the man she met was Terry Coats, one of my murder victims. They were in a relationship in Edinburgh last year, a few months ago, whenever she flew there. I'll send you down an image for you to show to your taxi driver, but I'll send you Montell's as well, just in case I'm wrong.'

'Thanks. Is there anything else we can do?'

'Yes, there is. You might talk to the manager at Wister Air's Manchester office and ask him what, if anything, he knows about Karman. I need to understand why she wound up dead. On the basis of what I know so far, I don't quite get it.'

Forty-Three

'Where's DI Haddock?' Lottie Mann asked, noting Jackie Wright's new location as she took off her coat and slung it over the back of a chair.

'Moved office,' Marlon Honeyman replied. 'The DCC was in earlier and had a fit of reorganisation. He's moved into the meeting room; he said you're welcome to join him in there.'

'Decent of him,' she said, 'but I'll stay with my guys. That said, what are you doing here, Marlon? You worked yesterday; you're entitled to be off today. Haddock didn't ask you to come in, did he?'

The DC shook his head. 'No, it's my choice. I started something yesterday and I want to be the one that finishes it.'

'That's commendable, Marlon, but I've got to tell you, you don't need to prove yourself to me. You've impressed me from day one.'

'I know that, boss, and I appreciate it but . . . I'm a black boy frae Castlemilk; I have to prove myself to everybody else. Not everybody's moved into the twenty-first century; fact is, I've come across one or two that are still living in the nineteenth.'

'Come on,' Mann protested, 'it's not that bad. Look at me, I'm walking proof that things have changed.'

'Sure, boss, you are. You're also a six-feet-tall female and you're scary, so nobody's going to take the slightest chance that you might hear any of the things that are said behind your back. I'm a detective constable, and I'm a bloke, so folk tend not to be as cautious around me. I'm not talking about the senior ranks. I'm not saying that my colour or my social origins affect my promotion prospects. But if you think racism's been eradicated from a force this size, or even that it can be, you go and ask DS Singh. Okay, you might say that's true of society as a whole, and you'd be right, but this is the part that I function in, and I need to go the extra mile because of it.' He smiled. 'Also, I like Edinburgh,' he added.

She gazed down at him, then glanced at Cotter, a silent witness to the conversation. 'Is that right, John? Do they talk behind my back?'

'I'm new here, ma'am,' he said, 'and I'm English.'

'You're also male. Do they?'

'One or two maybe. Nothing to do with the job though.'

'Hah!' she laughed. 'So the fact that I've moved in with a man twenty years older than me who used to be my DS makes me the talk of the steamie? That's not exactly a surprise. I take it as a compliment to Dan, not a slur against me. But I know, Marlon, you're talking about something different. You might think nothing can be done about it, but there is. Any time you believe you've been the subject of a racist remark, report it to me, and I will take it straight to the bosses for investigation. That's not a suggestion, by the way, or an offer: it's an order. Maybe we can't beat it completely, but if we don't try we're all complicit, you included. Now, what's this task you have in hand?'

'I'm in the process of reviewing all the camera footage from the Edinburgh Airport bus from a week last Saturday.'

'Who are you hoping to find?' she asked, switching her attention to his computer screen.

'Inspector Montell, ma'am, and Anatoly Rogozin, the third victim.' He updated her on his discoveries of the day before.

'Actually, he's the fifth victim, chronologically.' All three detectives turned towards Haddock, who had moved silently behind them. 'Rogozin's linked by the gun that killed him to the death of a police officer in South Africa, and to that of a woman in Manchester; the weapon itself is linked directly to Inspector Griffin Montell.'

'Jeez,' Lottie Mann whispered. 'One of our own.'

'Two of our own,' the DI countered. 'Terry Coats was a cop too, and he wasn't an innocent bystander in all of this. We can't prove that yet, but we're close. Sorry, Marlon, I'm interrupting, keep doing what you're doing. Lottie, come on and I'll fill you and John in on the detail.'

The trio headed for Haddock's new office, leaving Honeyman to his video review. He carried on methodically; the bus service ran every ten minutes regardless of how full or empty each vehicle might be. On the Saturday before Christmas they were busy throughout the afternoon. The footage lacked an on-screen time clock, forcing the DC to examine every clip from the arrival of each bus on the stand to its departure.

'Do you want a coffee?' Tarvil Singh called to him. 'I can do that for ten minutes.'

Honeyman almost accepted the sergeant's offer, but sheer stubbornness made him persevere. He ran through two more excerpts. His bladder was on the point of forcing him to take a break when . . . 'What? Is it? Yes.'

Two men boarded the bus, showing their tickets to the

driver. The first was in his thirties, broad built, wearing a black knitted jacket; it appeared to be woollen and was certainly expensive, a designer label, the DC guessed. The second man was older, dragging a small suitcase and wearing a heavy overcoat. They walked towards the camera until they had passed out of its field of vision.

Honeyman paused the recording, went to the toilet and relieved himself. On the way back, he collected the coffee that he had declined earlier, and settled back into his chair, resuming his study as the bus pulled away.

Ten minutes later he knocked on the door of Haddock's office, stepping inside without waiting for a summons. 'Got them,' he announced, 'Montell and Rogozin, together on the bus. I followed them too until they got off. They weren't on board long. They only went to the first stop in fact, Drumbrae, I think it was called.'

'Drumbrae?' the DI repeated. 'Terry Coats' place is five minutes' walk from there. Finally, we've tied them together, Griff and Terry. Marlon, you are a star. Tell me, what was Montell wearing? I'm assuming Rogozin had on the coat he was killed in.'

'A black woollen jacket with a zipper.'

Haddock picked up his phone, found a number and called it. 'Arthur,' he said as it was answered, 'I need your team back into Terry Coats' place. Yes, I know they've been there before, but this time they'll know what they're looking for. We know who was there, we know what they were wearing, we just need to be able to prove it.'

Forty-Four

'This is the strangest investigation I have ever been on, gaffer,' Sauce said, his voice low as he glanced around Bar Italia; no more than half the tables were occupied but he had no wish to be overheard. 'It began with a double murder, but now I find that the victims were perpetrators themselves. It's an inquiry within an inquiry. We're making great progress at one level, but none at all at the other. What am I doing wrong?'

'Nothing,' Bob Skinner replied, as he wiped up the last traces of his lasagne with a piece of garlic bread. 'Are there any questions you haven't asked?'

'Not that I can think of.'

'Is there any part of any crime scene that the SOCOs haven't been over?'

'None that we know of.'

'In your search for the second car in Torphichen Place, have you been over all the available street camera footage?'

'Yes.'

'Have you interviewed all the friends and family members of the victims?'

'All that we can find, yes. Lottie and Cotter traced Terry Coats' mother last Thursday; she couldn't offer anything.

Likewise with his work colleagues; I had a team of DCs interview them. They knew him in the office; the men said he was capable, a couple of the women thought he was old school sexist.'

'What about the story he spun us when we caught him with Aisha? What about the shop he claimed she used to launder the gold coinage?'

'According to her, or so Coats said, the shop was owned by the same company as Wister Air. I've asked the airport's commercial management to give me a list of possibles from among their tenants, but they've still to come back to me.'

'What about the burner SIM card you found at Griff's?'

'One call made to another unregistered UK SIM.'

'Did anything in his papers, on his computer, on any device, give you a clue to who he might have called?'

'Not a scrap.'

'That all being the case, Sauce,' Skinner declared, 'the central part of your investigation can't be faulted. As for all the other stuff, where has it taken you?'

'We know now that Montell and Coats were acting in concert. I had a call from Inspector Ellis in Manchester; she has a taxi-driver witness who's identified Terry as the man who was waiting for Aisha Karman outside the Grange Hotel. She was killed with Griff's gun, which is absolute proof that they're a team.'

'Are you telling me that Coats shot her?'

'That's how it looks, gaffer,' Haddock replied. 'Do you doubt it?'

He shrugged. 'I don't see him as a killer, that's all. Did the taxi-driver witness say there was only one person waiting for her at the hotel?'

'Maybe Griff was in the car.'

'Would she have got in if he had been? I tend to doubt that.' He paused. 'Didn't you tell me she had sex just before she died?'

'Yes, but . . . Well . . . Okay, I get it. The English autopsy report did say that the body showed no signs of a struggle.'

Skinner leaned closer as another diner passed by their table on the way to the toilet. 'Then either I'm wrong, and Coats did have it in him to kill, or he took her to the place where he knew Griff would be waiting.' Unexpectedly, he shuddered and gazed out of the restaurant window, at the pedestrians and the traffic flow.

'What's up, gaffer?' his companion asked.

'I'm thinking about that man, and all the times he was alone with my daughter. It makes my blood run cold, Sauce. It makes me wish he was still alive, so I could kill him myself.' His eyes came back to Haddock. 'You've never had to fire a gun in the line of duty, have you? No, nor have ninety-nine out of a hundred police officers. I have, and even on the basis of a very brief acquaintanceship, that's what makes me confident that Coats didn't shoot the woman. He wasn't capable of it. Mind you,' he added with a twisted grin, 'I'd have said the same about Griff Montell, so don't listen to a bloody word I say.'

He leaned back as the waiter arrived to clear their table. 'Dessert, gentlemen? Or coffee?'

'Double espresso,' Skinner replied. 'Sauce?'

'Cappuccino, thanks.'

'So, what else have you established?'

'We know for sure how Griff got his gold and his gun into the country. His cousin DuPlessis told us he sent it to him on one of his company's cruise liners. He was vague about the dates but Tarvil did some checking and found that two and a half years ago Griff hired a car from Hertz, a big hatchback. When he brought it back two days later, the recorded mileage was consistent with a round trip to Southampton. The date coincided with the docking there of the Oceanic Aladdin, the ship DuPlessis named.'

'Do you know how many coins he collected?'

'Not for sure, no,' Haddock said. 'But apart from that we have established that on his first three years here, each time he went to South Africa to visit his kids, when he came back he disposed of forty Krugerrands to a licensed gold dealer in Glasgow. Do the sums, and that's around a hundred and twenty grand.'

'Yeah,' Skinner chuckled. 'Lucky for some, eh.'

Forty-Five

'Good lunch?' Singh asked.

'Always is in the Bar Italia,' Haddock replied. 'It's become big Bob's local when he's at the *Saltire* office. He was paying, which made it even better.'

'Mmm. My corned beef sandwiches went down really well. I made them myself, too. Washed down by a really nice Cotes du Pepsi. You've just missed your mate from Pretoria. He Zoomed you; I said you'd Zoom him back. Remember the days when you just phoned somebody?'

'Just about. The thing I remember most about them was that it was much easier to lie to someone.'

Haddock returned to his office; although he was still luxuriating in the space, he reflected on the reason he was enjoying it, and told himself that he would give it up in a second to Sammy Pye, if he could be brought back to health. Whether he would cede it so willingly to someone else, that was a different matter.

Settling into his chair, he switched on his computer and sent a Zoom meeting invitation to his South African colleague. Pollock responded within a minute, his face replacing Haddock's own on the screen. The Major seemed to be looking at him wide-eyed. 'What the hell is that building behind you?' he exclaimed. 'Since when did you have fucking Disneyland in Edinburgh?'

'The governors of that place wouldn't appreciate being compared to Mickey Mouse. You called me earlier?'

'Yes, sorry; I forgot the time difference. I have news for you. You were right about Griffin's gun. The one you have was indeed his service weapon on the day of the robbery. The serial number is still on our records, so I guess when we check them all, we'll find one that isn't. Obviously the inventory hasn't been reviewed for twelve years, an omission that we'll correct annually from now on.' He paused. 'In addition to that I have updates for you on both Anatoly Rogozin and Aisha Karman; they'll interest you, I think. How much do you know about Anatoly?'

'More than you might think,' Haddock confessed. 'He had a brother called Dimitri who was co-owner of a football club in Scotland. The other owner was a man named Cameron McCullough. As an aside, that's my partner's name too. She's his granddaughter and she was named after him. The Rogozin brothers have a remarkable distinction given that they were Russians. They were both murdered in Scotland.'

'Wow!' Pollock gasped. 'You have a knack for upstaging me, young man. You're not going to tell me that your wife's grandfather was involved in Dimitri's death, are you?'

He was about to correct the major's use of the word 'wife', but stopped himself; it sounded right. 'No, his killer was arrested fairly quickly. He was a guy with a grievance, no more.'

'What about Anatoly? Did he have a tie-up with him?'

'No. Cameron bought out his brother's share in the club.'

'How did Anatoly take that?' the major asked.

'I don't think he was best pleased, but nothing was made of it.'

'Still, has Mr McCullough been interviewed about the killing? Not by you, obviously.'

'Not by anyone.' Haddock saw his eyebrows rise in the small box in the corner of the screen. 'He disappeared, around the time of Griff's murder, and hasn't been seen since. He and his minder got into a car and drove off into the night.'

'Are you telling me he's a suspect?'

'Not directly. He was miles away when the killings happened.'

'Christ, he couldn't be dead too, could he?'

'In theory, he could,' Sauce admitted, 'but Grandpa McCullough's not your average man. Given his past connection to the Rogozins, sure he needs to be interviewed, but I don't believe he's involved.'

'Or you don't want to believe?' the major suggested.

'Oh no, I could, trust me; but I don't, that's all. Everybody in the game was already dead when he went away, so why would he bother?'

'How's your wife feeling about this?'

'Worried, but she feels the same about me. Cameron might be up to something but I don't believe it has anything to do with this. Now, what about your updates?'

'Yes, those. Anatoly had a place in Cape Town, owned by his airline, another in London, owned by a telecommunications company that he and his brother had part of, and another in Moscow that he inherited from Dimitri. His main South African business was Wister Air, which he bought ten years ago.'

'He bought it?'

'Yes,' the South African confirmed. 'He set up the company in North Cyprus, and used it to buy a small budget airline whose founder was doing okay until he made the mistake of cheating on his wife. Her father was the company's banker, and he didn't take it well. The airline went on the block and Anatoly's company bought it.'

'Not just Anatoly's company,' Haddock pointed out. 'There's another shareholder, an entity called Lente.'

'Mm, I didn't know that, but whoever it is, they're very much a sleeping partner. Anatoly ran Wister Air; Anatoly and nobody else.'

'What about Aisha Karman? What have you got on her?'

'She was Anatoly's girlfriend.'

'She was? But she was screwing Terry Coats whenever she landed in Edinburgh. It was Terry Coats she met on the day she disappeared.'

'Are you shocked?' Pollock chuckled. 'Being cabin crew gives you these opportunities. Not just cabin crew either. My ex-brother-in-law had offices in Durban and Bloemfontein, and a family in each. He still has the offices and the job, but hardly a rand to his name with two sets of kid support to pay. Anyway, the thing about Aisha: we got access to Anatoly's internet and his computer, and we found an email from her to him, sent two weeks ago, saying that she was in Edinburgh, and she needed to see him, urgently. He replied, saying he'd be there. He asked her to book them a suite in the Balmoral Hotel.'

'That would have been fucking clever on her part,' Haddock remarked, 'considering that at that time she was in a fridge in Manchester.'

Forty-Six

'Do you not find the air in Edinburgh too thin for your blood?' Dorward asked.

'Fuck off, Arthur,' Lottie Mann replied cheerfully. 'I'm a regular visitor to the capital city.'

'You don't strike me as the Festival type.'

'I'm not, but I'm a regular prosecution witness in the High Court.' From her position in the doorway she looked around the shambles that had been Terry Coats' living room. 'How are your people getting on here?'

'A hell of a lot better now we know what we're looking for. We're picking up quite a few fibre samples in the sitting room, and even more in the kitchen. The garden dustbin's interesting too. We didn't look at it on our first visit, because I didn't think it was relevant. I wish we had because it's a right bloody mess. Somebody's lit a fire in there.'

'Burning what?'

'I don't know for sure, because a lot of it's melted, but there's been a towel among it. Part of it survived, maybe because it was wet, and it looks like there are blood traces on it.'

'Rogozin's?'

'Lottie, please. Gimme time, okay?'

'Sorry. But at least we know his blood type,' she added, 'so it won't be a problem determining if it is.'

'That's if Sauce is right and he was here.'

'We can't be any more certain than we are. John Cotter went into the chippy round the corner. The guy behind the counter told him that Terry Coats was a regular. Good memory; he remembered that he was in on the evening Rogozin was killed, about five o'clock. He bought a fish supper, a haggis supper, and a single fish. Haggis supper; the Russian's last meal.'

'Single fish?'

'You know how it is, Arthur. There's always too many chips. The fish supper must have been Coats's. He had vinegar on it.'

'But no walnuts?'

The DCI frowned. 'Why the fuck would he have walnuts on a fish supper?'

'Who knows?' he retorted. 'To each her own, but I found a nutcracker on the kitchen table. Not that I really think it was used for cracking walnuts. I'm pretty sure I can see slivers of skin on it. Rogozin's fingers were broken, weren't they?'

'Yes,' Mann confirmed. 'Three of them, on his left hand.'

'Why that one rather than the right?'

'Tell me,' she challenged, patiently. 'The bus footage shows him handing over his ticket, with his right hand. I'm guessing that Montell and Coats wanted it to be usable when they had finished persuading him to do whatever they wanted.'

'For example, sign a document?'

'Arthur, we'll make a detective out of you yet.' She glanced around the room once again. 'When you're done here, we're going to need you to look again at Coats' car. I know the perpetrators are dead, but Rogozin is a murder victim and

Sauce and I need to make a report to the procurator fiscal, for the record. Even if he wasn't killed here, and I'm certain he was, he was dumped from a car. I'm guessing it was that one, but I need to be able to prove it.'

Forty-Seven

Skinner smiled at the camera that he knew was part of the doorbell as he pressed the button. Within, he heard a chain being unfastened, and then a creak as the heavy oak door swung open. 'You want to put a drop of oil on that hinge,' he said. 'I remember saying that last time I was here.'

'Your memory's better than mine, Bob,' Maggie Rose Steele said as she stood aside to admit him. 'I can't recall the last time you were here.' She sounded exhausted and her eyes lacked any sparkle.

'Is the wee one about?' Skinner asked, producing a parcel from a canvas bag. 'I brought her a present.'

'She's napping. She has playgroup until four, and she's usually tired when she gets back. What did you bring her?'

'Lego. Seonaid was getting into that at her age.'

'Lovely,' she said, with a hint of a smile. 'Dolls are out of fashion with Stephanie just now.'

He reached into the bag once again. 'I brought something for you too. They wrapped it in Toppings; I'm not that neat.'

She tore off the paper. 'What's this? *"The Invisible Spirit"* by Kenneth Roy,' she read. 'It's a tome,' she said, weighing it in her hand. 'Just what I need though, something that has nothing to do with the job. Thanks. Come into the kitchen. Intuition must have told me you were coming; I've just made a pot of coffee. Therapeutic,' she explained. 'I'm on medication and it's knocking me out.'

He followed her, taking a seat at a breakfast booth which was set with child's crockery. 'Thomas the Tank Engine gets everywhere,' he chuckled. 'We have something similar.'

'How are your brood?' Steele asked. 'We haven't really talked about personal stuff for ages. Remind me, what's your new one called?'

'Dawn. She'll be the sunset of our breeding programme, I promise. I never thought we'd have another, I admit, but she's a wee beauty, the most like Sarah of any of her three.' He took a sip from his coffee, then a mouthful, albeit with a wry expression. 'That's shit, Maggie.'

She sampled her own, wincing as it reached her taste buds. 'God, you're right. That packet's been in the cupboard for ages. Why did I give it to you, of all people?'

'Because you're on meds; your brain's switched off. Get yourself across the road to Sainsbury's tomorrow and do a decent shop.'

'I'd feel guilty, Bob,' she said. 'I'm on sick leave. It's not right to go out.'

'That's old-school thinking. You're not contagious, you're suffering from stress and depression. You won't cure that by sitting in the house. Get yourself back into the real world. Go shopping, go for walks in Holyrood park, take Stephanie to a matinee at the cinema. You need to get your life back.'

'I don't think I've had a life since Stevie died,' she admitted. 'We weren't together for long, he and I, and before that . . . I really fucked it up with Mario, Bob. You know, I don't think I've ever been a happy person.'

'If that's true, it's time you were.'

'How do I make that happen?' she asked him.

'You go looking for it. Mags, you've never dealt with Stevie's death. It's time you did. First, you need to move house. This place is like a mausoleum. It's dull, it's depressing, it's on a main road and it has hardly any garden. Stephanie needs a change and so do you.'

'I'm done with the job, Bob,' she murmured. 'You know that, don't you?'

'I think I do, and I blame myself.'

'Why, in God's name?'

'For not preparing you better for one thing. For not taking it myself, for another. I went off in the huff because I lost the political argument against unification. If I had taken it, maybe I could have set it up right, and made the fucking thing manageable. But I didn't, it isn't, and it's done this to you, for which, my dear, I am so, so, sorry.'

'What am I going to do, Bob? I'm forty-three, I'm a single mum, and I've been in the police all my adult life.'

'What would you like to do? You'll get early retirement on health grounds, no problem. If you take my advice, you'll finally take the damehood that goes with the job. That on its own will bring you lots of offers, and your CV will bring you even more. You might even find that one of them's from InterMedia.'

'Who'll take over from me? It's a poisoned chalice.'

He winked. 'Do not mistake me for someone who gives a fuck about that. I know who it won't be, but that's all. Before you go, though, there's one thing I would like you to do. The service is in danger of losing another very capable woman, and I don't want that to happen. We both know that last week, when your head was messed up, you made an error of judgement that put someone in an awful position. I want you to reach out to Noele McClair. I want you to visit her and I want you to keep her in the game. Whatever job she wants, give it to her. Don't ask her to step into Griff Montell's shoes at Torphichen Place, otherwise do the best you can. I should have done that for you when Stevie died, I should have taken you right out of the firing line and given you a nice comfy desk to drive, a nine-to-five sinecure that would have given you the opportunity of seeing out your career in a stress-free place.'

She looked at him for what seemed like a long time; her eyes offered a hint of a smile. 'Bob,' she said, when she was ready to reply, 'you wouldn't know a stress-free place suppose you were reincarnated as the Dalai Lama. But I'll find one, and I'll persuade Noele McClair that she's the only person in the service that could fill it. You're right; I do owe her one.'

Forty-Eight

Instinctively, Haddock stood and assumed a stance that approximated to attention, although the man who had stepped into his office was wearing civilian clothes.

'Detective Inspector,' the grey-haired newcomer began, extending a hand, 'or Sauce, as I hear they call you. Good morning, I'm ACC Lowell Payne. The DCC's told you about me, I think. With the chief being off, and him standing in for her, he's made me something akin to his vicar on Earth. I'm not trying to catch you out by turning up unannounced, I promise you. I was going to give you advance warning, but my phone was out of battery, and my car doesn't seem to be recharging it.'

'Welcome, sir,' Sauce replied as they shook. 'Can I see your warrant card, please?'

The assistant chief constable gasped, stared back at him, and then smiled as he drew his identification from within his shirt and displayed it. 'You're taking a chance,' he said. 'Bob Skinner told me you had balls, and that's not a compliment he hands out too often. But you're right, we've never met, so I should have worn uniform.'

'Sorry sir, I was just covering my arse, with you being in

charge of counter-terrorism and everything. Please, have a seat. What do you want to know?'

'Tell me how close you are to an arrest,' Payne responded.

'My team? Nowhere near it, I have to admit. In mitigation, we've cleared up two open investigations in England and in South Africa. We've established that Griffin Montell was responsible for three killings, the first personally and the others possibly acting in concert with former Detective Inspector Terry Coats. We've established that while in the South African Police Service Montell was a principal actor in a massive gold robbery, and that later he smuggled into this country an unknown but significant quantity of Krugerrands and a firearm, the gun that was used in all three homicides.'

'And he was my niece's occasional boyfriend,' the ACC murmured. 'You found that gun in a safe in his flat, I believe. I have been briefed by the DCC, Sauce; I just wanted to hear it from you.'

'We did,' Haddock confirmed, 'and we can prove that it was put back there after the murder of Anatoly Rogozin. We don't know for sure who did that, but we believe it was Coats. Montell was booked on the last shuttle to Heathrow, to catch the Johannesburg flight on the Sunday morning. In theory, that allowed time to meet Rogozin in the afternoon, take him to Coats' place, kill him, dispose of the body, and catch his plane. Tarvil Singh, my DS, has established that it was delayed by half an hour, but he still missed it. Tarvil spoke to a ground-crew employee who remembered him arriving at the gate as the flight was being pushed off the stand. He identified himself as a police officer, but there was nothing she could do.'

'What made him late?'

'Traffic. Apparently there was a pile-up on the city bypass, west-bound, at nine-forty on Saturday evening, just past the Lothianburn junction. Coming from Howgate, where the body was dumped, they'd have joined the by-pass at Straiton and been stuck there with no option but to wait for it to clear, which it did at five past ten. The operator of the drop-off zone at the airport has snooper cameras there to catch punters picking-up, contrary to the by-laws. We're hoping to get some footage of Coats dropping Montell off there. That might, just might, let us track Coats to somewhere near Griff's at the time the gun was dropped off. It's all fucking academic, of course, but it would be good to prove it.'

'Where did Montell go after he missed his flight?' Payne asked.

'This is only a guess, but I reckon that he laid low at Coats' place. He was supposed to be in South Africa, and he needed to appear to be there.'

'That makes sense,' the ACC conceded. 'So, the Rogozin killing. Can we consider that cleared up?'

'It's the fiscal's decision sir, you know that, but that's what my report will say. I've just had the latest feedback from Mr Dorward at Gartcosh. His forensics team can place the victim in Terry Coats' house on the night he was killed, they can prove that he was tortured there and we have his blood on an undamaged section of a towel that they tried to burn in an old steel dustbin. Also, we have fibres from Rogozin's Crombie coat in the boot of Terry Coats' car.'

'What about motive, Sauce? You're telling me the guy was tortured before he was killed. Have you got any idea what that was about?'

'Not much. I do know there was a link between him and Aisha Karman, the Manchester victim, and that her email was used to lure . . .' He grinned. '. . . one of my favourite words that, and I've never got to use it before . . . to lure him to Scotland. Why they wanted him here, that I don't know. However,' he continued, 'it's irrelevant. We can prove who killed him, miles beyond a reasonable doubt. If this was going to a jury, there would be no need to show a motive.'

'It won't go to a jury,' Payne accepted, 'but the Lord Advocate might decide that there needs to be a formal Fatal Accident Inquiry before a sheriff. Indeed I'd be surprised if there isn't, with a police officer involved. Does Rogozin have any family?'

'He has a nephew in Russia, his late brother Dimitri's son and heir, but he's eleven years old: an eleven-year-old who now owns part of an airline, I guess. Yes, the kid has a right to a form of justice for his uncle, and the Russian Embassy will have an interest too. It doesn't worry me though; I'll be happy giving evidence before any kind of a court.'

'But not about the murders of Montell and Coats?'

Haddock shook his head. 'No, sir, not yet, and that's a bugger. We're still in the dark there.'

Forty-Nine

'Is that us finished in Edinburgh?' John Cotter asked his boss. The day was grey, as he gazed out of her office window across open ground, towards the cantilevers of the main stand at Ibrox Stadium.

'Unless we're needed, but it's unlikely. ACC Payne called me half an hour ago. Marlon's staying there as he's in the middle of an internet search, but we're stood down. Worse luck maybe. Did you see what we've had reported from Airdrie by the North Lanarkshire division CID? A man's been found in a builder's merchant's warehouse there, crucified, dead as mutton.'

'Crucified?' Cotter repeated, aghast.

'He was nailed to a wall; hands, arms and ankles. Professor Scott's doing the post-mortem along the road at two and we are invited to attend. Very kind of him.'

The DS pointed to his computer screen. 'Does that mean we're no longer interested in this? I've had a message from Sauce Haddock; he's been told by traffic central control that Vito Tremacoldi's car's been found, in the multi-storey at Glasgow Airport.'

The DCI scratched her chin. 'At the airport? Rich man goes

missing with his minder. It's not exactly a serious crime, is it? It's not even in our area since he disappeared from Perthshire. If it's anyone's it's Sauce's, but,' she paused 'the boy's got enough on his plate, so, I'll tell you what, we'll take a run along there since it's handy, check it out and then head for the Queen Elizabeth Hospital for Graham Scott's autopsy.'

'Unless the victim's risen again by that time?'

'Shut the fuck up, John,' Mann said, but with a grin on her face.

With Cotter at the wheel, they joined the motorway; the traffic was light and no more than five minutes had elapsed when they reached the airport turn-off and saw their destination before them. The DS pushed the communication button at the car park entrance. 'Police,' he said, displaying his identification for the camera.

'You're looking for Level Four,' a disembodied voice advised as the barrier rose.

The access road to the car park was wide but it tested their car's turning circle as they rose from floor to floor. Mann breathed a sigh of relief as they turned off and into a long alley with cars parked tight on either side. 'You wouldn't expect this to be as busy,' Cotter remarked.

'Glasgow's a bigger city than Edinburgh by quite a way,' the DCI reminded him, 'even though the airport's smaller.'

As they turned into the second aisle, they saw two uniformed officers at the far end, standing beside a blue car. Cotter drew up just short of them. 'This is a big bastard,' he said, surveying the Jaguar. 'Do we know when it got here? The number plate should have been photographed on entry.'

'We weren't asked to find that out,' the older of the two constables replied.

'How was it found?' Mann asked her. 'Did the airport alert us?'

'No chance, ma'am. We did it the hard way, just cruising round. It was more by luck than judgement, for they only gave us the number. If we'd been told to look for a big blue Jag it would have made life a hell of a lot easier.'

'I'll feed that back,' the DCI promised. 'Thanks for the ma'am, by the way. I could be a plain DC, for all you know.'

The PC smiled. 'You're kidding. The whole of the Govan police office knows who you are. You're a legend.'

'Less of that,' Mann retorted. 'I'm too young to be a legend.'

'Now we're here, boss,' Cotter said, 'what do we do about it?'

'There's nothing we can do, John.' She peered through the front passenger window. 'It hasn't been reported stolen and we've got no reason to believe it's been involved in a crime. I can't see anything inside that would justify us breaking into it, and unless it's parked here illegitimately, which is bloody near impossible, we've got no grounds for having it towed. McCullough's wife may have her tights in a twist, but it's Tremacoldi's car and there is no Mrs Vito to report him missing.'

'Do you want to ask DI Haddock?'

'No, and I doubt very much that Sauce wants me to ask him either.'

'Sir Robert?'

'He's got no locus, and even if he did, I know what he'd say. Establish the time of arrival with the car park management, and instruct them to advise DI Haddock when the owner turns up to collect it, unless it was pre-booked and they already know when he's due back.' She checked her watch. 'PC . . .'

'Wood, ma'am; Victoria Wood.'

'Right, PC Wood, we've got to be somewhere soon, so I'd like you to do that for me. Find out whether the Jag is pre-booked. If it is, advise acting DCI Haddock of Serious Crimes in Edinburgh. If it isn't, ask the car park operator to do the same, without delay, when the system shows that the car's being collected.'

'Very good, ma'am. What if they don't come back?'

'We'll worry about that in a week . . . or rather, Sauce Haddock and Bob Skinner will.'

Fifty

'It's a terrible line,' the detective constable said. 'Let me call you back mobile to mobile.' He hung up and copied the number displayed on the website of TCOC into his handphone.

'That's much better; I can 'ear you now,' a male voice told him as his call was accepted. He had been expecting a thick accent, Turkish probably, and so the Cockney twang took him by surprise. 'My name's Ronnie Riley. Remind me, please sir, who you are. I didn't quite catch it earlier.'

'DC Marlon Honeyman, attached to Serious Crimes in Edinburgh. I'm involved in a major investigation . . .'

'That's in Scotland, is it?'

'It still was when I got up this morning, yes.'

'So how can I help the Scotch?'

The use of the term made Honeyman's hackles rise, but he forced them back into place. 'I'm trying to find out as much as I can,' he replied calmly, 'about a North Cyprus offshore company called Wister Air. It's the holding company for an airline of that name.'

'Yeah, that's one of ours. We set it up ten years ago for our client Mr Rogozin. A routine run-of-the-mill offshore company, nothing exceptional or dodgy about it. He could have done it anywhere but . . .' He stopped in mid-sentence and began another. 'Why are you asking about it now?'

'Because Mr Rogozin was murdered about a week and a half ago, here in Scotland.'

'Bloody 'ell!'

'We know who did it,' the DC continued, 'that's not in doubt, but we don't know why. My job is to find out as much as I can about him and his business dealings.'

'I'm not sure how much help I can give you,' Riley admitted. 'We help set these companies up, but very often that's the last we see of them. That's how it was with Wister Air.'

'What are the benefits?'

'Of an International Business Company? Massive. An IBC's only subject to one per cent income tax and corporation tax. It's exempt from VAT. The shareholders are exempt from any inheritance or income tax if they sell their shareholding. Even dividends are exempt from tax. Instead of taxes, an IBC only pays a fixed annual licensing fee of five thousand euros directly to the government. Plus, there's no restrictions on them taking money in and out of the country. And confidentiality's guaranteed.'

'I'm sold,' Honeyman chuckled. 'I understand there were two shareholders. Is that right?'

'Yeah, it is. Rogozin Enterprises, and a trust the name of which I can't bloody remember now.'

'Lente.'

'That's it! Spelt wiff a final "e". I remember asking what it meant and Rogozin telling me it means "slowly" in Latin. "Festina Lente", means don't be in a fuckin' rush or something like that. I've no idea where it were based, or even what its legal standing was. They were using a nominee so I didn't care as long as they paid the fee. Rogozin's company was based in Monaco.'

'Yes, I noticed that,' Honeyman said. 'It made me wonder why he bothered to go to Cyprus to set up Wister Air. Now you've explained the advantages, I understand it a hell of a lot better.'

'Sure, there's that, but also the company that Rogozin planned to buy was based there, so it made it easier all round.'

'The airline?'

'That's right. It was a nice little business and probably cheap at the price. The South African guy who ran it, 'is father-in-law sold it out from under him. He was a Russian too, as I remember.'

'Did that sale go through you?'

'No, that sort of transaction,' Riley explained, 'would go through lawyers licensed to practise here in North Cyprus, and would be lodged with the register of companies. I did hear about it though, through a mate of mine who was involved. The purchase price was fifty million euros. Not bad for an airline that was in profit already. But the really odd thing was, it was paid in gold.'

Fifty-One

Looking through the glass wall of what had become Jackie Wright's office, Tarvil Singh saw a smile spread across her normally impassive face as she gazed at her terminal. She looked across at him and started to rise, but he waved her back into her chair and headed for her instead. He stood in the doorway, unwilling to squeeze his bulk into the cramped little room. 'What's making your afternoon?' he asked.

'A result,' she replied, emphatically. 'You know I've been trying to identify which of the airport shops Terry Coats's girlfriend was fencing her Krugerrands through, if we're to believe the story he told Sir Robert.'

'Sure. He said it was owned by the same group who own Wister Air, didn't he?'

'That's right,' the DC agreed, 'and I've spent hours, days, trawling through every outlet at the airport, airside and groundside, trying to find it on that basis, with no success at all. Finally, I gave up on that and looked again, right across the board, with no preconceptions. Look what I found,' she turned her monitor towards him. 'It's a leather-goods shop, airside, showing on the current layout as being tucked in next to Wetherspoons. It's called MK Flight Accessories, an independent business, and the owner is a Mr Morris Karman.'

Her smile infected the DS. 'There's a coincidence,' he chuckled. 'Go on.'

She swung the screen to face her once more. 'Okay, we know that while Aisha was educated in South Africa, she actually had a British passport. Through that I got her place of birth which took me to her birth certificate. She was born in Portsmouth, father's name Steveland Karman, mother Serena Dixon. From there I went to Steveland and found that he has a brother named Morris, who's the same age as the one who shows up in Companies House as the owner of MK Flight Accessories. As well as the Edinburgh shop, the business has airport outlets in Manchester and Newcastle.'

'Crackin' good, Jackie,' Singh boomed. 'Did you find an address for Uncle Morris?'

'Only the one that's listed in Companies House; that needn't be his principal residence, but in this case I think it is. It's in Biggar, in South Lanarkshire, and conveniently in our territory. That means we can invite him to assist us with our enquiries without going through an English force.'

'Yes, we can lift him if we want,' the DS agreed, 'but we're only going on garbled hearsay from a dead man, so we should be gentler than that. Do you know where we can find him? Did you get that far?'

'I called the manager of the Edinburgh shop. She told me he's usually there on a Tuesday, but he called her this morning to say he has a heavy cold and he's having a day at home.'

'Captive audience,' the DS murmured. 'Get your coat, Jackie, I think you've earned a trip out of the office.'

Fifty-Two

'Do you agree with me, Sauce?' Lottie Mann asked. 'Tremacoldi's car should stay where it is?'

'Absolutely. It's there perfectly legally. My partner's step-granny might argue that it's relevant to a missing person investigation, but she'll need to get a lawyer to tell us, and that ain't going to happen. I'll tell her about it, but only as a family courtesy. The car park people are sure it wasn't pre-booked?'

'Yes, and they would know. Do you think that's significant?'

'Not for a minute,' Haddock said. 'Cameron's not the sort of guy who'd book a cheap deal. He'd just roll up and pay.'

'It's at the airport, so the assumption is they've flown somewhere. The ticket was issued at five fifty-eight; so they must have been on one of the first flights.'

'Can you fly out of Glasgow on New Year's Day?'

'Of course,' Mann said. 'Do you think this is the backwoods? There's Amsterdam, for a start. That's a very popular destination with middle-aged men out on the razzle.'

'Maybe so, but I don't see Grandpa slipping off for a few days in the canal-side brothels.'

'When he's got better at home?' she laughed. 'Is that what you're saying? I can tell you from bitter experience, that counts for eff all. Sauce, if you're under personal pressure over this with Cheeky, I can have a couple of guys go over all the passenger manifests from that day.'

'I'm not,' Haddock replied, instantly. 'And even if I was, I wouldn't use police manpower on a personal matter.'

'Bob Skinner would.'

'If I have to, I'll ask him, but I'm not there yet. Changing the subject, how about you? You happy to be home?'

'I was until a couple of hours ago,' the DCI said. 'John and I are just back from a post-mortem. The deceased was found in a warehouse in Airdrie when it opened up yesterday morning. What a mess! He'd been fixed to a wall with a nail gun, had his eyes and his genitals incinerated with a flame-thrower, and left hanging there.'

'Jesus, Mary and Joseph! Who did he upset, I wonder? What was the cause of death after all that?'

'Graham Scott decided that exsanguination was the likeliest, although he also said that it could have been shock. The femoral artery was cut after they had finished with him, so chances are he did bleed out. I only saw photos of the crime scene because I was with you on Monday, but it was a right bloody mess, literally.'

'Rather you than me with that one,' Haddock conceded. 'Have you got a name for him?'

'Walter Thomson, age thirty-seven, mixed race; he had a couple of convictions for violence, but he was suspected of a lot more, cases where the victims were too scared to speak. With the facial damage, he had to be identified by his fingerprints. He was muscle for hire in the East End of Glasgow, where we've never quite stamped out the old protection racket.'

'A gang killing?' Haddock suggested.

'Could be,' Mann agreed, 'but we've got nothing to point us in a specific direction. We don't even have an accurate time of death. A twelve-hour window stretching from about eight on old year's night into Wednesday morning.'

'The same time as Montell and Coats.'

'Possibly, but a completely different methodology. They were executed, this guy was tortured to death.' She sighed. 'Best get on with it, Sauce, I'm told that ACC Payne's coming in to see me tomorrow,'

'Is that right? You're getting more notice than I did. Let me know if there's any news about Tremacoldi's car.'

Fifty-Three

'As far as I know, Detective Sergeant Singh,' Morris Karman said, stiffly, 'what I did was not against the law. My poor niece told me that she was being given gold coins by her lover, Anatoly, the Russian man who owns the airline she worked for. Practically, they were no use to her in that form. She couldn't spend them and she lacked the knowledge to trade them on the gold market. She asked me to help and so I did. I was very fond of Aisha; I'm still in shock about what's happened to her. That's why I'm not at work today; I don't have a cold, as you can see. Tomorrow I'm driving down to Manchester; the police have asked me to identify her body formally. That's not something I'd ever imagine doing. I don't know how I'll handle it, I confess.'

'It won't take long,' the DS told him. 'DC Wright and I, we've both had to help people do that; I'm sure our English colleagues will make it as easy as they can for you.'

'You know who killed her? Have they caught him yet?'

'All I can say is that they're not looking for anyone in connection with Aisha's death. That might sound like police-speak, but it's the literal truth.' He paused as the little man nodded, pursing his lips. 'We need to ask you about the way you helped Aisha dispose of her . . . gifts.'

For the first time, Karman seemed hesitant; he turned his eyes towards the bay window of his sitting room, looking out across ploughed fields. 'I said I didn't believe I was doing anything illegal, Mr Singh. But if you have a different view, maybe I should consult a lawyer before we have this discussion.'

'You don't need to, we assure you. Look, we're Serious Crimes detectives; that means something. If you have sailed close to the wind, it's going to be minor at worst, and not within our remit. We're trying to build up a broad picture of what Aisha was doing and who she was doing it with. We're interested in the circumstances of her death, as part of a broader investigation. Our English colleagues are investigating her murder.'

'In that case, I'll trust you,' he said. 'I agreed to handle the coins for Aisha, but I didn't want to run the risk of being nailed for capital gains tax. To avoid that I came up with a formula that involved her tendering them at one of my shops as payment for an item, any item. A small amount of change would be given for the sake of appearances, then the staff would pass the coin to me. Effectively it became invisible, but legitimately, as a transaction had taken place and it had been accepted as payment. I would trade it in the normal way and give the money to Aisha.'

'Did this happen exclusively in Edinburgh?' Jackie Wright asked. 'Aisha flew into other airports, didn't she?'

'Yes, she did, but it was only done in Edinburgh. I'm there most frequently.'

'How many times was this done? How many coins did you trade for her?'

'Good question.' He frowned, searching his memory. 'Ten or eleven, I think. I can dig out the paperwork if you need it.'

'Not at this stage,' Singh said. 'Mr Karman, did the system stay confidential, or did anybody ever find out about it?'

'Once, it was mentioned to me by someone on the airport staff. I took it up with the shop manager and she investigated. The checkout girl had been talking out of turn. She was fired, but not for that, for helping herself to stock.'

'How close were your niece and the man Anatoly?'

Karman threw him a lazy smile. 'Do you mean was marriage in the offing? Not a chance. Aisha didn't even like the man all that much, but he was the boss, and he was generous with the K-rands.'

'They were a genuine gift? Are you sure about that? She wasn't giving him the money back?'

'That was the very first question I asked her, Sergeant. Was this money-laundering? She promised me that it was not, that they were hers to keep. She told me once that when he was drunk, he called them his *"slegte winste"*; that's Afrikaans for "ill-gotten gains" she explained.' He stopped; as the detectives watched, his face went pale. 'Are you going to tell me that she was stealing the coins from Anatoly and that's why she was killed?'

'No, we're not,' Singh assured him. 'I can't tell you too much, but he didn't know she was dead. We're satisfied that he had no part in it.'

'Are you sure?'

'Certain. Mr Karman, did Aisha ever mention to you a man named Terry Coats?'

'Ah,' he exclaimed, 'the stockbroker. Yes, she talked about him. She and Anatoly weren't . . . how can I put it? . . . exclusive.

I'm not saying she was promiscuous, God bless her, but she had more than one attachment. She met the man Coats by chance in Edinburgh Airport and they had a fling, I suppose you'd say. More often than not when she had a lay-over in Edinburgh, she'd come and stay with me, but when Coats came on the scene, she started to stop in hotels with him.'

'Did she tell him about the coins?' the DS asked.

'Yes, she did. I know this because she told me she had it in mind to ask him to invest her money when she had enough piled up.'

'Was she still seeing him when she died?'

'Yes, I believe so. Not so frequently, for her schedule was changed in the summer, but occasionally she still came through Edinburgh and they would meet up. Why do you ask about Coats? Is he a suspect?'

'You didn't happen to read a newspaper on the second of January, did you?'

'No,' Karman replied. 'The financial markets were closed and that's all I ever look at. Why? What would I have seen?'

'You'd have seen reports of Terry Coats being found shot dead on Wednesday morning, in Edinburgh, together with another man. Coats wasn't a stockbroker, Mr Karman, he was employed by Edinburgh Airport security, and before that he'd been a police officer in the west of Scotland. He was stalking your niece because he thought she was money-laundering.'

'But she wasn't, I tell you!' he exclaimed. 'I promise you, she wasn't . . . or if she was she didn't know it.'

Singh nodded. 'I believe you, Mr Karman,' he said. 'I accept that your niece was an innocent victim in this business; probably the only one. One last thing: the other man found dead with Coats, was named Griffin Montell, a serving police inspector. Did Aisha ever mention him?'

'No, she didn't, of that I'm also certain. I've never heard of him. If he was a police officer, damn it, he should have prevented her being killed!'

Fifty-Four

'There is nothing irregular about Wister Air,' the woman insisted. 'The European media like to portray the Turkish Republic of North Cyprus as a haven for criminals and gangsters, but I can assure you, sir, it is not. To be registered as an offshore company here, very strict conditions must be met. These are observed because the Register of Companies is directly overseen by government. Wister Air complies with the law.'

'That law, Ms Ecevit,' Marlon Honeyman said, 'doesn't seem to object to one of the owners hiding behind nominee directors.'

'If that owner is a registered company. But ultimately the owners of that company must be revealed; if it was set up in the TRNC they would be required to submit good character certificates from the police in their home country.'

'Okay, I get that, but where was Lente registered: the co-owner of Wister Air?'

'In the TRNC, of course,' Ms Ecevit replied. 'And now it is the sole owner of Wister Air.'

'It is?' Honeyman exclaimed. 'When did that come about?'

'On Monday of last week, when we received by email a

273

document transferring the holdings of Rogozin Enterprises to Lente. The document was signed by Anatoly Rogozin, as the law requires, and it was registered that same day. That's how it is now. Lente is now the sole owner of Wister Air.'

'What would the law say if it knew his signature had been obtained by torture?'

'That would need to be proved.'

'The first step to doing that is by finding who owns Lente. Can you tell me that?'

'I don't know,' Ms Ecevit admitted. 'You are a policeman from a foreign jurisdiction. I will need to consult the Ministry.'

'Then please do so. I'll call you back tomorrow.'

Fifty-Five

'You are sure about this, Inspector?' Pollock asked.

'It's what our man was told by someone on the ground,' Haddock said. 'If it's true, what are the chances of anyone else being involved?'

'I was planning to let him go this evening,' the major admitted, 'but if he was involved as you suggest, it moves him into another league. Listen, I know this happened in my jurisdiction, but would you like to take the lead in the interview? He doesn't know you, and he may not even know that you have no legal standing as far as he's concerned.'

The Scot smiled. 'If it helps you get a conviction and close a twelve-year-old case, then it'll be my pleasure.'

'Let's go for it. Constable,' he called to someone off camera, 'go get the man.'

While he waited for the prisoner to be brought to the interview room, Haddock moved around his office, closing the venetian blinds. He had barely resumed his seat when Tom DuPlessis appeared, handcuffed and looking more haggard than ever.

'What the fuck is this?' he protested. 'You guys, you are unbelievable. My lawyer said you can't hold me any longer.

Release me or I'll sue you; I will, I warn you.'

'I've already advised your lawyer that we have a new matter to discuss with you,' Pollock retorted. 'It relates to a murder investigation that my Scottish colleague is leading, and it's him you'll be talking to. Before we begin, I should tell you that extradition arrangements exist between the United Kingdom and South Africa and that, should he make such a request, I will be raising no objections. Be very careful what you say, sir, for if you are less than frank and honest with him, the consequences could be serious. Detective Inspector Haddock, it's all yours.'

'Thanks, Major.' He paused, looking, unsmiling and un-blinking, directly into the pinpoint of the camera, rather than at the face displayed on his screen. He thought of it as his best Bob Skinner stare, holding the pose as he counted silently to ten. 'Mr DuPlessis,' he began, his voice as cold as his eyes, 'a week ago, your cousin Griffin Montell was murdered, here in my city. I knew Griff as a colleague and, I thought, as a friend. We always insist that we treat every homicide victim with the same respect and that we investigate every crime with the same intensity, but the truth is . . . internationally, I'm sure . . . that when the victim's a police officer we pull out stops that sometimes we didn't even know existed. That's how it's been with Griff. Unfortunately, it's led us to discover things about him that we couldn't have suspected in our wildest fantasies, or even our drunkest, us being Scots. Your murdered cousin, my murdered friend, was a killer himself . . . a high-functioning psychopath, in the opinion of an eminent forensic psychologist. Before he ever came to Scotland, he killed a fellow SAPS officer in the course of a bullion robbery twelve years ago, one that's been unsolved until now. You've already admitted to us that you helped him smuggle to the UK both the weapon he used and an unknown number of gold coins, the proceeds of that robbery . . .'

'I told you already,' DuPlessis shouted, 'I didn't know what was in that box.'

'And we told you already, ignorance isn't absolution. The point is you did it, knowing that it was illegal, and you didn't bother to ask. You were right in what you said before; you were going to walk out of there tonight, because Major Pollock will need your testimony in closing the open file on the bullion robbery and in tying Griff to that crime. But what we've discovered since then in the course of our investigations here, puts you right back in the deepest of deep shit. The day after your cousin was murdered, the body of a man named Anatoly Rogozin was found in Scotland. He was an associate of Griff . . . indeed, Griff met him at the airport . . . and he'd been shot with the gun you smuggled into Scotland. So, you see, you're an accessory to murder both here and in your own country.'

'No!' DuPlessis shouted, panicking.

'Let me finish,' Haddock exclaimed. 'I'm not done yet. Rogozin's main business interest in South Africa was an airline called Wister Air. He purchased that ten years ago, through a company that he had established in North Cyprus, with another corporate entity called Lente. We didn't know for sure who owned that until earlier on today, when we discovered that on Monday of last week, the North Cyprus company registrar received a document, signed by Rogozin, transferring his stake in the company to Lente. That signature was obtained by torture. Rogozin must have been a tough guy, Griff had to break three of the fingers on his left hand before he signed.'

'I know nothing of this,' the prisoner screamed. 'You can't tie me to it.'

'Of course I can, if I want to,' Haddock laughed, 'but I still haven't got to the big finish. For that we have to go back ten years, to the day when Rogozin and Lente purchased the airline they rebranded as Wister Air, again in North Cyprus. It's still remembered there, even in that very unusual business environment, because the Russian owner . . . who was, incidentally, found dead himself in a snowdrift in Moscow six years ago . . . agreed to be paid in gold coinage, valued at fifty million euros.' He stopped and drew a deep breath and looked straight into the camera once again. 'So this is where you have a choice, Mr DuPlessis. This is where you can tell Major Pollock and me how that gold got to the port of Famagusta, via Istanbul, as undoubtedly it did, or he can go all the way through the movements of your ex-employer's liners to find out which one of them was there at the time in question. If he has to do that you'll have no deal with him, and you'll find yourself on a flight to Scotland with no prospect of going home inside ten years, minimum. Your choice, but you don't have a lot of time to make it. My partner's booked us seats for *Star Wars* and Major Pollock's due on the first tee for an evening round.'

DuPlessis threw up his cuffed hands. 'Okay, okay, okay! I'll tell you. I met Rogozin, with Griff, ten years ago. Griff introduced him as a friend and he did all the talking, or most of it. He told me that he needed to move a significant cargo to North Cyprus and that Griff had suggested I could help him. He paid me a hundred thousand US dollars, and fifty thousand for my contact on board ship. But again, I didn't ask what I was moving, because I didn't want to fucking know!'

'Well, now you do, buddy,' Major Pollock said, off camera.

'What Mr Haddock said is right. You have five minutes to put your signature on that, in return for which I will treat you as a witness rather than an accused.'

'What about him?' the prisoner asked. 'What about Scotland?'

'Pal,' Haddock sighed, 'you're not worth the air fare.'

'Done,' DuPlessis sighed. 'Where do I sign?'

'I'll get a clerk and we can do that now,' the major replied. 'Hey, Sauce,' he added, 'you know what "Lente" means in Afrikaans?'

Fifty-Six

'**D**etective Constable Honeyman,' Ms Ecevit said, in clipped tones. 'The Minister himself has advised that I may give you the information you seek without any further formality.'

'Pleased to hear it,' the DC replied.

'Yes, the register is public. If you walked in from the street you could inspect it. However,' she continued, 'the Minister did make one stipulation, that I should do so in a video call, so that you may display your credentials as a police officer.'

If it's a public document, what's the point? he thought, but instead, recognising the universal practice of a tail being covered, he turned the WhatsApp call from audio to video. When Ms Ecevit appeared on screen, he was glad that he had. He has been expecting a sharp-nosed middle-aged spinster; instead he saw a high-cheekboned woman, possibly in her late twenties, with almond eyes and full lips, who reminded him of the photos of Sophia Loren that his grandfather had shown him when he was a boy. Obediently, he displayed his warrant card, holding it close enough to the camera for her to read the text, and the name.

'Thank you, Marlon,' she said. He could have sworn that

she fluttered her eyelashes. 'You're not what I was expecting. I thought you Scots all had big beards.'

'Only some of us. You're a surprise to me too.'

'Why?' she smiled. 'Did you think the same of Turkish women?'

'Absolutely not,' he insisted.

'Pinocchio, your nose is growing,' she laughed.

He knew that he had to move matters on, or he might fall in love. 'What's your first name?' he asked.

'Zehra.'

He sighed. 'Well, Zehra, I suppose we'd better get on with it.'

'I suppose,' she agreed, with as little enthusiasm as him. 'Did you use a personal mobile to make this call?'

'Yes,' he said, smiling as he understood the question, 'as a matter of fact I did.'

'In that case, I can tell you that the company known as Lente has two shareholders, both South African and both sharing the same birthday. Mr Griffin Montell, and Ms Spring Montell. I have no record of Mr Montell ever having been on North Cyprus, but ten years ago, when the company Wister Air acquired the airline business, Ms Montell was here. Her signature is on the document, alongside that of Mr Rogozin. I have a cousin who is Dutch,' she added. 'She told me that in Afrikaans, Lente means Spring.'

Fifty-Seven

'You realise this has nothing to do with us, Sauce?' ACC Lowell Payne said. 'Isn't it a waste of your time to be sitting in on this interview?'

'Sorry, sir, I don't think so,' Haddock countered. 'Griff Montell's lying in a drawer in the Cowgate, and I'm tasked with finding out who put him there and why. If there's any possibility that his death is related to something that happened in South Africa twelve years ago, I have a duty to explore it.'

Payne turned towards the man who sat at the far end of the conference table. 'Bob?'

Skinner shrugged. 'Why are you asking me, Lowell? I just called in for a nostalgic coffee in my old office, like Mario said I should do from time to time.'

'Piss off. I know why you're here; he told me. I know Sauce is right. I'd value your thoughts as his mentor, that's all.'

'Then I agree, he should accept Major Pollock's offer to let him sit in on the interview. Jesus, it's the least the guy could do; it's thanks to Sauce and his team that he's able to take the robbery off his open investigations list, so it's only right that he lets him bask in the glory. I want to hang around for it too,' he added, 'although Pollock needn't know I'm here. Mary

Chambers is a good friend as well as a valued colleague. She's gutted by what's happened. She had no more idea about Spring than we had about her brother.'

Haddock stared at him. 'You've spoken to her?'

'Of course, I've fucking spoken to her, Sauce,' Skinner retorted. 'She isn't under arrest and I just . . .'

'. . . wanted to satisfy yourself that she couldn't have known anything about it.'

'Yes, okay,' he conceded. 'And I did. The place they have in Pretoria was bought by Mary out of her retirement lump sum. If Spring had bought it, that might have worried me.'

'Did she splash the cash at all?' Payne asked.

'Let Sauce ask her about that. You ready to go?'

Haddock nodded. 'I've just received the Zoom invite.' He went to his mouse and clicked to join the meeting, as the ACC moved in behind him. A few seconds later, his screen changed, showing Pollock, full face. 'Good morning, Major,' the DI said. 'My Assistant Chief Constable, Mr Payne, is joining us; he's my reporting officer.'

'He's welcome,' the South African said. 'Sauce, Ms Montell and I have had a full and frank discussion, and she accepts that it is in her best interests to admit her role in the robbery, given that we can now link her directly to seven hundred million rand that was paid by her company and that of Mr Anatoly Rogozin, in gold, for the business now known as Wister Air. We believe that to have been most of the proceeds of the robbery in which her brother Griffin participated, and she has confirmed this. Ms Montell has given a statement which she wishes to read after which she will be prepared to answer questions, on the understanding that they will not lead to her extradition to the United Kingdom. Mr Payne, as senior officer present do you agree to that?'

'Provided that she doesn't incriminate herself in any crime in my jurisdiction, yes.'

'I won't,' a female voice called out. 'Let's get on with it.' The camera swung round, and its position was adjusted until she was in mid-screen. The woman was dressed in a yellow jump-suit. Her face was a mask, her expression impassive. It occurred to Skinner, who was watching from the side, well out of the field of view of the camera, that she was in a mixture of shock and denial.

'My name is Spring Montell,' she began. 'My twin brother was Griffin Montell, who was murdered in Scotland last week. Although I have been in a relationship with a woman for some time, I am in fact bisexual. Twelve years ago, I had a relationship with a man named Anatoly Rogozin, a Russian national, whom I met through my cousin Tom DuPlessis. Tom was involved in smuggling narcotics into South Africa for Anatoly.' As she paused, Haddock and Skinner had identical thoughts: *She just threw him right under the bus.*

'Through me,' she continued, 'Anatoly met my brother; Griff knew what he did, but had no interest in chasing drug-dealers, not then. He was a street cop and wide with it. One night, the three of us were together, a little drunk, when Anatoly asked Griff if it was true that he sometimes escorted shipments from the Mint to the gold depository. Griff said yes, and not only that, he was the guy who decided the route that the van would take. But he never knew, he said, whether it was actually carrying coinage; that was how the system worked. Then Anatoly said, "What if I could tell you?" He said he had a contact inside the Mint who knew when the real shipments were going out. Griff said that would be interesting. That was how the robbery was planned, and it was how it was executed. The contact gave Anatoly the word that coins would be carried that day, Griff chose the quietest route and the getaway van was waiting for him. Obviously, Fannie DeWalt had to be a casualty; there was no other way. Anatoly sourced a pistol, identical to Griff's service weapon, and that was swapped at the scene for the gun that killed Fannie. Griff kept the original afterwards. It was the only way he could be certain that no trace of it would ever be found. The crew of the van tried to surrender but they were killed. Once the gold had been offloaded into the other van, Griff was shot, in the upper arm, a flesh wound, and then, very carefully along the side of the head. It was only when the gold reached Anatoly's safe house that they realised how much they had, three times what we expected. It was agreed that they would sit on it until they had worked out how they could dispose of it. They waited for two years; by then the police investigation had cooled, and also the financial crash had made the haul all the more valuable by making gold more of a haven. Then the Wister Air deal became possible. Anatoly's Russian friend, who was as crooked as he was, offered to sell him the business in Northern Cyprus, and he was happy to be paid in gold rather than currency. Griff set up Lente as discreetly as he could, with me as a co-owner, and together with Anatoly we went through with the sale. The rest of the coins were split three ways, and when we agreed that it was safe, with Tom's help, Griff and I moved our shares to Scotland. With him a cop and me living with one, we agreed it could never be safer. What I did not know was that Griff had brought the gun, or that it would be used in two more killings. That's all.'

Haddock reclined in his chair. 'Did you have a continuing relationship with Anatoly Rogozin?' he asked.

'Only through our shared ownership of Wister Air,' Spring replied. 'Physically, that ended immediately after the robbery. For several years after that, I had no personal involvements. I didn't want anybody getting close to me.' She surprised the Scots by smiling. 'Then I met Mary and discovered that I preferred batting for the other team.'

'Did Ms Chambers know anything of this? Ever?'

'Nothing. Ever. I swear.'

'What happened to the Krugerrands you moved two years ago?'

'Most of them are still in my safe deposit box in Edinburgh. Over the last couple of years I laundered some of them through my design business. I invented clients and sent them invoices which they settled. Those were the accounts that Mary saw, but not the tax man, ever.'

'Did you know that your brother was planning to kill Anatoly Rogozin and steal his share in the business?' Payne asked.

She gazed into the camera with a grin of open mockery on her face. 'No, I did not, sir. And if I did, I wouldn't be so fucking stupid that I'd tell you and put myself in handcuffs on the next Wister Air flight to Edinburgh.'

Haddock intervened. 'Did you ever meet Terry Coats, the man who was killed with your brother?'

'I never heard his name until you mentioned it.'

'What about Aisha Karman?'

'Who's she?'

'Miss Montell, she was your employee.'

Fifty-Eight

'Did she take an active part in the robbery?' June Crampsey asked.

'I don't know, but by her own admission she benefited from it,' Bob Skinner replied, 'so she's done. Major Pollock will hold a press conference in Pretoria tomorrow, announcing that the bullion robbery investigation has been closed, twelve years after it began. He'll announce Spring Montell's arrest and hopefully he'll incriminate her brother and Anatoly Rogozin.'

'Why isn't he doing it today? He has her confession.'

'He thinks he knows who the contact in the Mint was. He's arresting her now. Rogozin put himself about with the ladies, it seems.'

'What can we report?'

'I'm giving you a heads-up about Pollock's announcement. Nobody else has that, so you can alert our South African correspondent, and be ready to run the story on our online edition as soon as it's broken. But not before. Understand? Not before.' He read her thoughts in her eyes. 'I know, June, in theory we could run it now, but that would compromise my friends and me. Our rivals might make us the story if we did that; they'd accuse us of having insider information and they'd be bloody right. As it is, you'll be ready as soon as Pollock has finished speaking tomorrow; I'm pretty sure you can watch him on a streamed South African news service. The fact is, if any journalist had followed up Montell's murder and asked the right people the right questions, here and in Pretoria, they'd be where you are now, more or less. If the guy Darke was as good as he thinks he is and didn't spend so much time pissing off senior police officers, he could have got there.'

The *Saltire* editor's expressive eyes narrowed. 'The same thought occurred to me,' she admitted. 'Where can we go with it tomorrow, after the South African's made his statement?'

'You can incriminate Griffin Montell, for starters. You can also tie him to Rogozin's murder by saying that the police aren't looking for anybody else in that context.'

'What about the woman in Manchester?' she asked. 'Can we mention that?'

'That's less straightforward. Pollock won't mention her in his statement because it isn't connected to his investigation. When the story breaks, ACC Payne will be available to comment, either directly or attributably through the press office.'

'Not Sauce?'

'No. Lowell's fronting up. You know the score, he won't be able to tell you anything that hasn't been reported to the Crown Office, but by that time the Rogozin case should have gone there. If he chooses to volunteer that police in England have evidence that links his death to an open homicide, that will open the door.'

'Will he do that?'

Skinner raised his eyebrows. 'That'll be his decision, June. If he asks my advice, I'll say do it, because it'll deflect the media's attention away from the big issue.'

'What's that?'

'The fact that Sauce and his team still don't have a fucking clue who killed Griff and Terry Coats.'

'Then the *Saltire* must ask that question,' she insisted. 'Darke's got to put it to Payne.'

He looked at her. 'You know that I don't like Darke,' he admitted. 'Your choice, but I don't think his tone is right for the *Saltire*. However, he is where he is and you're right, if anybody is going to ask that question it should be him, but . . .'

'You'd like him to work that out for himself?'

'Got it in one.'

'Okay, this is how we'll play it. I'll pull Lennox Webster, Darke's predecessor, back on to the crime team and brief her to do the story around the Pollock press conference. If it is available streamed, she can watch it. Then they can both handle the follow-up with Payne. If he doesn't ask the big question, she will.'

Skinner grinned. 'Sounds like a plan. Can I make another suggestion?'

Crampsey smiled back. 'Make it and I'll tell you.'

'Have Lennox do an in-depth interview with Mary Chambers. Once her relationship with Spring Montell becomes public knowledge, and it will, the red-tops will be after her, big time. This is one time I don't mind using my insider position, not in the slightest. I'll speak to Mary first, then if she's okay with it, put the two of them together. Agree?'

'Very much so. It's even worth a plane fare for Lennox if Ms Chambers chooses to stay in Pretoria. Sir, you're starting to think like a journalist.'

'I always did,' he replied. 'That's why I was usually one step ahead of them when I was in the job.'

He stepped back into his office, checking his watch and thinking of calling Sarah to see whether she was free for lunch. His phone was in his hand when it sounded; he looked at the screen wondering whether she had beaten him to the punch but saw that the caller was not his wife, but his oldest son.

'Dad,' Ignacio said. 'There's a package here for you; it's just been dropped off by a courier. It's marked for your immediate attention. I had to sign for it on a screen, and I saw the sender's name, Deacon and Green. I looked it up; it's a law firm.'

'Yes, I know it. Nacho, are you doing anything just now?'

'Pilar and I are studying, but . . .'

'Aye sure,' he chuckled.

'Seriously!'

'Sure, I'll believe you. Look, get dressed, get in your car, the pair of you, put it in the boot and bring it to me, here, to the *Saltire* office. Don't open it. Get that? Don't. There'll be a couple of pizzas in it for you.'

Fifty-Nine

'Chief!' Noele McClair exclaimed. It had taken a few seconds for recognition to dawn; the woman on her doorstep was wearing jeans and a Barbour jacket, over a thick roll-necked sweater and her red-grey hair was ruffled by the wind. 'Come in, for God's sake. It's blowing a hoolie out there.'

Margaret Steele stepped inside, relieved that she had been welcomed, that the door had not been slammed in her face. 'Thanks, Noele,' she said, softly, as she handed over her jacket and stepped into a warm sitting room. 'I've come to apologise. I put you in a terrible position last week by asking you to come to Torphichen Place. I should never have done it; I wasn't thinking clearly. The deputy chief went bananas when he found out. We had a similar experience the two of us, just as we were getting together. We used to be married,' she explained. 'You probably don't know that. Mario was shot and I was there; I was quietly hysterical. I know you and Terry were at the other end of your relationship, but I should have been much more sensitive.'

'We were beyond the other end,' McClair replied. 'It was completely in the past. Terry had become pathetic; he was a loser, and I never actually wanted to see him again. Now I learn from Sauce that he might actually have been a murderer as

291

well, because he was the last person seen with his bit on the side before she died.' She paused, her hand moving to her lips as if she was making a belated attempt to stop her words. 'God,' she whispered, 'listen to me, calling her that. The poor girl, she didn't deserve that. Why was she killed, do you know? Does anybody?'

'Not for certain, no. But I don't know the detail of the case anymore. I've benched myself, Noele. I'm taking time off for a period of reflection, and re-bonding with my daughter.'

'Much the same as I'm doing with Harry.'

'How's he taking it?'

'Not great. He's struggling to get used to not seeing his dad again. We think kids are durable, but they're not.'

Steele nodded. 'I know. Stephanie came home crying from nursery one day. She'd been asked by a well-meaning helper to tell the other kids what she remembered about Stevie. She remembers nothing, because he died before she was born. All I can do is show her photos, and I don't even have many of them, because we weren't together long.' She paused, looking at the floor for a few seconds before re-engaging. 'I've got a second motive for coming here today. Bob Skinner told me something that's disturbing me.'

'That I'm chucking the job?' McClair ventured.

'Yeah, that. I'm sorry if you feel he broke a confidence, but . . .'

'I don't. At the time I'd have shouted it to the street, if it had been awake.'

'Did you mean it?'

'I don't know. I really don't know,' she admitted.

'Well, while you're deciding . . .' Steele smiled. It occurred to McClair that she had never seen her do so. 'I'm on sick leave; it will probably turn out to be permanent, but I can still do stuff, or tell Mario to do it. I'm going to transfer the station inspector from Haddington into Griff Montell's old job in Torphichen Place, and I would like to move you there, on promotion of course. While you're considering your future, it might help you to do so in less stressful surroundings than CID. It's an office job, and it's just over the hill.'

'Maybe I'm over the hill too.'

'I don't believe that,' she said. 'This experience, and my thoughtlessness, hasn't killed you, so it can only make you stronger. The job and its location, are ideal for a single mother.'

'Can I ask you one thing, chief?' McClair ventured. 'Are you suggesting this to clear your conscience?'

Steele nodded. 'In part, yes; I'll admit there is that, but most of all, it makes eminent sense. You're eligible for promotion, your appraisals are all first class, and you can be spared from CID.'

McClair's face twisted into something that might have been a grin, but then again might have been an expression of anguish. 'In that case, yes, thank you,' she murmured. 'I really thought I was back in the lifeboat with Griff, having been tipped over the side by Terry. Now I'm paddling as hard as I can to stay afloat. You're right, chief. If I have a reason to get up in the morning in addition to my son, it can only do me good, so if you can make that opportunity happen, I'll be very pleased and grateful. Now, my mother left me one of her speciality quiches. It's not great, but would you like a chunk?'

'I'd love it, on condition that you stop calling me "chief". I'm trying to distance myself from that. Call me Margaret; everyone else, apart from my sister, calls me Maggie or Mags, when I really do prefer my name as it was given.'

Sixty

He gazed at the brown envelope that lay on his desk, labelled, as Ignacio had said, 'Sir Robert Skinner. For immediate attention'. It was secured by a metal clasp, and whatever it contained was bulging its sides. He picked it up and shook it, for a second time, then felt it, gently. Laying it back down, he called the young intern from Girona whose services he shared with June Crampsey. 'Can you get me John Deacon, please, Artic? He's a partner in Deacon and Green, the law firm. You might remember, they annoyed me with a vexatious defamation claim last year, just after you joined us.' He replaced the phone and he waited, gazing at the two messengers. 'A mystery,' he murmured. 'I don't like mysteries.'

'I thought that solving mysteries was what you did,' Pilar ventured.

He grinned. 'That doesn't mean to say I have to like them. Some of them turned out to be very messy. I'm glad they're behind me . . . at least I thought they were.'

As he spoke the phone rang. He snatched it up. 'Mr Deacon for you,' Paco announced.

'Thanks.' He waited as the call was connected. 'Mr Deacon, Bob Skinner here. I gather you're the source of a package

294

that was delivered to my home an hour ago.'

'That's correct,' the lawyer confirmed.

'And you can vouch for its contents?'

'I can.'

'It might have been helpful to call me before it was dispatched; that way it would have come to the right place, important if it's as urgent as the label implies. What is it? Who's trying to make a quick buck out of the *Saltire* this time?'

'That has never been the motive of any of my clients, Sir Robert, and certainly not this one.'

'Who is that?' Skinner asked. 'I need to know before I open the package. I don't have a scanner in the office. Why have they sent whatever it is through you anyway?'

'That was my client's choice.'

'What's in the envelope?'

'I don't know. I'm simply obeying my client's instructions.'

'You don't fucking know?' he roared. Facing him, Pilar gasped, alarmed. Ignacio winced. 'You've just told me you could vouch for it!'

'Do I detect a touch of paranoia, Sir Robert?' The solicitor's voice carried more than a hint of a sneer.

'You detect experience, Mr Deacon,' he snarled, 'the effect of a lifetime of dealing with people whose every move had malice aforethought . . . and quite a few of them were lawyers. Listen chum, you'd better pray that there's nothing harmful in this package. If there is, and you had it delivered to my home . . . Do you have the faintest idea of how angry I will be, when I descend on your office?'

'You're not a police officer any longer,' Deacon blustered.

'That won't fucking stop me, although I will have a couple of them with me just to keep you safe. Now, before I decide to bypass you altogether and go straight to the Law Society with a complaint about your irresponsibility, tell me, who is your client?'

'Was, Sir Robert. Who was my client,' the lawyer replied, his attitude adjusted. 'He was Mr Terry Coats. I'm sure the name means something to you. On Monday morning of last week, he called at my office. He was unannounced, but I agreed to see him. He gave me that package and instructed me that in the event of his death, whatever the circumstances, I should have it delivered to you. I would have done it sooner, but my wife and I brought in the New Year in New York. We flew last Monday afternoon and this is my first day back in the office, which is why you haven't received it before now. It was only when I got back to Edinburgh yesterday afternoon and caught up with the newspapers that I found out that he really had died. Look, if you had issues with Mr Coats, I'm sorry.'

'I've had a couple in the past, but they're history. Okay, Mr Deacon, I'm about to open the package. I'm intrigued now; if I need to speak to you again, I'll call you back.' He replaced the telephone in its cradle. 'Kids,' he said, 'just step out into the corridor for a second, just to be safe. I don't really think this is anything nasty. I felt like tearing that bastard a new one, that was all.'

'Dad,' Ignacio exclaimed. 'Are you sure?'

He smiled. 'Yes, I'm sure, on you go. From the feel of it I'm pretty sure I know what it is.'

The pair stepped outside. In spite of his certainty, he ignored the metal clasps that closed the envelope and slit it at the other end. He shook out the contents; two items fell on to the desk. A voice recorder, which he had anticipated, and a key, which he had not. 'Well, well, well,' he murmured. 'Terry Coats speaks from beyond the grave. Okay,' he called out. 'You can come back in now.'

'What do you think will be on it?' Ignacio asked, as he saw the recorder.

'I've no idea,' his father replied, 'but I don't want you two here when I play it.' He took his wallet from his jacket, extracted five twenty-pound notes and handed them across the desk. 'There's a table in the Bar Italia; that'll cover anything you'll fancy. Nacho, no drink, you're driving. Pilar? You barely look old enough, so if you want a glass of anything alcoholic, you'd better have ID. Thanks, both of you.'

She gazed at him. 'Can't we listen to it?' she entreated.

He laughed. 'Rolling those eyes might work on my son . . . it worked with me for his mother, which is why he's here . . . but I'm an old dog now; I know all the tricks. Go on, the pair of you, enjoy your lunch.'

He waited until he heard the sound of the lift doors opening before picking up the recorder. It was a Philips model, low-end with few special features; he guessed that it might have been bought with one purpose in mind. Having used similar models on which the sound quality on replay had not been reliable, he found a cable in a desk drawer and connected the small machine to his computer. He pressed the 'play' button.

'Bob, my instruction to Deacon was to destroy this if I was arrested and charged. If you, or anyone else, is listening to it he's either broken his word or Griff Montell's decided I'm too much of a risk, and I'm dead.'

Terry Coats' voice had a metallic echo, but it was clear and loud, so audible that he turned down the computer volume to avoid it being heard through the wall by Paco.

'My intention was that if I had been arrested I would take

my chances with the court, and give evidence against Griff. He must have worked that out for himself, so this is my confession, made to you, because I know that you'll use it in a way that will protect Harry as far as you can. Just don't let Noele hear it, that's all I ask. She hates me already and she'll use it to poison my son against me.'

Skinner paused the recording and whistled. 'That's a big ask, Terry,' he murmured, as if he was in the room. 'If I have to give this to the police it'll be their call who hears it.' He pushed 'play' once again.

'I'm entrusting this to you because in a way what's happened to me is your fault,' the dead man's voice continued. 'When you and young Haddock caught me with Aisha, and I told you how it had come about, it was you who sent me to talk to Montell. You suggested that it might get me back into the police and that he might be interested in helping me as it would give him a way back into CID. Then, you cunt, you went and shopped me to Noele. You really do owe me one, Skinner. I thought I could talk to you bloke to bloke, but obviously not.'

He paused the recording again. He had told Coats that it had been a police decision to let Coats' wife in on his liaison; she was a serving officer in Serious Crimes and it would have been difficult, if not impossible, to keep the story from her. 'I owe you fuck all, Terry,' he hissed at the ghost in the room. 'If you hadn't been dipping your wick in that woman none of this would have happened, and you might still be living quietly in Fenton Barns.' He was still seething as he restarted the player.

'Things got messy after that for a while. It was a few weeks before I took my story to Griff,' the tinny narrative continued, 'not in his office obviously, but in a quiet corner of Ryrie's

Bar in Haymarket. He heard me out, without saying anything. Finally, he said that he needed to get back to the office,
that he'd think about it and that I should come to his place that
night to talk tactics. I was seeing Aisha that afternoon, so I said
it would have to be the next day, but he said no, to put her off,
to tell her that a meeting had come up. I did that. I put her off
until her next layover, and I went to Griff's. He sat me down,
he gave me a drink and he left the room. When he came back,
he was carrying a metal box. He put it down on the coffee table
and he told me to open it. When I picked it up it was fucking
heavy. That's because it was full of gold coins, fifty of them. He
told me they were Krugerrands, that each one was worth over a
grand. Then, Bob, he switched on the telly, turned up the
sound and produced a fucking pistol from his pocket, and he
told me that I was either going to walk out of there carrying
those coins, or I wasn't going to walk out at all. I caught on
straight away. I said to him, "That robbery you told me about in
South Africa, that was fucking you!" He didn't deny it, he didn't
have to. He was as calm as you like. It was like he'd turned into
Michael fucking Corleone. I said to him, "You realise I could
take these straight to Bob Skinner." He said, calm as you like,
"Then I'd have to kill him too." That's when I knew for sure he
was deadly fucking serious. I took the money, but not before
he told me there were strings attached. He was interested in
Wister Air and the fact that Aisha worked for it. He said she had
made up the story about the money-laundering, and the bit
about the airline owning the shop as well. He told me to find
out the truth. I saw Aisha a couple of times after that, and I
quizzed her gently. Finally, she admitted that she was being
given the coins by another boyfriend, by her boss in fact, the
Russian who owned the airline. I told Griff; he didn't say

anything, or ask me anything about the guy. I know now that was because he knew him already.'

Skinner paused the recording for the third time, considering what he had heard and guessing ahead. He stepped across his office, fixed himself a coffee and then resumed.

'When he had thought about it, Griff said he wanted to meet Aisha. He said there were a couple of things he wanted to ask her. The problem was, she and I were in a sort of a hiatus. Her routes had been changed, and she wasn't flying into Edinburgh for a while. She did tell me, though, that she'd be coming into Liverpool in a week or so, then flying out of Manchester next day, and suggested that we meet up in her hotel when she was there. By that time it was the beginning of November. I drove down there, with Griff, but he said he didn't want to be seen talking to her. He had a look at the map and found a remote spot. He said I should drop him here, pick Aisha up and bring her to him. I did that, but I didn't tell her about him; all I said was I wanted to go for a drive first. She was fine with that. We drove there but when we arrived, there was no sign of Griff. We were on our own, and she was horny, so we had sex. We were barely done when he appeared, opened the rear door and put a bullet in her head, without a word. I screamed, man. I was going to go for him, Bob, I really was, but he put the gun against my head and said if I wanted it to look like a murder suicide that could be arranged. Bob, you have no idea what that man was really like. He even smiled and thanked me for having left my DNA in her. He told me I was tied in for good now and he was right. I hadn't known, but I'd set her up to be killed. I was fucked, man, and I knew it. We left her body there, took her clothes and everything else with us and put them in a bin in a motorway service area south of Carlisle, apart from her airline ID, her passport and her jewellery. Griff gave me another twenty coins after that. Most of the first lot had gone, on the deposit on my house and to pay off bookies. The key I've left you is for my locker at Harcourt Golf Club, in West Lothian. You'll find Aisha's stuff there, with the coins that are left and with a letter for Harry. I want you to keep that for him, until he's old enough to have it. Not that I've finished my story yet. At the beginning . . .'

He paused the recorder as he heard a sound in the corridor. 'Fuck me, Terry,' he whispered, falling silent as his door opened and Alex stepped into the room.

Sixty-One

'He wouldn't let me hear it, Dominic,' she said. 'All he said was that it was Terry Coats' confession, to his involvement with Griff and his complicity in two murders. His complicity,' she repeated. 'I take that to mean that, according to Coats, Griff pulled the trigger on both of them. I'm still struggling to believe it, despite what's emerged since he was killed. He couldn't really have been that evil, could he?'

'He could, Alex,' Jackson replied, 'and he was. I never met the man, but on the basis of what I've been told and read, I see him as a classic case of a predator without a conscience. As I told you, I knew someone like him when I was inside,' he added. 'He made me feel better about myself.'

'How come? What do you mean?'

'He helped me come to terms with what I had done in my youth. Meeting him and talking with him led me to look at myself and confront my own excruciating guilt. I realised that he was irredeemable, but that I wasn't. I wasn't rehabilitated in prison, Alex. I was purged.'

'Can you purge me?' she asked.

'You don't need it.'

'I feel as if I do. I let that man into my life, whenever I

chose. Worse, I let him into me. I indulged myself with him, I used him as it suited me . . .'

'Just as he did with you,' Jackson pointed out.

'That makes us both the same,' she countered.

'No, it doesn't, not in any way.'

'It does in my eyes,' she insisted. 'I suppose I suspected there was something different about Griff, but it suited me not to explore it, to leave it under the surface. It suited me because I am a spoiled, self-indulgent cow. I always have been. When Andy Martin and I got together the first time, he was my dad's right-hand man . . . and he was ten years older than me. In most walks of life, fucking the boss's daughter can be seriously damaging to your career prospects, but I didn't care about that. I wanted him and I took him. When he and I were engaged, I saw someone else and I had a piece of him too, only he got caught up in one of my dad's investigations and I got found out. Then I got pregnant by Andy and I had a termination without ever telling him.' She paused, her eyes glistening, then carried on, the words tumbling out. 'I'll never have a child, Dominic, I can sense that now, and I don't deserve to. That split us up, Andy and me, but at the first opportunity I took him back. I took him away from his wife and two kids. He couldn't stand the guilt in the end, but you know what? It never bothered me, at least it hasn't until right now, because I have never really cared about anyone or anything other than myself. Tell me I'm wrong,' she challenged him.

'No,' he said, quietly. 'I won't, because you make a very good case against yourself, and someone who's more objective than I am might well agree with you. But as I said earlier, you don't need me to purge you, because you're in the process of doing that right now. The time you've spent with me has been all about that. You came here because you were lost and bewildered but you didn't know why. I did; I could see that you were filled with self-loathing, but I couldn't help. You had to work it out for yourself, like I did in prison.'

'Is there any of it left in you?'

'No,' he replied. 'Not anymore. I still hate what I was, but to tell you the truth, I quite like what I've become.'

'And I need to start to earn my own respect,' she murmured, 'which is why, I think, it's time for me to go back to my own place. I've got one more confession, Dominic. There was one night, one sleepless night, when I stood naked on the other side of your bedroom door, ready to open it and step through. But, thank Christ, I realised that if I did I'd be betraying your trust and my dad's, and I'd be destroying my self-respect for ever.'

He smiled. 'Yes, thank Christ you did, for I might have closed the door behind you. Do you think I'm perfect?'

Sixty-Two

'At the beginning of last week, last Tuesday, Griff told me to meet him at his place, at lunchtime. While I was there, he used his laptop to access police missing-persons reports in the Manchester area. He found a photograph of Aisha, dead, and a "Do you know this woman?" post. He'd already accessed her email account on her phone . . . it had her date of birth as her password. How stupid was that? . . . and used it to send Anatoly Rogozin a message saying that she needed to see him in Scotland, urgently, because she believed that he had been compromised, over certain events twelve years ago. Those were the words he used. Rogozin replied right away, almost instantly. He said he would be on the Wister Air flight on Saturday afternoon, and that she should meet him. Then Griff booked himself a flight to South Africa, British Airways. I asked him why; all he said was that he owed his sister a visit, and his kids. On the Saturday, he told me to be at my place in the afternoon. He didn't tell me why, just to be there. I was watching the racing on Sky, and watching myself lose on the second leg of a four-horse accumulator, when he arrived with a bloke in a Crombie overcoat. It was Rogozin. The guy looked slightly bewildered. Griff introduced me and said I was the cousin of

Aisha who'd sent him, Griff, to pick him, Anatoly, up, and that she'd be there any minute. I went along with it; I even went to the chippy for three suppers when he told me to. When I got back, everything was still kosher. We ate the suppers in the kitchen. Rogozin liked his haggis, and he even had some Irn Bru, after Griff made a joke of it. Then in an instant, it all changed. Griff said, "Anatoly, bad news. Aisha's not coming. She's dead. Dead because you compromised us, yourself, everything, by handing out K-rands like chocolate money when you were pissed. Your *slegte winste*, for fuck's sake! She could have been a SAPS undercover officer for all you knew! So here's what's going to happen," he said, and he produced a piece of paper. "You're going to sign over your share of the airline to Spring and me, right here, right now. Do it and you might just catch your flight home." Rogozin tried to stand up but Griff knocked him back down. Then he turned on the radio loud, picked up a nutcracker, grabbed the guy's left hand and broke his middle finger. Rogozin screamed like a bastard, but he wouldn't sign, so Griff broke another finger. I wanted to stop him, but I knew he wouldn't just be breaking my fingers, so I just stood and watched. He signed after the third one, on the dotted fucking line. I thought, okay, that it was over and we could all have a drink, that's how panicky I was. But no, while Rogozin was nursing his hand, Griff picked up a cushion, pulled his gun from the back of his belt and shot him in the fucking head, twice. Poor bastard barely knew what hit him. Maybe that was as well. Rogozin had crapped himself while his fingers were being broken, and I nearly did too, because I thought it was me next, but he just said, "Sorry about that, Terry, but it had to be done. We need to get him out of here, then you need to take me to the airport. I've got a plane to catch." There was a wee bit of blood. He mopped that up with a kitchen towel. He gave it to me and told me to burn it and the cushion in the dustbin later on, then we carried the body into the garage and put it in the boot of my car. I drove us out of the city, south past Straiton and Ikea, and through Auchendinny. It was quiet out there; no cars about. We were just short of a village when he told me to take a left turn and stop there a couple of hundred yards along. We waited for a minute just to be sure, and then we got Rogozin out and hid his body in a field behind a stand of trees. We'd removed anything we thought might identify him before we left the house. When we were back in the car I just drove straight on, but he told me to turn right around and head for the fucking airport, pronto. It had taken us longer than he'd thought. Then his grand plan really went tits up. We went back on to the by-pass at Straiton, right into a fucking tail-back from an accident. We could see blue light in the distance and we knew we were going nowhere until it was clear. I reckoned then that he'd blown his flight, but he stayed calm and eventually we got through. While we waited, he told me I had to put the gun back in his safe. He wrote down the combination, gave me his keys and said he could switch off the security from his phone. We got to the airport, into the drop-off, he gave me the gun, and he jumped out. I could have shot him then, and taken my chances, but I was too fucking scared to think straight. He missed the flight, of course. He turned up at my place back of midnight. I was drunk by then. He said he couldn't be seen at home, so he'd have to stay there for all the time he was supposed to be in South Africa. On the Monday, he said he needed to use my computer to send the document Rogozin had signed to Cyprus. I said okay, and I persuaded him that I needed to do a food shop. While I was out, I bought this recorder. I used it to make this statement. I'm about to put it in the package that you'll have received by now, Bob, and give it to John Deacon, my lawyer. I'm quite convinced that Griff will kill me, sooner or later, or that at least he'll try. There's always the possibility that the police will actually do their job and trace Rogozin's murder to us, but I doubt that. We're both pros and we haven't made any mistakes.' The voice stopped, as if the confession was over, until there was a long sigh, and Coats resumed.

'So, Bob, that's the story, and since you've heard it, I'm dead. I'm handing it all to you because I can't think of anyone who's better equipped to ensure that psycho Montell gets what's coming to him, preferably heavy calibre in the back of the head. When you get a chance, tell Harry his dad will always love him,' Terry Coats' voice faltered; he had been on the verge of tears, 'but that he should always look up to his mum,' he continued, 'and do what she says.'

Skinner switched off the recorder and laid it on Haddock's desk, beside Aisha Karman's possessions and a sealed envelope with 'Harry' scrawled across it in a shaky ballpoint script. 'It's all yours,' he said, 'apart from this.' He picked up Coats' letter to his son and put it in his pocket.

'I should really look at that,' the DI said.

'Maybe, but you're not going to. It's going into my safe for the next ten years, or until I decide that the boy's ready for it.'

Sixty-Three

'What will Sauce do with the recording?' Sarah asked. Bob's call had taken her by surprise; his excitement was obvious, but normally he would have contained it until they were both at home. She had listened, silently, as he had told her about the package that Terry Coats had sent him from the dark vale of death.

'If he takes my advice,' her husband said, 'he'll give it to Lowell Payne and let him deal with it. Obviously, a report on the death of Anatoly Rogozin will have to go to the Crown Office. In common parlance there is a thing known as the buck, and my guess is that the fiscal will pass it as fast as he can to his boss, the Crown Agent, and so on, until it winds up on the desk of our new Lord Advocate. On the face of it, there are two options. Will she hold the simple line that nobody else is being sought in connection with the death and close the case with no further action? That will lead the media to assume that it was a suicide; most of them won't even report it, or they'll give it page five treatment at best. Alternatively, will she order a full-scale Fatal Accident Inquiry with evidence led in public before a jury?'

'Which do you think she'll choose?'

'I could argue that she doesn't have a choice. The statute says that she has the discretion not to hold an FAI when, if I remember the wording right, the circumstances have been adequately established in criminal proceedings: repeat, proceedings, not just by an investigation. Obviously, she isn't going to fancy a public hearing that reveals that the police service had within its ranks a ruthless, cold-blooded killer. She won't want it, the Justice Secretary won't want it and the First Minister sure as hell won't want it with an election coming up in a year's time. The shit will spray over everybody, me included, because I was the guy who recruited him, and advanced him within the service. I was taken in as completely as everyone else. If you can see yellowy stuff on my face, it's egg.'

'You can prevent that, can't you?' she said. 'You're on good terms with the First Minister.'

Bob grinned. 'Yes,' he conceded, 'I could, but I'm not going to. The *Saltire* will run a piece tomorrow demanding that an FAI into Rogozin's death takes place. We'll run the piece and then we'll report on the South African Pollock's press briefing where he's expected to out the Montells and Rogozin as the people behind the unsolved bullion heist. After that, the Lord Advocate will announce a formal inquiry before the Sheriff, of that I'm certain.'

'What makes you that sure?'

'She'll do it because I'll tell her that if she tries to hush it up, the paper will publish the text of Terry Coats' confession in full and embarrass her right out of her brand-new office.'

Sarah frowned. 'But you said you gave the recording to Sauce.'

He nodded. 'And so I did, but I made a copy. It was addressed to me, not the police, and it isn't *sub judice* since there won't be a prosecution, the principals all being dead. I'll be a witness to the authenticity of the tape and after the hearing, we will indeed publish it, both in text and audio form online.'

'What will Mario say?'

'He's already said it, a resounding "Go for it". He'll say the same to the Lord Advocate.'

'So, case closed?'

'Hell, no,' he laughed. 'The purpose of Sauce's investigation is to solve the murders of Griff Montell and Terry Coats. In that respect he hasn't taken a single step forward. This whole business has been a diversion.'

'What does he do now?' she asked. 'Bob, the poor lad's been hung out there to dry.'

'Not exactly. The question hasn't changed that much. Apart from each of them having a vested interest in killing the other one, who else wanted them dead?'

'Do you have any ideas?'

'One,' he admitted, 'but for now I'm keeping it to myself. I'm sure Sauce will get there without my help.'

Sixty-Four

'Sauce,' Arthur Dorward sighed. 'My team's been there twice already. We've gone over the house centimetre by centimetre; we've found everything there is to find. What's changed that you want me to do it all again?'

'What's different is,' Haddock replied, 'I know now that Griff Montell was effectively hiding out there after missing his flight to South Africa. He couldn't take the chance of being seen in Edinburgh, and he certainly could not take the chance of hiding out in his own place, in a block of flats in the middle of Stockbridge. I don't think he'd have gone out; in fact, I'm sure he wouldn't. That tells me that he was probably killed there, and if not, abducted from there. But it wasn't his home; it was Terry Coats' place, and no bugger knew he was there. So, whoever killed them both went there looking for Terry.'

'How would they know where Terry lived?' Dorward asked.

'Research document number one, Arthur. He had a landline phone, and he wasn't ex-directory. The internet tells you all the T. Coats entries in Edinburgh and they can be cross-checked against the electoral register and the valuation roll. I've just done the first part myself. I need you to go back in now, and

312

look for identifiable traces of anyone who shouldn't have been there.'

'The house had previous owners, Sauce. He hadn't lived there very long.'

'In that case, we'll eliminate them.'

Dorward sighed again. 'Okay, I'll do it; first thing tomorrow the team'll go back in there. While we're at that, what will you be doing, Clouseau?'

'I'll be talking to Noele,' he replied. 'I should have given her a call before now.'

Sixty-Five

Skinner was halfway up the Aberlady straight, behind the winking light of a lone cyclist, when his phone sounded and his screen told him that Lottie Mann was calling. He considered rejecting her call; unusually he found that he was tired of business that should no longer have been his, but he knew that the DCI was self-reliant and would not be calling on a whim.

'What can I do for you?' he asked, trying to keep the tiredness from his voice.

'Nothing,' she replied cheerily. 'I thought I should let you know that Cameron McCullough is back. Tremacoldi's car checked out of the Glasgow Airport car park two hours ago, but the buggers only just got round to telling us.'

'How many passengers?'

'I don't know. I suppose I could access video if it was necessary, but the ticket was paid with Cameron's credit card so at least we can assume he was in it.'

'Thanks for letting me know. Two hours, you said?'

'Yes.'

'In that case he should be home by now, and Mia will be attaching electrodes to his nuts.'

'Unless she knew where he was all along and the whole thing was just a charade.'

'Why would they do that, Lottie?' Skinner asked.

'Maybe he was up to something they both wanted to keep from the rest of the family,' she suggested. 'Especially Sauce's partner, given her connection to him.'

'No,' he said. 'I don't see that. If it was a charade, Mia would have called the police and made a noise. But she didn't, she called Ignacio asking if he'd heard from him. She's cunning and devious, but not that much. He'll have a story, Lottie, and I'm sure I'll hear it soon enough, but right now, I don't give one.'

'I could find out what flight they were on.'

'So could I with one phone call to my friends in Thames House, but I really can't be arsed. Let it lie. Thanks again.'

He ended the call, overtook the cyclist, and drove carefully through Aberlady's overcrowded main street. He had reached the nature reserve car park when curiosity crept up on him. 'Call Cameron McCullough mobile,' he commanded. He was unsure if the call would be connected, but after half a minute it was.

'Where the fuck have you been, and do you need paramedics?' he asked.

'We were at Big Bozo's stag, in the Ice Hotel, in Norway, up near the Russian border,' McCullough replied. 'We took a private jet out of Glasgow with a couple of other guys. It was the easiest way of getting there. I didn't tell Mia I was going. I couldn't have or she'd have wanted to come. The Ice Hotel's on her bucket list.' His voice was a hoarse whisper. 'I'll need to take her now for sure, and I'll hate every fucking minute of it. It's fucking freezing up there.'

Skinner laughed, out of sheer surprise. 'It would be, you stupid . . . That's why they call it the Ice Hotel. I like Stacey Kent and I like the song, but it's never made me want to go there. Who the fuck is Big Bozo anyway?'

'A footballer Merrytown sold to Everton just after I joined the board. He retired at the end of last season, and now he works for us part-time, as a scout. It was quite a turn-out, I'll tell you.'

'And quite a fucking alibi too,' Skinner chuckled.

'What do you mean? Why would I need an alibi, man?'

'You haven't spoken to Mia yet?'

'No, we're only just back at the Lodge. We had trouble getting through Glasgow. The Kingston Bridge was choc-a-bloc.'

'Then I'll leave it to her to explain, once she's cleaned up the blood. Good luck with that one, Cameron.'

He was still grinning when he stepped indoors.

Sixty-Six

'Sauce,' Noele McClair declared, 'the fact that Terry died with me hating him isn't relevant. It doesn't affect my thinking in any way. I'm a serving police officer and it's my job to assist you in every way I can. You're asking me to name people who might have wanted to see him dead, but I can't. Bob Skinner phoned me last night and told me what's going to be in the press over the next few days and weeks, but even knowing that I can't help you. I wish I could, because I'd like to put in a plea in mitigation for the guy that shot them. No,' she said, correcting herself quickly, 'I shouldn't say that. I never wanted to see Terry dead. I said I hated him, but to be honest I didn't really. I was angry with him, and I'd never have taken him back, but really he was a victim of his own weaknesses, for slow horses and fast women. He was a walking cliché. You know, he was best man at another cop's wedding, before we were together, when he was a plod, and he felt it his duty to shag the bridesmaid. So he did. I heard the story from the bridegroom, not him. She was the bride's sister, their father was a superintendent in East Kilbride, where both lads worked, and he caught them at it, round the back of the Stuart Hotel, trousers round ankles, dress up round waist.' In spite of herself, Noele smiled, glancing away from her phone's camera. 'The man didn't know what to do. If he'd filled in a PC at his own daughter's wedding the story would have come out. In the end, he turned and walked away, then made sure that he and Terry never worked within miles of each other again.' She laughed, sadly. 'That was the thing about him; he got away with all sorts of stuff because he had this natural charm about him, with other people. Not at home, though. There he was the opposite, depressed and depressing. Griff, on the other hand, he was completely different. Reserved around others, outgoing and sharing with me.' In an instant her humour vanished. 'Do you know what I'm wondering now, Sauce? Can you guess?'

'I think so,' Haddock replied. 'You're wondering whether he came on to you because you were Terry's ex, to increase his hold over him.'

'Exactly. Silly me, he had me believing I was a desirable woman, while he saw a sad sex-starved single mum with stretch marks and saggy tits.' Haddock shuffled in his chair. 'Sorry,' she said, 'I'm embarrassing you.' She grinned again, briefly. 'Actually, they're not bad . . . and I put cream on the stretch marks. I will survive, Sauce,' she promised. 'I'm still standing, and I have a future. Those two are history, and I'm over them.'

Sixty-Seven

'He said less than I'd expected,' June Crampsey complained, as the streamed press briefing ended, six thousand miles away from Edinburgh. 'He didn't name Griff or Rogozin as participants in the robbery. Without that statement, I'm stuck with a story that says, "Edinburgh woman charged with gold robbery". I want more than that. Fuck it, Bob, we're in the exclusives business here.'

'I guess,' Skinner said, 'that whatever the South African equivalent of the Crown Office is has told him not to say anything that could be prejudicial to a trial. Spring might have confessed yesterday, but this morning she'll have every sharp defence brief in the country offering his services. We have our story, June, regardless of what Pollock did or didn't say. Nobody is going to sue us if we run it, because it's undeniably true. The only question is whether we could find ourselves in contempt of a South African court by using the story on our internet edition. We should take legal advice on that, but while we're doing it, Lennox Webster can be writing her story, based on what Pollock said and what I've told her, identifying me only as a source outside the police service.'

'What about ACC Payne?' Crampsey asked. 'What will he do in the light of the briefing?'

'Nothing yet. There's nothing for him to react to because neither Griff nor Rogozin were named. But as soon as Lennox's story runs there will be. Our piece this morning calling for the FAI into Rogozin's murder hasn't attracted much attention, but with the story it becomes relevant. While she's at work, tell Jack Darke to call Jane Balfour in the police's Edinburgh press office and put two questions, one about progress in the Coats-Montell investigation, the other asking for a reaction to the *Saltire*'s call for an FAI into Rogozin. That'll go to Lowell; let's see what he volunteers.'

'Which will be what you've told him to volunteer, let's hope.'

'I haven't told him anything, June. I can't be seen as his puppet-master, especially not because we have a family connection through Alex's mother. I don't even know if Sauce has let him hear the Coats' tape yet.'

'What if he stonewalls it?' she countered. 'Gives Jack a po-faced "no comment" on the FAI question and "no progress" on the Torphichen Place investigation?'

'You tell me,' Skinner said. 'You're the editor.'

'We run the story anyway,' she declared, 'incriminating Montell in the murder of Rogozin and describing it as a quarrel among thieves, and tying them both to South Africa, and we say that they're both suspects in the Aisha Karman murder. Then we say that police refused to back the FAI call.'

'No,' he replied firmly. 'That pretty much nails me down as the source. Our rivals would go to town on that and Sauce would be caught up in it. We have to rely on Lowell, and be prepared for him to issue a general press statement if he does decide to give Darke a full and frank answer.'

'Do you think he would do that?'

'I think he will do that, because if I was Mario McGuire, it's what I would tell him to do.'

'Speaking of Mario McGuire,' Crampsey said, holding up a printout. 'What do you think of this? It's a release from the police communications department saying that Chief Constable Steele is taking an extended leave of absence on health grounds. All media enquiries to Peregrine Allsop, Director of Communications.'

'I think it's a good time to be slipping out a three-day-old story. Allsop's got something right, for once.'

'You knew?'

'Of course, I bloody knew! I chose not to tell you, that's all.'

'Will she be back?'

'No comment.'

Sixty-Eight

'What did you tell him, sir?' Haddock asked.

'I gave him the story his editor was hoping for,' ACC Lowell Payne replied. 'I told him that diligent enquiries by our officers had uncovered evidence linking Griff Montell and Anatoly Rogozin to a twelve-year-old multi-million-pound robbery in South Africa, and also evidence incriminating Montell and Terry Coats in the murder of Rogozin and in another crime under investigation in Manchester. Of course, he asked me what that evidence was, but I said that he'd have to wait for that until the FAI takes place into Rogozin's death. The Crown Office will announce that this afternoon. That last thing I said was that he had an hour to get the story out on the internet before Jane Balfour issues a general press release. Against that background, he's not going to give a bugger that there's been no progress in discovering who killed Montell and Coats themselves.'

'That's not quite true, sir,' the DI corrected him, with a smile that was a mix of smugness and relief. 'Just before you got here, I had a briefing from Arthur Dorward by video link from Gartcosh.'

'Was he as pleased with himself as you seem to be?' Payne asked.

'For now, although he did tell me that if I send him back to Terry Coats' flea-pit one more time, I'll be a victim myself.'

'I'll defend you from him the best I can,' the ACC promised. 'Run me through each search and the circumstances.'

'Yes sir, they were like this. The first search was focused on Coats himself and his activities in the house. Through that we established that Montell had been there, but nothing more than that. On the second visit we knew that Montell had taken Rogozin there from the airport, so we looked for evidence of his presence there and of his murder. We got results on both counts, and they closed that part of the investigation. It was only then that Sir Robert received the recording from Coats that told us Montell had been hiding out there after he missed his flight to Johannesburg. That's why I asked Arthur to take his people in there for a third time.'

'So,' Payne said. 'What did he find that's made you both so happy?

'With the brief they had the third time,' the DI explained, 'they went further and looked in the garage. They hadn't gone in there before, and that's where they scored. It was roomy: there was plenty of space for Coats' estate car and more. In there they found traces of blood, from two men. In addition, they recovered brain tissue, and a bullet embedded in the wall with part of an eyeball. That's where Montell and Coats were killed, sir, no question about it. I've got officers out there now, doing door-to-door interviews with the neighbours, to see if anyone saw or heard anything around midnight.'

'Heard anything above the sound of fireworks and Jools Holland's bloody *Hootenanny*?' the ACC chuckled. 'Good luck with that one. But well done the pair of you, we really needed progress.'

Haddock's grin widened. 'And there's more,' he declared. 'In the garage they recovered a single fingerprint that didn't belong to either of the victims, or to Rogozin either. They ran a check, and it's been identified as belonging to a man named Raymond Bright. We might actually have a suspect. All we need to do now is find him.'

Sixty-Nine

The owner of the crime scene was less than pleased. 'When are you lot going to take your tape away and let me use my premises again?' he asked. 'You're costing me money.'

'If your warehouse had been a bit more secure, Mr Jessop,' Mann shot back, 'maybe none of it would have been necessary. My crime-scene investigators are still laughing at how easy it must have been to pick the padlock you had on it. One of them said that it would have held up a first-year student at burglary school for about a minute and a half.'

'We sell those things,' William Jessop protested. 'They're perfectly adequate.'

'Do you sell long-shafted screwdrivers too?' John Cotter asked. 'That's all it would take to get past it.'

'Okay,' the merchant grumbled. '*Mea culpa*. I'll know better next time.'

'Once DS Cotter and I have had a look at the scene,' the DCI told him, 'we can lift the restriction, and you can get a specialist cleaner in here. *Festina lente*,' she added.

'Who? I've never heard of them. I'll look for them in Yellow Pages.'

'Clearly not a fluent Latin speaker,' she chuckled as the proprietor walked away.

'Why? Did you just tell him to fuck off, boss?'

'Yes, but not to be in a rush about it. So, what are we looking at here, John?' she continued, as they walked towards the wall where the victim had died. The smooth white paint was disfigured by several holes where he had been nailed up, and by lines of dried blood leading down to a great dark red circle on the floor. 'A messy death, that's for sure. More than that; there was real feeling behind it, a punishment killing if ever I've seen one. What do we know?' she asked aloud. 'Forensically, it's a fucking nightmare. From a fingerprint viewpoint it looks as if the whole of Monklands has been through here, none of them with gloves on.' She consulted her omnipresent notebook. 'The victim's name was Walter Thomson, aged thirty-seven, known to the police. Several convictions and three spells inside, the last being two years in the Bar-L, out of a four-year sentence for a ram-raid in a jewellers in Paisley. Released on parole three years ago, three arrests since then but no convictions, no charges, even. Time of death, early on the morning of January the first, cause of death, probably exsanguination, according to Graham Scott.'

'When did the warehouse close for the holidays, boss?'

'The Friday before Christmas,' Mann replied. 'Twelve days before he was killed. Ligature marks on his wrists and ankles, plus the fact that he was severely dehydrated and Graham reckoned that he hadn't eaten for at least seventy-two hours before he died, indicates that he was left here for a while before his captors decided to deal with him.'

'Whatever their issue with him was,' Cotter observed, 'it must have been serious. I'm glad we weren't on the scene before he was removed. Seeing the photos and being at the autopsy was bad enough. Was he reported missing, did the local CID say?'

'No, because he wasn't missed. He lived with a twenty-two-year-old prostitute, Trudy George; he left her with enough of her earnings to buy drugs but no more, so she wasn't going to be making any nine-nine-nine calls. I need you to check her background, though. If she has any male relatives who decided that enough was enough, we need to be looking for them. You get on with that, and we'll let Mr Jessop get back to business. When you tell him, find out the make of that padlock. I want to be bloody sure that I never buy one.' She paused, smiling. 'It's nice to be back on the uncivilised side of Scotland, isn't it, John? Edinburgh's far too genteel for me.'

Seventy

'Raymond Bright?' Skinner repeated, gazing at the face on his computer screen. 'It means nothing to me, Sauce, and if he was an Edinburgh criminal it probably would.' Outside, the rain was turning to sleet, and he found himself looking forward to the following week's InterMedia board meeting in Girona with even more enthusiasm than usual. He had persuaded Sarah to come with him, the clincher being the use of the company's new Gulfstream jet.

'No, gaffer,' Haddock said. 'He's Glasgow. He's fifty-one years old; he has two convictions in his teens for assault, then did five years in his early twenties for an attempted murder in Easterhouse, a few years after the ice cream wars. There are no convictions on his record after that until thirteen years ago when he was sentenced to eighteen years for drug offences, again in the East End of Glasgow. He had several failed applications for parole, until he was finally released four months ago.'

'How does he relate to Terry Coats?'

'That's the thing. He doesn't; not that I can see. All of Bright's convictions were for offences in the same area. He was known to be active in the drugs trade, not at the top of the tree

328

but quite high up, again always in the East End. When he was active Terry Coats was stationed in Ayrshire, in uniform at first, latterly in CID. He was never part of any specialist units that might have brought him into contact with Bright, and Bright's record has nothing in it that connects through to Ayrshire. Terry did work in North Lanarkshire, but not until Bright was inside.'

'Has he been lifted yet?'

'I've asked Lottie Mann if she can do that. Bright operates in her area, and technically she's still attached to the Torphichen Place investigation. She's caught up in a new investigation of her own, a crucifixion in Airdrie . . .'

'You're kidding me,' Skinner exclaimed. 'Is she looking for a Billy Connolly fan?'

'What?' Haddock stared at him, bemused.

'It was a famous comedy sketch: the live version was recorded in Airdrie.' His protégé continued to stare. 'Never mind,' he sighed, 'before your time. Come to think of it, it was almost before mine. Have you been in touch with Mary Chambers?' he asked, changing the subject.

'No, gaffer, I haven't. Should I? Are you saying she might have known something about Spring and Griff's other lives?'

'No, I'm not. Am I suggesting you should be asking her that? Am I suggesting that if I was in charge of your investigation I would be looking at her financial affairs, to see if there's anything inexplicable there? Am I suggesting that if you don't, the fiscal might ask whether you were turning a blind eye because she used to be your station commander? You tell me?'

'Point taken, boss. Am I thinking that maybe I should call her up for a sympathetic chat and let her tell me anything she needs to? Yes, I am and, yes, I will.'

'You do that, and fairly soon, because we have a *Saltire* reporter flying out there this evening to interview her. If there is anything, emm,' he hesitated for a second, 'unfortunate, it would be good to have a hint of it before we run a nice cosy sympathetic feature and make an editorial arse of ourselves.'

'Jesus, gaffer,' Haddock laughed, 'you're good at walking on both sides of the street at the same time.'

Seventy-One

'This used to be bandit country, John,' Lottie Mann said, as they approached the address they had been given by the probation service. 'It looks all right now, but you can bet your life that some of those bandits are still there. A new generation maybe, but the same principles apply. It's a sort of parallel universe, the counter-cultures in cities, the world you can see, the one that runs the schools and empties the bins, and the one that you can't, the one that meets other needs, life-threatening cravings that it creates and then satisfies, whether the customers can afford it or not. I fucking hate people like Raymond Bright. Every time I lock one of them up, a happier woman goes home than the one who woke up that morning.' She pressed the bell in the centre of the bright-blue-painted front door of the terraced house.

And waited. In vain.

'How do we get round the back?' Cotter asked.

'Through that door there, son.' The gruff voice came from their left, from the house next door. Its owner was in his sixties, grey-haired and in want of a shave. 'But there's nae point. Him and Phoebe are away.'

'Do you know where they are, Mr . . . ?'

'Grimm, son, Joe Grimm. Aye, they're away at their place in Tenerife. They left last Friday, so they'll be back the morra. Raymond was looking forward tae it. He hasnae seen it for a while, but youse'll know that.'

'Do you know who they're flying with, Joe?' Mann asked. 'There can't have been too many options at this time of year.'

'Ryanair, out of Prestwick. Raymond was lookin' forward tae seein' the Elvis Presley bar again. That's if it's still there.'

'Thanks.' She paused. 'You realise, don't you?, that if for any reason they don't get on the return flight, you'll be the first person we talk to.'

'Nae worries,' he assured her, 'but ye never talked to me the day, right?'

'Right.'

The detectives turned and walked back to their car. 'I'll get on to the airline,' Cotter said, 'just to make sure he wasn't sending us in the wrong direction.'

'He wasn't,' the DCI assured him. 'I don't imagine he likes having Bright as a next-door neighbour. Do we know who Phoebe is?'

'She's his sister. Bright's never been married, and neither has she.'

'We'll be waiting for them, then . . . the morra.' She smiled in anticipation. 'Nice and quiet; I'll make sure we have two big plain-clothes lads just past passport control. We'll stay out of sight until they're in custody, then we'll have them driven straight through to Edinburgh.'

'Both of them?'

'Of course. There were two people involved, remember. Two cars drove into Torphichen Place, one drove away, with the driver of Coats' car as a passenger. We'll take Phoebe as well, until she proves it wasn't her.'

She was fastening her seatbelt when her phone buzzed, signalling an incoming email. She took it out and read it; as she did, her eyes widened. 'This is the full background report on Walter Thomson that I asked for,' she told Cotter. 'As fry went, he was pretty small, so he didn't rate a criminal-intelligence file, but what a gem just fell out of his past!'

Seventy-Two

Skinner gazed at the screen of his iPhone as the image of his youngest daughter was replaced by the name of an incoming caller. 'Mary Chambers,' he murmured. 'Now, why am I not surprised by that?'

'How are you holding up?' he asked, as he accepted her call.

'I'm still in shock, but now I'm just a wee bit concerned. Bob, am I somehow a suspect in this awful business?'

'Why are you asking me?' he replied. 'You know I'm long retired.'

'I also know you're mentoring Sauce Haddock, and others. Griff told Spring; he wasn't happy about anyone being given special treatment ahead of him. I just had a call from Sauce, and I suspect you knew about it before it was made.'

'Maybe,' he conceded. 'Mary, you were one of the best officers I ever worked with in CID. You know that certain questions have to be asked, even when they know the answers. No, you are not a suspect and I doubt that Sauce came close to suggesting that you were. I'll ask you straight out . . . which he probably didn't . . . did you ever suspect that Spring had access to funds that she hadn't told you about?'

'No. She said that she and Griff had an investment through

334

an offshore trust fund that would mature when they were forty-five. She said it was an inheritance from an uncle that had always been managed for them by an agent. She was always flush with cash, yes, but she told me that her design business was flourishing. She showed me her accounts and they bore that out. Okay, I know now they were phoney, but I had no reason to doubt her, or to suspect anything.'

'What about Griff?'

'You mean did I know that he had a gun in his safe and a medium-sized fortune in cash and gold? No, I didn't. You knew him as well as I did. You'll remember the explosion when Spring came out and he found out about us, but once he had got over that he was never anything but pleasant towards me. Okay,' she added, 'he was never going to be like a brother, but he didn't freeze me out either. We didn't talk much but he did let the odd thing slip, mostly about his frustration at being promoted into uniform. He said he only accepted it because he thought it would be short term. He got it into his head that Mario McGuire had manipulated him out of CID.'

'He could have got back into CID any time he liked,' Skinner told her. 'All he had to do was accept a move to Inverness.'

'He never told me that!'

'He never told anybody that.'

'The reporter you're sending out,' Chambers said, suddenly. 'Will she be asking me this kind of question?'

'No,' he replied. 'Lennox will be asking you about yourself rather than about them. The feature will be sympathetic, as I know she promised.'

'Can she be stopped?'

'I suppose she can, if you don't want to go through with it.'

'It's not that,' she confessed. 'I want to go home. I'll talk to her, no problem, but I would rather do it in Edinburgh. This place is a nightmare for me just now. There are press photographers in the street outside. Louis Pollock has promised to keep them in order, but I feel like a prisoner in my own home.'

'Will Pollock let you come back?'

'He'll have to arrest me to stop me. If he needs me as a witness I'll return, but I have no evidence to offer him.'

'Then go for it. I'll ask June Crampsey to tell Lennox to cancel her flight . . . unless . . .' He stopped as a possibility occurred to him. 'Maybe she still could go out there, but to interview Spring instead. I wonder how Pollock would react to that? You book your flight, Mary: your meeting with Lennox Webster will still happen, but maybe not for a day or two.'

'Jesus, Bob,' she said. 'You're turning into a journalist.'

'If I am,' he said to his empty office after the call had ended, 'there will be nobody with better sources.'

He unlocked his desk drawer and removed a small green notebook with a gold House of Commons crest on the cover. It had been a gift from Aileen de Marco, his former wife, and it contained a list of telephone numbers, landline and mobile, that were too sensitive to be included in his handphone directory.

He turned to the third page and called an entry that was prefixed 'DAD'.

'Just when I thought my day couldn't get any worse,' Dame Amanda Dennis sighed, 'I get a call from my favourite trouble magnet. What have you got for me?'

'Nothing,' he told the head of the Security Service. 'You don't pay me for my consultancy services, so I want something in kind. It's well below your pay grade so it shouldn't be a problem. There's a name that's been run past me. I know nothing about him, but I'd like to know everything.'

'Is he a threat to national security?'

'I doubt it very much, but if I'm wrong I'm sure you'll let me know. You got a pen handy? It's quite a long name.'

Seventy-Three

'Sauce, I'm busy here,' Skinner complained, frowning at the face on his screen. 'I've got our IT manager coming to make a presentation any minute now.'

'Sorry, gaffer,' Haddock said. 'I just thought I should let you know that I spoke to Mary Chambers. Your reporter can do the cosy piece you talked about. She's in shock. I tried to make it as gentle as I could. I hope I succeeded.'

'You may have fallen a bit short. She called me, for reassurance as much as anything else. Don't worry about having upset her, 'cos you didn't. She understood you had to ask her, given that Rogozin's murder happened here, and Spring could have had advance knowledge.'

'I'm working on that. We still don't know why Griff had that prepaid phone, but I've asked Jackie to get hold of Spring's mobile records. If he used it to call her in advance of sending the email that lured Rogozin to Scotland and to his death, and I can prove it, she'd be implicated.'

'Forget it,' Skinner said. 'You'd need to extradite her, and I think you'd find that the South Africans won't be letting her go anywhere until they've done with her, which will probably be at least twenty years from now. Also this; he had an untraceable phone, so the chances are she had too. It's not worth it, Sauce.'

'There's justice, gaffer.'

'For whom? What's it worth to the Scottish taxpayer to prove that she knew in advance that her brother was going to kill their co-conspirator in a crime on another continent? To do that, you'd need to keep your investigation open until she was available for a very expensive criminal trial which might not take place for years. As long as that was a possibility,' he pointed out, 'the Crown wouldn't be able to hold the FAI into Rogozin's murder, and the Aisha Karman file in Manchester might have to stay open too. There's justice, Sauce, but there's pragmatism too. If I were you, I'd tell Jackie to stop looking.' As Haddock digested his advice, he carried on. 'Oh, by the way, the reporter didn't go; Mary's decided to come home as soon as she can get a flight. They'll meet here.'

'I can understand that,' the DI said. 'She sounded very low when we spoke, depressed even.' On screen, he smiled. 'It's my turn to change the subject. I checked out that Billy Connolly sketch; very funny but I doubt that he'd get away with it now. I also had some interesting feedback from Lottie. It's her investigation but she thought I should know. The crucifixion victim, his name was . . .'

'Barabbas?'

'No, he must have escaped. His name was Walter Thomson; he seems to have been a man of no great distinction, and Lottie still has no idea what got him executed Roman-style, but his last arresting officer was Detective Inspector Terry Coats.'

Skinner stared at the young detective's Facetime image. 'What was his name again?' he asked.

'Walter Thomson.'

'Fuck,' he whispered.

'No, Walter Thomson.'

'Don't piss about, Sauce, and don't go anywhere either. I'm coming to see you.'

'What about the IT manager?'

'Sod her, she can wait. This is much more important.' He ended the call, and reached for his overcoat, which hung on a hook behind his desk. He was halfway into it when his mobile sounded on his desk. 'Dame Amanda,' he exclaimed, as he took the call, 'I didn't expect you to call me in person.'

Seventy-Four

'This isn't an airport, Lottie,' John Cotter remarked, 'it's a ghost town.'

'I know,' she agreed. 'It makes me sad. This used to be Scotland's only transatlantic airport. More than a few emigrants to Canada left from here, in aircraft with propellers on the wings that had to refuel before they reached Toronto. Nowadays, just look at it.'

'Why is it still open?'

'Ask the First Minister. Maybe it'll come into its own again when Brexit finally happens, I don't know.'

'What was old Joe, the neighbour, saying about Elvis?' the DS asked.

'My Dan would tell you that.' She felt a familiar frisson as she used the possessive. 'He's an Elvis buff. Legend has it that The King only set foot on British soil once, and it was here, when he was flying home after doing his national service in Germany. They've traded on it ever since.'

'Is it true?'

'There is another story, but I don't know that it's ever been verified. The one thing I know for sure is that Raymond Bright and his sister are on the flight that's coming in right now, so let's get moving.'

They walked into the baggage hall, showing their accreditation to the lone Customs official on duty, then made their way through the baggage hall, emerging at the police desk behind the Border Force check point. As Mann had requested, two large men in plain clothes were waiting there. One of them was middle-aged, the other much younger. She knew the former; he had worked on the same team as her ex-husband, before his fall from grace. For a second, she wondered how he would react, for Scott, her disgraced ex-husband, still had friends on the force, but he greeted her effusively.

'Lottie, how ye doing? Sorry, that should be, ma'am.' He touched his forelock.

'Only in front of strangers, Mac,' she laughed. 'I thought you were still in a black tunic.'

'I am, but I grab any excuse to wear a suit. I hear you're with Desperate Dan these days. That was a long time coming, but we all knew he was fond of you.'

'I wish you'd told me,' she said. 'It was a complete surprise to me when it happened.'

'This guy Bright we're here for. What's he done?'

'He's wanted for questioning about the New Year murder in Edinburgh.'

Mac's face darkened. 'Terry Coats?'

'That one, yes. Him and a serving inspector.'

'Indeed?' the veteran growled. 'In that case the van might hit a few bumps on the road on the way through there. I liked Terry; a bit of a spiv, but an okay guy. He didn't deserve what he got from that chief constable. On yis go now,' he said, as the first passengers began to appear at the end of a long corridor, 'get out of sight and let us collect him for you. At least we know he's not goin' to be armed, getting off a flight.'

'If there was any chance of that,' she said, 'you would be too.'

To their right was a double door, no more than four yards along a corridor. Mann and Cotter stepped back into it and waited. The flow of passengers was slow but steady; almost invariably they were couples, a few with children, but mostly middle-aged or elderly. Some were tanned, others showed various skin tones from pale pink to bright red. Nearly all were dressed for the weather conditions they had left rather than those that awaited them outside. The only exceptions were two Asian families, whose women and children were covered from head to toe.

The detectives waited in their alcove, impatient at first, then tense as the human tide crept past them. 'Are you certain they were on the plane, boss?' Cotter muttered. 'I didn't see any air bridges when we got here. They'll have walked across the tarmac. Is it possible that they've slipped out of the queue and found another way out?'

'Anything's . . .' Mann began until she was silenced by a glance and an imperceptible nod from the senior constable. As they looked on, two figures stepped into their eyeline, without noticing them. Phoebe Bright looked ten years older than the passport photo they had sourced. Raymond, her brother, was twelve years older than his last arrest photograph, but aside from greying hair around the temple, he was little changed: around six feet tall, heavily built with a thick jaw that gave him a simian look.

Mac and his colleague stepped across, blocking the passageway. 'Mr Bright, Miss Bright,' the senior man said.

'Would you come with us, please? Our colleagues would like a word with you.'

Glancing to his left, Raymond Bright noticed Mann and Cotter for the first time. His small eyes flared with anger. With unexpected speed, he dropped his cabin bag, head-butted Mac, spun on his heel and headed for the waiting detectives. Cotter moved towards him; he was much smaller and was swept aside easily, but in the time he had gained for her, the DCI had drawn an extendible baton. She went low with her first stroke, back hand, smashing an exposed kneecap below Bright's cargo shorts, then high on the follow-through, catching him on the side of the head and sending him crashing in a heap at her feet.

'That was not clever,' she told him, very quietly, as the DS snapped cufflinks around his wrists. 'In fact, you'll have a ninety-mile drive to reflect on just how stupid it was, given that the officer you just nutted will be one of your escorts.'

Seventy-Five

'Sorry, Sauce,' Skinner said as he stepped into the office, 'I had an unexpected call, one that I had to deal with.' To Haddock's surprise he was not alone. 'The good news is,' he continued, 'it's given ACC Payne the time to get here from the Secret Bunker.' The nickname that the lower ranks had bestowed on the police service national headquarters had found its way into the public domain. 'What I've got to tell you, you'd have to report to him anyway, so this speeds things up.'

'So what is it?' the DI asked, with the faintest sign of impatience, 'and how does it relate to Walter Thomson, the dead man in Airdrie?'

From inside his overcoat, as he removed it, Skinner produced a green folder, and laid it on the meeting table. 'Come and sit along here,' he said, 'and I'll explain.' He waited until Payne and Haddock were in place, facing him, then carried on. 'Lowell,' he began, glancing at the ACC, 'you'll remember my predecessor as Chief Constable of Strathclyde.'

Payne nodded. 'Only too well,' he confirmed. 'Antonia Field, parachuted in from south of the border. Everyone in Scotland knew that she saw the job as a stepping stone on the way to being Commissioner of the Metropolitan Police.

345

Nobody could stand her, but equally, nobody would have wished her fate on her either.'

'That's right. The only way that I'd have ever gone after the job as chief of the national force would have been to stop her getting it.' Skinner turned to Haddock. 'Sauce, how much do you know about the circumstances behind Terry Coats' resignation from Strathclyde, before it was wound up?'

'I know he was outed by a blog, Brass Rubbings, that focused on police corruption and general misbehaviour. It claimed that he had protected a criminal from prosecution because he was a source of useful information that had led to him putting various people away. It got wider press coverage and Chief Constable Field decided to throw Coats under the bus. She offered him a transfer that she knew he wouldn't accept, a uniform job in Oban. Noele was CID then, in North Lanarkshire like him, but she wasn't offered a move. He quit, as she knew he would, and he was bitter about it until the day he died.'

'That's correct,' Skinner agreed, 'but you left out one crucial consequence of the Brass Rubbings report. Its author, Austin Brass, was ruthless, or reckless, or stupid enough, depending on how you looked at him, to name Coats' informant. As a result, the man was found murdered, chopped up and fitted into a suitcase. The crime was never solved and the connection to the blog story was hushed up.' He opened the green folder and pushed it across the table.

'When I took over from Toni Field,' he continued, 'I found this file in a secure cabinet in my new office. It tells the whole story, but a casual read doesn't make Field look too good because it includes the fact that Coats was exonerated by an investigation by the professional standards department, yet she went ahead with axing him anyway, to preserve her own reputation. What it also includes is the name of the victim. He was called Alan Mason, a small-time criminal from Airdrie, in North Lanarkshire, and he was twenty-two years old. No one was ever charged with his murder but there was one outstanding suspect, a man who had done time as a result of information given by Mason to Terry Coats. His name? Walter Thomson.'

Lowell Payne whistled. 'Bloody hell, Bob,' he gasped. 'We have Coats and this man connected to Mason's death and murdered within hours of each other.'

'That's right. And,' he added, 'you have a suspect for Coats under arrest.' He smiled at Haddock. 'Join the dots, Sauce. Join the fucking dots.'

'I will, gaffer,' the DI replied. 'But can I ask you, how come you've still got the file?'

'I've got it because I kept it, lad. Nobody else seemed to want it, but I had a feeling that one day someone would. So . . . there you are.'

Seventy-Six

'You did us all a favour, Lottie,' Haddock said, 'when you cracked Bright so hard with that baton that the doctor wouldn't let us interview him until this morning. We've got more to put to him now.'

'Maybe that wasn't me,' she pointed out. 'Letting Big Mac ride with him in the van was a risky decision.'

'Big Mac?' Skinner repeated.

'Aye. His name's McDonald and he's big, so what else were they ever going to call him? I didn't have much choice though. I couldn't let Phoebe go in the van without a female escort, so she had to come with John and me.'

'Whatever,' Haddock continued, 'it let us execute the search warrant on their house. There's no way back from that. Tarvil,' he called out to the sergeant, 'go get him, please.' He turned to Mann. 'You and me in there, Lottie, yes?' She nodded assent. 'John, you, Tarvil, and Sir Robert can watch on video. Is his lawyer here?'

Singh stopped in the doorway. 'He said he didn't want one, Sauce.'

'Fuck that!' the DI exclaimed. 'He's been cautioned, so he's entitled to a solicitor present. He's having one, like it or not.

I'm not having him claiming later on that it was denied. Bugger! I want to get on with it; now we've got a delay. Can we whistle one up here?' He looked at Skinner. 'Gaffer, is Alex busy today?'

'It's Saturday, Sauce,' he reminded his protégé. 'But even if it wasn't, no way would she sit alongside a guy accused of murdering her boyfriend. The Law Society would shit itself collectively at the thought. Her associate, Johanna DaCosta, on the other hand, she might be available. Want me to check it out?'

'Please do. It'll be a legal-aid case, but we can top up today's fee if necessary.'

Skinner whistled. 'Wow! She can book her Caribbean holiday right now.'

Seventy-Seven

'Are you sure you don't mind?' the young solicitor advocate asked. 'Things might have come to light about him but even so you and he . . .'

'Johanna,' Alex Skinner exclaimed, 'he was a friend, at least I thought he was, and he was a good shag, but that's it. We were not romantically inclined, ever. My father is right that the Law Society might argue that we were close enough for it to cloud my judgement when to comes to acting for Bright, but you didn't know him and you're an associate of my firm, not my employee. You earn your own fees from your own work. There's no reason why you shouldn't accept Bright's instruction. That's if he gives it to you. Dad told me that he waived his right to legal advice; it may be that you'll get to Fettes and he'll still refuse to engage you. If he does, Sauce will ask you to sign a statement that you offered your services but the prisoner refused. That's all he really wants; he doesn't give a stuff whether Bright has a lawyer beside him.'

'If you say so, Alex,' DaCosta decided. 'I'll take it on. The police statement I read this morning said that two people had been arrested. What about the other one?'

'That was Bright's sister. They thought she might have been his accomplice, but she's been released on simple police bail. I see no other distractions, on you go.'

Seventy-Eight

'Aye, fine,' Raymond Bright grunted. 'As long as youse are payin' her.' He looked up towards the camera in a corner of the interview room, and tapped the side of his head, gingerly touching a purple lump. 'I hope youse all see this.'

'For the record, Ms DaCosta,' Lottie Mann said, 'your client had to be restrained at the airport. He's been cautioned in respect of an assault on a police officer and, be sure, he will be charged with that in addition to anything that happens after this interview. But I don't imagine that a three-month sentence on top of thirty years will be much of a bother to him.'

'Let's carry on,' Haddock declared. 'We've been delayed long enough. Mr Bright—'

'Haud on,' the prisoner exclaimed. 'What about oor Phoebe? Where's she?'

'She's at home,' the DI advised him. 'She was detained because we thought she might have been your accomplice. When we discovered that she has an eye condition that means she couldn't possibly have driven the second vehicle, she was released on bail. That doesn't mean she's off the hook though. If we find out that she was aware of your plan to murder Mr Coats and Inspector Montell, she may still face charges.'

'Can they do that?' Bright asked his solicitor. 'Let her oot and then haul her back in again?'

'They have that power,' Johanna DaCosta confirmed.

'Okay, let's get straight to the point,' Haddock continued. 'While we were following concussion protocol yesterday, it gave us time to search your home, in accordance with a warrant granted by a sheriff. We removed certain items of your clothing for scientific testing. This revealed traces of blood, which on first examination matched Inspector Montell's. DNA analysis is still being done, but I'm going to hazard a guess that'll confirm it was his. In addition to that we found these.' He paused to reach down and take a plastic evidence bag from the floor. 'As you can see, these are three distinctive gold coins, called Krugerrands. On each of them we've found fingerprints; they were partials but there are enough points of similarity for us to match them with those of Terry Coats. That means we can tie you to both murder victims, Mr Bright. In addition to that, we've got video footage of a man getting out of Mr Coats' car, just before twelve-thirty a.m. on January the first, after it had been parked in Torphichen Place in Edinburgh, outside the police station where Inspector Montell worked. The driver was wearing clothes similar to those we took from your house. He also wore a black balaclava. Not unlike this one.' He reached down once more and produced another evidence bag. 'It was also recovered from your house; to be precise, from a garden waste recycling bin, where it was wrapped around these.' He went to the floor for a third time and came up with a heavy revolver. 'This, or something similar,' he said, 'was used as far back as the Boer War, and in dozens if not hundreds since then. It's a Webley Mark Six, point four five five calibre, the same as the bullet that was recovered from Terry Coats' garage.

It's in good enough shape that we were able to match it to this gun.' He reached down for the last time. 'Finally there's this, a nine-millimetre Luger pistol, possibly from a later war. Ballistic tests have determined that it's the weapon used to kill Terry Coats.' He leaned back in his chair. 'In the face of all that, Mr Bright, do you have anything to say? If you want, I'll give you time for a private word with Ms DaCosta before you answer.'

'No thanks,' he grunted. 'I'm saying nuthin' until youse can explain to me why I'd want tae kill two fellas I've never met, one of them a polis and the other one ex-filth.'

'Okay,' Haddock replied, amiably. 'There's someone else here who can do that. Sir Robert,' he called out, 'would you like to join us now?'

Bright stared, frowning, at the door of the interview room until it opened and a tall middle-aged man with close-cropped steel-grey hair stepped through it, carrying a green folder. He picked up a chair from a corner of the room and set it down between the two detectives.

'For the recording,' Mann declared, 'Sir Robert Skinner has entered the room.'

'Skinner,' the prisoner repeated; for the first time, he seemed nervous. 'You were the big polis were ye, no? But ye're no' a polis any mair. What are you doin' here? Can they dae that?' he asked DaCosta.

'They can,' Skinner replied on her behalf, showing her a police warrant card in his name, with the designation 'Special Constable'.

'Yes, Mr Bright,' she agreed, 'they can.'

'You were asking about motive,' the newcomer said. He laid his folder on the desk, took out a photograph and slid it across. 'He's your motive. His name was Alan Mason. He was nineteen when that was taken.' He paused and displayed a second glossy print. Bright recoiled as he looked at it. DaCosta winced.

'He was twenty-two when this was taken, just before the autopsy that followed his murder. He was killed, after he'd been named online as a police source of criminal intelligence, having passed information to then Detective Inspector Terry Coats . . . information that put several people in prison.'

'If he wis a grass,' Bright blustered, 'fair enough.'

Skinner laughed. 'Give it up, Raymond,' he chuckled. You know what I'm going to say next. We've got your DNA, and naturally, his is on the database too. Alan Mason was your son, Mr Bright. There's no point in denying it. Grass or no grass, he was your boy, and you blamed Terry Coats for him being murdered. And you killed him,' he continued, 'for a very simple and traditional reason, revenge. The only thing I don't get is why, when Alan's birth was registered, he was given your middle name, rather than your surname. Okay, there's no record of you and his mother being married, but if you didn't want to lumber him with being Raymond Bright's son, why not just give him her name? She was Abigail Richardson, according to his birth certificate.'

'That's what she wanted, okay,' Bright snapped, banging his fists on the table. 'Aye, okay,' he shouted. 'Clever bastards all of you. Terry fuckin' Coats got my son killed and Terry fuckin' Coats paid for it.'

'Unfortunately,' Haddock said, 'so did another man, one who had nothing to do with it.'

'The other fella . . .' Bright's eyes narrowed. 'If Ah'd known he was there, Ah might no' have gone that night; Ah might've put it off for a bit. There was somethin' about that guy, and Ah'm no just talking about him bein' a polis. The way he looked at me, I knew that if he'd had the gun I'd have been fuckin' dead in a second. He made a mistake though. He told me he was a cop. Funny thing, though, he said that if we saw sense and fucked off, there would be no more said about it. Ah told him it was too late for that. He said we wouldn't fuckin' dare. Ah dared all right. We turned up the telly in the hoose, took them into the garage, then when the bells started, well, Ah gave the guy nae chance, shot him right through the back o' the heid. He never knew a thing. Coats did though. Ah let him realise what was coming, although the job was done before the bells wis finished.'

'Why did you leave the bodies outside Inspector Montell's station?' Haddock asked.

Bright's eyebrows rose. 'Was it? I knew there was a big polis station in the middle o' the town, so we went there. That wis the only reason. An' that's the whole story.'

'Not quite,' Skinner said. 'Who shot Coats? He was killed with a different weapon, and why would you carry two? No, he was shot by your accomplice. If it wasn't your sister, who was it? Tell us and it might get you a few years off your life-sentence tariff.'

'That Ah'll never do,' Bright declared. 'Ma boy might have been a grass, but Ah'm no'. Go on, charge us an' let's get this over wi'.'

'Not so fast,' Mann intervened. 'We haven't got to Walter Thomson yet.'

'Thomson?' Bright snorted. 'Why should you lot care about fuckin' Thomson? He wisnae a polis.'

Seventy-Nine

'He didn't deny it when I put Thomson's murder to him,' Lottie Mann insisted.

'No, he didn't,' Skinner agreed, reaching for the mug that sat on a coaster on Haddock's table. 'He laughed at you and said, "No comment".'

'He knew who Walter Thomson was,' she argued. 'He knew he'd been murdered.'

He countered. 'Thomson did his time in Shotts Prison; Bright spent part of his sentence there too and they coincided. They met, for sure. Thomson's death was reported in the Scottish press. You can buy the *Daily Record* in Tenerife, so you can't hold his knowledge of the crime against him.'

'Logistically, it's feasible,' the DCI persisted. 'Thomson's time of death is uncertain because of the time that elapsed before he was found, plus the temperature in the unheated warehouse and the way he was killed. There's evidence that he was bound, though, before he was nailed up. Bright and his accomplice could have picked him up before they killed Coats and Montell and left him there to be finished off later, when that was done. We've got opportunity. If we find his DNA and fingerprints at the scene, haven't we got him?' she challenged.

'You'll have a case, no denying that.' Skinner smiled. 'But if I'm the defence counsel, I'm going to ask if you've looked at Bright's background. He's got a day job. He's a self-employed builder. So it's quite natural that his DNA, his fingerprints, and maybe even a sample of his urine on a toilet bowl in the gents should be found at a builder's merchants. Then if I really want to make you squirm in the witness box, Lottie, I'm going to produce a receipt for goods purchased there a few days before it closed for the holidays.'

Haddock intervened. 'Come on, gaffer! He did it, for fuck's sake. It's obvious he did it. Find the physical evidence of his presence, and I bet you we do, and the most cautious, arse-covering fiscal in Scotland would go to court with that.'

He shrugged. 'You're right, Sauce. He'd probably get a conviction too. It's just . . .' He paused as the door behind him opened, turning to look over his shoulder.

'DS Singh said I'd find you here,' Johanna DaCosta murmured. Her gaze settled on Lottie Mann. 'My client wants to see you,' she told her. 'He's decided that he wants to make a statement confessing to the murder of Walter Thomson. He knows he's going to get the maximum tariff for Montell and Coats, so he's thinking that it'll be more or less a freebie.' She smiled, and her cheeks turned pale pink. 'He's asked me to represent him in the High Court,' she added shyly.

Skinner grinned at her. 'It'll be good experience for you, Johanna, but I'll tell you: the clouds could part, a dove could fly down from heaven and land on your client's shoulder, but he still won't be getting out before he's eighty-five.'

Eighty

'Gaffer, Bob, what the fuck do you want that for?' Haddock hissed. Mann, Cotter and DaCosta had gone, leaving them alone in the DI's office.

'You don't need to know. You just need to trust me; both of you.'

'What authority have you got?'

'Which one would you like? My Special Constable warrant or my Thames House card. Just ask her for me. I'm not asking you to do anything furtive; I need her consent. I doubt that anything will come of it. Even if I'm wrong about that, it won't affect her personally. It will either eliminate a possibility or it will . . . Look, if she insists I will explain why I want it, but I'd rather she didn't. It'll help me answer a question that's bugging me; you know what I'm like with them.'

'Bob, she's pregnant. Will that have any effect on whatever you're up to?'

'None. Congratulations though, you're a dark horse. Sauce,' he sighed. 'If she won't, I'll understand. If she will . . .'

Eighty-One

'So it's happy endings all round,' Sarah said. 'Sauce has cracked his first big solo case, Noele McClair has a nice promotion, Maggie Steele has decided that there is happiness in the world, and best of all Alex seems to have found herself again.'

'Happy isn't the word I'd choose,' Bob replied. 'Satisfactory on those four counts, yes, but Terry Coats and Griff Montell are still dead and so are seven other people. Then there's the collateral damage.'

'Seven? How do you work that out?'

He counted them off, a finger at a time. 'Anatoly Rogozin, the co-conspirator in the robbery, Fannie DeWalt, the cop Griff shot, the two security guards who died there, Aisha Karman, the unlucky flight hostess, Alan Mason, the boy that was hung out to dry by Brass Rubbings, and Walter Thomson, who almost certainly killed him.'

'And the collateral?'

'Spring Montell, who is probably as sociopathic as her twin, and Mary Chambers, who's back in Scotland looking at the wreckage of what she thought was a happy retirement.'

'I suppose,' she conceded. 'The Montell twins must have

had huge strength of will. To pull off such a big robbery, to dispose of the proceeds in the way they did, and then to live normal lives. I wonder what their end game was?'

'Spring told the South African prosecutor that they intended to disappear when they were forty-five; to sell the airline at a huge profit, buy new identities, go off to a bolt hole, and never be seen again.'

'That sounds . . .'

'Almost incestuous? Yeah, don't fucking go there. Enough's enough.' He winced. 'The final irony,' he sighed, 'was that it all went wrong for them through Griff being an innocent bystander . . . No! Definitely not innocent, but he was just in the wrong place at the wrong time.'

'And now it's all over?'

'They think it is. Some people are on the pitch,' he chuckled, quoting an iconic piece of football commentary.

'So why do I suspect that it might not be?' Sarah asked.

'It isn't. There are people still at liberty with blood on their hands. Raymond Bright confessed to the murders of Coats and Montell, and of Walter Thomson, but he didn't act alone. He had a partner in crime, the person who drove him away, in a Renault with false plates, after he dumped the bodies outside the police station. The plates were found in a rubbish bin in Polwarth, but the car never did turn up. The team's first thought was that it might have been his sister out to avenge her nephew, but she's half blind. She can't see well enough to ride a bike, let alone drive a getaway car, and she certainly couldn't put a bullet through the middle of someone's forehead from far enough away not to leave any scorch marks around the wound.'

'No,' she agreed. 'That was a very neat job.' She touched her forehead just above her nose. 'Very professional, special forces style. Do you think that it might have been Bright, with another gun?'

'No chance. Why would he need another? He'd just spread Griff's brains all over the garage. No, there was somebody else, and my gut tells me that it wasn't just an underworld pal who owed Bright a favour. This was a personal crime, retribution. It was natural to suspect Phoebe Bright, the principle was correct. Okay, it wasn't her, but you know, she wasn't poor wee Alan's only family member.'

Eighty-Two

'He wants what?' Cheeky Davis exclaimed.

'A sample of your DNA,' her partner repeated.

'Why the hell would he want that? Does he think I'm a fucking criminal just because I'm Goldic McCullough's niece?'

'Not for a second, love. I can promise you that. He said he needs it to help him answer a question. He wouldn't tell me what it is, but he said that he would tell you, if you really want to know. Look, my darling, the only thing I can tell you for sure is that if he wants this it must be to help him uncover a truth, because that's what he's all about. Look at how easily he's slipped into his media work. It's an extension of what he did in his other career. He's a truth seeker.'

'Sometimes we might not like the truth, Sauce,' she whispered.

'But that doesn't make it go away.'

'Okay,' she said. 'I'll do it for you, because you're one of those people too, and that's part of why I love you. On one condition though; whatever it is my DNA helps him discover, I don't want to know. Ever.'

Eighty-Three

'So how was the Ice Hotel really?' Skinner asked.

Cameron McCullough smiled. 'Truth? It really was fucking freezing, like I said. But we were all so full of schnapps that we barely knew it.'

His two guests laughed.

'I'm glad you guys decided to come tonight,' he continued. 'You know you've always had an open invitation, Bob, both you and Harold. No better night to take me up on it than a mid-week postponement against the champions. Too bad about the result, but at least my team put up a decent show.' He swivelled his chair until it faced the window that overlooked the football pitch. 'This room's the chairman's hideaway,' he said. 'It's just like one of your interview rooms, mirrored glass that nobody can see through. I could watch the whole game from here, but I need to let the customers see me, wearing the scarf and all. Usually I'd be putting myself about in the boardroom as well, at the post-match reception. What is it about football and meat pies?' he asked. 'I've had God knows who in that room next door, the Chairman of Barcelona, three international team managers, the President of UEFA and they've all wolfed down the pies.'

Haddock held up the remnants of his. 'They are pretty damn good, though.'

McCullough winked at him. 'Even without the sauce?'

'You know, Cameron, I really hate that stuff,' he confessed. 'I can think of nothing more disgusting than a fish supper smothered in HP.'

'You'll get on well with your future stepmother-in-law. She's very much a vinegar person. It was a nice suggestion that I should ask her along tonight. Mia's teeth were a bit clenched when I told her, but having Ignacio here as your driver mollified her. They can't stand each other, Mia and Inez. I shouldn't say this to you, Harold, but my daughter Inez is an irredeemable twat. She was a breech birth and from that time on she never stopped being awkward. Cheeky's gran and I brought her up, you know; she barely saw her mother until she was eight. I'm not surprised Cheeky didn't come tonight. They've barely spoken since that time Inez got her into trouble.'

'It wasn't that,' Haddock told him. 'I didn't tell Cheeky that Inez was coming. Her problem is she's off her food at the moment; the very sight of those pies would have been too much for her.' He smiled, diffidently. 'I might as well tell you now; the secret won't keep much longer. You're going to be a great-grandpa.'

His host stared at him, wide-eyed, then exploded in a huge guffaw. 'That's amazing! Harold, Sauce, that is terrific, I couldn't be happier for both of you, and aye and sure, for me. I don't know how Mia's going to handle being the youngest great-granny in Scotland.' He reached across and placed a hand on Haddock's sleeve. 'Anything you need, son, anything you want. There's nothing I wouldn't do for that girl.'

'Other than telling her she had a brother for twenty-two years of her life?'

'What the fuck do you mean, man?' McCullough stared at Skinner, stunned by his words.

'Yes, gaffer, what are you saying?'

The other two men ignored him, as their eyes locked together, unblinking. As Haddock looked at them, McCullough seemed to shed one persona, letting another emerge.

The pair had met face to face on perhaps a dozen occasions, but never before had Skinner been offered even a glimpse of the man who had worn such a fearsome reputation in his home city. 'You know, Cameron,' he replied. 'You know exactly what I mean. Sauce doesn't, though. He's still a relative innocent, not quite the finished article. To use an old cliché, I may have taught him everything he knows, but I hadn't taught him everything I know, not until now. His last lesson is this: never stop asking questions until you are absolutely one thousand per cent certain that there are no more left unanswered. You have to chase evil, you have to chase the truth of it, right down to the roots.'

'Bob?' Haddock whispered.

'Alan Mason,' Skinner said, his gaze never leaving McCullough. 'The boy that Terry Coats died for was Cheeky's half-brother.'

'What?'

'You heard me. His mother wouldn't let him have his father's name . . . that doesn't even appear on Alan's birth certificate . . . but she wouldn't let him have hers either. The reason? She was so afraid of her own father, of what he might do if he found out, that she didn't even put her own name on his birth certificate. What has Cheeky told you about her father, Sauce?'

'She said that he ran off as soon as her mother found out she was pregnant,' Haddock replied. 'She never knew who he was. Inez wouldn't even tell her his name; she never has.'

'Okay,' Skinner said, 'this is what I know. There was a missing person reported in Dundee twenty-eight years ago, seven months before Cheeky was born. He was a seventeen-year-old boy; his name was Samuel Trott and the report was filed by his aunt. It's very unusual for boys that age to vanish without trace, but the Tayside cops don't seem to have looked too hard for him. Indeed, he's still missing. You can ask Inez about him if you want. He was a year ahead of her at Morgan Academy. I have a notion that Inez remembered him when she registered her son's birth. When she did that, she called herself Abigail Richardson.' He looked at McCullough. 'Tell him who Abigail was, Cameron.'

'He doesn't have to,' Haddock said. 'I know. Granny Abby, that's what Cheeky calls her, whenever she talks about her.'

Skinner nodded. 'The DNA sample you got from Cheeky last week, Sauce, that's the proof. There's a close match between hers and Alan Mason's profile; that was kept on file after his cremation.' He paused, turning to his young friend. 'Get out of here now and leave us to talk. That's all you have to know, and Cheeky never needs to. Go and find Inez and don't let her out of your sight.'

Without argument, Haddock left the room.

'You're a bastard of the first order, Bob Skinner,' McCullough growled as the door closed. His eyes were still volcanic.

'That's been said before, Cameron. You might need to come up with a better description in a few minutes, after I've finished.'

'Have you not done enough, man?'

'Fuck no, I've barely started. First off, how did you get here tonight?' he asked.

'Mia drove us.'

'Not Vito Tremacoldi? I was looking forward to meeting him.'

McCullough reached out to the table at his side and poured himself another two fingers of Lagavulin. 'No,' he said, 'I let him go back to Italy. I was giving him a few months' trial in the job, but he never settled here. The language was a problem too.'

'Really?' Skinner exclaimed. 'I thought mercenaries needed a decent command of English.' He smiled, took a photograph from his jacket and tossed it on to the table. It showed the upper body of a man in camouflage colours, with a shaved head and very blue, very cold, eyes. 'Don't bullshit me, Cameron. I had Tremacoldi checked out by people with resources way beyond yours. I know everything about the man, including the details of certain deniable jobs that he's done for intelligence services, Britain's included. So I'm finding it just a wee bit strange that you hired him around the time Raymond Bright got out of jail, and that you let him go a few days after Terry Coats and Walter Thomson were both taken care of.'

'Go on then,' McCullough snapped, 'spell it out.'

'When did Inez run off?'

'Two years after young Cameron was born,' he replied. 'Sammy Trott's in Australia, by the way,' he added. 'He's a flooring contractor in Melbourne, well off too. His parents were dead, and he lived with an aunt he couldn't stand, so I flew him out there and got him a job with one of my suppliers. He doesn't know he has a child; he was told that Inez was having an abortion. I did the lad a favour, Bob, I really did. I liked him and my daughter was trouble from the day she was born. I mean that literally, too.' His eyes narrowed; Skinner read pain in their depths. 'Her birth wrecked Abby downstairs. She could never have any more kids. She died when Cameron was fifteen. She had surgery on her waterworks and developed sepsis; that was another gift from Inez.'

'You really hate your daughter, don't you?'

'Vehemently. But I love hers. When Inez did her runner, aged eighteen, when Cameron was two, I didn't chase after her. But I did find out early on that she'd met a Weegie bloke at one of the clubs I had then and gone off with him. I found out also that he'd been dealing drugs there. I had him punished for that, severely, but I left the pair of them to get on with it.'

'When did she come back?' Skinner asked.

'When her son was four. She didn't want to be stuck with him, so she left him with Bright and his sister. If she had brought him with her, I'd have acknowledged him, but she didn't. After she came home, I kept her on the periphery of young Cameron's life; effectively Abby and I were the lassie's parents. I never met my grandson, ever, but that was the choice that Inez made.'

'It wasn't Bright's choice?'

'Bob, I could have squashed Raymond Bright, had him sent a lot further away than Australia, but he wasn't worth the investment. Inez went off with him to Glasgow and her fucking vinegar chips. I'd had enough, so I left her to get on with it. I took her back when she finally ran away from him, to get off the drugs, and I made fucking sure that he was taken off the street by your lot not long after that. The boy stayed with his aunt, but I kept them fed and clothed. He grew up a toerag though; he was in bad company, in and out of court, and eventually . . . You know what happened to him.'

His face contorted with what seemed to Skinner to be genuine pain. 'Now,' he exclaimed, 'you're going to ask me if I feel guilty about just leaving the kid to it. Yes, of course I fucking do, and when I heard that Bright was finally up for release, I made sure he felt guilty too.'

'And Inez?'

'Who knows what Inez feels? Who knows what's in that woman's head?'

'She drives a Renault, doesn't she?'

'Yes, a Megane. A company car registered to the radio station. Why do you ask?'

'Like the one with false plates that picked up Bright in Torphichen Place.'

McCullough's eyes found his once again. 'That was a Megane? Oh Jesus,' he gasped. 'You're saying that she . . .'

'Yes, I am, but the police won't trace the car now. They haven't been able to place it in Airdrie either, outside the warehouse where Walter Thomson was crucified. They've tried,' he added, 'but the false plates were dumped in Edinburgh, having been stolen off a car there. Now why would anyone have done that, before,' he emphasised the last word, 'going on to commit another murder? And yet,' he continued, 'that's a crime of which Bright's insisting he's guilty. And everybody's happy to believe him; Lowell Payne the ACC, Lottie Mann, and Sauce too; they're all happy because it's a nice neat finish, guilty pleas all round. Even the Lord Advocate's happy, because it will save her the cost of a trial.'

He reached out, topped up McCullough's malt and refilled his own glass with a Spanish red that he knew must have cost two hundred euros a bottle.

'They're all so fucking delighted,' he continued, 'that they're not looking at you at all. They're not asking about the missing time between you and Tremacoldi leaving Black Shield Lodge and checking into the Glasgow Airport car park for your private jet to Big Bozo's bloody stag do. A two-hour journey that took a shade over three hours.'

He raised his glass and took a sip, savouring the quality of the Pesquera Reserva, wondering why one vintage could be so superior to another. 'And you know what, Cameron?' he said, 'I'm not asking either.'

'You going to tell me why not?'

'Sure. It's because I have no wish to lob a missile into young Sauce's career, or to darken the happiest time of your granddaughter's life. I'm sure it was you, Cameron; it had to be. Your Inez might be a determined woman, but Bright is not the most subtle guy in the world. Plus,' he laughed, 'I question whether, even together, they were capable of nailing a big man to a warehouse wall. Yes, they might have had it in them to burn his balls off with a blow torch, or Inez might, but would either of them know how to bleed someone out through the femoral artery? Maybe not. Tremacoldi would though; he'd have been capable of all of it.'

He drank a little more wine, then replenished it.

'Here's what I'm saying. You never acknowledged Alan as your grandson, but nonetheless he was; he was your blood. When he died in the way he did, I see you consumed by guilt, and determined that those who were behind his killing should pay. That included the cop who used him. It might have included Austin Brass too, the blogger who named him as a grass, but he had enemies all over the place and one of them got to him first.'

His gaze seemed to drill into McCullough. 'You weren't going to do it yourself, though,' he continued. 'No, you waited for Alan's father to finish his prison sentence so that you could use him to get even. Cameron, I believe that everything Raymond Bright did was at your prompting. There will be nothing on paper, no orders given, just hints and indications, but nonetheless, I reckon you set it in motion, everything. Apart, that is,' he added, 'from the death of Griff Montell. That was a major complication, one that you couldn't influence; I doubt that you'd have approved that. God, I hope not!

'As for Walter Thomson,' he continued, 'the world knew he killed Alan Mason. It couldn't be proved, but that didn't bother you and Raymond Bright. I believe that Bright picked up Thomson at the weekend before Hogmanay, after the warehouse had closed for the holidays, that he abducted him and left him there, tied up and helpless, waiting for whatever was going to happen to him. And I'm suggesting that turned out to be your man Vito Tremacoldi, your mercenary, with you parked out of sight all the while, maybe listening to the screams but knowing that on Hogmanay, that night of all nights, the polis would be elsewhere, keeping drunks in order, and knowing too that you wouldn't be leaving any trace of yourself on the premises, and that Vito wouldn't either, because he's a professional.'

McCullough raised his eyebrows and stared at him, with a trace of mockery in his eyes. 'And here was me believing,' he chuckled, 'that cops' greatest weakness is that they have no imagination.'

'I'm not a cop any longer,' Skinner replied. 'I was always a bit more than that anyway. None of that is imagination; it's a logical conclusion. It fits you too, Cameron. I have you sussed as a guy who'd always wait outside while the bad stuff was being done. It's part of the reason why you've been Teflon all these years: you had that fearsome reputation, and secretly you liked it, I'll bet, but inside you were just a wee bit Chicken Little, afraid that the sky would fall on you. The manner of Thomson's death fits that to a T.'

'You believe that and you're just going to let it lie? You? The mighty, incorruptible Bob Skinner?'

'Yes, I am, as much as I fucking hate it. But,' he added, 'only because it's unproveable, and because Bright's already confessed to killing Thomson, being done beyond redemption for Coats and Montell. It would fit my scenario if he's been incentivised by whatever you're going to pay his sister.'

He turned his attention back to his glass.

'I could, of course,' he murmured, 'tell the whole story to my editor at the *Saltire* and let her use her judgement on whether to run it or not. She's a brave woman, June, so she would . . . and I doubt that a defamation action would follow. Man, you've spent decades building your reputation, but it would be gone in the time it took your bankers and business associates to read the *Saltire* article.'

'So fuck off and do it!' McCullough shouted, anger fuelling his bravado.

'I'm prepared to,' Skinner said, 'but before we get there we have one more thing to discuss.' He paused. 'Cameron, it would be nice to think that your granddaughter might never get to hear of her brother, of how he was treated and what happened to him, but I fear it's inevitable that she will. There's one person who would tell her, if ever she feels guilty enough or, more likely, vindictive enough . . . and that I can well imagine. It's probably a miracle she hasn't done it already.'

'You're talking about Inez.'

'Exactly. So you see, Cheeky has to be told, and I reckon that if you want your relationship to survive, you should be the one to do the telling, rather than Sauce, or me, or my newspaper, if that's how this plays out. Are we agreed on that?'

'Yes,' McCullough said, quietly. 'Yes, we are. I'll tell her about her dad too; I might as well get it all over with. She'll explode, but she'll get over it eventually. She's as pragmatic as me in her own way.' He glowered at Skinner. 'Now are we done?'

'No, not quite,' he replied, 'because this goes along with it: it absolutely sticks in my throat that your daughter should walk away from three murders. In fact, I can't allow it.'

'Jesus, are you asking me to kill her?' he exclaimed.

'Don't be daft, man,' Skinner laughed, 'I'm not a barbarian. Just listen, will you: the only thing I don't believe about this business is that you knew that Bright would use an accomplice, even less that you knew who it would be. You proved that to me a few minutes ago, by the way you reacted when I told you about the car.'

McCullough sat silent, waiting.

'What I haven't told you yet,' he continued, 'is that forensics recovered a viable DNA sample from the second firearm that was found at Bright's house, the Luger that killed Terry Coats. There's no match for it yet, but that's only because my friend Arthur Dorward hasn't compared it with the profile of Alan Mason and found that there's a maternal match. Whether I tell him to do that, or whether we run the *Saltire* story instead, that's down to you. So, Cameron, this is my question. Does Inez pay the price for your continuing good name, such as it is and will be? Does she go to jail for the murder of Terry Coats, and for Montell and Thomson?'

'Is this blackmail, Bob?' McCullough asked.

Skinner gazed at him, contemplating his feelings about the man. He knew that he was more than a legitimate businessman, but was he capable of such savagery? He was convinced that he had procured Coats' murder and, unknowingly, Montell's, but his vision of how Walter Thomson had died was no more than a theory, and he was much less sure of it than he had let McCullough believe.

'Hell, no,' he replied, quietly. 'It's only this. Most of your life's been a closed book, Cameron. Just this once, I need you to open it, and get your hands dirty, because it's the right thing to do. Well? Do I call Dorward?'

Grandpa McCullough drained his malt and nodded.

Evidence-Based Practice

Guest Editor

ALYCE A. SCHULTZ, RN, PhD, FAAN

NURSING CLINICS OF NORTH AMERICA

www.nursing.theclinics.com

Consulting Editor
SUZANNE S. PREVOST, RN, PhD, COI

March 2009 • Volume 44 • Number 1

SAUNDERS an imprint of ELSEVIER, Inc.

W.B. SAUNDERS COMPANY

A Division of Elsevier Inc.

1600 John F. Kennedy Blvd., Suite 1800 ● Philadelphia, PA 19103-2899

http://www.theclinics.com

NURSING CLINICS OF NORTH AMERICA Volume 44, Number 1
March 2009 ISSN 0029-6465, ISBN-13: 978-1-4377-0508-9, ISBN-10: 1-4377-0508-1

Editor: Katie Hartner
Developmental Editor: Theresa Collier

Nursing Clinics of North America (ISSN 0029-6465) is published quarterly by Elsevier Inc., 360 Park Avenue South, New York, NY 10010-1710. Months of issue are March, June, September, and December. Business and Editorial Offices: 1600 John F. Kennedy Blvd., Suite 1800, Philadelphia, PA 19103-2899. Periodicals postage paid at New York, NY and additional mailing offices. Subscription price per year is, $133.00 (US individuals), $273.00 (US institutions), $228.00 (international individuals), $334.00 (international institutions), $184.00 (Canadian individuals), $334.00 (Canadian institutions), $70.00 (US students), and $115.00 (international students). To receive student/resident rate, orders must be accompanied by name of affiliated institution, date of term, and the signature of program/residency coordinator on institution letterhead. Orders will be billed at individual rate until proof of status is received. Foreign air speed delivery is included in all *Clinics* subscription prices. All prices are subject to change without notice. **POSTMASTER:** Send address changes to *Nursing Clinics*, Elsevier Periodicals Customer Service, 11830 Westline Industrial Drive, St. Louis, MO 63146. **Customer Service: 1-800-654-2452 (US). From outside the United States, call 1-314-453-7041. Fax: 1-314-453-5170. E-mail: JournalsCustomerService-usa@elsevier.com** (for print support) and **JournalsOnlineSupport-usa @elsevier.com** (for online support).

Nursing Clinics of North America is covered in *EMBASE/Excerpta Medica, MEDLINE/PubMed (Index Medicus), Social Sciences Citation Index, Current Contents, ASCA, Cumulative Index to Nursing, RNdex Top 100,* and Allied Health Literature and International Nursing Index (INI).

Printed in the United States of America.

Contributors

CONSULTING EDITOR

SUZANNE S. PREVOST, RN, PhD, COI
Associate Dean, Practice and Community Engagement, University of Kentucky,
Lexington, Kentucky

GUEST EDITOR

ALYCE A. SCHULTZ, RN, PhD, FAAN
President, EBP Concepts, Alyce A. Schultz & Associates, LLC, Chandler, Arizona

AUTHORS

REBECCA ALLEGRETTO, RN, BSN
Clinical Nurse Coordinator, Thoracic Surgery, Ronald Reagan University of California
Los Angeles Medical Center, Los Angeles, California

JACQUELINE J. ANDERSON, MSN, RN
Director, Nursing Programs Quality, Division of Nursing, The University of Texas MD
Anderson Cancer Center, Houston, Texas; and Former Director, Nursing Research,
St. Luke's Episcopal Hospital, Houston, Texas

RENEE APPLEBY, RN
Unit Director, Cardiothoracic Surgery Unit, Department of Nursing, Ronald Reagan
University of California Los Angeles Medical Center, Los Angeles, California

JAQUELINE M. ATTLESEY-PRIES, MS, RN
Nurse Administrator, Nursing Practice Resource Division, Department of Nursing,
Mayo Clinic Rochester, Rochester, Minnesota

KAREN BALAKAS, PhD, RN, CNE
Associate Professor, Goldfarb School of Nursing at Barnes-Jewish College,
St. Louis, Missouri

DORA BRADLEY, PhD, RN-BC
Vice President, Nursing Professional Development, Baylor Health Care System,
Corporate Office of Chief Nursing Officer, Dallas, Texas

KATHERINE BRADY-SCHLUTTNER, MS, RN-BC
Nursing Education Specialist and Assistant Professor, Education and Professional
Development Division, Department of Nursing, Mayo Clinic Rochester, Rochester,
Minnesota

BARBARA B. BREWER, PhD, RN, MALS, MBA
Director of Professional Practice, John C. Lincoln North Mountain Hospital, Phoenix,
Arizona

MELANIE A. BREWER, DNSc, RN, FNP-BC
Director, Nursing Research, Scottsdale Healthcare, Scottsdale, Arizona

M. KATHLEEN BREWER, PhD, ARNP, BC
Associate Professor, University of Kansas School of Nursing, Kansas City, Kansas

KAREN BURKETT, MS, RN, CNP
Evidence-Based Practice Mentor, Center for Professional Excellence-Research and Evidence-Based Practice, Cincinnati Children's Hospital Medical Center, Cincinnati, Ohio

PAULETTE BURNS, PhD, RN
Dean, Harris College of Nursing and Health Sciences, Texas Christian University, Fort Worth, Texas

SUE CULLEN, RN, MSN
Director of Education, Education Department, Acadia Hospital, Bangor, Maine

JOHN F. DIXON, MSN, RN, CNA, BC
Nurse Researcher and Interim Director, BUMC Center for Nursing Education and Research, Baylor University Medical Center, Dallas, Texas

SUE ELLIS-HERMANSEN, RN, MS
President, Omicron Xi Chapter At-Large, Sigma Theta Tau International Honor Society; and Director of Learning Resource Center/Lecturer, School of Nursing, University of Maine, Orono, Maine

DOREEN K. FRUSTI, MSN, MS, RN
Chair, Department of Nursing; and Co-Director, NQF Scholars Program, Department of Nursing, Mayo Clinic Rochester, Rochester, Minnesota

PAULETTE GALLANT, RN, MSN, CNL
Clinical Nurse Leader, Maine Medical Center, Portland, Maine

ANNA GAWLINSKI, RN, DNSc, CS-ACNP
Director of Evidence-Based Practice, Department of Nursing, Ronald Reagan University of California Los Angeles Medical Center; and Adjunct Professor, University of California Los Angeles School of Nursing, Los Angeles, California

MARCELLINE R. HARRIS, PhD, RN
Nurse Administrator/Nurse Researcher, NQF Scholars Program Director, Division of Nursing Informatics and Nursing Health Sciences Research, Department of Nursing, Mayo Clinic Rochester, Rochester, Minnesota

BARBARA HIGGINS, RNC, PhD
Chair of Nursing, Department of Nursing, Husson College, Bangor, Maine

CYNTHIA HONESS, RN, MSN, CCRN, ACNS-BC
Cardiology Clinical Nurse Specialist, Center for Clinical and Professional Development, Department of Nursing, Maine Medical Center, Portland, Maine

KATHLEEN KEANE, RN BSN, CCRN
Clinical Nurse II, Cardiothoracic Intensive Care Unit, Maine Medical Center, Portland, Maine

KELLY LANCASTER, RN, BSN, CAPA
Maine Medical Center, Scarborough Surgery Center, Scarborough, Maine

PHYLLIS LAWLOR-KLEAN, RNC, MS, APN/CNS
Advanced Practice Nurse, Neonatal Intensive Care Unit, Advocate Christ Medical Center/Hope Children's Hospital, Oak Lawn, Illinois

CHERYL A. LEFAIVER, PhD, RN
Professional Nurse Researcher, Advocate Christ Medical Center/Hope Children's Hospital, Oak Lawn, Illinois

CHERYL N. LINDY, PhD, RN-BC, NEA-BC
Director, Nursing and Patient Education and Research; and Magnet Project Director, St. Luke's Episcopal Hospital, Houston, Texas

GINA LONG, DNSc, RN
Director of Nursing Research, Division of Nursing, Mayo Clinic College of Medicine, Mayo Clinic Arizona, Mayo Clinic Hospital, Phoenix, Arizona

LISA ENGLISH LONG, MSN, RN, CNS
Director, Evidence-Based Practice, Center for Professional Excellence-Research and Evidence-Based Practice, Cincinnati Children's Hospital Medical Center, Cincinnati, Ohio

JUNE MARSHALL, RN, MS, NEA-BC
Director, Center for Nurse Excellence, Medical City Hospital, Dallas, Texas

SUSAN McGEE, MSN, RN, CNP
Evidence-Based Practice Mentor, Center for Professional Excellence-Research and Evidence-Based Practice, Cincinnati Children's Hospital Medical Center, Cincinnati, Ohio

PAMELA S. MILLER, RN, PhD(c), ACNP, CNS
Doctoral Candidate, University of California Los Angeles School of Nursing, Los Angeles, California

MARILYN MOKRACEK, MSN, RN, CCRN, NE-BC
Nurse Manager, Neurosciences Services; and Chair, Best Practice Council, St. Luke's Episcopal Hospital, Houston, Texas

CAROL MULVENON, MS, RN-BC, AOCN
Clinical Nurse Specialist, Pain Management, Palliative Care, Oncology, St. Joseph Medical Center, Kansas City, Missouri

JULIE NEUMANN, MS, RN
Nursing Education Specialist and Instructor, Education and Professional Development Division, Department of Nursing, Mayo Clinic Rochester, Rochester, Minnesota

MARIANNE OLSON, PhD, RN
Evidence-Based Practice Specialist, Nursing Research and Evidence-Based Practice Division, Department of Nursing, Mayo Clinic Rochester, Rochester, Minnesota

JOE ONG, RN, BSN
Staff Nurse Evidence-Based Practice Fellow, Clinical Nurse III, Cardiothoracic Surgery Unit, Department of Nursing, Ronald Reagan University of California Los Angeles Medical Center, Los Angeles, California

DORRIN PATILLO, RN-B
Director of Staff Education, Education Department, Dorothea Dix Psychiatric Center, Bangor, Maine

TERI BRITT PIPE, PhD, RN
Director of Nursing Research; and Associate Professor, Division of Nursing, Mayo Clinic College of Medicine, Mayo Clinic Arizona, Mayo Clinic Hospital, Phoenix, Arizona

PATRICIA POTTER, PhD, RN, FAAN
Research Scientist, Siteman Cancer Center at Barnes-Jewish Hospital at Washington University Medical Center, St. Louis, Missouri

ELIZABETH PRATT, MSN, RN, ACNS-BC
Clinical Nurse Specialist, Barnes-Jewish Hospital, St. Louis, Missouri

GAIL REA, PhD, RN, CNE
Professor, Goldfarb School of Nursing at Barnes-Jewish College, St. Louis, Missouri

SARINA ROCHE, RNC, DNSc
Director of Nursing, Department of Nursing, Eastern Maine Community College, Bangor, Maine

CINDY SCHERB, PhD, RN
Clinical Nurse Researcher, Nursing Research Division, Department of Nursing, Mayo Clinic Rochester, Rochester, Minnesota

ALYCE A. SCHULTZ, PhD, RN, FAAN
President, EBP Concepts, Alyce A. Schultz & Associates, LLC, Chandler, Arizona

JEAN SMITH, RNC, BSN, MSN (c)
Manager of Clinical Operations, Neonatal Intensive Care Unit, Advocate Christ Medical Center/Hope Children's Hospital, Oak Lawn, Illinois

ANN E. SOSSONG, RN, PhD
Associate Professor/Undergraduate Coordinator, School of Nursing, University of Maine, Orono, Maine

ALANNA STETSON, RN, BSN, BC
Staff Developer, Education and Training Center, Eastern Maine Medical Center, Eastern Maine Healthcare, Brewer, Maine

J. WAYNE STREET, RN
Director, Trauma Center, Luther Midelfort, Eau Claire, Wisconsin

TANIA D. STROUT, RN, BSN, MS
Associate Director of Research, Maine Medical Center, Department of Emergency Medicine, Portland, Maine

PAULA THERIAULT, RN, MBA
Director of Education, Education Department, St. Joseph Hospital, Bangor, Maine

JANE A. TIMM, MS, RN
Informatics Nurse Specialist/NQF Scholars Project Manager, Nursing Research Division, Department of Nursing, Mayo Clinic Rochester, Rochester, Minnesota

SHARON TUCKER, PhD, RN
Nurse Administrator/Clinical Nurse Researcher, Nursing Research Division, Department of Nursing, Mayo Clinic Rochester, Rochester, Minnesota

WENDY TUZIK MICEK, PhD, RN
Director of Nursing Research and Professional Development, Advocate Christ Medical Center/Hope Children's Hospital, Oak Lawn, Illinois

DIANE TWEDELL, DNP, RN
Nurse Administrator, Education and Professional Development Division, Department of Nursing, Mayo Clinic Rochester, Rochester, Minnesota

LAURA WASZAK, RN
Nurse Clinician II, Neonatal Intensive Care Unit, Advocate Christ Medical Center/Hope Children's Hospital, Oak Lawn, Illinois

SUSAN MACE WEEKS, MS, RN, CNS-P/MH, LMFT, LCDC
Director, Center for Evidence-Based Practice and Research, Texas Christian University, Fort Worth, Texas

ROSANNA WELLING, RN, BSN, MBA
Clinical Operations Assistant, Neonatal Intensive Care Unit, Advocate Christ Medical Center/Hope Children's Hospital, Oak Lawn, Illinois

JENNIFER WILLIAMS, MSN, RN, ACNS-BC, CEN, CCRN
Clinical Nurse Specialist, Barnes-Jewish Hospital, St. Louis, Missouri

Contents

Preface   xv

Alyce A. Schultz

Unique Partnership and Collaborative Arrangements

**Evidence Equals Excellence: The Application of an Evidence-Based
Practice Model in an Academic Medical Center**   1

Karen Balakas, Patricia Potter, Elizabeth Pratt, Gail Rea,
and Jennifer Williams

> An evidence-based practice (EBP) program that is designed to develop
> mentors in both clinical and academic settings has the potential for trans-
> forming a health care organization. This article describes an innovative
> program, Evidence Equals Excellence, which consists of two components:
> a clinical practice component for health care clinicians and an academic
> program for baccalaureate and graduate nursing students. The develop-
> ment of EBP mentors creates a core group of clinicians who can assist fel-
> low staff members apply evidence at the bedside. An academic program
> prepares new graduates to partner easily with clinical mentors to support
> and initiate successful practice changes.

**A Collaborative Approach to Building the Capacity for Research and
Evidence-Based Practice in Community Hospitals**   11

Barbara B. Brewer, Melanie A. Brewer, and Alyce A. Schultz

> The use of best evidence to support nursing practice and the generation of
> new knowledge to use in practice are hallmarks of excellence. Nurses at
> the bedside, however, often lack the resources and knowledge necessary
> to change the traditional nursing culture to one in which the use of evi-
> dence is incorporated into daily care. This article describes the experience
> in two hospitals using a program designed to give nurses the skills needed
> to engage in evidence-based care.

**Development of an Evidence-Based Practice and Research Collaborative
Among Urban Hospitals**   27

Susan Mace Weeks, June Marshall, and Paulette Burns

> This article describes the development of an evidence-based practice and
> research collaborative among urban hospitals. The collaborative began as
> a mechanism to support the incorporation of evidence-based practice and
> research in the acute care practice setting. This article discusses the

development of the collaborative, as well as the challenges, success, and future goals from both the academic and practice perspectives.

Renewing the Spirit of Nursing: Embracing Evidence-Based Practice in a Rural State   33

Ann E. Sossong, Sue Cullen, Paula Theriault, Alanna Stetson, Barbara Higgins, Sarina Roche, Sue Ellis-Hermansen, and Dorrin Patillo

> A group of nursing leaders from several organizations in the central and northern regions of the state established the Maine Nursing Practice Consortium (MNPC). The MNPC has created educational opportunities through workshops that assist nurses with the development and implementation of evidence-based practice (EBP) in rural Maine. Through collaboration and consultation with EBP leaders, members have ignited a spirit of inquiry and gained the support of nurses from varied backgrounds to engage actively in EBP initiatives. This article briefly summarizes the process of establishing these collaborative partnerships, describes some of the outcomes from the workshops, and describes the organizational and individual commitment that was essential to the work.

Implementing a Health System–Wide Evidence-Based Practice Educational Program to Reach Nurses with Various Levels of Experience and Educational Preparation   43

Teri Britt Pipe, Jane A. Timm, Marcelline R. Harris, Doreen K. Frusti, Sharon Tucker, Jaqueline M. Attlesey-Pries, Katherine Brady-Schluttner, Julie Neumann, J. Wayne Street, Diane Twedell, Marianne Olson, Gina Long, and Cindy Scherb

> This article describes a system-wide evidence-based practice (EBP) educational initiative implemented with a geographically, educationally, and clinically diverse group of nurses with the intent of increasing their EBP skill set and efficacy as local change agents and leaders. The overall scope of the larger National Quality Forum Scholar Program is described, and then the focus is narrowed to describe the EBP components of the initiative with case examples and lessons learned.

Evidence-Based Practice at the Point-of-Care

Promotion of Safe Outcomes: Incorporating Evidence into Policies and Procedures   57

Lisa English Long, Karen Burkett, and Susan McGee

> This article describes the process of incorporating evidence into policies and procedures, resulting in the establishment of evidence as a basis for

safe practice. The process described includes use of the Rosswurm and Larrabee model for change to evidence-based practice. The model guided the work of evidence-based practice mentors in developing a template, system, and educational plan for dissemination of evidence-based policies and procedures into patient care.

Staff Nurses Creating Safe Passage with Evidence-Based Practice 71

Dora Bradley and John F. Dixon

Patient safety is one of the most critical issues for health care today. The escalating need to decrease preventable complications serves as a significant catalyst to identify and use evidence-based practice (EBP) at the bedside. Decreasing preventable complications requires a synergistic relationship between the nurses at the bedside and nursing leadership. This article presents an overview of the concepts and the specific structures and processes used at Baylor Health Care System to increase the use of EBP and improve patient safety.

A Nursing Quality Program Driven by Evidence-Based Practice 83

Jacqueline J. Anderson, Marilyn Mokracek, and Cheryl N. Lindy

St. Luke's Episcopal Hospital in Houston established a best-practice council as a strategy to link nursing quality to evidence-based practice. Replacing a system based on reporting quality control and compliance, this Best Practice Council formed interdisciplinary teams, charged them each with a quality issue, and directed them to change practice as needed under the guidance of the St. Luke's Episcopal Hospital Evidence Based Practice Model. This article reviews the activities of the Best Practice Council and the projects of teams assigned to study best practice in (1) preventing bloodstream infection (related to central lines), (2) preventing patient falls, (3) assessing and preventing pressure ulcers, and (4) ensuring good hand-off communication.

Development and Implementation of an Inductive Model for Evidence-Based Practice: A Grassroots Approach for Building Evidence-Based Practice Capacity in Staff Nurses 93

Tania D. Strout, Kelly Lancaster, and Alyce A. Schultz

Evidence-based practice (EBP) is an essential component of the development of nursing science and has importance for today's clinical nurses. It benefits patients, organizations, and the nursing discipline, as well as having personal and professional benefits for individual clinicians. As interest in EBP has grown, so has the need for educational programs designed to develop the scholarly skills of the nursing workforce. The Clinical Scholar Model is one grassroots approach to developing a cadre of clinical nurses who have the EBP and research skills necessary in today's demanding health care delivery environments.

Effect of a Preoperative Instructional Digital Video Disc on Patient Knowledge and Preparedness for Engaging in Postoperative Care Activities   103

Joe Ong, Pamela S. Miller, Renee Appleby, Rebecca Allegretto, and Anna Gawlinski

This project determined the effects of developing and implementing a pre-operative instructional digital video disc (DVD) on patients' level of knowledge, preparedness, and perceived ability to participate in postoperative care activities. Content areas that were incorporated into the preoperative instructional DVD included: pain management, surgical drainage, vital signs, incentive spirometry, cough and deep breathe, chest physiotherapy, anti-embolism stockings/sequential compression device, ambulation, diet/bowel activity/urine output, and discharge. A system was created to ensure that patients consistently received the preoperative instructional DVD prior to surgery. The instructional media product was found to be effective in increasing pre-operative knowledge and preparedness of patients and their families. Nurses reported higher levels of knowledge and engagement among patients and their families related to postoperative activities.

The Clinical Scholar Model: Evidence-Based Practice at the Bedside   117

Cynthia Honess, Paulette Gallant, and Kathleen Keane

The Clinical Scholar Model serves as an effective framework for investigating and implementing evidence-based practice (EBP) changes by direct care providers. The model guides one in identifying problems and issues, key stakeholders, and the need for practice changes. It provides a framework to critique and synthesize the external and internal evidence. Three EBP projects conducted at a large tertiary care facility in northern New England illustrate the process of using the Clinical Scholar Model.

Using Evidence to Improve Care for the Vulnerable Neonatal Population   131

Cheryl A. Lefaiver, Phyllis Lawlor-Klean, Rosanna Welling, Jean Smith, Laura Waszak, and Wendy Tuzik Micek

The facilitation of evidence-based practice (EBP) in the clinical setting is important to ensure patients receive the best care possible. This article highlights changes in open visitation and feeding readiness practices that occurred in a Magnet-designated facility neonatal ICU. The examples demonstrate ways to bring evidence to the bedside within an environment that supports EBP at all levels of nursing leadership.

From the Bedside to the Boardroom: Resuscitating the Use of Nursing Research　　**145**

Carol Mulvenon and M. Kathleen Brewer

　　This article describes the process used by a multi-institutional organization to engage nurses in using and conducting nursing research using the Clinical Scholar Model. The challenges faced on the journey to engage nurses in questioning their practice and searching for answers are highlighted. Key resources necessary for a successful outcome are identified.

Index　　**153**

FORTHCOMING ISSUES

June 2009
Long-Term Care
Linda Dumas, PhD, RN, ANP,
Guest Editor

September 2009
**Legal and Ethical Issues: To Know,
To Reason, To Act**
Dana Bjarnason, RN, MA, CNA, PhD
and Michele A. Carter, PhD, RN,
Guest Editors

December 2009
Women's Health
Ellen Olshansky, DNSc, RNC, FAAN,
Guest Editor

RECENT ISSUES

December 2008
**Technology: The Interface to Nursing
Educational Informatics**
Elizabeth E. Weiner, PhD, RN-BC, FAAN,
Guest Editor

September 2008
Vulnerable Populations
Marcia Stanhope, RN, DSN, FAAN,
Lisa M. Turner, MSN, APRN, BC,
and Peggy Riley, RN, MSN,
Guest Editors

June 2008
Oncology Nursing: Past, Present, and Future
Marilyn Frank-Stromborg, MS, EdD, JD, FAAN,
and Judith Johnson, PhD, RN, FAAN,
Guest Editors

THE CLINICS ARE NOW AVAILABLE ONLINE!

Access your subscription at:
www.theclinics.com

Preface

Alyce A. Schultz, RN, PhD, FAAN
Guest Editor

Over 150 years ago, Florence Nightingale taught us that one of the most important practical lessons we can give student nurses is to always observe: teaching them what to observe; how to observe; and which symptoms are important for indicating improvement, decline, or neglect. She further instructed that as nurses, we should not spend our time collecting voluminous amounts of data that we do not use to improve the care we provide to our patients and that handwashing prevents the spread of infection.[1] How can we still be struggling with using our keen observation skills to improve care, collecting data that we do not use and spending millions of dollars attempting to sustain the evidence-based practice of handwashing?

If you have ever attempted to execute practice changes in your setting, particularly if the changes required support from multiple disciplines and administration, you know how complicated and challenging implementing evidence-based practice can be. Critique and synthesis of a body of research literature and changes in practice that are dramatic changes from the traditional way of care further challenge change efforts. In an effort to implement short-term solutions, quick fixes are put into practice, with practices steeped in tradition or "the way we have always done things." Senge and colleagues[2] directed us to pay more attention to long-term solutions with our practice issues, using programs that promote a sustainable change, creating and sustaining a learning environment in which point-of-care providers have the resources and knowledge necessary to improve patient outcomes through the use of best evidence. Building the capacity for evidence-based practice at the point-of-care provides a long-term solution to changing patterns of thinking and providing evidence-based care.

Medicine is often credited with the initiation of evidence-based practice; yet, in the mid- to late 1970s, researchers at Western Institute of Collegiate Education in Nursing (WICHEN) studied barriers to the use of research in nursing practice, the same barriers we find today. The Conduct and Utilization of Research in Nursing project examined the research evidence supporting or changing the care we were providing and published 10 practices that had sufficient scientific evidence. The definition for using research in practice at that point in time was research utilization. Concurrently, Dr. Archie Cochrane admonished his fellow physicians for their lack of research

Nurs Clin N Am 44 (2009) xv–xvii
doi:10.1016/j.cnur.2008.10.011
0029-6465/08/$ – see front matter © 2009 Elsevier Inc. All rights reserved.

utilization in guiding their practice decisions. In the 1990s, Sackett and colleagues expanded thinking for incorporating more sources of evidence than just research findings in making clinical decisions regarding care. The Institute of Medicine's landmark reports *To Err Is Human* and *Crossing the Quality Chasm: A New Health System for the 21st Century* brought a new awareness to the important decision-making issues of quality and safety facing patients and clinicians alike in our complex health care system.[3] Building on the 3 decades of work in nursing and medicine, the thrust from regulatory and credentialing agencies, and the nationwide efforts to build centers of nursing excellence supported by the Magnet Recognition Program from the American Nurses Credentialing Center, evidence-based health care has become the mantra for managing and changing our practice in the twenty-first century.

Use of the best evidence to support nursing practice and the generation of new knowledge to use in practice are the hallmarks of excellence across the nation and the globe. Yet, studies continue to find that nurses at the bedside are limited in the resources and knowledge necessary to change the traditional nursing culture to one in which the use of evidence is incorporated into daily care.[4] In the hectic world of today's nurse, finding the time to explore clinical and administrative questions systematically often takes a back seat to ever increasing demands of patient care and the work environment. This issue provides a wide array of examples representing the current thinking in and the efforts for establishing evidence-based health care, with continual improvement of patient outcomes.

The issue is organized around two themes, although, as you are likely to note in your reading, there is overlap between and among the articles. The first theme offers a multiplicity of unique partnerships and collaborative efforts used to facilitate evidence-based practice within educational and service settings. The articles within this section describe a unique program within a large academic medical center that addresses nursing education and nursing practice, one example of various joint agreements between an academic institution and clinical settings with multiple benefits, two collaborative strategies among multiple academic centers and multiple health care facilities (one in an urban setting and one in a rural setting), and, finally, a unique Web-based program used by a large multisite health care system to meet the needs of its staff in multiple geographic sites.

The second theme provides a rich collection of point-of-care exemplars. These exemplars include a template for planning and implementing strategies for evidence-based policies and procedures and a synergistic professional practice model that incorporates evidence-based practice and a nursing quality model that drives evidence-based care. Examples of the background on clinical questions, the search and synthesis of the evidence, and improvements in patient outcomes provide evidence-based ideas for use in other settings or opportunities for replication projects addressing important, relevant, common practice issues in a diversity of patient populations. This section concludes with a reflective article on challenges and opportunities in implementing the conduct of research and the use of evidence throughout a nursing department in a health care system.

Several models and frameworks for promoting and sustaining evidence-based practice are available for guidance on your journey toward improvement in patient care based on the best evidence. The articles in this section provide you with the references for a diverse group of models that can be used and further tested by individuals and small groups in addition to organizational models that can facilitate assessing and changing the larger work environment. Clearly, one model does not fit all organizations and all work settings or units. Selection of a model based on your workforce mix and resources is an important initial step in creating and sustaining a work environment in which the spirit of inquiry thrives and the best available evidence is incorporated into daily decisions for health care.

Almost 30 years ago, at a conference sponsored by the WICHEN entitled "Promoting Nursing Research as a Staff Nursing Function," Dr. Janelle Krueger declared that if research were ever to be valued and used, staff nurses must know how to read and conduct research studies because they are the individuals who know the important clinical questions. Dr. Krueger went on to say there would never be enough doctorally prepared nurses at the bedside to ask the questions. My own journey into creating an environment in which direct care providers would have the knowledge and support needed to conduct their own research and utilize these scientific findings, along with their expert knowledge, was sparked by her words. It is indeed an honor to bring you an issue packed with the knowledge transfer work of nurse educators, administrators, advanced practice nurses, and bedside staff.

It has been a privilege to serve as the guest editor of this timely issue on evidence-based practice. Building the capacity for evidence-based practice at the point of care provides a long-term solution to changing patterns of thinking through promotion of the use of evidence and generation of new knowledge. Sustaining a learning environment in which point-of-care providers have the resources and knowledge necessary to improve patient outcomes through the use of best evidence requires unique partnerships with academic programs and within and among health care systems. Nursing leadership must be knowledgeable and support the resources needed in the future work environment. I hope that this issue provides you with many ideas for the future.

Alyce A. Schultz, RN, PhD, FAAN
EBP Concepts
Alyce A. Schultz & Associates, LLC
5747 West Drake Court
Chandler, AZ 85226

E-mail address:
alyceaschultz@gmail.com

REFERENCES

1. Nightingale F. Notes on nursing: what it is, and what it is not. New York: D. Appleton and Company; 1898. Available at: http://www.gutenberg.org/etext/12439. Accessed July 24, 2008.
2. Senge P, Kleiner A, Roberts C, et al. The dance of change: the challenges of sustaining momentum in learning organizations. New York: Doubleday; 1999.
3. Committee on the Quality of Health Care in America, Institute of Medicine. Crossing the quality chasm: a new health system for the 21st century. Washington, DC: National Academies Press; 2001.
4. Pravikoff DS, Tanner AB, Pierce ST. Readiness of US nurses for evidence-based practice. Am J Nurs 2005;105:40–51.

Evidence Equals Excellence: The Application of an Evidence-Based Practice Model in an Academic Medical Center

Karen Balakas, PhD, RN, CNE[a], Patricia Potter, PhD, RN, FAAN[b],*,
Elizabeth Pratt, MSN, RN, ACNS-BC[c], Gail Rea, PhD, RN, CNE[a],
Jennifer Williams, MSN, RN, ACNS-BC, CEN, CCRN[c]

KEYWORDS

• Clinical • Education • Evidence-based practice • Mentoring
• Practice change

Within today's health care environment, there are numerous initiatives for health care organizations to adopt evidence-based practice (EBP) as a framework for the ongoing development and improvement of clinical practice. EBP is a problem-solving approach to clinical practice that integrates the conscientious use of best evidence in combination with a clinician's expertise and patient preferences and values in making decisions about patient care.[1,2] Patient safety and economic initiatives have triggered efforts at adopting EBP models within health care organizations to reduce patient injury, control costs, and improve the quality of patient care. Accrediting agencies such as The Joint Commission and credentialing programs such as the Magnet Recognition Program have incorporated research and EBP as underlying themes necessary for organizations to ensure health care excellence. In two quality-related reports, the Institute of Medicine[3] emphasized the importance of applying EBP to ensure the use of best practices and improve the education of health care professionals.[4]

[a] Goldfarb School of Nursing at Barnes-Jewish College, Mailstop 9060697, 4483 Duncan Avenue, St. Louis, MO 63110, USA
[b] Siteman Cancer Center at Barnes-Jewish Hospital at Washington University School of Medicine, Box 8100, 660 S. Euclid, St. Louis, MO 63110, USA
[c] Barnes-Jewish Hospital, Mailstop 9059360, 1 Barnes-Jewish Hospital Plaza, St. Louis, MO 63110, USA
* Corresponding author.
E-mail address: pap1212@bjc.org (P. Potter).

Nurs Clin N Am 44 (2009) 1–10
doi:10.1016/j.cnur.2008.10.001
0029-6465/08/$ – see front matter © 2009 Elsevier Inc. All rights reserved.

EVIDENCE-BASED PRACTICE IN AN ACADEMIC SETTING

In a large academic medical center, various levels of bureaucracy and associated decision processes often make change difficult. To implement an EBP program with promise of permanence, EBP must become part of the cultural fabric of an organization. An EBP program that is designed to develop mentors in both clinical and academic settings has the potential for transforming a health care organization. The EBP program at Barnes-Jewish Hospital at Washington University Medical Center and the Goldfarb School of Nursing at Barnes-Jewish College is innovative. The program, Evidence Equals Excellence (EEE), focuses on the education and mentoring of clinicians and nursing students to foster a level of clinical inquiry needed to make EBP a philosophy of clinical practice.

Barnes-Jewish Hospital at Washington University Medical Center is an academic teaching hospital licensed for 1200 beds. The hospital enjoys a long relationship with the Goldfarb School of Nursing at Barnes-Jewish College. The hospital also has a long-standing involvement in nursing research, and the school of nursing faculty routinely has partnered with the hospital in research and educational programs. In the fall of 2005, an EBP team of clinicians, faculty, and a nursing research scientist developed EEE, a unique EBP program. The program has two components: a clinical practice component for health care clinicians and an academic program for baccalaureate and graduate nursing students. The EBP model used in the EEE program is adapted from the Advancing Research and Clinical Practice through Close Collaboration model created by Melnyk and Fineout-Overholt[2,5] at Arizona State University. The goal of the EEE program is to develop evidence-based practice mentors and clinicians who are equipped to lead the effort in using evidence to improve nursing practice.

DEVELOPING THE EVIDENCE EQUALS EXCELLENCE PROGRAM

The impetus for the EEE program began when team members attended the Arizona State University's EBP mentorship program, a 5-day immersion program designed to prepare organizational leaders and mentors in changing organizational cultures through the promotion, implementation, and sustainability of EBP. The strength of the Arizona State model for EBP lies in its adaptability to any health care organizational structure. It does not require a major change in an organization's infrastructure.

At Barnes-Jewish Hospital, a shared governance model is in place with unit practice committees on each nursing unit (many are multidisciplinary) and a central practice committee that meets monthly. The hospital also has a large presence of advanced practice nurses who, when trained on EBP principles, provide a solid staff resource for making practice changes. With a sound infrastructure in place, the EEE program prepares mentors who then can assist staff in making practice changes relatively quickly.

Members of the EEE team quickly became champions of EBP principles, an important characteristic needed to guide the EBP process for an organization.[6] The team had a vision: to develop an EBP program for the hospital and school that can generate clinical EBP mentors who champion practice changes at the nursing unit level. From the beginning, the EEE team was committed to making its work both fun and challenging. Among the five members were clinicians, educators, previous managers and directors of nursing, and researchers. The variety of talent contributed to lively planning meetings and a continuous source of ideas necessary to make the program relevant and current. The EEE program is always changing because of the new ideas team members offer for program, course, and individual mentor development.

The Clinical Program

The clinical practice component consists of a 2-day multidisciplinary seminar for mentors, a semiannual refresher program for mentors, and a 4-hour class (the Champions Class) for clinicians. The team members are the faculty for the program and a library scientist from Washington University.

Two-day seminar

The 2-day seminar is structured along the six-step model from the Arizona State University program (**Box 1**). An introduction to EBP is followed by individual lectures and group work on each of the six steps (**Box 2**). The seminar is highly participative. Before the seminar, participants are asked to submit clinical questions regarding their area of interest so that faculty can integrate questions relevant to participants in the appropriate presentations. For example, participants spend 2 hours learning how to develop clinical questions, using a population of interest/intervention of interest/comparative intervention/outcome (PICO) format. Questions framed in a PICO format improve success in obtaining relevant articles during a literature search. During the seminar participants have the opportunity to rephrase their own questions as well as those of their colleagues. The aim of this exercise is to help participants develop questions that will lead to EBP projects on their work units.

A particularly popular presentation in the seminar is "Searching the Literature." A library scientist uses participant questions to demonstrate literature searches. Using popular databases such as PubMed, MEDLINE, the Cumulative Index to Nursing and Allied Health Literature (CINAHL), and the Cochrane Library, participants learn advanced search techniques that prepare them to search the literature for the best scientific evidence. In everyday clinical practice, it is imperative for an EBP mentor to be able to retrieve a few relevant articles that pertain to a clinical question or problem. The advanced search techniques include approaches in using search limits and search filters and tips on navigating different databases.

The seminar also includes presentations on research methods and on critiquing the evidence that give participants the opportunity, through group work, to recognize different study designs in the literature and how to review journal articles. The group process expedites the review, gives the participants experience in working within a group to review articles, and helps participants realize that most clinicians need help in appraising research articles. Participants receive copies of critical appraisal guidelines (developed by Melnyk and Fineout-Overholt) for the different types of research (eg, randomized, controlled trials or quasi-experimental or qualitative studies).

In the presentation on "How to Make Evidence Work at the Bedside," a faculty member, who is one of the clinical specialists, shares stories about actual EBP

Box 1
The six steps of evidence-based practice

1. Ask a burning clinical question
2. Collect the best evidence
3. Review the evidence critically
4. Integrate the evidence
5. Evaluate outcomes
6. Communicate results

Box 2
Outline for the Evidence Equals Excellence seminar

Day 1

Evidence-based practice: the path to excellence

Developing PICO questions

Research designs

Searching the literature for evidence

Laboratory practice: searching evidence

Day 2

Appraisal of the evidence

Being a change agent for EBP

Panel of EBP mentors

Outcomes measurement

Making EBP work at the bedside

---

programs implemented by her unit mentors. The seminar also includes a panel presentation by previous mentors, who discuss ongoing projects and share stories of their experiences in implementing EBP. These two presentations are very popular because they allow the participants to hear stories from past mentors about actual EBP projects, the challenges and barriers to implementation, and the approaches that result in successful implementation.

Refresher program

To date more than 100 nurses, social workers, respiratory therapists, and radiology technologists have attended the EEE seminars. A series of semiannual refresher programs keeps the mentors informed about current EBP activities and opportunities. These programs are valuable in giving mentors time to discuss strategies for work-unit implementation. Mentors discuss ongoing projects, the approaches used to involve staff, and project outcomes. Frequently mentors share ideas that have relevant applications for other units attempting similar projects. For example, several units have introduced hourly nurse rounds as an EBP fall-prevention project. The approaches for improving staff compliance with a rounding protocol on one unit can be useful for staff on other units as well.

The champions class

An abbreviated version of the EEE seminar was designed to educate bedside clinicians who are unable to commit to a mentoring role. After identifying the critical components from the 2-day EEE seminar, the two clinical nurse specialists on the EEE team coordinated the Champions Class. They encourage proficient staff from all disciplines to attend. Shift changes dictate the scheduling of classes, and attendees request specific dates amenable to staffing schedules. The class commences with an overview of EBP, emphasizing the knowledge explosion in nursing and the initiatives leading to a mandate of EBP. The class highlights the basics of EBP and prepares staff to become competent in EBP language, to partner with mentors, and to support best-practice implementation.

The EEE team recognizes the need for change agents to create a culture of EBP. Duck's Change Curve Model shows that group change requires individual change, and the greater the number of individuals involved, the more difficult effecting change will be.[7] Thus, hospital mentors require multiple champions to support their belief in the value of applying EBP and their initiatives in doing so.

Staff members are eager to implement best practices but may be overwhelmed by the thought of conducting a literature search and appraising the studies. Changing the hospital's culture to one that envelops EBP requires support and enthusiasm from clinicians at all levels. The EEE team asks mentors who graduate from the seminar to recruit expert staff members from their work units to attend the 3-hour Champions Class. Through the Champions Class, the program prepares a considerable number of caregivers who learn to understand the significance of searching for and using best evidence in practice. Ploeg and colleagues[8] highlighted 10 published studies that focused on facilitators and barriers to implementing best practice. The authors noted that one of the most common themes was the presence of change champions. The involvement of bedside clinicians is critical to change the environment to one that embraces clinical inquiry or the questioning and evaluating of best practices.

The Champions Class adapts content for relevance to the participants' clinical backgrounds, and the clinical nurse specialists encourage interactive discussion of traditional but not necessarily evidence-based practices that are ingrained in the hospital. As in the mentor seminar, the participants submit clinical questions before the class. The faculty discusses how to establish a culture of clinical inquiry by asking relevant clinical questions. The faculty then assists the participants in formulating their questions using the PICO format. Staff with little research experience report that they have difficulty searching the literature. Structuring their questions in the PICO format helps the participants outline their clinical question clearly and simplifies the search. The participants are most engaged when the discussion leads to the identification of practice issues and how they can use EBP to improve clinical outcomes.

Conducting the Champions Class has led the faculty to recognize that nurses are seeking a guide that will help them make decisions that are accurate and timely to apply evidence in the practice setting.[9] The class ends with an emphasis on working with the EBP mentors and resources available in the hospital. The clinical nurse specialists encourage participants to access the EBP intranet Web site, which provides staff with the steps of EBP, links to search engines, and EBP mentors and their ongoing projects.

Successful implementation of an EBP practice culture relies heavily on knowledge and belief in the value of EBP. More than 50 staff members representing the disciplines of nursing, respiratory therapy, and social work have attended the Champions Class to date. These EBP advocates have been involved in numerous projects throughout the hospital. Champions participate in journal clubs and quality improvement initiatives identified through their unit practice committees. Examples of projects by mentors and champions include the implementation of bedside reporting, a new tube-feeding protocol, fall-prevention rounds, and family presence during resuscitation efforts. As more disciplines participate in the class, participants are able to share their applications of best practice and encourage others to employ these changes in their work areas. Most importantly, participants learn the EBP language and promote discussion of why they choose specific practices. Participants become engaged in applying research and are able to communicate effectively with other disciplines, notably physicians. An educated staff increases scholarly discussions and elevates professionalism among the disciplines.

The Academic Program

During the past decade there has been a paradigm shift in teaching from a traditional nursing curriculum to one that supports and prepares nurses to practice in an evidence-based environment.[10–12] Following the Institute of Medicine's Quality Chasm series,[3] the Health Professions Educational Summit[13] identified five core competencies that all educators need to address within a curriculum:

Providing patient-centered care
Working in interdisciplinary teams
Employing EBP
Applying quality improvement
Using informatics

Many schools have responded to this mandate and incorporated EBP into their programs. It is far easier, however, to talk about the need to teach EBP than it is actually to accomplish the task.

Across the country, research courses have been revised to address the steps of EBP,[14–16] and additional courses have been developed to support further student development in the use of EBP.[15,17,18] Informatics courses are invaluable in helping students learn to search the literature effectively and in introducing databases such as The Cochrane Library (which contains four databases), CINAHL, MEDLINE, and PubMed. Clinical decision making relies on the ability to access and appraise research results; thus, education in how to find the best available evidence is critical for EBP. Some research courses teach students how to construct an evidence-based analysis and may incorporate a journal club to help teach appraisal skills.[10,18] Courses with a clinical component frequently incorporate assignments that include creating an answerable PICO question, requiring students to search the literature to find an answer, and communicating their findings.[15]

In the fall of 2005, the hospital and college collaborated in sponsoring a conference on EBP and invited Drs. Melnyk and Fineout-Overholt from Arizona State University. The hospital recently had achieved Magnet status and was working with the college to promote baccalaureate education among the nursing staff. As part of that initiative, the hospital was preparing to fund the education of 200 nurses. Following the conference, a special workshop was facilitated by the speakers for the Goldfarb School of Nursing faculty to learn how to incorporate EBP into a curriculum. The faculty on the EEE team elected to help lead the effort to revise the Registered Nurse/Bachelor of Science in Nursing (RN-BSN) curriculum to incorporate EBP for a new cohort of nurses from the hospital who would be taking the program in an online format.

The faculty and clinicians on the EEE team collaborated to explore ways to engage RN-BSN graduates in EBP upon completion of their academic program. Because the graduates would be learning the essential skills necessary for EBP, changes would have to be made in the hospital environment so the graduates could have the opportunity to apply their knowledge and continue to practice evidence-based nursing. This partnership of educators and clinicians, through the EEE program, has promoted change within the hospital with the development of EBP mentors and champions. The ultimate goal of the academic program is to partner new graduates with unit-based EBP mentors to support and initiate successful practice changes.

Initially, EBP was incorporated fully into the school's online RN-BSN curriculum. Although faculty had brought the curriculum outline back from the immersion workshop at Arizona State University, the faculty as a whole worked to develop each of the courses. Faculty divided into teams and applied the concepts learned in previous workshops with the guidance of faculty mentors. As students begin the program, they are introduced to change theory and models for EBP. Assignments within the beginning courses focus on the construction of PICO questions and how to search the literature effectively. The nursing research course is positioned early in the curriculum to emphasize the steps of EBP and to help students learn how to appraise studies critically. In the course, students develop a PICO question and then construct an evidence-based analysis to arrive at an answer. In subsequent nursing courses, students are challenged to begin projects within their work setting to illustrate EBP. For example, students have created PICO question boxes on their units, developed posters to illustrate the steps of EBP, and participated in EBP projects with mentors who attended the EEE seminar.

The incorporation of EBP into the online curriculum generated positive feedback from students and faculty. As a result, each of the courses within the remaining baccalaureate programs has been redesigned with a new description, course outcomes, and assignments that support the development of EBP. Faculty members strive to create at least one assignment within each course that furthers understanding and application of EBP. Students develop PICO questions in each of the clinical courses and share the evidence they find to answer their questions with peers and the nursing staff on their practicum unit. During one of the semesters, students worked with managers from the community outreach department of a local pediatric hospital to determine whether the programs being offered in the community were evidence based. Students shared their findings with the hospital management and were able to see the impact of their analysis as changes were proposed for the programs.

The graduate program also was revised to emphasize EBP and the new role expectations for advanced-practice nurses. Students continue to develop PICO questions as they complete clinical hours and now are expected to use their findings to guide decision making at point of care. Students have revised clinical protocols, such as the guideline now used at a National Cancer Institute–designated cancer center for central venous catheter dressing changes in neutropenic patients. Some of the evidence-based analyses that students have completed have led to research studies on their units. For example, students were interested in the use of chewing gum to promote gastrointestinal motility in postoperative colorectal patients. They concluded that the evidence was not strong enough to support a practice change and now are conducting a study to confirm their findings.

Communicating the results is an important component of EBP and is part of the academic programs. Students have developed posters and papers that have been presented at local and statewide research conferences. Developing a poster and an abstract with an evidence-based analysis is an assignment in the graduate research course. The capstone project for the graduate program reflects the application of EBP and supports the student's role as an EBP mentor and change-agent upon graduation.

A CASE STUDY: MAKING EVIDENCE-BASED PRACTICE WORK AT THE BEDSIDE

EBP can be infused into the work culture of a hospital department in multiple ways. Strategies for implementation include developing policy and procedures, creating work teams focused on nursing interventions, integrating EBP concepts into employee performance expectations, and purposeful recruiting of new employees who are familiar with EBP concepts. Within the emergency department (ED), all these approaches have been embraced and used to enhance the nurse's role as an active and informed partner in patient care.

The policies and procedures in the ED are developed and reviewed annually for currency and relevance. As part of this process the procedure and references are verified using the PICO method to assure that all changes and updates are evidence based. An example of this practice involved the revision of the triage policy to include an alcohol screening by the nursing staff. Recent guidelines[19,20] demonstrated the value of including a brief alcohol consumption screen by the nurse and pairing it with a short intervention. This screen was added to the triage policy along with a list of resources for individuals who may be at risk for binge drinking or alcoholism. The nurse provides the list of resources to the patient upon completing the screen. The next step in this process will be the full implementation of the brief intervention by the nurse when a patient has a positive screening. A rewarding finding from this practice implementation has been seeing patients who screened positively for at-risk alcohol consumption and who were admitted later asking for assistance and resources. The initial screening seems to stimulate the conversation about alcohol use and to encourage at-risk individuals to consider assistance.

The value in demonstrating that nursing polices and practices are evidence based has created a culture in the department in which staff members routinely seek out the evidence that supports treatment decisions. All members of the treatment team are encouraged to inquire about the evidence supporting a practice, especially when nurses and physicians are discussing the plan of care. In addition, the physician residency program supports and encourages the use of EBP. The physicians host a monthly EBP journal club that all physicians and ED nursing staff are welcome to attend. The topics reflect ongoing developments in clinical practice, and the forum is used to explore new treatment approaches the department is considering adopting. This support has led to a practice environment that encourages open discussion and values the input from all team members.

The clinical nurse specialist in the ED, who is an EEE faculty member, developed a cadre of staff nurses in both formal and informal leadership roles as EBP mentors. Ten direct-care nursing staff members have attended the EEE seminar in the past 2 years. As this group formed, they began to develop unit-specific patient care questions and, as a team, used the tools they had acquired at the workshop. The team began by identifying a single practice question: what is the evidence to support a practice change for supported family presence during medical resuscitation? The group reviewed the current literature and developed a consensus document in support of the practice. The team determined that family presence should be implemented in the ED and then sought administrative support. Providing the nursing and physician leadership with an evidence-based position statement facilitated the formal implementation of the program. The ED EBP team then identified the opportunity to develop the project into a formal research study regarding the staff beliefs about the practice of family presence. After seeking Human Studies Committee approval, the team distributed the pre-implementation survey and used the results to develop and expand the education and training plan. A post-implementation survey was distributed 6 months after the initial survey to evaluate whether changes had occurred in the department. Statistically significant improvement ($P < .05$) in staff members' willingness to have family present at the bedside during resuscitation or invasive procedures was achieved.

The changes regarding family presence are an excellent example of the impact of EBP in patient care. The group continues to grow and address other concerns in the department including skin care, the effective use of capnography, and the use of noninvasive technology to assess tissue oxygenation and stroke volume. The team communicates their findings to the department via posters, monthly newsletters, e-mail, and through the unit practice committee.

The ED EBP team members participate actively on specific disease process–focused committees within the department. As members of those core clinical practice treatment teams, they are able to represent the larger nursing staff and can address issues brought forward using an EBP approach. Examples of clinical practice teams that benefit from this input are the acute stroke tissue plasminogen activator reperfusion team, acute myocardial treatment team, pneumonia treatment team, and sepsis treatment team. Focusing the teams on an EBP framework has streamlined and standardized care among the large numbers of nursing and physician staff, resulting in positive patient outcomes that have been sustained over time.

Approaching recruitment and retention through an EBP model also has led to changes. Potential candidates for the ED are assessed to determine their level of familiarity with EBP concepts and how these concepts are related strategically to their position in the department. One successful example of this philosophy was the hire of a new graduate nurse who had attended the college's RN-BSN program that emphasized EBP. He had used EBP throughout his academic program to identify clinical patient care issues and address the appropriate nursing interventions with evidence support. Once graduated, he actively sought a department that would embrace excellent clinical nursing practice and incorporate evidence into its care structure. Consequently, he chose the ED. During his first year as a nurse in the ED, he became involved in the use of evidence-based protocols for the management of the patients who had suffered an acute myocardial infarction and of septic patients. He was able to identify multiple opportunities to develop and implement EBP as they relate to fall prevention in the ED and is redesigning the current standards. He will attend the EEE mentorship workshop in the future to develop further his literature searching strategies and to focus his clinical practice questions.

Actively engaging the staff in the practice of EBP has implications for retention.[21,22] As part of the performance appraisal process, employees in the ED receive feedback on their individual performance in relation to the core clinical practice measures. Meeting those measures is a role expectation in the unit. The nurses report that they feel a sense of ownership of the EBP process and subsequent practice changes. Promoting a sense of autonomy has decreased the staff turnover and created a positive environment.

SUMMARY

The application of EBP within a large, academic medical center requires an infrastructure to support practice change as well as the development of clinicians and students who become adept at using EBP principles. The partnering of clinicians and academic faculty in developing an EBP program brings together multiple talents and perspectives to create a program that is innovative, dynamic, and diverse. The EEE program has been successful in preparing clinicians to apply EBP principles and in creating an environment where they can successfully make changes to improve practice, quality of care, and patient and staff satisfaction.

ACKNOWLEDGMENT

The authors acknowledge the support of JoAnn O'Neill, RN, in the review of this article.

REFERENCES

1. Sackett DL, Straus SE, Richardson WS, et al. Evidence-based medicine: how to practice and teach EBM. London: Churchill Livingstone; 2000.
2. Melnyk BM, Fineout-Overholt E. Making the case for evidence-based practice. In: Melnyk BM, Fineout-Overholt E, editors. Evidence-based practice in nursing &

healthcare: a guide to best practice. Philadelphia: Lippincott, Williams & Wilkins; 2005. p. 3–24.

3. Institute of Medicine. Crossing the quality chasm: a new health system for the 21st century. Washington, DC: National Academy Press; 2001.

4. Greiner AA, Knebel E, editors. Health professions education: a bridge to quality. Washington, DC: National Academy Press; 2003.

5. Melnyk BM, Fineout-Overholt E. Consumer preferences and values as an integral key to evidence-based practice. Nurs Adm Q 2006;30(2):123–7.

6. Fineout-Overholt E, Levin RF, Melnyk BM. Strategies for advancing evidence-based practice in clinical settings. J N Y State Nurses Assoc 2005;35(2):28–32.

7. Duck JD. The change monster: the human forces that fuel or foil corporate transformation and change. New York: Crown Business; 2001.

8. Ploeg J, Davies B, Edwards N, et al. Factors influencing best-practice guideline implementation: lessons learned from administrators, nursing staff, and project leaders. Worldviews Evid Based Nurs 2007;4(4):210–9.

9. Newhouse R, Dearholt S, Poe S, et al. Evidence-based practice: a practical approach to implementation. J Nurs Adm 2005;35(1):35–40.

10. Burke L, Schlenk E, Sereika S, et al. Developing research competence to support evidence-based practice. J Prof Nurs 2005;21(6):358–63.

11. Callister L, Matsumura G, Lookinland S, et al. Inquiry in baccalaureate nursing education: fostering evidence-based practice. J Nurs Educ 2005;44(2):59–64.

12. Fineout-Overholt E, Johnson L. Teaching EBP: a challenge for educators in the 21st century. Worldviews Evid Based Nurs 2005;2(1):37–9.

13. Committee on the Health Professions Education Summit. Health professions education: a bridge to quality. Washington, DC: The National Academies Press; 2003. Available at: http://books.nap.edu/openbook.php?record_id=10681&;page=1. Accessed April 7, 2008.

14. Ciliska D. Educating for evidence-based practice. J Prof Nurs 2005;21(6):345–50.

15. Brancato V. An innovative clinical practicum to teach evidence-based practice. Nurse Educ 2006;31(5):195–9.

16. Ferguson L, Day R. Evidence-based nursing education: myth or reality? J Nurs Educ 2005;44(3):107–15.

17. Courey T, Benson-Soros J, Deemer K. The missing link: information literacy and evidence-based practice as a new challenge for nurse educators. Nurs Educ Perspect 2006;27(6):320–3.

18. Killeen M, Barnfather J. A successful teaching strategy for applying evidence-based practice. Nurse Educ 2005;30(3):127–32.

19. Academic ED SBIRT Research Collaborative. The impact of screening, brief intervention, and referral for treatment on emergency department patients' alcohol use. Ann Emerg Med 2007;50(6):699–710.

20. Desy PM, Perhats C. Alcohol screening, brief intervention, and referral in the emergency department: an implementation study. J Emerg Nurs 2008;34(1):11–9.

21. Beecroft PC, Dorey F, Wenten M. Turnover intention in new graduate nurses: a multivariate analysis. J Adv Nurs 2008;62(1):41–52.

22. Erenstein CF, McCaffrey BC. How healthcare work environments influence nurse retention. Holist Nurs Pract 2007;21(6):303–7.

A Collaborative Approach to Building the Capacity for Research and Evidence-Based Practice in Community Hospitals

Barbara B. Brewer, PhD, RN, MALS, MBA[a],*,
Melanie A. Brewer, DNSc, RN, FNP-BC[b], Alyce A. Schultz, RN, PhD, FAAN[c]

KEYWORDS

- Evidence-based practice • Models • Staff nurses

The use of best evidence to support nursing practice and the generation of new knowledge to use in practice are the hallmarks of excellence across the nation and the globe. Studies, however, continue to find that nurses at the bedside are limited in the resources and knowledge necessary to change the traditional nursing culture to one in which the use of evidence is incorporated into daily care.[1]

In the hectic world of today's nurse, the time needed to explore clinical and administrative questions systematically often is usurped by the ever-increasing demands of patient care and the work environment. In an effort to implement short-term solutions, quick fixes are put into practice as nurses focus on the "domain of action," continuing with traditional and multiple patterns of practice or, alternately, using a single article or hearsay to change practice, rather than focusing on the "domain of enduring change" by creating changes in attitudes and beliefs (eg, learning skills necessary to make organizational changes).[2] Creating and sustaining a learning environment in which point-of-care providers have the resources and knowledge necessary to improve patient outcomes through the use of best evidence focuses on the domain of enduring

[a] John C. Lincoln North Mountain Hospital, 250 E. Dunlap Avenue, Phoenix, AZ 85020, USA
[b] Nursing Research, Scottsdale Healthcare, 9003 E. Shea Boulevard, Scottsdale, AZ 85260, USA
[c] EBP Concepts, Alyce A. Schultz & Associates, LLC, 5747 W. Drake Court, Chandler, AZ 85226, USA
* Corresponding author.
E-mail address: barbara.brewer@jcl.com (B.B. Brewer).

Nurs Clin N Am 44 (2009) 11–25
doi:10.1016/j.cnur.2008.10.003
0029-6465/08/$ – see front matter © 2009 Elsevier Inc. All rights reserved.

change. Building the capacity and skills for evidence-based practice (EBP) at the point of care provides a long-term solution to changing patterns of thinking and promotes evidence-based care.

In its first 12 years of existence, a unique program designed to build the research capacity of point-of-care providers resulted in 16 publications co-authored by staff nurses, more than 40 posters, and 50 paper and symposium presentations at local, regional, national, and international conferences by staff nurses, recognition by nine professional nursing societies, including the Innovation in Clinical Excellence award from Sigma Theta Tau International and *Nursing Spectrum*, and three internal and four external grants.[3] The Clinical Scholarship resource paper first published by Sigma Theta Tau International in 1999 provided the overarching principles for the development of the Clinical Scholar Model (CSM) (**Fig. 1**).[4]

DEVELOPMENT OF THE CLINICAL SCHOLAR MODEL

The role of a clinically focused nurse researcher is to mentor nurses in the conduct and use of research and other forms of evidence. Since its inception in 1993, the clinical nursing research program at Maine Medical Center, a tertiary care hospital with more than 600 beds in northern New England, has promoted the professional growth of curious and creative direct-care nurses through education and mentorship by the nurse researcher on the conduct of research and the use of evidence in practice. Clinical nurses who already were asking clinical questions and wanting to change the way they currently were practicing were the first participants; they were eager to learn how to critique the research literature and integrate their findings to improve patient care. The practice of research utilization evolved to incorporating all forms of evidence when determining changes in nursing practice. The definition of EBP, adapted from the work of Stetler,[5] as used in the program, was

> the interdisciplinary approach to health care practice that bases decisions and practice strategies on the best available evidence including research findings, quality improvement data, clinical expertise, and patient values; considering feasibility, risk or harm, and costs.

External evidence is provided by empiric studies. Internal evidence may be data from quality improvement projects, program evaluations, satisfaction surveys, risk management, and other sources. These data are integrated and synthesized through the lens of clinical experts and are applied based on patient and family values and preferences. In nursing, implementing and sustaining EBP usually requires an organizational change and always requires the support and flexibility of management.

Clinical Scholar Model
Promoting the Spirit of Inquiry

- *Observe & Reflect*
  - *Analyze*
    - *Synthesize*
      - *Apply and Evaluate*
        - *Disseminate*

Fig. 1. The Clinical Scholar Model. (*Data from* STTI Resource Paper, 1999; and *Courtesy of* Alyce A. Schultz, RN, PhD, FAAN, Chandler, AZ.)

The CSM is an inductive model for mentoring point-of-care providers in the conduct of research and the implementation of evidence, diffusing EBP into the culture, and creating an organizational change in the work environment. The clinical questions are conceived by nurses at the bedside; using their questions as the context, the nurses are taught to find, critique, synthesize, and implement the evidence into their practice. The CSM facilitates responsibility and accountability for all nurses to base their care on evidence. It is decentralized, is predicated on "building a community of EBP mentors at the bedside," and fully supports the notion that for research to be translated into practice effectively, it must be read, understood, and valued by the direct-care provider.

Clinical scholarship promotes changing one's way of thinking from a task orientation to one of inquiry, reflection, and critical thinking.[4] Clinical scholarship does not mean that nurses must always be conducting research and publishing their findings, but it does mean that nurses must always be questioning their practice. Accordingly, clinical proficiency is not the same as clinical scholarship: performing a task consistently based on a written procedure does not make it scholarly unless the nurse questions whether the procedure needs to be performed in the first place.[4] Clinical scholars are innovators, the "out-of-the-box" thinkers who are always questioning their practice and who use their knowledge and the research to provide, teach, and manage patient care, based on knowledge rather than the rules. They seek information from multiple sources, continuously look for new sources of knowledge, and reflect on this information in planning the most effective care. They never stop asking "why?" They recognize that although their years of experience provide expertise in their area, there always is new information on the horizon, and that new information must be synthesized with the traditional ways of performing care.

Clinical scholarship requires strong skills in observation, analysis of varying forms of data, synthesis of the data/findings from all sources of evidence, application and evaluation of the synthesized results in practice, and dissemination of the information and sharing it with others so that the efforts are not duplicated needlessly in similar practice arenas. Each of these areas of the CSM was used to develop and refine the Clinical Scholar Program.

THE CLINICAL SCHOLAR PROGRAM

The Clinical Scholar Program is based on the CSM. The program is a series of six or seven workshops designed to build the capacity of nurses and other point-of-care providers in conducting research and in using research and other forms of evidence in practice.

Observation and Reflection

By using observation and reflection in their daily work, point-of-care providers can recognize patient responses to treatment and the cues that suggest that current practice is not effective. By cultivating these observational skills, Clinical scholars move beyond just observation to asking the important clinical questions. Other prompts that might generate researchable clinical questions include changes in quality outcome or risk management data, scorecard reports, knowledge shared by a new staff member, new knowledge learned at a conference, family concerns about a particular patient's response to a nursing or interdisciplinary intervention, or new regulatory requirements for reducing nurse-sensitive patient outcomes. Ultimately, the question is written in the population of interest/intervention of interest/comparative intervention/outcome (PICO) format. The scholar then completes a library search for articles addressing the intervention/innovation, outcomes, or both.

Analysis and Critique

The scholars learn to critique the various types of research designs, including qualitative studies, quantitative studies, and meta-analyses. The important components of a study are put into an evaluation table, including, if appropriate, the statistical outcomes that relate to the intervention or outcome of interest. It is important to be able to differentiate quickly between published articles that are and are not research. The purpose of this learning is to prepare the scholars to synthesize all the evidence later and determine its strength to support practice changes. These workshops include methods of searching for and evaluating published guidelines and systematic reviews. The scholars also begin the process of identifying sources of internal data for baseline data collection and ultimately for monitoring continuous improvement of outcomes.

Synthesis of the Evidence

Synthesis of the internal and external evidence is critical in determining whether the evidence is strong enough to change practice without increasing risk or harm to the patients, to improve outcomes without significantly increasing the costs of care, and to determine the feasibility of implementation in the practice setting. The strength of the evidence is determined through amalgamation of the study designs, the statistical and clinical relevance of the findings, the quality of study methods, and the consistency of the results across studies. The findings are put in synthesis tables that clearly show the reliability of study outcomes based on similar interventions. Multiple synthesis tables may be required to answer a single clinical question, depending on how interventions have been applied and outcomes have been defined.

Application and Evaluation

The synthesized results are used to develop or change a clinical guideline, policy, procedure, or pathway. Throughout the process, attention is paid to team development, team membership, and consideration of challenges that may inhibit implementation of the new ideas. In this phase of the CSM, a pilot implementation plan is developed that addresses the need to educate nonmembers of the project or study team, to plan for systematic data collection, and to assure fidelity of the intervention. Outcome data form the basis for adopting the new practice throughout a facility or system, for discarding the new practice, or for adapting and re-evaluating the practice further before adoption.

Dissemination

A research study or an evidence-based practice change is not complete until the results have been disseminated to a professional audience, either through presentation, publication, or both. The last workshop addresses writing an abstract for poster or podium presentation, followed by a day of presentations to the administrators and other point-of-care providers in the facility. The projects and studies are presented at their point of progress.

THE FIRST CLINICAL SCHOLAR PROGRAM

The first Clinical Scholar Program was conducted in at Maine Medical Center by a cadre of 10 staff nurse and clinical nurse specialist innovators who had worked with the model explicitly and implicitly for almost a decade. Fifty nurses started the six-part series, and 45 nurses (90%) completed the program. Fourteen clinically focused projects were developed. Of these 14 projects, 10 were completed, and eight have been presented at local, regional, national, and international conferences. One nurse was recognized for her study by the American Nephrology Nurses Association in 2005. All the original Clinical Scholar facilitators have completed a master's degree or currently are enrolled in a graduate program.

Collaboration, Cooperation, and Accomplishments

The Clinical Scholar Program is the format for EBP and research fellowships in multiple settings. The successes and challenges in a community hospital and a freestanding pediatric hospital are described here.

Building Evidence-Based Practice Capacity in a Community Hospital

John C. Lincoln North Mountain Hospital (JCLNMH) is a 266-bed community hospital with a Level I trauma center. It was the first hospital in Phoenix, AZ to receive Magnet designation. The hospital is part of a health network containing two hospitals, physician practices, and a longstanding mission to the community, demonstrated through multiple social and health services incorporated in the Desert Mission, which is the social service division of the network.

Nursing leadership began building its capacity for EBP as part of its Magnet journey. Evidence was incorporated into policies, procedures, and protocols, but many still contained textbook references and manufacturer guidelines as their only sources of evidence. Additionally, there were minimal levels of nursing research and quality improvement activities. Many nurses were long tenured in the organization and had received their nursing education more than a decade earlier. As a result, there was confusion regarding the components of EBP and minimal, if any, experience using computer-based databases for locating relevant literature.

Leadership recognized that transforming the organizational culture to embrace evidence as a way of informing daily patient care would require further knowledge and skill development in the nursing staff, accessibility to evidence resources at the point of care, and the commitment of financial resources in the form of dedicated time for study and project work. Furthermore, leadership recognized the need to accelerate the pace for transformation to build a cadre of nurses who could help to promote and implement research and EBP.

Recognition of the need to accelerate the pace of transformation was not enough to change practice. Moving forward was limited by the educational level of the nursing staff, which primarily was at the associate degree level. Only 30% of direct-care nurses were prepared at the baccalaureate level. Many of the nurses had been educated before the advent of computer-based databases. As a result, nurses had limited skills in searching, critiquing, and synthesizing literature. Few of the nursing staff were prepared at the master's level, so it was not possible to mentor less-skilled staff by drawing on internal expertise. The staff members who held master's degrees held managerial and educational positions.

Creative partnerships
Building capacity for EBP in bedside nurses requires individual skill development as well as leadership and an organizational culture that promotes and supports its

use.[6] Melnyk[7] suggests that once excitement about learning and applying new skills related to EBP wanes, the presence of mentors may support sustainability of EBP within an organization. Nursing leadership at JCLNMH was committed to improving nursing staff skills in EBP. Building skills and providing staff support fell within the responsibilities of the director of professional practice, who was a doctorally prepared nurse researcher. The director, newly hired in mid-2005, was accountable for nursing research, EBP, and oversight of the Magnet program. She had the skills to find and evaluate evidence for practice and was comfortable providing content to staff nurses. She felt a sense of urgency to accelerate the transformation of the culture from tradition based to evidence based. As a result, she thought it prudent to find a model that could be used to define the curriculum and reduce the time needed for content development. The JCLNMH was fortunate to be located near a university with faculty who were internationally known for their expertise in EBP; therefore she investigated options for adjunct faculty opportunities while learning more about potential resources and support from the university.

Faculty at Arizona State University had developed two EBP models, Advancing Research and Clinical Practice through Close Collaboration (ARCC) and the CSM, both of which are built on mentors who facilitate the diffusion of EBP through an organization. A major difference between the two models is that Melnyk and Fineout-Overholt's ARCC model uses advanced-practice nurses as mentors, whereas Schultz' Clinical Scholar Model uses bedside nursing staff as mentors.[8] The CSM was better suited to the limited number of advanced-practice nurses within the JCLNMH.

About this time, an opportunity arose that facilitated the development of a creative partnership between the hospital and the university. The university recently had developed an EBP post-master's certificate program. One of the courses in the program was an online course in outcomes management, which was an area of expertise of the hospital's nurse researcher. A partnership was formed through which the hospital's nurse researcher taught the outcomes course for the university, and in exchange the university provided a series of workshops taught by a faculty member. The partnership was of benefit to both parties: the hospital enjoyed the university faculty's expertise, and the university enjoyed the expertise of the hospital's nurse researcher, without exchanging money. The nurse researcher invited the developer of the CSM to present information about projects completed by bedside nurses. Nurses who attended the presentation were excited. Many had questions, began thinking of ideas they could investigate, and wanted more information. Most of the individuals who composed the first cohort of scholars attended this session.

Developing content and setting expectations

Once the partnership had been established, the content, dates, and times for the workshops were developed jointly. Most of the workshops were based on the CSM, but content regarding change theory was added. Change theory was incorporated to provide tools nurses could use to introduce practice changes and obtain support for the practice changes from other staff. As noted earlier, these practice changes require organizational changes that many staff nurses never have orchestrated.

Once the dates and content for workshops had been determined, expectations for clinical scholars and nursing leadership were established. An EBP fellowship was established by the nurse researcher, who acted as the mentor for all fellows. In collaboration with members of the Clinical Research Committee, an application for the fellowship was developed that asked about the applicant's education level, exposure to EBP projects, and ideas for potential projects. Selection criteria for the fellowship also were discussed with members of the committee. Two selection criteria were recommended: all applicants must be in good disciplinary standing and must hold a minimum of a bachelor's degree. The goal was to begin with a cohort of 10 to 15 fellows.

Nurses interested in applying for the fellowship were given a list of the expectations they would be required to meet if selected. All fellows were expected to attend all workshops, to complete a project, and to submit an abstract to a conference. Nursing leadership had agreed to give each fellow 12 hours of paid release time during the pay period of the workshop. Fellows could use the time to attend the workshop and complete individual or group work on their projects. To date two cohorts of fellows have completed the Clinical Scholar series of workshops. The following sections summarize the experience for each cohort.

The first cohort
Information about the fellowship was shared with clinical directors, members of shared leadership, charge nurses, and through fliers distributed to all nursing units. Twenty-three staff nurses, clinical educators, and clinical directors completed applications. Ten of the applicants had earned a bachelor's or master's degree in nursing science, three held bachelor's degrees in areas other than nursing, one held a non-nursing master of science degree, and five held an associate degree in nursing. Four of the applicants who held an associate's degree were pursuing a bachelor's degree in nursing. Rather than turn away applicants who were excited about the possibility of developing new skills in EBP, all were accepted into the fellowship. Of the 23 accepted, 21 began the fellowship. Two nurses dropped out before the first session because they could not commit to attending all workshops. Nineteen nurses completed the series.

The fellows were from four hospital units: two critical care units, a medical unit, and a medical-surgical unit. Although unplanned, the limited number of units resulted in common project interests among the fellows, greater accessibility to discuss progress and ideas among themselves between workshops, and increased visibility on their units of the fellows' excitement in gaining new skills in clinical inquiry.

From the start, the fellows were full of enthusiasm for the new skills they were gaining. The energy levels during the workshops were palpable. With each workshop, the level of dialogue increased. Scholars discussed such things as the literature they were or were not finding, changes being made to their questions as they delved more deeply into the literature, their surprise regarding the limited availability of research for many of their topics, and the positive responses they were experiencing on their units as they shared what they were learning with the other staff. **Table 1** contains project information for the two cohorts that have completed Clinical Scholar workshops. Projects generally focused on improving care for patient populations admitted to the units represented by the fellows.

The second cohort
During the fall of 2007, fellowships began for the second cohort of scholars. Applications were distributed using the same process as with the first cohort. Interest continued to be high and resulted in 22 applications from staff nurses, clinical educators, and clinical directors. All applicants began the workshops; 18 completed the series. Fellows in the second cohort were from obstetrics, medical, medical-surgical, surgical, perioperative services, and critical care units. Unlike the first cohort, half of whom were critical care nurses, the second cohort contained only one critical care nurse. Educational levels were mixed; as happened in the first group, those who had had previous exposure to research courses or literature searches helped those who were less

Cohort	Specialty	Project
Table 1		
Summary of John C. Lincoln North Mountain Hospital clinical scholar program projects		
1	Critical care	Effect of ambient music versus headphones on stress in patients after coronary artery bypass graft
1	Critical care	Effect of chlorhexidine oral care on reducing ventilator associated pneumonia
1	Critical care	Use of an EBP protocol to standardize care and reduce pulmonary complications in patients after coronary artery bypass graft
1	Critical care	Understanding nurse barriers to using EBP protocols to reduce the prevalence of pressure ulcers in critical care patients
1	Medicine/surgery	Reducing falls in hospitalized patients
1	Medicine/surgery	Using Caring Theory to improve work environment for nurses
2	Medicine/surgery	Methods of cross-contamination of *Clostridium difficile* in hospitals
2	Medicine/surgery	Evidence-based smoking cessation intervention for nurses
2	Obstetrics	Using chart audits to change practice in nursing staff
2	Medicine/surgery	Reducing musculoskeletal injuries in nursing staff
2	Medicine/surgery	Effect of a centralized orientation unit on sense of belonging and satisfaction of new graduate nurses
2	Medicine/surgery	Predictors of readmission within 30 days of patients who have community-acquired pneumonia

experienced. To a person, regardless of educational level and prior experience, fellows reported that they learned new information from the workshops and felt much more confident about their skills.

Based on feedback received from the first cohort, changes were made in the spacing between workshops and the emphasis placed on some topics. Workshops for the first cohort were not spaced apart evenly but were spaced to allow more time for evaluating and synthesizing evidence. Two months were planned to provide balance with reading articles, work, and school schedules for many fellows. Participants recommended allowing less time in the future because they felt they lost momentum during the long interval between sessions. They also reported that they tended to leave homework until close to the next session, so having more time between sessions was not helpful. As with the first series, most of the workshops were taught by the faculty member, searching was taught by the hospital librarian, and change theory was taught by the hospital's nurse researcher, who served as the mentor for all projects.

Scholars from the first cohort served as support for the second group. They reported their experiences and the progress they were making on their projects. When the second cohort began meeting, projects from the first group were at different stages of maturity. In fact, projects ranged from being ready for institutional review board approval to a change in topic requiring beginning a new search for literature.

Challenges and solutions
One of the challenges faced with both cohorts was maintaining momentum between workshops. As stated earlier, some slowing of momentum was related to the length of the interval between workshops. Some was related to the inability of group members to schedule time to work together and the inherent frustration caused by scheduling

difficulties. As with any group, different members had different levels of energy for the project work and different levels of commitment involving other aspects in their lives, such as family or school assignments. Some groups were better able than others to find ways to work together productively.

Another challenge involved providing support for those who had steeper learning curves. Despite frequent offers by the nurse researcher to provide help to those who were having difficulty with searching, evaluating, or synthesizing literature, few individuals in the first cohort asked for help. As a result, time was not always used efficiently when groups did meet, and progress on projects slowed. In an attempt to avoid this situation with the second cohort, more structure was added to the fellowship. Project groups were asked to meet with the nurse researcher between workshops covering evaluation and synthesis of the literature and to review their evaluation and synthesis tables with the nurse researcher so problems could be identified and resolved in a more timely way.

The development of synthesis tables was difficult to master and problematic for all individuals in both cohorts. Fellows tended to summarize their evaluation tables rather than integrate them into a synthesis of all evidence. A technique that helped the second cohort clarify where there was misunderstanding was the use of workshop time to review preselected articles together. Attendees were asked to work within their groups to develop a synthesis table for each outcome addressed in the articles. They were asked to specify how each outcome was measured and to evaluate whether measurement was consistent across studies. They then were asked to synthesize the evidence for each outcome. Tables were reviewed as a group so everyone could see how to synthesize correctly the evidence provided in the articles. The exercise worked so well that the first cohort was scheduled for a "booster" workshop in which they repeated this process. Again, attendees found the exercise very useful in identifying where they did not understand how to distill information from multiple studies into a cogent recommendation for practice change based on the strength and quality of the evidence.

Group process issues plagued project teams in both cohorts. This program may have been the first time that some nurses had worked in this type of group situation. Some nurses were better than others in dealing with group conflicts and resolving issues among group members. Some groups were able to divide the work by assigning pieces to each group member; others believed each member should do each part. Based on the experiences of the first two cohorts, a workshop taught by experts in organizational development and containing content on group process, managing group conflict, assigning workload, and similar issues will be added to the next series of workshops.

Personal and organizational outcomes
Nurses who completed the series of workshops gained confidence in asking relevant clinical questions, searching literature for best evidence, critiquing research articles, critiquing systematic reviews and published guidelines, and synthesizing multiple sources of evidence on a topic. Many have stated that what they have learned has made them feel more empowered in their own practice and more confident of their ability to find answers to their questions. Some have incorporated information from internal evidence into the way they personally manage patients.[9]

As noted earlier, many of the participants were in school during the time they attended the Clinical Scholar workshops. One participant, who also was a member of the clinical research committee, decided to return to school to obtain her bachelor's degree because she was concerned that she would not be accepted to participate in the fellowship unless she did. She had ignored the recommendation of her nurse manager on multiple previous occasions but changed her mind once she feared she would miss the opportunity to be part of the fellowship.[10] Three members of the first cohort decided to return to school for master's degrees as a result of their participation in the fellowship. Several members of both cohorts currently are in school pursuing master's degrees.

As a condition of participation, fellows agreed to prepare and submit abstracts to conferences. To date, five abstracts have been submitted by fellows. Two were accepted for podium presentations at national conferences,[9,11] and three have been submitted for consideration for an upcoming conference. It was the first time any of the staff nurses had presented at a conference. Each year the hospital presents a series of exemplar awards to nurses during Nurses' Week. In 2007, one of the nurses selected for a podium presentation was recognized with the Student of the Year exemplar; in 2008, a different nurse presenter was recognized with the EBP and Research exemplar.

Organizational outcomes include multiple research and EBP projects that will improve patient outcomes and the work environment for nurses. A second outcome has been recognition of the investment the organization has made in its nursing staff. Information about the program and the experience of participants has been reported in *NurseWeek*, *American Nurse*, and at a national Magnet conference. Nursing leadership is proud of the accomplishments and will continue to invest in the program.

The Clinical Scholar Program in a Children's Hospital

In an effort to build capacity to deliver safe, high-quality health care to acutely ill infants and children, nursing leadership at Phoenix Children's Hospital, a 300-bed pediatric hospital, determined that a practical approach was needed to create an environment of evidence-based care (EBC). Executive leadership fully supported advancing evidence-based decision making in clinical practice across disciplines. The need to improve outcomes for patients and families was well recognized among bedside care providers, and several were eager to discover new strategies to improve care. Most bedside clinicians rarely accessed the available online library resources or contacted the medical librarian, however, and many were unaware of the existence of the medical library. The first step toward improving outcomes required educating bedside clinicians in finding and using the best available clinical and scientific evidence for practice.

Phoenix Children's Hospital recently had expanded from "a hospital within a hospital" to a freestanding 300-bed facility. Establishment of the nursing leadership team and of policies and guidelines for practice and the development of a complete staff for each unit were well underway. Approximately 23% of the nurses in the institution held a bachelor's degree or higher. These factors supported the need for EBC and also created challenges for implementation in a new facility.

During her faculty interview at a local university, an internationally recognized expert in EBP and the developer of the CSM presented "Creating the Spirit of Inquiry Using the Clinical Scholar Model." Her presentation and the discussion that followed resonated with bedside nurses and with the nursing leadership team. The CSM provided a framework for (1) educating nurses and other care providers to find, critically appraise, synthesize, implement, and evaluate the best evidence for practice, (2) conducting research when no evidence was available, which often is the case in pediatric and neonatal care, (3) disseminating findings, and (4) creating a cadre of mentors to encourage the spread of evidence-based skills and knowledge to improve outcomes.[3] Nursing leadership and bedside nurses chose the CSM as a roadmap to excellence for the care of children and their families.

Collaboration with university faculty

A collaborative partnership was established with a college of nursing at a local university to support implementation of the CSM. The partnership involved a joint appointment for three individuals (two nursing faculty from the university, each with 25% appointment at the hospital, and a faculty appointment for the hospital's nurse researcher at 50% time) to complete the one full-time nursing research position supported by the hospital. The faculty included the developer of the CSM and an expert in neonatal clinical care and research. In year two of the partnership, the neonatal faculty member accepted a faculty position out of state, and subsequently the partnership included one faculty member and the nurse researcher. The neonatal faculty member has continued to support projects at the hospital with neonatal nurses.

The joint appointment model was chosen to implement the CSM in this clinical environment for several reasons. Leadership at Phoenix Children's Hospital and at Arizona State University had begun to develop collaborative partnerships for advancing pediatric nursing education and for research. The Chief Nurse Executive for the hospital was enthusiastic about the opportunity to have an EBP expert as part of the nursing research team, and, with the Dean of the College of Nursing, established an agreement to exchange faculty time for teaching and mentored research opportunities for the nurse researcher, which would enhance further opportunities for bedside clinicians to participate in relevant clinical nursing research. Funding for one full-time equivalent position was paid to the university in exchange for the faculty collaboration.

Program implementation

The Clinical Scholars Program, based on the CSM, was initiated at the hospital in 2005. Information on the program was presented to all bedside clinicians (nurses, respiratory therapists, pharmacists, and other allied health providers) who held bachelor's or master's degrees. This decision was based on the assumption that persons with a bachelor's degree would have taken a research course and basic statistics. The EBP faculty member led the Clinical Scholars Program workshops at the hospital. All three program faculty met with new clinical scholars as they developed and implemented projects. The diverse backgrounds of the faculty supported the scholars in a variety of interest areas.

Scholar selection process

Initially, the selection of the scholars occurred through individual expression of interest via an e-mail to the nurse researcher with a signed statement of support from their unit manager. Participants were selected if they committed to attend each of the six workshops in addition to the time required to complete assignments following the workshop (eg, reading the articles, searching for evidence, conducting evidence appraisal and synthesis, participating in group discussion, and project development). The responsibility for requesting time away from clinical care to participate in each workshop and to complete assignments belonged to the individual scholar. Unfortunately, several participants missed workshops because of scheduling conflicts and lack of staff to cover bedside patient care needs. Additional time for team meetings and project development outside of the workshops was rarely possible.

The selection process has evolved with each successive workshop series to the current formal application process. The application, adapted from JCLNMH, includes (1) a description of the potential scholar's interest in and expected outcomes for participation in the program; (2) area of interest for an EBP project with inclusion of a PICO question; (3) a letter of support from the unit manager including confirmation of release time for workshop attendance and time required to work on the proposed project (8 hours of workshop participation and 4 hours of reading/review time); and (4) a statement signed by the participant confirming agreement to prepare for and attend all workshops. Potential scholars complete and submit the application packet for review by the faculty approximately 1 month before the beginning of the program. Selection is based on successful completion of the packet. Preference is given to applicants who have completed a bachelor's degree, but no applicant has been denied entry to the program because of educational level. The number of scholars in any workshop series is limited to 20.

Program mentors

Initially, five master's and one doctorally prepared nurse met with program faculty to discuss their role as mentors for the scholars. Each expressed interest in and commitment to helping facilitate the program and mentor bedside clinicians in the processes of EBP and research. Unfortunately, most were unable to participate in the program because of lack of available time away from their clinical roles. One neonatal nurse practitioner attended four of the workshops and, together with the other faculty, supported the development of a research study in the neonatal ICU (NICU).

The first workshop series

Scholars participating in the first series of workshops were from various disciplines and educational backgrounds, including associate's degree, bachelor's and master's prepared nurses, bachelor's prepared dieticians, associate's degree and master's prepared respiratory therapists, and a pharmacy intern. The clinical scholars worked in teams with shared interest areas whenever possible. The topic and PICO question chosen were negotiated among the group members. Of the initial 22 participants, 10 completed the program, including one dietician and nine nurses. Various reasons were given for lack of participation, but most were related to the requirements of their clinical roles. Specifically, the need to work overtime in the winter months, lack of staff coverage to enable participants to take the time away from the care unit, and last-minute schedule changes caused by colleagues' illness contributed to absenteeism.

The first series of seven all-day workshops were held semi-monthly. This format was based on previous experience with implementation of the Clinical Scholar Program at another hospital. The timeframe between workshops may have been too long to support momentum and interest, because most participants did not complete reading assignments or work together in their groups between sessions. Additionally, management support seemed to decrease between workshops. Communication with the scholars was challenging, because e-mail was not consistently available to all employees during this time.

Despite the challenges, the first series of workshops led to further discussion and awareness of the need for evidence to guide practice. Three scholars who completed the program presented posters or podium presentations at national symposia, and one presented at an international conference the next year. A randomized, controlled trial implemented by NICU staff and including the initial team of nurses, dieticians, and the neonatal faculty member, is still in progress. Other successes include the testimonials of the clinical scholars about their experiences in the program as they encouraged other staff to participate. Nursing leadership and management also noted motivation and additional interest among staff in asking clinical questions about their practice.

The second workshop series

The second workshop series differed from the first in several respects. Selection occurred through an application process, as described previously. Scholars in the second series were attending either a Registered Nurse-Bachelor of Science in Nursing program or a master's program with pediatric or neonatal nurse practitioner coursework. The timeframe between workshops was shortened to 6 weeks, and an additional workshop was held at the end of the series to assist scholars with abstract writing. Of the 18 scholars who began the program, 16 completed it. Although attendance during the second series was significantly better than in the first series, obtaining release time to complete reading assignments and work on projects with team members was still a challenge. Manager support for workshop participation and project development increased in most clinical areas but continued to lag in others.

After program completion, the clinical scholars continued to work on their projects. Two groups have initiated research studies, and three evidence-based projects have been initiated. Interest in conducting EBC has continued to escalate among scholars who have completed the program in terms of discussions with peers, in encouraging others to participate in the Clinical Scholars Program, and in searching for and using evidence to guide practice.

The third workshop series
The format of the third workshop series was seven 8-hour workshops held monthly with additional time for discussion of project development so that the scholars might share ideas and learn from the work of their colleagues. Most of the workshop content was didactic presentation and discussion regarding the principles and practice of finding, appraising, synthesizing, applying, and measuring the best available internal and external evidence. Preparation for project implementation, including presentation to the institutional review board by the scholars, was a key component. Of the 10 bedside nurses and nurse educators who began the program, 9 nurses recently completed it. The clinical scholars had baccalaureate degrees or currently were enrolled in a Registered Nurse-Bachelor of Science in Nursing program. **Table 2** summarizes examples of the projects initiated or completed by the clinical scholars for each series of workshops.

Program outcomes and conclusions
Through collaboration with Arizona State University and EBP experts, the Clinical Scholars Program has been successful in enhancing the use of evidence to guide practice at Phoenix Children's Hospital. In addition to improving outcomes for patients and families through the use of evidence in practice, those who have completed the program have begun to mentor others in beginning to question their current practice. The nurses and dietician who completed the program have graduated from bachelor's and master's programs, and two have been accepted in doctoral programs.

The clinical scholars have participated in events at the hospital to highlight program outcomes, including Nursing Grand Rounds and podium and poster presentations during Nurses' Week. In addition, scholars have submitted proposals and made presentations to the hospital institutional review board. One scholar now is participating in a national collaborative to study best practices related to risk assessment and prevention of falling. Scholars who have completed the program have initiated journal clubs (oncology and NICU), and nine have submitted or presented their work at regional, national, and international conferences. These presentations illustrate how bedside clinicians can use evidence and develop different ways of thinking and questioning clinical practice. The Clinical Scholars Program has been successful in leading the effort to change the delivery of clinical practice to enhance both the quality and safety of health care for children in the Southwest.

Table 2
Summary of Phoenix Children's Hospital clinical scholar program projects

Series	Specialty	Project
1	Neonatal	Effects of holding infants during gavage feeding
1	Medicine/surgery	Development of an evidence-based pediatric guideline for assessing risk and preventing falls
2	Airway	Evaluation of an evidence-based car seat challenge test for children on ventilators
2	Pediatric ICU	Evaluation of an evidence-based sedation protocol for critically ill children
2	Neonatal ICU	Evaluation of an evidence-based ventilator-associated pneumonia protocol
2	Emergency	Descriptive study of Zofran and oral fluid therapy for children who have acute gastroenteritis
2	Oncology	Implementation of a symptom management checklist for children with cancer
3	Oncology	Phenomenologic study of the educational experience of parents of children who have acute lymphocytic leukemia
3	Neonatal ICU	Evidence-based protocol for administering low dose medications in low birth weight infants
3	Oncology	Discussion of fertility options by oncology providers
3	Pulmonary	Outcomes of patient education
3	Emergency	Personal protective equipment compliance in the emergency department

CONCLUSIONS AND IMPLICATIONS FOR PRACTICE AND RESEARCH

Practicing as a clinical scholar distinguishes a job from a career in nursing. To sustain excellence, clinicians must be involved actively in the selection and collection of quality improvement data and the critique and synthesis of evidence. Collaboration among multiple disciplines is paramount for the decision making necessary for clinical research and EBP. Involvement in the Clinical Scholar Program has renewed the spirit of nursing. A translational research study is planned to evaluate the outcomes of the CSM as compared with the usual methods for promoting the spirit of inquiry.

ACKNOWLEDGMENT

The authors acknowledge the support of the Department of Nursing at Maine Medical Center, Portland, ME during the development and early implementation of the Clinical Scholar Model. The collaborative efforts in the community hospitals would not have been possible without the vision of the Dean at Arizona State University, College of Nursing and Healthcare Innovation, and the chief nurse executives, nursing managers, and nursing colleagues within the direct-care settings.

REFERENCES

1. Pravikoff DS, Tanner AB, Pierce ST. Readiness of U.S. nurses for evidence-based practice: many don't understand or value research and have had little or no training to help them find evidence on which to base their practice. Am J Nurs 2005; 105(9):40–52.

2. Senge PM. The fifth discipline: the art and practice of the learning organization. 1st edition. New York: Doubleday/Currency; 1990.
3. Schultz AA. Clinical scholars at the bedside: an EBP mentorship model for today. Excellence in Nursing Knowledge; 2005. p. 4–11.
4. Clinical scholarship task force: clinical scholarship resource paper. Available at: http://www.nursingsociety.org/aboutus/Documents/clinical_scholarship_paper.pdf. Accessed June 3, 2008.
5. Stetler CB. Updating the stetler model of research utilization to facilitate evidence-based practice. Nurs Outlook 2001;49(6):272–9.
6. Rycroft-Malone JO. Evidence-informed practice: from individual to context. J Nurs Manag 2008;16:404–8.
7. Melnyk BM. The evidence-based practice mentor: a promising strategy for implementing and sustaining EBP in healthcare systems. Worldviews of Evidence Based Nursing 2007;4:123–5.
8. Fineout-Overholt E, Melnyk BM, Schultz A. Transforming health care from the inside out: advancing evidence-based practice in the 21st century. J Prof Nurs 2005;21(6):335–44.
9. Alber D, Brewer BB, Berkley C, et al. 2008. Collection and analysis of fall risk characteristics in hospitalized adults. Presented at the Ninth Annual EBP Conference. Glendale (AZ), February 14, 2008.
10. Ratner T. Evidence-based practice 101. Available at: http://include.nurse.com/apps/pbcs.dll/article?AID=/20080114/SW02/80111033. Accessed May 30, 2008.
11. Brewer BB, Schultz AA, George N, et al. 2007. A community hospital's path to bedside nurse competence in EBP. Presented at the Eleventh National Magnet Conference. Atlanta (GA), October 5, 2007.

Development of an Evidence-Based Practice and Research Collaborative Among Urban Hospitals

Susan Mace Weeks, MS, RN, CNS-P/MH, LMFT, LCDC[a],*,
June Marshall, RN, MS, NEA-BC[b], Paulette Burns, PhD, RN[c]

KEYWORDS

- Evidence-based practice • Research • Collaboration
- Nursing research • Community partnerships

The Texas Christian University (TCU) Center for Evidence-Based Practice and Research (CEBPR) was established in the Harris College of Nursing and Health Sciences in June, 2006. Originally funded by an internal TCU grant, the CEBPR was developed as a point of connection between nursing faculty members and the clinical agencies where student practicum experiences occur. There was a growing focus on evidence-based practice and research occurring among the area hospitals, motivated largely by the hospitals' pursuit of the American Nurses Credentialing Center's Magnet designation. It was recognized that nursing faculty members had expertise in the areas of evidence-based practice and research that would be useful to hospitals focusing efforts in these realms.

One activity that occurred during the first year of the TCU CEBPR's existence was the sponsorship of an internationally recognized expert who has gained acclaim for her ability to engage direct-care nurses in both evidence-based practice and research. Dr. Alyce Schultz is known for her ability to create enthusiasm and commitment in the individuals to whom she speaks. She was invited to come to the TCU campus, and arrangements were made for her to present also at five area hospitals. Each hospital decided on the setting and the audience to whom she would speak and made arrangements to provide nursing continuing education credits. During a 3-day period, Dr. Schultz spoke to more than 500 nurses in the Dallas-Fort Worth area.

[a] Center for Evidence-Based Practice and Research, Texas Christian University, TCU Box 298620, Fort Worth, TX 76129, USA
[b] Center for Nurse Excellence, Medical City Hospital, 7777 Forest Lane, Dallas, TX 75230, USA
[c] Harris College of Nursing and Health Sciences, Texas Christian University, TCU Box 298625, Fort Worth, TX 76129, USA
* Corresponding author.
E-mail address: s.weeks@tcu.edu (S.M. Weeks).

Nurs Clin N Am 44 (2009) 27–31
doi:10.1016/j.cnur.2008.10.009
0029-6465/08/$ – see front matter © 2009 Elsevier Inc. All rights reserved.

nursing.theclinics.com

The director of the TCU CEBPR escorted Dr. Schultz to each of her speaking engagements. While traveling between two of the sites, they began to brainstorm ways to build on the enthusiasm that had developed during the presentations. One of the ideas that emerged from the discussion was the development of a collaborative of hospitals focused on evidence-based practice and research. From this idea, the TCU Evidence-Based Practice and Research (EBPR) Collaborative was born.

The initial goal of the TCU EBPR Collaborative was quite simple: to increase connections between area hospitals in an effort to increase evidence-based practice and research. One of the initial concerns was whether competing hospitals could collaborate effectively. Fortunately, that concern has not been a problem. The hospitals involved in the Collaborative have been very willing to share their successes and struggles. From the beginning, the Collaborative has been open to any individual or any agency wishing to participate. Announcements of meetings are distributed by e-mail, and recipients are encouraged to share the announcement with others. Within the first 6 months, nurses from 30 hospitals and three universities had become involved in the Collaborative.

ACTIVITIES

The first meeting of the TCU EBPR Collaborative was held in June, 2007. The hope was for an attendance of 10 to 15 individuals; in fact, more than 20 nurses attended. The first meeting was held on the TCU campus and was focused on sharing the idea of the Collaborative, sharing ideas of EBPR projects that seemed to be successful, and brainstorming future projects for the Collaborative.

The second meeting was held in August, 2007 at an area hospital that volunteered to host the meeting because of its central location between Dallas and Fort Worth. The attendance at this meeting increased to more than 40 individuals. During this meeting, each hospital was encouraged to describe a specific idea or project that had infused EBPR successfully in its practice setting. The projects described ranged from the situation, background, assessment, and request (SBAR) method of hand-off communication to a presentation titled "Pico de Practice" that focused on the population/intervention/comparison/outcome (PICO) method of formulating clinical questions. A highlight of the second meeting was a presentation by an intensive care staff nurse who shared how he had changed practice related to the use of oral-gastric tubes as a result of a clinical question he had investigated. Hearing the excitement of a staff nurse who had implemented an evidence-based practice change effectively was inspiring to the attendees.

At the end of the second meeting, a decision was made to form two taskforces from the Collaborative. One taskforce would focus on the development of a series of workshops and mentoring opportunities for direct-care nurses to increase their knowledge and skills related to evidence-based practice (referred to as an "EBP Fellowship"). The second taskforce would focus on joint research projects focusing broadly on "Research about Nurses." During October, 2007 both taskforces met on the TCU campus, and reports from these two meetings were given during the third meeting of the Collaborative, which occurred in November of 2007.

The third meeting also was held at a hospital centrally located between Dallas and Fort Worth. In addition to hearing from the two taskforces, additional sharing of EBPR projects and ideas occurred. The CEBPR director had conducted a brief survey among chief nursing officers (CNOs) of participating hospitals to assess their ability to provide salary and other financial support for an EBP Fellowship for direct-care nurses. The results of this survey were announced, and options based on the

CNOs' willingness to support the Fellowship were discussed. One specific idea that evolved from this meeting was the desire to host a CNO speaker from a Magnet-recognized hospital system. This CNO had made an earlier offer to the TCU Dean of Nursing and Health Sciences to speak at an area nursing event, and the Collaborative was excited to have this CNO share her thoughts about fostering and supporting evidence-based practice and research in a hospital setting. A decision was made to invite this CNO to speak at the next Collaborative meeting and to invite area CNOs to attend the meeting. The desired outcome was to learn from this Magnet CNO and to garner continued support among area CNOs for the activities of the TCU EBPR Collaborative.

In February 2008, Joyce Batcheller, CNO of the Seton Family of Hospitals in Austin, Texas, gave a presentation to the TCU EBPR Collaborative on the topic of "Resources to Support Evidence-Based Practice and Research in the Hospital Setting." More than 100 nurse leaders from hospitals in the Dallas-Fort Worth area attended the event. The event continued the excitement about promoting evidence-based practice and research in area hospitals and also helped the nurse leaders understand the human and financial resources needed to create a culture of evidence-based nursing practice.

CHALLENGES

The challenge initially thought most likely to be a problem for the TCU EBPR Collaborative, establishing cooperation among competitors, has not emerged as an issue of concern. Instead, each agency involved in the Collaborative has been willing to share ideas, support, and motivation with other Collaborative members. Perhaps the open, inclusive nature of the Collaborative has helped foster this spirit of sharing. Other challenges that have been faced are the distance between agencies and the ever-present challenge of communication. Both these challenges have been addressed by using electronic communication as the primary means of communication between meetings. An electronic distribution list is maintained by the TCU CEBPR, and notices are sent to Collaborative members through this electronic distribution list. TCU also has agreed to provide a Web-based portal that will allow members of the Collaborative to post and comment on shared documents and to post questions and ideas on a discussion board.

A potential challenge for the TCU EBPR Collaborative was addressed successfully through open communication. The area hospital trade organization (Dallas-Fort Worth Hospital Council, DFWHC) decided to form a group of nurse researchers focused on joint research a few months after the beginning of the TCU Collaborative. The announcement of the DFWHC nursing research group was sent to nurse researchers in area hospitals, many of whom already were involved in the TCU Collaborative. Several of the nurse researchers who received the DFWHC announcement expressed their desire to remain committed to the TCU Collaborative and focused on the projects currently being developed rather than participating in a separate initiative. As the organizer of the TCU Collaborative, the TCU CEBPR director was included on the replies that several of the nurse researchers sent to the DFWHC organizers and quickly reached out to the DFWHC organizers to invite their involvement in the TCU Collaborative. The DFWHC was supportive of the TCU Collaborative and, after an initial meeting to explore interest, decided to focus its efforts through the TCU group. The DFWHC has continued to support the TCU Collaborative in several ways, including distribution of Collaborative meeting notices, offers to attend Web-based conferences, and making Collaborative members aware of joint hospital data already being collected by the DFWHC Data Initiative. Through this sharing, Collaborative members learned that extensive joint data, of which many members were unaware, already is available to members of the TCU Collaborative.

HOSPITAL PERSPECTIVE

Chief nurse executives, Magnet project directors, and nurse researchers in Magnet-designated organizations and those on the "Journey to Excellence" feel both a responsibility for and a commitment to evidence-based practice, nursing research, and community partnerships with local colleges of nursing. One of the difficulties in this particular urban area is that relationships between academia and service do not exist within systems and must be facilitated, implemented, and sustained by forging partnerships between nurse leaders in university and health care system settings to share scarce faculty resources across settings and accomplish mutual goals.

As members of the TCU EBPR Collaborative, the perspective of area hospitals is that the Collaborative serves as an excellent vehicle for networking with other nurse leaders who share common vision and purpose. The Collaborative offers the possibility of working together to create training programs in evidence-based practice and research and to collaborate on multisite clinical studies while efficiently capitalizing on the wealth of nursing talent in a large, diverse metropolitan area. Despite the competitive nature of this environment, nurses can come together around the table to share both unique and similar perspectives regarding the issues that affect both patients and nurses. This Collaborative provides a forum for brainstorming ideas and sharing best practices and eventually may make possible the implementation of multisite projects with greater scientific rigor than could be accomplished by any one of these organizations acting alone.

One of the difficulties in contracting with a single entity or individual for nursing research consultation is that the organization may be limited by the specific clinical expertise and research experience of a single individual and academic setting. With the rich diversity of nurse researchers, expert clinicians, and organizations within the Collaborative, the members are connected efficiently to a broader environment of resources and possibilities for partnerships.

In light of limited internal and external funding and organizational resources, this initiative connects nursing experts in efficient ways to assist members in identifying evidence-based best practices that result in quality patient outcomes and therefore provides a beneficial solution for all involved. A single entity or individual cannot provide sufficient infrastructure to support the same level of evidence-based practice and research education and consultation that is possible through a large collaborative effort such as that offered by the TCU EBPR Collaborative. Individuals responsible for evidence-based practice and research programs in area organizations feel fortunate to be part of an initiative of this magnitude that brings nurse leaders, clinicians, and researchers together to foster scientific inquiry, educate direct-care nurses about evidence-based practice and research, and create safe environments for patients.

SUCCESSES

The activities of the TCU EBPR Collaborative have resulted in many benefits. TCU has enjoyed a long-standing positive relationship with numerous clinical agencies, and those relationships have been strengthened even further through the Collaborative. The Collaborative is a tangible demonstration of the university's commitment to improving nursing practice and patient care in area hospitals. This commitment has been reciprocated by the hospitals' support of the Collaborative and their use of TCU nursing faculty members as consultants for EBPR projects. Another benefit has been a strengthened relationship between nursing faculty members from three different universities who are providing EBPR consultation services to various hospitals. The joint pool of talent among these faculty members, as well as among the nurse researchers employed by area hospitals, is significant and provides a wealth of opportunity for joint support and projects. Hospitals that are on the Magnet journey have been mentored by other hospitals that are already Magnet-designated, and hospitals with current Magnet designation have received encouragement and ideas from their peer agencies.

An encouraging milestone occurred during the third meeting of the TCU EBPR Collaborative when a poster that had been presented at a recent national nursing conference was discussed. The poster described a similar collaborative that had developed among Magnet-designated hospitals in a much larger urban setting. In comparison, the TCU Collaborative developed quickly over a 6-month period with significantly more hospitals as members. Another unique feature of the TCU Collaborative was the inclusion of faculty members from three universities, as well as the actual sponsorship of the Collaborative by the primary university.

FUTURE GOALS

The future goals of the TCU EBPR Collaborative are categorized in three primary realms: continued sharing of best practices, development of an EBP Fellowship for direct-care nurses, and joint benchmarking and research. The EBP Fellowship planning is progressing, and it is anticipated that the Fellowship will begin in the fall of 2008. TCU faculty members and nurse researchers from area hospitals have offered to serve as the faculty and facilitators of the Fellowship. Support such as facilities, continuing education credit, and other supplies will be requested from hospitals whose direct-care nurses participate in the EBP Fellowship. In addition, there will be a fee for each participating nurse to cover the additional costs of the Fellowship.

A goal that is not as well defined at this point is the joint benchmarking and research. An area of interest is joint research about nurse-sensitive indicators and the possible opportunity to benchmark at the regional level. The DFWHC Data Initiative has offered to provide opportunities for shared data, and additional projects probably will develop. One idea being considered is a research project regarding the relationship of nurse-sensitive indicators to nursing turnover and vacancy.

The meetings of the TCU EBPR Collaborative have been highly valued as forums for sharing, brainstorming, and problem solving. It is anticipated that this type of collegial exchange will remain one of the most valued aspects of the Collaborative. In addition, the hosting of speakers who are recognized experts from outside the Dallas-Fort Worth area is seen as an area of focus for future events.

SUMMARY

ecor   ngly more complex, the tendency is to engage in
                       efine processes, and attempt to control closely
                       Collaborative has been a successful example
                       torming, was allowed to evolve, and gradu-
                       vor. The initial concern about the attempt to
                       as not proved to be an issue. During the ini-
                       O in attendance responded to the concern
                       laborative could be successful if it focused
                       what was right for nurses. With those prior-
                       ion have been resolved quickly. The Collab-
                       y affecting patient safety and quality of care

Renewing the Spirit of Nursing: Embracing Evidence-Based Practice in a Rural State

Ann E. Sossong, RN, PhD[a],*, Sue Cullen, RN, MSN[b],
PaulaTheriault, RN, MBA[c], Alanna Stetson, RN, BSN, BC[d],
Barbara Higgins, RNC, PhD[e], Sarina Roche, RNC, DNSc[f],
Sue Ellis-Hermansen, RN, MS[g], Dorrin Patillo, RN-B[h]

KEYWORDS

- Evidence-based practice • Quality care
- Collaborative partnerships • Consortium
- Barriers • Rural state

The nursing profession has been challenged to develop and implement improved patient care outcomes that are supported by research findings. These efforts are supported by the Institute of Medicine's (IOM) report that identifies a health care safety crisis, citing an increase in preventable deaths in the United States.[1,2] The IOM (2001) report clearly calls for nursing and other health care disciplines to care for patients using best evidence and encourages professionals to move practice more quickly to the application of research findings in the clinical setting.[3,4] The IOM report highlights the need to restructure health care delivery to create systems that are both patient centered and evidence based.[3] Organizations in which health care takes place must be dynamic and adaptive to appropriate internal and external feedback based on

[a] School of Nursing, 5765 Dunn Hall, University of Maine, Orono, ME 04469, USA
[b] Education Department, Acadia Hospital, 268 Stillwater Avenue, Bangor, ME 04401, USA
[c] Education Department, St. Joseph Hospital, 360 Broadway, Bangor, ME 04401, USA
[d] Education and Training Center, Eastern Maine Medical Center, Eastern Maine Healthcare, Whiting Hill, Brewer, ME 04412, USA
[e] Department of Nursing, Husson College, One College Circle, Bangor, ME 04401, USA
[f] Department of Nursing, Eastern Maine Community College, 354 Hogan Road, Bangor, ME 04401, USA
[g] Omicron Xi Chapter At-Large, Sigma Theta Tau International Honor Society, School of Nursing, 5765 Dunn Hall, University of Maine, Orono, ME 04469, USA
[h] Education Department, Dorothea Dix Psychiatric Center, 656 State Street, Bangor, ME 04401, USA
* Corresponding author.
E-mail address: ann.sossong@umit.maine.edu (A.E. Sossong).

Nurs Clin N Am 44 (2009) 33–42
doi:10.1016/j.cnur.2008.10.010
0029-6465/08/$ – see front matter © 2009 Elsevier Inc. All rights reserved.

nursing.theclinics.com

evidence but structured enough to maintain order in a complex and ever-changing system.

When a complex institutional system is organized purposefully to be dynamic, clinical practice is transformed more easily to ensure patient safety and quality of care. Such systems contain mechanisms for continual feedback on selected outcomes, as well as regular and frequent searches for solutions to problems that have been identified. Evidence-based practice (EBP) is an essential part of the strategy used to accomplish this positive transformation. As Melnyk and Fineout-Overholt[5] purport, "EBP is a problem-solving approach to practice, one that cultivates an excitement for implementing the highest quality care as well as a spirit of inquiry and life-long learning." Acknowledging the role of EBP is an essential step in achieving quality outcomes.

An informal interdisciplinary group of educational leaders began to meet at the University of Maine in 2006 to undertake a dialogue about how to accomplish a transformation to EBP that ensures patient safety and improved quality of care. Members of the group represented the nursing honor society, acute and critical access hospitals, mental health institutions, and university and college schools of nursing in central and northern regions of Maine. Collaborative efforts to introduce and implement EBP in these areas in Maine were deliberate and focused, although initially there was no clear vision of the outcome.

This article provides insight into the formative processes of the group, discusses the collaborative efforts of the group, and describes the outcomes. The IOM challenge to implement EBP is addressed as a central theme, and a process has been established that continually revisits the quality of that transformational implementation, even in the more remote areas of Maine.

THE JOURNEY BEGINS

Nursing leaders must form strong informal and formal networks in any geographic area if high standards of care are to be met and maintained. It could be argued that successful and effective links in these networks are more important in a large rural state like Maine than in more densely populated ares of the country. Frequent interactions between educators and health care institutions are necessary simply because of the need for agreements regarding clinical articulation and professional development programs within and among representative organizations. Discussions during these interactions revealed a common desire to integrate EBP in health care organizations and academia, but no one had a clear idea how to accomplish this goal. The shared value of incorporating EBP into agency or institutional policies helped the group stay focused and led to discussion about the need to change nursing culture to reflect this value. Central to the conversation was the need to clarify challenges and barriers to change from each participant's perspective.

All members of the interdisciplinary group previously had attended a program in which Alyce Schultz,[6] RN, PhD, had spoken about a successful Clinical Scholar Model (CSM) and mentorship program for EBP in the southeastern (more urban) part of Maine. Dr. Schultz's earlier presentations had familiarized the group with examples of clinical scholarship initiatives. The group also was familiar with other clinical scholar models, such as the ACE Star Model of evidence-based nursing practice,[7] the Stetler model of research use to promote EBP,[8] and the Iowa Model of EBP to promote quality.[9] Each of the models emphasize "clinical scholarship as an intellectual process, steeped in curiosity that challenges traditional nursing practice through observation, analysis, synthesis, application, and dissemination."[7] The success of earlier educational programs in southeastern Maine was attributed to the use of the CSM along with teamwork and collaboration. The nursing leaders realized this same team-work and collaborative spirit had to be essential elements in the process, regardless of locale, if they were to engage the nurses in EBP.[10,11]

Another element in creating and maintaining a culture of clinical excellence required more attention to additional collaborative partnerships with major stakeholders (eg, leadership from tertiary health care centers and critical access hospitals). Partnerships between nursing and these institutional representatives focusing on improvements in patient care afford educational leaders more opportunities to design educational programs that facilitate the integration of shared values of EBP. These steps are a logical part of the process for cultivating professional pride and excitement.[6] Through these collaborative efforts, educational leaders are able to establish a more deliberate and organized approach for creating a culture of change by gaining the support of key organizational leaders in cultivating a spirit of inquiry. The value placed on inquiry (versus tradition or simple habit) will lead nurses to acquire a better knowledge base for practice, which is a necessary step to inform and facilitate better patient outcomes.

PAVING THE WAY

As in any endeavor of this magnitude, barriers surfaced that required patience and perseverance to overcome. Some of these obstacles were expected, and others were encountered during the team-building process. Those in more rural areas were relatively unfamiliar with the meaning of EBP. Some of the nurses in the group identified lack of time to explore and adopt protocols reflecting EBP as a barrier to change. Other nurses who were fully engaged in research projects did not recognize the ways in which their findings were applicable and were hesitant to share results with colleagues. These experiences were consistent with the findings of Nagy and colleagues,[12] who found four major obstacles to the use of EBP in their study of nurse's beliefs about the conditions that hinder or support evidence-based nursing. These major obstacles include "nurses' lack of belief in the use of evidence to guide practice, lack of organizational support, lack of time to use evidence effectively in practice, and lack of knowledge in the use of evidence."[12]

Competitive tension also existed between various organizational and educational leaders. Nursing initiatives in the different settings customarily were developed without input from others, and this pattern did not foster collaborative thinking or efforts. Introspection during the group meetings led to the realization that such initiatives had been seen as responses to internal conditions of the institution rather than processes that better might be seen as reactions to broader national or state-wide events. Long-standing rivalries and a history of actions directed at local-only interests led to ineffective support for collaborative efforts between administration in health care and academic settings. As honest dialogue progressed, the goal of creating a clinical scholar environment for nursing emerged. The group energy that resulted from this positive dynamic was certainly a factor that fed the change process.

It is necessary to inform organizational leaders of the importance of EBP as part of the process of reinforcing the changes needed in institutional culture. Literature on systems change emphasizes the need to avoid the roadblocks and pitfalls that often hinder staff-driven initiatives and to promote organizational champions. Even though sustaining EBP is a difficult task, the difficulty does not detract from the value of the endeavor.[13] Champions of this cultural change surface through strategic initiatives to provide optimal outcomes for patients, thereby creating a culture of excellence.

THE PROCESS OF SOLIDIFYING A COLLABORATIVE PARTNERSHIP

The first step in establishing this partnership was to acknowledge the underlying competitive tension between the various organizations. The shared value for evidence-based nursing practice gave participants a common connection from which to build the trust needed to conduct this dialogue. Members in the group agreed that Dr. Schultz would be ideally suited to guide the task ahead. She was familiar with the culture, challenges, and historical relationships between and among institutions represented in the group. Her credibility as an expert in successfully establishing a CSM allowed members of the group to welcome her guidance.[14]

The CSM is a logical process of implementing research and therefore sustaining the use of evidence in nursing practice. This model requires strategies for organizational support and teamwork.[14] Dr. Schultz's previous success in implementing the CSM with the assistance of several point-of-care nurse researchers was recognized nationally and internationally. her enthusiasm and familiarity with the process instilled a belief that the initiative to cultivate and institute EBP was not only desirable but also was attainable.

Meetings were held in which Dr. Schultz and other southern Maine colleagues graciously shared their experiences with the CSM. These brainstorming sessions led to the decision to hold an inquiry-based learning workshop as a necessary means of institutionalizing EBP. All participants needed greater familiarity with the notion of both doing and teaching EBP; that familiarity in turn would reinforce the connections that were necessary for successful long-term change. The workshop would help the group develop a common language for educational goals that would be appropriate for nurses and administrators. Sessions within the workshop needed to provide opportunities for nurses to gain an understanding of what EBP was (and was not) and to evaluate and appraise critically the quality of research findings. Likewise, workshop sessions were needed to provide administrators with guidance on how to support EBP institutionally and ultimately infuse research findings into the practice environment by using an EBP model.

The agencies to which individual members of the group belonged were asked for contributions to cover the expense involved in the workshop. There was support from representative organizations for the workshop, although resources were limited. Dr. Schultz generously donated her time and expertise to the endeavor, and the seeds for creating a comprehensive event to cultivate EBP in rural Maine were planted.

THE WORKSHOP: PROMOTING EVIDENCE-BASED PRACTICE THROUGH A SPIRIT OF INQUIRY: 2007

The theme of the 1-day workshop promoting EBP through a spirit of inquiry. The educational leaders in the group worked closely with Dr. Schultz, who then was the Associate Director for the Advancement of Evidence-Based Practice at Arizona State University, College of Nursing and Health care Innovation. In the spring of 2007 the well-attended workshop was held in central Maine, a location that was reasonably accessible to the target audience. Participants came from many of the state's rural health care organizations. Most of the conference attendees were staff nurses, although several organizations were represented by administrators.

An introductory session in the workshop addressed the dynamics of managing change, with attention to the feasibility and sustainability of EBP. An element in this portion of the workshop was the need to identify the characteristics of a transformational leader—a role model who leads nurses to question practice and rewards changes and innovation. These mentors "walk the talk" by continually asking for the evidence, strengthening their knowledge and skills related to reading and appraising research, and demonstrating willingness to change practice if evidence contradicts beliefs.[15] Another early task was to address the need for innovative leaders who could create an infrastructure to support EBP. The interactive workshop allowed participants to explore their values in relation to the characteristics of a transformational leader and to identify strategies for change within their own institution's culture.

The structured sessions in the workshop included collaborative exercises designed to stimulate ideas for research projects among the participants. Examples of studies focusing on the patient/nurse interface at the point of care were used to assist participants in conceptualizing clinical issues. Participants also were assisted in easily identifying sources for existing evidence and methods for evaluating the quality of that evidence. A medical librarian was an invaluable resource for this part of the workshop. The librarian provided detailed and specific information about how to locate and select the best refereed research articles supporting EBP and how to locate and evaluate clinical practice guidelines. The importance of addressing the use and implementation of these guidelines in nursing practice was considered separately, with time allowed for specific questions that might arise at a particular institution. Workshop participants were introduced to the essential requirements and strategies for implementing EBP and to barriers to implementation previously identified in the literature.[9]

Another feature in the workshop was the "Evidence in Action" panel. This discussion panel included expert nurses, a director of clinical research, and a physician at a large tertiary center in central Maine. The "spirit of inquiry" theme was reinforced by the panel participants reminding attendees that many institutional protocols had been developed by nurses as they tried to improve patient care. Panelists and attendees acknowledged that there had been an ongoing, although less formal, level of nursing research supporting EBP in their organizations that affected quality improvement processes. Participants saw that change was possible and that the mechanisms for such change already were partially in place. The major learning objective for the workshop was to recognize the value of incorporating research findings into practice guidelines that would result in improvements in clinical outcomes. Workshop attendees also were expected to communicate their readiness to implement EBP in their respective work settings.

THE MAINE NURSING PRACTICE CONSORTIUM

Nursing leaders debriefed after the EBP workshop expressed the need to establish a more permanent collaborative group, resulting in the formation of the Maine Nursing Practice Consortium (MNPC). The MNPC has evolved and continues to be a valuable resource helping bridge the cultural differences between research-rich urban health science centers and the smaller medical centers and critical access hospitals that constitute the more rural Maine health care systems. Following the first workshop, the MNPC members worked diligently with nurses in their respective institutions to promote EBP. They met regularly to share the progress of EBP initiatives, and more formal arrangements were made between and within institutions to implement EBP. Members were committed to promoting the goals of the partnership and to working to maintain the momentum for the spirit of inquiry. Professional pride in accomplishments was evident among those who played a part in the first workshop, and a sense of shared achievement provided a base from which to set clear goals for continued evidence-based efforts of the MNPC.

Shared values among MNPC members had to be agreed upon before collegial relationships could be established between the nurse educators and the health care providers and administrators of the health care systems. In most cases, increased and improved communication between the nursing leaders was a necessary step in incorporating EBP into regular dialogue among nurse educators, nurses at the bedside, and administrators in institutional settings where health care is provided. Educational workshops as well as collaborative partnerships such as the MNPC were essential to advance nursing in the quest for optimal patient care outcomes.

FIRST YEAR ACCOMPLISHMENTS

Organizational commitment to the collaborative efforts was stronger after the workshop, as measured by offers of time and financial support for the mission of instituting EBP. Nurses who attended the conference began searching literature pertinent to their nursing projects, no doubt aided by the knowledge shared at the conference. Nursing leaders who participated in the workshop development worked more collaboratively, using teamwork to advance the goals of safety and quality patient care. A shared appreciation of the value of EBP, continually reinforcing the language and processes aimed at a spirit of inquiry, was leading inevitably to outcomes recommended by professional, accrediting, and regulatory organizations at all levels.

More collaborative avenues developed as a direct result of increased organizational understanding of the components of EBP. Experiential opportunities for senior nursing students were initiated, providing them with beginning skills and knowledge in the research process and use of evidence that they can incorporate into their own EBP. A Nursing Research Fellowship is being sought for graduate nursing students.

There is lively dialogue at area hospitals aimed at identifying ways in which staff can implement EBP routinely on the various clinical units. One study, "Patients' and Nurses' Perceptions of Caring," recently completed by academic faculty and staff nurses, represents the first successful research collaboration. The impetus for the study was the increased emphasis hospitals place on marketing their institutions as the best place to come for care. What constitutes excellent care is difficult to define, especially from the patient's perspective. To implement true patient-centered care, it is essential to incorporate the patient perspective on caring. This study provided evidence about what both patients and nurses perceived as "care." Findings from this collaborative study have been presented nationally and internationally and have been well received. The process provided the leadership of the hospital with the chance to acknowledge the significance of nursing contributions in improving patient satisfaction and quality of care. This study was the first independent nursing study conducted at this central Maine hospital, because nursing studies previously had required physician sponsorship. When the proposal for this study was submitted to the institutional review board for approval, the clinical research director worked with academic faculty to change the policy to allow nurses to engage in research that promotes EBP without physician sponsorship.

Another successful outcome of these collaborative activities is visible at the world's only psychiatric hospital with Magnet designation. This psychiatric and substance abuse facility in central Maine now formally and institutionally embraces nursing practices that are evidence based. The facility's chief nursing officer attended the 2007 workshop and strongly supported the spirit of inquiry. This Magnet hospital uses nursing leadership teams to infuse the principles of EBP through research. The concept has permeated the institution and includes advanced-practice registered nurses and staff nurses in the collaborative process.

The educational workshop sessions promoted a change in the perception of what constitutes research, identified research activities as "doable" by nurses, and incorporated the value of practice based on evidence for all who attended. Perhaps the most fundamental outcome is the recognition that EBP is part of the professional role of all nurses, whether they are brainstorming about what research is needed, searching for supporting evidence to inform a particular practice, writing a proposal, or gathering data as part of a clinical project. Examples of evidence-based projects inspired by the 2007 workshop are varied (eg, constipation-relieving remedies for patients on methadone therapy, intravenous fluid hydration for postprocedure electroconvulsive therapy for patients suffering from headaches, and nurses and EBP in a successful school re-entry project), but all represent the movement toward a "spirit of inquiry."

The successful outcomes from the workshop have contributed immeasurably to a change in the perception of the role of nurses as researchers and change agents for EBP in their respective institutions. There is greater confidence in nurses' ability and greater institutional support for the establishment of an environment for research leading to evidence-driven practice. Clearly, there has been a shift from lip service about the value of EBP to acknowledgment of the responsibility of all nurses at all levels for creating a favorable institutional setting in which nurses implement EBP. Change in systems and practice stimulated by the workshop sessions has been brought to bear in this geographically large but rural environment. Success from the initial workshop led to the development of the second EBP workshop in April 2008.

RENEWING THE SPIRIT OF NURSING: 2008

Sensing a renewed spirit, the MNPC members designed the second EBP workshop to provide novice nurses the opportunity to speak about and showcase their work. Workshop organizers believed that the focus on accomplishments would convey effectively the value placed on EBP. The recognition of achievements energized and encouraged nurses to continue to direct their energy toward systematic evaluation and promotion of EBP. Nurse researchers well versed in the use of EBP strategies who had presented in the 2007 workshop returned to evaluate and recognize achievements and build more clear connections between EBP and a higher quality of patient care.

Jane Kirschling, RN, DNS, Dean and Professor of University of Kentucky, College of Nursing, and former Dean at the University of Southern Maine, provided the keynote address at "Renewing the Spirit of Nursing by Embracing EBP 2008." She reinforced the call for EBP and emphasized the implications of national initiatives on nursing practice. Expanding on the previous workshop initiatives, she helped the participants identify their expanded roles, influence, and responsibility to assure that nursing practice is examined critically and is assessed systematically to provide quality care. Interactive sessions enabled the nurses to gain further insight in how the national initiatives from organizations such as the Agency for Health Care Research and Quality, National Quality Forum, National Database of Nursing Quality Indicators, and Quality and Safety in Nursing Education affect decisions made by leaders in changing health care systems in their institutions.

The language of these initiatives encompassed EBP to generate measurable, optimal patient outcomes. The participants acknowledged that they shared a common change, because all the national nursing initiatives mirrored their efforts to promote optimal patient care by changing systems and practices, with the ultimate goal of ensuring

---

Box 1
Selected EBP projects presented at "Renewing the Spirit of Nursing: 2008"

Implementation of sucrose for neonatal procedural pain

Nursing role: nonpharmacologic interventions for insomnia

Providing behavioral health care in primary practice settings: co-location pilot project

Inflammatory bowel disease in children: an overview for the pediatric health care provider

Health Lifestyles Group: nursing practice improves patient outcomes

Therapeutic hypothermia following out-of-hospital cardiac arrest

Psychiatric emergency response team outcomes

---

safety and improving quality outcomes through best evidence. These national initiatives have opened doors previously closed to nursing, and the participants recognized that there are greater opportunities for nurses to assume a leadership role in a dynamic, challenging, and increasingly complex health care system.

OUTCOMES OF THE 2007 AND 2008 WORKSHOPS

Advances in EBP in central and northern Maine as a result the 2007 and 2008 workshops are evident when considering the quality and the quantity of projects presented by staff nurses in 2008 (**Box 1**). Positive outcomes in the "Renewing the Spirit of Nursing 2008" workshop were evident in the outcomes of the projects presented by nurses and in staff nurses' active participation. Enthusiasm for the change was expressed through verbal and written communications and evaluations that demonstrated increased knowledge regarding EBP, greater familiarity with national initiatives concerning EBP, and individual contributions to organizational changes.

LESSONS LEARNED

MNPC members have categorized their experiences into six major lessons for the development of EBP in rural Maine. These insights may prove useful to other groups of leaders who are committed to a similar vision for promoting collaborative efforts among academic institutions and health care systems in rural settings.

1. Communication among nurses in clinal practice, nurse educators, and those in administrative positions is essential for the creation of a dialogue for change in the culture of nursing. Collaboration is based on effective communication.
2. Clear professional nursing goals can supersede individual organizational goals when competing factions in nursing can overcome rivalry.
3. Logistic challenges to meetings for participants in wide geographic areas can be overcome when all members commit to participation in a manner that acknowledges individual circumstances.
4. When the ultimate goal is to provide the safest and highest-quality nursing care to the citizens in rural areas, funds and material resources will not be a prohibitive factor to progress.
5. Patience and respect for colleagues are essential qualities for a collaborative team process, regardless of the goal.
6. The driver for change must be the common goal of patient safety and quality care, not individual or institutional advantage.

SUMMARY

A group of nursing leaders from several organizations in the central and northern regions of the state established the MNPC. Their efforts renewed the spirit of nursing through a commitment to collaborate on the adoption and integration of EBP in each clinical and educational setting. Regular meetings with this goal in mind led to the design of workshops focusing on the establishment and continued promotion of EBP. Trust was established within and between organizations, geographic and traditionally competitive barriers were addressed, and members of the MNPC led a number of evidence-based initiatives.

Staff nurses acknowledged the value of their evidence-based unit improvement projects and proudly showcased these results. Faculty members in schools of nursing continue to pursue better methods for integrating EBP in undergraduate and graduate nursing courses. Faculty members also incorporate national initiatives into classroom discussions as well as clinical practice settings. Nursing administrators likewise are embracing EBP and strongly support nurses in their quest to improve patient care by revising practices through mechanisms based on the best evidence.

Renewing the spirit of nursing through EBP was a challenge that was met in central and northern Maine through the collaborative efforts of committed nursing leaders. The consortium members created a synergy for valuing, using, teaching, and adding to the professionalism of nursing through EBP. The incorporation of EBP as a fundamental concept in nursing practice was given a tremendous boost with a modest beginning of respectful dialogue that has led rural Maine nurses in academia and practice institutions to excel. Members of the MNPC will continue to foster collaborative efforts that support and strengthen EBP endeavors in rural Maine. Excellence in clinical care and improvement of patient outcomes result from applying the intellectual process in the application of new scientific knowledge. There is reason to believe that EBP also can become a reality in the even more rural areas of Maine, and this goal is more likely to be realized if team spirit and collaborative effort play a key part in the process.

ACKNOWLEDGMENT

The authors acknowledge Carol Wood, EdD, Graduate Coordinator, School of Nursing, University of Maine, Orono, ME, for her editing and support.

REFERENCES

1. Kohn LT, Corrigan JM, Donaldson MS, editors. To err is human: building a safer health system. Washington, DC: National Academy Press; 2000.
2. Aspden P, Corrigan JM, Wolcott J, editors. Patient safety: achieving a new standard for care. Washington, DC: The National Academies Press; 2004.
3. Committee on the Quality of Health Care in America. Crossing the quality chasm: a new health system for the 21st century. Washington, DC: National Academy Press; 2001.
4. Finkelman A, Kenner C. Teaching IOM: implications of the Institute of Medicine reports for nursing education. Silver Spring (MD): American Nurses Association; 2007.
5. Melnyk BM, Fineout-Overholt E. Evidence-based practice in nursing & healthcare: a guide to best practice. Philadelphia: Lippincott Williams & Wilkins; 2005.

6. Schultz AA. Origins and aspirations: conceiving the Clinical Scholar Model. Excellence in Nursing Knowledge 2005;6:1–4. Available at: http://www.nursingknowledge.org/Portal/Main.aspx?PageId=3512&IssueNo=6. Accessed May 17, 2008.

7. Stevens KR. ACE Star Model of EBP: knowledge transformation. Academic Center for Evidence-based Practice, The University of Texas Health Science Center at San Antonia; 2004. Available at: www.acestar.uthscsa.edu. Accessed June 19, 2008.

8. Stetler CB. Updating the Stetler model of research utilization to facilitate evidence-based practice. Nurs Outlook 2001;49(6):272–9.

9. Titler MG, Kleiber C, Steelman VJ, et al. The Iowa model of evidence-based practice to promote quality care. Crit Care Nurs Clin North Am 2001;13(4):497–509. Available at: http://www.ncbi.nlm.nih.gov/pubmed/11778337. Accessed May 17, 2008.

10. Schultz AA. Implementation: a team effort. Nurs Manage 2007;38(6):12–4. Available at: http://www.nursingcenter.com/Library/JournalArticle.asp?Article_ID=718987. Accessed May 17, 2008.

11. Schultz AA. The Clinical Scholar Model: promoting interdisciplinary EBP teamwork at the point of care. Presented at the 18th International Nursing Research Congress Focusing on EBP. Vienna, Austria, July 12, 2007. Available at: http://stti.confex.com/stti/congrs07/techprogram/paper_33398.htm. Accessed May 17, 2008.

12. Nagy S, Lumby J, McKinley S, et al. Nurses' belief about the conditions that hinder or support evidence-based nursing. Int J Nurs Pract 2001;7:314–21.

13. Stetler CB, Caramanica L. Evaluation of an evidence-based practice initiative: outcomes, strengths and limitations of a retrospective, conceptually-based approach. Blackwell Synergy-Worldviews Evid Based Nurs 2007;4(4):187–99.

14. Schultz AA. Clinical scholars at the bedside: an EBP mentorship model for today. Excellence in Nursing Knowledge 2005;6:1–8. Available at: http://www.nursingknowledge.org/Portal/Main.aspx?PageId=3512&IssueNo=6. Accessed May 17, 2008.

15. Schultz AA. Sustainability of EBP: learning organizations. Presented at Promoting Evidence Based-practice Through a Spirit of Inquiry. Eastern Maine Community College, Bangor (ME), April 6, 2007.

Implementing a Health System-Wide Evidence-Based Practice Educational Program to Reach Nurses with Various Levels of Experience and Educational Preparation

Teri Britt Pipe, PhD, RN[a],*, Jane A. Timm, MS, RN[b],
Marcelline R. Harris, PhD, RN[c], Doreen K. Frusti, MSN, MS, RN[b],
Sharon Tucker, PhD, RN[b], Jaqueline M. Attlesey-Pries, MS, RN[d],
Katherine Brady-Schluttner, MS, RN-BC[e], Julie Neumann, MS, RN[e],
J. Wayne Street, RN[f], Diane Twedell, DNP, RN[e], Marianne Olson, PhD, RN[b],
Gina Long, DNSc, RN[a], Cindy Scherb, PhD, RN[b]

KEYWORDS

- Evidence-based practice • Leadership
- Nursing professional development • Practice innovation
- Informatics • National Quality Forum

The NQF Scholars Program was funded by the Mayo Clinic Rochester Board through the Incented Investment in Mayo's Future.

[a] Nursing Research, Division of Nursing, Mayo Clinic College of Medicine, Mayo Clinic Arizona, Mayo Clinic Hospital, Nursing Administration, 5777 E. Mayo Boulevard, Phoenix, AZ 85054, USA

[b] Nursing Research Division, Department of Nursing, Mayo Clinic College of Medicine, Mayo Clinic Rochester, 200 SW 1st Street, Rochester, MN 55905, USA

[c] Division of Nursing Informatics and Nursing Health Sciences Research, Department of Nursing, Mayo Clinic Rochester, 200 SW 1st Street, Rochester, MN 55905, USA

[d] Nursing Practice Resource Division, Department of Nursing, Mayo Clinic Rochester, 200 SW 1st Street, Rochester, MN 55905, USA

[e] Education and Professional Development Division, Department of Nursing, Mayo Clinic Rochester, 200 SW 1st Street, Rochester, MN 55905, USA

[f] Nursing Trauma, Luther Midelfort, 1221 Whipple Street, Eau Claire, WI 54701, USA

* Corresponding author.

E-mail address: pipe.teri@mayo.edu (T.B. Pipe).

The work of nursing always has changed with the times, remaining rooted in theoretic and ethical foundations but being flexible enough to expand and meet new challenges. The emerging and future work of nursing requires a growing agility to allow the practitioner to move between disparate knowledge areas and to integrate cognitive skill sets in creative and innovative ways. Three of these areas of knowledge are clinical informatics, evidence-based practice (EBP), and nursing-sensitive quality methodologies. Until recently these content domains have been absent from the academic and service education curricula. When content has been provided, these three domains have been learned and applied separately. In the evolving health care arena, it became apparent to Mayo Clinic Nursing that preparing nurses with expertise in all of these content areas would position the health care system to deliver the best scientifically grounded care for patients and to communicate clinical information and outcomes of care effectively for the mutual benefits of the patient, nurse, and the organization. Thus, the departments and divisions of nursing embarked on a system-wide educational initiative to expand the knowledge of nursing leaders in clinical informatics, EBP, and nursing-sensitive quality methodologies as well as the skills needed to translate this knowledge into optimal impact at the point of patient care. Intramural funding was secured to develop, execute, and evaluate the initiative.

The system designed and implemented a 1-year curriculum for nurses that focused on the three content domains of clinical informatics, EBP, and quality methodologies. This article describes a system-wide EBP educational initiative implemented with a geographically, educationally, and clinically diverse group of direct care nurses with the intent of increasing their EBP skill set and their efficacy as local change agents and leaders. In this article, the overall program is described, and then the focus is narrowed to describe the EBP components of the initiative with case examples and lessons learned. Although the National Quality Forum (NQF) Scholars Program was much broader in scope, only the EBP components of the program are presented as examples.

NATIONAL QUALITY FORUM SCHOLARS INITIATIVE

The initiative was named the "NQF Scholars Program." This name was selected to denote the rigorous academic preparation combined with the context of nursing-sensitive quality indicators published by the National Quality Forum.[1] The vision was to expand the knowledge of nursing leaders to translate best practices into optimal impact at the direct point of patient care through focusing on the NQF nursing-sensitive measure set.[1] The result envisioned was enhanced effectiveness in nursing practice by decreases in unnecessary variation across all of the systems' health care facilities guided by a shared mission of doing what is best for the patient.

The approach described in this article is a departure from the local hospital–based efforts that have been presented elsewhere.[2–8] In the past, the efforts designed to improve EBP knowledge and skills were directed primarily at the local organizational level; this initiative provided the opportunity to broaden the scope and coordination of efforts to a system-wide perspective that encompassed nursing professionals across Mayo Clinic's five-state health care enterprise, including the affiliated multistate health care system. The essence of this program was to create and apply rigorous academic preparation with the primary focus on patient quality and safety from a nursing perspective.

The model guiding the EBP portion of the curriculum was the Clinical Scholar Model.[9] The Clinical Scholar Model promotes a spirit of inquiry and willingness to change the processes and tasks of patient care and the theories framing practice based on rigorous, systematic appraisal of the evidence guided by nursing clinical judgement. The approach is one of mentorship that supports nurses in becoming responsible, account-able change agents for providing patient care based on the best evidence available.[9]

NQF SCHOLARS: A PROGRAM DESCRIPTION

Numerous organizations, including the Institute of Medicine, the NQF, and the Joint Commission on Accreditation of Healthcare Organizations, have recognized that EBP, performance measurement sets, and health information technologies are critical to improving the quality and safety of health care. The current program was developed and implemented to prepare registered nurses to be NQF scholars by combining cur-riculum from each of these concepts (**Table 1** provides a curriculum overview and pro-totypical schedule). This program was designed to establish a critical foundation for the future of nursing across the Mayo Health System by addressing the five core com-petencies recommended by the Institute of Medicine, which also include key factors that are known to affect directly the recruitment and retention of nurses:[10]

- Demonstration of the highest quality of care using nursing-sensitive outcome measures
- Demonstration of organizational support for ongoing learning and EBP
- Practicing nurse involvement in key processes
- Exposure to the research foundations for practice
- Access to and use of information technologies in the workplace

Table 1
Nursing National Quality Forum Scholar Program: schedule at a glance

Dates	Activity	Location
Month 1	Quality Conference Networking event "Sustaining the Gains" for Cohort 1 Scholars "Setting the Stage for NQF Scholars" for Cohort 2 Scholars	Central site
Months 2–4	Informatics AMIA 10 × 10 online course	Local setting
Months 5–6	Informatics synthesis Networking event Evidence-based practice overview	Central site
Months 6–7	Summer assignment: information gathering at local setting about related initiatives and contacts	Local setting
Month 8	Evidence-based practice kick-off System-wide quality model Data governance presentation Evening networking event	Central site
Months 8–11	Online evidence-based practice course via virtual classroom (12 modules) Statistical concepts Translating course concepts into National Quality Forum project/project development	Local setting
Months 11–12	Virtual meeting for project presentations and National Quality Forum leadership role Project implementation	Local setting
Month 12	Nursing Research Conference Evening recognition/social event	Central site

SPECIFIC PROGRAM GOALS

The specific aims of the NQF Scholars Program were to prepare practicing nurse scholars to

1. Serve as local leaders and champions of nursing-focused and/or nursing-relevant NQF measure sets and their associated EBP
2. Use Web-based tools on the system-wide intranet for collecting evidence, conducting analysis, sharing information, and benchmarking
3. Bring forward and apply informatics principles at their sites

The program development team consisted of the chief nurse executive with oversight of the entire organizational system, faculty members with expertise in the three content domains, and administrative project planners whose role it was to coordinate the efforts of the entire team and manage the logistics of the program from enrollment to evaluation. A steering group consisting of members of the program development team and other key nursing leaders guided the initiative in a strategic and effective direction. Members of the faculty and the administrative project planners met regularly to plan curriculum and the delivery of the program. There was intentional overlap between groups. Much of the work of the teams was accomplished via teleconference and e-mail communication because of scheduling demands and geographic separation. A description of the EBP portion of the overall curriculum is delineated in **Box 1**.

The program was inspired by the existence of gaps in linkages between clinical information systems, best EBP interventions, and nursing-sensitive patient quality outcomes. The curriculum was designed to bridge the knowledge gaps between these areas and to provide participants with the leadership skills vital for transforming their learning into sustainable practice innovations. Because of the number of metrics included in the NQF nursing-sensitive measure set, it was decided that only one NQF measure would be used as an exemplar for each NQF scholar cohort to unify effort and learning using one specific clinical issue. The objective was to teach specific skills that then could be generalized when approaching other nursing-sensitive measures.

DESCRIPTION OF THE INTENDED PARTICIPANTS

Candidates were identified by the chief nurse executive in each of the participating organizations and had nurse manager support for participation. Nurses were recruited based on their interest and commitment to the yearlong program as well as on their leadership potential. Individuals who currently were in leadership positions and desired the expanded knowledge in the curricular content as well as nurses who showed promise in becoming enduring change agents and who had informal and/or formal leadership influence were prime applicants.

In year one (2007–2008), 51 nurses from across all sites participated with a focus on hospital-based nursing. In year two (2008–2009), an additional 40 nurses from across all sites were enrolled, and the focus was on clinic-, homecare-, and long-term care–based nursing. The number of nurses recruited for the project depended on availability and workload at their respective sites.

PROGRAM IMPLEMENTATION

The program began in the winter with an orientation meeting at the most central and largest site within the system. In a face-to-face session participants were introduced to the components of the NQF Scholars Program and became aware of resources,

---

Box 1
EBP content outline

1. Discuss the history of EBP

2. Discuss goals and processes of EBP as compared with the conduct of nursing research and nursing quality initiatives

3. Outline the importance of EBP to professional nursing practice in terms of the American Nurses Association Social Policy Statement

4. Describe the use of evidence in achieving positive NQF outcomes

5. Formulate a clinical/educational or administrative question using a structured format

6. Identify accurate search strategies and applicable databases for addressing evidence-based nursing practice questions

7. Select research articles applicable to the clinical question from the library search.

8. Practice skills for evaluating and critiquing individual research articles and groups of articles.

9. Practice skills of literature synthesis verbally and in writing, assessing levels and quality of evidence.

10. Evaluate and compare published guidelines.

11. Select the appropriate outcome measure (evaluation of published scales).

12. Critique systematic reviews.

13. Apply the process of critically appraising the literature into a "clinical bottom line."

14. Describe conceptual and implementation models that guide evidence-based nursing practice.

15. Describe how theories of change and diffusion of innovation can be used to support EBP.

16. Describe implementation strategies.

17. Identify specific organizational, provider, and patient barriers and facilitators to implementing EBP processes and policies.

18. Describe feasible evaluation frameworks for selected EBP initiatives.

19. Identify ways that leadership strategies can be combined with EBP methods to ensure translation of evidence in to practice in an effective and sustainable fashion.

20. Describe how to evaluate a practice change and know that it is sustainable.

---

such as online learning tools and library services. NQF scholars were provided an overview that included an orientation to clinical informatics, the basics of NQF quality metrics, and fundamental elements of EBP. The second day, participants attended a Nursing Research Conference that focused on EBP.

The initial 10-week content session was an online graduate course on clinical informatics offered through the Oregon Health and Science University in partnership with the American Medical Informatics Association (AMIA), an AMIA 10 × 10 program that emphasizes EBP.[11] The informatics coursework was concluded when the NQF scholars came back to the central site for a 2-day face-to-face meeting. During this meeting, the faculty for the EBP course introduced the curriculum outline and provided the first module of content. Delivery method of the 12-module EBP course primarily was online asynchronously, with some synchronous meetings available as well. All sessions were recorded to allow later playback.

Because the curriculum was designed with the NQF metrics in mind, one metric of interest was chosen for all of the scholars to work on for the remainder of the course: the incidence and point prevalence of pressure ulcers for cohort one and the prevalence of falls and of falls with injury for cohort two. The scholars also received a summer assignment designed to help them learn more about local resources and personnel involved with informatics, EBP, and quality initiatives (see Appendix). The intention behind this assignment was to lighten the workload for the scholars at this point in the curriculum and to achieve a connection with quality improvements already occurring in their respective sites.

The next face-to-face meeting occurred in the fall when the scholars had completed several EBP modules. A module was delivered during a 2-day meeting, and work sessions were offered for online scholarly inquiry. Groups of scholars formed to work on various projects related to pressure ulcers. Content was delivered during this 2-day meeting on quality methodologies, human factors, leadership, and project development.

After the EBP modules were completed, the scholar groups continued to meet locally to incorporate content from the EBP course along with informatics and quality measures into their pressure ulcer projects. In the mid-winter a virtual meeting was arranged between the scholars and some of the faculty so that the scholars could report on the progress of the pressure ulcer-related EBP projects and quality initiatives and the faculty could provide leadership and mentorship content formally. A secondary outcome of these presentations was the excitement of learning about different products sites were using for pressure ulcers and the possibility of purchasing these products for the other sites as well as the recognition of the work that had been accomplished thus far.

In the spring, the first cohort of scholars met for their final planned face-to-face meeting to celebrate their accomplishments, to initiate mentoring work with the second cohort of NQF scholars who were in the initial phase of their curriculum, and to develop plans for sustaining their knowledge and skills. This meeting intentionally coincided with a large, system-wide quality conference that held many opportunities for participant networking and communicating about the NQF Scholars Program with other disciplines. Virtual seminars are planned quarterly to sustain the ongoing work of the first cohort of NQF scholars.

CASE EXAMPLES: NQF SCHOLAR EVIDENCE-BASED PRACTICE PROJECT TEAMS

As described earlier in this article, the NQF scholars formed local work groups that focused on specific, local clinical issues relevant to the assessment, prevention, or treatment of pressure ulcers. The teams formulated a question using the population of interest/intervention of interest/comparative intervention/outcome (PICO) format, searched and synthesized the pertinent literature, and designed a plan to translate the evidence into nursing practice. The results of the literature synthesis were used in various ways, including being posted on the shared drive for use by all NQF scholar groups. Also, the work of the groups has been used to inform and guide the enterprise-wide pressure ulcer initiative. Local efforts have varied and continue to emerge. Specific examples of clinical questions that were identified by the NQF scholar groups are

- How does nursing knowledge affect early recognition of pressure ulcers?
- Will providing a standardized education program for patients and families decrease the incidence of preventable pressure ulcers?
- In immobile, bedridden patients, does the use of Granulex help prevent skin breakdown?

- Does a Web-based teaching module with hyperlinked video recordings increase interrater and intrarater reliability among staff nurses and wound, osteotomy, and continence nurses for differentiating pressure ulcers from moisture-associated skin lesions?
- Is there an instrument (incorporating oxygenation perfusion and/or fluid balance) that is more accurate than the Braden Scale for Predicting Pressure Sore Risk in assessing risk for developing pressure ulcers in critically ill patients?
- In hospitalized patients at risk for developing pressure ulcers, do "just in time" electronic reminders decrease the incidence of pressure ulcers as compared with current practice?
- In adult hospitalized patients, is the Braden Scale for Predicting Pressure Sore Risk the most effective scoring instrument for assessing the risk of developing pressure ulcers?

The group projects often resulted in the scholars accessing all the three major curricular areas of informatics, EBP, and nursing-sensitive measures. In the words of one NQF scholar,

Our local project focused around the evidence on pressure ulcer risk assessment scales. In examining how we were using informatics to assist with our project, we discovered that reports were being generated weekly related to pressure ulcers. As we progressed through the project, the group sought out other ideas in how to use an electronic health record. In the future, we would like to incorporate decision support for the nursing staff when documenting on pressure ulcers – such as recommended interventions that are based on the best evidence.

LEADERSHIP/MENTORSHIP

The systematic translation of best evidence into clinical practice was a primary overarching goal of the NQF Scholars Program, particularly the EBP component. Content knowledge and EBP skills are critical in attaining this goal, but they are not sufficient to initiate and sustain meaningful change; leadership skills are required to gain momentum to initiate, implement, evaluate, and sustain practice innovations. Likewise, clinical informatics and quality improvement initiatives are successful both because individuals have the cognitive skills in place and because leaders have exerted effective influence to make enduring changes in practice. Nurses at all levels of the system are considered leaders. Therefore, the development of leadership skills was included in the program content. Leadership was introduced in the first face-to-face meeting and was included in the EBP modules. During the final session, cohorts one and two had the opportunity to participate in a "speed mentoring" activity designed to initiate mentoring relationships between the cohorts. In this exercise cohort two participants had a short, timed (3 minutes) chance to interact with cohort one participants to investigate possible opportunities for shared learning or mentoring. The activity was completed in a lighthearted but focused manner.

CHALLENGES

Transitioning from a focus on the individual organization to a system-wide scope brought new challenges and opportunities. Providing education and support in a health care system–wide manner expanded the capacity for organizational learning and also presented new complexities that were distinct from previous hospital- and clinic-based approaches. These challenges, opportunities, and complexities, along with suggestions for future directions are discussed here.

First, the program participants were geographically dispersed across the Southeast, Southwest, and Midwest areas of the continental United States. Participants were in different time zones, different organizational structures and cultures, and various communication systems. Participants came from varied clinical settings and roles with widely differing responsibilities and reporting structures. To address this challenge, a great deal of flexibility was built into the educational delivery system. Web-based formats were used whenever possible, and distinct individual modules that could be accessed in a variety of settings were provided. Because the participants worked in the same system but in different locations, there was the benefit of a common infrastructure and support network for computer access and Web-based technologies. A second strategy for meeting this challenge was providing periodic face-to-face meetings at the most central location so that participants would have the opportunity to get to know each other, develop relationships, and network. Many of the instructional modules were provided in asynchronous formats, but several synchronous sessions also were posted in the spirit of "office hours" so that participants could ask questions of the instructor and project planners in a real-time format.

Another challenge in program delivery was that the participants had various levels of clinical expertise and different educational backgrounds, many of which did not include EBP or research coursework. Some participants came from organizations with strong nursing research and EBP infrastructures and processes in place; other nurses had access to more limited resources. To address the issue of varied preparation, the course was designed at the postgraduate level, but resources for more basic content areas were available. Textbooks on EBP and nursing research were provided for each participant as reference resources. In addition, project planners and faculty were available by e-mail and telephone for questions and assistance. Web-based resources also were made available, and a tutorial regarding electronically available library resources was included in one of the face-to-face sessions. In many cases, nurses who were more expert in EBP or in critiquing and using research in practice paired with more novice participants to help them understand the concepts. The major project was accomplished in a group setting to facilitate informal mentoring and to maximize the expertise of all members.

Participants not only came from diverse geographic settings and educational backgrounds; they also represented varied clinical positions and professional roles. This variety presented a challenge in crafting the curriculum and assignments in a way that would be pertinent to every participant, but the situation also had advantages, because participants could view issues from a variety of perspectives. Part of the EBP course was a group project focused on the development of a PICO question, appropriate search and critique of the literature, design of a synthesis table, and formulation of an implementation plan. The project groups met the challenges of diversity by optimizing the positives: coordinating schedules, using asynchronous communication (usually e-mail), and using each other's unique strengths. Group members had to keep themselves and each other accountable for group assignments.

A major challenge for the faculty and participants was the ability to tie the three domains of EBP, clinical informatics, and nursing-sensitive quality measures together in a meaningful way, regardless of clinical role of the participant. Within the curriculum, threads of statistical methods, leadership skills, and Web-based tools also were woven across the three major content domains. It was important that the curricular domains were standardized in their delivery but flexible enough to accommodate diffusion of innovation within several different organizational cultures represented by the nurses from different sites. Much of the program content synthesis remained to be evaluated formally at the end of the 1-year program, but participants anecdotally reported that they were starting to see ways that they could integrate EBP, clinical informatics, and nursing quality metrics into their everyday work processes. For example, one NQF scholar group began formal meetings with their local hospital-based wound ostomy nursing team to disseminate the synthesized literature about the pressure ulcer severity rating system currently in use. Additionally, participants noted that they were more aware of the presence of these content areas in their practice, although they might not have been attuned to them before participating in the program.

Perhaps one of the most challenging aspects of the program was the short timeline for implementing the curriculum. Internal funding was received for the 2-year project, and work began immediately to put together the curriculum and instructional delivery systems. The compressed timeframe led the faculty and planning team to be focused and innovative in their approaches and to use time wisely. The faculty and steering group wanted the content for all three areas to be rigorous and externally valid, so a variety of academic programs and providers was explored. For the EBP portion of the curriculum, it was important to provide content that was theoretically grounded, that had scholarly merit and clear clinical relevance, and that highlighted the role of the direct-care nurse in leading EBP initiatives with institutional support. Fortunately, the EBP course and the clinical informatics course were available from external entities; the organization contracted with these individuals and organizations to provide the content, while the faculty and planners managed the delivery and coordination of the curriculum. Formative curriculum and evaluation strategies are in place to modify the curriculum for subsequent cohorts. Adaptations will include integrating the content more completely across modules, sustaining collaborative work groups that emphasize EBP, and more completely introducing and reinforcing leadership content within the program.

In the future, efforts for leadership and mentorship education will be more explicit, systematic, and intentional. Expectations that scholars will pursue leadership, mentorship, and a sustained scholarship role as a result of the program will be expressed and reinforced from the beginning and will be integrated into follow-up online working groups. Even though leadership potential was among the criteria for participation in the program, some participants came into the program with strong leadership skills, and others were relative novices. In retrospect, leadership training is an aspect of the program that could be strengthened in the future. There is great untapped potential in arranging the sharing of leadership skills among scholars at different levels of experience and expertise across the system. Leadership skills are likely to play a key role in program sustainability.

FACILITATING FACTORS

Many factors worked together to make this initiative successful. The program had organizational support from the highest levels of administration that translated into endorsement, time allocation, and financial resources. At every level a high value was placed on developing nursing workforce knowledge and competencies for future generations of the nursing profession. The benefits were articulated in potential impact on outcomes of patient care (safety, effectiveness, and quality) and in workforce optimization (nursing satisfaction, retention, and professional development).

Fiscal resources were critical in providing time for the nurses to participate, including travel expenses to attend all-site meetings, curricular fees for the content provided, textbooks, and online educational support. Personnel resources for a project planning team consisted of three individuals who coordinated participant communication and enrollment, provided meeting schedules and agendas, managed the instructional design and technology resources, and provided administrative oversight of the continuing education aspects of the program. Continuing education units were awarded to participants, and one of the program planners served as coordinator of this process. Program faculty scheduled time to meet, plan, and evaluate the curriculum as it was developed.

High levels of motivation and expertise of participants and faculty served as catalysts for program implementation. The organization had access to information technology expertise and resources that facilitated the actual delivery of the education and helped bridge the geographic distance among participants. Fortunately, recognized experts in the content areas were available both within the system and from highly respected external entities. Faculty members had broad professional networks on which to draw when planning how the content areas should be provided.

LESSONS LEARNED

Many valuable lessons emerged.

- The project planning team was vital in meeting the timeframes of the program and for coordinating workflows.
- Face-to-face meetings with participants, planning team, and faculty were important for building connections, networking, developing leadership skills, and conveying the larger context of the work.
- Choosing a clinically relevant issue (eg, pressure ulcers) as the focus for the EBP projects served to unify the work of the clinically diverse nurse participants.
- Work groups helped participants divide the effort and understand how to make it most meaningful clinically.
- The diverse roles of participants were turned into a benefit: sharing complementary expertise.
- Work groups sometimes met virtually because of scheduling challenges. This practice was not always ideal, but technology support helped greatly.
- The instruction was available online through a shared portal server (Sharepoint) and a meeting/educational delivery application (Interwise), so it was possible for geographically dispersed participants to interact effectively.
- The compressed timeframe for the curriculum kept the momentum going, but participants sometimes needed more time to synthesize their learning and translate it in clinically meaningful ways.
- Participants expressed the need for consistently communicated expectations regarding the time and resources needed to complete assignments.
- There was a need for stronger and more formal preparation for leadership/change agent portion of the curriculum. Even with the best EBP content, strong leadership skills are essential to bring about practice transformation based on best evidence.
- Participants valued faculty presence and availability.
- The outcomes and future roles sometimes were vague. There was not always a definite answer to the question, "How will I use this in my job right now?"
- There was a need to manage, incorporate, and treat the modules as an integrated curriculum; the three content areas are not "plug and play."
- Setting participant expectations was very important; an identified need was to build in a spirit of comfort with ambiguity and preparation for an unknown and largely unpredictable future, because nursing roles are evolving constantly.

SUMMARY AND CONCLUSIONS

This article has described the implementation of a system-wide curriculum for nurses incorporating the content domains of informatics, EBP, and quality methodologies focused on a nursing-sensitive performance measure set. Transitioning the focus from individual organization to a system-wide approach meant that the implementation required innovative strategies to optimize outcomes despite disparate geographic locations, nursing education, and professional expertise of the participants. The diversity of the participants greatly enriched the outcomes of the program, both in the projects that were designed and in the collegial relationships that were formed. The system-wide approach was facilitated by the resources of time, technology, personnel expertise, rigorous course content, and leadership support across the system. Future challenges include making the program sustainable for the long term, developing leadership content and teaching modalities that meet varying levels of learner need, completing formal evaluations of the curriculum and outcomes, and discerning which components of the program are best suited for different nurse constituents.

APPENDIX. DEPARTMENT OF NURSING NQF SCHOLARS PROGRAM SUMMER ASSIGNMENT
Purposes

There are three purposes for this summer assignment: (1) to begin to establish dialogues and relationships within each site related to data, evidence-based practice, and the NQF nurse-sensitive measure set; (2) to begin to create a bridge between the didactic content from the informatics module to the data activities that enable collection of NQF nurse-sensitive measures, and (3) to lay a foundation for the evidence-based practice content that will start in the late summer.

Assignment

First, meet with the Chief Nursing Officer at your site and identify a plan for meeting with key stakeholders (eg, quality department, practice committees, and others) to identify the key efforts at your site related to data sources for the NQF nurse-sensitive measures, the underlying practices that are associated with the NQF nurse-sensitive measures, and any technologies that are used at your site that contain information related to NQF nurse-sensitive measures or the practices you might associate with an NQF nurse-sensitive measure.

Example

One of the NQF nurse-sensitive measures is concerned with the point prevalence of pressure ulcers. It would be helpful if you could determine how data about pressure ulcers are collected at your site. Who combines that data across units? What types of order sets or practice guidelines did you previously identify related to pressure ulcers at your site? Try to connect with the individual or group working on that order set. Ask whether the data are being converted to an electronic format and if information will be included in the electronic medical record. Find out who is submitting information about pressure ulcers to various reporting groups (including NQF nursing measures). Are there individuals and/or committees working on best practices concerning pressure ulcers?

The questions in **Table 2** are intended as sample questions to help you get the dialogue started.

Table 2		
Examples of Contacts	Sample Discussion Topics/Questions You Might Ask the Contact Person	Notes
Chief nursing officer	What are we doing with the NQF nurse-sensitive measures we are currently collecting? My expectations/ideals about the NQF scholars program are [fill in the blank!]. What are your expectations of my involvement in this program? Do you see overlap between the NQF nurse-sensitive measures and other quality and evidence-based projects? Do you see opportunities for information technologies to enhance the capture of data related to NQF measures? What opportunities do you see for information technologies to enhance specific areas of our practice? Who would you suggest I talk with this summer so that I can get a more complete picture of the connection between quality measures, the NQF nurse-sensitive measures (specifically, evidence-based and best practices), and the use of information technology to support?	
Staff that work with quality initiatives (within nursing and for your institution)	In what ways do the NQF nurse-sensitive measures overlap with other measures currently being collected in the organization? How are the data for NQF measures being collected? Who is collecting the data? What electronic systems are used throughout the collection, analysis, and reporting NQF nurse-sensitive and related measures? Is a quality model used in our quality department?	
Information technology staff	How do you identify what vocabulary or terminology to use when developing or modifying applications?	
Practice analysts	Is much modification of applications done here? If so, how do you get a sense of the business need for making those modifications?	
Informatics staff	How do you develop an understanding of the process flows that need to be supported in specific applications? Is there a template or standard set of information that would be useful for you to have before engaging in conversations with clinicians about software modifications? How are priorities set for information technology at our site?	
Other persons or roles that may assist in projects (eg, nursing and medicine practice colleagues)	Do we have project managers? How do you organize to "get the work done" on a specific project? How would you recommend I go about identifying key stakeholders for any practice project?	

REFERENCES

1. National Quality Forum (NQF). National voluntary consensus standards for nursing-sensitive care: an initial performance measure set. Washington, DC: NQF;2004. Available at: http://www.qualityforum.org/pdf/nursing-quality/txNCFINALpublic.pdf. Accessed May 20, 2008.
2. Tucker S, Derscheid D, Odegarden S, et al. Evidence based training for enhancing psychiatric nurses' child behavior management skills. J Nurses Staff Dev 2008; 24(2):75–85.
3. Neumann J, Brady-Schluttner K, Street W. Developing nursing scholars: implementation of a multi-faceted, integrated staff development project. Presented at the Second Annual National Database Of Nursing Quality Indicators Conference. Orlando, January 30–February 1, 2008.
4. Neumann J, Brady-Schluttner, Timm J. Nursing professionalism: accountablity and image. National Quality Forum Scholars Program poster presentation, Mayo Clinic Rochester. Rochester, April 8, 2008.
5. Neumann J, Brady-Schluttner K. NQF scholars engaging in excellence in nursing practice. A journey. Defining Excellence Magnet ANCC National Magnet Conference. October 15–17, 2008.
6. Pipe T, Cisar N, Caruso E, et al. Leadership strategies: inspiring evidence-based practice at the organizational and unit levels. J Nurs Care Qual 2008;23(3): 266–72.
7. Pipe T. Optimizing nursing care by integrating theory-driven evidence-based practice. Journal of Nursing Care Quality 2007;22(3):234–8.
8. Pipe T, Wellik K, Buchda V, et al. Implementing evidence-based nursing practice. Med Surg Nursing 2005;14(3):179–84.
9. Schultz A. Clinical scholars at the bedside: an EBP mentorship model for today. Online Journal of Excellence in Nursing Knowledge. Available at: http://www.nursingknowledge.org. Accessed May 28, 2008.
10. Institute of Medicine, Keeping patients safe: transforming the work environment of nurses, committee on the work environment for nurses and patient safety, Page A (ed.). Institute of Medicine of the National Academies, 2004. The National Academies Press, Washington, DC Available at: www.nap.edu. Accessed May 20, 2008.
11. American Medical Association of Informatics web site. Available at: http://www.amia.org/10x10. Accessed, May 20, 2008.

Promotion of Safe Outcomes: Incorporating Evidence into Policies and Procedures

Lisa English Long, MSN, RN, CNS*, Karen Burkett, MS, RN, CNP, Susan McGee, MSN, RN, CNP

KEYWORDS

• Evidence • Policies • Procedures • Outcomes • Safety

Policies and procedures (P&Ps) provide guidance in the care nurses provide to patients and families. The goal of achieving safe practice can be obtained through the use of P&Ps. To further enhance the effect of P&Ps on patient care, incorporation of evidence provides documentation of safe and best practice. The addition of evidence to P&Ps requires the development of a process to ensure consistency, rigor, and safe nursing practice.

This article describes the process of incorporating evidence into P&Ps, resulting in the establishment of evidence as a basis for safe practice. The process described includes use of the Rosswurm and Larrabee[1] model for change to evidence-based practice. The model guided the work of evidence-based practice mentors in developing a template, system, and educational plan for dissemination of evidence-based P&Ps into patient care.

ASSESS

Point-of-care nurses focus on the use of current best evidence to guide their practice. Caring for patients also involves the use of P&Ps, which provide the direction to implement procedures, patient education, and evaluation of interventions in an approach that focuses on safety. For P&Ps to be based on best practice, evidence must be integrated. The addition of evidence to P&Ps requires the development of a process to ensure consistency, rigor, and safe nursing practice.

Evidence-Based Practice, Center for Professional Excellence-Research and Evidence-Based Practice, Cincinnati Children's Hospital Medical Center, 3333 Burnett Avenue, ML 11016, Cincinnati, OH 45229, USA
* Corresponding author.
E-mail address: lisa.long@cchmc.org (L.E. Long).

Nurs Clin N Am 44 (2009) 57–70
doi:10.1016/j.cnur.2008.10.013
0029-6465/08/$ – see front matter © 2009 Elsevier Inc. All rights reserved.

To ensure integration of evidence in the P&Ps of a large midwestern pediatric academic medical center, evidence-based practice mentors were charged with reviewing, updating, and incorporating evidence into 32 P&Ps over a 6-month time frame. Within the medical center, evidence-based practice mentors are advanced practice nurses with additional education in evidence-based practice. The focus of the mentors is to collaborate with nursing staff in addressing clinical issues. The role of the mentors involves education, facilitation, implementation, and evaluation of evidence in practice. The mentors within this organization have approached evidence work from a unit-based and systems perspective.

To begin the assessment phase, internal and external data about current practices were gathered to determine organizational readiness for change to an evidence-based P&P process. The institution did not at this point have a clear definition of evidence-based policies or procedures. Within the institution, definitions of policy, procedure, and standard were inconsistent from policy manual to policy manual and from division to division.

Internal to the organization, within the nursing division, multiple online policy manuals were used by staff. These manuals were selected from nursing divisional policy manuals and critical care unit manuals. The nursing P&P manual for the division included over 100 P&Ps. Policy manuals within the many critical care units often included a greater number of P&Ps than in the divisional manual. In each of the P&Ps, references were noted; however, the references were not leveled and graded. To provide a logical starting point, senior nursing leadership determined early that the focus of the work would be to evidence base the divisional nursing P&P manual.

Internal data suggested an auspicious approach to implementing a change. First, there was recognition from the senior leadership team that policies based on evidence would sustain best practices, promote improved patient outcomes, and were a necessary requirement for Magnet recognition. Second, with support from senior leadership, the divisional Nurse Practice Council (NPC) adopted a goal to evidence base P&Ps but struggled with how to operationalize that goal. Third, the evidence-based practice mentor team, who were asked to lead this process, recognized that "evidence-based policies are outcomes that can be derived from the EBP process."[2]

External data included reports from the Institute of Medicine that supported the proposed change. At a national level, the Institute of Medicine reports discussed the importance of safety in health care and the use of evidence in decision making within the practice arena.[3] In discussions with health care organizations about the use of evidence within P&Ps, the evidence-based practice mentor team noted that inconsistencies existed, especially in the referencing and leveling and grading of the evidence. Most institutions used either textbooks or published procedure manuals for a reference to provide some evidence for procedural policies. Overall, those references were not leveled and graded.

LINK

Evidence-based practice mentors addressed the rationale for the aspiration to develop P&Ps based on evidence. The vision and mission of the organization's focus on safety and best practice and the institution's current Magnet journey supported the need for evidence to be integrated into P&Ps.

Linking the problem of a lack of evaluated evidence embedded in policy to measurable outcomes was a critical element in this process. Outcomes are often defined within the all-encompassing concepts of patient, nurse, cost, and organizational effects. Identifying an outcome that was specific and measurable was needed to drive the process of incorporating evidence into nursing practice. The recent attention at this institution to the National Patient Safety Initiatives[4] guided the evidence-based practice mentor team to patient safety. Patient safety outcomes became the focal point around which all clinical questions were centered.

To reach the desired outcomes, the five steps of evidence-based practice were used as a guide to the evidence process.[2] These steps include the following:

1. Asking the burning clinical questions
2. Collecting the most relevant and best evidence
3. Critically appraising the evidence
4. Integrating all evidence with one's clinical expertise, patient preferences, and values in making a practice decision or change
5. Evaluating the practice decision or change

Use of these steps guided formulation of the clinical question, the search for evidence, and evaluation of the evidence to make a recommendation relevant to each policy or procedure reviewed. These steps also informed the evaluation of the proposed process of embedding evidence into P&Ps.

SYNTHESIS

The five steps of evidence-based practice were a model for the evidence work guided and facilitated by the evidence-based practice mentors. The mentors engaged in the process of designing a change so that P&Ps were based on evidence. The standardized language of PICO (population, intervention, comparison, outcome) was used to formulate the clinical question "Among nurses, does the use of evidence versus traditional care improve patient safety outcomes?"

Systematic search strategies were employed including multiple databases and keywords pertinent to the PICO question. Databases searched included CINAHL, PubMed, Medline, and the National Guidelines Clearinghouse. Search terms were *nurses, patients, safety,* and *improved outcomes*.

Findings from the literature search and subsequent evidence review demonstrated positive outcomes such as improved staff satisfaction,[5] patient care,[6] and cost outcomes[7] when using evidence in clinical practice; however, no research studies related to the general concept of patient safety and the use of evidence were found. Although it may be implied that improved safety can result from using evidence in practice, it has not been studied. The National Patient Safety Initiatives[4] suggest that patient safety improves with the use of evidence in practice. In addition, third party payers request evidence to support reimbursement provided to health care organizations for patient care. The answer to the clinical question was "When nurses use evidence versus traditional care in clinical practice, many nurse satisfaction, cost, and patient care outcomes are improved." No research findings supported the use of evidence to improve patient safety. Although research is needed in the area of safety, the research evidence related to satisfaction, cost, and patient care outcomes plus the clinical expertise related to safety support the concept of embedding evidence into P&Ps.

DESIGN

The proposed change would lead to the integration of evidence into 32 divisional nursing P&Ps. To accomplish the change to evidence-based P&Ps, a well-defined process was needed to maintain consistency within the work led by the evidence-based practice mentors. To initiate this process, the evidence-based practice mentor team defined "evidence-based P&Ps" as P&Ps supported by leveled and graded references, with a clinical question focusing on the safety of each policy or procedure. The revised or new P&Ps included a recommendation based on a safety-related evidence search, appraisal, and synthesis.

To begin the process, identification of an evidence-based procedure book that could serve as the main reference for the nursing division's P&P manual was undertaken by the evidence-based practice mentors. The goal was to identify a procedure manual with integrated evidence. Mentors identified stakeholders to serve on the team to review and recommend a manual, including point-of-care staff accountable for the P&Ps. A nine-member point-of-care review team was composed of point-of-care nurses, a medical librarian, and evidence-based practice mentors. This team rated online pediatric evidence-based procedure manuals. A textbook evaluation instrument[8] had been adapted for use in evaluating pediatric content, online format, and evidence-based qualities of nursing procedure manuals. Through the use of this instrument, one manual was selected from three that were reviewed.

The selection of a procedure manual with integrated evidence provided guidance in integrating evidence within P&Ps. It was imperative that references listed within the chosen manual had been reviewed in a rigorous process that included the leveling of each study and grading of the body of evidence. When this did not appear in the manual, the institutional definition of evidence-based P&P provided guidance and clarification.

The next action needed to attain the outcome of evidence-based P&Ps was the development of a template to provide a consistent format. To address this need, a leadership group was formed consisting of senior nursing leaders, legal services, NPC leaders, policy and procedure committee members, and the evidence-based practice mentor team. The template format was similar to the previously used process for organizing P&Ps. The key difference was the availability of current, synthesized evidence related to pertinent safety issues of each policy or procedure. A supplementary document template was developed to maintain a record of the review date and process. This template included the names of the review team members, the reference list with levels, the grade of the body of evidence, the recommendation for practice based on the evidence review, and a key to the appraisal system used (**Box 1**).

In addition to the policy name, number, and date of origin and review, the template includes five main headings: policy, purpose, guideline for procedure, references, and implementation. The template includes cues to the definitions of the headings and the information that should be included under each one. The "policy" heading cue indicates that this section answers the question "What is this policy (procedure)?" This section defines who is licensed to enact the policy or to perform the procedure.

Box 1
Summary of nursing policy, procedure, and standards review process

Policy #/Name:

Review Team:

PICO Question:

References (with Level & Grade):

    (Level __ Evidence)

    [Strength of the Body of Evidence as of (most recent review date): Grade]

Courtesy of EBP Mentor Team, Cincinnati Children's Hospital Medical Center, Cincinnati, OH; with permission. Copyright, © 2007, EBP Mentor Team.

The "purpose" heading cue is the question "Why does this policy exist?" The team considers if there is a regulatory, safety, or process requirement for the topic under consideration. If not, a recommendation might be made to the pertinent committee to delete the policy or procedure. If the group determines there is a need, this section of the template includes the aim of the P&P or the desired outcome.

The "guideline for the procedure" provides the steps that are required to perform an activity, answering the question "How do I follow this policy?" If there is a corresponding procedure in the online procedure manual, a link to that procedure is created. Any recommended variation to the online procedure is identified by a symbol inserted into the relevant document. If there is no corresponding online procedure, the steps to perform the procedure are listed within the policy or procedure template.

The fourth heading in the template is the "reference" list. Identification of the quality level of the individual article is noted at the end of each citation, answering the question "Is the study valid, reliable, and applicable to the population of interest?" At the end of the reference list, the review team provides a grade for the body of the evidence and answers the question "What are the quality, quantity, and consistency of the evidence that speaks to the PICO question?" Tables of the quality level and grading systems are included within the template.

The final template heading of "implementation" addresses how the policy or procedure will be implemented. The intention of this heading is to answer the question "Who is responsible for this policy?" For example, nursing procedures are typically maintained by the NPC. If a policy affects more than one discipline, the responsible group would be the Interdisciplinary Practice Committee. Minimally, P&Ps are reviewed every 3 years. If a need to make a change based on new research evidence occurs, a practitioner brings this to the attention of the responsible group for earlier review. This process can be initiated by any staff member, beginning the task of developing evidence-based P&Ps.

In addition, the template includes reference lists with each reference leveled and graded. When using the accepted manual or online resources, it was noted that many resources did not engage in the rigorous process of leveling each study and grading a body of evidence. This discovery led to the definition of an evidence-based policy or procedure that raised the standard for evidence evaluation. The development of a template supported the definition of an evidence-based P&P as a policy or procedure that was focused on patient safety. In addition, the goal for the evidence to be leveled and graded was evident within the template. This definition made explicit three key components: (1) the focus of the evidence search and evaluation would be patient safety outcomes; (2) the evidence would be leveled and graded for quality, quantity, and consistency of the findings; and (3) the strength of the evidence would provide a recommendation to support or refute the need for a change in practice.

Successful template development led to a systematic selection of 32 P&Ps for revision or development by point-of-care review teams. P&Ps were grouped by clinical area or condition (eg, all policies on documentation or all procedures related to vascular access) and divided among the evidence-based practice mentors. The mentors had the primary responsibility for overseeing completion of the evidence work on each of the 32 policies. Grouping of related policies or procedures allowed the evidence-based practice mentors to identify evidence that overlapped and consider consolidation of P&Ps if appropriate. For example, if there was strong evidence of the effectiveness of chlorhexidine gluconate to reduce infections for central venous catheters and peripheral intravenous catheters, the evidence could be embedded in each procedure.

This phase of the practice change outlined a "sequence of activities in a descriptive format."[1] The sequenced actions were set in motion once the point-of-care review teams were formed. The teams would begin a review of the current policy or procedure and weigh it against the procedure from the manual with integrated evidence. If there were slight changes needed to the policy, it could be customized for current practice and the evidence embedded with references that were leveled and graded. For online procedures that required small changes, a link to the online procedure reference was provided; however, if too many amendments were required to the online procedure manual, it was abandoned, and the P&P template was used independently to construct a new policy or procedure. In an effort to keep the policy or procedure concise, the supplementary document was used to summarize the policy or procedure review process.

When the mentors had lists of P&Ps for review, each identified the appropriate stakeholders for every topic and formed P&P review teams. These teams were comprised of clinicians familiar with the policy or procedure based on their use within the clinical setting. Nursing staff accountable for the practice guided by that procedure or policy were the obvious choice for review team members. Others potential review team members were advanced practice nurses, clinical managers, education coordinators, or outcome managers. The purpose of the additional clinical staff was the expertise they offered in relation to the P&P under review. The evidence-based practice mentors as part of the team located and evaluated the evidence. The team reviewed the revised P&P for accuracy, clarity, and applicability to practice.

In support of the shared governance structure within the organization, upon completion of the P&P, one of the evidence-based practice mentors would forward the P&P in the new template along with the supplementary document to the divisional NPC. The NPC would review the document and approve it for placement within the P&P manual.

Table 1	
Sample of policies and procedures with clinical questions	
Policy or Procedure Name	**PICO Question Related to Patient Safety**
Policy	
Bed placement	Among hospitalized children, does restriction of co-bedding versus co-bedding of adults and children reduce the risk of suffocation or injury?
Patient classification system	Among hospital nurses, does use of a patient classification system tool increase safety and effectiveness in staffing standards?
Student nurses	In providing care to pediatric patients, does allowing nursing students to administer medications lead to an increase in medication errors versus medication errors among experienced nurses?
Procedure	
Central venous catheters	Among hospitalized children, does use of chlorhexidine gluconate scrub versus Betadine and alcohol scrub decrease the incidence of catheter-related infections?
Intramuscular injections	Among infants requiring an intramuscular injection, does use of a long needle versus short needle reduce localized reactions?
Healing touch	For hospitalized children, does the use of healing touch by certified healing touch practitioners have any adverse effects compared with hospitalized children who are not treated with healing touch?

Table 2	
Levels of evidence	
Level	**Description**
I	Systematic review or meta-analysis of RCTs or evidence-based practice guidelines based on RCTs
II	At least one well-designed RCT
III	Well-designed controlled trials without randomization (quasi-experimental)
IV	Well-designed case-control and cohort studies
V	Systematic reviews of descriptive and qualitative studies
VI	One descriptive or qualitative study
VII	Expert opinion or reports of expert committees

Abbreviation: RCT, randomized controlled trial.
Adapted from Melnyk BM, Fineout-Overholt E. Evidence-based practice in nursing & healthcare: a guide to best practice. Philadelphia: Lippincott; 2005; with permission.

To introduce the new process of embedding evidence into P&Ps to the nursing staff, an educational plan was developed by the mentors in collaboration with leadership of the NPC. The education was provided to members of NPC and to the nurse educators group, unit-based educators responsible for communicating and educating staff about practice changes on each unit.

IMPLEMENTATION

Implementation of the new process began with the evidence-based practice mentors identifying the 32 P&Ps to be reviewed. The online procedure manual had been selected by the nine-member point-of-care review team.

For the manual to reflect the practice in a consistent manner, the template developed by the leadership group was used with each P&P under review. This template was the blueprint for the content and format of evidence-based P&Ps. Using the template, evidence-based policies or procedures were developed that ranged from policies on bed placement and patient classification systems to procedures on central venous catheters and healing touch.

With the systems and process developed, synthesizing the evidence for the P&Ps commenced. This step meant finding answers to the clinical questions formulated from key patient safety concerns for each policy or procedure (**Table 1**). "The purpose

| Box 2 |
| Grading the strength of the body of evidence |

A. Level I evidence

B. Consistent findings from levels II, III, IV, or V

C. Inconsistent findings from levels II, III, IV, or V

D. Little or no evidence or level VI only

E. Level VII

Data from Schiffer CA, Anderson K, Bennett C, et al. ASCO special article. Platelet transfusion for patients with cancer: clinical practice guidelines of the American Society of Clinical Oncology. J Clin Oncol 2001;19(5):1519–38.

Table 3
Integrated table (evidence summary) for PICO question "Among pediatric hospitalized patients requiring a central venous catheter, does use of chlorhexidine gluconate scrub versus Betadine and alcohol scrub decrease the incidence of catheter-related infections?"

Citation/Funding	Sample/Research Design	Independent Variable/ Intervention	Dependent Variable/ Outcome	Significant Results	Limitations/ Gaps	Generalizability	Level of Evidence
Citation: Pratt RJ, Pellowe CM, Wilson JA, et al. Epic2 national evidence-based guidelines for preventing health care–associated infections in NHS hospitals in England. J Hosp Infect 2007;665(Suppl):S1–64 Funding: British government	Sample: Development team a nurse-led multi-professional team of researchers and specialist clinicians Research design: guideline	N/A	Outcome: infection associated with central venous catheters	1) Decontaminate the skin site with a single patient use application of alcoholic chlorhexidine gluconate solution (preferably 2% chlorhexidine gluconate in 70% isopropyl alcohol) before the insertion of a central venous access device. (Class A recommendation: a systematic review of randomized controlled trials or a body of evidence that consists principally of studies rated as 1+, is directly applicable to the target population, and demonstrates overall consistency of results)	Guideline recommendations not tested, but audit criteria identified	Yes, except to children less than 1 year of age	Level I

Citation	Sample/Design		Outcome		Comments		Level
Citation: Morgan LM, Thomas DJ. Implementing evidence-based nursing practice in the pediatric intensive care unit. J Infusion Nurs 2007;30(2):105–12. Funding: no source identified	Sample: PICU staff at major pediatric hospital Research design: descriptive study	N/A	Outcome: incidence of catheter-related bloodstream infections in children	2) Use a single patient use application of alcoholic povidone-iodine solution for patients with a history of chlorhexidine sensitivity. Allow the antiseptic to dry before inserting the central venous access device. (Class D/GPP recommendation: a recommendation for best practice based on the experience of the guideline development group)	1) Mean rate decrease to 3.0 per 1000 CVC days (2006) from 5.2 per 1000 catheter days (2005) with CVC practice bundle and monitoring performance, including skin antisepsis at catheter insertion site with 2% chlorhexidine	Statistical analysis methods, power calculations, and variables not clearly described	Yes	Level VI

(continued on next page)

Table 3
(continued)

Citation/Funding	Sample/Research Design	Independent Variable/ Intervention	Dependent Variable/ Outcome	Significant Results	Limitations/ Gaps	Generalizability	Level of Evidence
Citation: Infusion Nurses Society. Infusion nursing standards of practice. J Infusion Nurs 2006; 29(1 Suppl): S1–92 Funding: no source identified	Sample: Development team a committee of RN experts Research design: guideline	N/A	Outcome: infusion nursing practicecriteria for infection control and safety compliance of access site preparation	1) Antiseptic solutions that should be used include alcohol, chlorhexidine gluconate, povidone-iodine, and tincture of iodine, as single agents or in combination. Formulations containing a combination of alcohol and chlorhexidine gluconate or povidone-iodine are preferred. 2) Use of chlorhexidine gluconate in infants weighing <1000 g has associated with contact dermatitis and should be used with caution in this patient population. 3) For neonates, isopropyl alcohol or products containing isopropyl alcohol are	Recommendations not explicit or tagged by level of evidence. Development strategy not discussed. Key stakeholders and guideline developers unknown. Unknown if guideline subjected to peer-review and testing.	Yes	Level II

Citation: Lee OK, Johnston L. (2005). A systematic review for effective management of central venous catheters and catheter sites in acute care pediatric patients. Worldviews on Evidence Based Nursing 2005;2(1):4–13. Funding: no source identified	Sample: Randomized and nonrandomized controlled trials investigating catheter management strategies in prevention of CVC complications in hospitalized children 0–18 years Research design: systematic review	Intervention: type of skin preparations/ antiseptic/ antimicrobial ointment	Outcome: catheter-related bloodstream infections in pediatric hospitalized patients	not recommended for access site preparation. Povidone-iodine or chlorhexidine gluconate solution is recommended but requires complete removal after the preparatory procedure with sterile water or sterile 0.9% sodium chloride (USP) to prevent product absorption. 1) CVC sites prepped and cleansed daily with chlorhexidine gluconate versus povidone-iodine solutions showed no significant differences in catheter-related bacteremia overall. Subgroup analysis of patients <12 months old showed higher rate of bacteremia in povidone-iodine group versus chlorhexidine gluconate group, but was not statistically significant.	Meta-analysis of the study results not feasible due to differences in intervention and outcome measures. Statistical power calculations not done on individual study. Variable dressing techniques confounded results of individual study.	Yes	Level I

(continued on next page)

Table 3
(continued)

Citation/Funding	Sample/Research Design	Independent Variable/ Intervention	Dependent Variable/ Outcome	Significant Results	Limitations/ Gaps	Generalizability	Level of Evidence
Citation: O'Grady NP, Alexander M, Dellinger EP, et al. (2002). Guidelines for the prevention of intravascular catheter-related infections. Pediatrics 2002;110(5):1-24. Funding: US government	Sample: Development team a multidisciplinary team of medicine and nursing Research design: guideline	N/A	Outcome: intravascular catheter-related bloodstream infections	1) Disinfect clean skin with an appropriate antiseptic before catheter insertion and during dressing changes. Although a 2% chlorhexidine-based preparation is preferred, tincture of iodine, an iodophor, or 70% alcohol can be used. (Category IA recommendation: strongly recommended for implementation and strongly supported by well-designed experimental, clinical, or epidemiologic studies) 2) No recommendation can be made for the use of chlorhexidine in infants aged 2 months. (Unresolvedissue: no recommendation; practices for which insufficient evidence or no consensus regarding efficacy exist)	Development strategy and process to identify, select, and combine evidence was not described. Guideline recommendations not tested.	Yes	Level II

Abbreviations: CVC, central venous catheter; GPP, good practice point.
Courtesy of Alvce A. Schultz, PhD, RN, FAAN, Chandler, AZ.

of synthesizing research studies is to determine whether the strength of the evidence supports a change in practice."[1] At this phase of the process, the steps of evidence-based practice were used to guide the literature search, collection of the best evidence, and critical appraisal. An example of the evidence synthesis relevant to a policy or procedure is consideration of the clinical question for central venous catheters.

The PICO question identified was "Among pediatric hospitalized patients requiring a central venous catheter, does use of chlorhexidine gluconate scrub versus Betadine and alcohol scrub decrease the incidence of catheter-related infections?" Employing multiple search databases, three guidelines, one systematic review, and one descriptive study were collected. Because only studies can be appraised, the published expert opinion was summarized but not appraised. The studies were appraised and leveled for quality using the rapid critical appraisal tools from Melnyk and Fineout-Overholt.[2] One systematic review (level I), three guidelines (levels I and II), and one descriptive study (level VI) were appraised and assigned a quality level using the system for levels of evidence (**Table 2**). The body of evidence, or synthesis of all the studies collectively, was graded for quality, quantity, and consistency of the results using an adapted system (**Box 2**).[9] The grade for this body of evidence on chlorhexidine gluconate was grade B, that is, consistent findings from evidence levels II, III, IV, or V. A recommendation was made in support of continuing the practice of using chlorhexidine gluconate as an antiseptic agent in preventing catheter-related infections in pediatric patients undergoing insertion of a central venous catheter (**Table 3**).

The NPC, after viewing a demonstration, adopted the developed process that integrated leveled and graded evidence in conjunction with an online pediatric procedure manual into P&Ps. For members of the NPC to disseminate an educational plan and maintain the practice change, the evidence-based practice mentors conducted education sessions for council members. The education provided served as a plan for council members in collaboration with the educator group to further develop into a process for educating all staff regarding evidence-based P&Ps. Outcomes to be addressed are the effects of evidence-based P&Ps on patient safety, cost, length of stay, nurse work time, and flow.

INTEGRATE AND MAINTAIN

Outcomes of the process for integrating evidence into P&Ps consisted of development of an evidence-based P&P template, completion of 32 P&Ps that were evidence based, education provided to the NPC and unit educators group, and development of a plan to educate the entire nursing staff about the integration of evidence into P&Ps. The process outcome of a template to guide incorporation of evidence into P&Ps was approached with the goal of enhancing the safe provision of patient care. An additional outcome from the process included the completion of 32 P&Ps that were evidence based by mentors in collaboration with experts in the content area. The P&Ps, once completed, were submitted to the NPC to approve and disseminate to health care staff within the organization.

This dissemination will aid in the integration and maintenance of the practice change related to evidence-based P&Ps. Communication of the recommended change to stakeholders, including nurses at the point-of-care, will continue to occur through educational endeavors by the nurse educators in the form of education sessions, Power Point presentations on unit online sites, and group e-mails. Monitoring of the process and evaluation of outcomes will continue within the organization through follow-up of NPC members.

SUMMARY

The process of developing P&Ps that are based on evidence involves multiple steps performed by experts in both evidence-based practice and content areas. P&Ps based on evidence can support consistency in nursing practice. Consistency can promote safety in the care of children and families, supporting the strategic plan of the organization and the national health care agenda of safety and promotion of evidence-based decision making at the point-of-care.

REFERENCES

1. Rosswurm MA, Larrabee JH. A model for change to evidence-based practice. Image J Nurs Sch 1999;31(4):317-22.
2. Melnyk BM, Fineout-Overholt E. Evidence-based practice in nursing & healthcare: a guide to best practice. Philadelphia: Lippincott Williams & Wilkins; 2005.
3. Finkelman A, Kenner C. Teaching IOM. Implications of the Institute of Medicine reports for nursing education. Silver Spring (MD): American Nurses Association; 2007.
4. The Joint Commission. 2008 National Patient Safety Goals. May 28, 2008.
5. Dawes M. On the need for evidence-based general and family practice. Evid Based Med 1996;1:68-9.
6. Heater B, Becker A, Olson R. Nursing interventions and patient outcomes: a meta-analysis of studies. Nurs Res 1988;37:303-7.
7. Goode CJ, Tanaks DJ, Krugman M, et al. Outcomes from the use of an evidence-based practice guideline. Nurs Econ 2000;18(4):202-7.
8. Sicola V, Chesley DA. Development of the Texas Textbook Evaluation Tool (T-TET). Nurse Educ 1999;24(2):23-8.
9. Schiffer CA, Anderson K, Bennett C, et al. ASCO special article. Platelet transfusion for patients with cancer: clinical practice guidelines of the American Society of Clinical Oncology. J Clin Oncol 2001;19(5):1519-38.

Staff Nurses Creating Safe Passage with Evidence-Based Practice

Dora Bradley, PhD, RN-BC[a],*, John F. Dixon, MSN, RN, CNA, BC[b]

KEYWORDS

- Evidence-based practice • Professional practice models
- PARIHS • Transformational leadership • Synergy

Patient safety is one of the most critical issues for health care today.[1-5] The escalating need to decrease preventable complications serves as a significant catalyst to identify and use evidence-based practice (EBP) at the bedside. Decreasing preventable complications requires a synergistic relationship between the nurses at the bedside and nursing leadership. By virtue of their place relative to the patient, nurses are positioned to prevent errors and poor care decisions and also to assume a leadership role in advancing the use of evidence to promote safety and quality care.[1,2,6] Further, nursing leaders must be able to provide a unified perspective of nursing's contribution by highlighting the linkages among the practice environment, evidence-based nursing practice, quality of patient care, and outcomes.[1,7] At Baylor Health Care System (BHCS) the Professional Nursing Practice Model (PNPM) is used in conjunction with the Promoting Action on Research Implementation in Health Services (PARIHS) framework[8] to develop and implement critical strategies that have increased significantly the use of EBP to improve nursing practice and to promote "safe passage," the optimal outcome of nursing.[9]

The urgency of employing EBP at the bedside has never been greater. By putting into operation the PARIHS concepts of evidence, facilitation, and context together with the BHCS PNPM model, BHCS has created a number of structures and processes necessary for engaging nurses in EBP activities that promote safe passage for patients. This article presents an overview of the concepts and the specific structures and processes used to increase the use of EBP and improve patient safety.

[a] Nursing Professional Development, Baylor Health Care System, Corporate Office of Chief Nursing Officer, 2001 Bryan Tower, Suite 600, Dallas, TX 75201, USA
[b] BUMC Center for Nursing Education and Research, Baylor University Medical Center, 3500 Gaston Avenue, Dallas, TX 75246, USA
* Corresponding author.
E-mail address: dora.bradley@baylorhealth.edu (D. Bradley).

Nurs Clin N Am 44 (2009) 71–81
doi:10.1016/j.cnur.2008.10.002   nursing.theclinics.com

CREATING URGENCY FOR EVIDENCE-BASED PRACTICE

In recent months, the Centers for Medicare and Medicaid Services (CMS) has promoted a culture of progressively greater provider accountability.[4] Building on the Institute of Medicine report, *To Err is Human: Building a Safer Health System*,[3] the CMS created a plan that will deny extra reimbursement for hospitals if a patient develops a preventable complication during the hospitalization. Currently the plan to be implemented in October 2008 includes eight non-reimbursable conditions, and that number may increase significantly by 2010. These reimbursement issues, coupled with the increasing public awareness of errors and avoidable hospital complications occurring throughout the nation, have created a new sense of urgency for hospitals to find ways to prevent complications. Consequently, hospitals are being compelled to allocate significant resources to identifying and implementing strategies and processes that will decrease the occurrence of avoidable complications. Even though complications are everyone's concern, it makes sense to focus on supporting nursing efforts, because nurses typically are closest to the patient and many of these non-reimbursable conditions (eg, pressure ulcers, catheter-associated urinary tract infections, and falls with injuries) are nurse-sensitive outcomes.[10] Therefore, it is imperative that nurses be able to employ the most effective actions to prevent these outcomes.

In the recent Agency for Healthcare Research and Quality (AHRQ) publication, *Patient Safety and Quality: An Evidence-Based Handbook for Nurses*,[1] the Director of AHRQ and the President and Chief Executive Officer of the Robert Wood Johnson Foundation stated that "high-quality health care can be achieved through the use of evidence and an enabled and empowered nursing workforce." Consequently, the need to empower and support nurses to identify and use EBP related to patient safety has a significant likelihood of resulting in better patient outcomes and also in a substantial return on investment.

So what does nursing need to do? Nursing generally has stressed the importance of patient safety but has not always been able to articulate the nursing practices that are designed to prevent harm and create safe passage of patients.[1] Florence Nightingale set the stage for using evidence and data to make decisions about patient safety and prevention. After Nightingale, however, nursing's knowledge development seems to have been based more on tradition than on evidence. Now there is increasing evidence that some tradition-based practices may not promote the type of outcomes they once were thought to do.[11,12] Conversely, there is substantial verification that specific evidence-based nursing practices can decrease patient complications and adverse events.[1,11] Therefore, if nursing's identification and use of EBP can decrease complications, it is imperative that hospitals and nursing leadership create structures and processes to promote the development and implementation of evidence-based nursing practices. Not implementing EBP could be considered unethical.

FACTORS INFLUENCING THE IMPLEMENTATION OF EVIDENCE-BASED PRACTICE

Because of external forces, hospitals will need to make aggressive changes in current practices to ensure that patients do not experience avoidable complications during hospitalization. To meet fiscal goals, organizations must look at the growing evidence demonstrating the significant link between the identification and implementation of EBP and improved patient outcomes.[1,4,5] Therefore, the allocation of resources for the creation of effective structures and processes to support EBP will be critical both to patient safety and to the fiscal goals of the organization. To create a supportive environment, organizations need to identify and develop strategies that have the highest potential of influencing the successful implementation of EBP. The PARiHS

framework[8,13] purports that successful implementation of EBP at the bedside relates directly to the functions of evidence, facilitation, and context. The function of evidence reflects knowledge sources, which include research, clinical experience, patient experience, and local data and information. Facilitation is a function that relates to assisting with the implementation of EBP and is operationalized in the role, skills, and attributes of the facilitator. Context function represents the culture, leadership, and evaluation processes in the environment where practice changes need to occur.

Using the PARIHS framework as a guide to decrease complications and improve quality, nursing leaders must transform infrastructures in the work environment to integrate EBP into bedside nursing practice. Successful implementation of EBP at the bedside requires nurses to have ready access to meaningful information and data, specifically library access, patient preference information, and meaningful quality data. In addition, allocation of funds and other resources is critical to support the development of EBP expertise and credible practice changes. To create an "EBP context," transformational nursing leaders must work with staff to create a vision for EBP at the bedside, create opportunities for nurses to question practice, promote risk-taking, and value questioning of practice.[14] In addition, strategies that support development and create opportunities for recognition are critical to the effort. Some examples are advancement programs that promote the use of EBP, nurse councils in which nurses make decisions to change practices based on evidence, and methods to create ongoing feedback. By operationalizing the functions of the PARIHS framework in conjunction with defined practice models, nursing leaders have the means to integrate EBP at the bedside and improve patient outcomes.

BAYLOR HEALTH CARE SYSTEM PROFESSIONAL NURSING PRACTICE MODEL

The system's chief nursing officers adopted the BHCS PNPM in 2005 (**Fig. 1**). At its core is the American Association of Critical-Care Nurses (AACN) Synergy Model for Patient Care.[9] The Synergy Model is based on studies of practice and clearly articulates the importance of the linkage between nurse competencies and patient needs, regardless of practice specialty. The premise of the Synergy Model is that when patient needs are matched to nurse competencies, synergistic nursing practice results in safe passage defined as "an optimal outcome of nursing."[9] BHCS has expanded on the original definition by describing safe passage as "an optimal outcome of nursing. Nurses promote safe passage for their patients by using knowledge of patient needs and the health care environment to assist them to transition through the health care encounter without any preventable complications or delay."[15]

The patient's need for safe passage is a catalyst for EBP. Within the Synergy Model,[9] there are eight areas of patient need and eight nurse competencies. The nurse competencies have operational definitions that are defined further on a continuum from baseline competence to expert level. The areas of patient need reflect a holistic assessment going beyond the physiologic system approach of the traditional medical model. This holistic approach includes distinctive areas best addressed by the unique contributions of nursing practice through interventions such as facilitation of learning, responsiveness to diversity, and creation of supportive and healing therapeutic environments. The model also reflects the importance of nurses being autonomous, having the authority to change or modify their practice, and the expectation that nurses take accountability for their actions and the resulting outcomes. In addition, the model recognizes that nursing practice does not occur within a vacuum but rather interacts with a complex work environment that surrounds it. To address this phenomenon, BHCS incorporated the AACN's Healthy Work Environment Standards[16] as part of

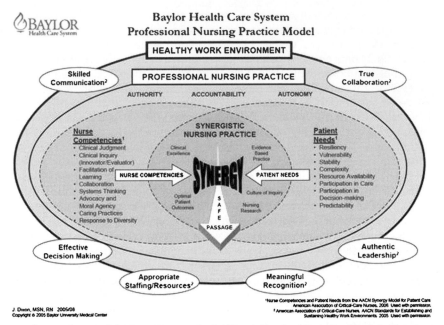

Fig. 1. The Baylor Health Care System Professional Nursing Practice Model (*Courtesy of Baylor Health Care System, Dallas, TX; with permission.*)

the PNPM. To promote synergistic nursing practice, the immediate work environment must be one that supports the development of a culture of inquiry, expects clinical excellence and optimal patient outcomes, and fosters nursing research and EBP. The PNPM provides a framework for professional practice and clearly articulates important concepts and linkages suitable for EBP projects and research.

ENGAGING NURSES IN EVIDENCE-BASED PRACTICE TO PROMOTE SAFE PASSAGE

BHCS has used specific strategies to engage nurses in EBP while assisting them to promote safe passage of their patients. By applying the PARIHS functions of evidence, facilitation, and context to the PNPM concepts, BHCS has been able to operationalize a number of the successful strategies that link EBP, nursing practice, and patient outcomes.

Evidence

Increasing the staff nurses' access to evidence, including research, data, and benchmarking information, was the first essential strategy. The BHCS library provides outstanding services and resources in support of Baylor's evidence-based nursing practice, nursing research efforts, and nursing practice specialties. The library's online resources, including more than 250 full-text nursing journals, dozens of full-text nursing books, and a wide variety of literature databases, are available from any computer in the BHCS network. The librarians are available for customized classes, one-on-one training sessions, researching tough questions, and performing literature searches—all free of charge to any nurse. These resources have been used to explore and support changes in both administrative and clinical practices.

With increased awareness of EBP and the implementation of Baylor's professional nursing advancement program ("Achieving Synergy in Practice through Impact, Relationships, and Evidence," ASPIRE), Cumulative Index of Nursing and Allied Health Literature (CINAHL) searches increased by 17% from 2006 to 2007 (2007 = 6806), CINAHL sessions increased by 26% (2007 = 2140), and access to nursing journals increased by 12% (2007 = 3752).

To understand patient preferences as a source of evidence, nurses have used patient satisfaction data and unit interviews. A number of nurses have conducted focus groups to identify patients' preferences for various aspects of care and learning. The neonatal ICU (NICU) nurses completed an EBP project to determine the best practices for discharge-to-home education of parents with potentially fragile infants. Over the years, the NICU nurses had compiled a very comprehensive discharge education program. They were challenged to identify whether their current practices were truly evidenced based. They reviewed the literature and found some important differences in their approach, especially for the younger parents. To identify patient/family preferences, they sought information from families attending the annual NICU day. They discovered that much of the material they were providing to families was based on what the staff thought was critical, not on what the family really needed. Consequently, the NICU made significant evidence-based changes to the discharge education program.

As in many other large facilities, access to meaningful local data and reports has been somewhat difficult at times. BHCS leadership, however, is committed to transparency, and therefore nursing leadership, staff, and others have spent considerable time creating staff nurse access to unit-based data. Now, unit data are available with trends and comparisons to other like units, the hospital, the system, and national benchmarks, when available. This effort has yielded a number of EBP projects related to falls, urinary tract infections, ventilator-acquired pneumonia, and pressure ulcers. These projects have resulted in decreased complication rates and have provided the foundation for changes in practice on individual units and frequently across units and multiple facilities within the BHCS.

Facilitation

To facilitate the ongoing growth of EBP, the goal has been to assist managers and staff in gaining the skills and knowledge necessary to recognize the need for change and the steps they need to take to get the desired outcomes. Consequently, a Research and EBP series was developed. In 2007 and 2008, experts in the areas of EBP and research were invited to provide education and consultation at various venues throughout BHCS. Some of the topics presented included creating a culture of inquiry, determining a clinically significant problem and writing the clinical question, evaluating and critiquing primary studies and systematic reviews, and linking EBP and research to patient outcomes. Groups and individuals also participated in private consultations to refine their projects. The result was a significant increase in both EBP projects and research studies. Most of the projects focused on improving patient outcomes and decreasing complications conceptualized within the PNPM.

The Evidence-Based Nursing Practice and Nursing Research Council was created to facilitate practice changes and the ongoing development of EBP and research skills. The charge of this council is to "develop and validate knowledge to advance the science and practice of nursing through the promotion and support of Evidence-Based Nursing Practice (EBNP) and Nursing Research at Baylor." The Council is responsible for (1) providing a setting to evaluate nursing practice against best practices and current evidence; (2) recommending the implementation of specific nursing protocols, procedures, and guidelines to promote best practice; (3) improving patient care, safety, and outcomes; and (4) serving as a clearinghouse for evidence-based nursing practice and nursing research projects. Membership is primarily staff nurses from all nursing specialties but also includes representatives from education, management, and advanced practice. This council makes evidence-based recommendations for practice and policy changes to the Staff Nurse Advisory Council.

To provide a consistent approach, several key structures have been adopted to facilitate EBP. The Iowa model serves as a guideline for identifying and processing triggers for potential EBP projects.[17] Questions are formulated using the PICO format, but with a slight modification. An "S" has been added to PICO to represent "Safe Passage and Synergy," thus ensuring that the question links to the BHCS PNPM (**Fig. 2**). The strength of the evidence is graded using the Stetler level of evidence table.[18]

Two practice changes that the EBP council facilitated are practices in the insertion and routine care of urinary catheters and eliminating saline instillation before suctioning into endotracheal tubes. Both these practices tie directly to EBP and Safe Passage: evidence is being used to direct practice to minimize the risk of preventable complications and delays so that the patient can continue to move along the health care continuum.

Context

The focus on decreasing patient complications and the use of EBP has been a "strategic direction" for the entire BHCS during the last few years. There has been a major effort to cascade these strategic goals for EBP and patient safety in a meaningful way to the unit level. Because of this focus on EBP and safety, resources are allocated to this initiative for all patient care disciplines. Within the nursing departments, a number of hospitals in the Baylor Healthcare System are seeking Magnet designation, providing tremendous contextual support for EBP initiatives.[7]

Recent revisions in nursing job descriptions include expectations for the staff nurse in the area of clinical inquiry. Specifically the staff nurse is expected (1) to question and evaluate practice and provide EBP; (2) to create practice changes through research use and experiential learning; and (3) to support the implementation of changes and EBP. These expectations are reflected in the regular performance appraisals.

Other contextual factors include EBP as a focus during nursing orientation and new graduate internships. Nursing leaders promote the expectation for use of evidence in practice through an introduction in nursing orientation. There is a strong focus on EBP in all the internship programs. The recent revision of internship goals and outcomes reflects the practice model and includes a significant focus on EBP (**Table 1**) Learning content is included in both didactic and clinical practice. Unit or service-line educators evaluate the achievement of outcomes on the unit through the completion of specific learning activities. The preceptor, clinical nurse specialist, and/or unit educator keys in on a specific "why is it done this way" question asked by the nurse intern. The nurse intern is expected to use the unit computer to access articles related to the practice. to review the data and to create a method for sharing findings with other nurses on the unit. The nurse educator and/or clinical nurse specialist validates the results.

LINKING NURSING EVIDENCE AND PATIENT OUTCOMES

BHCS has created a number of strategies to identify opportunities support EBP. One of the most important programs is the professional nursing advancement program, AS-PIRE. ASPIRE was created in 2005 to recognize the registered nurse's unique contributions to patient outcomes. The program defines nursing practice as the integration of

PICO-S

Asking Your Burning Clinical Question

Whether doing an evidence-based practice review or conducting a nursing research study, you start with a question. If your question is focused and well-thought out then your efforts will be easier because you will have a clear direction of how to proceed.

<u>Burning Clinical Questions</u> can arise from a number of triggers such as:

...**data** (e.g., quality, risk management, financial, benchmarks) ...a **clinical problem or process** you identify

...**standards and guidelines** from national nursing organizations ...a recently **published article**

To help create a focused, well-thought out question, we are using the PICO-S format. The better you craft your question, the clearer it is to determine specific steps you need to take.

P	I	C	O	S
Patient or Problem	**Intervention**	**Comparison**	**Outcome(s)**	**Synergy & Safe Passage**
• Define who will make up this population, addressing who will be included and, if appropriate, who will be excluded • Define what the problem is	• Define the intervention	• Define who/what will be used as the comparison, could be another group like a control group or themselves if doing a pre- then post- test with the same group	• Define what outcomes are to be measured and how these will be measured	• Identify which patient needs and/or nurse competencies align with this initiative • Think about how this project will contribute to Safe Passage
Example				
Patients to be fed using a nasogastric tube	Verification of nasogastric tube placement	Current practice versus the evidence	Correct placement of nasogastric tube.	Safe Passage - Feeding delivered into the gut. Patient Need – *Vulnerability* – at risk for inappropriate placement Nurse Competency – *Clinical Judgment* – refined assessment

Fig. 2. Baylor Health Care System PICO-S question template. (*Courtesy of* Baylor Health Care System, Dallas, TX; with permission.)

knowledge, skills, experience, and attitudes that, when linked to the patient needs and characteristics, creates a synergistic process that results in safe passage and optimal outcomes.

The program has three levels, colleague, mentor, and leader. The scope and level of outcomes differentiates the three levels. There are a number of components that must be completed. First are the required elements, which address experience, education, certification, EBP, learning opportunities, and nursing's unique contribution to outcomes. Many have used the required EBP activity as the overall direction and support for the other activities of their plans. **Table 2** shows the requirements and expected evidence for EBP at each level.

There are four areas of development: clinical practice, leadership, education, and best practices. Each of these areas is linked specifically to one or more of the eight

Nurse Competency	Key Criteria/Interactions to Identify	Learning Content	Outcomes
Table 1 Baylor health care system competency expectations for nursing interns			
Clinical inquiry (innovator/evaluator)	Incorporates evidence-based practice/best practices into daily care	Exposure to evidence-based practice/research	By completion of orientation, the interns will identify questions related to practice and be able to access research/best practices in their field of expertise. They will do this by:
	Accesses unit QI data/infection rates and explains how best practices contribute to patient safety	Resources to access	Recognizing the evidence based/best practices used in their specialty areas
	Questions practice and accesses online resources to identify research findings	ASPIRE	Questioning why practices in health care are "done this way"
		Professional organizations	Accessing the online Health Sciences Library and locating research articles related to their practice questions
		Educational offerings	Recognizing systems in place to improve practice (nursing councils)
		Certification	

Courtesy of Baylor Health Care System, Dallas, TX; with permission.

nurse competencies of the Synergy model. The nurse chooses to develop one activity from each area. In addition, two optional activities can be used to replace some of the specialty development areas. For example, the nurse can conduct a formal research study approved by the institutional review board in which the nurse is the principal investigator or can write and submit a formal manuscript for publication in a national nursing journal.

The outcomes of the ASPIRE program have been outstanding. Through clinical narratives, nurses have documented the ways their intentional nursing actions have had a positive impact on patient or unit outcomes. As would be expected in a large academic medical center, medical practice is predominant. The EBP review has required staff to focus on nursing practice's unique contribution to patient care. Some of the initial plans identified medical practices or procedures as the EBP focus, but through mentoring and coaching, staff members were able to translate these foci into nursing practice. For instance, one nurse wanted to conduct an EBP review on anesthesia given

| Table 2 | | |
| ASPIRE: three levels of requirements for evidence-based nursing practice | | |
Colleague	Mentor	Leader
Assists with the identification of a patient or practice problem by gathering, analyzing baseline information, and presenting recommendations for considerations to Unit-based Partnership Council	Uses an evidence-based nursing practice review to create or validate a practice and formally presents findings to Unit-based Partnership Council	Implements and evaluates an evidence-based nursing practice change and formally presents to housewide Best Care Partnership Council
Evidence: Overview of baseline information, collection method, analysis and recommendations presented to partnership council; minutes from council	Evidence: Provide evidence-based indicators used to evaluate nursing practice and the results; minutes of partnership council	Evidence: Description of the process used to implement change and the resulting outcomes; minutes of partnership council

Modified from Baylor Health Care System; with permission.

during circumcision. Anesthesia is not determined or administered by nurses. Discussion with the nurse revealed that her interest lay predominantly pain management for infants undergoing circumcision. With help in crafting her question and redirecting her energies, she was able to identify nursing practices to support effective pain management of infants undergoing this procedure.

Many of the EBP projects addressed in the ASPIRE projects are based on situations that bedside practitioners encounter on a routine basis. Some of these practices include difficult intravenous starts in cold procedural areas, ineffective assessment of the risk for falls or pressure ulcers, inadequate patient and family teaching practices, and many others. Consistent with this culture of inquiry, these individuals now ask why a practice is followed and what evidence supports current practices. As a result, nurses are thinking about the evidence that supports daily nursing practices. In addition, the process of participating in ASPIRE is helping strengthen further the EBP knowledge and skills of staff, advancing the culture of inquiry.

Positive Patient Outcomes

Two of the many examples of the work nurses have done are described here in more depth. One nurse decided to look at the safe passage of patients who had a prior history of lymphadenectomy or mastectomy and who were undergoing some other type of surgical procedure. The vulnerability she identified was that these patients could not participate in their care or decision making when sedated; thus, they could not tell practitioners not to use their affected arm. From her own family members' experiences, she knew that this situation could create fear and anxiety. She decided that there had to be a better way inform all health care practitioners encountering the patient of the existence of these affected extremities. From her efforts in examining communication and handoff practices in the literature and benchmarking with other hospitals, she initiated the pink bracelet pilot project. In the day surgery hospital, a pink armband was placed on the affected extremity of patients who had a known history of lymphadenectomy or mastectomy. The reaction from patients was so extremely positive that several asked to meet the nurse who had developed this program. After the pilot, one patient who returned for an additional day hospital procedure refused to go to the operating room until she had her pink bracelet. As a result, the pink bracelet identification project is being used system-wide, and this nurse now is the principal investigator on a nursing research study to measure the bracelet's effect in reducing anxiety and fear.

The second example of positive change in practice based on inquiry and evidence occurred in one of the ICUs. A nurse identified that a coordinated plan for initiating weaning of patients from ventilators was lacking, thus making the patients vulnerable for potential complications and delays. She began her exploration by reviewing the literature, where she found a reliable and valid method for assessing readiness to wean from the ventilator.[19] Through her research, she learned that most practitioners focus on a only few primary pulmonary factors. Using this baseline knowledge assessment, she instituted a series of learning interventions. Postassessments demonstrated a significant increase in staff's knowledge of pulmonary and nonpulmonary factors that affect readiness to wean. Additionally, she applied the weaning-readiness screening tool and identified a number of patients who met the readiness criteria but had not been provided with a weaning trial. These missed opportunities resulted in delay in weaning and extubation, an outcome contrary to safe passage. The results of her nursing intervention have been shared with the critical care service line, and plans now are underway to consider routine implementation of the screening tool for all mechanically ventilated patients.

In both these ASPIRE projects, the nurses identified patients who were vulnerable and had a high potential for complications or adverse reactions. They responded with EBP initiatives and collected measurable data on nursing's unique contribution to outcomes and safe passage. A recent evaluation of the ASPIRE program found that nurses across the system identified evidence-based nursing practice as an essential element of current nursing practice and thought it should continue to be a required element.

SUMMARY

Focusing on the development of evidence, context, and facilitation functions within the practice environment is likely to assist nurses in identifying and implementing EBP. In addition, by demonstrating their ability to decrease complications and improve patient outcomes, nurses can demonstrate their significant contribution to patient care and organizational stewardship. The true challenge, however, still may be in getting nurses to realize that EBP can empower them to demonstrate the significant impact on outcomes and the safe passage of their patients.

REFERENCES

1. Hughes RG. Patient safety and quality: an evidence-based handbook for nurses. Rockville (MD): Agency for Healthcare Research and Quality; 2008. AHRQ Publication No. 08-0043.
2. Clancy CM, Farquhar MB, sharp BA. Patient safety in nursing practice. J Nurs Care Qual 2005;20(3):193–7.
3. Kohn LT, Corrigan JM, Donaldson MS, editors. To err is human: building a safer health care system. Washington, DC: National Academy Press, Institute of Medicine; 1999.

4. Centers for Medicare and Medicaid Services Office of Public Affairs. CMS proposes to expand quality program for hospital inpatient service in FY 2009 [April 14, 2008 press release]. Available at: http://www.cms.hhs.gov/apps/media/press/release. asp?Counter=3041&;intNumPerPage=10&checkDate=1&checkKey=2&srchType =3&numDays=90&srchOpt=0&srchData=quality&keywordType=All&chkNews Type=1%2C+2%2C+3%2C+4%2C+5&intPage=&showAll=1&pYear=&year= 0&desc=&cboOrder=date. Accessed May18, 2008.
5. Leape LL. Advances in patient safety: from research to implementation. In: Implementation issues, Vol 3. Rockville (MD): Agency for Healthcare Research and Quality; 2005. AHRQ Publication No. 05-0021-3.
6. Institute of Medicine. Keeping patients safe: transforming the work environment of nurses. Washington, DC: National Academies Press; 2004.
7. American Nurses Credentialing Center. Overview of ANCC magnet recognition program new model [brochure]. Available at: http://www.nursecredentialing.org/ model/MagnetModel.pdf. Accessed June 19, 2008.
8. Rycroft-Malone J. The PARIHS framework: a framework for guiding the implementation of evidence-based practice. J Nurs Care Qual 2004;19(4):297–304.
9. Curley MA. Patient–nurse synergy: optimizing patients' outcomes. Am J Crit Care 1998;7(1):64–72.
10. National Quality Forum. Nation consensus standards for nursing-sensitive care: an initial performance measure set. Washington, DC: National Quality Forum; 2004.
11. Rauen CA, Chulay M, Bridges E, et al. Seven evidence-based practice habits: putting some sacred cows out to pasture. Crit Care Nurse 2008;28(2):98–124.
12. Nursing staffing and patient outcomes in the inpatient setting: report. Washington, DC: American Nurses Association; 2000.
13. Cummings GC, Estabrooks CA, Midodzi WK, et al. Influence of organizational characteristics and context on research utilization. Nurse Res 2007;56(4S): S24–39.
14. McCormack B, Kitson A, Harvey G, et al. Getting evidence into practice: the meaning of "context". J Adv Nurs 2002;38(1):94–104.
15. Dixon JF, Bradley D. Implementing a synergistic professional nursing practice model. In: Curley AQ, editor. Synergy: the unique relationship between nurses and patients. Indianapolis (IN): Sigma Theta Tau; 2007. p. 119–28.
16. AACN standards for establishing and sustaining health work environments: a journey to excellence. Aliso Viejo (CA): Amreican Association of Critical-Care Nurses; 2005.
17. Titler MG, Kleiber C, Steelman VJ, et al. The Iowa model of evidence-based practice to promote quality care. Crit Care Nurs Clin North Am 2001;13(4):497–509.
18. Stetler C. Updating the Stetler model of research utilization to facilitate evidence-based practice. Nurs Outlook 2001;49(6):272–8.
19. Burns SM, Earven S, Fisher C, et al. Implementation of an institutional program to improve clinical and financial outcomes of mechanically ventilated patients: one-year outcomes and lessons learned. Crit Care Med 2003;31(12):2752–63.

A Nursing Quality Program Driven by Evidence-Based Practice

Jacqueline J. Anderson, MSN, RN[a,b],
Marilyn Mokracek, MSN, RN, CCRN, NE-BC[c,d],
Cheryl N. Lindy, PhD, RN-BC, NEA-BC[e,*]

KEYWORDS

• Nursing quality • Best practice • Evidence-based practice

St. Luke's Episcopal Hospital in Houston established a best-practice council as a vehicle for identifying critical issues at the hospital and focusing on improving outcomes. Committed to convene, charge, and direct small interdisciplinary work teams, this Best Practice Council replaced the traditional nursing-quality council. The traditional nursing-quality program had focused on nursing documentation compliance rather than on quality improvement. Under that program, the nursing staff completed monthly chart reviews and submitted the audits as part of the nursing service quality program. However, the unit manager rarely audited nursing documentation for compliance with organizational policies. The nursing staff was required to review nursing documentation and collect data on peers. Completion of the audits was a requirement to receive a "meets" score on the staff nurse annual performance evaluation. Therefore, each nurse manager was required to track the completion of the quality audits and follow up with those whose audits were incomplete. The program consumed an extensive amount of time of both nursing staff and unit management. The nursing staff

[a] Division of Nursing, Unit 82, The University of Texas MD Anderson Cancer Center, 1515 Holcombe Boulevard, Houston, TX 77030, USA
[b] Nursing Research, St. Luke's Episcopal Hospital, 6720 Bertner Avenue, MC4-278, Houston, TX 77030, USA
[c] Neurosciences Service, St. Luke's Episcopal Hospital, 6720 Bertner Avenue, MC4-278, Houston, TX 77030, USA
[d] Best Practice Council, St. Luke's Episcopal Hospital, 6720 Bertner Avenue, MC4-278, Houston, TX 77030, USA
[e] Nursing and Patient Education and Research, St. Luke's Episcopal Hospital, 6720 Bertner Avenue, MC4-278, Houston, TX 77030, USA
* Corresponding author. Nursing and Patient Education and Research, St. Luke's Episcopal Hospital, 6720 Bertner Avenue, MC4-278, Houston, TX 77030, USA.
E-mail address: 77030janderson@mdanderson.org (J.J. Anderson).

Nurs Clin N Am 44 (2009) 83–91
doi:10.1016/j.cnur.2008.10.012
0029-6465/08/$ – see front matter © 2009 Elsevier Inc. All rights reserved.

did not see value in the completion of the audits because rarely was any action taken to improve the outcome findings. The time-intensive tasks of auditing charts left no opportunity for staff to become involved in actual improvement projects.

Unit outcomes data were reported to the nursing directors and filtered to the nurse managers with assignments for developing action plans to correct variances in their department data. Quality scores determined by nursing audits were often inconsistent with outcomes data reported through other departments. The traditional program also resulted in several teams working on the same problem completely unaware that another department had already identified the problem and implemented a practice change.

The main purpose of the Best Practice Council was to investigate clinical outcomes variances and provide clinically relevant direction to enhance patient care. The aim of the council was to legislate and standardize practice change across the hospital based on evidence of best practice. The council developed mechanisms to share best practices and eliminate duplicate efforts.

BEST PRACTICE COUNCIL

The Best Practice Council consisted of nursing leaders and staff nurses committed to enhancing patient outcomes through evidence-based practice. The council established work teams based on areas identified for performance improvement. Team leaders were identified and interdisciplinary team membership was assigned from multiple units. Teams were given clearly defined goals and responsibilities with the requirement to provide a progress report at the monthly Best Practice Council meeting. Each team was charged with identifying the problem or opportunity for improvement through the development of a problem statement. Each team assessed current practice and outcomes data, reviewed the current research, and made recommendations for changes to policies and practice. Once the best practice was identified and tested within the organization's culture, the team made recommendations for evaluation to ensure continued success. The Best Practice Council reviewed and tracked each team's performance and made recommendations for organizational implementation of "best practice" for each specific topic. According to the original plan, once a team's goals were met, the team would be disbanded and new teams would be created.

The team leader was responsible for scheduling the team meetings, developing the agenda, and ensuring that minutes were recorded. The first meetings were dedicated to getting the team organized. The team leader reviewed the quality data with the team, clarified the problem or opportunity for improvement, and developed a list of available and potential resources that might be required. The team completed a review of the literature related to the clinical issue. Based on the results and the action required, the team developed measurable goals and a timeline for completion of the project.

ST. LUKE'S EVIDENCE BASED PRACTICE MODEL

The teams each used the St. Luke's Evidence Based Practice Model (**Fig. 1**) as a guide. Adopted by the hospital's Division of Nursing in 2006, the model was developed for research use in the mid-1990s by the hospital's nurse researcher and Nursing Research Council. The original model was based on the Iowa Model of Evidence Based Practice to Promote Quality Care.[1]

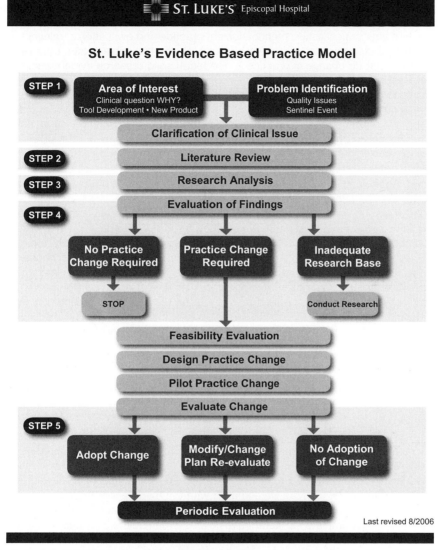

Fig. 1. St. Luke's Evidence Based Practice Model. (*Courtesy of* St. Luke's Episcopal Hospital, Houston, TX; with permission. Copyright © 2006, St. Luke's Episcopal Hospital.)

The model was updated in 2006 to favor an evidence-based practice approach. Melnyk and Fineout-Overholt,[2] in outlining the process for comparison, identified five key steps to the process of evidence-based practice:

1. Ask the burning question.
2. Collect the most relevant and best evidence.
3. Critically appraise the evidence.
4. Integrate the evidence with one's clinical expertise, patient preferences, and values in making a practice decision or change.
5. Evaluate the practice decision or change.[2]

These fives steps were highlighted in the model as shown in **Fig. 1**.

As a guide for each team, the St. Luke's Evidence Based Practice Model enumerates the steps that lead to each major decision that must be made. The first decision is reached after critical assessment of current practice and evaluation of relevant literature. Three outcomes are possible at this point. The first possible outcome is a recommendation that no change in practice is needed. If solid research evidence supports the current practice, then the decision is to make no changes. The second potential outcome is the finding that sufficient evidence supports making a change. The third potential outcome is the finding that evidence is insufficient to determine best practice and that the team needs to conduct further research to answer the question at hand.

When evidence supports change, the subsequent steps of the model lead the individual or team through the steps of designing and implementing that change. The final decision comes after completing a pilot and evaluating the impact of the practice change. Again, any of three outcomes are possible. The result of the pilot may demonstrate that the intended impact was not achieved and, for a variety of reasons, the change in practice may not be practical. The proposed change is then not adopted for the time being and the team returns to the literature to research alternative solutions. The second and rare outcome is that the practice change worked perfectly, exactly as expected, and is ready to be put into practice as a permanent and house-wide change. The third and more common outcome is that additional modifications are needed and another pilot called for. This step is repeated until the practice change consistently produces the required results and is ready for implementation across the hospital setting. This process mirrors the organizational quality improvement model and each team presents its results using the plan–do–check/study–act design.

USING OR IMPLEMENTING THE BEST PRACTICE MODEL

After the Best Practice Council completed the initial step of problem identification, each team was established based on quality outcome data that reflected potential areas for improvement. The director of nursing research was assigned to assist each team leader in getting the teams started. The director explained the evidence-based practice model to team members and described the steps each team needed to follow in working through the process. The first meeting was used to clarify the clinical issue and develop key search terms. At subsequent meetings, the relevant literature and a method for analysis were shared with the members of the team.

In critiquing literature and drawing conclusions, each team acted differently. Some teams elected to complete the literature review as a team. Others divided the literature and reviewed the studies as smaller groups within the team. Each team had a different experience with the literature. For example, the members assigned to the Pressure Ulcer Best Practice Team reviewed an abundance of literature from a number of different disciplines. In contrast, the Communication Hand-Off Best Practice Team found several studies related to team communication and emergency situations in other industries, but little evidence on communication between shifts or among departments within hospitals. The conclusions reached by each team after reviewing evidence and making comparisons to current practice are discussed below.

The Best Practice Council expected that each team would require 4 to 6 months to assess current practice and data results, review the current research and evidence related to the practice, and make recommendations for changes in policy and practice. Once the work of the current teams was completed, new teams for new target areas would be identified. The team members used the evidence-based practice model described above to focus concerns and questions, search for relevant evidence, and determine the applicability and feasibility of necessary changes. The first teams were assigned to study best practice in (1) preventing bloodstream infection (related to central lines); (2) preventing patient falls; (3) assessing and preventing pressure ulcers; and (4) ensuring good hand-off communication. The activities of the teams are described below.

Bloodstream Infection Prevention Best Practice Team

The Blood Stream Infection Prevention Best Practice Team focused on bloodstream infections related to the presence of central lines in the intensive care unit (ICU). In September 2006, when this team was formed, there were 11 ICUs in the institution. Five of the units ranked within the top 10th percentile in the National Nosocomial Infections Surveillance database, which provides the infection control benchmarks.[3] The remaining units were still well below the 50th percentile. An interdisciplinary team was formed with staff nurses, nurse managers, infection control practitioners, a critical care clinical nurse specialist, a nurse researcher, and an intravenous therapy nurse. Through use of the evidence-based practice model, the team conducted an extensive literature review, which was enhanced by the use of an annotated bibliography from the Institute for Healthcare Improvement[4] and of guidelines to prevent catheter-related infections from the Centers for Disease Control and Prevention.[5] Information from the literature was synthesized and compared with the current policy and procedures regarding insertion and care of central lines. The practices of the ICUs that ranked within the top 10th percentile were also evaluated for best practice. The team found that in comparing policy to best practice, only two minor revisions needed to be made. The policy was revised to include regular "dead end" cap changes and end the practice of placing a gauze over the insertion site underneath the clear dressing. The team also found a critical gap in the process of ensuring proper procedures: The bedside nurse was powerless to stop an insertion if any step in the proper process was omitted. To correct this problem, the team introduced a checklist to empower the nurse to assess and intervene if necessary.[6] Meanwhile, in reviewing practices in all of the hospitals's ICUs, the team found that the ICU with lowest infection rate used a sign to indicate the day the dressing needed to be changed. All of the hospital's ICUs came to adopt each of these changes—implementing the "dead-end" cap, ending the use of gauze over the insertion site, introducing a checklist, and posting signs calling for dressings to be changed. The bloodstream infection rates are reported monthly. The rate has improved and, with the exception of two units, remains well below the benchmark of the 50th percentile.

Fall Prevention Best Practice Team

The Fall Prevention Best Practice Team was assembled to identify innovative approaches to prevent falls. Team members included nursing staff and management, physical therapists, radiologists, clinical nurse specialists, and nursing researchers. A review of current practice revealed that fall risks were being assessed using the Hendrich II Fall Risk Assessment Tool,[7] which was completed every shift. The review also found that the rates of both falls and falls with injury were increasing. The interdisciplinary team determined that innovative strategies needed to be developed for patients identified at high risk of falling. A review of the literature initially revealed 131 research articles. After research criteria were limited to include only those articles from the past 3 years that focused on innovative interventions and that had scientific merit, 9 research studies were selected. These studies, all related to fall prevention, focused on (1) patient assessment,[8–11] (2) patients' needs for excessive toileting and effects of medications,[9,10] (3) staff, patient, and family education,[8,12,13] and (4) ability of nursing staff to implement innovative interventions.[8,10,11,13–16] Three primary interventions were piloted and subsequently implemented house-wide. The first intervention was the use of colored nonskid socks for patients at high risk of falling. The use of yellow socks in addition to a yellow sign posted on door to the patient's room and on the front of the chart alerted other hospital staff that the patient was at high risk of falling. If a patient had fallen in the hospital, he or she received red socks. Anyone seeing a patient in the hall with red socks knew the patient should always be accompanied and not left alone. Second, a safety huddle was added to the change-of-shift communication procedure on each unit. The patients at high risk of falling were identified and labeled as a "community patient." Every staff member was expected to respond immediately to these patients' call lights. Third, for reporting falls, an algorithm was developed that included an immediate fall debriefing. This algorithm provided timely critical information that is often forgotten when reporting is delayed. These interventions created a heightened staff awareness and focus on fall prevention rather than fall-risk assessment. After implementation, the fall rate decreased 18% and the rate of falls with injury was reduced by 30%.

Pressure Ulcer Prevention Best Practice Team

Before the formation of the Pressure Ulcer Best Practice Team, quarterly pressure ulcer prevalence studies showed that rates of hospital-acquired pressure ulcers at St. Luke's were below national benchmarks. Even so, the interdisciplinary team chose to focus on further decreasing this percentage and on addressing prevention. Represented on the team were nursing, pharmacy, physical therapy, and nutrition services. Nursing representatives included staff nurses, nurse managers, advanced practice nurses, and certified wound ostomy nurses. After reviewing the literature, the team found that staff education was the key to a thorough skin assessment and the implementation of interventions to prevent skin breakdown.[17-23] With the assistance of nurse managers from each of the acute and critical care units, staff nurses were identified to be skin resource nurses. These nurses were divided into teams to collect the quarterly pressure ulcer prevalence data. They were given extensive instruction on pressure ulcer staging and interrater reliability was established. In addition, these staff nurses assisted with the further education of staff nurses on the use of the Braden Scale assessment to assess patients at risk of skin breakdown and to implement measures to prevent breakdown based on the Braden subscale assessment.[24] If skin breakdown did occur, staff nurses were instructed about how to describe these pressure ulcers using common terminology, including location, depth, status of wound bed, and appearance of wound edges and surrounding skin. The team also worked with representatives from information systems. Nurses now send reports daily to nutrition indicating which patients have low albumin. Those patients then receive early treatment. An on-line incident report has been developed to facilitate early reporting of skin breakdown. At this writing, the incidence reporting is still being piloted. Pressure ulcer prevalence has decreased since this initiative began. Ulcers equal to or greater than stage II have decreased 18%.

Hand-Off Communication Best Practice Team

The Hand-Off Communication Best Practice Team was established to develop a comprehensive plan for more effective communication hospital-wide. Patients interact with multiple caregivers and departments on a daily basis. During many of these interactions, caregivers make observations or collect data that must be consistently and accurately passed on to other caregivers. To improve the process of sharing information, a team was formed with staff and managers from nursing, perioperative services, diagnostic testing areas, emergency department, transportation, social services, and case management. Hand-off communication is defined as the interactive process of passing patient-specific information from one caregiver to another or from one team of caregivers to another for the purpose of ensuring the continuity and safety of the patient's care.[25] Two related initiatives had already been implemented successfully in nursing. One was the use of the communication technique represented by the acronym SBAR for *situation*, *background*, *assessment*, and *recommendation*.[26,27] The technique is designed to ensure that nurses, in communicating with physicians, provide useful and clear information in an efficient way. The nurse first describes the situation, then summarizes the background, then provides an assessment, and finally makes a recommendation. The team recommended that the SBAR technique used successfully by nurses be implemented by caregivers hospital-wide. The other initiative was the use of a universal transfer report upon transfer to another level of care. To exceed the standard outlined in The Joint Commission National Patient Safety Goal #2,[28] the team identified a need for a standardized house-wide approach to hand-off communication that included the opportunity to ask and respond to questions. After an extensive literature review of published best practices on hand-off and team communication, the team created three report forms. The forms are based on the patient's destination and the level of information required. The most comprehensive form is the preoperative checklist,[29] which is the written report and checklist to be completed before the patient entered the operating room. The preprocedure checklist was created for invasive testing and includes an area for a return report to be completed by the staff in the testing department. The third form was the trip ticket that provides a written report for transfer of the patient to a noninvasive testing or examination area. Change-of-shift reporting[30-33] and a verification process before invasive procedures—known as a "time-out"[34,35]—are also critical communication events. A template was created for change-of-shift report. The elements of a "time-out" were identified on a sticker that could be placed in the patient's chart for procedures performed at the bedside. To educate staff, the team produced a video that demonstrated both the use of the change-of-shift report template and how to conduct a proper time-out. The checklists, trip ticket, change-of-shift report, and time-out stickers have improved communication among caregivers and enhanced patient safety. After the initial implementation of the new forms and processes, chart reviews and observations revealed a 89% compliance with the changes. Through ongoing record review and unit rounding, the current compliance is 93%.

SUMMARY

The replacement of the traditional nursing quality council with the Best Practice Council has helped St. Luke's Episcopal Hospital regain the focus of its nursing quality efforts. The structure provided to the teams by the Evidence Based Practice Model gave the hospital a consistent roadmap for solving quality problems. The success of the teams can be attributed to clear directions, an aggressive timeline, and the short-term commitment required of team members. The teams have remained focused and on track. Each team met their original goals. In the spirit of continuous quality improvement—and despite the original plan for them to disband after meeting goals—each team continues to meet and has identified new projects and goals to work toward. Meanwhile, new teams have formed to address additional areas for improvement identified through review of outcomes data by the Best Practice Council.

REFERENCES

1. Titler MG, Klieber C, Steelman V, et al. Infusing research into practice to promote quality care. Nurs Res 1994;43(5):307–13.

2. Melnyk B, Fineout-Overholt E. Evidence based practice in nursing & healthcare: a guide to best practice. Philadelphia (PA): Lippincott, Williams, Wilkins; 2005.
3. National Center for Preparedness D, and Control of Infectious Diseases. National Nosocomial Infections Surveillance System (NNIS). Centers for Disease Control and Prevention. Available at: http://www.cdc.gov/ncidod/dhqp/nnis.html. Accessed June 25, 2008.
4. Improvement IfH. Getting started kit: prevent central line infections. IHI. Available at: http://www.ihi.org/nr/rdonlyres/2ab66d90-c8e0-4a22-82a4-55ea9d93f94e/0/centrallineinfectionsbibliography.doc. Accessed June 25, 2008.
5. O'Grady N, Alexander M, Dellinger E, et al. Guidelines for the prevention of intravascular catheter-related infections. MMWR 2002;51(No. RR-10). Centers for Disease Control and Prevention. Available at: http://www.cdc.gov/mmwr/preview/mmwrhtml/rr5110a1.htm. Accessed June 25, 2008.
6. Wall R, Ely E, Elasy T, et al. Using real time process measurements to reduce catheter related bloodstream infections in the intensive care unit. Qual Saf Health Care 2005;14(4):295–302.
7. Hendrich A. The AHI Fall Prevention Program with the Hendrich II Fall Risk Model©. Available at: http://www.ahincorp.com/hfrm/index.php. Accessed June 25, 2008.
8. Szumlas S, Groszek J, Kitt S, et al. Take a second glance: a novel approach to inpatient fall prevention. Jt Comm J Qual Saf 2004;30(6):295–302.
9. Krauss M, Evanoff B, Hitcho E, et al. A case-control study of patient, medication and care-related risk factors for inpatient falls. J Gen Intern Med 2004;20(2):116–22.
10. Mills P, Neily J, Luan D, et al. Using aggregate root cause analysis to reduce falls and related injuries. Jt Comm J Qual Patient Saf 2005;31(1):21–31.
11. Vassallo M, Vignaraja R, Sharma J, et al. Predictors for falls among hospital inpatients with impaired mobility. J R Soc Med 2004;97(6):266–9.
12. Ray W, Taylor J, Brown A, et al. Prevention of fall-related injuries in long-term care: a randomized controlled trial of staff education. Arch Intern Med 2005;165(19): 2293–8.
13. Haines T, Bennell K, Osborne R, et al. Effectiveness of targeted falls prevention programme in subacute hospital setting: randomised controlled trial. BMJ 2004;328(7441):676–82.
14. Jeske L, Kolmer V, Muth M, et al. Partnering with patients and families in designing visual cues to prevent falls in hospitalized elders. J Nurs Care Qual 2006; 21(3):236–41.
15. Dempsey J. Falls prevention revisited: a call for a new approach. J Clin Nurs 2004;13(4):479–85.
16. Healey F, Monro A, Cockram A, et al. Using targeted risk factor reduction to prevent falls in older in-patients: a randomised controlled trial. Age Ageing 2004;33(4):390–5.
17. Bryant R, Nix DE. Acute & chronic wounds: current management concepts. 3rd edition. St. Louis (MO): Mosby Elsevier; 2007.
18. Courtney B, Ruppman J, Cooper H. Save our skin: initiative cuts pressure ulcer incidence in half. Nurs Manage 2006;37(4):36–45.
19. Lyder C, Grady J, Mathur D, et al. Preventing pressure ulcers in Connecticut hospitals by using the plan-do-study-act model of quality improvement. Jt Comm J Qual Saf 2004;30(4):205–13.
20. National Pressure Ulcer Advisory Panel. Updated staging system. Available at: http://www.npuap.org/pr2.htm. Accessed October 9, 2007.
21. Scanlon E, Stubbs N. Pressure relieving devices for treating heel pressure ulcers (Protocol). Cochrane Database Syst Rev 2005, 2006;(4):CD005485.10.1002/14651858.

22. Whittington K, Briones R. National prevalence and incidence study: 6-year sequential acute care data. Adv Skin Wound Care 2004;17(9):490–4.

23. Young T, Clark M. Re-positioning for pressure ulcer prevention. (Protocol). Cochrane Database Syst Rev 2003, 2006;(4):CD004836. 10.1002/14651858.

24. Braden B, Bergstrom N. Braden scale for predicting pressure sore risk. Available at: http://www.bradenscale.com/braden.PDF. Accessed June 25, 2008.

25. Joint Commission Resources. Improving handoff communications: Meeting National Patient Safety Goal 2E. Joint Commission International Center for Patient Safety. Accessed June 25, 2008.

26. Kaiser Permanente of Colorado. SBAR technique for communication: a situational briefing model. Institute for Healthcare Improvement. Available at: http://www.ihi.org/IHI/Topics/PatientSafety/SafetyGeneral/Tools/SBARTechniqueforCommunicationASituationalBriefingModel.htm. Accessed June 25, 2008.

27. Haig K, Sutton S, Whittington J. SBAR: a shared mental model for improving communication between clinicians. Jt Comm J Qual Patient Saf 2006;32(3):167–75.

28. National Patient Safety Goals. The Joint Commission. Available at: http://www.jointcommission.org/PatientSafety/NationalPatientSafetyGoals/. Accessed June 25, 2008.

29. Lingard L, Espin S, Rubin B, et al. Getting teams to talk: development and pilot implementation of a checklist to promote interprofessional communication in the OR. Qual Saf Health Care 2005;14(5):340–6.

30. Benson E, Rippin-Sisler C, Jabusch K, et al. Improving nursing shift-to-shift report. J Nurs Care Qual 2007;22(1):80–4.

31. Lamond D. The information content of the nurse change of shift report: a comparative study. J Adv Nurs 2000;31(4):794–804.

32. Strople B, Ottani P. Can technology improve intershift report? What the research reveals. J Prof Nurs 2006;22(3):197–204.

33. Thompson D, Holzmueller C, Hunt D, et al. A morning briefing: setting the stage for a clinically and operationally good day. Jt Comm J Qual Patient Saf 2005;31(8):476–9.

34. Anonymous. Best practices for preventing wrong site, wrong person, and wrong procedure errors in perioperative settings. AORN J 2006;84(Suppl 1):S13–29.

35. Saufl N. Universal protocol for preventing wrong site, wrong procedure, wrong person surgery. J Perianesth Nurs 2004;19(5):348–51.

Development and Implementation of an Inductive Model for Evidence-Based Practice: A Grassroots Approach for Building Evidence-Based Practice Capacity in Staff Nurses

Tania D. Strout, RN, BSN, MS[a],*, Kelly Lancaster, RN, BSN, CAPA[b],
Alyce A. Schultz, RN, PhD, FAAN[c]

KEYWORDS
- Evidence-based practice • Nursing • Nursing practice
- Clinical scholarship • Clinical scholar • Clinical scholar model

WHAT IS EVIDENCE-BASED PRACTICE?

Sackett and colleagues'[1] definition states that evidence-based practice (EBP) is "the integration of best research evidence with clinical expertise and patient values." Their definition is an important departure from a previous one, "the conscientious, explicit, and judicious use of current best evidence in making decisions about the care of individual patients." The updated approach presents a synergy among three essential components: a research evidence, the expertise of clinicians, and the values of the patients they serve.[2] It acknowledges the tensions that exist in developing a balance

[a] Maine Medical Center, Department of Emergency Medicine, 321 Brackett Street, Portland, ME 04102, USA
[b] Maine Medical Center, Scarborough Surgery Center, 84 Campus Drive, Scarborough, ME 04074, USA
[c] EBP Concepts, Alyce A. Schultz & Associates, LLC, 5747 W. Drake Court, Chandler, AZ 85226, USA
* Corresponding author.
E-mail address: strout@mmc.org (T.D. Strout).

Nurs Clin N Am 44 (2009) 93–102
doi:10.1016/j.cnur.2008.10.007
0029-6465/08/$ – see front matter © 2009 Elsevier Inc. All rights reserved.

nursing.theclinics.com

between clinical expertise, developed over years of practice at the bedside, and scientific evidence that may or may not be generalizable to patients. This approach also gives credence to a voice formerly silent—that of patients and their families. It takes into account their cultures, ethnicities, ideas about health and wellness, and all the other unique attributes that make them who they are. An additional EBP definition includes concern for feasibility, risk or harm, and costs.[3]

This article discusses the development and implementation of one model for EBP education, the Clinical Scholar Model, within a framework relevant for the practicing clinical nurse.[4]

CULTURAL READINESS

Maine Medical Center (MMC) is a 606-bed tertiary-care referral center hospital located in Portland, Maine currently employing approximately 1500 registered nurses. MMC nurses participate in a shared governance model that encourages participation in nursing councils where information is exchanged and consensus-based decisions are made by clinical and administrative nurses. As noted by Broom and Tilbury,[5] when staff nurses are involved in decision-making processes, they become empowered, engaged, and have a sense of control over their professional practice.

When the Clinical Scholar Model was being developed, many individual nursing research and EBP projects were in process, with small groups of nurse clinicians being mentored through the projects one-on-one by the hospital's nurse researcher. Accolades and recognition for completed projects were mounting, and administrative support for nursing research was growing throughout the institution. In addition, nurses were encouraged to continue this work by interdisciplinary colleagues, who also began to collaborate on many projects.

As described by Kingdon,[6] windows of opportunity for large-scale change can exist when forces align. For MMC, consensus around various clinical problems and consensus around research and EBP as solutions for those problems came together. The developing professional practice environment and the chief nursing officer's commitment to developing the infrastructure necessary to support EBP came together as elements essential for success.[7,8] The alignment of these forces and the emerging Clinical Scholar Model created the cultural readiness necessary to support the catalyzing changes that full implementation of the model would bring.

DEVELOPMENT OF CLINICAL SCHOLAR MODEL

As the environment at Maine Medical Center became increasingly ready for transformational change, it became clear that a larger number of nurses with basic EBP skills would be necessary to act as front-line change agents and mentors within the clinical setting. Many nurses were coming forward with clinical questions deserving consideration; few, however, were prepared to begin to answer these important questions.

Years earlier, the words of Dr. Janelle Krueger planted the seeds for the development of the model. At one of the nation's first nursing research conferences, Dr. Krueger introduced the idea of research as a staff nurse function and promoted the notion that clinical staff are truly in a position to be able to link research and practice.[9] Vital to the formal development of the Clinical Scholar Model were some of the ideas presented in the Conduct and Utilization of Research in Nursing (CURN) project, change theory concepts discussed by Everett Rogers, and the synthesis of ideas about scholarship disseminated by Sigma Theta Tau, International in the *Clinical Scholarship Resource Paper*.[10–12] The wellspring of innovative ideas developed by clinical nurses within the institution, the visionary and creative leadership of the nurse researcher, and administrative support intersected to encourage development of the model.

Early work on the model addressed not only what its goals and essential components would look like but also how the model would be applied in clinical settings. Key competency areas, including literature search, review and critique, research ethics, project design, proposal development, and computer proficiency, were identified. These skills were to be developed in the Clinical Scholar Program, constructed as didactic sessions followed by hands-on time for mentored work and practice by the participants. The initial series of workshops featured lectures delivered by the nurse researcher, other nationally known nurse scholars, and clinical scholars from within the institution.

Essential to the development of the model and workshop series was a strong desire to adhere to the ethical principles of the conduct of research. The interconnectedness of research conduct, quality, and EBP was identified. Ethical obligations to the potential subjects were primary considerations (**Fig. 1**).[3] For example, for each clinical

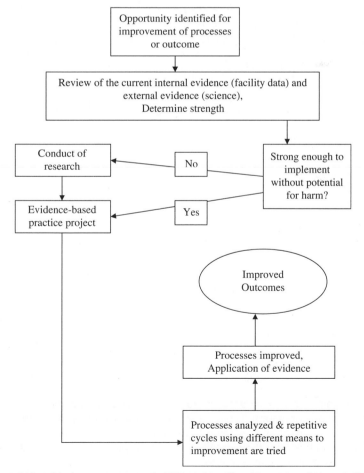

Fig. 1. Interrelationship between research, EBP, and quality. (*Courtesy of* Alyce A. Schultz RN, PhD, FAAN, Chandler, AZ.)

question or potential project, a comprehensive review of the current scientific literature was conducted. When strong and pertinent evidence for a particular practice was present in the literature, nurses were encouraged not to conduct additional research activities but to undertake projects aimed at applying existing evidence to practice and evaluating outcomes following the change. The program's developers and participants believe that it is their ethical obligation to minimize risk to potential subjects by conducting research only when it is truly necessary and to honor the contributions of previous research subjects by applying evidence gained through their participation where appropriate. Nurses participating in the Clinical Scholar Program were strongly encouraged to seek institutional review board review for all nursing EBP and quality improvement projects to ensure compliance and to retain the ability to share results outside of their own institution.

THE MODEL
Description of the Clinical Scholar Model

The Clinical Scholar Model is predicated on the development of a cadre of point-of-care nurses who become clinical scholars, committed to patient care, knowledge development, research translation, and evidence implementation. **Fig. 2** depicts the Clinical Scholar Model used by nurse scholars in the conduct of their research, EBP, and quality improvement projects.

Goals of the Clinical Scholar Model

The Clinical Scholar Model incorporates four central goals. The first is to challenge current practices within the discipline of nursing.[9] The second goal is for clinical nurses to be able to speak and understand the language of research, featuring research-related discussion as a component of day-to-day dialogue. Third, the model seeks to encourage the critical appraisal, critique, and synthesis of current evidence. The final goal of the model is for clinical scholars to serve as mentors to other staff nurses involved in journeys to scholarship through the creation of mentoring partnerships between experienced and novice scholars. The structure provided by these goals is important in providing clarity of purpose and a sense of direction for those working within the model's framework.

Essential Components of the Clinical Scholar Model

The essential components of the model are grounded in the Sigma Theta Tau, International *Clinical Scholarship Resource Paper*.[9,12] It requires the use of observation and scientifically based methods to identify and solve clinical problems. Clinical scholars must analyze both internal and external evidence that substantiates or refutes a current practice. Evidence is synthesized by evaluating its level, quality, quantity, consistency, and strength. Findings are applied, and results are disseminated in poster and oral presentations as well as in the published scientific literature.

IMPLEMENTATION OF THE CLINICAL SCHOLAR MODEL

Implementation of the Clinical Scholar Model began with the development of a series of Clinical Scholar workshops. Ten clinical nurses and the nurse researcher worked to organize and implement six full-day workshops aimed at providing other nurses the knowledge to with which they could begin to develop their own scholarship-in-practice. While the clinicians learned basic evidence-based practice skills, the nurse-mentors learned new methods for knowledge sharing and developing the mentor–mentee relationship and continued to develop their own EBP skills.

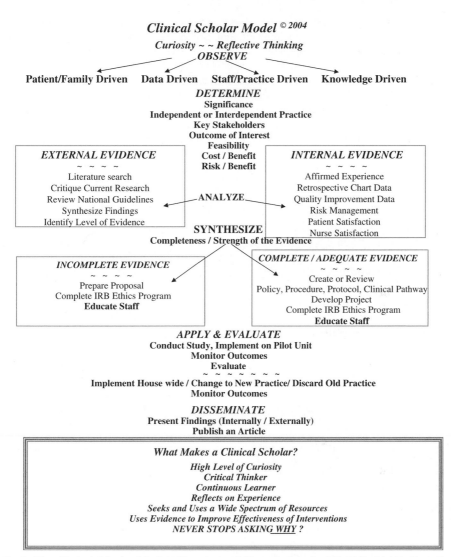

Fig. 2. The Clinical Scholar Model. (*Courtesy of* Alyce A. Schultz RN, PhD, FAAN, Chandler, AZ.)

Because each workshop day was designed to include both didactic and practical time, participants spent a portion of each session applying the skills they had just reviewed. Practical time was conducted within a small-group framework and was facilitated by the nurse mentors. Group discussion, team collaboration, and experiential sharing were encouraged, particularly with review and debriefing at the end of each day. To promote continued practice and project development during the time between workshops, homework assignments were chosen to reinforce and challenge newly developed skills.

At the conclusion of the workshop series, each emerging scholar produced and delivered an oral presentation describing the project he/she had developed during the year. By the end of the first set of workshops, 14 new nursing research, EBP, or quality improvement projects had emerged. These projects ultimately were completed and resulted in many national and international poster and podium presentations, as well as in multiple scientific publications. Several projects received awards from discipline-specific nursing organizations. Most importantly, the results of the different projects were incorporated into daily clinical practice and were adopted by nurses on many units throughout the institution. Along with the integration of these practice changes, EBP and clinical scholarship truly became woven into the tapestry of nursing practice at MMC.

All major change initiatives require administrative support for lasting success, and the Clinical Scholar Model is no exception. Administrators in the department of nursing were invested in and supportive of the development and implementation of this model. Funding for the workshops, including costs for external speaker honoraria, refreshments, and printing, came from the department of nursing and research institute budgets. In addition, funding for workshop attendees was required from the individual nursing units. Each participant was supported with 8 hours of paid time to attend the scheduled workshops and 4 additional hours per month to complete project work. Given that 50 nurses attended the first series of workshops and that replacements needed to be hired to cover nurses' scheduled clinical duties, the contributions of the nursing units were substantial. Clearly, these activities were seen as being in alignment with the institutional values and initiatives.

WHO IS THE CLINICAL SCHOLAR?

Sigma Theta Tau's *Clinical Scholarship Resource Paper* describes clinical scholarship as[12]

> *an approach that enables evidence-based nursing and development of best practices to meet the needs of clients efficiently and effectively. It requires the identification of desired outcomes; the use of systematic observation and scientifically based methods to identify and solve clinical problems; the substantiation of practice and clinical decisions with reference to scientific principles, current research, consensus-based guidelines, quality improvement data, and other forms of evidence; the evaluation, documentation, and dissemination of outcomes and improvements in practice through a variety of mechanisms including publication, presentations, consultation, and leadership; and the use of clinical knowledge and expertise to anticipate trends, predict needs, create effective clinical products and services, and manage outcomes.*

Clinical scholars connect with these words; they are at the core of their identities as nurses. They are a piece of the scholars' daily functioning: meeting needs effectively, substantiating practice, using evidence, and managing outcomes. As nurses evolve as clinical scholars, the symbiotic relationship between scholarship and practice becomes rich and nourished.

What does the clinical scholar look like? What distinguishes his/her practice? The clinical scholar possesses a high level of curiosity. S/he is the nurse on the unit who not only questions traditional practices and wonders how a practice could be done better next time but deliberates over whether a practice needs to be performed at all. S/he thinks critically to solve complex problems and is not satisfied with a temporary fix. Clinical scholars make time to reflect on their practice, because this activity renews the professional spirit and generates clarity of purpose.

Clinical scholars seek out and use a wide variety of resources in their work, drawing on expert clinicians and scholars alike. They use both internal and external evidence to improve the effectiveness of their interventions, and they find creative ways to incorporate clinical expertise and patient preferences into their care. Most importantly, clinical scholars possess a passion for learning, are never satisfied with the status quo, and never stop asking, "Why?": "Why do we remove intravenous lines based on their time in situ?" "Why don't we use buffered lidocaine for our intravenous starts?" "Why do our open-heart patients recall being intubated?" These are all examples of questions explored by clinical scholars at MMC.

Importantly, as Dr. Melanie Dreher explained in the *Clinical Scholarship Resource Paper*, clinical scholarship is not the same thing as clinical proficiency.[12] She writes that performing a nursing procedure well, even with expertise, does not make it scholarly unless the practitioner also is questioning whether the procedure needs to be performed in the first place or whether there is a better way to accomplish the same objective. Clinical scholarship involves inquiry and a willingness to scrutinize one's own practice. It involves looking for a better way and refusing to accept any practice simply because it has always been done in a particular way.

Clinical scholars are some of nursing's most transformational leaders. They have a vision for the future of health care that excites and converts followers; they can see the big picture and work to help others share in this vision. They sell and model their vision of improved outcomes in their daily actions, both on and off their units. They are invested in this goal and work to bring their patient's agendas forward, but they also recognize and accept the inevitable challenges and setbacks that happen along the way. Clinical scholars face these obstacles with poise and grace. They create trust. They are expert at forging new relationships. They are charismatic, confident, and believe fully in themselves. Clinical scholars are constantly at the forefront; they are innovators who create the path and always can be depended upon to lead the charge. Their commitment to all that they do is unwavering, and they remember take time to provide others with praise, support, and rewards. Clinical scholars live the words of Mahatma Gandhi, "We must be the change we wish to see in the world."

SUSTAINING THE CLINICAL SCHOLAR MODEL

Through its focus on the development of new clinical scholars who can act as EBP mentors to their colleagues in the future, the Clinical Scholar Model is self sustaining. The Clinical Scholar workshops provide a nurturing, rich environment for nurses to create and develop extended networks of professional contacts and colleagues to draw upon for future mentoring. In return for this gift of professional growth, many scholars embrace the opportunity to "pay it forward" by assisting others in their own journeys while continuing to refine their own skill sets through new projects.

Incorporating basic principles of change theory also can assist in sustaining the Clinical Scholar Model. Everett Rogers'[11] *Diffusion of Innovations* provides a useful framework for considering the spread of evidence adoption through health care organizations. His work suggests that innovative change spreads through a society (in this case a health care organization) in an S-shaped curve, with early adopters incorporating the technology first, early and late majorities adopting the innovation next, followed by the final 16% of the population known as "laggards." He further theorized that the rate or speed of technology adoption is affected by the speed at which the adoption takes off and the speed at which later growth occurs. The intensity of the Clinical Scholar Program and the relatively fast pace at which an initial group of clinicians can be educated supports a speedy initial adoption of EBP. The steadier, consistent pace at which those initial clinical scholars act as mentors to new groups reinforces constant growth in the model and supports its continuation in a given organization.

Change theory gives additional assistance by anticipating and planning for resistance to innovation during individual projects and to the new and expanded roles fulfilled by nurses participating in scholarship programs. Completing a probability of adoption assessment, as outlined by the CURN project, is one way to begin thinking about potential sources of resistance to change. The CURN authors also provide useful insights into organizational change, for creating a climate prepared for change, and identifying sources of resistance to change that can be applied with the Clinical Scholar Model.[10]

Maintaining a focus on improvement in patient- and family-centered outcomes also helps sustain the Clinical Scholar Model. Although projects may revolve around issues of importance to nursing as a discipline (eg, on retaining nurses or on nursing education), most concentrate on improving health-related outcomes for patients. When outcomes remain measurable and focused in a way that is so central to the institutional mission of care provision, administrative leaders and clinicians alike can see the value in and give support to the program.

Demonstrating and celebrating programmatic benefits and the benefits of EBP is another effective means of creating support for and sustaining interest in the Clinical Scholar Model. Sharing specific project results at a nursing research day, spreading the news of abstracts presented or awards received, and highlighting successes of the workshops as a whole focuses positive attention on the program. This attention sustains support for the model by creating buy-in from leadership and by providing positive reinforcement for those who will serve as mentors in the future. In addition, recognizing contributions to important programs such as the Magnet Recognition program and the National Database of Nursing Quality Indicators garners support for and sustains the model.

In today's environment of limited health care budgets, financial support for programs such as the Clinical Scholar Model can be limited. Financial investment in the program is essential, and clinical nurses can work successfully toward funding individual projects in support of the larger model. Consideration of the financial implications of any project is an important step in evaluating the probability of adoption of the practice. Evaluating the monetary costs of projects and interventions is essential, and including financial outcomes data whenever possible is a key to providing evidence of benefit in this area. In seeking project funding, clinical nurses without advanced training and with limited access to nurses who have advanced degrees can form creative partnerships with local universities or schools of nursing; these environments are rich with academically prepared nurses who are willing to mentor in this area.

CLINICAL EXEMPLAR: AN EVIDENCE-BASED PRACTICE PROJECT
Observing

Traditionally, criteria for ambulatory surgical discharge have required that patients take oral fluids before discharge home. Nurses in the ambulatory surgery unit at MMC encouraged early intake of oral fluids to ensure that patients met discharge criteria. This practice often led to postoperative nausea and vomiting and frequent use of expensive rescue antiemetics. Additional sequelae were a requirement for increased nursing care hours and delayed discharge for patients.

Frequently, nursing staff would contact physician colleagues to obtain permission to discharge patients without any significant oral fluid intake, providing that patients met the remaining discharge criteria. With the use of shorter-acting anesthetics, many patients were ready for discharge before they were thirsty or ready to drink. The requirement for taking oral fluids was not clearly defined and resulted in wide variations in practice among physicians and nursing staff. Frustrated with the lack of a standardized practice, nurses frequently found themselves asking why they were continuing a practice that seemed to be a source of dissatisfaction for patients, families, and staff alike.

Analyzing

A team of three nurses from the ambulatory surgery unit participated in the Clinical Scholar Program to learn the skills necessary to initiate a practice change, in this case to define further the practice regarding the necessity of mandatory oral fluid intake following ambulatory surgery. Using the Clinical Scholar Model as a framework for supporting the work, the team searched the external evidence for published studies that determined the relevance of oral intake as discharge criteria for adult and pediatric patients. The search yielded five studies and one published clinical guideline. Team members reviewed and critiqued the national guidelines and determined the strength of the published research using a critique form.[13] The internal evidence consisted of anecdotal reports describing patient, family, and nurse experiences and satisfaction; this qualitative evidence was included as part of the group's analysis.

Synthesizing

The outcome variables reviewed in the selected studies included the occurrence of emesis, length of stay, and postoperative complications. The study findings indicated that without mandatory oral intake, there was reduced postoperative vomiting, reduced length of stay, and no significant difference in complications during the first 24 hours following discharge. The project team determined that there was adequate evidence to move forward and make a policy change in discharge criteria.

The MMC ambulatory surgery discharge criteria were updated to reflect the evidence. Oral fluid intake became optional, with exceptions made by physician prescription. Patients needed to demonstrate the ability to swallow and were evaluated for minimal nausea and vomiting before discharge. Nursing staff no longer forced oral fluid intake against patients' wishes or delayed discharge for lack of oral intake.

Applying and Evaluating

Following the policy update and staff education, the practice change was implemented in the ambulatory surgery unit. Quality improvement data were collected, and outcomes were monitored. Evaluation of data after implementation demonstrated no negative outcomes related to the elimination of mandatory oral fluid intake following ambulatory surgery.

Disseminating

The findings from this project were presented to the ambulatory surgery unit and to the MMC community at an annual Nursing Research Conference and to the larger nursing community at a statewide conference. As a result of experience gained in the Clinical Scholar Program, staff nurses were able to identify a clinical issue and make a change that led to positive outcomes for patients, their families, and their nursing colleagues. This success fueled continued motivation for development as clinical scholars. MMC ambulatory surgery nurses now have the knowledge and expertise to use EBP to improve patient outcomes.

SUMMARY

EBP is an essential component of the development of nursing science and has importance for today's clinical nurses. It benefits patients, organizations, and the nursing discipline, as well as having personal and professional benefits for individual clinicians. As interest in EBP has grown, so has the need for educational programs designed to develop the scholarly skills of the nursing workforce. The Clinical Scholar Model is one grassroots approach to developing a cadre of clinical nurses with the EBP and research skills necessary in today's demanding health care delivery environments.

ACKNOWLEDGMENT

The authors acknowledge the generous support of the department of nursing at Maine Medical Center during the development and implementation of this work. Without the backing of our nursing administrators, managers, and clinician colleagues, this work would not have been possible; to each of them we offer our most sincere thanks. In addition, we offer our thanks to the nurses, patients, and physicians who collaborated on the mandatory oral hydration project.

REFERENCES

1. Sackett DL, Straus SE, Richardson WS, et al, editors. Evidence-based medicine—how to practice and teach EBP. New York: Churchill Livingstone; 2000.
2. Sackett DL, Rosenberg WM, Gray JA, et al. Evidence based medicine: what it is and what it isn't. BMJ 1996;312(7023):71–2.
3. Schultz AA. Research, evidence-based practice, and quality improvement in a clinical setting. Phoenix (AZ): Alyce A. Schultz; 2007.
4. Schultz AA. Clinical scholars at the bedside: an EBP mentorship model for today. ENK: Excellence in Nursing Knowledge Feb 2005.
5. Broom CM, Tilbury MS. Magnet status: a journey not a destination. J Nurs Care Qual 2007;22(2):113–8.
6. Kingdon JW. Bridging research and policy: agendas, alternatives, and public policies. New York: Harper Collins; 1984.
7. Titler MG, Everett LQ. Sustain an infrastructure to support EBP. Nurs Manage 2006; 37(9):14–6.
8. Stetler CB, Brunell M, Giuliano KK, et al. Evidence-based practice and the role of nursing leadership. J Nurs Adm 1998;28(7/8):45–53.
9. Schultz AA. Origins and aspirations: conceiving the clinical scholar model. ENK: Excellence in nursing knowledge 2005.
10. Horsley JA, Crane J, Crabtree MK, et al. Using research to improve nursing practice: a guide. Philadelphia: WB Saunders Company; 1983.
11. Rogers EM. Diffusion of innovations. 5th edition. New York: Free Press; 2003.
12. Clinical Scholarship Task Force, Sigma Theta Tau International. Clinical scholar resource paper 1999. Available at: wwwnursingsociety.org. Accessed April 9, 2008.
13. Gallant P. Analysis: what's all the speak about critique? ENK: Excellence in Nursing Knowledge 2005.

Effect of a Preoperative Instructional Digital Video Disc on Patient Knowledge and Preparedness for Engaging in Postoperative Care Activities

Joe Ong, RN, BSN[a], Pamela S. Miller, RN, PhD(c), ACNP, CNS[b],
Renee Appleby, RN[a], Rebecca Allegretto, RN, BSN[c],
Anna Gawlinski, RN, DNSc, CS-ACNP[a],*

KEYWORDS

- Patient education • Preoperative instructional digital video disc
- Evidence-based practice

Health care delivery systems have been restructured in recent years to focus on achieving high-quality outcomes for patients by using the most cost-effective methods.[1] Optimizing outcomes for patients undergoing surgery requires the collaborative and coordinated efforts of physicians, nurses, and allied health personnel.[2] Preoperative teaching serves as a standard of nursing practice within the surgical setting.[3] Providing patients with supportive preoperative teaching that incorporates the most useful information about postoperative activities within a confined time frame has been a challenge.[1] The psychologic burden placed on patients in the preoperative

This work was supported by funding provided by the Ronald Reagan University of California Los Angeles Women's Auxillary.

[a] Department of Nursing, Ronald Reagan University of California Los Angeles Medical Center, Los Angeles, CA 90095, USA

[b] University of Los Angeles School of Nursing, Los Angeles, CA 90095, USA

[c] Thoracic Surgery, Ronald Reagan University of California Los Angeles Medical Center, Los Angeles, CA 90095, USA

* Corresponding author. Ronald Reagan University of California Los Angeles Medical Center, Los Angeles, CA 90095, USA.

E-mail address: agawlinski@mednet.ucla.edu (A. Gawlinski).

Nurs Clin N Am 44 (2009) 103–115
doi:10.1016/j.cnur.2008.10.014
0029-6465/08/$ – see front matter © 2009 Published by Elsevier Inc.

period may be underestimated, and this burden lessens patients' ability to comprehend and contribute to the postsurgical plan. Patients have a defined learning curve for understanding the intricacies of the surgical procedure and facilitating their own recovery after surgery. The effectiveness of preoperative teaching depends, in part, on the learning needs, style, and preference of the patient. The amount of information conferred to patients may be overwhelming.[2] As a result, the patient may require repeated or frequent reinforcement. Once the patient has had the opportunity to grasp the information, additional questions may arise. Nurses are in a key position to provide preoperative teaching and respond to patients' questions and concerns.[2] Advancements in technology have provided nurses with the opportunity to improve and intensify preoperative educational strategies.

SCOPE OF THE PROBLEM IN EXISTING PRACTICE

In general, preoperative teaching should include significant information about the surgery and issues that patients are anticipated to face in the perioperative and postoperative periods. Surgical procedures expose patients to pain, bodily injury, and potential death.[4] Preoperative teaching readily and effectively enables patients to cope with their surgery, reduces the duration of hospitalization, elevates satisfaction, minimizes postsurgical complications, and augments patients' psychologic well-being.[4]

Preoperative teaching has been administered in various ways and formats:[2] verbal instruction, printed materials, demonstrations, and videotapes. Routine dissemination of information by means of verbal instruction with supplemental written material (information packets) has been the basis for preoperative teaching for decades. Such factors as degree of attentiveness, emotional aptitude, intellectual level, learning disabilities, and language or cultural barriers can affect patients' ability to assimilate the information.[2]

Currently, substantive inconsistencies are apparent in preoperative instruction for thoracic surgical patients who are scheduled to undergo such procedures as esophagectomy or lung volume reduction surgery. Ideally, a written preoperative instructional handout was to be given during each patient's preoperative surgical visit. Baseline data indicated that 23 (92%) of 25 patients did not receive the written handout. This lapse has resulted in a lack of knowledge and preparedness that prevents patients from immediately engaging successfully in postoperative self-care activities (eg, ambulation and pain management), which can lead to increases in patients' anxiety, postoperative complications, and length of stay in the hospital. Thus, the challenge was to develop structures and processes that would enable thoracic surgical patients to receive thorough preoperative teaching consistently.

An evidence-based project that included development of postoperative thoracic surgery information in a standardized format by using state-of-the-art digital video disc (DVD) technology was implemented. This staff nurse–driven project illustrates the contribution of preoperative teaching to improving patients' outcomes. The evidence-based literature and the evaluation of an audiovisual medium dedicated to providing patients with valuable information on the spectrum of care activities after thoracic surgery are discussed.

EVIDENCE-BASED LITERATURE

Preoperative teaching has been defined in the literature as an "interactive process of providing information and explanations about surgical processes, expected patient behaviors, and anticipated sensations and providing appropriate reassurance…to patients who are about to undergo surgery."[1] Postoperative care refers to nursing activities performed during the patient's postoperative phase. Preoperative teaching not only provides patient-specific information about what to expect during the postoperative period but influences the attitudes and behaviors of patients with respect to their postoperative care.[1,5]

Little experimental or quasiexperimental research has explored the impact of preoperative instruction in patients undergoing thoracic surgery. Most studies have explored its impact among selected patients undergoing such procedures as cardiac surgery,[6] orthopedic surgery,[7] reproductive surgery,[4] and cancer surgery.[8] Published reports describe a positive relation between preoperative teaching and improved outcomes for patients and indicate that preoperative teaching is a cost-effective approach.[7] **Table 1** lists the relevant studies reviewed for this project and their respective level of evidence.

In a qualitative study by Doering and colleagues[6] of patients' perceptions of the quality of nursing and medical care during hospitalization after cardiac surgery, patients wanted to know what they could honestly and realistically expect during their postoperative recovery. Specific information embedded within the preoperative education provided by nurses can assist patients in understanding the level of their participation that is required during recovery. Meeting the informational and physical needs of patients is imperative.[6] Well-informed patients are more likely to experience positive outcomes and to have higher levels of satisfaction with their care. Such patients have the confidence to carry out behaviors necessary for successful postoperative outcomes.[4] Additional evidence supports the use of video-teaching versus routine care: video-teaching resulted in decreases in postoperative complications (eg, atelectasis) and length of stay among patients undergoing coronary artery bypass graft surgery.[9]

Stern and Lockwood[10] conducted a systematic review of randomized controlled trials investigating preoperative instruction of patients and the effect of such instruction on patients' understanding of, knowledge of, and ability to perform postoperative activities. On the basis of limited rigorous studies, these researchers concluded that preoperative teaching before admission and the use of preoperative videos improved patients' knowledge and skill.[10]

The teaching must take into consideration the emotional state of the patient and the patient's ability to cope,[11] factors that often may be overshadowed by feelings of anxiety or fear about the impending procedure.[2] The evidence supports the benefit of preoperative teaching in reducing anxiety and complications and in improving recovery. Studies have shown an inverse relation between preoperative teaching and postoperative anxiety, wherein improved outcomes were exemplified not only by lower levels of anxiety but by shorter stays in the hospital.[12]

Brumfield and colleagues[5] conducted a descriptive study to isolate important content areas in preoperative teaching as reported by patients and nurses in ambulatory surgery settings. Patients and nurses strongly favored the inclusion of situational information (eg, explaining activities, explaining events), patient role information (eg, anticipated behaviors), and psychosocial support (eg, emotional descriptors) in preoperative teaching. Patients undergoing ambulatory surgery preferred for this teaching to occur before admission. Early instruction targeted toward patients' priorities seems to be critical to enhancing postoperative outcomes.[5] Similar needs of patients were identified in the inpatient surgical setting.[13]

Fitzpatrick and Hyde[14] reported that nurse-related factors, such as individual knowledge and experience, may influence the preoperative education received by patients. This influence is particularly evident among novice nurses or nurses who are new to the clinic or unit. The diversity in degree of knowledge and experience

Table 1
Levels of evidence for the review of the literature

Authors	Level of Evidence
Bernier and colleagues, 2003	Level V: evidence from observational studies with consistent results (eg, correlational, descriptive studies)
Whyte and Grant, 2005	Level VI: evidence from expert opinion, multiple case reports, or national consensus reports
Lewis and colleagues, 2002	Level V: evidence from observational studies with consistent results (eg, correlational, descriptive studies)
Oetker-Black and colleagues, 2003	Level II: evidence from one or more randomized controlled trials with consistent results
Brumfield, and colleagues, 1996	Level V: evidence from observational studies with consistent results (eg, correlational, descriptive studies)
Doering and colleagues, 2002	Level V: evidence from observational studies with consistent results (eg, correlational, descriptive studies)
Johansson and colleagues, 2005	Level I: evidence from well-designed data meta-analysis or well-done systematic review with results that consistently support a specific action (eg, assessment, intervention, or treatment)
Evrard and colleagues, 2005	Level V: evidence from observational studies with consistent results (eg, correlational, descriptive studies)
Shaban and colleagues, 2002	Level IV: evidence from one or more quasiexperimental studies with consistent results
Stern and Lockwood, 2005	Level I: evidence from well-designed data meta-analysis or well-done systematic review with results that consistently support a specific action (eg, assessment, intervention, or treatment)
Doering and colleagues, 2000	Level II: evidence from one or more randomized controlled trials with consistent results
Devine and Cook, 1983	Level I: evidence from well-designed data meta-analysis or well-done systematic review with results that consistently support a specific action (eg, assessment, intervention, or treatment)
Yount and Schoessler, 1991	Level V: evidence from observational studies with consistent results (eg, correlational, descriptive studies)
Fitzpatrick and Hyde, 2006	Level V: evidence from observational studies with consistent results (eg, correlational, descriptive studies)
Thomas and colleagues, 1999	Level V: evidence from observational studies with consistent results (eg, correlational, descriptive studies)
Hathaway, 1986	Level I: evidence from well-designed data meta-analysis or well-done systematic review with results that consistently support a specific action (eg, assessment, intervention, or treatment)

possessed by nurses can produce inconsistent and ineffective preoperative preparation for patients. Addressing this challenge requires an organizational commitment to address internal practices[14] and might best be accomplished through structured preoperative education across the board.

Evrard and colleagues[8] surveyed 108 postsurgical oncology patients who had watched a preoperative DVD. The DVD content included general information pertaining to the hospital environment and postoperative complications in addition to specialized surgery-specific information. The survey asked patients to evaluate the following DVD content areas: (1) access to the information, (2) presentation, (3) patients' perception, and (4) global satisfaction. Seventy-one percent of the patients reported that the DVD provided a positive and encouraging experience, and 83% recommended its use as a preoperative teaching tool. Interestingly, among the 14 patients who experienced complications, only 21% thought that they had received thorough information from the DVD and only 12% believed that they were well prepared to handle postoperative complications. Notably, the patients were allowed to view the DVD only in the clinical setting and were unable to take the DVD home to review. This limitation undermines any chance for patients to reinforce the information and improve recall.[8]

Earlier research using meta-analyses (eg, Hathaway[15]) supported the value of traditional preoperative instruction to improve postoperative outcomes. Modern-day video technology has emerged as a suitable tool for relaying practical information in a timely manner. The visual and auditory emphasis of standardized educational videos provides an additive effect to traditional written preoperative instruction, an additive effect that increases recall.[16] Use of audiovisual materials, such as DVDs, benefits patients because they are able to refer back to and review the information at their convenience. The richness of this multimedia tool provides a venue for answering basic questions that come up after preoperative discussions with the surgeon or nurses. The timing of teaching is best when the DVD is viewed at home before the surgical procedure, in a less stressful environment. Preoperative teaching should be provided near the time of surgery. Teaching should not be provided too early; otherwise, patients are more likely to forget.

PURPOSE OF EVIDENCE-BASED PROJECT

The purpose of this evidence-based practice project was to determine the effects of developing and implementing an innovative preoperative instructional DVD on patients' level of knowledge, preparedness, and perceived ability to participate in postoperative care activities at a university-affiliated public medical center.

INTERVENTION FOR PROJECT IMPLEMENTATION

After gaps in existing preoperative teaching practice were identified and the literature was reviewed, this project was developed on the basis of the principles identified in the Iowa Model of Evidence-Based Practice.[17] The design used convenience sampling methods to survey a group of registered nurses from the medical observation unit before and after the intervention and to survey a group of thoracic surgical patients after the intervention.

This project had two intervention phases. The first intervention was to redesign the delivery of preoperative instruction by developing a preoperative instructional DVD for thoracic surgical patients that was evidence-based and prepared patients to engage in postoperative care activities. The staff nurse collaborated with the director of the medical observation unit on developing the DVD. Thoracic surgeons, clinic staff, and the nurse specialist were consulted about the content of the video. The development of the DVD necessitated scripting, filming, editing, and replication. Partnership with a production crew resulted in the production of a user-friendly DVD. The following content areas of the preoperative teaching program were incorporated into the instructional DVD: pain management, surgical drainage, vital signs, incentive spirometry (IS), cough and deep breathing, chest physiotherapy (CPT), TED hose (antiembolism stockings)/sequential compression device (SCD), ambulation, diet/bowel activity/urine output, and discharge. Patients and staff nurses from the medical observation unit and thoracic surgeons were participants in the DVD. The final DVD was reviewed and approved by all key persons who had a stake in the process.

The second phase of the intervention implemented the delivery process for the preoperative instructional DVD to be given to patients. The system was changed to ensure that all patients were consistently provided with a preoperative instructional DVD. The staff nurse worked in partnership with the clinic staff and nurse specialist to assist in providing patients with the DVD and obtaining survey results. All nursing personnel involved in preoperative teaching and postoperative patient care were taught about the project and inclusion of the DVD. This process included providing each thoracic surgical patient with a preoperative packet during the preoperative clinic visit. The packet included a copy of the 14-minute DVD and a written survey to evaluate the patient's self-reported knowledge and preparedness for surgery. Patients were provided mailing instructions to return the completed survey. Nurses were instructed to complete surveys before and after the intervention that documented the nurses' assessment of patients' knowledge and preparedness to engage in postoperative care activities.

POSTINTERVENTION RESULTS

Data were analyzed by using descriptive statistics and Student's *t* tests.

Registered Nurses

Before and after the intervention, registered nurses completed a six-item survey to assess patients' knowledge of and preparedness to engage in postoperative care activities. The survey included questions related to the nurses' demographic characteristics.

Demographic characteristics of the 18 registered nurse participants indicated that most of the nurses were female (n = 16 [89%]) and rotated between the day shift and night shift (n = 16 [89%]). Most nurses possessed between 1 and 5 years of total nursing experience (n = 16 [89%]) and had between 1 and 5 years of experience in the medical observation unit of the University of California, Los Angeles (UCLA; n = 15 [83%]). At the time of the project, nearly all nurses served as a clinical nurse level II on the clinical ladder system (**Table 2**).

Based on the Likert scale (1 = not knowledgeable to 4 = very knowledgeable), nurses' response to the question "How knowledgeable do you feel your thoracic surgical patients were about each of the following important aspects of postoperative care?" indicated a significantly higher level of knowledge after the intervention for aspects of surgical drainage, IS, cough and deep breathing, and TED hose/SCDs ($z = -3.461, -2.899, -3.095$, and -2.960, respectively; $P \le .004$; **Fig. 1**). Nurses also reported significant increases in knowledge about general care (mean: 1.94 versus 3.06; $P < .001$) and pain management (mean: 2.17 versus 3.22; $P < .001$) after the intervention.

Based on the Likert scale (1 = not engaged to 4 = very engaged), nurses' response to the question "How engaged do you feel your thoracic surgical patients were about

Table 2
Demographic characteristics of the nurses who completed surveys before and after the intervention

Variable	Sample (N = 18)	%
Title		
Clinical nurse I	1	5.6
Clinical nurse II	16	88.9
Clinical nurse III	1	5.6
Shift		
Days	1	5.6
Nights	1	5.6
Rotate	16	88.9
Gender		
Male	2	11.1
Female	16	88.9
Years of nursing experience		
<1	1	5.6
1–5	16	88.9
>10	1	5.6
Years of experience in the UCLA medical observation unit		
<1	2	11.1
1–5	15	83.3
6–10	1	5.6

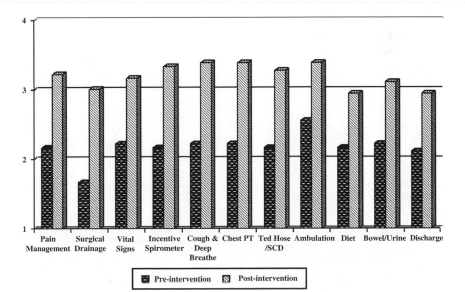

Fig. 1. Mean level of patients' knowledge of postoperative care activities reported by nurses surveyed before and after the intervention. Asterisks indicate significant difference (P<.004) from before to after the intervention. PT, physiotherapy.

each of the following important aspects of postoperative care?" indicated a significantly higher level of understanding after the intervention for aspects of IS, cough and deep breathing, and TED hose/SCDs ($z = -3.411, -3.255$, and -2.804, respectively; $P \leq .007$; **Fig. 2**). Nurses reported a significant increase in overall knowledge of patients and engagement of patients and their families ($P \leq .004$).

Nurses were provided with the opportunity to respond with comments at the end of the survey. **Box 1** and **2** cite a few of the nurses' anecdotal comments before the intervention and after the intervention respectively. Responses are best summed up by the response of one nurse who stated that "Giving patients/family members information regarding what to expect of them in regards to postoperation activities will empower them to be in control of their care."

Patients Undergoing Thoracic Surgery

After a review of the DVD, patients were surveyed for their knowledge and perceived ability to participate in postoperative care activities. Patients (n = 15) who participated in this project were predominantly older than 60 years of age (n = 12 [80%]) and English-speaking (n = 14 [93%]). Fifty-three percent were female (n = 8), and 47% were male (n = 7). Most patients had undergone lung surgery (**Table 3**).

Based on the Likert scale (1 = I do not understand to 4 = I understand very well), on the postintervention survey, patients' response to the question "How much do you understand about each of the following after viewing the preoperative DVD?" indicated

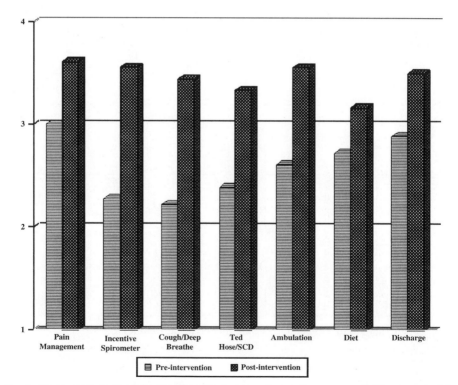

Fig. 2. Mean engagement levels of patients in postoperative care activities reported by nurses surveyed before and after the intervention. Asterisks indicate significant difference ($P<.007$) from before to after the intervention.

Table 3
Demographic characteristics of the patients undergoing thoracic surgery who completed surveys after the intervention

Variable	No. (N = 15)	%
Age, years		
18–30	1	6.7
31–40	1	6.7
41–60	1	6.7
>60	12	80.0
Gender		
Male	7	46.7
Female	8	53.3
Primary language		
English	14	93.3
Other	1	6.7
Type of surgery		
Esophageal	1	6.7
Lung	10	66.7
Other	3	20.0

Box 1
Comments by nurses before the intervention

- "We need to properly evaluate whether the thoracic patient and family have fully understood the concepts and components of postoperative care. It's not enough for the person giving the instructions to hand out pamphlets as reading materials to patients and assume that they'll follow them postoperatively."

- "Patients usually do not expect to walk three times daily and are surprised as to how much work we want them to do. Teaching them preoperatively about the post-op activities would be beneficial. The whiteboards marking their progress with ambulation, CPT, and IS (like a scoreboard) also help to remind them of these activities. Letting them know that the family can help also assists in getting activity done. Most times, the family is unsure of where they can help. Specifically telling them they can assist with CPT and IS engages them more in patient care. Visual demos—most helpful in telling patients, for example, to inflate lungs with the IS."

- "Patients…post-op 3 or 2…still do not know much of any of their post-op therapies or if they did not know, they did not know why they were doing what they were doing. They were sort of knowledgeable of the purposes of the SCDs and TEDs, but the incentive spirometer, they would just breathe in real fast and they said they were exercising their lungs but when demonstrating how to do it, they were just breathing in and out really fast. When I did chest PT, I asked if they know why I was doing it and they all said they did not know. But after instruction that it is to loosen up secretions, they were more enthusiastic to do it."

- "Educated in the medicating…This is not to intimidate the patient/family but to empower them from the very beginning."

- "Patients and their families need reinforcement when it comes to teaching. Although they are somewhat knowledgeable overall, they need to be reminded to follow through with post-op care."

> **Box 2**
> **Comments by nurses after the intervention**
>
> - "The instructional DVD was very useful in educating thoracic patients with regards to their role and expectations after surgery."
> - "Patients as well as family were very knowledgeable about pain medication, CPT, IS, Ambulation . . . . Relatives were very involved in patients' care."
> - "This DVD was very helpful in preparing patients in becoming familiar with what to expect after surgery. When the nurses did their teaching it was nice when the patient and/or family members were not hearing things for the first time. It is really hard for a patient to hear things for the first time during the overwhelming period post op."
> - "I believe that patients and patients' families are more knowledgeable regarding on what they need to do and what they expect during hospitalization post operatively."

high mean scores for all areas of postoperative care (**Fig. 3**). When asked about their ability to participate in postoperative care after viewing the preoperative DVD, scores indicated patients thought that they were able to participate or able to participate a great deal in all areas (**Fig. 4**). Patients reported that the preoperative DVD was effective overall in preparing them and their family members for postoperative care activities. One patient commented that "it was extremely helpful to be able to take the DVD home." Another patient reportedly "had one long surgery at UCLA in January of 2007" and further stated, "this DVD was not available at the time...I have another longer surgery in September of 2007, and this has been helpful."

DISCUSSION

Elevated scores for knowledge, engagement, and understanding may be attributable to the incorporation of the DVD in the preoperative teaching. A quality instructional media product was developed, implemented, and found to be effective in increasing preoperative knowledge and preparedness of patients and their families. Nurses

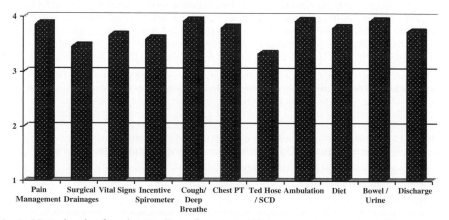

Fig. 3. Mean levels of understanding of postoperative care activities reported by patients surveyed after the intervention. PT, physiotherapy.

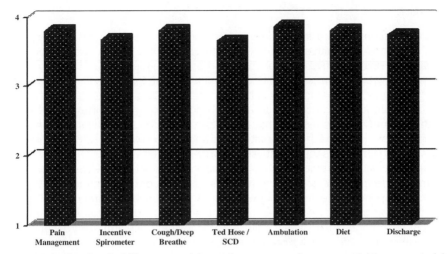

Fig. 4. Mean levels of ability to participate in postoperative care activities reported by patients surveyed after the intervention.

reported higher levels of knowledge and engagement of patients and their families related to postoperative activities. The supposition is that use of the DVD would increase knowledge and provide useful information to enhance the level of involvement of patients in their postoperative activities. The accessibility of information about postoperative care provided opportunities for viewing by the patient and family members. This format enabled patients to review the information numerous times at their own pace. It is not known whether this format influenced outcomes, such as length of stay. It is assumed, however, that the more active patients are in their own care, the more likely they are to progress toward short-term and long-term goals.

This important evidence-based practice project emphasized the value of incorporating DVDs as a part of the preoperative teaching process. The findings delineate the necessity for providing patient-specific postoperative care instruction before patients undergo thoracic surgery. "The goal of patient teaching is to improve patients' understanding of their disease process and the operation that they are about to experience, with the goal of enlisting their active participation in the healing process."[2] This goal is best reached through the collaborative efforts of the health care providers involved in the patients' care. In turn, an eager and well-informed patient can become a participating member of the health care team.[2]

The development of the preoperative DVD was based on existing evidence-based literature and the needs of patients after thoracic surgery. As a result, the findings of this project and the DVD may be limited in generalizability to a small sample of patients and nurses in acute thoracic surgical settings. The magnitude of the effect of the intervention may be too small to detect. Replication of this study with a larger sample size is warranted. A potential effect of time is related to the nurse and patient survey assessments after the DVD intervention. Changing the system was a challenge. The clinic, which is located offsite, lacks an infrastructure to ensure the distribution of preoperative teaching and educational materials. The outcomes of this project clearly delineate the benefits of implementing a preoperative DVD in an effort to meet postoperative care goals, however. This project enhanced thoracic surgical patients' knowledge of, engagement in, and understanding of their postoperative care activities.

SUMMARY

Patients' outcomes were improved by changing the system so that patients were consistently provided with a preoperative instructional DVD. The connection between the patient's postoperative experience and preoperative teaching is intimately linked. This evidence-based project clearly demonstrates that for patients who have had thoracic surgery, and perhaps patients in other acute surgical settings, the need for information about their postoperative care and potential complications obligates health care providers to ensure that patients receive the information they need to engage in their care. Health care practitioners should consider providing this information in a DVD format to supplement verbal and written instruction. A DVD provides an effective and efficient method of distributing important postoperative care information and may enhance patients' ability to recall key aspects of their preoperative instruction. In turn, patients are well equipped to exert confidence and empowered control over their performance of clinically relevant activities after surgery. Perhaps the greatest advantage is the patient's ability to access and view the instructional DVD easily within the confines of his or her home as opposed to a medical office or hospital room.

ACKNOWLEDGMENTS

The authors thank the thoracic surgeons (Drs. Cameron, Lee, Maish, and Maharaja) and Martha Martinez for their generous support. They also thank the DVD production crew, particularly Nancy Williams and Brian Williams, for their professional and understanding work. Finally, they thank to the patients and clinical staff in the medical observation unit who generously provided their time and experience.

REFERENCES

1. Bernier MJ, Sanares DC, Owen SV, et al. Preoperative teaching received and valued in a day surgery setting. AORN J 2003;77(3):563–72, 575–8, 581–2.
2. Whyte RI, Grant PD. Preoperative patient education in thoracic surgery. Thorac Surg Clin 2005;15(2):195–201.
3. Lewis C, Gunta K, Wong D. Patient knowledge, behavior, and satisfaction with the use of a preoperative DVD. Orthop Nurs 2002;21(6):41–3.
4. Oetker-Black SL, Jones S, Estok P, et al. Preoperative teaching and hysterectomy outcomes. AORN J 2003;77(6):1215–8, 1221–31.
5. Brumfield VC, Kee CC, Johnson JY. Preoperative patient teaching in ambulatory surgery settings. AORN J 1996;64(6):941–6, 948, 951–2.
6. Doering LV, McGuire AW, Rourke D. Recovering from cardiac surgery: what patients want you to know. Am J Crit Care 2002;11(4):333–43.
7. Johansson K, Nuutila L, Virtanen H, et al. Preoperative education for orthopaedic patients: systematic review. J Adv Nurs 2005;50(2):212–23.
8. Evrard S, Mathoulin-Pelissier S, Larrue C, et al. Evaluation of a preoperative multimedia information program in surgical oncology. Eur J Surg Oncol 2005; 31(1):106–10.
9. Shaban M, Salsali M, Kamali P, et al. Assessment the effects of respiratory exercise education in acute respiratory complication and the length of patient hospitalization, for undergoing coronary artery by-pass surgery in Kermanshah Emam Ali Hospital. HAYAT: J Faculty Nurs Midwifery 2002;15:12–20 [in persian]. Available at: http://journals.tums.ac.ir/abs.aspx?org_id=59&culture_var=en&journal_id=10&segment=fa&issue_id=66&manuscript_id=577.

10. Stern C, Lockwood C. Knowledge retention from preoperative patient information. Int J Evidence-Based Healthcare 2005;3(3):45–63 Available at: http://www3. interscience.wiley.com/journal/118719400/abstract.
11. Doering S, Katzlberger F, Rumpold G, et al. Videotape preparation of patients before hip replacement surgery reduces stress. Psychosom Med 2000;62(3): 365–73.
12. Devine EC, Cook TD. A meta-analytic analysis of effects of psychoeducational interventions on length of postsurgical hospital stay. Nurs Res 1983;32(5):267–74.
13. Yount S, Schoessler M. A description of patient and nurse perceptions of preoperative teaching. J Post Anesth Nurs 1991;6(1):17–25.
14. Fitzpatrick E, Hyde A. Nurse-related factors in the delivery of preoperative patient education. J Clin Nurs 2006;15(6):671–7.
15. Hathaway D. Effect of preoperative instruction on postoperative outcomes: a meta-analysis. Nurs Res 1986;35(5):269–75 [editorial].
16. Thomas R, Deary A, Kaminski E, et al. Patients' preferences for video cassette recorded information: effect of age, sex and ethnic group. Eur J Cancer Care (Engl) 1999;8(2):83–6.
17. Titler MG, Kleiber C, Steelman VJ, et al. The Iowa model of evidence-based practice to promote quality care. Crit Care Nurs Clin North Am 2001;13(4): 497–509.

The Clinical Scholar Model: Evidence-Based Practice at the Bedside

Cynthia Honess, RN, MSN, CCRN, ACNS-BC[a],*, Paulette Gallant, RN, MSN, CNL[b],
Kathleen Keane, RN, BSN, CCRN[c]

KEYWORDS
- Evidence-based practice • Staff nurse
- Clinical scholar • Clinical scholar model
- Bedside evidence-based practice

THE CLINICAL SCHOLAR MODEL: EVIDENCE-BASED PRACTICE AT THE POINT OF CARE

The innovative design of the Clinical Scholar Model[1] enables nurses to question and reflect on traditional practices at the bedside. Maine Medical Center (MMC), a tertiary care center with more than 600 beds in northern New England, used the model to support staff nurses in developing an evidence-based practice (EBP) culture. The model empowered staff nurses to be curious, reflective, and question traditional practices. The three EBP projects described here evolved from the clinical curiosity of staff nurses. Each of the projects used the Clinical Scholar Model to guide the process of identifying, implementing, and evaluating clinical practice changes and outcomes. These projects illustrate how staff nurses use their critical thinking skills to observe, analyze, and synthesize evidence and determine its applicability to the clinical practice setting.

REDUCING THE LENGTH OF BED REST FOLLOWING A CARDIAC CATHETERIZATION OR PERCUTANEOUS CORONARY INTERVENTION

A core group of cardiology nurses used the Clinical Scholar Model as a framework to identify issues surrounding the optimal duration of bed rest for patients following a cardiac catheterization or percutaneous coronary intervention (PCI). The time the nurses spent on this project and attending the Clinical Scholar Program workshops to guide learning of EBP was supported by the nursing director.

[a] Center for Clinical and Professional Development, Department of Nursing, Maine Medical Center, 22 Bramhall Street, Portland, ME 04102-3175, USA
[b] Maine Medical Center, Richards 1, 22 Bramhall Street, Portland, ME 04102-3175, USA
[c] Cardiothoracic Intensive Care Unit, Maine Medical Center, 22 Bramhall Street, Portland, ME 04102-3175, USA
* Corresponding author.
E-mail address: honesc@mmc.org (C. Honess).

Nurs Clin N Am 44 (2009) 117–130
doi:10.1016/j.cnur.2008.10.004
0029-6465/08/$ – see front matter © 2009 Elsevier Inc. All rights reserved.
nursing.theclinics.com

The optimal duration of bed rest following a cardiac catheterization or PCI is not known. Duration of bed rest postprocedure may vary from as little as 2 hours to as much as 12 hours. Maintaining bed rest is an effort to avoid complications at the vascular entry point for the procedure, which usually is the femoral artery and/or vein. Vascular complications range from bleeding at the femoral access site, hematomas of varying sizes, arterial-venous fistula, and pseudoaneurysms.[2]

Potential discomforts arise for the patient remaining on bed rest for any length of time. These discomforts include inability to flex the leg in the femoral area on the procedural side, head of the bed elevated to only 30°, and log rolling from side to side. Back and leg pain may occur related to the inability to move freely in bed or to have the head of bed elevated. Bed rest also can present problems in urinary elimination because of the change in urination habits. These issues are related significantly to patient and family satisfaction with the hospital stay and to hospitalization costs associated with pain medications, urinary catheters, and nursing care time.

Approximately 2000 patients per year experience a cardiac catheterization or PCI at MMC, and traditionally these patients remained on bed rest for 6 hours. Patients and family are the primary stakeholders in this practice, but other stakeholders include staff nurses, physicians, and nursing administrators. Garnering support from all the stakeholders was an important first step in examining the current practice regarding the duration of bed rest and in exploring the feasibility and safety of decreasing the duration of bed rest to 4 hours. For patients and families, the benefits of reducing the duration of bed rest include early ambulation, a potential decrease in pain medication usage, and adequate elimination.

The nursing staff, as stakeholders in reducing the length of postprocedure bed rest, saw an opportunity to change practice using the latest evidence and as an opportunity to improved documentation. A new postprocedure documentation tool including specific features addressing assessments for the development vascular complications over time was developed to introduce and implement this practice change.

Nursing administrators are involved in examining the feasibility of proposals for practice changes. Presenting the cost benefits of a shorter duration of bed rest to nursing administrators helped gain their support. The potential cost savings would be realized in reduced needs for analgesia and assistive equipment and shorter patient stay.

Gaining support from physician stakeholders involved multiple presentations of the results of synthesized research studies with components that paralleled the practices for these cardiac procedures at MMC. The physicians were especially concerned with the risks of vascular complications. Synthesis of the primary external evidence showed that the duration of bed rest could be reduced without increasing vascular complications.

Search and Analysis of the External Evidence

A literature search was conducted in MEDline and the Cumulative Index of Nursing and Allied Health Literature (CINAHL) using the keywords "cardiac procedures," "bed rest duration," "amounts of anticoagulation," "early ambulation," "and vascular complications." Thirty research studies were found; five studies included the variables of interest.

The five studies were critiqued using a research critique table.[3] Three of the studies were randomized, controlled trials, and two were quasi-experimental. Variables of interest included bed rest duration of 2 to 6 hours,[2,4–7] femoral access sheath dwell time of approximately zero to 6 hours following the procedure,[2,4–7] a femoral sheath size of 6 to 8 F,[2,4–7] and varying amounts of anticoagulant administered during selected cardiac procedures.[2,4-7] All studies evaluated were of acceptable quality.

Synthesizing the Internal and External Evidence

Following critique of the studies, four tables based on the variables of interest were developed to synthesize and compare the results in each of the five studies. **Table 1** is an example of a single synthesis table based on length of bed rest. Each table had the same column headings, and findings were compared with current practices within the institution.

Decreasing the length of bed rest from 6 to 4 hours without increasing vascular complications was the major goal of this evidence-based project. The studies most closely paralleling the practices at MMC were those that compared results in a control group remaining in bed for 6 hours and an interventional group that remained in bed for 4 hours. The other synthesis tables tabulated vascular complications incorporating the other variables of sheath dwell time, sheath size, and anticoagulation.

The rate of vascular complications following a cardiac catheterization or PCI was low at MMC. Events considered as complications included bleeding, hematoma, and arterial-venous fistula developing during sheath removal or at some point during bed rest. These complications were considered as internal evidence in the result of decreasing bed rest from 6 to 4 hours. External evidence[2,4-7] provided an overall complication rate of 6% related to bleeding and hematoma, higher than the current complication rate MMC.

As key stakeholders in this project, the physicians were concerned about a possible increase in vascular complications. The synthesis tables demonstrating the strength of the evidence for reducing bed rest after sheath removal from 6 hours to 4 hours convinced the physicians that the practice change would not increase the potential for risk or harm. After reviewing the framework of the Clinical Scholar Model, the cardiology team gave the project their support.

A proposal to move ahead with this EBP was drafted. The draft was based on strength of the evidence from the research studies regarding vascular complications following a reduction of bed rest from 6 to 4 hours. The provisions for bed rest were prescribed by physicians through an order set for postcardiac catheterization or PCI care.

Implementing and Evaluating: A Pilot Study

A pilot study for bed rest duration was planned to test this practice change and to assess the rate of vascular complications. As bedside clinicians, nursing staff were valuable stakeholders in the implementation and monitoring of this practice change. The cardiac interventional department identified as the pilot unit was a demanding area for nursing care. The nursing staff had been removing femoral access sheaths and establishing hemostasis in the procedural area for the past 5 years and was expert in assessing the presence of vascular complications. Their participation was needed to implement the change and successfully decrease the duration of bed rest.

A postprocedure documentation tool was developed to incorporate assessment of the femoral access site and other components that might potentiate a vascular complication. The first assessment served as a baseline for the access site condition. An area for treatment of a vascular complication was included; the designated methods for achieving hemostasis were manual compression or the use of a mechanical device. Vital signs and further assessments were entered on the documentation tool at regular intervals. The countdown to ambulation began when the femoral access sheath was removed, based on the activated clotting time being within the designated

Table 1
Length of bed rest

First Author[ref]	Sample Research Design	Independent Variable/ Intervention	Dependent Variable Outcome	Significant Results	Limitations/Gaps	Generalizability (AHRQ Levels of Evidence)
Vlasic W, et al[2]	Randomized, controlled trial N = 299 n = 99: 2 hr BR n = 99: 4 hr BR n = 101: 6 hr BR	BR: 2, 4, or 6 hr	Vascular complications Major: transfusion, surgical repair, ultrasound guided compression, prolonged hospital stay Minor: requiring site compression, hematoma < 5 × 5 cm, bleeding (soaking two 4 × 4 inch gauzes)	2-hr group 3% hematoma 4% rebleeding 1% pseudoaneurysm and surgical repair 4-hr group 6% hematoma 3% rebleeding 6-hr group 5% hematoma 2% rebleeding	Trial became unblinded after hemostasis	Yes (A)
Keeling A, et al[4]	Randomized, controlled trial N = 71 Experimental group: n = 51: 4 hr BR Control group: n = 20: 6 hr BR	4 hr of bed rest versus 6 hr of bed rest	Vascular complications	4-hr group98% without complication. One patient had a small amount of oozing after multiple procedures and ACT > 200 at the time of sheath pull.	Incomplete data collection because of inability to place patients in the control group: doctors ordered 4 hr of bed rest	Yes (B)
Koch K, et al[5]	Descriptive N = 300 patients	2 hr bed rest	Vascular complications Bleeding at ambulation Late bleeding: ambulation to 48 hr Hematoma > 5 × 5 cm Arterial-venous fistula Pseudoaneurysm	2-hr group 1.7% bleeding at ambulation 3% hematoma > 5 × 5 cm No late bleeding	Patients taking oral anticoagulants or heparin before the procedure were excluded Use of compression bandage	No (B)

Koch K, et al[6]	Quasi-experimental N = 830 n = 420: 4 hr BR n = 410: BR overnight	Experimental group = 4 hr of bed rest Control group = Bedrest overnight	Vascular complications Bleeding at ambulation Late bleeding: ambulation to 48 hr Hematoma > 5 × 5 cm Arterial-venous fistula Pseudoaneurysm	4-hr group: 2.3% all complications 4-hr to overnight group: 2.2% all complications	Patients taking oral anticoagulants or heparin before the procedure were excluded Non randomized use of compression bandage	No (B)
Bogart M, et al[7]	Randomized, controlled trial N = 200 Experimental: n = 100: 4 hr BR Control: n = 100: 6 hr BR	Experimental group: 4 hr BR Control group: 6 hr BR	Vascular complications Rebleeding Hematoma Arteriovenous fistula Pseudoaneurysm Limb ischemia Thrombosis of femoral artery Hematoma: Small (< 5 cm) Medium (6–10 cm) Large (> 10 cm)	4 hr group: 1% small hematoma 6-hr group: 2% rebleeding 1% pseudoaneurysm	After cardiac catherization, 79% of patients in the experimental group and 71% of patients in the control group received heparin during the procedure	Yes (B)

Abbreviations: ACT, active clotting time; AGCHR, Agency for Health care and Research Quality; BR, bed rest.

range. The method for compression of the femoral access site following sheath removal was identified on the form. The final assessment was an observation of the femoral access site 15 minutes after initiating activity. Exclusions to ambulation at 4 hours were hypertension, sedation, and the development of bleeding or hematoma during bed rest. The postprocedure documentation tool was used to collect quality improvement data at different points in time as well as to provide assessment guidelines.

One of the goals of this EBP project was the absence of vascular complications when bed rest was reduced. After pilot testing for 6 months, there had been no increase in vascular complications. This outcome was communicated to physicians and nursing through cardiology staff and nursing staff meetings. Order sets for post-cardiac procedural care were adapted to reflect the 4 hours of bed rest.

Using the framework of the Clinical Scholar Model as a guide, this nurse workgroup identified a clinical practice issue and the evidence needed to support a successful practice change after PCI. It was estimated that over a 1-month period this change in practice resulted in a saving of 300 hours of nursing time, time that could be spent providing patient education and other nursing care. Audits for the development of vascular complication continue with the postprocedure record.

Dissemination

The core group of cardiology nurses involved in this EBP project shared their reflections on the Clinical Scholar Model and this project with their colleagues at the hospital and at national and international research conferences. The practice of reduced bed rest is sustained by the change in order sets and the postprocedure record. Nursing staff directly sustain the practice of reduced bed rest following a cardiac catheterization or PCI through efforts to avoid vascular complications while maintaining patient comfort.

REDUCING POSTOPERATIVE NAUSEA AND VOMITING IN PATIENTS UNDERGOING OPEN-HEART SURGERY

The following project illustrates using the Clinical Scholar Model in a different setting at MMC, the cardiothoracic ICU (CTICU). Bedside nurses are astute observers of patients' experiences and responses in health and illness. As a part of their critical thinking processes, staff nurses continuously ask questions about their practice and reflect on the efficacy of their interventions. The richness of the bedside nursing practice and the questions generated are fertile ground for beginning the process of changing nursing practice based on supporting evidence.

Staff nurses in the CTICU observed that many of their patients experienced postoperative nausea and/or vomiting (PONV) during the recovery period. The nurses questioned the current practice protocol. Some of the questions they asked were

Is treatment of PONV enough?
Should we be doing more to prevent PONV?
Is our current rescue treatment with ondansetron adequate?
What are the most efficacious pharmacologic measures for prevention and treatment of PONV?
Are there nonpharmacologic treatments for PONV?

A practice-driven clinical question was formulated: "Is the current protocol we use to treat postoperative nausea and vomiting evidence based?" Three staff nurses formed a core nurse workgroup and explored this question. These nurses already were attending the workshops in the Clinical Scholar Program, and the time they spent at the workshops and working on the project was supported by the CTICU nursing director.

Search and Analysis of the External Evidence

The nurse workgroup began with a search for external evidence. Prevalence studies of PONV in patients undergoing open-heart surgery (OHS) showed that this clinical issue was a common problem in this population.[8] The focus of the search turned to the efficacy of pharmacologic treatment strategies for PONV. The challenges of the search became apparent when simple searches in multiples databases revealed thousands of individual articles on various aspects of treatment and prevention of PONV. In this case, there was substantial external evidence, and the primary challenge was how to sift through and synthesize the information relevant to the clinical question.

The Clinical Scholar workshops supported the nurse workgroup in exploring the literature and learning about the levels of evidence that supported practice change. With a well-designed approach[9] to grading the evidence, it became clear that there were meta-analyses, as well as individual studies, that discussed the treatment and prevention of PONV. Unlike the Agency for Health care and Research Quality level of evidence table used in the previous example, the levels of evidence used to grade the reviewed evidence included well-designed quantitative studies, meta-analyses, qualitative research, quality improvement data, and expert opinion. Additional evidence in the form of consensus clinical guidelines was reviewed by the core nurse workgroup. The use of these broad sources of evidence to examine the clinical question strengthened the basis with which they approached the clinical issue[10] and contributed with an approach that was patient centered.

Recognizing the utility of a guideline in summarizing clinical information, the nurse workgroup identified a clinical guideline[11] that addressed the key issues identified in their meetings. They critiqued the guideline using a framework suggested by Brown[12] and gained insight into an overview of the process for addressing PONV in a clinical setting. The evidence reviewed demonstrated that the process of preventing and treating PONV was well studied and well understood. Risk-assessment studies[13,14] indicated that patients after OHS were at risk for PONV because of a variety of factors, including the length of the surgery and the use of postoperative narcotics. With use of the guideline, it also became clear that prophylaxis involves treatment of the patient before induction of anesthetic as well as treatment in the postoperative phase. The nurse workgroup realized anesthesiologists would be key stakeholders in the project, and they invited a physician colleague to join the project. The anesthesiologist brought important contributions to the workgroup through his knowledge of individual studies[15] that pertained to the efficacy of steroids for PONV in the OHS population. Another stakeholder who joined the core workgroup was a pharmacist dedicated to the ICU setting; his knowledge of the drug therapies and formulary options at MMC was very helpful. Other key stakeholders included the nursing director of the unit, the CTICU staff nurses who implemented a pilot of the project, the cardiothoracic surgeons, and their physician assistants. Building consensus on recognizing the need for EBP change involved the entire culture of the CTICU.

Synthesizing the Internal and External Evidence

The nurse workgroup saw that PONV was common in their postoperative patients, so they conducted a preliminary 2-week chart audit on the OHS cases. Using antiemetic usage as a flag for PONV, they noted that 50% of patients required treatment for PONV in the first 3 days after surgery. Quality-improvement audits gathered from patients before discharge indicated that patients reported nausea as a major problem postoperatively. This site-specific internal evidence validated the concerns of the staff nurses and supported the need for further exploration of the clinical question.

The external evidence[11] indicated that prevention of PONV should begin for patients before induction of anesthesia via the administration of dexamethasone. Another prophylactic dose of antiemetic, ondansetron, should be administered in the immediate postoperative period. Further rescue therapy for treatment of breakthrough PONV followed a key principle called "multimodal treatment": that is, should breakthrough PONV occur, it should be treated with a pharmacologic agent with a mechanism of action different from that of the previously used agents. For this reason, prochlorperazine was added to the protocol for treatment of breakthrough PONV.

Implementation and Evaluation

Through a review of the evidence and interdisciplinary collaboration with representatives from anesthesia and pharmacy, a new evidence-based protocol was developed for preventing and treating patients experiencing PONV after OHS. Nurses and physicians from the CTICU were invited to review the proposed changes and share their concerns. The proposal for change was submitted to and reviewed by the hospital's institutional review board. Detailed baseline data before protocol implementation provided a basis of comparison for evaluating the protocol's efficacy. The use of this new protocol and analysis of data before and after protocol implementation showed that patients experienced a significant decrease in the incidence and prevalence of PONV in the CTICU. Implementation of the protocol resulted in a 50% overall reduction in patient episodes of PONV from the day of surgery to 4 days after surgery. The protocol was most effective in reducing PONV on the day of surgery and on postoperative day one. Cost analysis showed that the new protocol did not increase the amount of ondansetron used and provided better patient outcomes.

Dissemination

The nurse workgroup involved in this study shared its findings at the unit and hospital level and at national and international conferences. Along with its findings, it proposed suggestions to enhance project sustainability. These suggestions included embedding the data collection and data analysis of the protocol into systems already in place in the clinical microsystem, thereby enhancing the ability continually to review and improve delivery at the point of care.

The systematic process of studying this clinical question using the Clinical Scholar Model provided these clinical scholars with answers as well as even more questions about the clinical experiences of their patients. The protocol developed was effective in treating early-onset PONV, but after OHS many patients also experience later-onset PONV or PONV that persisted throughout their hospital stay. More research in this area is needed to understand the effectiveness of treatments and interventions. In addition, as new therapies evolve, the evidence supporting practice will change. The challenge for clinical scholars is to review and re-evaluate the evidence as it is disseminated; clinical knowledge is evolving at a pace that brings a wealth of both quantitative and qualitative knowledge to the bedside.

IMPROVING GLYCEMIC CONTROL IN AN OPEN-HEART SURGERY PROGRAM

For several years, the Clinical Scholar Model has been used as a format for identifying an issue, assessing internal and external evidence, synthesizing the evidence, implementing and evaluating a change in practice, and disseminating the results in the stepdown (intermediate care) unit for patients after OHS. In addition to dissemination, an interdisciplinary team recently evaluated the sustainability of a practice change and subsequent outcomes. In 2004A the cardiothoracic surgical team at MMC instituted a continuous insulin infusion (CII) protocol in the OHS population, but adherence to the CII protocol (ie, a blood glucose goal of 110 mg/dL in the ICU patients and 150 mg/dL for patients in the step-down unit) had never been evaluated. Also, it had not been determined whether the rates of deep sternal wound infection (DSWI) had been reduced after implementation of the CII protocol.

Search and Analysis of the External Evidence

This protocol was based on the research studies conducted by Furnary,[16–18] which showed that using a CII for 72 hours postoperatively on all patients undergoing heart surgery reduced DSWI and mortality. Before Furnary's[16–18] studies, only diabetics were treated with insulin, and the insulin usually was given subcutaneously. Van Den Berghe's[19] research on patients in intensive care concluded that patients who had abnormal glucose tests had a much higher risk of infection and mortality. In addition, in their position statement the American College of Endocrinology[20] recommended a blood glucose of 110 mg/dL or below be maintained for all patients in surgical intensive care.

Synthesizing the External and Internal Evidence

Based on the evidence supporting the use of CII in patients undergoing heart surgery, the cardiothoracic team developed a protocol based on the work of Furnary.[18] The protocol was developed and initiated in both the CTICU and the step-down unit. The protocol was initiated upon the patient's arrival at the ICU, and it was continued for 96 hours postoperatively. The nursing staff, the doctors, and the physician assistants received minimal education on the use of the protocol, and the protocol was received with skepticism and uneasiness related to the fear of hypoglycemia. Also, there was no plan for an evaluation of the success or failure of the protocol. The only data point collected was the incidence of DSWI, which remained unchanged at 3%. The clinicians' prevailing perception was that the use of the CII would guarantee good glucose control. Random checks of glucose levels in the cardiac surgery population showed glucose levels consistently were above 200 mg/dL, levels that were alarming. In addition, the CII protocol was not followed in either the ICU or the step-down unit.

Implementation and Evaluation

The initial goal of the glucose project was to determine nurses' adherence to the CII protocol. The original team members included a staff nurse, a physician assistant, and a physician. As the glycemic control project progressed, other team members were added to obtain their expertise; at various times, the team included a dietician, staff nurses, data analysts, medical students, a clinical nurse specialist, perfusionists, and anesthesiologists.

In the initial glycemic control protocol, the target glucose level was 110 mg/dL or less in the CTICU and 150 mg/dL or less in the step-down unit, based on evidence from the work of Furnary[16–18] and Van den Berghe.[19] As part of the ongoing quality improvement program, a data collection tool was developed and approved by the MMC institutional review board that included the name, age, and gender of the patient; the procedure performed; the patient's height, weight, and fasting blood sugar; diagnosis of diabetes; transfusion of blood products; all glucose recordings; and treatment for 96 hours. Blood product information was collected because there is ongoing evidence that patients undergoing heart surgery who receive blood products are at increased risk for mortality and infection.[21] Following completion of each phase of the glycemic control project, the data analyst for the Northern New England Cardiovascular Disease Study Group provided additional information on length of stay, DSWI, and mortality.

Body mass index (BMI) and hemoglobin A1c were added as data points in subsequent phases. BMI is a more definitive measure of obesity than height and weight. Abnormal BMIs in patients correlate with higher glucose levels even when the patients do not have a diagnosis of diabetes.[22,23] Hemoglobin A1c was added in the preoperative order set for all patients undergoing heart surgery to give the practitioner information about previous control of a patient's diabetes and/or to indicate a need for further testing for diabetes if the preoperative test was abnormal.[24,25] In previous studies, the risk for infection was highest in the first 72 hours following surgery.[16–18] The team decided to collect data on 150 patients, approximately one eighth of the annual adult heart surgery population. A proposal was developed and sent to the institutional review board for review and approval. After approval, data were collected on 157 consecutive patients undergoing heart surgery.

Evaluation of the Glycemic Control Project: Phase One

Findings from the first phase showed that the mean glucose levels ranged from 128 to 158 mg/dL in the first 96 hours postoperatively, the CII protocol was stopped prematurely in the first 24 hours postoperatively, and the full CII protocol was not followed. In addition, the DSWI rate during the 3 months of the glycemic study was 3.3%, as compared with a target rate of less than 1%. As a result of these findings, the CII protocol was revised, and intensive education on diabetes and hyperglycemia was presented to the nurses in the critical care and step-down units, the physician assistants, and cardiothoracic physicians. It was hypothesized that education would increase both knowledge and comfort level with the CII protocol. The education was done both formally through short educational sessions and informally through discussions on glucose control and use of the protocol. Education was accomplished by physicians, a physician assistant, a unit-based educator, and a diabetic clinical nurse specialist. Daily discussions with nurses, physicians, and physician assistants focused on efforts for reducing DSWI through the implementation of good glycemic control. This approach with education conducted by a team was successful in reaching coworkers.

Revisions, Implementation, and Monitoring: Phase Two

In phase two, the target glucose range for patients in the critical care and the step-down units was increased from 110 mg/dL in the ICU and 150 mg/dL in the step-down unit to 150 mg/dL in both units. This change was made to increase the comfort level of the heart surgery team with a future goal of decreasing the upper limit of glucose to 120 mg/dL.

Many things happened during the second phase of this project. In response to multiple complaints about the three-page length of the CII protocol, three medical students developed a nomogram. This user-friendly, color-coded one-page format was well received by nurses, physician assistants, and doctors and has continued to be used with minor changes based on the findings during the subsequent phases of the glycemic control project. During this second phase, patients remained on the CII protocol for 96 hours. Phase two mean glucose levels from admission to the operating room to 96 hours postoperatively were found to be in the range of 124 to140 mg/dL. No DSWI occurred during 6 months. One of the findings from phase two was the number of abnormal glucose levels in both the known and unknown diabetic population at the 96-hour mark: 25% of the patients were prediabetic or new type 2 diabetics with previously undiagnosed diabetes. This finding created a new dilemma, because most of these patients would be discharged within 24 to 48 hours.

A New Dilemma With a Creative Solution

There were ongoing discussions among physicians, nurses, and physician assistants about how to solve the new problems that arose from the findings in the glucose study. As a result, a team met with to find a solution that (1) would not increase length of stay but would provide a safety net for the patient and (2) would not increase the workload of the staff nurse. A collaborative team including dieticians, dietary aides, nurses, physicians, a diabetic nurse specialist, Lifescan representatives, a laboratory representative, and physician assistants convened to look at both the dietary and discharge needs of the patients. Providing more dietary options for patients and providing new diabetics with a free glucometer and educational materials were two of the decisions made by this collaborative group. In addition, information about poorly controlled diabetics and new diabetics was sent to the patients' primary care physicians.

Revisions, Implementation, and Monitoring: Phase Three

Following minor revisions in the nomogram for the CII protocol and the development of an insulin infusion start chart to differentiate dose amounts depending on a patient's blood glucose nadir, phase three of the glucose project was conducted. In addition to determining compliance with the CII protocol, data for the discharge plan were collected for the newly diagnosed and poorly controlled diabetics.

During phase three data collection, the cardiothoracic team found several alarming issues:

1. An increase in leg infections
2. No change in mediastinitis or mortality rates
3. Lack of standardization for patients transitioning off the CII protocol
4. Several incidences of hypoglycemia in discharged patients, with one patient readmitted to the hospital with seizures

These findings led to three changes: re-education of nurses about the importance of glucose control, development of a transition protocol to be used when the CII protocol is discontinued, and a preoperative order for hemoglobin A1c for all patients undergoing cardiac surgery.

Changes in practice were made within 1 month. Delays in surgery that occurred because of double-digit hemoglobin A1c and abnormal glucose levels resulted in patients being treated aggressively to bring glucose levels down to a normal level before surgery. Based on the results from Funary's research,[16–18] the risk for DSWI from hyperglycemia diminished by postoperative day three. Because of these findings at the end of phase three of the study, the team decided to discontinue the CII protocol on the morning of postoperative day three.

Plans for Phase Four

Furnary[22] used a CII tight glycemic protocol in the first 72 hours postoperatively when patients were at highest risk for DSWI. Based on Funary's findings, the team decided to discontinue the CII protocol on the morning of postoperative day three. A transition protocol was developed for use when the CII protocol was discontinued: to standardize the approach for glucose levels above 150 mg/dL, short-acting insulin was administered subcutaneously for correctional coverage. In addition, patients who had a previous diagnosis of diabetes resumed their preoperative regimen on the evening of postoperative day two or on the morning of postoperative day three. The exceptions to this approach were patients who were taking Metformin Hcl and had an elevated creatinine level, diabetic patients who were poorly controlled, and newly diagnosed diabetics. The transition protocol will be evaluated in phase four of the hyperglycemia project.

The cardiothoracic team is aware that ongoing assessment of the CII protocol is needed to reduce each patient's risk for mortality and morbidity following cardiac surgery. In addition to reducing the DSWI rate, the team has developed a consistent approach for glycemic control in the heart surgery population.

Interdisciplinary Respect and Collaboration

The greatest accomplishment to date has been the collaboration among all team members in identifying problems or issues involving the cardiothoracic population. This interdisciplinary team allows all voices to be heard in a nonpunitive atmosphere. This collaborative model has thrived and been sustained for 3 years with the ultimate goal of providing patients with best possible outcomes. The same collaborative approach has been used to implement oral care, prevent pressure ulcers, improve wound care, and develop a ventricular assist device protocol. Informal bi-weekly 30-minute meetings are held to identify any issues within the cardiothoracic patient population and/or issues with staff relationships. Doctors, nurses, physician assistants, management, nursing assistants, and other disciplines are invited to attend. The relationship among the team members filters to the daily work environment, where communication is key to providing the best possible outcomes for patients. Opinions about a patient's condition are heard, and complications are averted because of this unique model. This collaborative model now is being used to implement glycemic control in all inpatient areas throughout the hospital.

SUMMARY

Using the Clinical Scholar Model, staff nurses can evaluate the evidence supporting clinical practice at the point of care. Following the model through the steps was easy for a novice bedside researcher. This model gave clinical staff nurses an avenue for conducting nursing research and implementing evidence-based changes that are meaningful in their daily practice. In addition, the process increased collaborative conversations among health care providers, patients, and families about evidence-based care.

The Clinical Scholar Model serves as an effective guide for investigating and implementing EBP change at the bedside. It assists in identifying problems and issues, the key stakeholders, and the need for change in practice. These three projects, although identifying different clinical issues, followed the format of the Clinical Scholar Model. The completed projects improved patient outcomes. These projects illustrate some real-life examples of bringing this process to the clinical setting and of using the Clinical Scholar Model in practice.

ACKNOWLEDGMENTS

C.H. acknowledges the invaluable assistance of Trudy Kent, RN, BSN, Sue Chenoweth, RN, BSN, and Sara Kovacs RN, BSN. K.K. acknowledges the invaluable assistance of Bethany Drabik, RN, BSN, CCRN, and Anne Marie Gray, RN, BSN, CCRN.

REFERENCES

1. Schultz A. Origins and aspirations: conceiving the clinical scholar model. Excellence in Nursing Knowledge 2005;1–4 [online publication].
2. Vlasic W, Almond D, Massel D, et al. Reducing bed rest following arterial puncture for coronary interventional procedures. J Invasive Cardiol 2001;13:788–92 A.
3. Gallant P. Analysis: what's all the speak about critique? Excellence in Nursing Knowledge 2005;1–5 [online publication].
4. Keeling A, Fisher C, Haugh K, et al. Reducing time in bed after percutaneous transluminal coronary angioplasty. Am J Crit Care 2000;9:185–7 B.
5. Koch K, Piek J, de Winter R, et al. 2Hr ambulation after PCI with a 6 F guiding catheter and low dose heparin. Heart 1999;81:53–6 B.
6. Koch K, Piek J, de Winter R, et al. Early ambulation after coronary angioplasty and stenting with 6F guiding catheters and low dose heparin. Am J Cardiol 1997;80: 1084–6 B.
7. Bogart M, Bogart D, Rigden, et al. A prospective randomized trial of early ambulation following 8F diagnostic cardiac catheterization. Catheter Cardiovasc Interv 1999;47:175–8 B.
8. Mace L. An audit of post-operative nausea and vomiting, following cardiac surgery: scope of the problem. Nurs Crit Care 2003;8(5):187–96 B.
9. Stetler C, Brunell M, Giuliano K, et al. Evidence-based practice and the role of nursing leadership. J Nurs Adm 1998;28:45–53.
10. Rycroft-Malone J, Seers K, Titchen A, et al. What counts as evidence in evidence-based practice? J Adv Nurs 2004;47:81–90 B.
11. Gan T, Meyer T, Apfel C, et al. Consensus guidelines for managing postoperative nausea and vomiting. Anesth Analg 2003;97(1):62 B.
12. Brown SJ. Knowledge for health care practice: a guide to using research evidence. Philadelphia: W.B. Saunders Company; 1999.
13. Apfel C, Kranke P, Eberhart A. Comparison of predictive models for postoperative nausea and vomiting. Br J Anaesth 2002;88:234–40 B.
14. Koivuranta M, Laara E, Alahuhta S. A survey of postoperative nausea and vomiting. Anaesthesia 1997;52(5):443–9 B.
15. Halvorsen P, Raeder J, White PF, et al. The effect of dexamethasone on side effects after coronary revascularization procedures. Anesth Analg 2003;96:1578–83 A.
16. Zerr K, Furnary A, Grunkemeier G, et al. Glucose control lowers the risk of wound infection in diabetics after open heart operations. Ann Thorac Surg 1997;63: 353–61.
17. Furnary A, Zerr K, Grunkemeier G, et al. Continuous intravenous insulin infusion reduces the incidence of deep sternal wound infection in diabetic patients after cardiac surgery procedures. Ann Thorac Surg 1999;67:352–62.
18. Furnary A, Guangqiang G, Grunkemeier G, et al. Continuous insulin infusion reduces mortality inpatients with diabetes undergoing coronary artery bypass grafting. J Thorac Cardiovasc Surg 2003;125(5):1007–21.
19. Van den Berghe G, Wouters P, Weekers F, et al. Intensive insulin therapy in critically ill patients. N Engl J Med. 2001;345(19):1359–67.
20. American College of Endocrinology. Position statement on inpatient diabetes and metabolic control. Endocr Pract 2004;10(1):1–6.
21. Ferraris V, Ferraris S, Sibu S, et al. Perioperative blood transfusion and blood conservation in cardiac surgery: the Society of Thoracic Surgeons and the Society of Cardiovascular Anesthesiologist clinical practice guideline. Ann Thorac Surg 2007;83:S27–86.

22. Gandhi GY, Nuttall GA, Abel MD, et al. Intraoperative hyperglycemia and perioperative outcomes in cardiac surgery. Mayo Clin Proc 2005;80(7):862–6.
23. Rady MY, Johnson DJ, Bhavesh P, et al. Influence of individual characteristics on outcome of glycemic control in intensive care patients with or without diabetes mellitus. Mayo Clin Proc 2005;80(12):1558–67.
24. American Diabetes Association. Clinical practice recommendations 2008. Diabetes Care 2008;31:S38–41.
25. Dailey G. Assessing glycemic control with self-monitoring of blood glucose and hemoglobin A1c measurements. Mayo Clin Proc 2007;82(2):229–36.

Using Evidence to Improve Care for the Vulnerable Neonatal Population

Cheryl A. Lefaiver, PhD, RN[a,*], Phyllis Lawlor-Klean, RNC, MS, APN/CNS[b],
Rosanna Welling, RN, BSN, MBA[b], Jean Smith, RNC, BSN, MSN (c)[b],
Laura Waszak, RN[b], Wendy Tuzik Micek, PhD, RN[a]

KEYWORDS

- Neonatal intensive care nursing
- Evidence-based practice implementation
- Evidence-based practice facilitation
- Parental visitation • Feeding readiness

The movement of evidence-based practice (EBP) into the clinical setting has become important to ensure that patients receive the best nursing care possible. Although the need to incorporate evidence into bedside care may be apparent, there is not a magic recipe for successfully implementing the use of evidence at the bedside. This article describes practical ways to overcome barriers and facilitate the implementation of evidence through two examples in a Magnet-designated 650-bed not-for-profit teaching medical center, Advocate Christ Medical Center in Oak Lawn, IL, within the specialty care environment of a 37-bed level III co-perinatal center neonatal ICU (NICU).

Barriers to the use of research have been studied extensively. Nurses are limited mainly by inadequate time on the job to implement new ideas, a lack of awareness of research findings, and insufficient time to read research.[1–4] Consistent with the literature, a study of 336 nurses in the Advocate Christ Medical Center using the Funk BARRIERS research tool[1] identified the greatest barrier to using research as being inadequate time to read research. Open-ended comments identified several specific suggestions to facilitate the use of research: having as a standardized format to critique the literature, having results of research more available, and having assistance available to help nurses understand the results of research. Findings from the literature as well as the authors' institutional research suggest that staff nurses

[a] Advocate Christ Medical Center/Hope Children's Hospital, 4440 West 95th Street, Oak Lawn, IL 60453, USA
[b] Neonatal Intensive Care Unit, Advocate Christ Medical Center/Hope Children's Hospital, 4440 West 95th Street, Oak Lawn, IL 60453, USA
* Corresponding author.
E-mail address: Cheryl.Lefaiver@advocatehealth.com (C.A. Lefaiver).

Nurs Clin N Am 44 (2009) 131–144
doi:10.1016/j.cnur.2008.10.005
0029-6465/08/$ – see front matter © 2009 Elsevier Inc. All rights reserved.

nursing.theclinics.com

perceive the use of research as the explicit use of published research reports and expect health care organizations to bear responsibility for facilitation.

Melnyk and Fineout-Overholt[5] defined research use as the incorporation of research findings from a single study and defined EBP as a process involving the synthesis of the best available evidence, including research, clinical expertise, and patient preferences. Nurses in the clinical setting often relate to the meaning of EBP more readily than to the what they assume the meaning of the term "research" to be. Staff nurses, however, do not understand clearly the distinction between EBP and research. The assumption often is that "evidence" equals published research reports. Nurses certainly will be disenchanted if they assume that practice is founded exclusively on research, because so much of nursing practice has not been formally studied. Kitson and colleagues[6] and Rycroft-Malone and colleagues[7] challenge the assumption that evidence should rely primarily on original research. The authors propose that knowledge generated from evidence can be gained from the sources of (1) research, (2) clinical experience, (3) patients, clients, and caregivers, and (4) the local context and environment.[7] It is important for nurses to accept a broader definition of what constitutes evidence, particularly in specialty clinical areas such as the NICU where nursing research is limited. As the primary care providers within a health care environment, nurses must realize that they have influence because of their experience, interaction with patient and family, and the context of the care environment.

CLINICAL NURSING RESEARCH

Nurses practicing at the bedside often generate the best clinical questions because they are the link between research and practice. Both clinical projects described in this article originated from nursing staff who questioned current practice. The ideas were developed in response to practice issues, and broad sources of evidence were sought to guide project implementation, evaluation, and modification. Nurses are capable of developing ideas for change in practice, but the environment must be one where nurses feel safe to share their ideas and have the opportunity to explore and influence change in practice.

The health care environment is changing constantly. Staff nurses constitute the largest component of the health care delivery system and should have input about how they practice every day. McCormack and colleagues[8] described the concept of "context" as a necessary component for the integration of evidence into the practice setting. The authors likened the environmental context to the practice setting and suggested that a specific culture within the setting underpins the working of the organization. Findings from the Funk[1] BARRIERS survey substantiate the importance of the organizational culture, because nurses largely perceive elements of the setting, such as inadequate time to implement new ideas, as barriers to research facilitation. Therefore, if nurses are expected to use evidence in practice, leaders must create a culture where nurses feel encouraged and valued for their contributions.

Although an organization's culture is intangible, the availability of resources is one tangible way for nurses to see the value of the use of evidence at the bedside. Facilitation of EBP within a supportive culture depends largely on the access to and strategic use of resources. Resources such as access to a library and electronic research databases are necessary, but the right people are indispensable for the process of EBP facilitation. Skills and attributes required of an effective facilitator include being flexible, energetic, a catalyst for change, sensitive, a team builder, and a good communicator.[9] The role of EBP facilitation can be delegated to a variety of leaders in an organization. At Advocate Christ Medical Center, EBP facilitation is led strategically by the director of nursing research and is operationalized by the professional nurse researcher and the clinical nurse specialists (CNSs). Several strategies have led to the successful facilitation and implementation of EBP.

ROLE OF THE PROFESSIONAL NURSE RESEARCHER

The nurse researcher is employed full time, with 100% of services provided for the staff of the organization. A distinct advantage to having a dedicated person responsible for the facilitation of EBP is the protected time to work directly with nurses from all practice settings and at varying skill levels. Furthermore, this person participates on multiple hospital councils and provides a voice for the incorporation of evidence throughout the organization. Harvey and colleagues[9] describe the facilitator as being concerned with doing for others or enabling others. The nurse researcher in this organization facilitates by enabling others, as well as by doing for others when necessary. One-on-one meetings between the nurse researcher and nurses interested in pursuing EBP projects have been a very successful way to educate staff and monitor progress through evolution of the projects. The education can be tailored to the specific needs of the nurses working on the project, and the personal interaction helps the staff know that their project is meaningful. Naturally, individual meetings may seem an inefficient method for distributing information about EBP to the entire organization. Therefore, in addition to individual meetings with project leaders, the nurse researcher meets with various clinical teams who will be working on EBP projects and collaborates with CNSs who strengthen the message of EBP. The extension of the EBP culture is accomplished when nurses who have been involved in a practice change share their positive experiences with others. Furthermore, CNSs employed on each nursing unit reinforce the EBP culture at the unit level.

ROLE OF THE CLINICAL NURSE SPECIALIST

The second edition of the "Statement on Clinical Nurse Specialist Practice and Education" (2004) states, "The essence of CNS practice is clinical expertise based on advanced knowledge of nursing science."[10] Additionally, it states, "The context for CNS practice is the specialty. The specialty directs specific knowledge and skill acquisition; thus, the specialty area shapes the core competencies of clinical expertise."[10] These are two very powerful statements when working with a nursing staff of 140 in a specialty clinical environment. Guiding others into action can be done in many different ways, but the authors' most successful avenue has been mentoring through the use of leadership, collaboration, and consultation skills. The traditional CNS model incorporates the subroles of practitioner, educator, researcher, consultant, administrator, and change agent. As the researcher, the CNS promotes scientific inquiry by integrating relevant nursing research into practice, assists staff incorporating EBP into bedside practice, and expands the scientific base of nursing practice by participating in or conducting original clinical research. These actions assimilate within the patient/client sphere, nursing and nursing practice sphere, and the organizations and systems sphere of CNS practice competencies. All of these components are important during the evolution of an idea and throughout the actual implementation of an EBP change at the bedside.

In the Advocate Christ Medical Center, each nursing unit has a leadership dyad comprised of a manager of clinical operations (MCO) and a CNS. This leadership structure helps the facilitation of EBP, because the MCO is accountable for the management of the staff time and operational activities, and the CNS is accountable for implementation of practice modifications and professional development. The following description of two EBP changes provides some insight into the role of unit nursing leadership in helping staff implement EBP changes in the NICU. Fortunately, the NICU staff is very motivated and willing to work with their peer group, a fundamental necessity for success in the implementation of an EBP change. Change does not happen overnight. Mentoring others through change entails leadership preparation, encouragement, and candor about the repetition that usually is needed to change practice.

The motivation or desire to create change may come from various avenues. The NICU projects evolved from a different impetus, but in both circumstances support from unit nursing leadership was essential for success. The practice change in open visitation evolved from parental requests and a medical center safety initiative to include the patient in the shift report. The feeding readiness EBP project evolved from supporting two staff nurses' attendance at a professional conference regarding the subject and then allowing them to explore the use of their new knowledge. Guidance from the CNS and MCO included support of staff involvement, development of an implementation plan, and encouragement to expand the complexity of the projects. The need for assistance from the nurse researcher emerged as the projects progressed; in particular, the researcher provided guidance in submitting the feeding readiness project to the institutional review board (IRB) and assistance in analyzing data during the evaluation of the projects. Unit nursing leadership and staff partnership was invaluable for the success of the projects and for the affirmation of EBP within the unit where the changes have been implemented.

CHANGE IN OPEN VISITATION PRACTICE
Background

In the NICU, a nurse-to-nurse bedside report has been the standard practice for shift change report. In 2007, however, throughout the medical center, the bedside report was changed to include the patient and family in the plan of care as a safety strategy. About the same time, the NICU was in the midst of a large reconstruction plan. Previously, the NICU had multiple beds in one large room, and parents were not allowed to be in the unit during report because of concerns related to patient privacy. After reconstruction, the square footage per bed space tripled, and the beds were separated into three rooms or pods. The coincidence of the NICU construction and the hospital bedside report initiative provided the impetus for the Unit Council shared governance members to examine the bedside report process critically and to explore opportunities for improvement. It was the opportune time to consider an open, less restrictive parent/family visitation policy.

Development of a Searchable Question

The Unit Council chair and co-chair were part of the hospital council that was assisting with the development of the educational components for bedside report. The NICU MCO, CNS, and Unit Council chair and co-chair attended all hospital training sessions addressing the implementation of bedside report. Additionally, the Unit Council chair worked with the librarian and CNS to review the literature related to open visitation in NICUs. To target the search for information specific to the NICU, a searchable question was developed: "Would parental satisfaction be improved if open visitation were permitted in the NICU?" The MCO and the CNS met with the Unit Council to outline an action plan for open visitation based on the search findings, allowing parental involvement in shift report and medical rounds.

Literature Review

The review of the literature showed that the needs of the family must be considered during visitation. The concept of family-centered care in the 1980s first identified family members as care partners.[11] Family-centered care is defined as including families in patient care during medical rounds as well as in the shift report. Including the family in the report provides them an opportunity for education as well as involvement in the patient's care.[12] Inviting the family to participate as a care partner also fosters a trusting relationship between the nurse and family.[13] Family-centered care can be enhanced by using an unrestricted, open visitation policy. Visitation for families who have infants in the NICU needs to be structured for the family, and not the staff.

Ward[14] studied the perception of family needs by surveying parents of infants in a NICU. Using the NICU Family Needs Inventory, Ward found that being able to visit any time was ranked within the top five of the most important needs of these parents. In another study, the amount of visitation in a NICU was correlated with infant and family demographics.[15] The babies with a greater number of hospital days with visitors were more likely to be brought for follow-up appointments than babies with greater number of no-visitor days.[15] Franck and Spencer[16] measured the length of visitation time and the type of activities conducted by mothers and fathers visiting 110 infants in the NICU. Visitation patterns showed the average amount of parental time spent at the bedside was about 2 hours.[16] These findings suggest that visiting meets an important need for parents and also improves outcomes for the infant.

Involving families in shift report and medical rounds allows the parents to feel valued and increases their satisfaction with the health care facility.[17] Ward[14] found that parents' greatest needs were to know exactly what was being done for their infant and to have questions answered honestly. Open visitation is one way to allow parents to identify the best time to visit their infant to see what care is being provided. If parents feel comfortable with the staff, they may want to spend more time at the bedside with their infant, and their presence can generate good communication and have beneficial effects on the infants' outcome.[13]

Evidence also suggests that nursing attitudes toward open visitation may not be positive. Nurses who are comfortable with the status quo may find it difficult to challenge and change an existing practice.[18] Nurses have been opposed to open visitation for three reasons: (1) nurses have varying levels of comfort performing their work with parents at the bedside, (2) nurses believe that parents will be at the bedside continuously and interfere with patient care, and (3) nurses believe that open visitation may lead to the disclosure of sensitive information.[18] Kowalski and colleagues[19] found that 63% of interviewed nurses reported relief when parents were not present during change of shift activities, suggesting that open visitation practices should allow for breaks for parents and nurses, support nurses' judgment of the practice, and maintain confidentiality.

Implementation

A combination of information was used to design the open visitation practice change, including the hospital education materials for improved bedside reporting and the evidence in support of open visitation. The Unit Council modified the hospital education materials for the open visitation changes in the NICU. The material included (1) role playing for social parenting issues that indicated the need for a discussion to occur away from the bedside; (2) positive comments regarding the oncoming nurse so parents felt comfortable with the shift transition; (3) a script to seek permission to include the parents and any additional visitors, if desired, in daily medical rounds; and (4) when it was appropriate to ask visitors to leave. The Unit Council members used the research to persuade staff who were not supportive of the practice change. The members of the Unit Council divided the staff to provide individual education for every staff member. The education included information about the changes to the visitation practices, role playing of anticipated problems, and notification of the date when the unrestricted visitation practice would start.

In addition to the nursing staff, the neonatologists were involved in the open visitation practice change. Initially, the Unit Council chairs met with the physicians to discuss the change for visitation and the educational plan for staff. Then, the unit nursing leadership met with the interdisciplinary team (neonatologists, pharmacy, dietary, chaplain, social work, and other areas) to inform them of the project progress and to discuss any questions. The entire group was receptive to the concept of open visitation, and the neonatologists believed that having parents available to participate in their child's rounds would be helpful for their communication with the parents.

Evaluation

The success of open visitation in the NICU was evaluated using quantitative and qualitative methods. Initially the plan was to obtain feedback using the Press Ganey patient satisfaction survey, but not enough surveys were returned to provide an adequate amount of reporting data. Therefore using the information from the literature, a 12-item satisfaction survey with a five-point Likert scale ranging from very poor to very good was developed to measure parents' satisfaction with the care in the NICU (**Table 1**). The survey was mailed to all families of discharged infants with a postage-paid return envelope. Surveys were returned to a central hospital location where results were tabulated and sent to the NICU MCO. Survey results showed the reaction to open visitation was overwhelmingly positive. Before the institution of open visitation, the patient satisfaction surveys frequently included negative comments about the visitation hours and how parents were kept out of the unit during procedures and medical rounds and at shift change. Since the implementation of open visitation, the parent satisfaction survey results have been extremely positive. From February to May 2008, 100% of parents who responded (n = 29) strongly agreed that it was easy to visit their infant in the NICU.

Additional feedback has been received through communication with parents and open-ended comments on the satisfaction survey. Parents who had experienced the NICU before open visitation noted the improvement in the visitation practice and commented on how it made the NICU more family friendly. The MCO now receives calls from families at other health care facilities asking if they can transfer their baby to this NICU because the family wants open visitation. Actual comments from parents on the satisfaction surveys confirm the positive effect of the change. One response stated: "The doctors and nurses were fabulous! Everyone we came in contact with was friendly, helpful, and supportive. Also, the constant communication was great and helped ease our worries! We also liked the 24/7 visiting hours."

The open visitation practice has been a huge success and has been a source of satisfaction for NICU parents. In addition, the staff has found the change to be positive. Because nurses spend less time addressing parental concerns related to visitation, they have been able to focus on other patient-satisfaction initiatives, such as teaching kangaroo care, guiding parents to create scrap books, and assessing feeding readiness.

CHANGE IN FEEDING READINESS PRACTICE
Background

One of the many challenges premature infants must master before discharge is successful oral feeding. This process might sound like a simple one, because full-term

Table 1 Neonatial ICU parent survey					
Component of Care	Very Poor	Poor	Fair	Good	Very Good
Care nurses provided to your infant					
Care neonatologists provided for your infant					
Care given to your infant by respiratory therapy, physical therapy, occupational therapy, speech therapy, lactation consultants, and other departments.					
Comfort measures and pain relief provided for your baby					
Nurses and physicians kept you up to date and informed about your infant's progress					
Support, assistance, and privacy were provided for you to breastfeed, care for, or kangaroo your infant					
Ease of visiting the baby					
Opportunity to participate In planning for and providing care for your baby					
Nursing staff provided information and education on your infant's condition(s) and health care needs					
Friendliness/courtesy of the nurses					
Discharge classes prepared you for taking your baby home					
Would recommend Advocate Christ Medical Center/Hope Children's Hospital to a family member or friend					
What most impressed you					
Suggestions for improvement					

newborns usually feed orally with the bottle or breast immediately after birth. Oral feeding, however, requires various skills and reflexes that are still immature in the preterm infant.

Once the onset diagnosis and any other disease process that brought the preterm infant into the unit is resolved, the infant can be categorized as a stable patient or a "feeder-grower" patient. It is now the infant's job to feed, gain weight, and prepare for discharge, not easy tasks to master. Specifically, the infant must learn to suck, swallow, and breathe (SSB) in sequence, without or with minimal drops in heart rate and oxygen desaturations.

Transitioning to oral feedings for the preterm infant requires the caregiver to measure and assess the infant's feeding readiness. Two staff nurses who attended a local conference were introduced to an evidence-based approach for using the infant's behavioral cues while instituting oral feedings. After returning from the conference and observing the customary practice in the unit, it was clear that the practice of advancing feedings was inconsistent and may not have been based on the best evidence. The leadership support of staff attendance at this conference ultimately led to the development and completion of a yearlong project that resulted in a positive change in patient care practice. Two staff nurses led the project to educate staff about the evidential practice of oral feeding and implemented a practice change in the NICU.

Development of a Searchable Question

The first step of this process was to identify systematically the patient care problem in the NICU. The problem was using proper support and feeding techniques to promote adequate nutrition and growth during the infant's transition to oral feedings. The identification of the patient care problem evolved from the questioning of two staff nurses who saw a discrepancy between what was presented at a conference as current evidence and the actual practice on the patient care unit. Working with the NICU CNS and the medical center nurse researcher, the nurses developed a researchable question: "Do preterm infants whose feedings are advanced based on a feeding protocol, compared with current practice, achieve adequate growth and nutrition and have a decreased length of stay?" Once the question was developed, the staff of the unit, in partnership with the CNS, nurse researcher, and librarian, searched for the evidence to provide guidance for the project.

Literature Review

The appropriate time to discharge a preterm infant home is determined by the competency of oral feedings, but there has not been a standard time to initiate the oral feeding process.[20] In the past, the basis for initiating feeding was determined by postconceptual age, weight, and behavioral characteristics such as being able to suck on a pacifier.[21–23] Medical advances have enabled the survival of infants born at earlier gestational ages; thus oral feedings may be introduced before the SSB sequence is present. Some preterm infants have been able to bottlefeed successfully at an age previously believed too early, because the practice was modified in an attempt to decrease length of stay in the NICU.[21,22]

The synactive theory of development as described by Als[24,25] describes the maturational process of behavioral organization in the preterm infant. The framework of this theory addresses the combination of the physiologic and behavioral systems and the way the infant's maturation works to maintain equilibrium between environmental stressors while coping with physiologic demands. This theory suggests that infants function through the "integrated activity of 3 subsystems; autonomic, motoric, and behavioral states."[24,25]

There are physiologic reasons that oral feeding can safely occur before the presence of SSB. Oral feeding for a preterm infant is a high-acuity task,[20,21,23,26–28] and it can be achieved through repetition[21] and the use of positive opportunities.[22,23] Evidence shows that the nurse's role is crucial for the infant to achieve feeding competence.[20–23] Nurses must recognize the initial state of the infant regarding readiness and understand appropriate interventions if the infant becomes distressed during feedings. Nurses also need to provide proper support for the infant during the feeding, which includes encouraging positive feeding experiences. Therefore, it is imperative for the nurse to understand infant cues to feeding readiness when the infant is transitioning to oral feeding.

Readiness often is described as the readiness to feed from a bottle when it is offered.[22] Several factors can contribute to the infant's readiness. Some of these factors are severity of illness, neurologic maturation, and ability to organize autonomic, motor, and behavioral state systems.[20–22,28,29] Depending on the severity of illness, the oral feeding process can be complicated, and the transition period can be lengthened.[22,29] The premature infant's brain is still developing before 34 weeks' gestation, and immaturity of the brain is an important factor in the lack of SSB coordination that makes oral feeding imsuccessful.[21] Typically sucking-swallowing occurs by 28 weeks' gestation, and SSB coordination begins by 32 to 34 weeks.

Several studies have shown that specific behaviors can be observed in infants who are ready for oral feeding. White-Traut and colleagues[28] used secondary analysis of an observational study to find that feeding efficiency can be predicted by the number of feeding-readiness behaviors (FRBs) that the infant exhibits immediately before the feeding. Kinner and Beachy[30] examined nurses' decisions concerning management of feeding in preterm infants in three metropolitan NICUs. Using a self-report questionnaire, the NICU staff nurses ranked factors indicating feeding readiness, behavioral, physiologic, and physical factors, and factors leading to decreasing or eliminating nipple feeds. Results of the study indicated that 54% of nurses worked in units that had guidelines for initiating nipple feeds, and 96% of nurses stated that their units were flexible when it came to managing schedules.[30] The findings suggest that assessment of FRBs can assist nurses in predicting when the infant is ready to begin oral feedings.

Feeding skills evolve continually, even after discharge. Many mothers have expressed concern and have lost confidence in caring for the infant once they are at home.[26] Another approach in aiding the preterm infant to master oral feeds is to involve the parents early in the neonate's stay so the parents can learn to recognize behavioral cues.[20] A structured tool to assess and document the infant's feeding readiness can be used to measure the ability to maintain autonomic stability, engagement, and motor skills before feeding, during feeding, and after feeding.[22,29] The tool can be used both to monitor the infant's progress and as an educational approach when interacting with parents.[27]

Initial skills in premature infants can change over the course of the feeding and between feedings.[27] The Early Feeding Skills Assessment (EFS)[27] is a 36-item observational measure of feeding skills that can be used to assess feeding readiness from the initiation to maturation of oral feeds. The assessment consists of three sections. Section one assesses the infant's state of alertness, oxygen saturation, and energy level; section two assesses the four critical skills domains needed for feeding; and the final section evaluates the impact of the feeding on the infant's alertness, energy level, and physiologic system.[27] The purpose of using the EFS is to give caregivers an ongoing, systematic way to evaluate the infant's strengths and weaknesses and to create individualized feeding care plans for premature infants in the NICU.

Implementation

The evidence supported the use of FRBs as a guide for advancement to oral feedings. The next steps for the team included the assessment of the staff's current practice beliefs, the development of a thorough educational program, and the integration of a FRBs assessment instrument into the standard care processes of the NICU. Because the team aimed to measure patient outcomes to evaluate the effectiveness of the change and hoped to share the results outside the organization, the project protocol, surveys, and methods were approved by the organization's IRB. The CNS and nurse researcher encouraged the team to submit this project to the IRB. By completing the IRB application, the team gained experience about the research process and writing skills needed to develop the literature review. In addition, two surveys were used during the implementation of the project, the EFS[27] and the Oral Feeding Survey.[31] The staff took responsibility for contacting the authors of the tools and asking permission to use their instruments. The authors of the surveys were very willing to share their surveys and personal experience.

To understand the baseline staff knowledge of evidence related to feeding readiness, the Oral Feeding Survey[31] was distributed to the entire staff. The Oral Feeding Survey was designed to measure the criteria that staff use to evaluate whether to initiate or advance to oral feedings in preterm infants. The survey includes nine questions with 34 items identifying cues to begin (eg, observed sucking, strong gag reflex), advance (eg, coordination of SSB, physiologic stability), or decrease (eg, fatigue, poor sucking) oral feedings.

The staff respondents included 117 registered nurses, 18 patient care associates, and seven neonatologists, a 48% response rate from the entire staff. Descriptive analysis of the survey items showed that only 60% of the staff considered behavioral cues when beginning oral feedings (**Fig. 1**). Much of the staff used traditional cues when making decisions to begin oral feedings (**Fig. 2**). Based on the results of the survey and the support of the evidence for change, a standardized educational feeding program was designed to emphasize the use of FRBs, consistent oral feeding techniques, the use of a common language between caregivers, and discharge teaching for parents. The material provided in the teaching sessions included a brief synopsis on the physical growth of the infant, the infant's behavioral cues, and the new feeding protocol. The feeding protocol included a standard feeding assessment schedule,

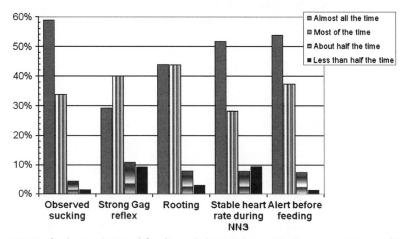

Fig. 1. Criteria for beginning oral feedings: behavioral cues. NNS, non nutritive sucking.

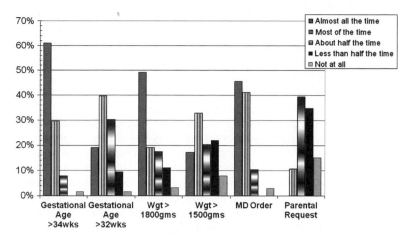

Fig. 2. Criteria for beginning oral feedings: traditional cues. MD, physician.

practice techniques for successful feeding, and educational strategies for parents. Mandatory teaching sessions were provided to the staff of the NICU. To accommodate all the nurses, the session was offered 16 different times over 3 months.

All attendees of the educational sessions were invited to take a pretest and a posttest. A total of 132 staff, including nurses, physicians, speech pathologists, and occupational/physical therapists, attended the education. Once the educational sessions were completed, the feeding protocol and EFS assessment instrument were integrated into the NICU documentation system. Nurses were instructed to use the assessment of FRBs consistently as a guide for assessing the infant's readiness to begin oral feedings. The EFS assessment tool was modified into a chart (**Box 1**) for the nurses to use as a checklist at the bedside. The feeding chart was and continues to be used as a reminder of infants' FRB cues and as a record of an infant's feeding patterns and physical reactions to each feeding, such as decreased heart rate, desaturations, and interventions. Nurses use the assessment data to notify doctors of the infant's readiness and to discuss the proper feeding order for the infant. With the education from the training courses and collaboration with the physicians to write orders according to the feeding protocol, the nurse has the autonomy to increase the oral feeding times based on the infant's FRBs and tolerance of previous feedings.

Box 1
Selected infant feeding assessment criteria
Engagement/readiness cues/feeding skills
Disengagement/distress cues/feeding difficulties
Interventions
Method of feeding
Amount taken/method
Total amount of feeding
Length of oral feeding (minutes)
Fed by parent/nurse

Physicians have been cooperative in implementing the feeding protocol for advancing the infant to oral feedings. The staff nurses are eager to remind the physicians to use the feeding protocol. Evidence that the change is evolving has been found in the orders written by physicians that now read "nipple per feeding protocol" instead of the previous order of "nipple BID" or "nipple 2 to 1."

Evaluation

The pretests and posttests suggested that a need for additional educational reinforcement could be anticipated. It has been approximately 5 months since the last teaching session. Informal evaluation of the change in practice occurred through visual assessment by the unit nursing leadership. Based on the evaluation of the staff's use of the EFS, additional education has been provided on an "as needed" basis. Formal evaluation has begun with a currently ongoing collection of infant length-of-stay data before and after the implementation of the practice change. In addition, the educational session posttest has been incorporated into the semiannual mandatory competencies and will be distributed 6 months after the initial education to assess the staff's level of retention.

The emphasis in this practice change was to shift the feeding paradigm from "volume" to "success." It took time for some nurses and physicians to appreciate the evidence that promoted interactions with the infant for successful feedings not necessarily based on the amount the infant ate. Since the practice change, the staff focuses on making the feeding experience positive so that the infant may continue to feed successfully without tiring and experiencing distress. In addition to the beneficial clinical impact from this practice change, the process of implementing an EBP change was a positive learning experience for the staff and the EBP leaders. The EBP leaders gained personal experience in teaching their colleagues, leading a group through change, and presenting their project at local nursing conferences.

SUMMARY

In a demanding clinical setting, it can be challenging to conduct EBP and follow through with a practice change. In an established Magnet organization that promotes nursing excellence, facilitating the use of EBP is no exception. This Magnet journey allowed the participants to examine the existing nursing research and EBP infrastructure, create positions, establish clean practices, and make improvements that would enable EBP. Early on, the medical center nursing leadership recognized, encouraged, and valued clinical inquiry and change. The chief nurse executive fosters a collaborative environment to deliver evidence-based patient care effectively.

EBP starts with a question, and who is better positioned than the bedside nurse, who lives in the practice environment, to question the day-to-day practices. It is important for nurses to feel supported when questioning practice and to be directed appropriately to translate the project into reality. Both EBP examples described demonstrate that with mentoring and facilitation passionate nurses can succeed in changing practice by using their skills and ability.

Consistent communication and awareness between the facilitator roles is critical so that the appropriate handoffs between the CNS and nurse researcher occur and maintain the project momentum. At the same time, nursing unit leadership needs to continue to provide staff support, time, and resources based on the phase of the project. When EBP project stories are shared with staff, the excitement becomes contagious, and the EDP program can grow, develop, and mature, reducing the gap between practice and research.

One never knows the potential of an EBP project. The benefits can affect individual practice, the organization, and reach as far as local, regional, national, and international practice. Where will your EBP project lead you?

REFERENCES

1. Funk SG, Champagne MT, Wiese RA, et al. BARRIERS: the barriers to research utilization scale. Appl Nurs Res 1991;4(1):39–45.
2. Hutchinson AM, Johnston L. Bridging the divide: a survey of nurses' opinions regarding barriers to, and facilitators of, research utilization in the practice setting. J Clin Nurs 2004;13(3):304–15.
3. Hutchinson AM, Johnston L. Beyond the BARRIERS scale: commonly reported barriers to research use. J Nurs Adm 2006;36(4):189–99.
4. Karkos B, Peters K. A Magnet community hospital: fewer barriers to nursing research utilization. J Nurs Adm 2006;36(7–8):377–82.
5. Melnyk BM, Fineout-Overholt E. Evidence-based practice in nursing & healthcare: a guide to best practice. Philadelphia: Lippincott Williams & Wilkins; 2005.
6. Kitson A, Harvey G, McCormack B. Enabling the implementation of evidence based practice: a conceptual framework. Qual Health Care 1998;7(3):149–58.
7. Rycroft-Malone J, Harvey G, Seers K, et al. An exploration of the factors that influence the implementation of evidence into practice. J Clin Nurs 2004;13(8): 913–24.
8. McCormack B, Kitson A, Harvey G, et al. Getting evidence into practice: the meaning of 'context'. J Adv Nurs 2002;38(1):94–104.
9. Harvey G, Loftus-Hills A, Rycroft-Malone J, et al. Getting evidence into practice: the role and function of facilitation. J Adv Nurs 2002;37(6):577–88.
10. National Association of Clinical Nurse Specialists Statement on clinical nurse specialist practice and education. 2nd edition. Harrisburg (PA): National Association of Clinical Nurse Specialists; 2004. p. 96.
11. Thomas LM. The changing role of parents in neonatal care: a historical review. Neonatal Netw 2008;27(2):91–100.
12. Griffin T. Facing challenges to family-centered care. I: conflicts over visitation. Pediatr Nurs 2003;29(2):135–7.
13. McGrath JM. Partnerships with families: a foundation to support them in difficult times. J Perinat Neonatal Nurs 2005;19(2):94–6.
14. Ward K. Perceived needs of parents of critically ill infants in a neonatal intensive care unit (NICU). Pediatr Nurs 2001;27(3):281–6.
15. Lewis M, Bendersky M, Koons A, et al. Visitation to a neonatal intensive care unit. Pediatrics 1991;88(4):795–800.
16. Franck LS, Spencer C. Parent visiting and participation in infant caregiving activities in a neonatal unit. Birth 2003;30(1):31–5.
17. Davidson JE, Powers K, Hedayat KM, et al. Clinical practice guidelines for support of the family in the patient-centered intensive care unit: American college of critical care medicine task force 2004–2005. Crit Care Med 2007;35(2):605–22.
18. Griffin T. The visitation policy. Neonatal Netw 1998;17(2):75–6.
19. Kowalski WJ, Lawson ML, Oelberg DG. Parent and nurse perceptions of confidentiality, rounding, and visitation policy in a neonatal intensive care unit. Neonatal Intensive Care 2003;16(3):46–50.
20. Thomas JA. Guidelines for bottle feeding your premature baby. Adv Neonatal Care 2007;7(6):311–8.

21. FernÃ¡ndez DÃ-az P, Rosales Valdebenito M. International connections. The transition from tube to nipple in the premature newborn. Newborn Infant Nurs Rev 2007;7(2):114–9.

22. Pickler RH. A model of feeding readiness for preterm infants. Neonatal Intensive Care 2004;17(4):31–6.

23. Shaker CS, Woida AM. An evidence-based approach to nipple feeding in a level III NICU: nurse autonomy, developmental care, and teamwork. Neonatal Netw 2007;26(2):77–83.

24. Als H. Toward a synactive theory of development: promise for the assessment of infant individuality. Infant Ment Health J 1982;3:229–43.

25. Als H. A synactive model of neonatal behavioral organization: framework for the assessment of neurobehavioral development in the premature infant and for support of infants and parents in the neonatal intensive care environment. Phys Occup Ther Pediatr 1986;6(3/4):3–53.

26. Reyna BA, Pickler RH, Thompson A. A descriptive study of mothers' experiences feeding their preterm infants after discharge. Adv Neonatal Care 2006;6(6): 333–40.

27. Thoyre SM, Shaker CS, Pridham KF. The early feeding skills assessment for preterm infants. Neonatal Netw 2005;24(3):7–16.

28. White-Traut RC, Berbaum ML, Lessen B, et al. Feeding readiness in preterm infants: the relationship between preterm behavioral state and feeding readiness behaviors and efficiency during transition from gavage to oral feeding. MCN Am J Matern Child Nurs 2005;30(1):52–9.

29. Ludwig SM. Oral feeding and the late preterm infant. Newborn Infant Nurs Rev 2007;7(2):72–5.

30. Kinneer MD, Beachy P. Nipple feeding premature infants in the neonatal intensive-care unit: factors and decisions. J Obstet Gynecol Neonatal Nurs 1994; 23(2):105–12.

31. Scotland J. The regional oral feeding protocol. Calgary, Canada: Calgary Health Region; 2004. p. 1–22.

From the Bedside to the Boardroom: Resuscitating the Use of Nursing Research

Carol Mulvenon, MS, RN-BC, AOCN[a],*, M. Kathleen Brewer, PhD, ARNP, BC[b]

KEYWORDS

- Clinical scholar model • Nursing research
- Clinical research • Implementing nursing research

It is impossible to pick up a nursing journal today and not find at least one article that mentions the importance of research. Providing care that has some science behind it just makes sense. Walk through a hospital in any community today and ask nurses about nursing research, and you probably will get a wide variety of responses ranging from "I don't understand research articles" to "I am a bedside nurse; I have no time for research." In that group of responses, one hopes, there will be a nurse who can describe a practice change based on research that has led to improved patient outcomes. One of the hallmark features of a profession has been described as "how its practitioners use knowledge to make a difference."[1] How then can one persuade the nurse who does not believe she needs to use or do research to move into the professional role of a nurse—one who not only uses existing knowledge but continues to expand the field by questioning practice and searching for answers? This task is not easy. Here is the story of how one organization is accomplishing this goal, one small step at a time.

A BRIEF HISTORY OF RESEARCH WITHIN THE ORGANIZATION

A nursing research committee was started at St. Joseph Medical Center, Carondelet Health System, in Kansas City, Missouri, in 2001. Membership consisted of four advanced-practice nurses and several motivated staff nurses who participated when they could get someone to cover their patient assignment on the floor. A purpose statement was developed, and the functions of the committee were described. It was determined that the promotion of evidence-based practice would

[a] Pain Management, Palliative Care, Oncology, St. Joseph Medical Center, Kansas City, MO 64114, USA
[b] University of Kansas School of Nursing, 3901 Rainbow Boulevard, Kansas City, KS 66160, USA
* Corresponding author. 4138 Blackjack Oak Drive, Lawrence, KS 66047.
E-mail address: cmulvenon@carondelet.com (C. Mulvenon).

Nurs Clin N Am 44 (2009) 145–152
doi:10.1016/j.cnur.2008.10.006
0029-6465/08/$ – see front matter © 2009 Elsevier Inc. All rights reserved.

nursing.theclinics.com

underpin nursing practice. The committee members also recognized the importance of educating nurses about how to use and conduct research. Within months of the committee's formation, an issue surfaced regarding the way blood pressure was taken. What better way to promote research and educate nurses than by conducting a study?

The agony of a good idea gone awry will not be described in detail. The limited research experience of the group quickly became evident. The investigation was begun before the question was completely defined. Operating from a quality improvement mindset, approval from an institutional review board was not obtained. Armed with enthusiasm and a problem clearly needing to be addressed, the group set out to assess baseline data, review the evidence, and make recommendations for change based on evidential findings. Valuable knowledge for the organization was obtained from this "study." Changes were made in how blood pressures were assessed. New equipment was purchased. Alas, this knowledge could not be shared with the broader nursing community because it was more of a quality improvement project than a formal study. Help was needed from an experienced researcher. For a period of time the committee collaborated with a local school of nursing, and a doctorally prepared nurse attended meetings. This informal relationship was vitally important in getting started, but it was evident that more structure was required and that a formal arrangement with a nurse researcher must be established.

As the committee struggled to find its way with the process of conducting research, education was provided for staff members about nursing research. The goal of this education was to emphasize why the practice should be guided by evidence and not based on the traditional views of the most outspoken nurse at the meeting. Attendance at educational programs was small and erratic. Nurses at all levels of practice continued to express feelings of intimidation regarding conducting research and using it to inform their practice. Frustration among the committee members mounted. Eye rolling was seen, and deep sighs were heard before, during, and after meetings. In Shared Leadership councils, policies were updated dutifully on a regular basis using the most current reference from the literature. No, the resources were not always evidence based, but they were published in journals.

Steps were being taken, the committee had been formed, a study had been undertaken, education was occurring, but the goal of promoting evidence-based practice was not being achieved at a desirable level. In retrospect it is easy to see that there was not a clear vision of what was to be achieved. "Promotion of research and the use of evidence" is not as specific as "nurses actively questioning their practice and becoming knowledgeable about how to find answers that are supported by evidence." This lack of direction made it impossible to plan and achieve what was desired. The same education process continued: a reiteration of what research is and why it is important. Unsurprisingly, nurses were not engaged with this approach.

Despite the lack of a clear vision and a plan, some key components were in place. From the outset, there was complete support from nursing administration. All clinical nurse specialists had research incorporated into their job descriptions. Nursing research and quality improvement was an integral part of the career advancement program. There was access to literature through the hospital library, and a skilled, approachable librarian served as an excellent resource for literature searches and obtaining articles as needed. There were computers in the clinical nurse specialists' offices as well as on all nursing units, and access to the Internet was available. Nursing research was included explicitly in the budget of the organization. One change that occurred in this time frame was the expansion of the committee to include nurses not from just one institution, but from two, encompassing all the nurses within the organization. This expansion created a few logistical challenges, but, more impor-tantly, the research committee members still felt that something vital was lacking.

RESUSCITATING THE VISION

If this were a fairy tale, we would tell you that one day the nursing research committee awakened and proclaimed "Enough of this time-wasting stuff that has gone on for the last 5 years. From this day forth, nurses within the organization will stop thinking that evidence-based practice means updating the reference list of policies and will begin to question practice actively and to learn a method through which practice can be changed. Everyone will like it and participate!" Oh no, enlightenment did not come like that. What did occur, though, was a case of excellent timing. The two integral components of a vital plan—a vision and a reliable process—somehow came together at just the right moment.

The vice president of nursing had heard about the Clinical Scholar Model at a training session that she attended to be come a new Magnet program appraiser.[2,3] The pre-senters reported a winning formula for bringing the bedside nurse and research to-gether in a large tertiary care hospital, with a nurse researcher as coordinator and facilitator of the program. Could an organization without a full-time researcher realistically implement a similar program? The presenter, who had initiated this point-of-care program, was invited as a keynote speaker to talk with the direct care nursing staff about research at the bedside and with managers about their role in creating the environment that would support this research. "We want nurses to see that research is important and something they can do," we told her. "We want you to put on your super hero cape and swoop down among the nurses and sprinkle fairy dust and get them fired up about research." Those may not have been the exact words, but that is what we wanted to ask for. This was a tall order, much to ask of a speaker who was coming in for 1 day and visiting each institution for 2 hours. But she did it. She used examples to which nurses could relate. She shared stories from the hospital where she worked, with research and evidence-based practice ex-amples that resonated with the nursing staff. She made the program seem like some-thing we could do. More than that, she somehow made staff nurses realize that nursing research was not stuffy and impossibly hard. Instead she made it relative. She used language that nurses understand. Attendance at the programs was high. Nurses remarked in their evaluations that they had "not gotten the connection" between research and practice before, but after hearing this presentation they did. The members of the nursing research committee saw a glimmer of hope. A clear vision had been provided.

The Clinical Scholar Model was selected as the foundation for how a nurse might evaluate and possibly change practice.[3] Once the model was selected, various institutions that had adopted the model were studied to determine how they had developed nurses in the role of clinical scholars. The goal was to determine how the nursing department at Carondelet Health system could individualize the model to work within both institutions using the current available resources. Simultaneously, the search was ongoing for a part-time nurse researcher. Time was a big factor. The program needed to be implemented while nurses still were enthusiastic about en-gaging in research.

The nursing research committee discussed putting together an education program for the nurses who would participate in the Clinical Scholar Program. But what would be the most effective way to prepare nurses to evaluate existing practices critically? The committee met. They discussed the issues. What should be included in the education for staff? Who should teach the classes? How would staff be mentored through the process? Merely providing a blueprint for transitioning from staff nurse to clinical scholar would not provide the support needed to sustain nurses through the pitfalls and frustrations that would arise in their investigations.

A search was conducted to find templates and educational material that had been used in other facilities to increase the conduct and use of research by point-of-care providers. A continuing education program was located on the Sigma Theta Tau International website (www.nursingknowledge.org). Instead of re-inventing the wheel, should we use this program? We contacted our speaker, because she had offered to provide additional consultation. Could this program work in our organization? She advised us, "try one and see what you think." How very sensible. A copy was purchased and completed. All the essential elements required in conducting a review of the literature and determining whether to make practice changes or conduct further research were included. A decision was made to use this curriculum, and it was purchased by the organization for all participants in the Clinical Scholar Program.

Around the time the decision to use the online program was made, a nurse researcher applied to the organization and was hired. At last, a voice of experience was available to provide direction and expertise when needed. The actualization of our vision was in sight.

FULFILLING THE VISION

Armed with clear vision (ie, that nurses would question their practice actively and would be knowledgeable about how to find answers that are supported by evidence), a reliable process (ie, the Clinical Scholar Program), and a ready guide (ie, our nurse researcher), we set out on our journey. An application was developed and sent to all the nurses in the organization, encouraging them to be a part of the Clinical Scholar Program. Most of the nursing research committee members made a commitment to participate in the online Clinical Scholar Program as well. There was discussion at the meetings about the number of nurses to enroll in the program. The enrollment of one or two nurses from every unit, or at least one or two nurses from every clinical area, would result in a very large number of participants. A suggestion was made to actively recruit individuals who were considered to be ready for this type of challenge. Others thought it might be best to start small and simply select individuals who applied for the program, rather than actively trying to recruit. Members of the committee would be involved actively in an investigation of their own. Although most committee members had conducted some research in the past, none thought they were experts. Could they actively assist a number of uncertain recruits while conducting their own investigation? After a thorough discussion, it was decided to keep the numbers small and to select nurses who were motivated and confident enough to submit an application on their own. Depending on the outcome of the first group of scholars, this program would continue in the future with increasing participation from nurses throughout the organization.

Nurses were selected for the program based on the merits of their completed application and the endorsement of their manager. With the guidance of the nurse researcher, the clinical scholar group would select issues to investigate and carry out the steps of the research process as they completed each part of the online program. In a group setting, participants would discuss and problem solve barriers they encountered in their quests to implement evidence-based practice.

The plan was for the education of the clinical scholars to unfold over a 3- to 5-month period, culminating with the annual nursing research fair to showcase work accomplished by clinical scholars as they worked to make evidence a tangible, meaningful part of everyday practice.

A DIARY OF THE CHALLENGES AND SUCCESSES
January 10, 2008

Applications have been reviewed, and the clinical scholars have been selected. A total of 10 individuals, including members of the nursing research committee, will participate in the program. Participants include five staff nurses, three clinical nurse specialists, a nursing administrator, and the nurse researcher. The plan is to have a poster forum this summer to showcase the work of the clinical scholars.

I am very glad to be moving beyond this never-ending cycle of trying to explain what research is and how we are supposed to be or are using it. I am ready to begin conducting investigations into issues so that we can show people better by doing things. I think most nurses learn best when they have an example they can see.

February 14, 2008

After a few snags all the participants in the clinical scholars program have been able to sign in and have begun the program. Time was spent discussing briefly what topics each participant may want to delve into deeper. Three members of the group are fairly certain about their topic. Six members have a vague idea or are trying to decide between two topics.

One of our members has dropped out of the program. She passed her materials on to another nurse at her facility. I will need to evaluate if he will be a good candidate for this program and be certain of his commitment. I am disappointed that we have already lost one of our staff nurse members and someone that I thought would be good in this role, but I am glad that she dropped out now instead of later after she had already started part of the program. I know there are likely to be more dropouts. I am not sure how you can prevent it. I thought I did a pretty good job of making clear what the expectations were and did not try to talk anyone into undertaking this program, knowing that it would be difficult to keep people in the program with all the other directions they are being pulled in. Today a blackboard or angel site for the research committee to use was discussed. I am excited about the ability for the participants in the program to communicate with each other in this way at their convenience. Time is always a big issue, and having everyone meet at the same time is hard.

March 13, 2008

The nurse researcher demonstrated the angel site that will be available for communicating informally among the group between meetings. Some have used this form of communication in school; others do not yet have a clear picture of how it will work but express a desire to be able to communicate electronically when they have the time. There was good discussion about three of the clinical scholars' topics.

A staff nurse from the operating room (OR) is interested in exploring the lack of a written record of the physician orders during the intraoperative period and the possible impact on the patient from a safety perspective. Potential ramifications discussed include the potential for duplicate orders or omissions in care. The discussion included steps that would be needed to get this information on the chart, what staff members in the OR think about this issue, and what the benefits of this change would be. Suggestions were provided regarding directions for a literature search and an investigation of the community standard.

The reduction of nursings' footprint in pharmaceutical waste is the topic a staff nurse in the ICU is exploring. Discussion centered on how and to what extent nurses contribute to the problem. The group is unsure of the process currently used by pharmacy to dispose of waste. A variety of ways that nurses can impact the issue were discussed, including educating patients about disposal of medications.

Open visitation in the postanesthesia care unit (PACU) has been of interest to a nurse from this department since she went to a national conference several years ago and heard about a hospital that allowed it. Benefits included very high levels of satisfaction from patients. This nurse is concerned about studying this topic because open visitation in the current physical environment of the PACU could infringe on patient privacy. There are mixed feelings about this issue among the nurses in the recovery room as well. Suggestions were made regarding a review of the available literature regarding ICU and pediatric visiting hours.

Unfortunately not everyone had a chance to discuss their topic. Next month the meeting will occur via a teleconference between our two facilities. I am concerned about the possible impact on discussion and the ability to communicate easily. All the clinical scholars have completed module one. A new staff nurse has replaced the one who was unable to continue. It is good to have a researcher here to assist with the development of individual questions and to focus more precisely on the issues. Keeping the group on target can be challenging. We only have 1 hour each month in which we get together formally to talk about this program. I struggle with the issue of making the meetings longer, but my experience tells me that longer meetings generally lead to more time wasting.

April 10, 2008

Today the meeting started with a discussion of the projects being considered by the members of the group who did not share last month.

An emergency department nurse who also is a clinical instructor has selected a topic regarding preceptors and their needs when precepting a student. She is working with a fellow instructor on this study, and they are applying for a clinical research grant. They have reached the point of seeking approval for this study from the Human Subjects Committee at the university. This study also will need to go to the Research Steering Committee at the hospital.

The orientation of patients as they are transported is the subject of interest to an ICU nurse. She wants to know if there is any validity to transporting a patient feet first. She reports that studies done regarding this practice have been conducted on healthy people. A member of the group mentioned reviewing research done comparing amounts of antiemetics used with patients who were loaded feet first or head first into medical evacuation helicopters.

The director of nursing in the clinical scholars group is exploring family-initiated rapid assessment team calls. She reports not finding research published on this topic. There are recommendations regarding the need for this practice in the literature, but no studies or guidelines exist. The group suggested looking at available literature on the topics of family presence in codes or family involvement in patient care. Evaluating material presented at conferences that may not yet be in literature also was discussed.

One of the clinical nurse specialists is focusing on early indicators of dehydration in the patient. Her focus is on early identification by the nurse and interventions to improve patient outcomes.

Another topic proposed is the co-administration of blood and opioids administered via a patient-controlled analgesia (PCA) pump. Blood bank standards and hospital policy generally do not allow the simultaneous administration of blood with any other products except normal saline. This prohibition can lead to poor pain control or the need for another intravenous site to continue the PCA. A search is underway to determine the rationale for this prohibition and the data that support the practice.

We are discussing ideas in real, not theoretic, circumstances. It feels different. Instead of talking but knowing no change will take place, we are appraising situations critically. It feels empowering instead of frustrating. The exchange of ideas among the group is invigorating. A call for abstracts has been received for the 11th Kansas Nursing Research Exchange. Can anyone be ready to submit an abstract by the deadline called for? Our nurse researcher assures us that we can. Writing abstracts remains a bit intimidating to those of us who have not done much of it. It's a good thing we have someone to encourage and help us.

May 8, 2008

Work progresses on the refinement of the questions at the heart of each clinical scholar's investigation. The study on preceptors' needs has been submitted to the Human Subjects Review Board and is awaiting word on approval. The review of literature for the pharmaceutical waste study has been completed. The next step is development of a survey with the help of our researcher.

The operating room nurse has become frustrated with her topic because she cannot find anything in the literature, but her enthusiasm for the program remains undampened. She has decided to tackle her initial topic of physician's orders in the OR from a quality improvement perspective and to work on the importance of normothermia in the perioperative patient for the Clinical Scholars Program. A committee member suggested a review of what is happening with normothermia in military hospitals. This milieu also was suggested as a resource for the issue of co-administration of blood and opioids.

The issue of open visiting hours in the postanesthesia care unit has become overwhelming for the nurse who wants to make this change happen. She reports that she does not know where to focus and feels that she will meet resistance no matter what she does. The nurse researcher helps her to focus on just one aspect of the issue—surveying the nurses in the department about reasons to allow visitors in the area and reasons not to let visitors in.

Another clinical nurse specialist reported on her topic of the prevention of deep vein thrombosis (DVT). Despite safety initiatives and efforts by hospitals aimed at preventing DVTs, some patients still develop them. Treatment in the acute phase focuses on anticoagulation and prevention of pulmonary embolism. These patients also are at risk for long-term complications, such as postthrombotic syndrome, venous insufficiency, and venous stasis ulcers, that can be extremely debilitating. The use of compression therapy following a DVT has been shown to reduce the incidence and severity of long-term complications, but most patients either are never counseled to wear them or choose not to comply. She plans to explore the reasons why patients do not use compression therapy after an acute DVT.

As work progresses among the clinical scholars, you can feel the excitement of the group. Although challenges have arisen, the group members remain engaged in the process. Chairing this committee has moved beyond the drudgery of research hanging around my neck like a ball and chain to feeling good about knowing the resources are there and we actually are in the process of undertaking investigations and doing it right. We are still working on the use of the angel site. I think it will be a good method of communication between our meetings. It seems hard to get what we need to get done in an hour, but everyone has other commitments as well.

WHERE WE ARE TODAY

Since the nursing research committee began to meet approximately 7 years ago, we have learned some tough lessons. Is it necessary and perhaps even helpful to go through the trial-and-error process to be where we are today? For those who subscribe to the "no pain—no gain" way of thinking, maybe it is. We like to think we are more enlightened than that. What rescued our nursing research committee from certain death was the coming together of the vision, a plan, and a ready resource. It helped immensely to have someone come to our organization and show us that what we wanted to do was possible. Seeing an example of how someone had accomplished it enabled us to believe we could, as well. Along with the vision, the Clinical Scholars Program is turning out to be a reliable roadmap. This structured approach for teaching nurses the steps needed to conduct an investigation the proper way feels right for us. The third and absolutely essential piece of our success is the nurse researcher who serves as our guide and mentor, encouraging us along the way and providing the expertise and support we need as we continue to grow and develop.

The group has committed to complete the Clinical Scholars curriculum by the summer of 2008. Several have completed it already and are moving full steam ahead on their projects. The decision to start with a small group of clinical scholars was a good one for us. A larger group would have made it very difficult to give each topic the time and attention warranted. We are just at the beginning of our journey, with much yet to accomplish. As our organization continues on the path of achieving our vision for research, this current group of clinical scholars will be able to mentor the next group and broaden the base of support for nursing research, one clinical scholar at a time.

REFERENCES

1. Hegyvary ST. To make a difference. J Nurs Scholarsh 2007;39(1):1–2.
2. Schultz AA. Nursing research, research utilization, evidence-based practice. Houston (TX): New Magnet Appraiser Workshop; 2007.
3. Schultz AA. Clinical scholars at the bedside: an EBP mentorship model for today. ENK: Excellence in Nursing Knowledge 2005.

Index

Note: Page numbers of article titles are in **boldface** type.

A

Academic medical centers, application of evidence-based practice model in, **1–10**
    case study, 7–9
    developing the program, 2–7
        academic program, 5–7
        clinical program, 3–5
Analysis, of evidence-based practice, and critique, in model for staff nurses, 14
    example of, in Clinical Scholar model, 101
Application, of evidence-based practice, example of, in Clinical Scholar model, 101
    in model for staff nurses, 14
Assessment, of evidence, to incorporate into policies and procedures, 57–58

B

Barnes-Jewish Hospital, Evidence Equals Excellence program at, **1–10**
Baylor Health Care System Professional Nursing Practice Model, staff nurses creating safe
    passage with, 73–80
        engaging nurses in evidence-based practice, 74–76
        linking nursing evidence and patient outcomes, 76–80
Bedrest, optimal length of, following cardiac catheterization or percutaneous coronary
    intervention, Clinical Scholar model in evaluation of, 117–122
Best practices, nursing quality program driven by evidence-based practice, **83–91**
        Best Practices Council, 84
        St. Luke's Evidence Based Practice Model, 84–86
        using or implementing best practice model, 86–89
            bloodstream infection prevention, 87
            fall prevention, 87–88
            hands-off communication, 88–89
            pressure ulcer prevention, 88
Bloodstream infections, prevention of, implementing best practices for, 87

C

Cardiac catheterization, reducing length of bed rest following, use of Clinical Scholar model
    in evaluation of, 117–122
Cardiology nursing, evidence-based practice in, improving glycemic control in open-heart
    surgery program, 124–128
    reducing length of bed rest following cardiac catheterization or percutaneous coronary
        intervention, 117–122
    reducing postoperative nausea and vomiting in patients undergoing open-heart surgery,
        122–124

Nurs Clin N Am 44 (2009) 153–160
doi:10.1016/S0029-6465(08)00097-2
0029-6465/08/$ – see front matter © 2009 Elsevier Inc. All rights reserved.

nursing.theclinics.com

Children's hospitals, experience with evidence-based practice model in, 20–24
Clinical nurse specialist (CNS), role of, in evidence-based practice, 133–134
Clinical practice. *See* Evidence-based practice.
Clinical Scholar Program, development and implementation of, **93–102**
 clinical exemplar: policy for oral fluids prior to patient discharge, 100–102
  analyzing, 101
  applying and evaluating, 101
  disseminating, 101
  observing, 100–101
  synthesizing, 101
 cultural readiness, 94
 definition of evidence-based practice, 93–94
 development of the model, 94–96
 implementation of, 96–98
 sustaining the model, 99–100
 the model, 96
  description, 96
  essential components of, 96
  goals, 96
 who is the clinical scholar, 98–99
 embracing evidence-based practice in a rural state, **33–42**
 in community hospitals, **11–25**
  development of model, 12–13
  experience at a community hospital, 15–20
  experience at a freestanding pediatric hospital, 20–24
 resuscitation of nursing research with, **145–152**
 three evidence-based projects using the model, **117–130**
  improving glycemic control in open-heart surgery program, 124–128
  reducing length of bed rest following cardiac catheterization or percutaneous coronary intervention, 117–122
  reducing postoperative nausea and vomiting in patients undergoing open-heart surgery, 122–124
Collaboration, among urban hospitals through Texas Christian University Center for Evidence-Based Practice and Research, **27–31**
 Maine Nursing Practice Consortium, **33–42**
Communication, hands-off, implementing best practices for, 88–89
Community hospitals, building capacity for research and evidence-based practice in, **11–25**
 Clinical Scholar Program, 13–14
  experience at a community hospital, 15–20
  experience at a freestanding pediatric hospital, 20–24
 development of clinical scholar model, 12–13

D

Design, of policies and procedures incorporating evidence-based practice, 59–63
Dissemination, of evidence-based practice findings, example of, in Clinical Scholar model, 101
 in model for staff nurses, 14
DVDs, preoperative instructional, effects on patient knowledge and preparedness, **103–115**

E

Education, nursing, application of evidence-based practice model in academic medical center, **1–10**

case study, 7–9

developing the program, 2–7

academic program, 5–7

clinical program, 3–5

National Quality Forum Scholars Initiative for practicing nurses, **43–55**

Education, patient, preoperative instructional DVD on postoperative care activities, **103–115**

discussion, 112–114

evidence-based literature, 104–107

intervention for project implementation, 107–108

postintervention results, 108–112

purpose of project, 107

scope of problem in existing practice, 104

Evidence Equals Excellence (EEE) program, in an academic medical center, **1–10**

case study, 7–9

developing the program, 2–7

academic program, 5–7

clinical program, 3–5

Evidence-based practice, 1–152

building capacity for, in staff nurses, **93–102**

clinical scholar model for, **117–130**

collaboration among urban hospitals for, **27–31**

health system-wide educational program for nurses in, **43–55**

in a rural state, **33–42**

in an academic medical center, **1–10**

in community hospitals, **11–25**

nursing quality program driven by, **83–91**

patient education with preoperative instructional digital video disc, **103–115**

promoting safe outcomes in, **57–70**

resuscitating use of nursing research, **145–152**

staff nurses creating safe passage with, **71–81**

to improve care for vulnerable neonatal population, **131–144**

F

Fall prevention, implementing best practices for, 87–88

Feeding readiness, in neonatal intensive care unit, evidence-based changes in practice, 136–142

Fluids, oral, prior to patient discharge, evidence-based practice resulting in policy change, 100–102

analyzing, 101

applying and evaluating, 101

disseminating, 101

observing, 100–101

synthesizing, 101

G

Glycemic control, improvement of in open-heart surgery program, 124–128

H

Hands-off communication, implementing best practices for, 88–89
Hospitals, academic medical centers. *See* Academic medical centers.
    community. *See* Community hospitals.
    urban. *See* Urban hospitals.

I

Implementation, of policies and procedures incorporating evidence-based practice, 63–69
Infections, bloodstream, prevention of, implementing best practices for, 87
Informatics, in National Quality Forum Scholars Initiative for practicing nurses, **43–55**
Integration, of policies and procedures incorporating evidence-based practice, 69

J

John C. Lincoln North Mountain Hospital, experience with Clinical Scholar program at, 15–20

L

Leadership, development of, in National Quality Forum Scholars Initiative for practicing nurses, 49
Linking, of evidence to outcomes, to incorporate evidence into policies and procedures, 58–59

M

Maine Medical Center, development of Clinical Scholar program at, 12–13, **93–102**
    three examples of staff nurses' projects using the Clinical Scholar model at, **117–130**
Maine Nursing Practice Consortium, embracing evidence-based practice in a rural state through, **33–42**
        lessons learned, 40–41
        Maine Nursing Practice Consortium, 37–38
            first year accomplishments, 38–39
        outcomes of workshops, 40
        process of solidifying a collaborative partnership, 36
        workshop on promoting evidence-based practice through a spirit of inquiry, 36–37
        workshop on renewing the spirit of nursing, 39–40
Mayo Clinic, National Quality Forum Scholars Initiative for nurses at, **43–55**
Mentoring, in an evidence-based practice model in an academic medical center, **1–10**
Mentorship, development of, in National Quality Forum Scholars Initiative for practicing nurses, 49
Models, Baylor Health Care System Professional Nursing Practice Model, 73–80
    Clinical Scholar Program, at St. Joseph's Medical Center, Kansas City, 147–149
        development of, **93–102**
        in community hospitals, **11–25**

three examples of staff nurses' projects using the, **117–130**
use to promote evidence-based practice in a rural state, 34–36
Evidence Equals Excellence program, **1–10**
National Quality Forum Scholars Initiative for practicing nurses, **43–55**
Promoting Action on Research Implementation in Health Services (PARHIS) framework, 71–73
St. Luke's Evidence Based Practice Model, 84–86

N

National Quality Forum Scholars Initiative, implementation by Mayo Clinic Nursing, **43–55**
    case examples from evidence-based practice project teams, 48–49
    challenges in, 49–51
    facilitating factors, 51–52
    intended participants, 46
    leadership and mentorship in, 49
    lessons learned, 52
    program description, 45
    program implementation, 46–48
    specific program goals, 46
    summer assignment (Appendix), 53–54
Nausea, postoperative, reduction of in patients undergoing open-heart surgery, use of Clinical Scholar model in evaluation of, 122–124
Neonatal intensive care nursing, using evidence to improve care in, **131–144**
    change in feeding readiness practice, 136–142
    change in open visitation practice, 134–136
    clinical nursing research, 132–133
    role of clinical nurse specialist, 133–134
    role of professional nurse researchers, 133
Nurse researcher, professional. *See* Researcher, professional nurse.
Nurses, staff. *See* Staff nurses.
Nursing education. *See* Education, nursing.
Nursing research. *See* Research, nursing.

O

Observation, example of, in Clinical Scholar model, 100–101
    reflection and, in evidence-based practice model for staff nurses, 13–14
Open-heart surgery, evidence-based practice in, improving glycemic control in patients undergoing, 124–128
    reducing postoperative nausea and vomiting in patients undergoing, 122–124
Oral fluids, *see* Fluids, oral.
Outcomes. *See also* Safety, patient.
incorporating evidence into policies and procedures for promotion of safe, **57–70**
    assess, 57–58
    design, 59–63
    implementation, 63–69
    integrate and maintain, 69
    link, 58–59
    synthesis, 59

P

Partnerships, among urban hospitals through Texas Christian University Center
   for Evidence-Based Practice and Research, **27–31**
Patient education. *See* Education, patient.
Patient safety. *See* Safety, patient.
Pediatric hospitals, experience with evidence-based practice model in, 20–24
Percutaneous coronary intervention, reducing length of bed rest following, use of Clinical
   Scholar model in evaluation of, 117–122
Phoenix Children's Hospital, experience with Clinical Scholar program at, 20–24
Policies, procedures and, incorporating evidence into, for promotion of safe outcomes,
   57–70
      assess, 57–58
      design, 59–63
      implementation, 63–69
      integrate and maintain, 69
      link, 58–59
      synthesis, 59
Postoperative care activities, effects of preoperative instructional DVD on patient
   knowledge and preparedness for, **103–115**
      discussion, 112–114
      evidence-based literature, 104–107
      intervention for project implementation, 107–108
      postintervention results, 108–112
      purpose of project, 107
      scope of problem in existing practice, 104
Postoperative nausea and vomiting, reduction of in patients undergoing open-heart
   surgery, use of Clinical Scholar model in evaluation of, 122–124
Preoperative instructions, effects of preoperative instructional DVD on patient knowledge
   and preparedness, **103–115**
Pressure ulcers, focus on, by evidence-based practice project teams in National Quality
   Forum Scholars Initiative, 48–49
prevention of, implementing best practices for, 88
Procedures, *see* Policies, procedures and.
Professional development, in National Quality Forum Scholars Initiative for practicing
   nurses, **43–55**
Promoting Action on Research Implementation in Health Services (PARHIS), 71–73

Q

Quality, nursing, program for, driven by evidence-based practice, **83–91**
      Best Practices Council, 84
      St. Luke's Evidence Based Practice Model, 84–86
      using or implementing best practice model, 86–89
         bloodstream infection prevention, 87
         fall prevention, 87–88
         hands-off communication, 88–89
         pressure ulcer prevention, 88

R

Reflection, observation and, in evidence-based practice model for staff nurses, 13–14

Research, nursing, building capacity for in community hospitals, **11–25**
 clinical, in neonatal intensive care unit nursing, 132–133
  role of clinical nurse specialist, 133–134
  role of professional nurse researcher, 133
 collaboration in, among urban hospitals through Texas Christian University Center for
  Evidence-Based Practice and Research, **27–31**
 resuscitating the use of, from bedside to boardroom, **145–152**
  brief history of research at St. Joseph's Medical Center, Kansas City, 145–147
  challenges and successes in, 149–151
  fulfilling the vision for, 148–149
  vision for, Clinical Scholar Model in, 147–148
  where we are today, 152
Researcher, professional nurse, role of, in evidence-based practice, 133
Rural areas, embracing evidence-based practice in, **33–42**
  lessons learned, 40–41
  Maine Nursing Practice Consortium, 37–38
   first year accomplishments, 38–39
  outcomes of workshops, 40
  process of solidifying a collaborative partnership, 36
  workshop on promoting evidence-based practice through a spirit of inquiry, 36–37
  workshop on renewing the spirit of nursing, 39–40

S

Safety, patient, incorporating evidence into policies and procedures, **57–70**
  assess, 57–58
  design, 59–63
  implementation, 63 69
  integrate and maintain, 69
  link, 58–59
  synthesis, 59
 staff nurses creating safe passage with evidence-based practice, **71–81**
  Baylor Health Care System Professional Nursing Practice Model, 73–80
   engaging nurses in evidence-based practice, 74–76
   linking nursing evidence and patient outcomes, 76–80
  creating urgency for, 72
  factors influencing implementation of, 72–73
St. Joseph's Medical Center, Kansas City, resuscitating the use of nursing research at,
 145–152
  brief history of research at, 145–147
  challenges and successes in, 149–151
  fulfilling the vision for, 148–149
  vision for, Clinical Scholar Model in, 147–148
  where we are today, 152
St. Luke's Hospital, Houston, Best Practices Council for nursing quality at, **83–91**
Staff nurses, evidence-based practice by, 1–152
  building capacity for, **93–102**
  clinical scholar model for, **117–130**
  collaboration among urban hospitals for, **27–31**
  creating safe passage with, **71–81**
  health system-wide educational program for, **43–55**

in a rural state, **33–42**
in an academic medical center, **1–10**
in community hospitals, **11–25**
nursing quality program driven by, **83–91**
patient education with preoperative instructional digital video disc, **103–115**
promoting safe outcomes in, **57–70**
resuscitating use of nursing research, **145–152**
to improve care for vulnerable neonatal population, **131–144**
Surgical patients, cardiology, evidence-based nursing practice in, improving glycemic
control in open-heart surgery program, 124–128
reducing length of bed rest following cardiac catheterization or percutaneous
coronary intervention, 117–122
reducing postoperative nausea and vomiting in patients undergoing open-heart
surgery, 122–124
effects of preoperative instructional DVD on patient knowledge and preparedness,
103–115
discussion, 112–114
evidence-based literature, 104–107
intervention for project implementation, 107–108
postintervention results, 108–112
purpose of project, 107
scope of problem in existing practice, 104
Synthesis, of evidence, example of, in Clinical Scholar model, 101
in evidence-based practice model for staff nurses, 14
to incorporate evidence into policies and procedures, 59

T

Texas Christian University Center for Evidence-Based Practice and Research, **27–31**

U

Urban hospitals, development of evidence-based practice and research collaborative
among, **27–31**
activities, 28–29
challenges, 29
future goals, 31
hospital perspective, 30
successes, 30–31

V

Visitation, parental, in neonatal intensive care unit, evidence-based changes in practice,
134–136
Vomiting, postoperative, reduction of in patients undergoing open-heart surgery, use of
Clinical Scholar model in evaluation of, 122–124

Moving?

Make sure your subscription moves with you!

To notify us of your new address, find your **Clinics Account Number** (located on your mailing label above your name), and contact customer service at:

E-mail: elspcs@elsevier.com

800-654-2452 (subscribers in the U.S. & Canada)
314-453-7041 (subscribers outside of the U.S. & Canada)

Fax number: 314-523-5170

Elsevier Periodicals Customer Service
11830 Westline Industrial Drive
St. Louis, MO 63146

*To ensure uninterrupted delivery of your subscription, please notify us at least 4 weeks in advance of move.